THE
1,000 page
TREASURY OF
CHILDREN'S
STORIES

First published in Great Britain in 1983 by
Octopus Books Limited

This edition published in the USA in 1987 by
Gallery Books
An imprint of W.H. Smith Publishers, Inc.
112 Madison Avenue, New York, New York 10016

ISBN 0-8317-0037-8

Printed in Czechoslovakia

THE

1,000 *page*

TREASURY OF CHILDREN'S STORIES

GALLERY BOOKS
An Imprint of W. H. Smith Publishers Inc.
112 Madison Avenue
New York City 10016

CONTENTS

THE LEFT-HANDED SWORD
E Nesbit

His name was Hugh de Vere Coningsby Drelincourt, and he lived with his mother in a queer red-roofed house incoherently built up against the corner of the old castle that stands on the edge of the hill looking out over the marshes. Once the castle and the broad lands about it had all belonged to the Drelincourts, and they had kept great state there. But they had been loyal to King Charles, and much went then. Later Hugh's father had spent what was left on lawyers, gaining nothing. And now only the castle itself was left, and some few poor fields. His mother was Lady Drelincourt by rights, and he himself, since his father was dead, was Sir Hugh, but there was no money to keep up the title, so she called herself plain Mrs Drelincourt, and he was just Hugh.

They lived very simply and kept cows and pigs, and Hugh did lessons with his mother and was very happy. There was no money to send him to school, but he minded that less than his mother did. It was a pleasant little house, and all the furniture in it was old and very beautiful, carved oak and polished apple-wood, and delicate lovely glass and china. But there was often only bread and cheese to put on the china plates, and cold water from the well in the castle courtyard to fill the Venice glasses.

There were relics too—an old silver bowl with raised roses round the brim, and a miniature or two, and a little sword that some boy Drelincourt had worn many many years ago. This sword Hugh had for his very own, and it hung over the mantelpiece in his bedroom. And the sword had been made for a left-handed little boy, because all the Drelincourts are left-handed.

Hugh used to wander about the old place, climb the old walls, and explore the old passages, always dreaming of the days when the castle was noisy with men-at-arms, and gay with knights and ladies.

Now the wild grasses and wallflowers grew in the rugged tops of the walls, and the ways to the dungeons were choked with fern and bramble. And there was no sound but the cooing of pigeons and the hum of wild bees in the thyme that grew over the mounds beyond the moat.

'You spend all your time dreaming,' his mother used to say, as she sat darning his stockings or mending his jackets, 'and the castle comes through all your clothes.'

'It comes through all everything,' Hugh would say. 'I wish I could see it as it was in the old days.'

'You never will,' said his mother, 'and isn't it beautiful enough as it is? We've got a lovely home, my son, and we've got each other.'

Then he would hug her and she would hug him, and he would try to pay more attention to his lessons, and not so much to the castle.

He loved his mother very much, and did many things to please her —lessons and errands and work about the house; and once when she was ill, and a silly woman from the village came in to do the housework, he mounted guard on the stairs all day, so that the woman should not disturb his mother with silly questions about where the soda was kept, and what dusters she was to use.

So now he tried to think less of the castle; but for all his trying the castle filled his life with dreams. He explored it and explored, till he thought he knew every inch of it.

One wall of Hugh's bedroom was just the thick, uneven stones of the old castle wall, against which the house was built. They were grey with time, and the mortar was crumbling from between them; the fires he had in the room in the winter, when he had colds, dried the mortar and made it crumble more than ever. There was an arch in this wall that had been filled up, in forgotten days, with heavy masonry. Hugh used to watch that arch, and wish it was a door that he could get through. He could not find the other side, though he had searched long and well. 'I expect it was only a cupboard,' his mother said, as she peeled the potatoes or made the puddings; 'I wouldn't worry about if it I were you.'

Hugh did not worry about it, but he never forgot it. And when the next winter he had one of those bad colds that made his mother so anxious, and caused him to be tormented with linseed poultices and water-gruel and cough-mixture and elder-flower tea, he had plenty of time to think, and he thought of the arch, and of nothing else.

And one night, when his mother had gone to bed, tired out with taking all sorts of care of him, he could not sleep, and he got out of bed and fingered the stones inside the arch as he had so often done before, to see if any one of them was loose. Before, none ever had been—but now . . . oh, joy! one was loose. The fire had dried the old mortar to mere dust that fell away as Hugh's fingers pulled at the stone—weakly, because his cold had really been a very severe one. He put out all the strength he could, however, and pulled and tugged and twisted, and shifted the stone, till it was quite loose in its place, and with the help of the poker he prised it out, and with difficulty put it on the floor.

He expected to seek a dark hole, through which a cold wind would blow; but no cold wind blew, and curiously enough, the hole was not dark. There was a faint grey light, like the light of daylight in a room with a small window.

Breathless and eager, he pulled out another stone. Then his heart gave a jump and stood still. For he heard something moving on the other side of the arch—not the wind or rustling leaves or creaking tree-boughs, but something *alive*. He was quite as brave as most boys, and, though his heart was going like a clock when you have wound it up, and forgotten to put on the pendulum, had the courage to call out:

'Hullo! who's there?'

'Me,' said a voice on the other side of the arch. 'Who are you?'

'Who are you, if it comes to that?' Hugh asked cautiously.

'Sir Hugh de Drelincourt,' said the voice from the hole in the wall.

'Bud thad's *by* dabe,' said Hugh with the cold in his head; and as he spoke another stone disappeared, and the hole was larger. Now in silence two pairs of hands worked at loosening the stones from the crumbling mortar.

'Ibe cobing through,' said Hugh suddenly; 'the hole's big edough.' And he caught the little sword from the wall, and he set his knee on the bottom of the hole and through he went.

Through into a little room whose narrow window showed the blue daylit sky—a room with not much in it but a bed, a carved stool, and a boy of his own age, dressed in the kind of dress you see in the pictures of the little sons of Charles I.

'Why, you're me!' the strange boy said, and flung his arms round him. And Hugh felt that he spoke the truth. Then a sudden fear caught at him; he threw off the other boy, and turned to go back quickly into his own room, with the dancing firelight and the cough-mixture and the elder-flower tea.

And then a greater fear wiped out the first, as a great wave might wash out a tear-mark on the sea-sand. For the hole in the wall was no more there. All the wall was unbroken and straight and strongly stony. And the boy who had been so like him was there no longer. And he himself wore the laced breeches, the little handsome silk coat, the silk stockings and buckled shoes of that other boy. And at his side hung his own little left-handed sword.

'Oh, I'm dreaming,' said Hugh. 'That's all right. I wonder what I shall dream next!'

He waited. Nothing happened. Outside the sun shone, and a rainbow-throated pigeon perched in the window preened her bright feathers.

So presently he opened the heavy door and went down a winding stair. At its foot was a door opening on the arched gateway that he knew so well. A serving-man in brown came to him as he passed through the door.

'You lazy young lie-a-bed,' he said, 'my lady has asked for you three times already——'

'Where is my lady?' Hugh asked, without at all knowing that he was going to ask it.

'In her apartments, where any good son would have been with her,' said the serving-man.

'Show me where,' said Hugh.

The serving-man looked at him, and nodded to a group of men in armour who stood in the gatehouse.

''Mazed,' he said, touching his forehead, ''mazed with the cannons and the shoutings and the danger, and his father cold in the chapel, and ... Come, lad,' he said, and took Hugh's hand in his.

Hugh found himself led into a long, low room, with a square wooden pattern on the ceiling, pictures along one side, and windows along the other. A lady, with long curls, a low-necked dress, and a lace collar, was stooping over an open chest from which came the gleam of gold and jewels. She rose as his shoes pattered on the floor.

'My son,' she said, and clasped him in her rich-clad arms, and her face, and her embrace, were the embrace and the face of his own mother, who wore blue cotton and washed the dishes in the little red-tiled castle house.

'All is lost,' said the lady, drawing back from the embrace. 'The wicked Roundheads have almost battered in the east wall. Two hours at least our men can keep them out. Your father's at peace, slain while you were asleep. All our wealth—I must hide it for you and for the upkeep of our ancient name. Ralph and Henry will see to it, while you and I read the morning prayers.'

Hugh is quite sure that in that long pleasant gallery, with the morning sun gay in the square garden outside, he and his mother read the prayers, while some serving-men staggered out with chest upon chest of treasure.

'Now,' his mother said, when the prayers were ended, 'all this is in the vault beneath your bed-chamber. We will go there, and I will lie down a little on your bed and rest, for, indeed, I am weary to death. Let no man enter.'

'No man shall enter. I will keep guard,' said Hugh, 'on the stairs without,' and felt proudly for his little sword at his side.

When they had come to that little room he kissed the silk-clad lady that was his mother, and then took up his station on the stairs outside.

And now he began to hear more and more loudly the thunder of artillery, the stamping and breathless shouting of fighting men. He sat there very still, and there was no sound from the chamber where his mother lay.

Long, very long, he waited there, and now there was no thought in him of its being a dream. He *was* Hugh de Drelincourt; the Round-heads were sacking his father's castle; his father lay in the chapel, dead,

13

The thrust was too fierce . . .

and his mother slept on the bed inside. He had promised that none should enter. Well, they should not.

And at long last came the clatter of mail on the stairs, and the heavy sound of great boots, and, one above another, heads in round steel caps, and shoulders in leather came round the newel of the little stair.

'A page-in-waiting,' cried the first man; 'where is your lady, my young imp?'

'My lady sleeps,' Hugh found himself saying.

'We have a word for your lady's ears,' said the round-capped man, trying to push past.

'Her ears are not to be soiled by your words,' Hugh was surprised to hear himself say.

'Don't thou crow so loud, my young cockerel,' the man said, 'and stand back, and make room for thy betters.'

The round caps and leather shoulders pushed upward, filling, crowding the staircase.

'Stand back!' they all cried, and the foremost drew a big sword, and pointed it, laughing, at the child.

' 'Tis thou shalt stand back!' Hugh cried, and drew his own little left-handed blade. A great shout of laughter echoed in the narrow staircase, and someone cried, 'Have a care, Jeremiah, lest he spit thee like a woodcock!'

Hugh looked at the coarse, laughing faces, and saw, without looking at it, the dear quiet face that lay in the room behind him.

'You shall *not* speak to her!' he cried, and thrust furiously with the little sword. The thrust was too fierce. It carried him forward on to the point of that big sword. There was a sharp pain in his side, a roaring in his ears: through it all he heard: 'This for our pains: a dead woman and a little child slain!' Then the roaring overpowered everything—the roaring and the pain, and to the sound of heavy feet that clattered down the stairs he went out of life, clutching to the last the little sword that had been drawn for her.

He was clutching the iron edge of his bed, his throat was parched and stiff, and the pain in his side was a burning pain, almost unbearable. 'Mother!' he called, 'Mother, I've had such a dreadful dream, and my side does hurt so!'

She was there even as he called—alive, living, tenderly caressing him. But not even in the comfort of her living presence, with the warmth of linseed poultices to the side that hurt, of warm lemon drink to the parched throat, could he tell a word of his dream. He has never told it to anyone but me.

'Now let this be a lesson to you, my darling,' his mother said; 'you must *not* climb about in those windy walls and arches, in this sort of weather. You're quite feverish. No wonder you've had bad dreams.'

But the odd thing is that nothing will persuade Hugh that this was only a dream. He says he knows it all happened—and indeed, the history books say so too. Of course, I should not believe that he had gone back into the past, as he says, and seen Drelincourt Castle taken by the Roundheads, but for one curious little fact.

When Hugh got well of his pleurisy, for that was the name the doctors gave to the pain that came from a dream sword-wound in his side, he let his mother have no peace till she sent for Mr Wraight, the builder at Dymchurch, and had all the stones taken out of that arch. And, sure enough, beyond it was a little room with a narrow window and no door. And the builder's men took up the stone floor, because nothing else would satisfy the boy, and sure enough again, there was a deep vault, and in it, piled on top of the other, chests upon chests of silver plate, and gold plate, and money, and jewels, so that now Lady Drelincourt can call herself by that gentle title, and Sir Hugh was able to go to Eton and to Oxford, where I met him, and where he told me this true tale.

And if you say that the mother of Hugh de Drelincourt, who died to defend his mother from the Roundheads, could not have been at all like the mother of little Hugh, who lived in the red-tiled castle house, and drank the elder-flower tea, and loved the left-handed sword that hung over his mantelpiece, I can only say, that mothers are very like mothers here, there, and everywhere else, all the world over, when all is said and done.

TWO MURDER MYSTERIES

Alice Monaghan

MADELAINE SMITH

In the late autumn of 1856, a tall, elegant young woman entered John Currie's pharmacy in Sauchihall Street in Glasgow. When asked what she required, the lady replied, 'Arsenic. To kill some rats.'

On hearing this, Mr Currie himself stepped forward and tried to convince the woman that another poison would do just as well. She insisted, gently, that she would rather have arsenic as she believed it to be the most efficient rat poison. Currie then explained that before he would sell it to her she would have to sign her name in the poison book. Would the young lady have any objections to doing so. 'No. None at all.'

Currie was impressed by the air of respectability and the openness of the young lady's manner, so he decided to go ahead with the sale. He carefully measured out one ounce of the arsenic and the young lady signed her name in the book, 'M. H. Smith.'

In June of the following year, the same M. H. Smith appeared in the High Court of Judiciary in Edinburgh on three charges; two of administering poison with intent to kill Pierre Emile L'Angelier and one of murdering the same man by poison.

The trial attracted a large amount of publicity and when the heavy wooden doors of the court swung open there was a rush for seats in the public gallery. The case had all the ingredients of the romantic novels that were so popular at the time. The daughter of a respectable and well-established architect had fallen in love with a penniless, young Frenchman of much lower social rank. However, her ardour had died and when she realised that he was not going to release her from her unofficial engagement in order that she could marry one of her own class, without threatening scandal, she had, with malice aforethought, decided to end his life in the most convenient manner.

The public waited expectantly for the trial to begin.

Two hours and twenty-five minutes after the public had been admitted, the clerk of the court's voice rang around the room. 'Court.'

The public in their benches and the legal gentlemen in the well of the court rose to their feet as the three judges moved in stately procession to their judicial chairs. They were Lord John Hope (The Lord Justice-Clerk), Lord Handside and Lord Ivory; dour, legal gentlemen not far above the accused in social rank, but well-known for their scrupulous fairness in matters judicial.

The public's eyes moved from the judges to a trapdoor in the floor. The door was opened and from the gloomy steps below there appeared a policeman followed by the accused. A murmur of sympathy swept around the court, and a few catcalls as well. The public were divided in their opinion of the attractive, slender young woman who had been described as a beauty.

Certainly, she was tall and graceful. Her dress was of elegant cut and colour, matching the rich, brown hair that was partially covered by a fashionable, veiled bonnet. When she raised the veil, the public saw that she was not beautiful. Handsome was a more appropriate description. Her nose was a trifle too large for true beauty, but her eyes were brilliant and her mouth was perfectly shaped.

The three charges were read out to her. She replied to each one in a steady, unemotional voice which was heard at the back of the crowded court.

'Not guilty.'

Again an audible whisper swept along the public gallery.

Over the next few days the story of Madelaine Smith and her romantic involvement with L'Angelier gradually unfolded.

A slender, attractive woman appeared from the gloomy steps

L'Angelier was not as 'French' as his name implied. He had been born on Jersey of French extraction. In his youth he drifted across Europe and eventually ended up, penniless, in Glasgow. He managed to find employment as a £50-a-year clerk in a local firm where he supervised the packing and despatch of the firm's goods. How he met Madelaine we do not know but he did meet her and the two became lovers.

Over a period of some months, a series of letters passed between the two. When these were read out in court, the public was astonished at the intimacy of the language used and several times Madelaine looked relieved when the Lord Advocate ordered that certain passages be omitted.

'Beloved Husband [!]' she wrote in one, 'This time last night you were with me. Tonight I am all alone . . . I love you more than ever . . . You are the only being I love.'

In another she wrote 'Beloved and best of husbands . . . the man I love and adore.'

For an impoverished clerk to receive such letters from the daughter of a wealthy architect, must have meant to him that his days of poverty would soon be over and that he would be married to his young lover. How his hopes must have been dashed when Madelaine became engaged to one of her own class, William Minnoch.

Madelaine wrote to L'Angelier breaking off their secret engagement. His reply was such to make Madelaine write, 'On my bended knees I write to you and ask you, as you hope for mercy at the judgement day, do not inform on me . . . Write to no one, Papa or any other . . . Do not make me a public shame.'

When L'Angelier had arrived in Glasgow he found lodgings at the home of David Jenkins, a joiner, and his wife Anne.

Anne Jenkins' evidence gave a graphic description of L'Angelier's illness. It seems that one day in February she had found the 'Frenchman' in bed suffering from violent nausea. She asked him why he had not called her and was told that he had been seized with such violent pain in the stomach that he had had to lie down to take his clothes off, crawl to bed, and was literally unable to summon up the energy to ring the bell.

Throughout the month he became ill again and again. The kindly Mrs Jenkins called a doctor to whom she said, 'He seems to become ill after being out. I must ask him the cause.' But before she could do so,

L'Angelier died – on 23rd March.

A post mortem revealed that L'Angelier had 82 grains of arsenic in his stomach. Dr Frederick Penny, Professor of Chemistry at Glasgow University replied 'four to six grains are generally regarded as sufficient to destroy life.'

Even more sensational evidence was given by a small, elderly spinster, Mary Perry, who attended the same church as L'Angelier and claimed to have acted as go-between for the two lovers. Under oath she told the court that L'Angelier said that during his secret visits to Madelaine, she served him chocolate and coffee as refreshment and that it was after taking these drinks that he became ill. On one occasion L'Angelier had told Mary Perry that 'if she, Madelaine, were to poison me I would forgive her. When Mary asked him why Madelaine would want to poison him, he replied, 'Perhaps she might not be sorry to be rid of me.'

Mr Currie's evidence that it was Madelaine Smith, sitting calmly in the box, who had purchased arsenic from him was, the prosecution claimed, conclusive that Smith had patched up her quarrel with L'Angelier having cold-bloodedly decided to murder him while pretending to be in love with him.

The prosecution had a strong case and one damning letter read out in court seemed to condemn Madelaine in her own words. 'You did look bad, Sunday night and Monday moring. I think that you got sick walking home so late – and the long want of food, so the next time we meet, I shall make you eat a loaf of bread.'

Would anyone planning poison have the cool nerve to implicate herself so clearly? Madelaine was certainly cool. As the evidence against her built up she remained totally calm, only once showing any sign of emotion, and that was when the Lord Advocate ruled certain parts of her letters as 'objectionable.'

Also, Madelaine admitted buying the arsenic. But would anyone planning murder openly sign her own name knowing that the purchase could be so easily traced?

When Madelaine was questioned by the police as to why she had bought arsenic she confessed that it was not for destroying rats, but for cosmetic reasons. Arsenic was a 'fashionable' cosmetic aid. Diluted down it was said to be good for the skin. Madelaine claimed that she was told about this by an old school friend, Augusta Guibeli. But Miss

Guibeli denied this under oath. The case against Madelaine seemed sure.

The prosecution summed up the case against her. She had written damning and indiscreet letters to her lover and in order to maintain her reputation and ensure her marriage to Minnoch she decided to kill him. She had purchased arsenic and given this to her lover in cups of coffee and chocolate. She had changed her story as to why she bought the arsenic. 'There is,' said Lord Advocate Moncrieff to the jury, 'but one course open to you, and that is to return a verdict of guilty.'

Madelaine's father had engaged as defence counsel, the Dean of the Faculty of Advocates. The Scottish legal system is different from that in England. An advocate is similar to a barrister and the Dean of the Faculty would be one of the leading and most prestigious lawyers of his day. The Dean's defence speech was masterly. He stressed that Madelaine was a girl of good family who had never, before she met L'Angelier, been the subject of even the merest whisper of gossip. He admitted that her affair had been corrupt and degrading, 'but would, without temptation, without evil teachers, a young girl fall into such depths of degradation?' Such influence, he claimed, could only come from one source – L'Angelier. The Dean painted him as a wastrel who had wormed his way into Madelaine's affections. There was evidence that L'Angelier had frequently suffered from stomach complaints. There was evidence, too, that he had boasted of being an arsenic eater. There was *circumstantial* evidence against Madelaine but the prosecution had failed to prove that Madelaine had been with the Frenchman on any occasion during the final bouts.

The judge summed up the case and the jury filed out. Less than half an hour later they returned. On the first charge of attempted murder she was found not guilty. Madelaine remained totally calm. The charge of attempted murder was found not proven as was the actual charge of murder. [Not Proven is a peculiarly Scottish verdict. It is generally taken to mean that the jury consider the accused guilty, but that the prosecution has failed to prove it. A prisoner is freed after such a verdict is returned.]

Madelaine gracefully accepted the congratulations of those in court who believed her innocent and seemed oblivious to the hoots of derision of those who thought her guilty.

The question as to whether Madelaine Smith was innocent or guilty has always fascinated those interested in crime. We shall never know for sure who killed L'Angelier. After the trial, Madelaine went to London where she married an artist. When he died she went to live in the United States where she died in 1927, aged 91.

JACK THE RIPPER

'It was too harrowing to be described . . . the most gruesome memory of the whole of my police career.' The writer was Detective Drew of the Metropolitan Police in London who later became famous as the policeman who arrested the infamous Doctor Crippen. The event he was writing about was the grisly murder of Mary Jeannette Kelly whose body was discovered on Saturday, 9th November, at quarter to eleven.

Mary Kelly was aged 25. She was Irish and she was a widow.

At about half past three on that Saturday morning two women who lived near Mary's small, ground-floor room at 13 Miller's Court in Whitechapel in London, heard the cry of 'Murder' but they paid little attention. When her body was discovered seven hours later the scene in the room well justified Detective Drew's comments. Her face had been mutilated in the most horrible manner and her throat had been cut. Parts of her body had been removed from her corpse and were spread around the room. In the opinion of Sir Melville Macnaughten, Head of Criminal Investigation, the murderer must have taken at least two hours over his 'hellish' job. Word soon spread around Whitechapel – Jack the Ripper had struck again.

★   ★   ★   ★

Whitechapel, in the East End of London, was as notorious as it was squalid. It was an area of sordid lodging houses and dirty pubs. Even in the sunshine of a sunny autumn day it had a threatening air about it, but at night when the mists blew off the river and swirled round the gas lamps, when the sound of raucous laughter and bawdy songs filled the damp and foggy gloom, when around each street corner there were women offering a few hours friendship for a few pennies, it was a place of threat and darkness. It was here that the terror of Jack the Ripper reigned for a few short weeks in the autumn of 1888.

In the cool hours of the early morning of Friday, 31st August, the body of Mary Anne Nichols was found. Her death was no loss to anyone for she was a 42-year-old penniless drunk; but the manner of her death shocked even the hardened mortuary attendant who 'dressed' the body. He was so sickened that he became violently ill. Mary Nichols' throat had been cut and there were severe abdominal injuries. Despite the horror of the crime, the police at first thought that it was 'just another murder' in an area where murder and brutal attack were not uncommon.

Then, eight days later, just before six o'clock in the morning of Saturday, 8th September, the body of 47-year-old Annie Chapman was found in the back yard of 29 Hanbury Street. Her injuries were almost identical to those of the luckless Mary Nichols, one difference being that several of Annie Chapman's internal organs had been removed – and removed with surgical skill!

The police suddenly realised that they had a madman on their hands. Horrified Londoners began to read the sensational headlines in the popular press. The residents of Whitechapel, hardened as they were to crime and violence, began to think twice about going out on their own at night and the population of London began to ask themselves questions about the handling of the case. Why were the bodies of the two victims not examined until after they had been washed and, perhaps, vital clues been lost? Why had Sir Charles Warren, the man in charge of the investigation, ordered that a recently chalked message be removed from the wall next to the scene of the crime? He justified this by claiming that he was protecting the public peace. Was he, Londoners asked, protecting more than the peace? Was the identity of the killer known to him, but if revealed would the ensuing scandal rock the establishment? Rumours began to fly around. It was said that the killer was none other than the Duke of Clarence, eldest son of the Prince of Wales and heir to the throne on his father's death! The duke was known to be 'unstable' and prone to fits of violence. Was Sir Charles protecting the monarchy? No one knows, but his handling of the case was such that he was forced to resign. But not before the murderer struck again.

Unfortunately Elizabeth Stride, known as 'Long Liz' was not one to think twice about going out alone at night. Her body was found on the last day of September by Louis Diemschutz whose horse shied at something in the road. The 'something' was the bleeding body of 'Long.

The 'something' was the bleeding body of Long Liz Stride

Liz'. So recently had she been murdered that blood was still warm from her gashed throat. Had the murderer been interrupted before he could begin to mutilate the body? The police believed so and chalked up murder number three to the Whitechapel killer.

A few hours after Louis Diemschutz had come upon Long Liz Stride's body, a fourth mutilated corpse was found. It was Catherine Eddows, a 43-year-old advanced alcoholic who suffered from Bright's disease. This disease affects the kidneys and those who suffer from it can easily be recognised by their peculiar bloated appearance.

Interestingly enough, as well as having had her throat cut and her body badly cut up, one of Catherine Eddows' kidneys had been removed! The police began to ask whether the murderer was a medical person, perhaps doing research into Bright's disease. Was the murderer familiar with his (or her) victim? Suspicion fell on Alexander Pedachenko.

He was a Russian doctor who worked in a clinic in the East End. Three of the murderer's victims had attended that clinic. He was questioned but was freed. However, many people, including Sir Basil Thomson, who was head of CID some years later, believed that he was guilty. Was it coincidence that shortly after he was released he returned to his native Russia and spent his last years in an asylum for the criminally insane having killed a Russian woman? Sir Basil believed not.

By the time that Elizabeth Stride and Catherine Eddows met their ghastly deaths the police had received a confession! Two days before these brutal murders the first of a series of callous letters was delivered at the Central News Agency. The letter finished with a dreadful poem:

I'm not a butcher, I'm not a kid,
Nor yet a foreign skipper,
But I'm your own true loving friend,
Yours truly – JACK THE RIPPER.

Within hours the name Jack the Ripper was being whispered in hushed, terrified tones in Whitechapel and soon spread into the rest of London. Who was this Jack the Ripper? The question was being asked in bars and shops, on buses and trains, and even in the fashionable drawing rooms of London society.

For the entire month of October, the Ripper was quiet. And then Mary Kelly's body was found. The Ripper had struck again – as he boasted in another letter to the Central News Agency.

Police investigations continued and one month later stopped as suddenly as the Ripper had struck. In December the body of a young lawyer, Montague John Druitt, was fished out of the River Thames. Druitt came from a good family who believed him to be insane. His name is mentioned in Sir Melville's files and all police investigations ceased on Druitt's suicide.

But was Druitt indeed the Ripper? There were plenty of other suspects. The Duke of Clarence was rumoured to be the killer. Certainly when he died in 1892 it was widely believed that he was demented and certain aspects of the police investigation have led 'Ripper hunters' to believe that there was a cover up of some sort being organised by the police. Were the police under orders from the Government, or even from the Palace, to hide the identity of the killer? Perhaps, but one fact has emerged from investigations – the Duke of Clarence could not have killed all the victims. When three of the Ripper's victims were murdered the duke was either shooting at Sandringham in Norfolk, or was in Scotland.

Several years after the Ripper had ceased to kill, a Doctor Thomas Neil Cream was tried and convicted of poisoning. On the scaffold he said 'I am Jack the . . .'' but before he could finish the sentence the rope closed around his neck and squeezed the life out of him. But Cream could not have been the Ripper as he was in prison while the Ripper was active.

Chief Inspector Abberline, one of the detectives working on the case, was convinced that the Ripper was Severin Klosowski (who later changed his name to George Chapman). Klosowski was a Polish barber who worked in Whitechapel. As a barber, he would have been used to working with the cut-throat razors that the police believed were used to cut the victims' throats. But Klosowski's guilt could never be proved.

Sir Basil Thompson was equally convinced that the Russian, Pedachenko, was the Ripper. After all he had had contact with three of the victims. As a doctor he would have had the skill to cut up the victims in the way in which they were dissected and, also, he may have been sufficiently interested in Bright's disease to remove a kidney from Catherine Eddows' body for examination.

There was also evidence against a deranged shoemaker called Kosminski. This was based on the fact that a leather apron similar to the ones that he wore, was found next to Annie Chapman's body.

Whoever it was, one thing is clear. We shall never know, for sure, exactly who Jack the Ripper was. Certainly, there were no more murders after Druitt's sodden body was dragged from the Thames. Was he the Ripper? If so, he took his dark secret to the murky depths of the river with him. If not, then someone else took the secret to his grave – for the only person who could know for sure the identity of Jack the Ripper was Jack the Ripper himself..

MR EVANS

Hayden McAllister

Philip Maddison and his cousin Stewart Johnson attended Sealyn School. Both boys were thirteen and shared the same desk in class, but whereas Philip was proficient only at English composition and Nature study, Stewart seemed to excel at most subjects.

According to Mr Tonks, their class teacher, the brown-haired Philip was a dreamer and didn't take his work seriously enough. Soon however, Mr Tonks's opinion would stand for nothing in the school for at the beginning of the autumn term a new teacher would be arriving to be Philip's class master. Rumour had it that the new teacher 'Mr Evans' was an ex-military man – but for the time being Philip wasn't too concerned with school, for it was still the summer break.

Both Philip and Stewart lived on the dockland housing estate and Philip's front door was less than three hundred yards from the North Sea. During the long summer evenings he would take his bicycle down to the beach and sometimes pedal, and sometimes walk along the shingle. He loved watching the fishing boats ploughing through the rough grey waters at full tide, followed by the hungry flocks of shrieking seagulls. On occasions when the tide was fully out he would kick his football along the sands.

To the east lay the dock area with two concrete piers stretching out like pincers. At the end of one pier was a lighthouse, while on the other stood a port beacon which acted as a warning light to guide vessels entering the docks at night. From his bedroom window Philip could see the beacon glowing like a red star above the North Sea.

Not far from the lighthouse was a barnacle-covered rock and sea-birds, more especially cormorants and shags, often perched there after feeding with fish sticking out of their gullets. These tall black birds looked for all the world like passengers queuing for a bus.

At low tide Philip would walk out to this rock and climb up and stand at the 'Cormorants Bus Stop' and gazing out to sea he would watch the empty coal ships in the offshore waters till the tides changed. Then the boats would steam into Sealyn Docks to collect their cargoes of coal. Railway trucks brought the coal to the port side from the local pits and the dock was fitted with loading bays and mechanical coal chutes, enabling the coal to be poured directly into the holds of the coal ships.

Coal was big business in Sealyn and the town boasted three pits. One high on Sealyn Hill Road beyond the school and the other two near the coast road. The one called Sealyn Old Colliery had coal shafts probing out nearly two miles underneath the sea. Philip's father worked as a miner there and it was thought that Philip would one day take a job at the Old Colliery. But Philip's secret ambition was to become a professional footballer and when Sunderland Football Club played their home matches he travelled to the Roker Park ground with his father and cousin Stewart. Naturally he roared with delight when his team scored – but he also tried to learn as he watched, committing to memory some of the moves the more skilful players made.

But when Philip concentrated on playing his own game, all those skilful moves seemed to 'stick in his head', and when he was challenged for the ball, he found it very difficult to put his ideas and theories into practice. In fact the harder he tried, the harder it became. Often he would trip over the ball or lose possession in a tackle, and he knew he would have to improve a great deal before he was even considered for the school team.

Meanwhile he plodded on with his lessons, taking special interest in English composition and Nature study. But as for geometry and algebra – *they* made his head spin, and quite often when he was supposed to be doing his lessons he'd be day-dreaming about football – or thinking of the beach on a summer's day.

But the arrival of Mr Evans – his new class teacher – was to change all that.

★   ★   ★   ★

Sealyn School was situated halfway up Sealyn Hill Road, partially in the shadow of Hill Top Pit. On two sides of the school lay asphalt playgrounds, while at the rear of the building the playing fields stretched almost to the railway embankment.

Many years ago a pupil had been injured on the railway tracks and now a tall metal fence topped with coiled barbed-wire separated the sports field from the main Newcastle to Middlesborough railway line.

In Philip's class there were the usual mixture of pupils: Chambers the 'Swot' who spent all his spare time studying at home. This admirable sense of dedication did not give him pride of place at the head of the class however – that distinction went to Malcolm Keenan, the 'Prof', who casually designed micro-wave ovens and intergalactic transporters on the rear pages of his exercise books. What was even more astonishing was the fact that his inventions worked – in *theory* at least. There was a well-founded rumour that Keenan was a 'genius'; but Nature – as if to balance her gifts – had given him a trait of professorial absent-mindedness and a huge shock of carrot red hair – which he often 'forgot' to comb. Nevertheless the 'Prof' always had top marks in Maths, Science, Geography, History etc. . . .

Next on the list of school chums was Stewart Johnson – Philip's counsin. 'Stewie' was the sportsman of the class *and* the school. He was captain of the cricket and football teams and could give any boy ten yards start and beat him over half a mile. He was also a good scholar and generally finished in the top five. John Smith was the poet, and 'Smithers' often used his talent to make rhymes about his class mates and the most hated teachers.

The bully of the class was Bill Baxter. He was a big-boned lad with squinting eyes set in a face the colour of uncooked dough. He lived on fear – other people's fear. Most of his classmates hated him. Baxter reckoned that if he made enough noise and trouble, people would sit up and take notice of him. He was the type of boy who liked torturing weaklings and animals, not realizing that this was an outward sign of his own inner brutality. But for all that he also had a better side to his nature, if you dug deep enough to find it.

The first morning of the new term found Philip walking towards school alone. He'd called for cousin Stewart but Mrs Johnson told him that Stewart was in bed with tonsilitis.

On the way up Sealyn Hill Road, Philip began wondering how Sunderland Football Club were faring on their North American tour. For such a big nation Philip thought it odd that the Americans couldn't produce a decent soccer team. Still on the subject Philip made up his mind to be his level best to get into the school eleven and the thought of a football training session that morning sent his blood racing. To put in a good performance during the first sports' session would certainly heighten his chances of getting into the team.

Slowly he climbed the road leading to the school. Ahead lay the pit cages, and one of the huge slag-heaps where the pit authorities dumped slate and shale and other non-combustible materials. Directly to his right lay the Sealyn Sports' Centre.

Suddenly a stone skidded past his feet. He looked around. Along one side of the perimeter fence of the club ran a narrow alleyway. There he saw Bully Boy Baxter throwing stones at a tin can which lay on the ground. Philip was about to pass on when he heard a reedy squeak. There was something trapped inside the can!

Before he realized what he was doing, Philip had taken the few paces necessary to reach the can. As he bent to pick it up Bully Baxter yelled: 'Hands off. That's mine!' Philip hesitated, then the tiny squeal of terror came again.

In a flash Philip had prised off the lid with his pocket knife. Inside was a tiny field mouse shivering with fear. Philip laid down the can and the field mouse scuttled to freedom into the long grass at the side of the boundary fence. The next moment Philip felt a heavy blow on his forehead, then he was staring up at the menacing figure of Bully Baxter.

'Now I'll teach you to mess up my games!' sneered Baxter.

'Why don't you pick on someone your own size?' retorted Philip.

'That's what all white-livered cowards say.'

'Look,' said Philip, steadying himself on one knee. 'I don't mind you picking on me. I was talking about the mouse.'

'I don't like mice,' said Baxter. 'I don't like anything that creeps or crawls. . . .'

'You mean you don't like anything that reminds you of yourself,' provoked Philip.

At this the bigger boy kicked out towards the crouching figure of Philip, but Philip saw the blow coming and moved to one side, grabbing Baxter's foot and twisting it as he did so. The bully crashed onto the pavement with a curse.

Being of lighter build, Philip regained his feet first and sprinted up the alley with Baxter lumbering behind. The next second Philip collided with another figure at the alley entrance and almost stuck out a fist, thinking it to be one of Baxter's cronies. But he looked up into the eyes of a tall man with a military bearing who gazed at both boys in a detached manner. 'You boys seem to be in a great big hurry,' he said. 'Why are you so keen to get to school? Do you enjoy sitting in class-rooms on summer days?'

'No', blurted Philip. 'I was – I thought I would be late.' The stranger then looked at Baxter with an amused expression, but Baxter merely scowled.

'Well let me assure you boys that you have more than a quarter of an hour before school begins – which should give you ample time to walk the fifty yards necessary – or hop – or do whatever you like, so long as you get there in one piece and *don't harm anyone or anything* on the way.' This latter sentence seemed to be directed at Baxter, who stared morosely at his boots.

'Thank you sir,' said Philip, making to pass the stranger.

'Oh. Don't thank me boy,' said the man with a smile. 'My advice is free. But did you thank the sun for shining this morning?'

'The sun?' Philip laughed. 'No, I didn't sir.'

'Then why thank me for mere words and then not thank the sun for its life-giving light?' Disconcerted, Philip replied. 'Never thought about it sir.'

'Well *do* think about it boy. Why do we take life for granted, seeing one side and never the other. I call this "Evans' law of relativity" .'

'I've heard of Einstein's law . . .' began Baxter, 'but never Evans – '
Then he stopped. 'Evans!' he gasped. Mr Evans!?'

'Then you must be our new class master sir,' said Philip after an
awkward silence. The man nodded but said nothing. 'Oh, I'm Philip
Maddison, sir, and this is Bull – er Bill Baxter,' said Philip by way of
introduction.

'Pleased to meet you boys,' said Mr Evans. 'Now perhaps you'd like
to give me your thoughts on school life as we walk towards the
playground?'

★　　★　　★　　★

The first lesson on Nature study with their new class master started
abruptly.

' What can you tell me about bees?' asked Mr Evans.

'They fly, sir,' said Stewart. Someone snorted.

'They do indeed,' said Mr Evans, ignoring the suppressed laughter.
'What else?'

'They sting,' said Baxter.

'But only when severely provoked,' added Philip.

'They buzz', said the 'Prof' absent-mindedly. Everyone laughed. 'I
once designed an inter-galactic fuel transporter sir,' he continued,
'based on the aerodynamic flight potential of a bee outside the earth's
gravitational field.'

'Does it work?' asked Mr Evans.

'Don't know sir. Haven't had a chance to try it.'

'Let me tell you something about bees, Professor,' said Mr Evans.
'According to the earthly laws of aero-dynamics, bees should *not* be
able to fly.'

'You're joking, sir!' said Smithers.

'No. I'm quite serious, Smith. Bees – by flying – are actually defying
the laws of aero-dynamics. Furthermore, when a bee finds, let's say a
patch of clover, he can fly back to the hive and let his fellow bees know
exactly where that clover is. He can tell them what variety of clover it
is, how far the clover is and in what direction they'll find the plants in
relation to the sun.' Mr Evans looked up. 'What have you got to say
about that Baxter?'

'Don't like bees sir. They sting.'
'Do you like honey Baxter?'
'Yes, sir.'
'Bees make honey, Baxter. . . . Now what does honey remind you of boys?'
'Goodness, sir,' said Philip.
'Sunshine,' said Smithers.
'Energy,' said Prof.
'Now these creatures whom Baxter doesn't like – creatures which cannot fly according to textbooks on aero-dynamics – do an intricate dance in their hives and relay complicated information to other bees about food sources. This is just one insight into the miraculous world of Nature. And this is what I want you boys to understand, that the world isn't a dead billiard ball flying around a light bulb called the sun. It's a vast and sensitive organism linked to the solar system which is in turn linked to the heavens. . . . As one poet called Francis Thompson said: "Thou canst not stir a flower, without the troubling of a star." '

'Now on Friday morning I want to explore this subject further by taking half the class out on a Nature Trail. The other half can join Mr Billington's art class and their turn will come next Friday.

'Now, Keenan. Using your scientific mind, could you explain how trees get water up to their higher branches?'
'Capillary action, osmosis and atmospheric pressure, sir.'
'Explain capillary action, please.'
'Well' said the Prof. 'If you dip a long strip of blotting paper into a cup of water – the water will slowly rise up the blotting paper. This is capillary action.'
'Very good explanation Keenan. But according to science, capillary action, osmosis and atmospheric pressure can push the water in a tree up to the height of about 100 feet. Yet some trees – like the Australian Eucalyptus can grow to the height of 300 feet. How they manage to pump the water so high still remains a mystery.'
The Prof looked glum. Apparently science didn't have all the answers. . . .

★　　★　　★　　★

Philip turned up on Wednesday evening at Baydon Colliery School to watch the Sealyn School team play a practice match. Secretly he hoped that someone might drop out of the team at the last moment and that he'd be asked to play. No one did, and by half-time Baydon Colliery led 1–0. It was a goal brilliantly engineered by their outside right who ran fifty yards down the wing, jinking past two players before centring the ball. The centre-forward threw himself at the ball, and connected amidst a ruck of players. The ball ricocheted off his shin and grazed a post before it ended up in the back of the net.

Philip heard a voice say, 'Brave lad', and turning he saw Mr Evans dressed in an old tweed jacket and smoking a briar pipe.

'Hello, sir. I didn't know you liked football.'

'I love the game, Maddison,' replied the teacher, enthusiastically. 'It has all the elements of classical drama, skill, unpredictability – a villain – a hero, with occasional moves which have an almost poetical beauty.

'Of course, there's not always a story-book ending, for the script isn't written beforehand. In football, fate and the elements always take a hand.' Mr Evans looked at Philip. 'But why aren't you playing, Maddison? You're not injured, are you?'

Philip blushed. 'I've never been able to make the grade, sir. I guess I'm just not good enough.'

'Why not? Do you practise?'

'Yes, sir. But although I know how to play in theory – I can't do it when I'm playing for real.' Mr Evans looked thoughtful. 'Well – I can spare a couple of hours on Saturday morning. If your parents are agreeable, I'll meet you down on Sealyn Beach around ten o'clock. I believe the tide will be out. . . . And bring your football.'

'Gosh! Thanks sir!'

★   ★   ★   ★

Friday morning, the day of the proposed 'Nature Trail', dawned clear and Philip was happy to do as Mr Evans suggested. . . . He thanked the sun for shining, for if it had been raining, the expedition would certainly have been cancelled.

Nine pupils – one half of the class – Bully Baxter, Stewart, Smithers, Stevie, Prof, Lanky, the Swot, Tubby and Philip accompanied Mr

Evans out of the school gate. It was only when they got around the corner and out of sight of the school that he announced: 'I've hired a mini-bus to take us to the Baydon Black Beach gentlemen.'

'The Black Beach!' gasped Stewart. 'But that's out of bounds sir!'

'I've received permission from the National Coal Board to explore the beach, so let's get cracking. I presume you've all brought your sandwiches?'

The Black Beach lay seven miles up the coast from Sealyn Sands. And while the Sealyn sands were a bright surf-washed yellow, the Black Beach was a bizarre mixture of colours. For twenty years coal and shale dust had been poured into the sea and the level of the sands at Baydon had been slowly raised as waves spread the coal dust up to the edge of the limestone cliffs. As time passed, the colour of the beach had turned black. Soon the shore became shelved until gradually the waves began to fall well short of the cliffs. Now the sea had been forced back to a distance of nearly a mile from the cliff face. Marram grass had sprung up, followed by wild sea flowers; Common Tamarisk, Sea Campion, Bloody Cranesbill, Purple Thistle, Green Seablite and Golden Samphire. There were also great clumps of bleached driftwood strewn upon the vast beach, and due to chemical reaction, oxides caused red blushes to appear on the blackened sands, and these colours were in turn mingled with green and yellow sulphur marks.

Rare birds and butterflies, completely undisturbed, had found their way to the strange beach and made it their home. Because of the high cliffs, no one could descend and the one straggling footpath was barred by a fence warning off any would-be trespassers. It was an untouched wilderness, a paradise for wild life.

The first thing the boys did under Mr Evans's supervision was to build a small bonfire under the lee of the shelving beach. As the wind blew off the land, it was sheltered and with the sun shining clear in the late August sky the air was pleasantly warm. The fire was built to boil water so that the boys could have tea with their sandwiches. As the logs burned, Mr Evans pointed to the strange colours of the flames; red, green and yellow – due to the wood being impregnated with sea salt. He also remarked on 'lambent' flames. These flames played on the surface of the driftwood without burning the surface. This phenomenon was due to gases escaping from the driftwood and igniting.

Oddly striped 'digger wasps' were their first discovery once their Nature Trail began in earnest. These insects dug themselves small holes in the cleaner sand. Mr Evans explained briefly the difference between wasps and bees, then set the boys out on a 'discovery' ramble.

Amongst lumps of shale and shingle almost at the water's edge, Baxter found a white flower strangely fragile and incongruous against the black shore. He called out with a yell to Mr Evans who identified it as Sea Campion. Baxter wanted to take a section to grow at home, but Mr Evans pointed out that the sea and sand didn't inhabit Baxter's front garden and that the plant would die in such an alien environment.

Mr Evans told the boys about sea currents, about whales and porpoises and how gigantic marine forests had been found near Tierra del Guego with monster sea-weed growing nearly six hundred feet high.

Were these plants related to Baxter's flower, asked the Swot?

'Everything is linked in some way or another,' said Mr Evans. 'When a man looks through a telescope he sees a cluster of objects in space. When he peers through a microscope he sees a similar pattern as if to show that the same agency is at work. A sparrow, without being taught, recognizes a kestrel as an enemy. A swallow can find its way to South Africa. A pigeon is born with a star map in his head and homing instinct within its breast. Not in its tiny brain,' added Mr Evans – 'but in the pigeon *spirit*.'

'I don't understand when you say everything is linked,' said Philip, puzzled.

'Look,' said Mr Evans. 'We all need the sun – otherwise we couldn't survive. It's the same for plants and animals, they'd die too. And when we eat our food it's a kind of sacrament – so long as we eat the plant or vegetable in the right way. This is why people used to say Grace before meal times.

'An apple will thank you if you eat it in the right way. If you don't – you'll get bellyache. Right Baxter?'

'Dunno sir.'

'Try it Baxter. Have any of you heard of the experiments with plants. How even the scientists have proved that plants are sensitive and feel things?'

'Science is the greatest of all arts,' murmured Keenan dreamily.

'Mmm. I'm not sure about that,' said Mr Evans. 'Remember,

'I love the game, Maddison,' replied the teacher, enthusiastically.

Professor, that poets knew that plants were sensitive at least two thousand years before the scientists actually proved it by experiment.'

Keenan blinked. 'What instruments did they use sir?' he asked, face lined with suspicion.

'Intuition, Professor. And sensitivity. They found in a deeper part of themselves something which was linked to all things – showing that we are all interrelated. Have you ever spoken to a tree or smiled at the sun, Keenan?'

Keenan took off his spectacles and polished them gravely. 'You're surely not serious, sir?'

'Trees are the highest vegetables on the earth, Professor, the humans the highest animals – so why shouldn't they be friends? And as for the sun – which scientist discovered that?'

'It was already there, sir,' said the Prof.

'Exactly,' smiled Mr Evans. 'And can you tell me what has been discovered that wasn't *already* there?'

Deep thought lines bit into the Professor's brow. 'Theoretically – nothing, sir,' he answered at last. 'Because to be discovered – it already *had* to be there.'

'You're learning fast, Professor. Next question – what or who put all the things discovered and all the things *to be* discovered there?'

'I've yet to discover that, sir.'

'Drop me a line when you do,' said Mr Evans with a wry smile.

For the rest of the morning Mr Evans tried to let each boy express himself in his own way. Smithers wrote poetry about his experiences at the Black Beach. The Prof compiled a scientific thesis on the relationship between the environment and the multitude of plants and creatures growing and living at Baydon. The Swot made a list of plants, birds, weeds and butterflies, helped by Stewart who copied and sketched leaf formations, colourings and characteristics of plant and bird life.

Baxter climbed up to a high ledge with some crayons and a sketch pad and sketched the unusual scene which unfurled before him. Philip wrote an essay titled 'My day on Baydon Beach' and described his own feelings as a new world unfolded before his eyes.

'Can we do this more often sir?' asked Philip as they got ready to leave the beach at lunchtime. 'Of course,' said Mr Evans. 'We'll get out as much as possible and visit the Wild Fowl Trust, the parks, woods and other areas of the beach. But if you've enjoyed yourselves, why not take the initiative and form small groups – learning to look after yourselves – discovering for yourselves. Or if you wish to go alone, take your note-pad and sketch book and keep your eyes open. Be observant and you'll be amazed at what life has to tell you.

'Most people are so busy thinking about their own petty affairs that they never "see" the amazing world of Nature. So look out for every thing from the star constellations in the heavens to the daisies in the fields – and if you do it gently without trying to grab at the beauty of life – its spirit may bring you a gift much more precious than gold.'

★   ★   ★   ★

'Why is it that everything becomes so much more interesting when Mr Evans is around?' asked Philip's mother at Saturday morning breakfast.

Philip shrugged. 'Because he's different I suppose.'

'Different!?' His dad looked over the top of his newspaper. 'In what way?'

' 'Cos he seems to make ordinary things come alive,' said Philip. 'Take that water in your tea-cup. Where did it come from?'

'Out of the tank of course,' answered his father in astonishment. 'Where else?'

'But before that it was in the river or the sea, and before that maybe as a cloud passing over Russia. . . .'

Philip's dad looked at his tea with new found suspicion. 'Russian tea, you mean?!'

'I don't mean that, dad,' protested Philip. 'Everything is linked Mr Evans says. If it wasn't for the sun there'd be no tea, or people to drink it. No cows in the field to eat the grass and make the milk. No sugar cane and tea plants in foreign countries and ships that fetch them here. All that goes into making your cup of tea dad.'

'Knowing all that doesn't make it *taste* any different though,' said Philip's dad.

★   ★   ★   ★

When Philip arrived on the beach Mr Evans was already there, scouring the horizon with his binoculars. But as soon as Philip approached he laid them down.

'Good morning! Now – about this football, young Philip!'

'Good morning sir. Thank-you for coming.'

First Mr Evans helped Philip practise passing, trapping and heading the ball, then after half an hour he smiled. 'That's fine! Now you try and get past me with the ball at your feet and I'll tackle you. . . .'

Straight away Philip blundered, either pushing the ball too far forward or getting caught in possession. At the sixth attempt a frown of concentration puckered Philip's face – but as usual, the harder he tried, the worse he played.

Finally Mr Evans picked up the ball and beckoned Philip to him. 'Now when you see Pelé or Best playing soccer – what strikes you?'

'Their skill sir?'

'Apart from that?'

'Don't know sir.'

'How "natural" they appear? You see they are *relaxed*, almost casual, for their game is *instinctive*. Your game Philip is all in your head. You've got to trust your body and the *moment* of challenge to show you what to do.'

'How do you mean sir?'

'Well – you know the usual technique – how to pass, trap and head a ball. But when it comes to beating your man, you hesitate. So learn to trust yourself. Throw away all the clever ideas and take the situation as it comes.

'In a man to man situation you can take your eyes off the ball. Make a move one way. Tempt your man. Watch him. Once you've thrown him off balance use that moment to push the ball past him – and he's left tackling your shadow. Come on – try it!'

An hour passed – but Philip didn't improve at all and at the end of two hours he doubted his ability more than ever. At least now he knew that Mr Evans wasn't a miracle worker.

A cloud crossed the sun and at the same time a big black shadow passed over Philip's secret dream to become a professional footballer. Finally, Philip grew tired and dispirited, until Mr Evans suggested they call it a day.

As they reached the coast road Mr Evans spoke: 'I'm thinking of starting a school newspaper Philip. We can use some of the material we collected on the Baydon Beach expedition for a start, and there'll be room for various articles, quizzes, drawings puzzles and short stories. As there was so much promise in your essay on your day at the Black Beach – perhaps you'd like to do a football report on the next game played by the school team?'

'Football reporter . . . ?' said Philip, half to himself. The dream had escaped from the shadows, and this time it was more realistic. . . .

'It's nothing much, I know,' prompted Mr Evans, 'But it'll be a beginning.'

'Yes sir,' said Philip. 'I'd like to write about football matches very much!'

As Philip walked home to his dinner the sun came out and a brighter dream glowed in his heart.

SOME WORDS WITH A MUMMY

Edgar Allan Poe

The *symposium* of the preceding evening had been a little too much for my nerves. I had a wretched headache, and was desperately drowsy. Instead of going out, therefore, to spend the evening, as I had proposed, it occurred to me that I could not do a wiser thing than just eat a mouthful of supper and go immediately to bed.

A *light* supper, of course. I am exceedingly fond of Welsh rabbit. More than a pound at once, however, may not at all times be advisable. Still, there can be no material objection to two. And really between two and three, there is merely a single unit of difference. I ventured, perhaps, upon four. My wife will have it five; but, clearly, she has confounded two very distinct affairs. The abstract number, five, I am willing to admit; but, concretely, it has reference to bottles of brown stout, without which, in the way of condiment, Welsh rabbit is to be eschewed.

Having thus concluded a frugal meal and donned my nightcap, with the serene hope of enjoying it till noon the next day, I placed my head upon the pillow, and through the aid of a capital conscience, fell into a profound slumber forthwith.

But when were the hopes of humanity fulfilled? I could not have completed my third snore when there came a furious ringing at the street-door bell, and then an impatient thumping at the knocker, which awakened me at once. In a minute afterward, and while I was still rubbing my eyes, my wife thrust in my face a note, from my old friend, Doctor Ponnonner. It ran thus:

'Come to me, by all means, my dear good friend, as soon as you receive this. Come and help us to rejoice. At last, by long persevering diplomacy, I have gained the assent of the Directors of the City Museum, to my examination of the Mummy—you know the one I mean. I have permission to unswathe it, and open it, if desirable. A few friends only will be present—you, of course. The Mummy is now at my house, and we shall begin to unroll it at eleven tonight.—Yours ever,

PONNONNER.'

By the time I had reached the 'Ponnonner', it struck me that I was as wide awake as a man need be. I leaped out of bed in an ecstasy, over-throwing all in my way; dressed myself with a rapidity truly marvellous; and set off, at the top of my speed, for the doctor's.

There I found a very eager company assembled. They had been awaiting me with much impatience. The Mummy was extended upon the dining-table; and the moment I entered, its examination was commenced.

It was one of a pair brought, several years previously, by Captain Arthur Sabretash, a cousin of Ponnonner's, from a tomb near Eleithias, in the Lybian Mountains, a considerable distance above Thebes on the Nile. The grottoes at this point, although less magnificent than the Theban sepulchres, are of higher interest, on account of affording more numerous illustrations of the private life of the Egyptians. The chamber from which our specimen was taken, was said to be very rich in such illustrations—the walls being completely covered with fresco-paintings and bas-reliefs, while statues, vases, and mosaic work of rich patterns, indicated the vast wealth of the deceased.

The treasure had been deposited in the Museum precisely in the same condition in which Captain Sabretash had found it—that is to say, the coffin had not been disturbed. For eight years it had thus stood, subject only externally to public inspection. We had now, therefore, the complete Mummy at our disposal; and to those who are aware how very rarely the unransacked antique reaches our shores, it will be evident, at once, that we had great reason to congratulate ourselves upon our good fortune.

Approaching the table, I saw on it a large box, or case, nearly seven feet long, and perhaps three feet wide, by two feet and a half deep. It was oblong—not coffin-shaped. The material was at first supposed to be the wood of the sycamore *(platanus)*, but upon cutting into it, we found it to be pasteboard, or, more properly, *papier-mâché*, composed of papyrus. It was thickly ornamented with paintings, representing funeral scenes, and other mournful subjects—interspersed among which, in every variety of position, were certain series of hieroglyphical characters, intended, no doubt, for the name of the departed. By good luck, Mr Gliddon formed one of our party; and he had no difficulty in translating the letters, which were simply phonetic, and represented the word, *Allamistakeo*.

We had some difficulty in getting this case open without injury; but, having at length accomplished the task, we came to a second, coffin-shaped, and very considerably less in size than the exterior one, but resembling it precisely in every other respect. The interval between the two was filled with resin, which had, in some degree, defaced the colours of the interior box.

Upon opening this latter (which we did quite easily) we arrived at a third case, also coffin-shaped, and varying from the second one in no particular, except in that of its material, which was cedar, and still emitted the peculiar and highly aromatic odour of that wood. Between the second and the third case there was no interval—the one fitting accurately within the other.

Removing the third case, we discovered and took out the body itself. We had expected to find it, as usual, enveloped in frequent rolls or bandages of linen; but, in place of these, we found a sort of sheath, made of papyrus, and coated with a layer of plaster, thickly gilt and painted. The paintings represented subjects connected with the various supposed duties of the soul, and its presentation to different divinities, with numerous identical human figures, intended, very probably, as portraits of the persons embalmed. Extending from head to foot, was a columnar, or perpendicular inscription, in phonetic hieroglyphics, giving again his name and titles, and the names and titles of his relations.

We found a sort of sheath made of papyrus.

Around the neck thus ensheathed, was a collar of cylindrical glass beads, diverse in colour, and so arranged as to form images of deities, of the scarabæus, etc., with the winged globe. Around the small of the waist was a similar collar or belt.

Stripping off the papyrus, we found the flesh in excellent preservation, with no perceptible odour. The colour was reddish. The skin was hard, smooth, and glossy. The teeth and hair were in good condition. The eyes (it seemed) had been removed, and glass ones substituted, which were very beautiful, and wonderfully life-like, with the exception of somewhat too determined a stare. The fingers and the nails were brilliantly gilded.

Mr Gliddon was of opinion, from the redness of the epidermis, that the embalmment had been effected altogether by asphaltum; but, on scraping the surface with a steel instrument, and throwing into the fire some of the powder thus obtained, the flavour of camphor and other sweet-scented gums became apparent.

We searched the corpse very carefully for the usual openings through which the entrails are extracted, but, to our surprise, we could discover none. No member of the party was at that period aware that entire or unopened mummies are not unfrequently met. The brain it was customary to withdraw through the nose; the intestines through an incision in the side; the body was then shaved, washed, and salted; then laid aside for several weeks, when the operation of embalming, properly so called, began.

As no trace of an opening could be found, Doctor Ponnonner was preparing his instruments for dissection, when I observed that it was then past two o'clock. Hereupon it was agreed to postpone the internal examination until the next evening; and we were about to separate for the present, when some one suggested an experiment or two with the Voltaic pile.

The application of electricity to a mummy three or four thousand years old at the least, was an idea, if not very sage, still sufficiently original, and we all caught it at once. About one-tenth in earnest and nine-tenths in jest, we arranged a battery in the doctor's study, and conveyed thither the Egyptian.

It was only after much trouble that we succeeded in laying bare some portions of the temporal muscle which appeared of less stony rigidity than other parts of the frame, but which, as we had anticipated, of course, gave no indication of galvanic susceptibility when brought in contact with the wire. This, the first trial, indeed, seemed decisive, and, with a hearty laugh at our own absurdity, we were bidding each other goodnight, when my eyes, happening to fall upon those of the Mummy, were there immediately riveted in amazement. My brief glance, in fact, had sufficed to assure me that the orbs which we had all supposed to be glass, and which were originally noticeable for a certain wild stare, were now so far covered by the lids, that only a small portion of the *tunica albuginea* remained visible.

With a shout I called attention to the fact, and it became immediately obvious to all.

I cannot say that I was *alarmed* at the phenomenon, because 'alarmed' is, in my case, not exactly the word. It is possible, however, that, but for the brown stout, I might have been a little nervous. As for the rest of the company, they really made no attempt at concealing the downright fright which possessed them. Doctor Ponnonner was a man to be pitied. Mr Gliddon, by some peculiar process, rendered himself invisible. Mr Silk Buckingham, I fancy, will scarcely be so bold as to deny that he made his way, upon all fours, under the table.

After the first shock of astonishment, however, we resolved, as a matter of course, upon further experiment forthwith. Our operations were now directed against the great toe of the right foot. We made an incision over the outside of the exterior *os sesamoideum pollicis pedis,* and thus got at the root of the *abductor* muscle. Readjusting the battery, we now applied the fluid to the bisected nerves, when, with a movement of exceeding life-likeness, the Mummy first drew up its right knee so as to bring it nearly in contact with the abdomen, and then, straightening the limb with inconceivable force, bestowed a kick upon Doctor Ponnonner, which had the effect of discharging that gentleman, like an arrow from a catapult, through a window into the street below.

We rushed out *en masse* to bring in the mangled remains of the victim, but had the happiness to meet him upon the staircase, coming up in an unaccountable hurry, brimful of the most ardent philosophy, and more than ever impressed with the necessity of prosecuting our experiments with vigour and with zeal.

It was by his advice, accordingly, that we made, upon the spot, a profound incision into the tip of the subject's nose, while the doctor himself, laying violent hands upon it, pulled it into vehement contact with the wire.

Morally and physically—figuratively and literally—was the effect electric. In the first place, the corpse opened its eyes, and winked very rapidly for several minutes, as does Mr Barnes in the pantomime; in the second place, it sneezed; in the third, it sat up on end; in the fourth, it shook its fist in Doctor Ponnonner's face; in the fifth, turning to Messieurs Gliddon and Buckingham, it addressed them, in very capital Egyptian, thus—

'I must say, gentlemen, that I am as much surprised as I am mortified, at your behaviour. Of Doctor Ponnonner nothing better was to be expected. He is a poor little fat fool who *knows* no better. I pity and forgive him. But you, Mr Gliddon—and you, Silk—who have travelled and resided in Egypt until one might imagine you to the manner born—you, I say, who have been so much among us that you speak Egyptian fully as well, I think, as you write your mother tongue—you, whom I have always been led to regard as the firm friend of the mummies—I really did anticipate more gentlemanly conduct from *you*. What am I to think of your standing quietly by and seeing me thus unhandsomely used? What am I to suppose by your permitting Tom, Dick, and Harry to strip me of my coffins, and my clothes, in this wretchedly cold climate? In what light (to come to the point) am I to regard your aiding and abetting that miserable little villain, Doctor Ponnonner, in pulling me by the nose?'

It will be taken for granted, no doubt, that upon hearing this speech under the circumstances, we all either made for the door, or fell into violent hysterics, or went off in a general swoon. One of these three things, was, I say, to be expected. Indeed each and all of these lines of conduct might have been very plausibly pursued. And, upon my word, I am at a loss to know how or why it was that we pursued neither the one nor the other. But, perhaps, the true reason is to be sought in the spirit of the age, which proceeds by the rule of contraries altogether, and is now usually admitted as the solution of everything in the way of paradox and impossibility. Or perhaps, after all, it was only the Mummy's exceedingly natural and matter-of-course air that divested his words of the terrible. However this may be, the facts are clear, and no member of our party betrayed any very particular trepidation, or seemed to consider that anything had gone very especially wrong.

For my part I was convinced it was all right, and merely stepped aside, out of the range of the Egyptian's fist. Doctor Ponnonner thrust his hands into his breeches pockets, looked hard at the Mummy, and grew excessively red in the face. Mr Gliddon stroked his whiskers and drew up the collar of his shirt. Mr Buckingham hung down his head, and put his right thumb into the left corner of his mouth.

The Egyptian regarded him with a severe countenance for some minutes, and at length, with a sneer, said—

'Why don't you speak, Mr Buckingham? Did you hear what I asked you, or not? *Do* take your thumb out of your mouth!'

Mr Buckingham, hereupon, gave a slight start, took his right thumb out of the left corner of his mouth, and by way of indemnification, inserted his left thumb in the right corner of the aperture above mentioned.

Not being able to get an answer from Mr B, the figure turned peevishly to Mr Gliddon, and, in a peremptory tone, demanded in general terms what we all meant.

Mr Gliddon replied at great length, in phonetics; and but for the deficiency of American printing-offices in hieroglyphical type, it would afford me much pleasure to record here, in the original, the whole of his very excellent speech.

I may as well take this occasion to remark, that all the subsequent conversation in which the Mummy took a part, was carried on in primitive Egyptian, through the medium (so far as concerned myself and other untravelled members of the company)—through the medium, I say, of Messieurs Gliddon and Buckingham, as interpreters. These gentlemen spoke the mother-tongue of the mummy with inimitable fluency and grace; but I could not help observing that (owing, no doubt, to the introduction of images entirely modern, and, of course, entirely novel to the stranger) the two travellers were reduced, occasionally, to the employment of sensible forms for the purpose of conveying a particular meaning. Mr Gliddon, at one period, for example, could not make the Egyptian comprehend the term 'politics', until he sketched upon the wall, with a bit of charcoal, a little carbuncle-nosed gentleman, out at elbows, standing upon a stump, with his left leg drawn back, his right arm thrown forward, with his fist shut, the eyes rolled up toward heaven, and the mouth open at an angle of ninety degrees. Just in the same way Mr Buckingham failed to convey the absolutely modern idea, 'Whig', until (at Doctor Ponnonner's suggestion) he grew very pale in the face, and consented to take off his own.

It will be readily understood that Mr Gliddon's discourse turned chiefly upon the vast benefits accruing to science from the unrolling and disembowelling of mummies; apologising, upon this score, for any disturbance that might have been occasioned *him*, in particular, the individual mummy called Allamistakeo; and concluding with a mere hint (for it could scarcely be considered more) that, as these little matters were now explained, it might be as well to proceed with the investigation intended. Here Doctor Ponnonner made ready his instruments.

In regard to the latter suggestions of the orator, it appears that Allamistakeo had certain scruples of conscience, the nature of which I did not distinctly learn; but he expressed himself satisfied with the apologies tendered, and, getting down from the table, shook hands with the company all round.

When this ceremony was at an end, we immediately busied ourselves in repairing the damages which our subject had sustained from the scalpel. We sewed up the wound in his temple, bandaged his foot, and applied a square inch of black plaster to the tip of his nose.

It was now observed that the Count (this was the title, it seems, of Allamistakeo) had a slight fit of shivering—no doubt from the cold. The doctor immediately repaired to his wardrobe, and soon returned with a black dress coat, made in Jennings' best manner, a pair of sky-blue plaid pantaloons, with straps, a pink gingham *chemise*, a flapped vest of brocade, a white sack overcoat, a walking cane with a hook, a hat with no brim, patent-leather boots, straw-coloured kid gloves, an eye-glass, a pair of whiskers, and a waterfall cravat. Owing to the disparity of size between the Count and the doctor (the proportion being as two to one), there was some little difficulty in adjusting these habiliments upon the person of the Egyptian; but when all was arranged, he might have been said to be dressed. Mr Gliddon, therefore, gave him his arm, and led him to a comfortable chair by the fire, while the doctor rang the bell upon the spot and ordered a supply of cigars and wine.

The conversation soon grew animated. Much curiosity was, of course, expressed in regard to the somewhat remarkable fact of Allamistakeo's still remaining alive.

'I should have thought,' observed Mr Buckingham, 'that is it high time you were dead.'

'Why,' replied the Count, very much astonished, 'I am little more than seven hundred years old! My father lived a thousand, and was by no means in his dotage when he died.'

Here ensued a brisk series of questions and computations, by means of which it became evident that the antiquity of the Mummy had been grossly misjudged. It had been five thousand and fifty years, and some months, since he had been consigned to the catacombs at Eleithias.

'But my remark,' resumed Mr Buckingham, 'had no reference to your age at the period of interment (I am willing to grant, in fact, that you are still a young man); and my allusion was to the immensity of time during which, by your own showing, you must have been done up in asphaltum.'

'In what?' said the Count.

'In asphaltum,' persisted Mr B.

'Ah, yes; I have some faint notion of what you mean; it might be made to answer, no doubt—but in my time we employed scarcely anything else than the Bichloride of Mercury.'

'But what we are especially at a loss to understand,' said Doctor Ponnonner, 'is, how it happens that, having been dead and buried in Egypt five thousand years ago, you are here to-day all alive, and looking so delightfully well.'

'Had I been, as you say, *dead*,' replied the Count, 'it is more than probable that dead I should still be; for I perceive you are yet in the infancy of galvanism, and cannot accomplish with it what was a common thing among us in the old days. But the fact is, I fell into catalepsy, and it was considered by my best friends that I was either dead or should be; they accordingly embalmed me at once—I presume you are aware of the chief principle of the embalming process?'

'Why, not altogether.'

'Ah, I perceive—a deplorable condition of ignorance! Well, I cannot enter into details just now; but it is necessary to explain that to embalm (properly speaking) in Egypt, was to arrest indefinitely *all* the animal functions subjected to the process. I use the word "animal" in its widest sense, as including the physical not more than the moral and *vital* being. I repeat that the leading principle of embalmment consisted, with us, in the immediately arresting, and holding in perpetual abeyance, *all* the animal functions subjected to the process. To be brief, in whatever condition the individual was, at the period of embalmment, in that condition he remained. Now, as it is my good fortune to be of the blood of the Scarabæus, I was embalmed *alive*, as you see me at present.'

'The blood of the Scarabæus!' exclaimed Doctor Ponnonner.

'Yes. The Scarabæus was the *insignium*, or the "arms", of a very distinguished and very rare patrician family. To be "of the blood of the Scarabæus", is merely to be one of that family of which the Scarabæus is the *insignium*. I speak figuratively.'

'But what has this to do with your being alive?'

'Why, it is the general custom in Egypt, to deprive a corpse, before embalmment, of its bowels and brains; the race of the Scarabæi alone did not coincide with the custom. Had I not been a Scarabæus, therefore, I should have been without bowels and brains; and without either it is inconvenient to live.'

'I perceive that,' said Mr Buckingham; 'and I presume that all the *entire* mummies that come to hand are of the race of Scarabæi.'

'Beyond doubt.'

'I thought,' said Mr Gliddon, very meekly, 'that the Scarabæus was one of the Egyptian gods.'

'One of the Egyptian *what*?' exclaimed the Mummy, starting to its feet.

'Gods!' repeated the traveller.

'Mr Gliddon, I really am astonished to hear you talk in this style,' said the Count, resuming his seat. 'No nation upon the face of the earth has ever acknowledged more than *one god*. The Scarabæus, the Ibis, etc., were with us (as similar creatures have been with others) the symbols, or *media*, through which we offered worship to the Creator too august to be more directly approached.'

There was here a pause. At length the colloquy was renewed by Doctor Ponnonner.

'It is not improbable, then, from what you have explained,' said he, 'that among the catacombs near the Nile, there may exist other mummies of the Scarabæus tribe, in a condition of vitality.'

'There can be no question of it,' replied the Count; 'all the Scarabæi embalmed accidentally while alive, are alive. Even some of those *purposely* so embalmed, may have been overlooked by their executors, and still remain in the tombs.'

'Will you be kind enough to explain,' I said, 'what you mean by "purposely so embalmed"?'

'With great pleasure,' answered the Mummy, after surveying me leisurely through his eye-glass—for it was the first time I had ventured to address him a direct question.

'With great pleasure,' he said. 'The usual duration of man's life, in my time, was about eight hundred years. Few men died, unless by most extraordinary accident, before the age of six hundred; few lived longer than a decade of centuries; but eight were considered the natural term. After the discovery of the embalming principle, as I have already described it to you, it occurred to our philosophers that a laudable curiosity might be gratified, and, at the same time, the interests of science much advanced, by living this natural term in instalments. In the case of history, indeed, experience demonstrated that something of this kind was indispensable. An historian, for example, having attained the age of five hundred, would write a book with great labour and then get himself carefully embalmed; leaving instructions to his executors *pro tem.*, that they should cause him to be revivified after the lapse of a certain period—say five or six hundred years. Resuming existence at the expiration of this time, he would invariably find his great work converted into a species of hap-hazard note-book—that is to say, into a kind of literary arena for the conflicting guesses, riddles, and personal squabbles of whole herds of exasperated commentators. These guesses, etc., which passed under the name of annotations, or emendations, were found so completely to have enveloped, distorted, and overwhelmed the text, that the author had to go about with a lantern to discover his own book. When discovered, it was never worth the trouble of the search. After rewriting it throughout, it was regarded as the bounden duty of the historian to set himself to work, immediately, in correcting, from his own private knowledge and experience, the traditions of the day concerning the epoch at which he had originally lived. Now this process of rescription and personal rectification, pursued by various individual sages, from time to time, had the effect of preventing our history from degenerating into absolute fable.'

'I beg your pardon,' said Doctor Ponnonner at this point, laying his hand gently upon the arm of the Egyptian—'I beg your pardon, sir, but may I presume to interrupt you for one moment?'

'By all means, *sir*,' replied the Count, drawing up.

'I merely wished to ask you a question,' said the doctor. 'You mentioned the historian's personal correction of *traditions* respecting his own epoch. Pray, sir, upon an average, what proportion of these Kabbala were usually found to be right?'

'The Kabbala, as you properly term them, sir, were generally discovered to be precisely on a par with the facts recorded in the unrewritten histories themselves; that is to say, not one individual iota of either was ever known, under any circumstances, to be not totally and radically wrong.'

'But since it is quite clear,' resumed the doctor, 'that at least five thousand years have elapsed since your entombment, I take it for granted that your histories at that period, if not your traditions, were sufficiently explicit on that one topic of universal interest, the Creation, which took place, as I presume you are aware, only about ten centuries before.'

'Sir!' said the Count Allamistakeo.

The doctor repeated his remarks, but it was only after much additional explanation that the foreigner could be made to comprehend them. The latter at length said, hesitatingly—

'The ideas you have suggested are to me, I confess, utterly novel. During my time I never knew any one to entertain so singular a fancy as that the universe (or this world, if you will have it so) ever had a beginning at all. I remember once, and once only, hearing something remotely hinted by a man of many speculations concerning the origin *of the human race*; and by this individual the very word *Adam* (or Red Earth), which you make use of, was employed. He employed it, how-

ever, in a generical sense, with reference to the spontaneous germination from rank soil (just as a thousand of the lower *genera* of creatures
are germinated)—the spontaneous germination, I say, of five vast
hordes of men, simultaneously upspringing in five distinct and nearly
equal divisions of the globe.'

Here, in general, the company shrugged their shoulders, and one or
two of us touched our foreheads with a very significant air. Mr Silk
Buckingham, first glancing slightly at the occiput and then at the
siniciput of Allamistakeo, spoke as follows—

'The long duration of human life in your time, together with the
occasional practice of passing it, as you have explained, in instalments,
must have had, indeed, a strong tendency to the general development
and conglomeration of knowledge. I presume, therefore, that we are
to attribute the marked inferiority of the old Egyptians in all particulars
of science, when compared with the moderns, and more especially with
the Yankees, altogether to the superior solidity of the Egyptian skull.'

'I confess again,' replied the Count, with much suavity, 'that I am
somewhat at a loss to comprehend you; pray, to what particulars of
science do you allude?'

Here our whole party, joining voices, detailed, at great length, the
assumptions of phrenology and the marvels of animal magnetism.

Having heard us to an end, the Count proceeded to relate a few
anecdotes, which rendered it evident that prototypes of Gall and
Spurzheim had flourished and faded in Egypt so long ago as to have
been nearly forgotten, and that the manoeuvres of Mesmer were
really very contemptible tricks when put in collation with the positive
miracles of the Theban *savants,* who created lice, and a great many
other similar things.

I here asked the Count if his people were able to calculate eclipses.
He smiled rather contemptuously, and said they were.

This put me a little out; but I began to make other inquiries in
regard to his astronomical knowledge, when a member of the company,
who had never as yet opened his mouth, whispered in my ear, that for
information on this head I had better consult Ptolemy (whoever
Ptolemy is), as well as one Plutarch *de facie lunæ.*

I then questioned the Mummy about burning-glasses and lenses,
and, in general, about the manufacture of glass; but I had not made

an end of my queries before the silent member again touched me quietly on the elbow, and begged me, for God's sake, to take a peep at Diodorus Siculus. As for the Count, he merely asked me, in the way of reply, if we moderns possessed any such microscopes as would enable us to cut cameos in the style of the Egyptians. While I was thinking how I should answer this question, little Doctor Ponnonner committed himself in a very extraordinary way.

'Look at our architecture!' he exclaimed, greatly to the indignation of both the travellers, who pinched him black and blue to no purpose.

'Look!' he cried, with enthusiasm, 'at the Bowling-green Fountain in New York! or, if this be too vast a contemplation, regard for a moment the Capitol at Washington, D.C.!'—and the good little medical man went on to detail, very minutely, the proportions of the fabric to which he referred. He explained that the portico alone was adorned with no less than four and twenty columns, five feet in diameter, and ten feet apart.

The Count said that he regretted not being able to remember, just at that moment, the precise dimensions of any one of the principal buildings of the City of Aznac, whose foundations were laid in the night of Time, but the ruins of which were still standing, at the epoch of his entombment, in a vast plain of sand to the westward of Thebes. He recollected, however (talking of porticoes), that one affixed to an inferior palace in a kind of suburb called Carnac, consisted of a hundred and forty-four columns, thirty-seven feet each in circumference, and twenty-five feet apart. The approach of this portico, from the Nile, was through an avenue two miles long, composed of sphynxes, statues, and obelisks, twenty, sixty, and a hundred feet in height. The palace itself (as well as he could remember) was, in one direction, two miles long, and might have been, altogether, about seven in circuit. Its walls were richly painted all over, within and without, with hieroglyphics. He would not pretend to *assert* that even fifty or sixty of the doctor's Capitols might have been built within these walls, but he was by no means sure that two or three hundred of them might not have been squeezed in with some trouble. That palace at Carnac was an insignificant little building after all. He (the Count), however, could not conscientiously refuse to admit the ingenuity, magnificence, and superiority of the fountain at the Bowling green, as described by the doctor. Nothing like it, he was forced to allow, had ever been seen in Egypt or elsewhere.

I here asked the Count what he had to say to our railroads.

'Nothing,' he replied, 'in particular.' They were rather slight, rather ill-conceived, and clumsily put together. They could not be compared, of course, with the vast, level, direct, iron-grooved causeways, upon which the Egyptians conveyed entire temples and solid obelisks of a hundred and fifty feet in altitude.

I spoke of our gigantic mechanical forces.

He agreed that we knew something in that way, but inquired how I should have gone to work in getting up the imposts on the lintels of even the little palace at Carnac.

This question I concluded not to hear, and demanded if he had any idea of Artesian wells; but he simply raised his eyebrows; while Mr Gliddon winked at me very hard and said, in a low tone, that one had been recently discovered by the engineers employed to bore for water in the Great Oasis.

I then mentioned our steel; but the foreigner elevated his nose, and asked me if our steel could have executed the sharp carved work seen on the obelisks, and which was wrought altogether by edge-tools of copper.

This disconcerted us so greatly that we thought it advisable to vary the attack to Metaphysics. We sent for a copy of a book called the 'Dial', and read out of it a chapter or two about something which is not very clear, but which the Bostonians call the Great Movement or Progress.

The Count merely said that Great Movements were awfully common things in his day, and as for Progress, it was at one time quite a nuisance, but it never progressed.

We then spoke of the great beauty and importance of Democracy, and were at much trouble in impressing the Count with a due sense of the advantages we enjoyed in living where there was suffrage *ad libitum* and no king.

He listened with marked interest, and in fact seemed not a little amused. When we had done he said that, a great while ago, there had occurred something of a very similar sort. Thirteen Egyptian provinces determined all at once to be free, and so set a magnificent example to the rest of mankind. They assembled their wise men, and concocted the most ingenious constitution it is possible to conceive. For a while they managed remarkably well; only their habit of bragging was prodigious. The thing ended, however, in the consolidation of the thirteen states, with some fifteen or twenty others, in the most odious and insupportable despotism that ever was heard of upon the face of the Earth.

I asked what was the name of the usurping tyrant.

As well as the Count could recollect, it was *Mob*.

Not knowing what to say to this, I raised my voice, and deplored the Egyptian ignorance of steam.

The Count looked at me with much astonishment, but made no answer. The silent gentleman, however, gave me a violent nudge in the ribs with his elbows—told me I had sufficiently exposed myself for once—and demanded if I was really such a fool as not to know that the modern steam-engine is derived from the invention of Hero, through Solomon de Caus.

We were now in imminent danger of being discomfited; but, as good luck would have it, Doctor Ponnonner, having rallied, returned to our rescue, and inquired if the people of Egypt would seriously pretend to rival the moderns in the all-important particular of dress.

The Count, at this, glanced downwards to the straps of his pantaloons, and then taking hold of the end of one of his coat-tails, held it up close to his eyes for some minutes. Letting it fall, at last, his mouth extended itself very gradually from ear to ear; but I do not remember that he said anything in the way of reply.

Hereupon we recovered our spirits, and the doctor, approaching the Mummy with great dignity, desired it to say candidly, upon its honour as a gentleman if the Egyptians had comprehended at *any* period the manufacturer of either Ponnonner's lozenges, of Brandreth's pills.

We looked, with profound anxiety, for an answer—but in vain. It was not forthcoming. The Egyptian blushed and hung down his head. Never was triumph more consummate; never was defeat borne with so ill a grace. Indeed, I could not endure the spectacle of the poor Mummy's mortification. I reached my hat, bowed to him stiffly, and took leave.

Upon getting home I found it past four o'clock, and went immediately to bed. It is now ten a.m. I have been up since seven, penning these memoranda for the benefit of my family and of mankind. The former I shall behold no more. My wife is a shrew. The truth is, I am heartily sick of this life, and of the nineteenth century in general. I am convinced that everything is going wrong. Besides, I am anxious to know who will be President in 2405. As soon, therefore, as I shave and swallow a cup of coffee, I shall just step over to Ponnonner's and get embalmed for a couple of hundred years.

PRINCE ANDREY'S WOUND

Leo Tolstoy

Prince Andrey, pale and haggard like every one else in the regiment walked to and fro in the meadow next to the oat-field from one boundary line to the other, with his hands clasped behind his back, and his eyes fixed on the ground. There was no need for him to give orders, and nothing for him to do. Everything was done of itself. The killed were dragged behind the line; the wounded were removed, and the ranks closed up. If any soldiers ran away, they made haste to return at once. At first Prince Andrey, thinking it his duty to keep up the spirits of the men, and set them an example, had walked about among the ranks. But soon he felt that there was nothing he could teach them. All his energies, like those of every soldier, were unconsciously directed to restraining himself from contemplating the horror of his position. He walked about the meadow, dragging one leg after the other, making the grass rustle, and watching the dust, which covered his boots. Then he strode along, trying to step on the traces of the footsteps of the mowers on the meadow; or counting his steps, calculated how many times he would have to walk from one boundary rut to another to make a verst: or cut off the flowers of wormwood growing in the rut, and crushing them in his hands, sniffed at the bitter-sweet, pungent odour. Of all the thoughts of the previous day not a trace remained. He thought of nothing at all. He listened wearily to the sounds that were ever the same, the whiz of the shells above the booming of the cannon, looked at the faces of the men of the first battalion, which he had gazed at to weariness already, and waited. 'Here it comes . . . this one's for us again!' He thought, listening to the whiz of something flying out of the region of smoke. 'One, another! More! Fallen' . . . He stopped short and looked towards the ranks. 'No; it has flown over. But that one has fallen!' And he fell to pacing up and down again, trying to reach the next boundary in sixteen steps.

A whiz and a thud! Five paces from him the dry soil was thrown up, as a cannon-ball sank into the earth. A chill ran down his back; he looked at the ranks. Probably a number had been struck: the men had gathered in a crowd in the second battalion.

'M. l'aide-de-camp,' he shouted, 'tell the men not to crowd together.'

The adjutant, having obeyed this instruction, was approaching Prince Andrey. From the other side the major in command of the battalion came riding up.

'Look out!' rang out a frightened cry from a soldier, and like a bird, with swift, whirring wings alighting on the earth, a grenade dropped with a dull thud a couple of paces from Prince Andrey, near the major's horse. The horse, with no question of whether it were right or wrong to show fear, snorted, reared, almost throwing the major, and galloped away. The horse's terror infected the men.

'Lie down!' shouted the adjutant, throwing himself on the ground. Prince Andrey stood in uncertainty. The shell was smoking and rotating like a top between him and the recumbent adjutant, near a bush of wormwood in the rut between the meadow and the field.

'Can this be death?' Prince Andrey wondered, with an utterly new, listful feeling, looking at the grass, at the wormwood, and at the thread of smoke coiling from the rotating top. 'I can't die, I don't want to die, I love life, I love this grass and earth and air . . .'

He thought this, and yet at the same time he did not forget that people were looking at him.

'For shame, M. l'aide-de-camp!' he said to the adjutant; 'what sort of—' He did not finish. Simultaneously there was a tearing, crashing sound like the smash of broken crockery, a puff of stifling fumes, and

Prince Andrey was sent spinning over, and flinging up one arm, fell on his face. Several officers ran up to him. A great stain of blood was spreading over the grass from the right side of his stomach.

The militiamen stood with their stretchers behind the officers. Prince Andrey lay on his chest, with his face sunk in the grass; he was still breathing in hard, hoarse gasps.

'Well, why are you waiting, come along!'

The peasants went up and took him by the shoulders and legs, but he moaned piteously, and they looked at one another, and laid him down again.

'Pick him up, lay him on, it's all the same!' shouted some one. They lifted him by the shoulders again and laid him on the stretcher.

'Ah, my God! my God! what is it? . . . The stomach! It's all over then! Ah, my God!' could be heard among the officers. 'It almost grazed my ear,' the adjutant was saying. The peasants, with the stretcher across their shoulders, hurried along the path they had trodden to the ambulance station.

'Keep step! . . . Aie! . . . these peasants!' cried an officer, seizing them by the shoulders, as they jogged along, jolting the stretcher.

'Drop into it, Frydor, eh?' said the foremost peasant.

'That's it, first-rate,' said the hindmost, falling into step.

'Your excellency? Eh, prince?' said the trembling voice of Timohin, as he ran up and peeped over the stretcher.

Prince Andrey opened his eyes, and looked at the speaker from the stretcher, through which his head had dropped, and closed his eyelids again.

One of the doctors came out of the tent with a blood-stained apron, and small, blood-stained hands, in one of which he had a cigar, carefully held between his thumb and little finger, that it might not be stained too. This doctor threw his head up, and looked about him, but over the level of the wounded crowd. He was evidently longing for a short respite. After turning his head from right to left for a few minutes, he sighed and dropped his eyes again.

'All right, immediately,' he said in reply to an assistant, who pointed him out Prince Andrey, and he bade the bearers carry him into the tent.

A murmur rose in the crowd of wounded men waiting.

'Even in the next world it's only the gentry who will have a good time,' said one.

Prince Andrey was carried in, and laid on a table that had just been cleared, and was being rinsed over by an assistant. He could not make out distinctly what was in the tent. The pitiful groans on all sides, and the excruciating pain in his thigh, his stomach, and his back distracted his attention. Everything he saw around melted for him into a single general impression of naked, blood-stained, human flesh, which seemed to fill up the whole low-pitched tent, as, a few weeks before, on that hot August day, the bare human flesh had filled up the dirty pond along the Smolensk road. Yes, it was the same flesh, the same *chair à canon,* the sight of which had roused in him then a horror, that seemed prophetic of what he felt now.

There were three tables in the tent. Two were occupied, on the third they laid Prince Andrey. For some time he was left alone, an involuntary witness of what was being done at the other tables.

Having finished with a Tatar, over whom a cloak was thrown, the doctor in spectacles came up to Prince Andrey, wiping his hands.

He glanced at his face, and hurriedly turned away. 'Undress him! Why are you dawdling?' he shouted angrily to the assistant.

His earliest, remotest childhood came back to Prince Andrey, when the assistant, with tucked-up sleeves, hurriedly unbuttoned his buttons, and took off his clothes. The doctor bent close down over the wound, felt it, and sighed deeply. Then he made a sign to some one. And the excruciating pain inside his stomach made Prince Andrey lose consciousness. When he regained consciousness, the broken splinters of his thighbone had been removed, the bits of ragged flesh had been cut off, and the wound bound up. Water was sprinkled on his face. As soon as Prince Andrey opened his eyes, the doctor bent over him, kissed him on the lips without speaking, and hurried away.

After the agony he had passed through, Prince Andrey felt a blissful peace, such as he had not known for very long. All the best and happiest moments of his life, especially his earliest childhood, when he had been undressed and put to bed, when his nurse had sung lullabies over him, when, burying his head in the pillows, he had felt happy in the mere consciousness of life, rose before his imagination, not like the past even, but as though it were the actual present.

And all at once a new, unexpected memory from that childlike world of purity and love rose up before Prince Andrey. He remembered Natasha, as he had seen her for the first time at the ball in 1810, with her slender neck and slender arms, and her frightened, happy face, ready for ecstatic enjoyment, and a love and tenderness awoke in his heart for her stronger and more loving than ever.

On Saturday, the 31st of August, the whole household of the Rostovs seemed turned upside down. All the doors stood wide open, all the furniture had been moved about or carried out, looking-glasses and pictures had been taken down. The rooms were littered up with boxes, with hay and packing paper and cord. Peasants and house-serfs were tramping about the parquet floors carrying out the baggage. The courtyard was crowded with peasants' carts, some piled high with goods and corded up, others still standing empty.

The voices and steps of the immense multitude of servants and of peasants, who had come with the carts, resounded through the court-yard and the house. The count had been out since early morning. The countess had a headache from the noise and bustle, and was lying down in the new divan-room with compresses steeped in vinegar on her head. Petya was not at home; he had gone off to see a comrade, with whom he was planning to get transferred from the militia to a regiment at the front. Sonya was in the great hall, superintending the packing of the china and glass. Natasha was sitting on the floor in her dismantled room among heaps of dresses, ribbons, and scarfs. She sat gazing immovably at the floor, holding in her hands an old ball-dress, the very dress, now out of fashion, in which she had been to her first Petersburg ball.

Natasha was ashamed of doing nothing when every one in the house was so busy, and several times that morning she had tried to set to work; but her soul was not in it; and she was utterly unable to do anything unless all her heart and soul were in it. She stood over Sonya while she packed the china, and tried to help; but soon threw it up, and went to her room to pack her own things. At first she had found it amusing to give away her dresses and ribbons to the maids, but afterwards when it came to packing what was left, it seemed a wearisome task.

'Dunyasha, you'll pack it all dear? Yes? yes?'

And when Dunyasha readily undertook to do it all for her, Natasha sat down on the floor with the old ball-dress in her hands, and fell to dreaming on subjects far removed from what should have been occupying her mind then. From the reverie she had fallen into, Natasha was aroused by the talk of the maids in the next room and their hurried footsteps from their room to the backstairs. Natasha got up and looked out of the window. A huge train of carts full of wounded men had stopped in the street.

The maids, the footmen, the housekeeper, the old nurse, the cooks, the coachmen, the grooms, and the scullion-boys were all at the gates, staring at the wounded men.

Natasha flung a white pocket-handkerchief over her hair, and holding the corners in both hands, went out into the street.

The old housekeeper, Mavra Kuzminishna, had left the crowd standing at the gate, and gone up to a cart with a tilt of bast-mats thrown over it. She was talking to a pale young officer who was lying in this cart. Natasha took a few steps forward, and stood still timidly, holding her kerchief on and listening to what the housekeeper was saying.

'So you have no one then in Moscow?' Mavra Kuzminishna was saying. 'You'd be more comfortable in some apartment.... In our house even. The masters are all leaving.'

'I don't know if it would be allowed,' said the officer in a feeble voice. 'There's our chief officer ... ask him,' and he pointed to a stout major who had turned back and was walking along the row of carts down the street.

Natasha glanced with frightened eyes into the face of the wounded officer, and at once went to meet the major.

'May the wounded men stay in our house?' she asked.

The major with a smile put his hand to his cap.

'What is your pleasure, ma'mselle?' he said, screwing up his eyes and smiling.

Natasha quietly repeated her question, and her face and her whole manner, though she still kept hold of the corners of the pocket-handkerchief, was so serious, that the major left off smiling, and after a moment's pondering—as though asking himself how far it were possible—he gave her an affirmative answer.

'Oh yes, why not, they may,' he said.

Natasha gave a slight nod, and went back with rapid steps to Mavra Kuzminishna, who was still talking with commiserating sympathy to the young officer.

'They may; he said they might!' whispered Natasha.

The officer in the covered-cart turned into the Rostov's courtyard, and dozens of carts of wounded men began at the invitation of the inhabitants to drive up to the entries of the houses in Povarsky Street. Natasha was evidently delighted at having to do with new people in conditions quite outside the ordinary routine of life. She joined Mavra Kuzminishna in trying to get as many as possible driven into their yard.

'We must ask your papa though,' said Mavra Kuzminishna.

'Nonsense, nonsense. What does it matter? For one day, we'll move into the drawing-room. We can give them all our half of the house.'

'What an idea! what next? The lodge, maybe, the men's room, and old nurse's room; and you must ask leave for that.'

'Well, I will ask.'

Natasha ran indoors, and went on tiptoe to the half-open door of the divan-room, where there was a strong smell of vinegar and Hoffmann's drops.

'Are you asleep, mamma?'

'Oh, what chance is there of sleep!' said the countess, who had just dropped into a doze.

'Mamma, darling!' said Natasha, kneeling before her mother and leaning her face against her mother's. 'I am sorry, forgive me, I'll never do it again, I waked you. Mavra Kuzminishna sent me; they have brought some wounded men in, officers, will you allow it? They have nowhere to go; I know you will allow it, . . .' she said rapidly, not taking breath.

'Officers? Who have been brought in? I don't understand,' said the countess.

Natasha laughed, the countess too smiled faintly.

'I knew you would let me . . . so I will tell them so.' And Natasha, kissing her mother, got up and went to the door.

In the hall she met her father, who had come home with bad news. 'We have lingered on too long!' said the count, with unconscious anger in his voice; 'the club's shut up and the police are leaving.'

'Papa, you don't mind my having invited some of the wounded into the house?' said Natasha.

'Of course not,' said the count absently. 'But that's not to the point. I beg you now not to let yourself be taken up with any nonsense, but to help to pack and get off—to get off tomorrow . . .'

And the count gave his butler and servants the same orders.

After dinner all the Rostov household set to work packing and preparing for their departure with eager haste. The old count, suddenly rousing himself to the task, spent the rest of the day continually trotting from the courtyard into the house and back again, shouting confused instructions to the hurrying servants, and trying to spur them on to even greater haste. Petya looked after things in the yard. Sonya was quite bewildered by the count's contradictory orders, and did not know what to do. The servants raced about the rooms, shouting, quarrelling, and making a noise. Natasha, too, suddenly set to work with the ardour that was characteristic of her in all she did. At first her intervention was sceptically received. No one expected anything serious from her or would obey her instructions. But with heat and perseverance, she insisted on being obeyed, got angry and almost shed tears that they did not heed her, and did at last succeed in impressing them.

The packing went on fast now, thanks to Natasha's supervision; everything useless was left behind, and the most valuable goods were packed as compactly as possible.

But with all their exertions, even late at night everything was not ready. The countess had fallen asleep, and the count put off their departure till morning and went to bed.

Sonya and Natasha slept in the divan-room, without undressing.

That night another wounded officer was driven along Povarsky Street, and Mavra Kuzminishna, who was standing at the gate, had him brought into the Rostov's yard. The wounded officer must, Mavra Kuzminishna thought, be a man of very great consequence. He was in a coach with the hood let down and a carriage apron completely covering it. An old man, a most respectable-looking valet, was sitting on the box with the driver. A doctor and two soldiers followed the carriage in another conveyance.

'Come into our house, come in. The masters are going away, the whole house is empty,' said the old woman, addressing the old servant.

'Well,' answered the valet, sighing, 'and indeed we have no hope of getting him home alive! We have a house of our own in Moscow, but it is a long way further, and there's no one living in it either.'

'Pray come in, our masters have plenty of everything, and you are welcome,' said Mavra Kuzminishna. 'Is the gentleman very bad, then?' she asked.

'There's no hope! I must ask the doctor.' And the valet got down and went to the vehicle behind.

'Very good,' said the doctor.

The valet went up to the coach again, peered into it, shook his head, told the coachman to turn into the yard, and stood still beside Mavra Kuzminishna.

'Lord Jesus Christ, have mercy!' she murmured.

Mavra Kuzminishna suggested the wounded man being carried into the house.

'The masters won't say anything . . .' said she.

But they had to avoid lifting him up the steps, and so they carried the wounded man to the lodge, and put him in the room that had been Madame Schoss's. This wounded officer was Prince Andrey Bolkonsky.

By two o'clock the Rostovs' four carriages, packed and ready to start, stood in the approach. The wagon-loads of wounded were filing one after another out of the yard.

The coach in which Prince Andrey was being taken drove by the front door, and attracted the attention of Sonya, who was helping a maid to arrange the countess's seat comfortably in her huge, high carriage.

'Whose carriage is that?' asked Sonya, popping her head out of the carriage window.

'Why, haven't you heard, miss?' answered the maid. 'The wounded prince; he stayed the night in the house, and is going on with us.'

'Oh, who is he? what's his name?'

The wounded officer was Prince Andrey Bolkonsky.

'Our betrothed that was . . . Prince Bolkonsky himself!' answered the maid, sighing. 'They say he is dying.'

Sonya jumped out of the carriage and ran in to the countess. The countess, dressed for the journey, in her hat and shawl, was walking wearily about the drawing-room, waiting for the rest of the household to come in and sit down with closed doors, for the usual silent prayer before setting out. Natasha was not in the room.

'Mamma,' said Sonya, 'Prince Andrey is here, wounded and dying. He is going with us.'

The countess opened her eyes in dismay, and clutching Sonya's arm, looked about her.

'Natasha,' she said.

Both to Sonya and the countess this news had for the first moment but one significance. They knew their Natasha, and alarm at the thought of the effect the news might have on her outweighed all sympathy for the man, though they both liked him.

'Natasha does not know yet, but he is going with us,' said Sonya.

'You say he is dying?'

Sonya nodded.

The countess embraced Sonya and burst into tears. 'The ways of the Lord are past our finding out!' she thought, feeling that in all that was passing now the Hand of the Almighty, hitherto unseen, was beginning to be manifest.

'Well, mamma, it's all ready. What is it? . . .' asked Natasha, running with her eager face into the room.

'Nothing,' said the countess. 'If we're ready, then do let us start.' And the countess bent over her reticule to hide her agitated face. Sonya embraced Natasha and kissed her.

Natasha looked inquisitively at her.

'What is it? What has happened?'

'Nothing, . . . oh, no, . . .'

Something very bad, concerning me? . . . What is it?' asked the keen-witted Natasha.

Sonya sighed, and made no reply. The count, Petya, Madame Schoss, Mavra Kuzminishna, and Vassilitch came into the drawing-room; and closing the doors, they all sat down, and sat so in silence, without looking at each other for several seconds.

The count was the first to get up. With a loud sigh he crossed himself before the holy picture. All the others did the same. Then the count proceeded to embrace Mavra Kuzminishna and Vassilitch, who were to remain in Moscow; and while they caught at his hand and kissed his shoulder, he patted them on the back with vaguely affectionate and reassuring phrases. The countess went off to the little chapel, and Sonya found her there on her knees before the holy pictures, that were still left here and there on the walls. All the holy pictures most precious through association with the traditions of the family were being taken with them.

In the porch and in the yard the servants who were going—all of whom had been armed with swords and daggers by Petya—with their trousers tucked in their boots, and their sashes or leather belts tightly braced, took leave of those who were left behind.

As is invariably the case at starting on a journey, a great many things were found to have been forgotten, or packed in the wrong place; and two grooms were kept a long while standing, one each side of the open carriage door, ready to help the countess up the carriage steps, while maids were flying with pillows and bags from the house to the carriages, the coach, and the covered gig, and back again.

'They will always forget everything as long as they live!' said the countess. 'You know that I can't sit like that.' And Dunyasha, with clenched teeth and an aggrieved look on her face, rushed to the carriage to arrange the cushions again without a word.

'Ah, those servants,' said the count, shaking his head.

The postillion started his horse. The right-shaft horse began to pull, the high springs creaked, and the carriage swayed. The footman jumped up on the box while it was moving. The carriage jolted as it drove out of the yard on to the uneven pavement; the other vehicles jolted in the same way as they followed in a procession up the street. All the occupants of the carriages, the coach and the covered gig, crossed themselves on seeing the church opposite. The servants, who were staying in Moscow, walked along on both sides of the carriages to see them off.

Natasha had rarely felt such a joyful sensation as she experienced at that moment sitting in the carriage by the countess and watching, as they slowly moved by her, the walls of forsaken, agitated Moscow.

Now and then she put her head out of the carriage window and looked back, and then in front at the long train of waggons full of wounded soldiers preceding them. Foremost of them all she could see Prince Andrey's closed carriage. She did not know who was in it, and every time she took stock of the procession of waggons she looked out for that coach. She knew it would be the foremost. In Kudrino, and from Nikitsky Street, from Pryesny, and from Podnovinsky several trains of vehicles, similar to the Rostovs', came driving out, and by the time they reached Sadovoy Street the carriages and cars were two deep all along the road.

When Natasha had been told that morning that Prince Andrey was seriously wounded, and was travelling with them, she had at the first moment asked a great many questions, how and why and where was he going; whether he were dangerously wounded, and whether she could see him. But after she had been told that she could not see him, that his wound was a serious one, but that his life was not in danger, though she plainly did not believe what was told her, she saw that she would get the same answer whatever she said, and gave up asking questions and speaking at all. All the way Natasha had sat motionless in the corner of the carriage with those wide eyes, the look in which the countess knew so well and dreaded so much. And she was sitting in just the same way now on the bench in the hut. She was brooding on some plan; she was making, or already by now had made some decision, in her own mind—that the countess knew, but what that decision was she did not know, and that alarmed and worried her.

'Natasha, undress, darling, get into my bed.'

For the countess only a bed had been made up on a bedstead. Madame Schoss and the two girls were to sleep on hay on the floor.

'No, mamma, I'll lie here on the floor,' said Natasha irritably; she went to the window and opened it. The moans of the adjutant could be heard more distinctly from the open window. She put her head out into the damp night air, and the countess saw her slender neck shaking with sobs and heaving against the window frame. Natasha knew it was not Prince Andrey moaning. She knew that Prince Andrey was in the same block of huts as they were in, that he was in the next hut just across the porch, but that fearful never ceasing moan made her sob. The countess exchanged glances with Sonya.

'Go to bed, darling, go to bed, my pet,' said the countess, lightly touching Natasha's shoulder. 'Come, go to bed.'

'Oh yes . . . I'll go to bed at once,' said Natasha, hurriedly undressing, and breaking the strings of her petticoats. Dropping off her dress, and putting on a dressing-jacket, she sat down on the bed made up on the floor, tucking her feet under her, and flinging her short, fine hair over her shoulder, began plaiting it. Her thin, long, practised fingers rapidly and deftly divided, plaited, and tied up her hair. Natasha's head turned from side to side as usual as she did this, but her eyes, feverishly wide, looked straight before her with the same fixed stare. When her toilet for the night was over, Natasha sank softly down on to the sheet laid on the hay nearest the door.

For a long while Natasha listened to the sounds that reached her from within and without, and she did not stir. She heard at first her mother's prayers and sighs, the creaking of her bed under her, Madame Schoss's familiar, whistling snore, Sonya's soft breathing. Then the countess called to Natasha. Natasha did not answer.

'I think she's asleep, mamma,' answered Sonya.

The countess, after a brief silence, spoke again, but this time no one answered her.

Soon after this Natasha caught the sound of her mother's even breathing. Natasha did not stir, though her little bare foot, poking out below the quilt, felt frozen against the uncovered floor.

A cricket chirped in a crack, as though celebrating a victory over all the world. A cock crowed far away, and another answered close by. The shouts had died away in the tavern, but the adjutant's moaning went on still the same. Natasha sat up.

'Sonya! Are you asleep? Mamma!' she whispered. No one answered. Slowly and cautiously Natasha got up, crossed herself, and stepped cautiously with her slender, supple, bare feet on to the dirty, cold floor. The boards creaked. With nimble feet she ran like a kitten a few steps, and took hold of the cold door-handle.

It seemed to her that something with heavy, rhythmical strokes was banging on all the walls of the hut; it was the beating of her own heart, torn with dread, with love and terror.

She opened the door, stepped over the lintel, and on to the damp, cold earth of the passage outside. The cold all about her refreshed her.

Her bare foot felt a man asleep; she stepped over him, and opened the door of the hut in which Prince Andrey was lying.

In that hut it was dark. A tallow candle with a great, smouldering wick stood on a bench in the further corner, by a bed, on which something was lying.

Ever since she had been told in the morning of Prince Andrey's wound and his presence there, Natasha had resolved that she must see him. She could not have said why this must be, but she knew their meeting would be anguish to her, and that made her the more certain that it must be inevitable.

All day long she had lived in the hope that at night she would see him. But now when the moment had come, a terror came over her of what she would see. How had he been disfigured? What was left of him? Was he like that unceasing moan of the adjutant? Yes, he was all over like that. In her imagination he was that awful moan of pain personified. When she caught sight of an undefined mass in the corner, and took his raised knees under the quilt for his shoulders, she pictured some fearful body there, and stood still in terror. But an irresistible force drew her forward. She made one cautious step, another, and found herself in the middle of the small hut, cumbered up with baggage. On the bench, under the holy images, lay another man (this was Timohin), and on the floor were two more figures (the doctor and the valet).

The valet sat up and muttered something. Timohin, in pain from a wound in his leg, was not asleep, and gazed, all eyes, at the strange apparition of a girl in a white night-gown, dressing-jacket, and nightcap. The valet's sleepy and frightened words: 'What is it? What do you want?' only made Natasha hasten towards the figure lying in the corner. However fearfully unlike a human shape that figure might be now, she must see him. She passed by the valet, the smouldering candle flicked up, and she saw clearly Prince Andrey, lying with his arms stretched out on the quilt, looking just as she had always seen him.

He was just the same as ever; but the flush on his face, his shining eyes, gazing passionately at her, and especially the soft, childlike neck, showing above the lay-down collar of the nightshirt, gave him a peculiarly innocent, childlike look, such as she had never seen in him before. She ran up to him and with a swift, supple, youthful movement dropped on her knees.

He smiled, and held out his hand to her.

'You?' he said. 'What happiness!'

With a swift but circumspect movement, Natasha came nearer, still kneeling, and carefully taking his hand she bent her face over it and began kissing it, softly touching it with her lips.

'Forgive me!' she said in a whisper, lifting her head and glancing at him. 'Forgive me!'

'I love you,' said Prince Andrey.

'Forgive . . .'

'Forgive what?' asked Prince Andrey.

'Forgive me for what I di . . . id,' Natasha murmured in a hardly audible, broken whisper, and again and again she softly put her lips to his hand.

'I love thee more, better than before,' said Prince Andrey, lifting her face with his hand so that he could look into her eyes.

Those eyes, swimming with happy tears, gazed at him with timid commiseration and joyful love. Natasha's thin, pale face, with its swollen lips, was more than ugly—it looked terrible. But Prince Andrey did not see her face, he saw the shining eyes, which were beautiful. They heard talk behind them.

Pyotr, the valet, by now wide awake, had woken up the doctor. Timohin, who had not slept all night for the pain in his leg, had been long watching all that was happening, and huddled up on his bench, carefully wrapping his bare person up in the sheet.

'Why, what's this?' said the doctor, getting up from his bed on the floor. 'Kindly retire, madam.'

At that moment there was a knock at the door; a maid had been sent by the countess in search of her daughter.

Like a sleep-walker awakened in the midst of her trance, Natasha walked out of the room, and getting back to her hut, sank sobbing on her bed.

From that day at all the halts and resting-places on the remainder of the Rostovs' journey, Natasha never left Bolkonsky's side, and the doctor was forced to admit that he had not expected from a young girl so much fortitude, nor skill in nursing a wounded man.

Terrible as it was to the countess to think that Prince Andrey might (and very probably, too, from what the doctor said) die on the road in her daughter's arms, she could not resist Natasha. Although with the renewal of affectionate relations between Prince Andrey and Natasha the idea did occur that in case he recovered their old engagement would be renewed, no one—least of all Natasha and Prince Andrey—spoke of this. The unsettled question of life and death hanging, not only over Prince Andrey, but over all Russia, shut off all other considerations.

A TERRIBLY STRANGE BED

Wilkie Collins

Shortly after my education at college was finished I happened to be staying in Paris with an English friend. We were both young men then, and lived, I am afraid, rather a wild life in the delightful city of our sojourn. One night we were idling about the neighbourhood of the Palais Royal, doubtful to what amusement we should next betake ourselves. My friend proposed a visit to Frascati's; but his suggestion was not to my taste. I knew Frascati's, as the French saying is, by heart; had lost and won plenty of five-franc pieces there, merely for amusement's sake, until it was amusement no longer, and was thoroughly tired, in fact, of all the ghastly respectabilities of such a social anomaly as a respectable gambling-house.

'For heaven's sake,' said I to my friend, 'let us go somewhere where we can see a little genuine, blackguard, poverty-stricken gaming, with no false gingerbread glitter thrown over it at all. Let us get away from fashionable Frascati's, to a house where they don't mind letting in a man with a ragged coat, or a man with no coat, ragged or otherwise.'

'Very well,' said my friend, 'we needn't go out of the Palais Royal to find the sort of company you want. Here's the place just before us, as blackguard a place, by all report, as you could possibly wish to see.' In another minute we arrived at the door and entered the house.

When we got upstairs, and had left our hats and sticks with the door-keeper, we were admitted into the chief gambling-room. We did not find many people assembled there. But, few as the men were who looked up at us on our entrance, they were all types—lamentably true types—of their respective classes.

We had come to see blackguards; but these men were something worse. There is a comic side, more or less appreciable, in all 'black-guardism'—here there was nothing but tragedy—mute, weird tragedy. The quiet in the room was horrible. The thin, haggard, long-haired young man, whose sunken eyes fiercely watched the turning up of the cards, never spoke; the flabby, fat-faced, pimply player, who pricked his piece of pasteboard perseveringly to register how often black won and how often red—never spoke; the dirty, wrinkled old man, with the vulture eyes and the darned greatcoat, who had lost his last sou, and still looked on desperately after he could play no longer—never spoke. Even the voice of the croupier sounded as if it were strangely dulled and thickened in the atmosphere of the room.

I had entered the place to laugh, but the spectacle before me was something to weep over. I soon found it necessary to take refuge in excitement from the depression of spirits which was fast stealing on me. Unfortunately I sought the nearest excitement by going to the table and beginning to play. Still more unfortunately, as the event will show, I won—won prodigiously, won incredibly; won at such a rate that the regular players at the table crowded round me; and, staring at my stakes with hungry, superstitious eyes, whispered to one another that the English stranger was going to break the bank.

The game was *rouge-et-noir*. I had played at it in every city in Europe, without, however, the care or the wish to study the 'theory of chances' —that philosopher's stone of all gamblers! And a gambler, in the strict sense of the word, I had never been.

But on this occasion it was very different—now, for the first time in my life, I felt what the passion for play really was. My success first be-wildered, and then, in the most literal meaning of the word, intoxi-cated me. Incredible as it may appear, it is nevertheless true, that I only lost when I attempted to estimate chances, and played according to previous calculation. If I left everything to luck, and staked without any care or consideration, I was sure to win—to win in the face of every recognized probability in favour of the bank. At first, some of the men present ventured their money safely enough on my colour; but I speedily increased my stakes to sums which they dared not risk. One after another they left off playing, and breathlessly looked on at my game.

Still, time after time, I staked higher and higher, and still won. The excitement in the room rose to fever pitch. The silence was interrupted by a deep-muttered chorus of oaths and exclamations in different languages every time the gold was shovelled across to my side of the table—even the imperturbable croupier dashed his rake on the floor in a fury of astonishment at my success. But one man present preserved his self-possession, and that man was my friend. He came to my side, and, whispering in English, begged me to leave the place, satisfied with what I had already gained. I must do him the justice to say that he repeated his warnings and entreaties several times, and only left me and went away after I had rejected his advice (I was to all intents and purposes gambling-drunk) in terms which rendered it impossible for him to address me again that night.

Shortly after he had gone a hoarse voice behind me cried, 'Permit me, my dear sir!—permit me to restore to their proper place two Napoleons which you have dropped. Wonderful luck, sir! I pledge you my word of honour, as an old soldier, in the course of my long experience in this sort of thing, I never saw such luck as yours!—never! Go on, sir—*Sacré mille bombes!* Go on boldly, and break the bank!'

I turned round and saw, nodding and smiling at me with inveterate civility, a tall man, dressed in a frogged and braided coat.

If I had been in my senses I should have considered him, personally, as being rather a suspicious specimen of an old soldier. He had goggling bloodshot eyes, mangy mustachios, and a broken nose. His voice betrayed a barrack-room intonation of the worst order, and he had the dirtiest pair of hands I ever saw—even in France. These little personal peculiarities exercised, however, no repelling influence on me. In the mad excitement, the reckless triumph of that moment, I was ready to 'fraternize' with anybody who encouraged me in my game. I accepted the old soldier's offered pinch of snuff, clapped him on the back, and swore he was the most honest fellow in the world, the most glorious relic of the Grand Army that I had ever met with. 'Go on!' cried my military friend, snapping his fingers in ecstasy. 'Go on, and win! Break the bank —*Mille tonnerres!* my gallant English comrade, break the bank!'

And I *did* go on—went on at such a rate that in another quarter of an hour the croupier called out, 'Gentlemen! the bank has discontinued for tonight.' All the notes and all the gold in that 'bank' now lay in a heap under my hands; the whole floating capital of the gambling-house was waiting to pour into my pockets!

'Tie up the money in your pocket-handkerchief, my worthy sir,' said the old soldier, as I wildly plunged my hands into my heap of gold. 'Tie it up, as we used to tie up a bit of dinner in the Grand Army; your winnings are too heavy for any breeches pockets that ever were sewed. There, that's it! Shovel them in, notes and all! And now, as an ancient grenadier, as an ex-brave of the French Army, what remains for me to do! I ask what? Simply this: to entreat my valued English friend to drink a bottle of champagne with me, and toast the goddess fortune in foaming goblets before we part!'

'Excellent ex-brave! Convivial ancient grenadier! Champagne by all means! An English cheer for an old soldier!'

'Bravo! the Englishman; the amiable, gracious Englishman, in whose veins circulates the vivacious blood of France! Another glass? Ah,— the bottle is empty! Never mind! *Vive le vin!* I, the old soldier, order another bottle!'

'No, no, ex-brave; never—ancient grenadier! *Your* bottle last time, *my* bottle this. Behold it! Toast away! The French Army!—The great Napoleon!—The present company! The croupier! The honest croupier's wife and daughters—if he has any! The ladies generally! Everybody in the world!'

By this time the second bottle of champagne was emptied. I felt as if I had been drinking liquid fire—my brain seemed all aflame. No excess in wine had ever had this effect on me before in my life. Was it the result of a stimulant acting upon my system when I was in a highly excited state? Was my stomach in a particularly disordered condition? Or was the champagne amazingly strong?

'Ex-brave of the French Army!' cried I, in a mad state of exhilaration, '*I* am on fire! how are *you*? You have set me on fire! Do you hear, my hero of Austerlitz? Let us have a third bottle to put the flame out!'

The old soldier wagged his head, rolled his goggle eyes, until I expected to see them slip out of their sockets; placed his dirty forefinger by the side of his broken nose, solemnly ejaculated, 'Coffee!' and immediately ran off into an inner room.

The word pronounced by the eccentric veteran seemed to have a magical effect on the rest of the company present. With one accord they all rose to depart. Probably they had expected to profit by my intoxication; but finding that my new friend was benevolently bent on preventing me from getting dead drunk, had now abandoned all hope of thriving pleasantly on my winnings. Whatever their motive might be, at any rate they went away in a body. When the old soldier returned and sat down again opposite to me at the table, we had the room to ourselves. I could see the croupier, in a sort of vestibule which opened out of it, eating his supper in solitude. The silence was now deeper than ever.

A sudden change, too, had come over the 'ex-brave'. He assumed a portentously solemn look, and when he spoke to me again his speech was ornamented by no oaths, enforced by no finger-snapping, enlivened by no apostrophes or exclamations.

'Listen, my dear sir,' said he, in mysteriously confidential tones, 'listen to an old soldier's advice. I have been to the mistress of the house —a very charming woman, with a genius for cookery!—to impress on her the necessity of making us some particularly strong and good coffee. You must drink this coffee in order to get rid of your little amiable exaltation of spirits before you think of going home—you *must*, my good and gracious friend! With all that money to take home tonight, it is a sacred duty to yourself to have your wits about you. You are known to be a winner to an enormous extent by several gentlemen present tonight, who, in a certain point of view, are very worthy and excellent fellows; but they are mortal men, my dear, sir, and they have their amiable weaknesses! Need I say more? Ah, no, no! you understand me ! Now, this is what you must do. Send for a cabriolet when you feel quite well again, draw up all the windows when you get into it, and tell the driver to take you home only through the large and well-lit thoroughfares. Do this, and you and your money will be safe. Do this, and tomorrow you will thank an old soldier for giving you a word of honest advice.'

Just as the ex-brave ended his oration in very lagubrious tones, the coffee came in, ready poured out in two cups. My attentive friend handed me one of the cups with a bow. I was parched with thirst, and drank it off at a draught. Almost instantly afterwards I was seized with a fit of giddiness, and felt more completely intoxicated than ever. The room whirled round and round furiously; the old soldier seemed to be regularly bobbing up and down before me like the piston of a steam-engine. I was half deafened by a violent singing in my ears; a feeling of utter bewilderment, helplessness, idiocy overcame me. I rose from my chair, holding on by the table to keep my balance, and stammered out that I felt dreadfully unwell, so unwell that I did not know how I was to get home.

'My dear friend,' answered the old soldier—and even his voice seemed to be bobbing up and down as he spoke—'my dear friend, it would be madness to go home in *your* state; you would be sure to lose your money; you might be robbed and murdered with the greatest ease. *I* am going to sleep here: *you* sleep here, too—they make up capital beds in this house—take one; sleep off the effects of the wine, and go home safely with your winnings tomorrow—tomorrow, in broad daylight.'

I had but two ideas left: one, that I must never let go hold of my handkerchief full of money; the other, that I must lie down somewhere immediately and fall off into a comfortable sleep. So I agreed to the proposal about the bed, and took the offered arm of the old soldier, carrying my money with my disengaged hand. Preceded by the croupier, we passed along some passages and up a flight of stairs into the bedroom which I was to occupy. The ex-brave shook me warmly by the hand, proposed that we should breakfast together, and then, followed by the croupier, left me for the night.

I ran to the wash-stand, drank some of the water in my jug, poured the rest out, and plunged my face into it, then sat down in a chair and tried to compose myself. I soon felt better. The change for my lungs from the stinking atmosphere of the gambling-room to the cool air of the apartment I now occupied; the almost equally refreshing change for my eyes from the glaring gaslights of the salon to the dim, quiet flicker of one bedroom candle, aided wonderfully the restorative effects of cold water. The giddiness left me, and I began to feel a little like a reasonable being again. My first thought was of the risk of sleeping all night in a gambling-house; my second, of the still greater risk of trying to get out after the house was closed, and of going home alone at night, through the streets of Paris, with a large sum of money about me. I had slept in worse places than this on my travels; so I determined to lock, bolt, and barricade my door, and take my chance till the next morning.

Accordingly, I secured myself against all intrusion, looked under the bed and into the cupboard, tried the fastening of the window, and then, satisfied that I had taken every proper precaution, pulled off my upper clothing, put my light, which was a dim one, on the hearth among a feathery litter of wood ashes, and got into bed, with the handkerchief full of money under my pillow.

I soon felt not only that I could not go to sleep, but that I could not even close my eyes. I was wide awake, and in a high fever. Every nerve in my body trembled—every one of my senses seemed to be pre-ternaturally sharpened.

What could I do? I had no book to read. I raised myself on my elbow, and looked about the room, which was brightened by a lovely moon-light pouring straight through the window—to see if it contained any pictures or ornaments that I could at all clearly distinguish.

There was, first, the bed I was lying in; a four-post bed, of all things in the world to meet with in Paris!—yes, a thorough clumsy British four-poster, with the regular top lined with chintz—the regular fringed valance all round—the regular stifling unwholesome curtains, which I remembered having mechanically drawn back againt the posts without particularly noticing the bed when I first got into the room. Then there was the marble-topped wash-stand, from which the water I had spilt, in my hurry to pour it out, was still dripping, slowly and more slowly, on to the brick floor. Then two small chairs.

Then the window—an unusually large window. Then a dark old picture, which the feeble candle dimly showed me. It was the picture of a fellow in a high Spanish hat, crowned with a plume of towering feathers. A swarthy, sinister ruffian, looking upward, shading his eyes with his hand, and looking intently upward—it might be at some tall gallows at which he was going to be hanged. At any rate, he had the appearance of thoroughly deserving it.

This picture put a kind of constraint upon me to look upward too—

at the top of the bed. It was a gloomy and not an interesting object, and I looked back at the picture. I counted the feathers in the man's hat— they stood out in relief—three white, two green. I observed the crown of his hat, which was of a conical shape, according to the fashion sup- posed to have been favoured by Guy Fawkes. I counted the feathers again—three white, two green.

While I still lingered over this very improving and intellectual em- ployment, my thoughts insensibly began to wander. The moonlight shining into the room reminded me of a certain moonlight night in England—the night after a picnic party in a Welsh valley. Every inci- dent of the drive homeward, through lovely scenery, which the moon- light made lovelier than ever, came back to me, though I had never given the picnic a thought for years; though, if I had *tried* to recollect it, I could certainly have recalled little or nothing of that scene long past.

I was still thinking of the picnic—of our merriment on the drive home—of the sentimental young lady who *would* quote *Childe Harold* because it was moonlight. I was absorbed by these past scenes and past amusements, when, in an instant, the thread on which my memories hung snapped asunder: my attention immediately came back to present things more vividly than ever, and I found myself, I neither knew why nor wherefore, looking hard at the picture again.

Looking for what?

Good God! the man had pulled his hat down on his brows!—No! the hat itself was gone! Where was the conical crown? Where the feathers—three white, two green? Not there! In place of the hat and feathers, what dusky object was it that now hid his forehead, his eyes, his shading hand?

Was the bed moving?

I turned on my back and looked up. Was I mad? Drunk? Dreaming? Giddy again? Or was the top of the bed really moving down—sinking slowly, regularly, silently, horribly, right down throughout the whole of its length and breadth—right down upon me as I lay underneath?

My blood seemed to stand still. A deadly paralysing coldness stole all over me as I turned my head round on the pillow and determined to test whether the bed-top was really moving or not by keeping my eye on the man in the picture.

The next look in that direction was enough. The dull, black, frowsy outline of the valance above me was within an inch of being parallel with his waist. I still looked breathlessly. And steadily, and slowly— very slowly—I saw the figure, and the line of frame below the figure, vanish as the valance moved down before it.

I am, constitutionally, anything but timid. I have been on more than one occasion in peril of my life, and have not lost my self-possession for an instant; but when the conviction first settled on my mind that the bed-top was really moving, was steadily and continuously sinking down upon me, I looked up shuddering, helpless, panic-stricken, beneath the hideous machinery for murder, which was advancing closer and closer to suffocate me where I lay.

I looked up, motionless, speechless, breathless. The candle, fully spent, went out; but the moonlight still brightened the room. Down and down, without pausing and without sounding, came the bed-top, and still my panic-terror seemed to bind me faster and faster to the mattress on which I lay—down and down it sank, till the dusty odour from the lining of the canopy came stealing into my nostrils.

At that final moment the instinct of self-preservation startled me out of my trance and I moved at last. There was just room for me to roll myself sideways off the bed. As I dropped noiselessly to the floor the edge of the murderous canopy touched me on the shoulder.

Without stopping to draw my breath, without wiping the cold sweat from my face, I rose instantly on my knees to watch the bed-top. I was literally spellbound by it. If I had heard footsteps behind me, I could not have turned round; if a means of escape had been miraculously provided for me, I could not have moved to take advantage of it. The whole life in me was, at that moment, concentrated in my eyes.

It descended—the whole canopy, with the fringe round it, came down—down—close down, so close that there was not room now to squeeze my finger between the bed-top and the bed. I felt at the sides, and discovered that what had appeared to me from beneath to be the ordinary light canopy of a four-post bed was in reality a thick, broad mattress, the substance of which was concealed by the valance and its fringe. I looked up and saw the four posts rising hideously bare. In the middle of the bed-top was a huge wooden screw that had evidently worked it down through a hole in the ceiling, just as ordinary presses are worked down on the substance selected for compression.

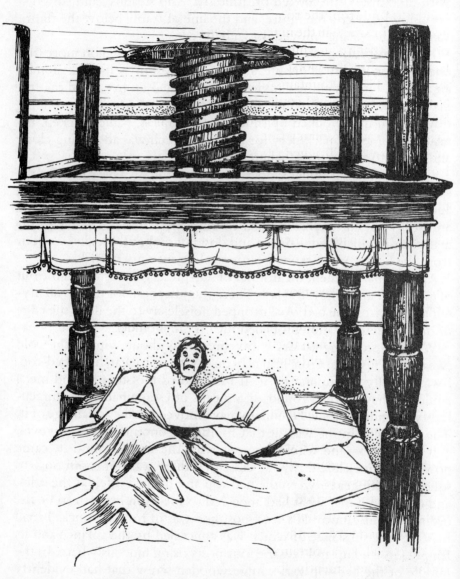

I looked up beneath the hideous machinery for murder, which was advancing closer and closer to suffocate me where I lay.

The frightful apparatus moved without making the faintest noise. There had been no creaking as it came down; there was now not the faintest sound from the room above. Amid a dead and awful silence I beheld before me—in the nineteenth century, and in the civilized capital of France—such a machine for secret murder by suffocation as might have existed in the worst days of the Inquisition, in the lonely inns among the Hartz Mountains, in the mysterious tribunals of Westphalia! Still, as I looked on it I could not move, I could hardly breathe, but I began to recover the power of thinking, and in a moment I discovered the murderous conspiracy framed against me in all its horror. My cup of coffee had been drugged, and drugged too strongly. I had been saved from being smothered by having taken an overdose of some narcotic. How I had chafed and fretted at the fever-fit which had preserved my life by keeping me awake! How recklessly I had confided myself to the two wretches who had led me into this room, determined, for the sake of my winnings, to kill me in my sleep by the surest and most horrible contrivance for secretly accomplishing my destruction! How many men, winners like me, had slept, as I had proposed to sleep, in that bed and had never been seen or heard of more! I shuddered at the bare idea of it.

But ere long all thought was again suspended by the sight of the murderous canopy moving once more. After it had remained on the bed—as nearly as I could guess—about ten minutes, it began to move up again. The villains who worked it from above evidently believed that their purpose was now accomplished. Slowly and silently, as it had descended, that horrible bed-top rose towards its former place. When it reached the upper extremities of the four posts, it reached the ceiling too. Neither hole nor screw could be seen; the bed became in appearance an ordinary bed again—the canopy an ordinary canopy—even to the most suspicious eyes.

Now, for the first time, I was able to move—to rise from my knees— to dress myself in my upper clothing—and to consider of how I should escape. If I betrayed, by the smallest noise, that the attempt to suffocate me had failed, I was certain to be murdered. Had I made any noise already? I listened intently, looking towards the door.

No! No footsteps in the passage outside—no sound of a tread, light or heavy, in the room above—absolute silence everywhere. Besides locking and bolting my door I had moved an old wooden chest against it, which I had found under the bed. To remove this chest (my blood ran cold as I thought of what its contents might be!) without making some disturbance was impossible; and, moreover, to think of escaping through the house, now barred up for the night, was sheer insanity. Only one chance was left me—the window. I stole to it on tiptoe.

My bedroom was on the first floor, above an *entresol*, and looked into the back street. I raised my hand to open the window, knowing that on that action hung, by the merest hair's-breadth, my chance of safety. They keep vigilant watch in a house of murder. If any part of the frame cracked, if the hinge creaked, I was a lost man! It must have occupied me at least five minutes, reckoning by time—five *hours*, reckoning by suspense—to open that window. I succeeded in doing it silently—in doing it with all the dexterity of a house-breaker—and then looked down into the street. To leap the distance beneath me would be almost certain destruction! Next, I looked round at the sides of the house. Down the left side ran the thick water-pipe—it passed close by the outer edge of the window. The moment I saw the pipe I knew I was saved. My breath came and went freely for the first time since I had seen the canopy of the bed moving down upon me!

To some men the means of escape which I had discovered might have seemed difficult and dangerous enough—to *me* the prospect of slipping down the pipe into the street did not suggest even a thought of peril. I had always been accustomed, by the practice of gymnastics, to keep up my schoolboy powers as a daring and expert climber, and knew that my head, hands, and feet would serve me faithfully in any hazards of ascent or descent. I had already got one leg over the window-sill when I remembered the handkerchief filled with money under my pillow. I could well have afforded to leave it behind me, but I was revengefully determined that the miscreants of the gambling-house should miss their plunder as well as their victim.

So I went back to the bed and tied the heavy handkerchief at my back by my cravat. Just as I had made it tight and fixed it in a comfortable place, I thought I heard a sound of breathing outside the door. The chill feeling of horror ran through me again as I listened. No! dead silence still in the passage—I had heard the night air blowing softly into the room. The next moment I was on the window-sill—and the next I had a firm grip on the water-pipe with my hands and knees.

I slid down into the street easily and quietly, as I thought I should, and immediately set off at the top of my speed to a branch Prefecture of Police, which I knew was situated in the immediate neighbourhood. A Sub-prefect and several picked men among his subordinates happened to be up, maturing, I believe, some scheme for discovering the perpetrator of a mysterious murder which all Paris was talking of just then. When I began my story, in a breathless hurry and in very bad French, I could see that the Sub-prefect suspected me of being a drunken Englishman who had robbed somebody; but he soon altered his opinion as I went on, and before I had anything like concluded, he shoved all the papers before him into a drawer, put on his hat, supplied me with another (for I was bare-headed), ordered a file of soldiers, desired his expert followers to get ready all sorts of tools for breaking open doors and ripping up brick-flooring, and took my arm in the most friendly and familiar manner possible to lead me with him out of the house. I will venture to say that when the Sub-prefect was a little boy, and was taken for the first time to the play, he was not half as much pleased as he was now at the job in prospect for him at the gambling-house!

Away we went through the streets, the Sub-prefect cross-examining and congratulating me in the same breath as we marched at the head of our formidable posse. Sentinels were placed at the back and front of the house the moment we got to it; a tremendous battery of knocks was directed against the door; a light appeared at a window; I was told to conceal myself behind the police—then came more knocks, and a cry of 'Open in the name of the law!' At that terrible summons bolts and locks gave way before an invisible hand, and the moment after the Sub-prefect was in the passage, confronting a waiter half-dressed and ghastly pale. This was the short dialogue which immediately took place:

'We want to see the Englishman who is sleeping in this house.'

'He went away hours ago.'

'He did no such thing. His friend went away; *he* remained. Show us to his bedroom!'

'I swear to you, Monsieur le Sous-prefect, he is not here! He——'

'I swear to you, Monsieur le Garçon, he is. He slept here—he didn't find your bed comfortable—he came to us to complain of it—here he is among my men—and here am I ready to look for a flea or two in his bedstead. Renaudin! (calling to one of the subordinates and pointing to the waiter) collar that man and tie his hands behind him. Now, then, gentlemen, let us walk upstairs!'

Every man and woman in the house was secured—the 'old soldier' the first. Then I identified the bed in which I had slept, and then we went into the room above.

No object that was at all extraordinary appeared in any part of it. The Sub-prefect looked round the place, commanded everybody to be silent, stamped twice on the floor, called for a candle, looked attentively at the spot he had stamped on, and ordered the flooring there to be carefully taken up. This was done in no time. Lights were produced, and we saw a deep raftered cavity between the floor of this room and the ceiling of the room beneath. Through this cavity there ran perpendicularly a sort of case of iron thickly greased, and inside the case appeared the screw which communicated with the bed-top below. Extra lengths of screw, freshly oiled; levers covered with felt; all the complete upper works of a heavy press—constructed with infernal ingenuity so as to join the fixtures below, and when taken to pieces again to go into the smallest possible compass—were next discovered and pulled out on the floor. After some little difficulty the Sub-prefect succeeded in putting the machinery together, and, leaving his men to work it, descended with me to the bedroom. The smothering canopy was then lowered, but not so noiselessly as I had seen it lowered. When I mentioned this to the Sub-prefect, his answer, simple as it was, had a terrible significance. 'My men,' said he, 'are working down the bed-top for the first time— the men whose money you won were in better practice.'

We left the house in the sole possession of two police agents—every one of the inmates being removed to prison on the spot. The Sub-prefect, after taking down my statement in his office, returned with me to my hotel to get my passport. 'Do you think,' I asked as I gave it to him, 'that any men have really been smothered in that bed as they tried to smother *me?*'

'I have seen dozens of drowned men laid out at the morgue,' answered the Sub-prefect, 'in whose pocket-books were found letters stating that they had committed suicide in the Seine, because they had lost everything at the gaming-table. Do I know how many of those men entered the same gambling-house that *you* entered, won as *you* won, took that bed as *you* took it, slept in it, were smothered in it, and were privately thrown into the river with a letter of explanation written by the murderers and placed in their pocket-books? No man can say how many or how few have suffered the fate from which you have escaped. The people of the gambling-house kept their bedstead machinery a secret from *us*—even from the police! The dead kept the rest of the secret for them. Good-night, or rather good-morning, Monsieur.'

One good result was produced by my adventure: it cured me of ever again trying *rouge-et-noir* as an amusement. The sight of a green cloth, with packs of cards and heaps of money on it, will henceforth be forever associated in my mind with the sight of a bed-canopy descending to suffocate me in the silence and darkness of the night.

A DREAM OF DEATH

James Hogg

Not very long ago, one William Laidlaw, a sturdy Borderer, went on an excursion to a remote district in the Highlands of Scotland. He was a tall and very athletic man, remarkably active, and matchless at cudgel-playing, running, wrestling, and other exercises for which the Borderers have been noted from time immemorial. To his other accomplishments he added an excellent temper, was full of good humour, and a most capital bottle-companion.

Most of our modern travellers would have performed the greater part of the journey he undertook in a steam-boat, a stage-coach, or some such convenience; but he preferred going on foot, without any companion excepting an old oaken cudgel, which had been handed down to him from several generations, and which, by way of fancy, had been christened 'Knock-him-down'.

With this trusty friend in his hand, and fifty pounds sterling in his pocket, he found himself, by the fourth day, in one of the most dismal glens of the highlands. It was by this time nightfall, and both William's appetite and limbs told him it was high time to look about for a place of repose, having, since six in the morning, walked nearly fifty miles.

Now, the question which employed his thoughts at this moment was whether he should proceed, at the risk of losing his way among the bogs and morasses for which this district is famed, or remain till daybreak where he was? Both expedients were unpleasant, and it is difficult to say which he would have adopted, when, about a mile to the left, a glimmering among the darkness attracted his notice.

It might have been a 'Will-o'-the-wisp', or the light of some evil spirit at its midnight orgies; but whatever the cause might be, it decided Mr Laidlaw as to his further operations. He did not reflect a moment upon the matter, but exercising 'Knock-him-down' in its usual capacity of walking assistant, he found himself in a few minutes alongside the spot from which the light proceeded. It was a highland cottage, built after the usual fashion, partly of stone and partly of turf; but without examining too minutely the exterior of the building, he applied the stick to the door with such a degree of force as he conceived necessary to arouse the inmates.

'Wha's there?' cried a shrill voice, like that of an old woman; 'what want ye at this hour of the night?'

'I want lodging, honest woman, if such a thing is to be got.'

'Na, na,' replied the inmate, 'you can get nae lodging here. Neither gentle nor simple shall enter my house this night. Gang on your ways, you're no aboon five miles frae the clachan of Ballacher.'

'Five deevils!' exclaimed the Borderer; 'I tell you I have walked fifty miles already, and could as soon find out Johnny Groat's as the clachan.'

'Walk fifty more, then,' cried the obstinate portress; 'but here you downa enter, while I can keep you out.'

'If you come to that, my woman,' said William, 'we shall soon settle the point. In plain language, if you do not let me in wi' your gude-will I shall enter without it,' and with that he laid his shoulder to the door, with the full intention of storming the fortress. A whispering within made him pause a moment.

'And must I let him in?' murmured the old woman to someone who seemed in the interior.

'Yes,' answered a half-suppressed voice; 'he may enter—he is but one, and we are three—a lowland tup, I suppose.'

The door was slowly opened. The person who performed this unwilling act was a woman apparently above seventy, haggard and bent by an accumulation of infirmity and years. Her face was pale, malignant, and wrinkled, and her little sharp peering eyes seemed, like those of the adder, to shoot forth evil upon whomsoever she gazed. As William entered, he encountered this aged crone, her natural hideousness exposed full to his gaze by the little rush-light she held up above her head, the better to view the tall Borderer.

'You want a night's lodging, say you? Ay, nae doubt, like many others frae the south, come to trouble honest folks.'

'There's nae need to talk about troubling,' said Laidlaw. 'If you have trouble you shall be paid for it; and since you are pleased, my auld lady, to talk about the south, let me say a word of the north. I have got money in my pouch to pay my way wherever I go, and this is mair than some of your bonnie highland lairds can say. Here it lies, my lady!' and he struck with the palm of his hand the large and well-replenished pocket-book which bulged out from his side.

'I want nane of your money,' said the old crone, her eyes nevertheless sparkling with a malicious joy; 'walk in; you will have the company of strangers for the night.'

He followed her advice, and went to the end of the cottage, near which, upon the floor, blazed a large fire of peat. There was no grate, and for chimney a hole in the roof sufficed, through which the smoke ascended in large volumes. Here he saw the company mentioned by the crone. It consisted of three men, of the most fierce and savage aspect. Two of them were dressed as sailors, the third in a sort of highland garb.

He had never seen any persons who had so completely the air of desperadoes. The two first were dark in their complexions, their black bushy beards apparently unshorn for many weeks. Their expressions were dark and ominous, and bespoke spirits within which had been trained up in crime. Nor were the red locks of the third, and his fiery countenance, and sharp, cruel eyes, less appalling, and less indicative of evil.

So near an intercourse with such people, and under those circumstances, would have thrown a chill over most hearts; but William Laidlaw was naturally a stranger to fear, and, at any rate, his great strength gave him a confidence which it was very difficult to shake;

he had, besides, a most unbounded confidence in scientific cudgel-playing, and in the virtues of 'Knock-him-down'.

These three men were seated around the fire; and when our traveller came alongside of them, and saluted them, not one returned his salutation. Each sat in dogged silence. If they deigned to recognize him, it was by looks of ferocious sternness, and these looks were momentary, for they instantly relapsed into their former state of sullen apathy.

William was at this time beset by two most unfortunate inclinations. He had an incorrigible desire, first, to speak, and secondly, to eat; and never had any propensities come upon so inappropriate a man. He sat for a few minutes absolutely nonplussed about the method of gratifying them. At length, after revolving the matter deeply in his mind, he contrived to get out with the following words:

'I have been thinking, gudewife, that something to eat is very agreeable when a body is hungry.' No answer.

'I have been thinking, mistress, that when a man is hungry he is the better of something to eat.' No answer.

'Did you hear what I was saying, mistress?'

'Perfectly weel.'

'And what is your opinion of the matter?'

'My opinion is, that a hungry man is the better of being fed.' Such was the old dame's reply; and he thought he could perceive a smile of bitter ridicule curl up the savage lips of his three neighbours.

'Was there ever such an auld hag?' thought the yeoman to himself. 'There she sits at her wheel, and cares nae mair for a fellow-creature than I would for a dead sheep.'

'Mistress,' continued he, 'I see you will not tak' hints. I maun then tell you plainly that I am the next door to starvation, and that I will thank you for something to eat.'

This produced the desired effect, for she instantly got up from her wheel, went to a cupboard, and produced a plentiful supply of cold venison, bread and cheese, together with a large bottle full of the finest whisky.

William now felt quite at his ease. Putting 'Knock-him-down' beside him, and planting himself at the table, he commenced operations in a style that would have done honour to Friar Tuck himself. Venison, bread and cheese disappeared like magic. So intently did he keep to his occupation that he neither thought nor cared about any other object.

Everything which came under the heading of eatable having disappeared from the table, he proceeded to discuss the contents of the black bottle which stood by. He probably indulged rather freely in this respect, for shortly after commencing he became very talkative, and seemed resolved, at all risks, to extract conversation from his mute companions.

'You will be in the smuggling trade, frien'?' said he, slapping the shoulder of one of his dark-complexioned neighbours. The fellow started from his seat, and looked upon the Borderer with an expression of anger and menace, but he was suddenly quieted by one of his companions, who whispered into his ear, 'Hush, Roderick; never mind him; the time is not yet come.'

'I was saying, frien',' reiterated Laidlaw, without perceiving this interruption, 'that you will be in the smuggling trade?'

'Maybe I am,' was the fellow's answer.

'And you are a fish of the same water?' continued William to the second, who nodded assent.

'And you, frien', wi' the red hair, what are ye?'

'Humph!'

'Humph!' cried the Borderer; 'that is one way of answering questions—humph, ay humph, very good; ha, ha, your health, Mr Humph!' and he straightway swallowed another glass of the potent spirit.

These three personages, during the whole of his various harangues, preserved the same unchanged silence, replying to his broken and unconnected questions by nods and monosyllables. They even held no verbal communication with one another, but each continued apparently within himself the thread of his own gloomy meditations. The night by this time waxed late; the spirit began to riot a little in the Borderer's head; and concluding that there was no sociality among persons who would neither drink nor speak, he quaffed a final glass and dropped back on his chair.

How long he remained in this state cannot be known. Certain it is, he was rather suddenly awakened from it by a hand working its way cautiously and gently into his bosom. At first he did not know what to make of this: his ideas were as yet unrallied, and by a sort of instinct he merely pressed his left hand against the spot by way of resistance. The same force continuing, however, to operate as formerly, he opened his eyes, and saw himself surrounded by the three strangers. The red-haired ruffian was the person who had aroused him—the two others, one of them armed with a cutlass, stood by. William was so astonished at this scene that he could form no opinion on the subject. His brain still rang with the strange visions that had crossed it, and with the influence of intoxication.

'I am thinking, honest man, that you are stealing my pocket-book,' was the first ejaculation he came out with, gazing at the same time with a bewildered look on the plunderer.

'Down with the villain!' thundered one of these worthies at the same instant; 'and you, sir,' brandishing his cutlass over the Borderer's head, 'resist, and I will cleave you to the collar.'

This exclamation acted like magic upon Laidlaw; it seemed to sober him in an instant, and point out his perilous situation.

The trio had rushed upon him, and attempted to hold him down. Now or never was the period to put his immense strength to the trial. Collecting all his energies, he bounded from their grasp, and his herculean fist falling like a sledge-hammer upon the forehead of him who carried the cutlass, the ruffian tumbled headlong to the earth. In a moment more he stood in the centre of the cottage, whirling 'Knock-him-down' around his head in the attitude of defiance. Such was now his appearance of determined courage and strength that the two ruffians opposed to him, although powerful men, and armed with bludgeons, did not dare advance, but recoiled several paces from their opponent.

He had escaped thus far, but his situation was still very hazardous, for the men, though baffled, kept their eyes intently fixed upon him, and seemed only to wait an opportunity when they could rush on with most advantage. Besides, the one he had floored had just got up, and with his cutlass joined the others. If they had made an attack upon him, his great skill and vigour would in all probability have brought one of them to the ground, but then he would have been assailed by the two others; and the issue of such a contest, armed as one of them was, could not but be highly dangerous.

Meanwhile the men, although none of them ventured to rush singly upon the Borderer, began to advance in a body, as if for the purpose of getting behind him.

'Now,' thought William, 'if I can but keep you quiet till I get opposite the door, I may show you a trick that will astonish you.'

So planning his scheme, he continued retreating before his assailants, and holding up his cudgel in the true scientific position till he came within a foot of the door; most fortunately it stood wide open. One step aside, and the threshold was gained—another, and it was passed.

In the twinkling of an eye, swift like a thunderbolt, fell 'Knock-him-down' upon the head of the most forward opponent and in another out bolted William Laidlaw from the cottage. The whole was the work of an instant. He who received the blow fell stunned and bleeding to the ground, and his companions were so confounded that they stood mute and gazing at each other for several seconds. Their resolution was soon taken, and in a mood between shame and revenge, they sallied out after the fugitive. Their speed was, however, employed in vain against the fleetest runner of the Cheviots, and they were afraid to separate, lest each might encounter singly this formidable adversary, who perhaps might have dealt with them in the same manner as Horatius did with the Curiatii of old. The pursuit continued but a short way, as the yeoman more than double distanced his pursuers in the first two minutes, and left them no chance of coming up with him.

It was by this time three in the morning. The intense darkness of midnight had worn away, and though the sun was yet beneath the horizon, a sort of reflected light so far prevailed as to render near objects visible. In the course of an hour the hill tops became exposed above the misty wreaths which hung heavily upon their sides, and which began to dissolve away and float slowly down the glen in pale columns.

In a short time a hue like that of twilight rendered distinctly visible the mountain boundaries of the vale. William walked onward with his usual speed. Such at last was his prodigious rapidity of movement that he utterly lost the use of his senses. He appeared to himself to fly rather than walk over the earth; his head became giddy, and it is difficult to say where his flight might have ended, when 'Knock-him-down' was suddenly swept from his hand. This in a moment arrested his speed, for such was his sympathy with this companion that he could not possibly get on, or even live without it.

'Knock-him-down, whare are ye?' was his first exclamation at the departure of his favourite. 'I say, Knock-him-down—whare are ye?' Here honest William sat down upon the heath to bemoan his misfortune. Now for the first time in his life he parted with all recollection. A strange, mysterious, indescribable ringing took place in his ears—the hills reeled—his head nodded once, twice, and again—and in a few seconds he dropped into a profound sleep.

This may be considered an epoch in the yeoman's life, for here he, for the first time, according to his own account, was visited by a dream. Out of the pale mist of the glen he imagined he saw approach him the very person to whose house he was bound. The aspect of this man was melancholy—his face deadly pale—and as he stood opposite to the Borderer and said, 'William Laidlaw,' the latter felt his flesh creep with an unutterable dread.

'William Laidlaw,' continued he, 'you are going to my house, but you will not find me at home. I have gone to a far country—Neil McKinnon and his two cousins sent me there. You will find my body in the pit near the Cairn of Dalgulish. The money you are bringing to me give to my poor family, and may God bless you!' Having pronounced these words the figure vanished, nor had the Borderer the power to recall it. He did not, however, awake, but lay in the same restless state till the sun, shining in all the splendour of an August morning, burst upon him.

William awoke a sober man. The morning was indeed beautiful. The sun shone in his strength, lighting up the vale with a flood of radiance. On the summits of the hills not a cloud rested—all was clear and lucid as crystal, and the untainted sky hung like a vault of pure sapphire over the thousand rocks and glens beneath.

The object which first arrested our friend's attention was 'Knock-him-down' stuck up in the middle of a gorse bush, and his immediate impulse was to relieve it from this inglorious situation. Having done this, stretched his limbs, and examined his pocket-book, which he found 'tight and well', he proceeded on his journey. He was naturally the reverse of superstitious, but somehow or other a train of unpleasant thoughts came over him, which he could not get rid of. His mind was so unaccustomed to thinking of any kind, and above all, to gloomy thinking, that he knew not what to make of the matter. He whistled and sang in vain to dispel the feeling. The same load hung upon his

The aspect of this man was melancholy, his face deadly pale . . .

mind, and oppressed it grievously.

In this train he found himself at length in front of the clachan of Ballacher. This small village was in possession of the individual to whom he was journeying. His dwelling, a large farmhouse, was in the centre; the cottages which surrounded it were occupied by his servants and tenants.

It was about midday when he entered the village. It was deserted, while a strange and subduing melancholy seemed to hang over it. He strode slowly on, but no human being made his appearance. At length a funeral procession, followed by many women and children, came silently up the middle avenue of the village. It might be a deception of his fancy, but he thought the looks of the mourners were more sad and more profoundly interesting than he had ever witnessed on any previous occasion. He followed the convoy to the cemetery, which was not far distant, and when the last shovelful of earth was thrown upon the grave, he inquired whose funeral it was.

'It is that of Allaster Wilson, our master,' was the reply.

'Good heaven! and how did he die?' cried William, deeply agitated.

'That no one knows,' answered an old man who stood by; 'he was found murdered; but a day will come when the Lord will cause his blood to be requited on his murderers.'

'And where was his body found?' said the astonished Borderer.

'In the chalkpit near the Cairn of Dalgulish,' replied the senior, and he wiped his aged eyes and walked slowly away.

William started back with horror and instantly recollected his dream. It was indeed the very individual to whose house he was journeying that he now saw laid in his grave. His first duty was to go to the bereaved family of his departed friend, and to comfort the widow and the fatherless. A tear rolled from his manly eye as he entered the mansion of sorrow; and when he saw the relict and the weeping family of his friend he thought his heart would have died within him. Having paid into their hands the money he owed them, and performed various offices of kindness, he bade them for the present adieu, and went to Inverness.

He had no business to transact there; his only object was to obtain the aid of justice in pursuit of the three men whom he supposed to be the murderers. Neil McKinnon was apprehended at the house where

Laidlaw first saw him; but though his guilt was strongly suspected, no positive proof could be adduced against him, and he was dismissed. The two other men were never heard of. It was supposed that they had gone on board a smuggling cutter which left Fort William, and afterwards perished, with all its crew, in the Sound of Mull.

The dream still continued to agitate the yeoman's mind to a great degree, and from being the gayest farmer of the Borders, he returned as thoughtful as a philosopher.

THE ALIBI

Anonymous

I wholly disbelieve in spirit-rapping, table-turning, and all supernatural eccentricities of that nature. I refuse credence to the best authenticated ghost story.

I can sleep in the gloomiest haunted room in the gloomiest haunted house without the slightest fear of a nocturnal visit from the other world.

But, although I scoff at white ladies and bleeding nuns, there is a species of supernatural occurrence in which I am, I confess, an unwilling and hesitating believer.

The circumstances I am about to relate are of this nature, and were told me by an intimate friend of mine, as having lately occurred to a relation of his own.

I give the story as he gave it to me, namely, in the words as nearly as possible of the principal actor in it.

Two years ago, towards the end of the London season, weary of the noise and bustle that for the last three months had been ceaselessly going on around me, I determined upon seeking a few days' rest and quiet in the country. The next evening saw me comfortably installed in a pretty farmhouse about two miles from a cathedral town. The little cottage in which I had taken up my quarters belonged to an old servant of my father's, and had long been a favourite resort of mine when wishing for quiet and fresh air.

The evening of the second day after my arrival was unusually close and sultry, even for the time of year. Weary with the heat, and somewhat sated with the two days' experience I had enjoyed of a quiet country life, I went up to my bedroom about half-past ten, with the intention of taking refuge from the *ennui* which was growing on me in a good long night's sleep. Finding, however, the heat an insuperable obstacle to closing my eyes, I got up, put on my dressing-gown, and, lighting a cigar, sat down at the open window, and dreamily gazed out on the garden in front of the cottage.

Before me several low, flat meadows stretched down to the river, which separated us from the town. In the distance the massive towers of the cathedral appeared in strong and bright relief against the sky. The whole landscape, indeed, was bathed in a flood of light from the clear summer moon.

I was gradually getting sleepy, and beginning to think of turning in, when I heard a soft, clear voice, proceeding apparently from some one just beneath my window, saying: 'George, George, be quick! You are wanted in the town.'

I immediately looked from the window, and although the moon still shone most brilliantly, somewhat to my surprise I could see no one. Thinking, however, that it was some friend of my landlord's who was begging him to come into the town upon business, I turned from the window, and, getting into bed, in a few minutes was fast asleep.

I must have slept about three hours, when I awoke with a sudden start, and with a shivering 'goose-skin' feeling all over me. Fancying that this was caused by the morning air from the open window, I was getting out of bed to close it, when I heard the same voice proceeding from the very window itself. 'George, be quick! You are wanted in the town.'

These words produced an indescribable effect upon me. I trembled from head to foot, and, with a curious creeping about the roots of the hair, stood and listened. Hearing nothing more, I walked quickly to the window, and looked out. As before, nothing was to be seen. I stood in the shade of the curtain for some minutes, watching for the speaker to show himself, and then, laughing at my own nervousness, closed the window and returned to bed.

The grey morning light was now gradually overspreading the heavens, and daylight is antagonistic to all those fears which under cover of the darkness will steal at times over the boldest. In spite of this, I could not shake off the uncomfortable feeling produced by that voice. Vainly I tried to close my eyes. Eyes remained obstinately open; ears sensitively alive to the smallest sound.

Some half-hour had elapsed, when again I felt the same chill stealing over me. With the perspiration standing on my forehead, I started up in bed, and listened with all my might. An instant of dead silence, and the mysterious voice followed: 'George, be quick! You *must* go into the town.'

The voice was in the room—nay, more, by my very bedside. The miserable fear that came over me I cannot attempt to describe. I felt that the words were addressed to me, and by no human mouth.

Hearing nothing more, I slowly got out of bed, and by every means in my power convinced myself that I was wide awake and not dreaming. Looking at myself in the glass on the dressing-table, I was at first shocked, and then, in spite of myself, somewhat amused by the pallid hue and scared expression of my countenance.

I grinned a ghastly grin at myself, whistled a bit of a polka, and got into bed again.

I had a horrible sort of notion that some one was looking at me, and that it would never do to let them see that I was the least uneasy.

I soon found out, however, that bed, in the circumstances, was a mistake, and I determined to get up and calm my nerves in the fresh morning air.

I dressed hurriedly, with many a look over my shoulder, keeping as much as possible to one corner of the room, where nobody could get behind me. The grass in front of my window was glistening with the heavy morning dew, on which no foot could press without leaving a visible trace.

I searched the whole garden thoroughly, but no sign could I see of any person having been there.

Pondering over the events of the night, which, in spite of broad daylight and common sense, persisted in assuming a somewhat supernatural aspect, I wandered across the meadows towards the river by a footpath which led to the ferry. As I drew near to the boatman's cottage I saw him standing at his door, looking up the path by which I was approaching. As soon as he saw me, he turned and walked down to his boat, where he waited my arrival. 'You are early on foot, my friend, this morning,' said I, as I joined him.

'Early, sir,' answered he, in a somewhat grumbling tone. 'Yes, it is early sir, and I have been waiting here for you this two hours or more.'

'Waiting for me, my friend—how so?'

'Yes, sir, I have; for they seemed so very anxious that you should not be kept waiting; they have been down from the farm twice this blessed night telling me that you would want to cross the ferry very early this morning.'

I answered the man not a word, and, getting into his boat, was quickly put across the water. As I walked rapidly up towards the town, I endeavoured to persuade myself that somebody was attempting to play a silly hoax upon me. At last, stopping at a gate through which I had to pass, I determined upon proceeding no further. As I turned to retrace my steps, suddenly the same shivering sensation passed over me—I can only describe it as a cold damp blast of air meeting me in the face, and then, stealing round and behind me, enveloping me in its icy folds.

I distinctly heard the words, 'George, George,' uttered in my very ear, in a somewhat plaintive and entreating tone.

I shuddered with a craven fear, and, turning hastily round, hurried on towards the town.

A few minutes' walking brought me into the market-place. It was evidently market day, for, in spite of the early hour, there was already a considerable bustle going on. Shops were being opened, and the country people were exposing their butter, poultry, and eggs for sale, and for about two hours I wandered among the busy and constantly increasing crowd, listening to every scrap of conversation that reached my ear, and vainly endeavouring to connect them with the strange summons that had roused me from my bed, and led me to the town.

I could hear nothing that interested me in any way, and, feeling tired and hungry, I decided on breakfasting at the hotel, which overlooked the market-place, and then taking myself back to the cottage, in spite of the mysterious voice.

The cheerful and noisy bustle of the market had indeed partly dissipated the morbid turn which my fancies had taken.

After I had breakfasted I lit my cigar, and strolled into the bar, where I talked for ten minutes with the landlord without elucidating anything of greater moment than that it was his (the landlord's) opinion that things were bad —very; that Squire Thornbury was going to give a great ball on the occasion of his daughter's approaching marriage; and that Mr Weston's ox was certain to carry off the prize at the next agricultural meeting.

I bade him good morning, and turned my steps homeward. I was checked on my way down the High Street by a considerable crowd, and upon inquiring what was the matter, was informed that the assizes were being held and that an 'interesting murder case' was going on. My curiosity was roused, I turned into the court-house, and, meeting an acquaintance who fortunately happened to be a man in authority, was introduced into the court, and accommodated with a seat.

The prisoner at the bar, who was accused of robbing and murdering a poor country girl, was a man of low, slight stature, with a coarse, brutal cast of features, rendered peculiarly striking by their strangely sinister expression.

As his small bright eyes wandered furtively round the court they met mine, and for an instant rested upon me. I shrank involuntarily from his gaze, as I would from that of some loathsome reptile, and kept my eyes steadily averted from him till the end of the trial, which had been nearly concluded the previous evening. The evidence, as summed up by the judge, was principally circumstantial, though apparently overwhelming in its nature. In spite of his counsel's really excellent defence, the jury unhesitatingly found him 'guilty'.

The judge, before passing sentence, asked the prisoner, as usual, if he had anything further to urge why sentence of death should not be passed upon him.

The unfortunate prisoner, in an eager, excited manner, emphatically denied his guilt—declared that he was an honest, hard-working, travelling glazier, that he was at Bristol, many miles from the scene of

*The unfortunate **prisoner** emphatically denied his guilt.*

the murder on the day of its commission, and that he knew no more about it than a babe unborn. When asked why he had not brought forward this line of defence during the trial, he declared that he had wished it, but that the gentleman who had conducted his defence had refused to do so.

His counsel, in a few words of explanation, stated that, although he had every reason to believe the story told by the prisoner, he had been forced to confine his endeavours in his behalf to breaking down the circumstantial evidence for the prosecution—that most minute and searching inquiries had been made at Bristol, but that from the short time the prisoner had passed in that town (some three or four hours), and from the lengthened period which had elapsed since the murder, he had been unable to find witnesses who could satisfactorily have proved an alibi, and had therefore been forced to rely upon the weakness of the evidence produced by the prosecution. Sentence of death was passed upon the prisoner, who was removed from the bar loudly and persistently declaring his innocence.

I left the court painfully impressed with the conviction that he was innocent. The passionate earnestness with which he had pleaded his own cause, the fearless, haughty expression that crossed his ill-omened features, when, finding his assertions entirely valueless, he exclaimed with an imprecation, 'Well, then, do your worst, but I am *innocent*! I never saw the poor girl in my life, much less murdered her,' caused the whole court, at least the unprofessional part of it, to feel that there was some doubt about the case, and that circumstantial evidence, however strong, should rarely be permitted to carry a verdict of 'guilty'. I am sure that the fervent though unsupported assertions made by the prisoner affected the jury far more than the florid defence made for him by his counsel.

The painful scene that I had just witnessed entirely put the events of the morning out of my head, and I walked home with my thoughts fully occupied with the trial.

The earnest protestations of the unfortunate man rang in my ears, and his face, distorted with anxiety and passion, rose ever before me.

I passed the afternoon writing answers to several business letters, which had found me out in my retreat, and soon after dinner retired to my room, weary with want of sleep the previous night and with the excitement of the day.

It had been my habit for many years to make every night short notes of the events of the day, and this evening, as usual, I sat down to write my journal. I had hardly opened the book when, to my horror, the deadly chill that I had experienced in the morning again crept round me.

I listened eagerly for the voice that had hitherto followed, but this time in vain; not a sound could I hear but the ticking of my watch upon the table, and, I fear I must add, the beating of my own coward heart.

I got up and walked about, endeavouring to shake off my fears. The cold shadow, however, followed me about, impeding, as it seemed, my very respiration. I hesitated for a moment at the door, longing to call up the servant upon some pretext, but, checking myself, I turned to the table, and resolutely sitting down, again opened my journal.

As I turned over the leaves of the book, the word Bristol caught my eye. One glance at the page, and in an instant the following circumstances flashed across my memory.

I had been in Bristol on that very day—the day on which this dreadful murder had been committed!

On my way to a friend's house I had missed at Bristol the train I had expected to catch, and having a couple of hours to spare, wandered into the town, and entering the first hotel I came to, called for some luncheon. The annoyance I felt at having some hours to wait was aggravated by the noise a workman was making in replacing a pane of glass in one of the coffee-room windows. I spoke to him once or twice, and finding my remonstrances of no avail, walked to the window and, with the assistance of the waiter, forced the man to discontinue his work.

In an instant I recalled the features of the workman. It was the very man I had seen in the felons' dock that morning. There was no doubt about it. That hideous face as it peered through the broken pane had fixed itself indelibly in my memory, and now identified itself beyond the possibility of doubt with the sinister countenace that had impressed me so painfully in the morning.

I have little more to add. I immediately hurried back to the town and laid these facts before the judge. On communicating with the landlady of the hotel at Bristol, she was able to prove the payment of a small sum on that day to a travelling glazier. She came to the town, and from among a crowd of felonsunhesitatingly picked out the convicted man as the person to whom she had paid the money.

The poor fellow, being a stranger at Bristol and having only passed two or three hours there, was utterly unable to remember at what houses he had been employed. I myself had forgotten the fact of my having ever been in that town.

A week later the man was at liberty. Some matter-of-fact people may endeavour to divest these circumstances of their, to me, mysterious nature by ascribing them to a disordered imagination and the fortuitous recognition of a prisoner condemned to die.

Nothing will ever efface from my mind the conviction that providence in this case chose to work out its ends by extraordinary and supernatural means.

Here ended his story. I give it you without addition or embellishment as he told it to me. It is second-hand, I confess, but hitherto I have never been fortunate enough to hear a story with anything supernatural in it that was not open to the same objection.

A TOUGH TUSSLE

Ambrose Bierce

One night in the autumn of 1861 a man sat alone in the heart of a forest in Western Virginia. The region was then, and still is, one of the wildest on the continent—the Cheat Mountain country. There was no lack of people close at hand, however; within two miles of where the man sat was the now silent camp of a whole Federal brigade. Somewhere about—it might be still nearer—was a force of the enemy, the numbers unknown. It was this uncertainty as to its numbers and position that accounted for the man's presence in that lonely spot; he was a young officer of a Federal infantry regiment, and his business there was to guard his sleeping comrades in the camp against a surprise. He was in command of a detachment of men constituting a picket guard. These men he had stationed just at nightfall in an irregular line, determined by the nature of the ground, several hundred yards in front of where he now sat. The line ran through the forest, among the rocks and laurel thickets, the men fifteen or twenty paces apart, all in concealment and under injunction of strict silence and unremitting vigilance. In four hours, if nothing occurred, they would be relieved by a fresh detachment from the reserve now resting in care of its captain some distance away to the left and rear. Before stationing his men the young officer of whom we are speaking had pointed out to his two sergeants the spot at which he would be found in case it should be necessary to consult him, or if his presence at the front line should be required.

It was a quiet enough spot—the fork of an old wood road, on the two branches of which, prolonging themselves deviously forward in the dim moonlight, the sergeants were themselves stationed, a few paces in rear of the line. If driven sharply back by a sudden onset of the enemy—and pickets are not expected to make a stand after firing—the men would come into the converging roads, and, naturally following them to their point of intersection, could be rallied and 'formed'. In his small way the young lieutenant was something of a strategist; if Napoleon had planned as intelligently at Waterloo, he would have won the battle and been overthrown later.

Second Lieutenant Brainerd Byring was a brave and efficient officer, young and comparatively inexperienced as he was in the business of killing his fellow men. He had enlisted in the very first days of the war as a private, with no military knowledge whatever, had been made first sergeant of his company on account of his education and engaging manner, and had been lucky enough to lose his captain by a Confederate bullet; in the resulting promotions he had got a commission. He had been in several engagements, such as they were— at Philippi, Rich Mountain, Carrick's Ford and Greenbrier—and had borne himself with such gallantry as to attract the attention of his superior officers. The exhilaration of battle was agreeable to him, but the sight of the dead, with their clay faces, blank eyes, and stiff bodies, which, when not unnaturally shrunken, were unnaturally swollen, had always intolerably affected him. He felt toward them a kind of reasonless antipathy which was something more than the physical and spiritual repugnance common to us all. Doubtless this feeling was due to his unusually acute sensibilities—his keen sense of the beautiful, which these hideous things outraged. Whatever may have been the cause, he could not look upon a dead body without a loathing which had in it an element of resentment. What others have respected as the dignity of death had to him no existence— was altogether unthinkable. Death was a thing to be hated. It was not picturesque, it had no tender and solemn side—a dismal thing, hideous in all its manifestations and suggestions. Lieutenant Byring was a braver man than anybody knew, for nobody knew his horror of that which he was ever ready to encounter.

Having posted his men, instructed his sergeants, and retired to his station, he seated himself on a log, and, with senses all alert, began his vigil. For greater ease he loosened his sword belt, and, taking his heavy revolver from his holster, laid it on the log beside him. He felt very comfortable, though he hardly gave the fact a thought, so intently did he listen for any sound from the front which might have a menacing significance—a shout, a shot, or the footfall of one of his sergeants coming to apprise him of something worth knowing. From the vast, invisible ocean of moonlight overhead fell, here and there, a slender, broken stream that seemed to plash against the intercepting branches and trickle to earth, forming small white pools among the clumps of laurel. But these leaks were few and served only to accentuate the blackness of his environment, which his imagination found it easy to people with all manner of unfamiliar shapes, menacing, uncanny, or merely grotesque.

He to whom the portentous conspiracy of night and solitude and silence in the heart of a great forest is not an unknown experience needs not to be told what another world it all is—how even the most commonplace and familiar objects take on another character. The trees group themselves differently; they draw closer together, as if in fear. The very silence has another quality than the silence of the day. And it is full of half-heard whispers, whispers that startle—ghosts of sounds long dead. There are living sounds, too, such as are never heard under other conditions: notes of strange night birds, the cries of small animals in sudden encounters with stealthy foes, or in their dreams, a rustling in the dead leaves—it may be the leap of a wood rat, it may be the footstep of a panther. What caused the breaking of that twig?—what the low, alarmed twittering in that bushful of birds? There are sounds without a name, forms without substance, translations in space of objects which have not been seen to move, movements wherein nothing is observed to change its place. Ah, children of the sunlight and the gaslight, how little you know of the world in which you live!

Surrounded at a little distance by armed and watchful friends, Byring felt utterly alone. Yielding himself to the solemn and mysterious spirit of the time and place, he had forgotten the nature of his connection with the visible and audible aspects and phases of the night. The forest was boundless; men and the habitations of men did not exist. The universe was one primeval mystery of darkness, without form and void, himself the sole dumb questioner of its eternal secret. Absorbed in the thoughts born of this mood, he suffered the time to slip away unnoted. Meantime the infrequent patches of white light lying amongst the undergrowth had undergone changes of size, form, and place. In one of them near by, just at the roadside, his eye fell upon an object which he had not previously observed. It was almost before his face as he sat; he could have sworn that it had not before been there. It was partly covered in shadow, but he could see that it was a human figure. Instinctively he adjusted the clasp of his sword belt and laid hold of his pistol—again he was in a world of war, by occupation an assassin.

The figure did not move. Rising, pistol in hand, he approached. The figure lay upon its back, its upper part in shadow, but standing above it and looking down upon the face, he saw that it was a dead body. He shuddered and turned from it with a feeling of sickness and disgust, resumed his seat upon the log, and, forgetting military prudence, struck a match and lit a cigar. In the sudden blackness that followed the extinction of the flame he felt a sense of relief; he could no longer see the object of his aversion. Nevertheless, he kept his eyes set in that direction until it appeared again with growing distinctness. It seemed to have moved a trifle nearer.

'Damn the thing!' he muttered. 'What does it want?'

It did not appear to be in need of anything but a soul.

Byring turned away his eyes and began humming a tune, but he broke off in the middle of a bar and looked at the dead man. Its presence annoyed him, though he could hardly have had a quieter neighbour. He was conscious, too, of a vague, indefinable feeling which was new to him. It was not fear, but rather a sense of the supernatural—in which he did not at all believe.

'I have inherited it,' he said to himself. 'I suppose it will require a thousand years—perhaps ten thousand—for humanity to outgrow this feeling. Where and when did it originate? Away back, probably, in what is called the cradle of the human race—the plains of Central

Asia. What we inherit as a superstition our barbarous ancestors must have held as a reasonable conviction. Doubtless they believed themselves justified by facts whose nature we cannot even conjecture in thinking a dead body a malign thing endowed with some strange power of mischief, with perhaps a will and a purpose to exert it. Possibly they had some awful form of religion of which that was one of the chief doctrines, sedulously taught by their priesthood, just as ours teach the immortality of the soul. As the Aryan moved westward to and through the Caucasus passes and spread over Europe, new conditions of life must have resulted in the formulation of new religions. The old belief in the malevolence of the dead body was lost from the creeds, and even perished from tradition, but it left its heritage of terror, which is transmitted from generation to generation—is as much a part of us as our blood and bones.'

In following out his thoughts he had forgotten that which suggested it; but now his eye fell again upon the corpse. The shadow had now altogether uncovered it. He saw the sharp profile, the chin in the air, the whole face, ghastly white in the moonlight. The clothing was grey, the uniform of a Confederate soldier. The coat and waistcoat, unbuttoned, had fallen away on each side, exposing the white shirt. The chest seemed unnaturally prominent, but the abdomen had sunk in, leaving a sharp projection at the line of the lower ribs. The arms were extended, the left knee was thrust upward. The whole posture impressed Byring as having been studied with a view to the horrible.

'Bah!' he exclaimed; 'he was an actor—he knows how to be dead.'

He drew away his eyes, directing them resolutely along one of the roads leading to the front, and resumed his philosophizing where he had left off.

'It may be that our Central Asian ancestors had not the custom of burial. In that case it is easy to understand their fear of the dead, who really were a menace and an evil. They bred pestilences. Children were taught to avoid the places where they lay, and to run away if by inadvertence they came near a corpse. I think, indeed, I'd better go away from this chap.'

He half rose to do so, then remembered that he told his men in front, and the officer in the rear who was to relieve him, that he could at any time be found at that spot. It was a matter of pride, too. If he abandoned his post, he feared they would think he feared the corpse. He was no coward, and he was not going to incur anybody's ridicule. So he again seated himself, and, to prove his courage, looked boldly at the body. The right arm—the one farthest from him—was now in shadow. He could barely see the hand which, he had before observed, lay at the root of a clump of laurel. There had been no change, a fact which gave him a certain comfort, he could not have said why. He did not at once remove his eyes; that which we do not wish to see has a strange fascination, sometimes irresistible. Of the woman who covers her face with her hands, and looks between the fingers, let it be said that the wits have dealt with her not altogether justly.

Byring suddenly became conscious of a pain in his right hand. He withdrew his eyes from his enemy and looked at it. He was grasping the tilt of his drawn sword so tightly that it hurt him. He observed, too, that he was leaning forward in a strained attitude—crouching like a gladiator ready to spring at the throat of an antagonist. His teeth were clenched, and he was breathing hard. This matter was soon set right, and as his muscles relaxed and he drew a long breath, he felt keenly enough the ludicrousness of the incident. It affected him to laughter. Heavens! what sound was that?—what mindless devil was uttering an unholy glee in mockery of human merriment? He sprang to his feet and looked about him, not recognizing his own laugh.

He could no longer conceal from himself the horrible fact of his cowardice; he was thoroughly frightened! He would have run from the spot, but his legs refused their office; they gave way beneath him, and he sat again upon the log, violently trembling. His face was wet, his whole body bathed in a chill perspiration. He could not even cry out. Distinctly he heard behind him a stealthy tread, as of some wild animal, and dared not look over his shoulder. Had the soulless living joined forces with the soulless dead?—was it an animal? Ah, if he could but be assured of that! But by no effort of will could he now unfix his gaze from the face of the dead man.

I repeat that Lieutenant Byring was a brave and intelligent man. But what would you have? Shall a man cope, single-handed, with so monstrous an alliance as that of night and solitude and silence and

He was crouching like a gladiator ready to spring at an antagonist.

the dead?—while an incalculable host of his own ancestors shriek into the ear of his spirit their coward counsel, sing their doleful death-songs in his heart and disarm his very blood of all its iron? The odds are too great—courage was not made for such rough use as that.

One sole conviction now had the man in possession: that the body moved. It lay nearer to the edge of its plot of light—there could be no doubt of it. It had also moved its arms, for, look, they are both in the shadow! A breath of cold air struck Byring full in the face; the branches of trees above him stirred and moaned. A strongly defined shadow passed across the face of the dead, left it luminous, passed back upon it and left it half obscured. The horrible thing was visibly moving. At that moment a single shot rang out upon the picket line—a lonelier and louder, though more distant, shot than ever had been heard by mortal ear! It broke the spell of that enchanted man; it slew the silence and the solitude, dispersed the hindering host from Central Asia, and released his modern manhood. With a cry like that of some great bird pouncing upon its prey, he sprang forward, hot-hearted for action!

Shot after shot now came in from the front. There were shoutings and confusion, hoofbeats and desultory cheers. Away to the rear, in the sleeping camp, was a singing of bugles and a grumble of drums. Pushing through the thickets on either side the roads came the Federal pickets, in full retreat, firing backward at random as they ran. A straggling group that had followed back one of the roads, as instructed, suddenly sprang away into the bushes as half a hundred horsemen thundered by them, striking wildly with their sabres as they passed. At headlong speed these mounted madmen shot past the spot where Byring had sat, and vanished round an angle of the road, shouting and firing their pistols. A moment later there was a roar of musketry, followed by dropping shots—they had encountered the reserve guard in line; and back they came in dire confusion, with here and there an empty saddle and many a maddened horse, bullet-stung, snorting and plunging with pain. It was all over—'an affair of outposts'.

The line was re-established with fresh men, the roll called, the stragglers were reformed. The Federal commander, with a part of his staff, imperfectly clad, appeared upon the scene, asked a few questions, looked exceedingly wise, and retired. After standing at arms for an hour, the brigade in camp 'swore a prayer or two' and went to bed.

Early next morning a fatigue party, commanded by a captain and accompanied by a surgeon, searched the ground for dead and wounded. At the fork of the road, a little to one side, they found two bodies lying close together—that of a Federal officer and that of a Confederate private. The officer had died of a sword thrust through the heart, but not, apparently, until he had inflicted upon his enemy no fewer than five dreadful wounds. The dead officer lay on his face in a pool of blood, the weapon still in his breast. They turned him on his back and the surgeon removed it.

'Gad!'said the captain—'it is Byring!'—adding, with a glance at the other, 'They had a tough tussle.'

The surgeon was examining the sword. It was that of a line officer of Federal infantry—exactly like the one worn by the captain. It was, in fact, Byring's own. The only other weapon discovered was an undischarged revolver in the dead officer's belt.

The surgeon laid down the sword and approached the other body. It was frightfully gashed and stabbed, but there was no blood. He took hold of the left foot and tried to straighten the leg. In the effort the body was displaced. The dead do not wish to be moved when comfortable—it protested with a faint, sickening odour.

The surgeon looked at the captain. The captain looked at the surgeon.

THE FISHERMAN
AND THE TURTLE

Anthea Courtenay

If he had not been late that morning, Urashima Taro would never have met the turtle. In the ordinary way he was up and away in his boat at first light, ahead of the others—and last home, too, for he was a good son and a conscientious fisherman. And something else, besides.

Urashima Taro was special. Though he was poor and uneducated and had never left his village on the southern coast of Japan, he had always known that he was in some way exceptional. It was not that he was remarkably handsome and strong, for he cared nothing for appearances; it was not that he was extraordinarily kind-hearted, for his kindness came so naturally that he was unaware of it. It was not the pride of his name, which means 'Son of the Island'. It was a kind of inner knowledge, almost like a memory—the knowledge that for him some special destiny was reserved. It was this that drew him so early to the sea and kept him out so late. Alone in his little boat his knowledge echoed around him, whispered in the wind, repeated in the wavelets lapping at the sides of his boat, hinted in the seabirds' cries. 'Urashima Taro is not like other men—for him there is more, much more!'

He would gaze up at the sky, and his soul would expand to meet the distance. Or he would look down into the dark waters, and a curious urge would come over him to plunge into their depths, as if some answer lay in their mystery. He spoke of these things to no-one.

That morning his mother, as she served his breakfast, had delayed him. 'Urashima, I must talk to you seriously. You are twenty years old, you are a fine, handsome young man—oh, don't pretend—I've seen the way the girls look at you! It's high time you got married.'

A handful of rice halfway to his lips, Urashima paused. Patiently, for he had heard all this before, he answered her. 'Mother, I honour you far too much to wish to change my way of life.'

'You are my only son, born to me late in life, and it's many years since your father was drowned. Soon I shall be growing old, I shall need a pair of young hands to help me. And *you* won't be young forever— one day you will need a son to take your fishing boat out to sea.'

'Oh, not for many years yet, mother. I'm strong and healthy—'

'And you work too hard and you take risks. What if anything happened to you? I should be all alone!'

'Nothing will happen to me, you worry too much!'

'Urashima Taro,' said she a touch impatiently. 'I am your mother, and I tell you it is time you got married!'

He smiled his charming smile and said, 'Mother, how could I find a wife worthy enough, when for twenty years I have lived with the most perfect woman in the world?'

He meant it, too; he loved his mother deeply. But the other reason he could not speak of to her: simple woman that she was, how could she understand that he must remain free to meet his Destiny?

He rose, wiped his fingers, and embraced her. 'Mother, I promise I'll think about what you have said. You know I would never do anything to hurt you.'

His mother sighed. 'I know. You always were a dear, good boy. Now, be careful. The seas were high last night—'

'I'll come home especially early tonight,' he promised, and set off through the village streets down to the beach and his beloved boat. As he turned the corner he looked back at his home. His mother stood in the doorway, looking after him, a little woman in black, with a brown, wrinkled face.

At first he ignored the voices shouting on the beach and would have gone straight to his boat had he not detected in the cries a harshness, the unmistakeable tone of boys tormenting someone or something weaker than themselves. He walked across the sand to the group of youths who danced and circled, half-mocking, half-afraid, round something he could not see. As he approached, one or two of them fell back: the village boys respected Urashima.

'What's going on?' He stepped into the circle. In the centre lay the giant turtle, upturned in its huge, heavy shell, its flippers waving helplessly in the air, its wrinkled neck stretched in useless effort.

'It was stranded,' said a boy. 'The storm must have washed it up last night. It'll make good soup.'

'And is that a reason to torment it?' said Urashima Taro severely, looking at the sticks and stones in their hands. 'We should respect life, especially the life of the sea that gives us our living.'

A youth shrugged. 'What's the difference? It's going to die anyway.'

'Then we should ask the poor creature's forgiveness, and thank it for the life it gives us in losing its own.'

He looked down at the turtle which had stopped its flapping at the sound of his voice, and was looking at him from its small black eyes.

'And just to teach you—this one we will not kill.' He bent and talked gently to the turtle, while the boys watched in silence. Then he gave a heave to its shell. But even his strength was not enough. 'Who will help me?'

Several boys helped him to drag the creature to the water's edge, where they carefully tilted it over. 'How strange,' thought Urashima Taro as he watched it swim away, gathering speed and strength as it went. 'Such a look it gave me—as though it really wanted to thank me.'

Then he strode off to his boat, and forgot the incident.

★   ★   ★   ★

He did not see the storm-clouds building on the horizon, nor become aware of the whirlwind until it was almost upon him. There was nothing he could do. He had truly intended not to be late; he had promised his mother, and he kept his promises. He had taken a good catch and could have returned. But some kind of daydream mood overtook him; he sat enjoying the silence and the loneliness, and wondering when and how his Destiny would come to him. He and his little vessel were flung this way and that; he felt as if a thousand boys with sticks were beating him on all sides. He clung to his boat until it shattered and was sucked down under the waves.

'Can this be my Destiny?' he cried aloud. 'To drown like so many others before me? If that's so, I refuse! I will live!'

'Yes,' said a voice beside him. 'Death is not for you. Come, quick, climb on my back.'

Swimming close to him was a turtle, the giant turtle of that morning. It did not surprise him that she should speak; he gripped the thick, solid shell above her neck and slid his body gratefully on to her back. Away they swam, away from the hurricane and away from the land. And from the turtle's wrinkled head the sweet, unearthly voice spoke. 'You saved my life, Urashima Taro. Such kindness must have its reward.'

And still he was not astonished that she spoke, only lulled and enchanted by the extraordinary beauty of her voice.

Without warning, the great creature dived. For a moment the fisherman's eyes, ears, nose, were full of salt water. A second or so later he found himself quite comfortable, not cold, not drowning, able to hear and answer the words of his strange mount.

As she swam effortlessly down and on, she spoke to him of the Kingdom under the sea from which she came, of the Sea God Ryugu, of the riches of his palace and the beauty of his daughter Otohime.

Was it really three days and three nights that they swam thus? So says the legend that they told afterwards. Time no longer existed. Urashima felt no hunger nor thirst, nor did he wish to sleep, though sometimes he had the sensation of a man returning from one dream only to lose himself in another. From time to time he wondered, 'Can this be my Destiny?' But the notion did not ring quite true, for he knew that when he met his Destiny he would be fully awake.

At last the towers and spires of the Sea God's palace rose before them, shimmering and glittering with a thousand precious stones, surrounded by underwater gardens: great banks of coral, from fingernail pink to ruby red, sea anemones of every shape and hue, and great, tree-tall seaweeds, purple, blue and green, moved by the waters in a constant dance.

Through vast doors they swam into a great white hall glittering with crystal and mother-of-pearl, with pillars that soared so high it was hard to distinguish the curve of the roof. Among them moved fishes of every shade of the rainbow, a kaleidoscope of undulating colours that made Urashima gasp: never in all his life at sea had he seen such fish.

The turtle gently stopped and let him slide from her back.

'Wait here,' she said. 'I shall not be long.' And she left him.

While he waited some graceful blue and green fishes with long, feathery tails floated in, carrying in their mouths a kimono of the finest silk shot with gold and silver threads. They nudged him gently until he had discarded his coarse fisherman's tunic and put on the kimono. Looking at himself, he laughed.

'This is not for me—this is a garment for a prince!'

'And a prince you shall be,' said the sweet voice of his companion. He turned round and saw in a doorway framed with shells and pearls a young woman more beautiful than he could ever have imagined. On the thick black hair that framed her oval face she wore a silver crown. As she glided towards him she smiled.

'I am Otohime, the Sea God's daughter. Sometimes I take the form of a turtle to visit the world outside—and this last time I might never have returned, but for you. My father has therefore given you permission to marry me—if that is your wish.'

'Is it your wish, lady?'

'What better husband could I ask for?' she said. 'Let us be married and live in joy forever—for those who dwell in the Sea God's Kingdom never grow old.'

This, then, must be my Destiny, thought Urashima Taro: to marry the most beautiful woman in the world and live, forever young, as a prince in the Sea God's Kingdom. He stretched out his rough, work hardened hand and in it took her long-fingered white one.

So they were married, and each day was more full of enchantment, as Urashima and Otohime grew closer, delighting in each other's company. Together they danced and sang, together they explored the rooms of the palace, each one more beautiful than the last. All the time that he lived there, there were always undiscovered rooms for Urashima and his bride to explore.

He gripped the turtle's back tightly as they swam away from the hurricane.

Only two things troubled him. One was the box that stood on the bureau in Otohime's chamber: a large box, containing three drawers, it was lacquered the colour of blood, and into its surface were inlaid curious designs in mother-of-pearl. When he asked Otohime what it contained she laughed at first and said, 'A secret!' But when he pressed her she replied, 'It contains the most precious thing in the world. Oh, my love, may you never have to open it.'

And she suddenly looked so sad that he dared not ask her about it again.

The second cause of faint unease he could not at first put his finger on: then, alone one day in a crystal courtyard he had not visited before, he realized what it was. He missed the sound of bird-song.

But such tiny shadows could not dim his happiness.

So three years passed.

*　　　*　　　*　　　*

'No!' He sat up in bed, wide awake. Beside him Otohime stirred and opened her dark eyes. 'What is it, my love? A nightmare?'

Urashima put his face in his hands. 'A dream! I dreamed of my mother, as she stood there looking after me the day I left home. Otohime, how could I? For three years I've lived here now, and I've never sent her a message, hardly given her a thought. Now she comes in my dreams to reproach me. I must go and see her!'

In the darkness he could not see the anxiety on his princess's face. Softly she stroked his brow and whispered, 'You have a new life now. . . . Are you not happy, here with me?'

'You know I am! But I have no right to happiness at her expense. My poor mother—I loved her so much, how could I have forgotten her? I must see her, reassure her.'

'Don't go! If you go, you will never come back.'

He turned and embraced her. 'Silly little one, of course I will. But I must go, just one visit to make sure she's all right, one visit, that's all. I can't be happy till I've seen her.'

'Ah, how is it that you men must always love the woman who is absent?' sighed Otohime. But she rose from their couch and went to her bureau. From it she took the lacquered box. 'If you must go,' she said,

'I will take you myself. Take this with you. Promise that you will only open it if you must.'

'Very well,' he said. He scarcely looked at the box now, his mind was all on his return.

'But I pray you may never have to,' she whispered.

He embraced her one last time. 'I'll come back safely, I promise. How could I ever leave you? My Destiny?'

But he felt a curious pang of doubt, as though, all unwillingly, he were lying.

★ ★ ★ ★

Three days and nights they travelled through the waters, Urashima Taro clinging to the back of his turtle princess. At last they broke surface and in the distance he could see the familiar outline of the shore, and his heart raced ahead of him so that he scarcely heard his wife's words or the sadness in her voice. At last they reached the sandy beach, and Urashima put his feet to the ground.

'You have the box?' she asked.

'I have it safe, don't worry.'

'I will wait for you here, then. Don't be too long.'

He patted the great domed shell affectionately. 'I won't, never fear.'

Eagerly he turned his footsteps to the village. As he walked, however, a strange uneasiness overcame him, a growing fear. For this was not his own village. Though the lines of the streets seemed the same, the houses were different; trees and gardens that he remembered well were no longer there. Had there been an earthquake in the last three years? A cold sensation gripped his stomach as he followed the line of the main street to where his home had stood. All he found was a patch of wild land strewn with rocks and stones; among them grasses and purple irises moved gently in the breeze.

'It is the wrong village,' he told himself, but he had already recognized the shape of the stone washbasin and the stepping stones of his mother's garden.

As he stood staring, an old peasant passed by.

'Good-day, father. Tell me—am I mistaken? I am looking for the house of Urashima Taro who left this village a few years ago. His mother—where is she?'

The old man's face creased in thought. 'Why, I remember that name,' he said. 'My grandmother used to tell me of an Urashima Taro who lived here once. Such a fine young man, he was quite a legend hereabouts. He was lost at sea one day—they never found his body, and his mother died soon after, of grief, they say. But that was—oh, that was three hundred years ago. You're a little late, young man.'

Three years . . . three hundred years! 'Oh, my poor mother!'

He sat down on the crumbling steps and began to weep. As he raised his sleeve to his eyes, his hand brushed against the princess's box. He took it in his hands: she had prayed he would never have to open it—was this what she had feared for him, known was in store for him—this stunning grief?

Three hundred years. . . . 'Only open it if you must!' Perhaps the box contained some magic spell that would wipe out those years, or perhaps enable him to see his mother one last time and ask her forgiveness. He only knew that he must open it.

In the velvet depths of the first drawer lay a white feather. He frowned; he knew it to be the feather of a crane, a symbol of long life. Was it there to mock him?

Anxiously he opened the second drawer; from it came a puff of smoke. As it coiled about him he felt a strange weakness overtake his limbs, his head felt too heavy for his neck, and his back began to curve forward. He looked at his hands and arms—but how wrinkled and dry they were, like the roots of dead trees. With what strength remained to him he opened the third drawer and drew from it the mirror that lay within, knowing the horror it would reveal. His face stared back at him, criss-crossed with a thousand lines, unrecognizable, the face of a man three hundred and twenty years old. He could never return to Otohime now.

'This, then, was my Destiny,' he thought. 'To have wounded and lost the two women I loved with all my heart.'

He cast the mirror from him. As it shattered on the stones, the crane's feather fluttered upwards, circled about him and came to rest on his shoulders.

Once more his limbs were transformed, long and slender his legs, his arms heavy with feathers. They began to beat, lifting him up, up, above the deserted garden and the ruined house. Light and urgent he flew, circling the garden three times, then higher, high above the village, above the seashore, his crane's wings gathering strength and skill, as he learned to rise and swoop with the wind.

Below him he saw the long stretch of sandy shore, children playing, a fisherman mending his nets. And the brown shape of a turtle, swimming slowly, sadly out to sea. He hovered above her until at last she dived.

Then he flew far out to sea, knowing that fatigue would not endanger him, that he had nothing to fear from winds and waves, that he would fly on forever, immortal. Urashima Taro had met his Destiny at last.

THE TELL-TALE HEART

Edgar Allan Poe

True! Nervous, very, very dreadfully nervous I had been and am; but why *will* you say that I am mad? The disease had sharpened my senses, not destroyed, not dulled them. Above all was the sense of hearing acute. I heard all things in the heaven and in the earth. I heard many things in hell. How then am I mad? Hearken! and observe how healthily, how calmly, I can tell you the whole story.

It is impossible to say how first the idea entered my brain, but, once conceived, it haunted me day and night. Object there was none. Passion there was none. I loved the old man. He had never wronged me. He had never given me insult. For his gold I had no desire. I think it was his eye! Yes, it was this! One of his eyes resembled that of a vulture—a pale blue eye with a film over it. Whenever it fell upon me my blood ran cold, and so by degrees, very gradually, I made up my mind to take the life of the old man, and thus rid myself of the eye for ever.

Now this is the point. You fancy me mad. Madmen know nothing. But you should have seen *me*. You should have seen how wisely I proceeded—with what caution—with what foresight, with what dissimulation, I went to work! I was never kinder to the old man than during the whole week before I killed him. And every night about midnight I turned the latch of his door and opened it—oh, so gently!

And then when I had made an opening sufficient for my head I put in a dark lantern all closed, closed so that no light shone out, and then I thrust in my head. Oh, you would have laughed to see how cunningly I thrust it in! I moved it slowly, very, very slowly, so that I might not disturb the old man's sleep. It took me an hour to place my whole head in the opening so far that I could see him lay upon his bed. Ha! would a madman have been so wise as this? And then when my head was well in the room I undid the lantern cautiously—oh, so cautiously—cautiously (for the hinges creaked), I undid it just so much that a single thin ray fell upon the vulture eye. And this I did for seven long hours, every night just at midnight, but I found the eye always closed, and so it was impossible to do the work, for it was not the old man who vexed me but his Evil Eye. And every morning, when the day broke, I went boldly into the chamber and spoke courageously to him, calling him by name in a hearty tone, and inquiring how he had passed the night. So you see he would have been a very profound old man, indeed, to suspect that every night, just at twelve, I looked in upon him while he slept.

Upon the eighth night I was more than usually cautious in opening the door. A watch's minute hand moves more quickly than did mine. Never before that night had I *felt* the extent of my own powers, of my sagacity. I could scarcely contain my feelings of triumph. To think that there I was opening the door little by little, and he not even to dream of my secret deeds or thoughts. I fairly chuckled at the idea, and perhaps he heard me, for he moved on the bed suddenly as if startled. Now you may think that I drew back—but no. His room was as black as pitch with the thick darkness (for the shutters were close fastened through fear of robbers), and so I knew that he could not see the opening of the door, and I kept pushing it on steadily, steadily.

I had my head in, and was about to open the lantern, when my thumb slipped upon the tin fastening, and the old man sprang up in the bed, crying out, 'Who's there?'

I kept quite still and said nothing. For a whole hour I did not move a muscle, and in the meantime I did not hear him lie down. He was still sitting up in the bed, listening; just as I have done night after night hearkening to the death watches in the wall.

Presently I heard a slight groan, and I knew it was the groan of mortal terror. It was not a groan of pain or of grief—oh, no! it was the low stifled sound that arises from the bottom of the soul when over-charged with awe. I knew the sound well. Many a night, just at midnight, when all the world slept, it has welled up from my own bosom, deepening, with its dreadful echo, the terrors that distracted me. I say I knew it well. I knew what the old man felt, and pitied him although I chuckled at heart. I knew that he had been lying awake ever since the first slight noise when he had turned in his bed. His fears had been ever since growing upon him. He had been trying to fancy them causeless, but could not. He had been saying to himself, 'It is nothing but the wind in the chimney, it is only a mouse crossing the floor', or 'It is merely a cricket which has made a single chirp'. Yes, he has been trying to comfort himself with these suppositions; but he had found all in vain. *All in vain*, because Death in approaching him had stalked with his black shadow before him and enveloped the victim. And it was the mournful influence of the unperceived shadow that caused him to feel, although he neither saw nor heard, to *feel* the presence of my head within the room.

When I had waited a long time very patiently without hearing him lie down, I resolved to open a little—a very, very little, crevice in the lantern. So I opened it—you cannot imagine how stealthily, stealthily—until at length a single dim ray like the thread of the spider shot out from the crevice and fell upon the vulture eye.

It was open, wide, wide open, and I grew furious as I gazed upon it. I saw it with perfect distinctness—all a dull blue with a hideous veil over it that chilled the very marrow in my bones, but I could see nothing else of the old man's face or person, for I had directed the ray as if by instinct precisely upon the damned spot.

And now have I not told you that what you mistake for madness is but over-acuteness of the senses? now, I say, there came to my ears a low, dull, quick sound, such as a watch makes when enveloped in cotton. I knew *that* sound well, too. It was the beating of the old man's heart. It increased my fury, as the beating of a drum stimulates the soldier into courage.

But even yet I refrained and kept still. I scarcely breathed. I held the lantern motionless. I tried how steadily I could maintain the ray upon

A single dim ray fell upon the vulture eye.

the eye. Meantime the hellish tattoo of the heart increased. It grew quicker and quicker, and louder and louder, every instant. The old man's terror *must* have been extreme! It grew louder, I say, louder every moment!—do you mark me well? I have told you that I am nervous: so I am. And now at the dead hour of the night, amid the dreadful silence of the old house, so strange a noise as this excited me to uncontrollable terror. Yet, for some minutes longer I refrained and stood still. But the beating grew louder, louder! I thought the heart must burst. And now a new anxiety seized me—the sound would be heard by a neighbour! The old man's hour had come! With a loud yell, I threw open the lantern and leaped into the room. He shrieked once—once only. In an instant I dragged him to the floor, and pulled the heavy bed over him. I then smiled gaily to find the deed so far done. But for many minutes the heart beat on with a muffled sound. This, however, did not vex me; it would not be heard through the wall. At length it ceased. The old man was dead. I removed the bed and examined the corpse. Yes, he was stone, stone dead. I placed my hand upon the heart and held it there many minutes. There was no pulsation. He was stone dead. His eye would trouble me no more.

If still you think me mad, you will think so no longer when I describe the wise precautions I took for the concealment of the body. The night waned, and I worked hastily, but in silence.

I took up three planks from the flooring of the chamber, and deposited all between the scantlings. I then replaced the boards so cleverly, so cunningly, that no human eye—not even *his*—could have detected anything wrong. There was nothing to wash out—no stain of any kind—no bloodspot whatever. I had been too wary for that.

When I had made an end of these labours, it was four o'clock—still dark as midnight. As the bell sounded the hour, there came a knocking at the street door. I went down to open it with a light heart,—for what had I *now* to fear? There entered three men, who introduced themselves with perfect suavity, as officers of the police. A shriek had been heard by a neighbour during the night; suspicion of foul play had been aroused; information had been lodged at the police office, and they (the officers) had been deputed to search the premises.

I smiled,—for *what* had I to fear? I bade the gentlemen welcome.

The shriek, I said, was my own in a dream. The old man, I mentioned, was absent in the country. I took my visitors all over the house; bade them search—search *well*. I led them, at length, to *his* chamber. I showed them his treasures, secure, undisturbed. In the enthusiasm of my confidence, I brought chairs into the room, and desired them *here* to rest from their fatigues, while I myself, in the wild audacity of my perfect triumph, placed my own seat upon the very spot beneath which reposed the corpse of the victim.

The officers were satisfied. My *manner* had convinced them. I was singularly at ease. They sat, and while I answered cheerily, they chatted of familiar things. But, ere long, I felt myself getting pale and wished them gone. My head ached, and I fancied a ringing in my ears; but still they sat, and still they chatted. The ringing became more distinct;—it continued and became more distinct: I talked more freely to get rid of the feeling: but it continued and gained definitiveness— until, at length, I found that the noise was *not* within my ears.

No doubt I now grew *very* pale;—but I talked more fluently, and with a heightened voice. Yet the sound increased—and what could I do? It was *a low, dull, quick sound—and much a sound as a watch makes when enveloped in cotton.* I gasped for breath—and yet the officers heard it not. I talked more quickly—more vehemently; but the noise steadily increased. I arose and argued about trifles, in a high key and with violent gesticulations; but the noise steadily increased. Why *would* they not be gone? I paced the floor to and fro with heavy strides, as if excited to fury by the observations of the men—but the noise steadily increased. O God! what *could* I do? I foamed—I raved—I swore! I swung the chair upon which I had been sitting, and grated it upon the boards, but the noise arose over all and continually increased. It grew louder— louder—*louder!* And still the men chatted pleasantly, and smiled. Was it possible they heard not? Almighty God!—no, no! They heard!— they suspected!—they *knew!*—they were making a mockery of my horror!—this I thought, and this I think. But anything was better than this agony! Anything was more tolerable than this derision! I could bear those hypocritical smiles no longer! I felt that I must scream or die!—and now—again!—hark! louder! louder! louder! *louder!*—

'Villains!' I shrieked, 'dissemble no more! I admit the deed!—tear up the planks!—here, here!—it is the beating of his hideous heart!'

137

NELSON'S LAST DAY

John Simpson

The cold rain came in such heavy squalls that not a solitary star showed above the restless sea. One moment the wind howled like a tormented hound; the next it died to a sigh in the night.

Nineteen miles off Cape Trafalgar, in the thin grey light that comes before dawn, silhouettes of twenty-six British men-of-war could be seen. They were all that stood between the hidden enemy fleet and a possible invasion of England. But where *was* the unseen Armada?

In such an atmosphere of nail-biting tension, none of the British sailors on board dared wager what the morrow would bring. Yet Vice-Admiral Nelson's sixth sense told him it would produce . . . a battle royal! Four times during the past week he'd predicted to Captain Hardy; 'The 21st will be our day!'

As dawn broke on that twenty-first day of October 1805, the rain suddenly stopped, the sky cleared, and the rising sun carved a pathway of burnished gold across the ocean. Only a heavy swell coming in from the vast Atlantic caused the three-masted men-of-war to roll slightly. Soon the white cliffs of Trafalgar would be seen on the eastern horizon, and already various look-outs were at their stations, eyes straining for a sight of land or enemy sail.

When Nelson left his sleeping quarters on his flagship HMS *Victory* that morning, he was dressed as usual in his admirals coat, but for some reason he did not wear his sword. That still lay on his cabin table below deck. It was to be the one time he fought in a battle without his sword. As he joined Captain Hardy on the poop he was in excellent spirits, and ready to face whatever adventure lay before him. Such was his mood that he declared to Hardy; 'Today, I'll not rest content unless we capture twenty enemy sail-of-the-line!'

Perhaps he was tempting providence, for within ten minutes of those words being spoken, a look-out on morning-watch, perched in the masthead of the HMS *Revenge* spotted a single sail on the eastern horizon. 'Enemy sail on the starboard bow!' he cried. Three minutes later the same sailor called again. This time in alarm. 'There's more than one of 'em! There's about forty of the devils!'

In fact there were thirty-three enemy ships in all; eighteen French and fifteen Spanish, under Admiral Pierre de Villeneuve, who commanded this huge squadron from his flagship *Bucentaure*. Soon, the eastern seascape was crowded with a legion of enemy masts bearing the colourful but ominous French and Spanish ensigns. It was the moment Nelson and the British crew had been waiting for, and hundreds of sleepy-eyed seamen scrambled up the hatchways to catch a glimpse of the hostile fleet.

Admiral Villeneuve had received orders to leave Cadiz Bay and land troops at Naples to strengthen Napoleon's waning military campaign in Southern Italy, but for some time he had hesitated before attempting to pierce the blockade of British ships. His orders were *not to go in search* of the enemy. But if his fleet should meet the British warships – then he was to fight to the death. Already the great Napoleon Boneparte had insulted him, calling him a coward. Well, he would show his Emperor; and what better way to do that than with a decisive victory over the British squadron?

So far there had been many encounters between his own ships and those of Lord Nelson, and each time because of successive setbacks, Napoleons plans to invade England had to be delayed. But now, if Villeneuve could crush the British war-dogs once and for all, then surely a victory would open wide the floodgates for a full-scale invasion of England.

The French Admiral looked through narrowed eyes at the distant

British fleet showing indistinct in the morning light. He estimated in his own mind that with the gentle northwest wind continuing to blow against his own ships it would take five hours before the rival squadrons would be close enough to engage in battle. Plenty of time to prepare. Time to call his captains together and remind everyone of them of their duty; especially the Spaniards! '*Vive le Empereur!*'

Six miles across the waves, on board HMS *Victory*, Lord Nelson's order was to hoist the signal, 'The British fleet are to sail in two columns.' Owing to the squalls of wind overnight, many ships had lost way. Now they began to close up and form two columns as part of Nelson's pre-arranged battle-plan.

Although the confrontation was still hours away, the gun crews began checking canons and bringing ammunition up from the magazines. Marines were cleaning their muskets; some of the men thinking what would be their last thoughts of their wives, children and sweethearts. Then they waited; tense and apprehensive as time ticked relentlessly away. One captain turned to his first lieutenant and calmly advised; 'You'd better wear silk stockings like me, for if you get shot in the leg it will be so much more manageable for the surgeon.'

At 9.30 a.m., the enemies were five miles apart, each ship showing full sail. British officers met over breakfast, but few could eat. There was a nervous expectancy in the air. Final plans were laid, for better or for worse. Then came the sound of the drum, beckoning the men to their posts, a little light headed after their pot of beer.

The ships of the combined fleets of Spain and France could be seen clearly now. Some flying the *tricolor*, others the red and yellow ensigns of Spain. At about eleven o'clock, the black snouts of the enemy guns slipped into view. Some of the Frenchmen were three-deckers, showing a terrifying one hundred and twelve guns. Young British hearts quailed at the sight. But the more experienced 'salts' merely grinned. They'd seen it all before. Someone called for a shanty to be sung and the sound of salt water ballads floated over the rippling water. Soon it would be the hissing noise of canonballs whipping through smoke filled air, the heaviest of which could smash right through three feet of solid timber, or leave a hole the size of a small football where a man stomach had been. Then there was chain shot, two half canonballs, to be fired at the rigging; or the raking grape-shot which could maim a dozen crew members in one firing. One hour more and all kinds of devilish destruction would be let loose.

Lord Nelson knew full well the fervid heat of battle. At Cape St Vincent he had directed his ship into action, alone and unsupported, and single-handed held two Spanish squadrons apart. At one time he was fighting seven enemy ships. Not content with such heroics, he managed to board and capture one enemy brig, and then from her deck board and take yet another!

The Battle of Cape St Vincent had earned Nelson a Knighthood – but all was not plain sailing in his naval career, for in his very next action, whilst engaged in an assault on Tenerife, a grapeshot smashed through his right elbow. Below the decks of his flag-ship in stifling heat, the arm was amputated. Nevertheless, further successful campaigns followed his recovery, and even before the approaching Battle of Trafalgar, Lord Nelson was England's most lauded hero.

Such a man as Nelson had destiny on his side. He commanded respect from officers and men alike. Every decision he made had to be carefully weighed, for its effect would be far reaching. Naturally he made mistakes, but these errors were by far eclipsed by his triumphs. However, his next decision on that sunlit morning off Cape Trafalgar was to prove most fateful. He decided that his own flagship HMS *Victory* would be *first* to break the enemy line.

Captain Hardy was appalled! He pointed out that Nelson, as the fleets commander-in-chief would be exposed to every possible danger. Not only canon and grape-shot, but musket fire too! But Nelson was absolutely convinced that only while he was *at the head* of an attack, could he exercise full control over the British squadron. He was adamant, and Hardy soon realized that further argument was useless. However, the Captain did point out that his commander made an excellent target for snipers, and he indicated the bright stars upon Nelsons splendid uniform, suggesting that perhaps His Lordship might change his coat? 'I agree Hardy,' returned Nelson, as he gazed upon the converging enemy. 'But it's too late now to be shifting a coat.' Then he turned calmly to his signals officer and ordered a communication to be sent to the whole fleet. It was the immortal message; 'England expects that every man will do his duty.' The very next order was; 'Prepare to engage the enemy in close action!'

By now the French and Spanish ships were 600 yards away and advancing menacingly in the battle formation of a crescent – as if to swallow up the British fleet in a crushing pincer movement.

Their broadsides turned to reveal rows of deadly iron barrels, ready at a given signal to discharge tons of venomous shot. Painted all colours, some ships had yellow sides, others blood red. A few were funereal black. Many sported decorative ribbons between their coloured decks. Some had carved figures on their prows. All looked proud, graceful and deadly, like cobras of the sea.

At twelve noon the first broadside was discharged.

Abruptly one French ship, the *Santa Ana* was towering over the British *Royal Sovereign* like a sword of Damocles. Yet miraculously, within a few minutes, the British guns had brought the *Santa Ana*'s masts crashing down.

Across the two fleets it was the same grisly tale of destruction. On almost every deck: Fire! Death! Headless bodies. A living nightmare. Flying splinters and grape shot. The stink of burnt flesh. The shrieking agony of wounded men. Disfigured corpses scattered everywhere, and the soft moans of the dying. This was the hideous outcome of war, and soon the salt waters were streaming with the blood of three nations.

At one broadside a hundred men would be shredded into mincemeat, with ropes and tackle lying in a twisted mess across the decks. The once varnished sides of the men o' war were now puckered with shot; the wounded piled high – and already there were as many dead as would sink three barges. The surgeon was the busiest man on board ship and if he died – then God help the wounded! In one private confrontation HMS *Revenge* had been rammed by a Spanish three-decker. The Spaniards bowsprit hung over the *Revenge*'s poop, with a whole party of men in her fore-rigging ready to board. Only the British marines with their rifles and carronades saved the day. But at that instant, with one minor battle won, a two-decked French ship appeared on the *Revenge*'s starboard side – while on the larboard bow yet another. Yet luck was still with the British ship for many of the French gunners shots struck their own ships, killing and wounding their compatriots.

Meanwhile, on board HMS *Victory*, death was already waiting in the wings for the gallant Nelson. He had but two hours to live. As his flagship attacked the enemy formation, the French and Spanish guns began an incessant raking fire. A shot struck the quarterdeck and passed between Lord Nelson and Captain Hardy. A splinter bruised the Captain's foot and tore the buckle from his shoe. Realizing that Hardy was not badly injured Nelson observed: 'This is much too frantic to last for long.'

The *Victory*'s mizzen mast was now gone. All her studding sails shot clean away. Thirty lay dead amidst the flying shot and thick acrid smoke. Nevertheless, *Victory* steered resolutely for a small gap in the enemy line. Passing directly between Admiral de Villeneuve's *Bucentaure*, and the Frenchman *Redoubtable*, HMS *Victory* was at the mercy of both her protagonists' guns. But with a defiant gesture, *Victory* fired double and treble shot into Villeneuve's great cabin windows, passing so close to the *Bucentaure* that her main yard-arm caught in the French leader's rigging. All her guns blazing, *Victory* pulverized the French commanders ship, putting at least thirty of her guns out of action. On the Frenchmans decks the dead were thrown back in heaps, with fresh shot further mangling the already mutilated bodies.

With *Bucentaure* behind her, the *Victory* moved into line with *Redoubtable*, and smashed the enemys masts to smithereens with devastating starboard broadsides. Now the English *Temeraire* joined the fray. Following the *Victory*, she was soon stationed on the opposite side of the *Redoubtable*, with the French *Fougueux* on her starboard bow. Four men o' war, two from each side were locked together in murderous combat.

Muskets spat from the mast-tops of the *Redoubtable*, decimating the *Victory*'s crew. Scarcely a sailor on the *Victory*'s foredeck escaped injury as Tyrolean snipers cooly picked off man after man. So close were the ships that there was the awesome prospect of the *Redoubtable* catching fire from the *Victory*'s blazing guns – and the possibility of the flames consuming both *Victory* and *Temeraire*.

With scenes of carnage on all sides, and the *Victory* filled with so many holes that she looked like a floating colander; Nelson ordered his marines to open fire on the snipers. The canons joined in this barbarous return of fire.

Suddenly *Redoubtable*'s main-mast swayed, seemed to falter, then came thundering down to smash across her decks. Only seconds afterwards her stern was stoved in. The rudder was fractured beyond repair. All the guns were broken or dismounted. Both sides of the ship were shattered. Most of the pumps were useless and the ladders which connected the decks were in ruins. Those same decks were littered with the victims of war. Yet still the survivors stubbornly cried; 'Vive le Empereur! Vive le Empereur!'

At 2 p.m. the French ship was so badly holed that she was in danger of sinking. At last her captain decided to surrender, ordering the colours to be hauled down. But even before this could be done with dignity, the main mast had crashed to the ground. Nearly 500 of *Redoubtable*'s crew were killed or wounded already and she was to have the worst casualty list in the battle.

Now, all over the frenzied waters, French and Spanish captains began striking their colours. Once *Victory* had broken the enemy line, it signalled the beginning of the end of the enemy.

Through blankets of thick smoke, fire balls descended. Men fought blindly on, others looked to survival. Nelson walked the *Victory*'s quarterdeck in the midst of that raging holocaust alongside Captain Hardy. He was in the act of turning. His eyes were directed towards the stern of the ship. Then the fatal musket ball was fired from the enemys mizzen top.

The ball struck the badge on his left shoulder and bit deep into his chest. He fell face down upon the deck. As Hardy approached, Nelson cried, 'They have done for me Hardy. My backbone is shot through!'

Captain Hardy immediately ordered two seamen to carry the Vice Admiral below. But before he left the deck Nelson still had the presence of mind to give an order regarding tiller ropes. He then covered his face with his handkerchief in the hope that his crew would remain ignorant of his injury. But within a minute, the news was all over the ship. Lord Nelson had been hit. In spite of this disaster, the great man had done enough . . . The tide of battle had turned.

*　　*　　*　　*

In a dim illumination cast by lantern candles, Nelson passed his last minutes. The Surgeon, Mr Beatty approached him and removed the handkerchief. Nelson looked up and muttered. 'Mr Beatty. You can do nothing for me. Attend to the others.' Beatty replied: 'I hope the

'*They have done for me,*' *cried Nelson.* '*My backbone is shot through.*'

wound is not as bad as Your Lordship imagines.' Nelson answered feverishly. 'Doctor, I told you – I am gone.'

Beatty probed at the wound in the half light. But when he discovered no injury to the skin of the Admiral's back, he realized that the musket ball must have lodged in the spine. He then inquired how His Lordship was feeling. 'I experience a gush of blood every minute within my breast.' said Nelson. 'I cannot feel the lower part of my body. I can hardly breathe. I believe my back is broken.'

These symptoms told Beatty that the wound was fatal. Although he tried to cheer his Admiral with hope, Nelson was not to be fooled. He sensed life ebbing from his body. But there were still questions to be answered! He had to hold on long enough to find out. He must speak with Captain Hardy. 'Will no-one bring Hardy to me?' he moaned. 'He must be killed? Surely Hardy is dead?'

But Captain Hardy was not only captaining the *Victory*, but also conducting the battle on behalf of Nelson. He would, he said, come below as soon as his duties allowed.

An hour gone and Hardy was at last bent over the broken body of Nelson. 'Well Hardy. How goes the battle?' 'Very well my Lord,' answered Hardy. 'We have fourteen of the enemys ships in our possession.' 'I trust none of our ships have lowered their colours?!' cried Nelson. 'None my Lord. Not one.' replied Hardy.

Twenty minutes after Captain Hardy had visited his wounded Admiral for a second time, Nelson's hands had grown quite cold. Soon, his heroic heart beat no more.

★   ★   ★   ★

The dismasted HMS *Victory* was now anchored. The sun was lowering in the western sky. All over the seascape, the ruins of once magnificent sailing vessels strove to stay afloat. Captains counted their dead. Crew members cleared up the wreckage and tended the wounded.

In the eerie quiet following the clamour of battle, the young midshipman of the watch on board HMS *Victory* pencilled in the log. 'Partial firing continued until 4.30, when a victory was reported to the Right Honourable Lord Nelson. He then died of his wound.'

So Nelson had been right. The 21st had been the day – a day of victory that became immortal.

CHERRY

Ann Lawrence

Cherry was the eldest child of a poor family that lived in Zennor some few years ago. She had nine younger brothers and sisters, all of whom grew up strong and healthy, which was God's blessing perhaps, but a sore puzzle to the parents, who had to put food in their bellies and clothes on their backs. Still, they were good-hearted, hard-working folk, and with a bit of kitchen garden, a pig and a few hens, they managed as well as most and better than many. They even sent all the children to the village school, at least until they could read and knew their times-tables, though there was more than one old gossip who said it was all fantasy. No good ever came of giving youngsters ideas above their station, they said.

In those days young girls generally went into service as soon as they left school, when they were about eleven or twelve years old, but Cherry was a sensible child, and her mother reckoned it was worth keeping her at home to help with the younger ones. When the second girl in the family was rising twelve, however, Cherry decided it was time she started to earn her living properly. Her mother was not that anxious to let her go—she had grown used to relying on her in so many ways—but Cherry says:

'Our Jenny'll be just as useful as ever I was, once she gets the chance.'

And off she sets for Towednack one spring morning, as bold as you like.

Only once she was up on the Downs and out of sight of home, her courage began to fail.

You would hardly credit it nowadays, but though Towednack was no more than five miles away, Cherry had never gone that far alone in all her fourteen years. (Come to that, with nine brothers and sisters, she had probably never been alone at all). It was not so surprising, then, if she suddenly felt lost out there on the bare hills, where the only works of man were the great standing stones set up by a forgotten people in a remote past, and the only voices to be heard were those of curlew and plover. By the time she came to the crossroads on the crest of the Downs, her heart was in her boots. She sat down on a boulder, ready to cry and with more than half a mind to turn back.

As she sat there, head in hands, trying to decide what to do, she heard the clink of harness. She looked up to see before her a fine-looking gentleman on a grey horse.

He was as pleasant-spoken as he was handsome, too.

'Can you tell me the way to Towednack, my dear?' he asks.

'Why yes, sir,' says Cherry, jumping up. 'I'm going there myself to look for a place.'

'Indeed?' says the gentleman. 'Then we may both be spared the journey. You want a situation; I want an honest girl to look after my child. Could you manage that?'

'I've nine younger brothers and sisters, so I think I might,' says Cherry modestly.

The gentleman laughs. His teeth show very white against his dark complexion.

'I think you might!' he says.

He dismounted and asked Cherry a few questions about her family and schooling. He commended her cleanly, tidy appearance, her neatly mended clothes, while she blushed, partly pleased by his approval, partly ashamed of her shabbiness. Finally he said he would engage her for a year and a day.

'And if we suit each other, we can extend the arrangement,' he says.

Cherry remembered little about that ride behind her new master, for his talk, always interesting and amusing, held her attention most of the time. Then again, she was tired from the excitement of leaving home, so maybe she dozed now and then. Quite soon after coming off the Downs, they turned off the road, between two stone pillars like tall gateposts, into a narrow lane. Steep banks rose on either side and trees arched overhead, so that it was like riding into a tunnel. A touch of unease brushed Cherry's mind, but it was dispelled at once as the gentleman began some new story of his travels, and she had only a vague impression of dark, winding ways, until they came to the ford. The stream flowed fast, but very dark and smooth. Once again something in her recoiled from a strangeness she could not name. But:

'Tuck your toes up, Cherry,' says her master cheerfully.

And the horse stepped quietly across.

The journey was nearly over then. After a short ride through open woodland they came to a gate in a high wall, through which they passed into a garden. Cherry glimpsed smooth grass, many different kinds of trees, banks of flowering shrubs, then they came to the front of the house.

As her master was helping her to dismount, the door opened, and a little boy ran out, shouting:

'Papa!'

Inside a week it was as if she had been there for ever. Her master was a widower called Mr Goodman, and the little boy's name was Aubrey. To her surprise there was only one other person in the house, an old woman, whom Mr Goodman introduced as Aunt Prudence, though Aubrey called her Granny. Cherry never did work out whether she really was related to them somehow, or was merely a servant like herself, for she addressed Mr Goodman with absolute freedom which was never rebuked, yet did all the cooking and most of the housework herself. She was a sharp-tongued old body, and Cherry was afraid of her at first. She snapped at the slightest mistake and invariably complained that she 'knew Robin would fetch home a fool', but she seemed to accept the girl in time. Cherry's principal occupation was looking after Aubrey, but she helped Aunt Prudence with any heavy work.

The nurseries were two long, low rooms at the top of the house.

Her master might have been amused to know that the day nursery surprised Cherry more than anything else in the house: the toys, the books, the huge rocking horse—that so many things should be provided for the diversion of one child was incredible to her. Aubrey himself puzzled her too, for he seemed so peevish and bored with all his treasures. Yet he responded readily to her pleasure in these things and the lively games she invented from them.

Aubrey was able to read a little, but still preferred to be read to, and at first this was the task Cherry dreaded, having never looked inside a book except at school. Indeed, she struggled through a page of print almost as painfully as the little boy. It soon came more easily to her, however, and her appetite for reading sharpened. In the evenings, after she had put her charge to bed, she began to work her way along his bookshelves: fairytales, nursery rhymes, simple history and geography, she absorbed them all, curled up in the big armchair in the day nursery.

Cherry and Aunt Prudence could hardly have managed the house between them, had not most of it been shut up. Only three rooms were in use on the ground floor. They took their meals in the big kitchen (Mr Goodman and Aubrey as well as Cherry and Aunt Prudence). Then there was a drawing-room, sparsely furnished, with white walls and long windows opening on the garden. Cherry thought it a strange, bare room, yet the rugs on the floor were richly patterned, and the curtains were figured with exotic foliage and flowers, reminding her of enchanted forests in Aubrey's books of fairytales.

The one other room she saw during her first weeks was the library, to which her master took her one morning. It was lined with books, with two large globes and something like the skeleton of a globe, made up of gilded hoops, standing in the middle of the floor, and a telescope set up at one of the windows.

'Use this room as you please,' says Mr Goodman.

As spring warmed to summer, Mr Goodman urged her to take Aubrey into the garden, and she discovered that there was no more help outside than in the house. The smooth-cut lawns and the supply of fresh vegetables suggested that there was at least a gardener, but Cherry found that her master did everything himself. He cut the grass with a mowing machine drawn by a donkey, on which Aubrey loved to ride, Cherry and his father walking on either side. Mr Goodman began to ask Cherry to help him whenever she was outdoors. He taught her a hundred things about plants and their uses, but even when the task was nothing more exciting than weeding in the kitchen garden, Cherry was happy.

One day when they are picking cherries, Mr Goodman on the ladder, Cherry standing at the foot of it holding a basket, he suddenly looks down at her and smiles.

'Pretty Cherry,' he says softly, and he pops a cherry into her mouth, already half-open with amazement.

The master was usually absent for a week or so every month. While he was away, some richness seemed to drain out of the house, as though it only truly lived when he was present. His return was the sun riding clear of a cloud. He never came empty-handed, either: there was always a package for Aunt Prudence's kitchen, a book or toy for Aubrey, and some pretty thing for Cherry too—a handkerchief, a bunch of ribbons, a string of beads. Aunt Prudence grumbled about spoiling and pampering, but she seemed to mean the little boy as much as his young nursemaid.

Years later, when she looked back to that time, it seemed as if it had always been spring or summer, but in fact the year passed from summer to autumn, and from autumn to winter, like any other. Towards the year's end Mr Goodman asked Cherry if she wanted to go home for Christmas, and she realised that she had never passed beyond the garden since she had arrived. Yet she had not felt enclosed.

'I suppose I could,' she says doubtfully. 'But I wouldn't want to, if it would put you out, sir,' she adds.

He smiles.

'I should miss you, Cherry,' he says.

'Then I'll stay,' says Cherry, blushing and looking at her toes.

He laughs under his breath and touches her cheek—oh, so gently—with the tips of his fingers.

Cherry thought they might have company at Christmas if at no other time, but still it was only the four of them, though they put up garlands of evergreens and Aunt Prudence brewed and baked as if to entertain half the county. After dinner they gathered round the fire

'Pretty Cherry,' he says softly, and he pops a cherry into her mouth.

in the drawing room, the enchanted forest shutting out the winter dusk, and Mr Goodman and Aunt Prudence told stories, turn and turn about, until Aubrey fell asleep in Cherry's arms. Carefully his father took him from her and carried him to bed. Cherry fetched milk and biscuits from the kitchen, then followed.

She meets her master at the foot of the stairs.

'Good night, sir,' she says, bobbing a little curtsy, and makes to pass.

But he stops her, one hand on her shoulder, the other tilting her face up to him.

'Pretty Cherry!' he whispers, and kisses her on the lips, so gently she can hardly believe it.

In the New Year Mr Goodman went away again, and Aunt Prudence was taken with a fit of spring-cleaning. She had Cherry running round, washing crockery and cleaning silver that had been stored away, while she herself went through the closed rooms.

Then one morning she says:

'Now we'll do the Gallery.'

And she leads Cherry through the part of the house she has never seen before.

The Gallery was a long room with windows all down one side, and a black-and-white chequered floor, that looked as slippery as glass. Cherry took one step inside, and stopped in her tracks. There were people everywhere—white and motionless.

'What's the matter, little simpleton?' cries Aunt Prudence. 'Never seen a statue before? Dear goodness! What did Robin think he was about, bringing you here?'

Cherry was annoyed with herself for giving the old woman an excuse to repeat her grumble. Of course she knew what statues were, though it was true she had never seen one before. She turned to without a word, as if it were any ordinary room, but she seemed to feel eyes watching her all the time. Eventually Aunt Prudence set her to polish a tall, narrow chest, covered with a mass of carving, that took a power of rubbing before it started to look good. Cherry rubbed so hard in the end, that the thing moved. It sighed, and gave a kind of groan. Already unnerved by the statues' stony gaze, Cherry fainted clean away.

When she came to herself, she was lying on a couch in the drawing-room. She heard voices: her master and Aunt Prudence. It seemed he was scolding the old woman for taking her into the Gallery.

'I expected you to know where to draw the line,' says he sharply.

'Oh, indeed?' says she, not a bit abashed. 'And how should I know that, when you don't know yourself?'

Then they both sensed that she was reviving. Aunt Prudence left the room, muttering to herself, while Mr Goodman sat on the edge of the couch and took Cherry's hands.

The weather turned mild: snowdrops and crocuses began to show. Spring stirred in the garden. For the first time Cherry felt restless. One night she woke with the sound of music in her ears. For a moment she thought she was dreaming, but it continued. She listened intently. It seemed to come from the part of the house that was shut up. She tiptoed along the landing to a window that overlooked the unoccupied wing. Light streamed from the windows of the Gallery.

Cherry asked no questions. She remembered the severity of her master's tone to Aunt Prudence, and dreaded to draw his anger on herself.

The spring burst into flower. Mr Goodman was at home more, and spent most of his time with Aubrey and Cherry. Yet somehow the perfect harmony had been disturbed, and she felt a current of unease beneath the quiet surface of their life. The last days of her agreed year of service ran swiftly away, like the last sand in an hourglass. Her master said nothing about renewing the contract, but his manner towards her was ever kinder and more attentive.

On a warm night the music woke her again. This time she resolved to see what was happening. As she crept along the passages, the music grew louder, mingled with talk and laughter. She crouched to look through the keyhole, and nearly cried out aloud.

It seemed to her that the marble people were moving freely about the Gallery, dressed as she remembered them, in strange, draped clothes or none at all. The music came, spritely and piping, from the tall chest that had frightened her. A lady in a green gown sat behind it, apparently playing it like a piano. Mr Goodman stood behind her, his hand resting lightly on her shoulder. When she stopped, she turned to him, smiling, and he bent to kiss her.

Cherry returned to the nursery with a heaviness inside that she did not understand.

Next day her master was laughing and affectionate as they worked in the garden, while Aubrey played at a little distance, but Cherry was withdrawn. At last he stopped.

'Come here, Cherry,' he says seriously.

She stands before him staring at the ground between them, but he lifts her chin and obliges her to look at him.

'What's the matter, Cherry?' he asks.

'Nothing,' says Cherry, but tears gather in her eyes.

'Tell me,' he coaxes. 'What can we do to make you happy again?'

'Teach me to play the music-box in the Gallery!' she blurts out, only thinking of how he kissed the lady in green.

Then his face becomes still and grave.

'What have you seen now, Cherry?' he says.

Cherry only shakes her head and cries. He puts his arm round her.

'Oh, my dear,' he says. 'I'm afraid Aunt Prudence was right—I shouldn't have brought you here.'

'Don't turn me away!' Cherry sobs.

'It's the end of your year,' says her master. 'And Aubrey goes to school soon, anyway. . . .'

Cherry left as she had come, mounted behind her master, but she saw even less of the way this time than before. She leaned against his back and heeded nothing. At the crossroads he dismounted and lifted her down.

'Here's your wages,' he says cheerfully, handing her a little purse, but she turns such a woeful face to him that his smile fades. He strokes her hair softly, touches her cheek. 'I had no choice,' he whispers. 'Pretty Cherry.'

He kisses her once more, and before she has blinked away her tears, he is gone.

Cherry's family was all agog to hear about her first year in service. At first her mother was disappointed by the vagueness of her account, but when she looked into the little purse, her disappointment changed to amazement and then suspicion.

'Mercy!' she cries, tipping twelve gold guineas out on the table.

'What's the matter?' says Cherry indifferently. 'Isn't it enough?'

'Enough?' says her mother. 'What could a girl like you do to earn so much?'

Then she began to question her closely about her master and how he had treated her. Cherry told her most things eventually, but just a little she kept to herself. Her mother did not know what to make of it. As the days passed she did not know what to make of Cherry either, she was so dreamy, so unlike herself, always wandering out on the Downs alone.

But the gossips thought they knew something, oh yes, though it was only old Mary Calineck who actually mentioned the Good Folk.

'Stuff and nonsense!' shouts Cherry's father. 'Find the girl another place and get her out of here quick, before the old fools turn her wits completely!'

Inside a week Cherry went off to be nursery maid in a big house over St Ives way. A Zennor lad called William was gardener's boy there, so she walked back with him when he returned from his Sunday off.

Cherry appeared to settle in easily, apart from a few early misunderstandings. She seemed not to realize, for instance, that servants were not expected to make free with the books in the library, but her mistress saw that she had not intended to be impertinent, and let her off with a sharp reprimand.

It did not take her long to recover her spirits. In fact her year in Mr Goodman's household soon began to seem like a dream. She realised now how unconventional that had been, and recognized the wisdom of her mother's advice to keep quiet about it. In a little while she hardly even thought about it, as she became drawn into the concerns of the other girls of her own age.

Every other Sunday she went home with William for the afternoon. In a little while the word was that Cherry and William were walking out. Cherry smiled and did not deny it.

William kissed her, hard, clumsy and earnest. Cherry turned away, blushing and giggling, but did not discourage him.

Only once did she show any sign of lingering strangeness or regret. It was on the Sunday a couple of years later, when William asked her to marry him, having been promoted to under-gardener the day before. She seemed surprised, and would not answer him, but begged to be left alone for a while.

She walked over the Downs. At the crossroads she loitered for some minutes, as if she were waiting for someone, then she set off down the hill, looking for two stone pillars, like gateposts, on either side of the entrance to a narrow lane, almost overgrown with trees. She went on for near an hour, until a farmhouse came in sight, but the lane was not to be found.

Cherry married William. He was a steady fellow. He certainly loved her—though he never touched her face with his finger tips, as if he feared to spoil its bloom, nor whispered 'Pretty Cherry!', half-laughing under his breath.

But then, Cherry never expected him to.

TO BUILD A FIRE

Jack London

Day had broken cold and grey, exceedingly cold and grey, when the man turned aside from the main Yukon trail and climbed the high earth-bank, where a dim and little-travelled trail led eastward through the fat spruce timberland. It was a steep bank, and he paused for breath at the top, excusing the act to himself by looking at his watch. It was nine o'clock. There was no sun nor hint of sun, though there was not a cloud in the sky. It was a clear day, and yet there seemed an intangible pall over the face of things, a subtle gloom that made the day dark, and that was due to the absence of sun. This did not worry the man. He was used to the lack of sun. It had been days since he had seen the sun, and he knew that a few more days must pass before that cheerful orb, due south, would just peep above the skyline and dip immediately from view.

The man flung a look back along the way he had come. The Yukon lay a mile wide and hidden under three feet of ice. On top of this ice were as many feet of snow. It was all pure white, rolling in gentle undulations where the ice-jams of the freeze-up had formed. North and south, as far as his eye could see, it was unbroken white, save for a dark hair-line that curved and twisted from around the spruce-covered island to the south, and that curved and twisted away into the north, where it disappeared behind another spruce-covered island. This dark hair-line was the trail—the main trail—that led south five hundred miles to the Chilcoot Pass, Dyea, and salt water; and that led north seventy miles to Dawson, and still on to the north a thousand miles to Nulato, and finally to St Michael on Bering Sea, a thousand miles and half a thousand more.

But all this—the mysterious, far-reaching hair-line trail, the absence of sun from the sky, the tremendous cold, and the strangeness and weirdness of it all—made no impression on the man. It was not because he was long used to it. He was a newcomer in the land, a *chechaquo*, and this was his first winter. The trouble with him was that he was without imagination. He was quick and alert in the things of life, but only in the things, and not in the significances. Fifty degrees below zero meant eighty-odd degrees of frost.

Such fact impressed him as being cold and uncomfortable, and that was all. It did not lead him to meditate upon his frailty as a creature of temperature, and upon man's frailty in general, able only to live within certain narrow limits of heat and cold; and from there on it did not lead him to the conjectural field of immortality and man's place in the universe. Fifty degrees below zero stood for a bite of frost that hurt and that must be guarded against by the use of mittens, ear-flaps, warm moccasins and thick socks. Fifty degrees below zero was to him just precisely fifty degrees below zero. That there should be anything more to it than that was a thought that never entered his head.

As he turned to go on, he spat speculatively. There was a sharp, explosive crackle that startled him. He spat again. And again, in the air, before it could fall to the snow, the spittle crackled. He knew that at fifty below spittle crackled on the snow, but this spittle had crackled in the air. Undoubtedly it was colder than fifty below—how much colder he did not know.

But the temperature did not matter. He was bound for the old claim on the left fork of Henderson Creek, where the boys were already. They had come over across the divide from the Indian Creek country, while he had come the roundabout way to take a look at the possibilities of getting out logs in the spring from the islands in the Yukon. He would be in to camp by six o'clock; a bit after dark, it was true, but the boys would be there, a fire would be going, and a hot supper would be ready. As for lunch, he pressed his hand against the protruding bundle under his jacket. It was also under his shirt, wrapped up in a handkerchief and lying against the naked skin. It was the only way to keep the biscuits from freezing. He smiled agreeably to himself as he thought of those biscuits, each cut open and sopped in bacon grease, and each enclosing a generous slice of fried bacon.

He plunged in among the big spruce trees. The trail was faint. A foot of snow had fallen since the last sled had passed over, and he was glad he was without a sled, travelling light. In fact, he carried nothing but the lunch wrapped in the handkerchief. He was surprised, however, at the cold. It certainly was cold, he concluded, as he rubbed his numb nose and cheek-bones with his mittened hand. He was a warm-whiskered man, but the hair on his face did not protect the high cheek-bones and the eager nose that thrust itself aggressively into the frosty air.

At the man's heels trotted a dog, a big native husky, the proper wolf-dog, grey-coated and without any visible or temperamental difference from its brother, the wild wolf. The animal was depressed by the tremendous cold. It knew that it was no time for travelling. Its instinct told it a truer tale than was told to the man by the man's judgement. In reality, it was not merely colder than fifty below zero; it was colder than sixty below, than seventy below. It was seventy-five below zero. Since the freezing point is thirty-two *above* zero, it meant that one hundred and seven degrees of frost obtained.

The dog did not know anything about thermometers. Possibly in its brain there was no sharp consciousness of a condition of very cold such as was in the man's brain. But the brute had its instinct. It experienced a vague but menacing apprehension that subdued it and made it slink along at the man's heels, and that made it question eagerly every unwonted movement of the man as if expecting him to go into camp or to seek shelter somewhere and build a fire. The dog had learned fire, and it wanted fire, or else to burrow under the snow and cuddle its warmth away from the air.

The frozen moisture of its breathing had settled on its fur in a fine powder of frost, and especially were its jowls, muzzle, and eyelashes whitened by its crystalled breath. The man's red beard and moustache were likewise frosted, but more solidly, the deposit taking the form of ice and increasing with every warm, moist breath he exhaled.

Also, the man was chewing tobacco, and the muzzle of ice held his lips so rigidly that he was unable to clear his chin when he expelled the juice. The result was that a crystal beard of the colour and solidity of amber was increasing its length on his chin. If he fell down it would shatter itself, like glass, into brittle fragments. But he did not mind the appendage. It was the penalty all tobacco-chewers paid in that country, and he had been out before in two cold snaps. They had not been so cold as this, he knew, but by the spirit thermometer at Sixty Mile he knew they had been registered at fifty below and at fifty-five.

He held on through the level stretch of woods for several miles, crossed a wide flat of nigger-heads, and dropped down a bank to the frozen bed of a small stream. This was Henderson Creek, and he knew he was ten miles from the forks. He looked at his watch. It was ten o'clock. He was making four miles an hour, and he calculated that he would arrive at the forks at half-past twelve. He decided to celebrate that event by eating his lunch there.

The dog dropped in again at his heels, with a tail drooping discouragement, as the man swung along the creek-bed. The furrow of the old sled-trail was plainly visible, but a dozen inches of snow covered the marks of the last runners. In a month no man had come up or down that silent creek. The man held steadily on. He was not much given to thinking, and just then particularly he had nothing to think about save that he would eat lunch at the forks and that at six o'clock he would be in camp with the boys. There was nobody to talk to; and, had there been, speech would have been impossible because of the ice-muzzle on his mouth. So he continued monotonously to chew tobacco and to increase the length of his amber beard.

Once in a while the thought reiterated itself that it was very cold and that he had never experienced such cold. As he walked along he rubbed his cheek-bones and nose with the back of his mittened hand. He did this automatically, now and again changing hands. But rub as he would, the instant he stopped his cheek-bones went numb, and the following instant the end of his nose went numb. He was sure to frost his cheeks; he knew that, and experienced a pang of regret that he had not devised a nose-strap of the sort Bud wore in cold snaps. Such a strap passed across the cheeks, as well, and saved them. But it didn't matter much, after all. What were frosted cheeks? A bit painful, that was all; they were never serious.

Empty as the man's mind was of thoughts, he was keenly observant, and he noticed the changes in the creek, the curves and bends and timber-jams, and always he sharply noted where he placed his feet. Once, coming around a bend, he shied abruptly, like a startled horse, curved away from the place where he had been walking, and retreated several paces back along the trail. The creek he knew was frozen clear to the bottom—no creek could contain water in that Arctic winter—but he knew also that there were springs that bubbled out from the hillsides and ran along under the snow and on top the ice of the creek. He knew that the coldest snaps never froze these springs, and he knew likewise their danger.

They were traps. They hid pools of water under the snow that might be three inches deep, or three feet. Sometimes a skin of ice half an inch thick covered them, and in turn was covered by the snow. Sometimes there were alternate layers of water and ice-skin, so that when one broke through he kept on breaking through for a while, sometimes wetting himself to the waist.

That was why he had shied in such panic. He had felt the give under his feet and heard the crackle of a snow-hidden ice-skin. And to get his feet wet in such a temperature meant trouble and danger. At the very least it meant delay, for he would be forced to stop and build a fire, and under its protection to bare his feet while he dried his socks and moccasins. He stood and studied the creek-bed and its banks, and decided that the flow of water came from the right. He reflected a while, rubbing his nose and cheeks, then skirted to the left, stepping gingerly and testing the footing for each step. Once clear of the danger, he took a fresh chew of tobacco and swung along at his four-mile gait.

In the course of the next two hours he came upon several similar traps. Usually the snow above the hidden pools had a sunken, candied appearance that advertised the danger. Once again, however, he had a close call; and once, suspecting danger, he compelled the dog to go on in front. The dog did not want to go. It hung back until the man shoved it forward, and then it went quickly across the white, unbroken surface. Suddenly it broke through, floundered to one side, and got away to firmer footing. It had wet its forefeet and legs, and almost immediately the water that clung to it turned to ice. It made quick efforts to lick the ice off its legs, then dropped down in the snow and began to bite out the ice that had formed between the toes. This was a matter of instinct. To permit the ice to remain would mean sore feet. It did not know this, it merely obeyed the mysterious prompting that arose from the deep crypts of its being. But the man knew, having achieved a judgment on the subject, and he removed the mitten from his right hand and helped tear out the ice-particles. He did not expose his fingers more than a minute, and was astonished at the swift numbness that smote them. It certainly was cold. He pulled on the mitten hastily, and beat the hand savagely across his chest.

At twelve o'clock the day was at its brightest. Yet the sun was too far south on its winter journey to clear the horizon. The bulge of the earth intervened between it and Henderson Creek, where the man walked under clear sky at noon and cast no shadow. At half-past twelve, to the minute, he arrived at the forks of the creek. He was pleased at the speed he had made. If he kept it up, he would certainly be with the boys by six. He unbuttoned his jacket and shirt and drew forth his lunch. The action consumed no more than a quarter of a minute, yet in that brief moment the numbness laid hold of the exposed fingers. He did not put the mitten on, but instead struck the fingers a dozen sharp smashes against his leg.

Then he sat down on a snow-covered lot to eat. The sting that followed upon the striking of his fingers against his leg ceased so quickly that he was startled. He had had no chance to take a bite of biscuit. He struck the fingers repeatedly and returned them to the mitten, baring the other hand for the purpose of eating. He tried to take a mouthful, but the ice-muzzle prevented. He had forgotten to build a fire and thaw out. He chuckled at his foolishness, and as he chuckled he noted the numbness creeping into the exposed fingers. Also, he noted that the stinging which had first come to his toes when he sat down was already passing away. He wondered whether the toes were warm or numb. He moved them inside the moccasins and decided that they were numb.

He pulled the mitten on hurriedly and stood up. He was a bit frightened. He stamped up and down until the stinging returned into the feet. It certainly was cold, was his thought. That man from Sulphur Creek had spoken the truth when telling how cold it sometimes got in the country. And he had laughed at him at the time! That showed one must not be too sure of things. There was no mistake about it, it *was* cold. He strode up and down, stamping his feet and threshing his arms, until reassured by the returning warmth.

Then he got out matches and proceeded to make a fire. From the undergrowth, where high water of the previous spring had lodged a supply of seasoned twigs, he got his firewood. Working carefully from a small beginning, he soon had a roaring fire, over which he thawed the ice from his face and in the protection of which he ate his biscuits. For the moment the cold of space was outwitted. The dog took satisfaction in the fire, stretching out close enough for warmth and far enough away to escape being singed.

When the man had finished, he filled his pipe and took his comfortable time over a smoke. Then he pulled on his mittens, settled the earflaps of his cap firmly about his ears, and took the creek trail up the left fork. The dog was disappointed and yearned back toward the fire. This man did not know cold. Possibly all the generations of his ancestry had been ignorant of cold, of real cold, of cold one hundred and seven degrees below freezing point. But the dog knew; all its ancestry knew, and it had inherited the knowledge. And it knew that it was not good to walk abroad in such fearful cold. It was the time to lie snug in a hole in the snow and wait for a curtain of cloud to be drawn across the face of outer space whence this cold came.

On the other hand, there was no keen intimacy between the dog and the man. The one was the toil-slave of the other, and the only caresses it had ever received were the caresses of the whiplash and of harsh and menacing throat-sounds that threatened the whiplash. So the dog made no effort to communicate its apprehension to the man. It was not concerned in the welfare of the man; it was for its own sake that it yearned back toward the fire. But the man whistled, and spoke to it with the sound of whiplashes, and the dog swung in at the man's heel and followed after.

The man took a chew of tobacco and proceeded to start a new amber beard. Also, his moist breath quickly powdered with white his moustache, eyebrows, and lashes. There did not seem to be so many springs on the left fork of the Henderson, and for half an hour the man saw no signs of any. And then it happened. At a place where there were no signs, where the soft, unbroken snow seemed to advertise solidity beneath, the man broke through. It was not deep. He wet himself halfway to the knees before he floundered out to the firm crust.

He was angry, and cursed his luck aloud. He had hoped to get into camp with the boys at six o'clock, and this would delay him an hour, for he would have to build a fire and dry out his foot-gear. This was imperative at that low temperature—he knew that much; and he turned aside to the bank, which he climbed. On top, tangled in the underbrush about the trunks of several small spruce trees, was a high-water deposit of dry firewood—sticks and twigs, principally, but also larger portions of seasoned branches and fine, dry, last year's grasses. He threw down several large pieces on top of the snow. This served for a foundation and prevented the young flame from drowning itself in the snow it otherwise would melt. The flame he got by touching a match to a small shred of birch bark that he took from his pocket. This burned even more readily than paper. Placing it on the foundation, he fed the young flame with wisps of dry grass and with the tiniest dry twigs.

He worked slowly and carefully, keenly aware of his danger. Gradually, as the flame grew stronger, he increased the size of the twigs with which he fed it. He squatted in the snow, pulling the twigs out from their entanglement in the brush and feeding directly to the flame. He knew there must be no failure. When it is seventy-five below zero, a man must not fail in his first attempt to build a fire—that is, if his feet are wet. If his feet are dry, and he fails, he can run along the trail for half a mile and restore his circulation. But the circulation of wet and freezing feet cannot be restored by running when it is seventy-five below. No matter how fast he runs, the wet feet will freeze the harder.

All this the man knew. The old-timer on Sulphur Creek had told him about it, and now he was appreciating the advice. Already all sensation had gone out of his feet. To build the fire he had been forced to remove his mittens, and the fingers had quickly gone numb. His pace of four miles an hour had kept his heart pumping blood to the surface of his body and to all the extremities. But the instant he stopped, the action of the pump eased down. The cold of space smote the unprotected tip of the planet, and he, being on that unprotected tip, received the full force of the blow. The blood of his body recoiled before it.

The blood was alive, like the dog, and like the dog it wanted to hide away and cover itself up from the fearful cold. So long as he walked four miles an hour, he pumped that blood to the surface; but now, it ebbed away and sank down into the recesses of his body. The extremities were the first to feel its absence. His wet feet froze the faster, and his exposed fingers numbed the faster; though they had not yet begun to freeze. Nose and cheeks were already freezing, while the skin of all his body chilled as it lost its blood.

But he was safe. Toes and nose and cheeks would be only touched by the frost, for the fire was beginning to burn with strength. He was feeding it with twigs the size of his finger. In another minute he would be able to feed it with branches the size of his wrist, and then he could remove his wet foot-gear and, while it dried, he could keep his naked feet warm by the fire, rubbing them at first, of course, with snow. The fire was a success. He was safe.

He remembered the advice of the old-timer on Sulphur Creek, and smiled. The old-timer had been very serious in laying down the law that no man must travel alone in the Klondike after fifty below. Well, here he was; he had had the accident; he was alone; and he had saved himself. Those old-timers were rather womanish, some of them, he thought. All a man had to do was to keep his head; and he was all right. Any man who was a man could travel alone. But it was surprising, the rapidity with which his cheeks and nose were freezing. And he had not thought his fingers could go lifeless in so short a time. Lifeless they were, for he could scarcely make them move together to grip a twig, and they seemed remote from his body and from him. When he touched a twig, he had to look and see whether or not he had hold of it. The wires were pretty well down between him and his finger-ends.

All of which counted for little. There was the fire, snapping and crackling and promising life with every dancing flame. He started to untie his moccasins. They were coated with ice; the thick German socks were like sheaths of iron halfway to the knees; and the moccasin strings were like rods of steel all twisted and knotted as by some conflagration. For a moment he tugged with his numb fingers, then, realizing the folly of it, he drew his sheath-knife.

But before he could cut the strings, it happened. It was his own fault or, rather, his mistake. He should not have built the fire under the spruce tree. He should have built it in the open. But it had been easier to pull the twigs from the brush and drop them directly on the fire. Now the tree under which he had done this carried a weight of snow on its boughs. No wind had blown for weeks, and each bough was fully freighted. Each time he had pulled a twig he had communicated a slight agitation to the tree—an imperceptible agitation, so far as he was concerned, but an agitation sufficient to bring about the disaster. High up in the tree one bough capsized its load of snow. This fell on the boughs beneath, capsizing them. This process continued, spreading out and involving the whole tree. It grew like an avalanche, and it descended without warning upon the man and the fire—and the fire was blotted out! Where it had burned was a mantle of fresh and disordered snow.

The man was shocked. It was as though he had just heard his own sentence of death. For a moment he sat and stared at the spot where the fire had been. Then he grew very calm. Perhaps the old-timer on Sulphur Creek was right. If he had only had a trail-mate he would have been in no danger now. The trail-mate could have built the fire. Well, it was up to him to build the fire over again, and this second time there must be no failure. Even if he succeeded, he would most likely lose some toes. His feet must be badly frozen by now, and there would be some time before the second fire was ready.

Such were his thoughts, but he did not sit and think them. He was busy all the time they were passing through his mind. He made a new foundation for a fire, this time in the open, where no treacherous tree could blot it out. Next, he gathered dry grasses and tiny twigs from the high-water flotsam. He could not bring his fingers together to pull them out, but he was able to gather them by the handful. In this way he got many rotten twigs and bits of green moss that were undesirable, but it was the best he could do. He worked methodically, even collecting an armful of the larger branches to be used later when the fire gathered strength. And all the while the dog sat and watched him, a certain yearning wistfulness in its eyes, for it looked upon him as the fire-provider, and the fire was slow in coming.

When all was ready, the man reached in his pocket for a second piece of birch bark. He knew the bark was there, and, though he could not feel it with his fingers, he could hear its crisp rustling as he fumbled for it. Try as he would, he could not clutch hold of it. And all the time, in his

The snow descended without warning on the man and the fire . . .

consciousness, was the knowledge that each instant his feet were freezing. This thought tended to put him in a panic, but he fought against it and kept calm.

He pulled on his mittens with his teeth, and threshed his arms back and forth, beating his hands with all his might against his sides. He did this sitting down, and he stood up to do it; and all the while the dog sat in the snow, its wolf-brush of a tail curled around warmly over its forefeet, its sharp wolf-ears pricked forward intently as it watched the man. And the man, as he beat and threshed with his arms and hands, felt a great surge of envy as he regarded the creature that was warm and secure in its natural covering.

After a time he was aware of the first faraway signals of sensation in his beaten fingers. The faint tingling grew stronger till it evolved into a stinging ache that was excruciating, but which the man hailed with satisfaction. He stripped the mitten from his right hand and fetched forth the birch bark. The exposed fingers were quickly going numb again. Next he brought out his bunch of sulphur matches. But the tremendous cold had already driven the life out of his fingers. In his effort to separate one match from the others, the whole bunch fell in the snow. He tried to pick it out of the snow, but failed.

The dead fingers could neither touch nor clutch. He was very careful. He drove the thought of his freezing feet, and nose, and cheeks, out of his mind, devoting his whole soul to the matches. He watched, using the sense of vision in place of touch, and when he saw his fingers on each side the bunch, he closed them—that is, he willed to close them, for the wires were down, and the fingers did not obey. He pulled the mitten on the right hand, and beat it fiercely against his knee. Then, with both mittened hands he scooped the bunch of matches, along with much snow, into his lap. Yet he was no better off.

After some manipulation he managed to get the bunch between the heels of his mittened hands. In this fashion he carried it to his mouth. The ice crackled and snapped when by a violent effort he opened his mouth. He drew the lower jaw in, curled the upper lip out of the way, and scraped the bunch with his upper teeth in order to separate a match. He succeeded in getting one, which he dropped on his lap. He was no better off. He could not pick it up. Then he devised a way. He picked it up in his teeth and scratched it on his leg. Twenty times he scratched before he succeeded in lighting it. As it flamed he held it with his teeth to the birch bark. But the burning brimstone went up his nostrils and into his lungs, causing him to cough spasmodically. The match fell into the snow and went out.

The old-timer on Sulphur Creek was right, he thought in the moment of controlled despair that ensued: after fifty below, a man should travel with a partner. He beat his hands, but failed in exciting any sensation. Suddenly he bared both hands, removing the mittens with his teeth. He caught the whole bunch between the heels of his hands. His arm muscles not being frozen enabled him to press the hand-heels tightly against the matches. Then he scratched the bunch along his leg. It flared into flame, seventy sulphur matches at once! There was no wind to blow them out. He kept his head to one side to escape the strangling fumes, and held the blazing bunch to the birch bark. As he so held it, he became aware of sensation in his hand. His flesh was burning! He could smell it. Deep down below the surface he could feel it. The sensation developed into pain that grew acute. And still he endured it, holding the flame of the matches clumsily to the bark that would not light readily because his own burning hands were in the way, absorbing most of the flame.

At last, when he could endure no more, he jerked his hands apart. The blazing matches fell sizzling into the snow, but the birch bark was alight. He began laying dry grasses and the tiniest twigs on the flame. He could not pick and choose, for he had to lift the fuel between the heels of his hands. Small pieces of rotten wood and green moss clung to the twigs, and he bit them off as well as he could with his teeth. He cherished the flame carefully and awkwardly. It meant life, and it must not perish.

The withdrawal of blood from the surface of his body now made him begin to shiver, and he grew more awkward. A large piece of green moss fell squarely on the little fire. He tried to poke it out with his fingers, but his shivering frame made him poke too far, and he disrupted the nucleus of the fire, the burning grasses and tiny twigs separating and scattering. He tried to poke them together again, but in spite of the tenseness of the effort, his shivering got away with him, and the twigs were hopelessly scattered. Each twig gushed a puff of smoke and went out.

The fire-provider had failed. As he looked apathetically about him, his eyes chanced on the dog, sitting across the ruins of the fire from him, in the snow, making restless, hunching movements, slightly lifting one forefoot and then the other, shifting its weight back and forth on them with wistful eagerness.

The sight of the dog put a wild idea into his head. He remembered the tale of the man, caught in a blizzard, who killed a steer and crawled inside the carcass, and so was saved. He would kill the dog and bury his hands in the warm body until the numbness went out of them. Then he could build another fire. He spoke to the dog, calling it to him; but in his voice was a strange note of fear that frightened the animal, who had never known the man to speak in such way before. Something was the matter, and its suspicious nature sensed danger—it knew not what danger, but somewhere, somehow, in its brain arose an appre-hension of the man. It flattened its ears down at the sound of the man's voice, and its restless, hunching movements and the liftings and shiftings of its forefeet became more pronounced; but it would not come to the man. He got on his hands and knees and crawled towards the dog. This unusual posture again excited suspicion, and the animal sidled mincingly away.

The man sat up in the snow for a moment and struggled for calmness. Then he pulled on his mittens, by means of his teeth, and got upon his feet. He glanced down at first in order to assure himself that he was really standing up, for the absence of sensation in his feet left him un-related to the earth. His erect position in itself started to drive the webs of suspicion from the dog's mind; and when he spoke peremptorily, with the sound of whiplashes in his voice, the dog rendered its custom-ary allegiance and came to him.

As it came within reaching distance, the man lost his control. His arms flashed out to the dog, and he experienced genuine surprise when he discovered that his hands could not clutch, that there was neither bend nor feeling in the fingers. He had forgotten for the moment that they were frozen and that they were freezing more and more. All this happened quickly, and before the animal could get away, he encircled its body with his arms. He sat down in the snow, and in this fashion held the dog, while it snarled and whined and struggled.

But it was all he could do, hold its body encircled in his arms and sit there. He realized that he could not kill the dog. There was no way to do it. With his helpless hands he could neither draw nor hold his sheath-knife, nor throttle the animal. He released it, and it plunged wildly away, with tail between its legs, and still snarling. It halted forty feet away and surveyed him curiously, with ears sharply pricked forward.

The man looked down at his hands in order to locate them, and found them hanging on the ends of his arms. It struck him as curious that one should have to use his eyes in order to find out where his hands were. He began threshing his arms back and forth, beating the mittened hands against his sides. He did this for five minutes, violently, and his heart pumped enough blood up to the surface to put a stop to his shivering. But no sensation was aroused in the hands. He had an impression that they hung like weights on the ends of his arms, but when he tried to run the impression down, he could not find it.

A certain fear of death, dull and oppressive, came to him. This fear quickly became poignant as he realized that it was no longer a mere matter of freezing his fingers and toes, or of losing his hands and feet, but that it was a matter of life and death with the chances against him. This threw him into a panic, and he turned and ran up the creek-bed along the old, dim trail. The dog joined in behind and kept up with him. He ran blindly, without intention, in fear such as he had never known in his life. Slowly, as he ploughed and floundered through the snow, he began to see things again—the banks of the creeks, the old timber-jams, the leafless aspens, and the sky.

The running made him feel better. He did not shiver. Maybe, if he ran on, his feet would thaw out; and, anyway, if he ran far enough, he would reach camp and the boys. Without doubt he would lose some fingers and toes and some of his face; but the boys would take care of him, and save the rest of him when he got there. And at the same time there was another thought in his mind that said he would never get to the camp and the boys; that it was too many miles away, that the freezing had too great a start on him, and that he would soon be stiff and dead. This thought he kept in the background and refused to consider. Sometimes it pushed itself forward and demanded to be heard, but he thrust it back and strove to think of other things.

It struck him as curious that he could run at all on feet so frozen that he could not feel them when they struck the earth and took the weight

But it was all he could do, hold the dog's body in his arms.

of his body. He seemed to himself to skim along the surface, and to have no connection with the earth. Somewhere he had once seen a winged Mercury, and he wondered if Mercury felt as he felt when skimming over the earth.

His theory of running until he reached camp and the boys had one flaw in it: he lacked the endurance. Several times he stumbled, and finally he tottered, crumpled up, and fell. When he tried to rise, he failed. He must sit and rest, he decided, and next time he would merely walk and keep on going. As he sat and regained his breath, he noted that he was feeling quite warm and comfortable. He was not shivering, and it even seemed that a warm glow had come to his chest and trunk. And yet, when he touched his nose or cheeks, there was no sensation. Running would not thaw them out. Nor would it thaw out his hands and feet.

Then the thought came to him that the frozen portions of his body must be extending. He tried to keep this thought down, to forget it, to think of something else; he was aware of the panicky feeling that it caused, and he was afraid of the panic. But the thought asserted itself, and persisted, until it produced a vision of his body totally frozen. This was too much, and he made another wild run along the trail. Once he slowed down to a walk, but the thought of the freezing extending itself made him run again.

And all the time the dog ran with him, at his heels. When he fell down a second time, it curled its tail over its forefeet and sat in front of him, facing him, curiously eager and intent. The warmth and security of the animal angered him, and he cursed it till it flattened down its ears appeasingly. This time the shivering came more quickly upon the man. He was losing in his battle with the frost. It was creeping into his body from all sides. The thought of it drove him on, but he ran no more than a hundred feet, when he staggered and pitched headlong.

It was his last panic. When he had recovered his breath and control, he sat up and entertained in his mind the conception of meeting death with dignity. However, the conception did not come to him in such terms. His idea of it was that he had been making a fool of himself, running around like a chicken with its head cut off—such was the simile that occurred to him. Well, he was bound to freeze anyway, and he might as well take it decently. With this new-found peace of mind came the first glimmerings of drowsiness. A good idea, he thought, to sleep off to death. It was like taking an anaesthetic. Freezing was not so bad as people thought. There were lots worse ways to die.

He pictured the boys finding his body next day. Suddenly he found himself with them, coming along the trail and looking for himself. And, still with them, he came around a turn in the trail and found himself lying in the snow. He did not belong with himself any more, for even then he was out of himself, standing with the boys and looking at himself in the snow. It certainly was cold, was his thought. When he got back to the States he could tell the folks what real cold was. He drifted on from this to a vision of the old-timer on Sulphur Creek. He could see him quite clearly, warm and comfortable, and smoking a pipe.

'You were right, old hoss; you were right,' the man mumbled to the old-timer of Sulphur Creek.

Then the man drowsed off into what seemed to him the most comfortable and satisfying sleep he had ever known. The dog sat facing him and waiting. The brief day drew to a close in a long, slow twilight. There were no signs of a fire to be made, and, besides, never in the dog's experience had it known a man to sit like that in the snow and make no fire. As the twilight drew on, its eager yearning for the fire mastered it, and with a great lifting and shifting of forefeet, it whined softly, then flattened its ears down in anticipation of being scolded by the man.

But the man remained silent. Later, the dog whined loudly. And still later it crept close to the man and caught the scent of death. This made the animal bristle and back away. A little longer it delayed, howling under the stars that leaped and danced and shone brightly in the cold sky. Then it turned and trotted up the trail in the direction of the camp it knew, where were the other food-providers and fire-providers.

THE DANCING ACADEMY

Charles Dickens

Of all the dancing academies that ever were established, there never was one more popular in its immediate vicinity than Signor Billsmethi's, of the 'King's Theatre'. It was not in Spring Gardens, or Newman Street, or Berners Street, or Gower Street, or Charlotte Street, or Percy Street, or any other of the numerous streets which have been devoted time out of mind to professional people, dispensaries, and boarding-houses; it was not in the West End at all—it rather approximated to the eastern portion of London, being situated in the populous and improving neighbourhood of Gray's Inn Lane.

It was not a dear dancing academy—four-and-sixpence a quarter is decidedly cheap upon the whole. It was *very* select, the number of pupils being strictly limited to seventy-five, and a quarter's payment in advance being rigidly exacted. There was public tuition and private tuition—an assembly-room and a parlour. Signor Billsmethi's family were always thrown in with the parlour, and included in parlour price; that is to say a private pupil had Signor Billsmethi's parlour to dance *in*, and Signor Billsmethi's family to dance *with*; and when he had been broken in in the parlour he ran in couples in the assembly-room.

Such was the dancing academy of Signor Billsmethi when Mr Augustus Cooper, of Fetter Lane, first saw an unstamped advertisement walking leisurely down Holborn Hill, announcing to the world that Signor Billsmethi, of the King's Theatre, intended opening for the season with a grand ball.

Now, Mr Augustus Cooper was in the oil and colour line—just of age with a little money, a little business, and a little mother, who, having managed her husband and his business in his lifetime took to managing her son and *his* business after his decease; and so, somehow or other, he had been cooped up in the little back parlour behind the shop on weekdays, and in a little deal box without a lid (called by courtesy a pew) at Bethel Chapel, on Sundays, and had seen no more of the world than if he had been an infant all his days; whereas Young White, at the gas-fitter's over the way, three years younger than him, had been flaring away like winkin'—going to the theatre—supping at harmonic meetings—eating oysters by the barrel—drinking stout by the gallon—even stopping out all night, and coming home as cool in the morning as if nothing had happened. So Mr Augustus Cooper made up his mind that he would not stand it any longer, and had that very morning expressed to his mother a firm determination to be 'blowed' in the event of his not being instantly provided with a street-door key. And he was walking down Holborn Hill, thinking about all these things, and wondering how he could manage to get introduced into genteel society for the first time, when his eyes rested on Signor Billsmethi's announcement, which it immediately struck him was just the very thing he wanted; for he should not only be able to select a genteel circle of acquaintance at once out of the five-and-seventy pupils at four-and-sixpence a quarter, but should qualify himself at the same time to go through a hornpipe in private society, with perfect ease to himself, and great delight to his friends. So he stopped the unstamped advertisement—an animated sandwich, composed of a boy between two boards—and having procured a very small card with the Signor's address indented thereon, walked straight at once to the Signor's house—and very fast he walked too, for fear the list should be filled up, and the five-and-seventy completed before he got there. The Signor was at home, and, what was still more gratifying, he was an Englishman! Such a nice man—and so polite! The list was not full, but it was a most extraordinary circumstance that there was only just one vacancy, and even that one would have been filled up that very morning, only Signor Billsmethi was dissatisfied with the reference, and being very much afraid that the lady wasn't select, wouldn't take her.

'And very much delighted I am, Mr Cooper,' said Signor Billsmethi, 'that I did *not* take her. I assure you, Mr Cooper—I don't say it to flatter you, for I know you're above it—that I consider myself extremely fortunate in having a gentleman of your manners and appearance, sir.'

'I am very glad of it too, sir,' said Augustus Cooper.

'And I hope we shall be better acquainted, sir,' said Signor Billsmethi.

'And I'm sure I hope we shall too, sir,' responded Augustus Cooper. Just then the door opened, and in came a young lady with her hair curled in a crop all over her head, and her shoes tied in sandals all over her legs.

'Don't run away, my dear,' said Signor Billsmethi; for the young lady didn't know Mr Cooper was there when she ran in and was going to run out again in her modesty, all in confusion-like. 'Don't run away, my dear,' said Signor Billsmethi, 'this is Mr Cooper—Mr Cooper, of Fetter Lane. Mr Cooper, my daughter, sir—Miss Billsmethi, sir, who I hope will have the pleasure of dancing many a quadrille, minuet, gavotte, country-dance, fandango, double-hornpipe, and faringaholka-jingo with you, sir. She dances them all, sir; and so shall you sir before you're a quarter older sir.'

And Signor Billsmethi slapped Mr Augustus Cooper on the back as if he had known him a dozen years—so friendly; and Mr Cooper bowed to the young lady, and the young lady curtseyed to him, and Signor Billsmethi said they were as handsome a pair as ever he'd wish to see; upon which the young lady exclaimed, 'Lor, pa!' and blushed as red as Mr Cooper himself—you might have thought they were both standing under a red lamp at a chemist's shop; and before Mr Cooper went away it was settled that he should join the family circle that very night —taking them just as they were—no ceremony nor nonsense of that kind—and learn his positions, in order that he might lose no time and be able to come out at the forthcoming ball.

Well; Mr Augustus Cooper went away to one of the cheap shoemakers' shops in Holborn, where gentlemen's dress-pumps are seven-and-sixpence, and men's strong walking, just nothing at all, and bought a pair of the regular seven-and-sixpenny, long-quartered, town mades, in which he astonished himself quite as much as his mother, and sallied forth to Signor Billsmethi's. There were four other private pupils in the parlour: two ladies and two gentlemen. Such nice people! Not a bit of pride about them. One of the ladies in particular, who was in training for a Columbine, was remarkably affable, and she and Miss Billsmethi took such an interest in Mr Augustus Cooper, and joked and smiled, and looked so bewitching, that he got quite at home and learnt his steps in no time. After the practising was over, Signor Billsmethi, and Miss Billsmethi, and Master Billsmethi, and a young lady, and the two ladies, and the two gentlemen, danced a quadrille—none of your slipping and sliding about but regular warm work, flying into corners, and diving among chairs, and shooting out at the door—something like dancing! Signor Billsmethi in particular notwithstanding his having a little fiddle to play all the time, was out on the landing every figure, and Master Billsmethi, when everybody else was breathless, danced a horn-pipe with a cane in his hand, and a cheese-plate on his head, to the un-qualified admiration of the whole company.

Then Signor Billsmethi insisted as they were so happy, that they should all stay to supper, and proposed sending Master Billsmethi for the beer and spirits, whereupon the two gentlemen swore, 'strike 'em wulgar if they'd stand that'; and they were just going to quarrel who should pay for it, when Mr Augustus Cooper said he would, if they'd have the kindness to allow him—and they *had* the kindness to allow him; and Master Billsmethi brought the beer in a can, and the rum in a quart-pot. They had a regular night of it; and Miss Billsmethi squeezed Mr Augustus Cooper's hand under the table; and Mr Augustus Cooper returned the squeeze and returned home too, at something to six o'clock in the morning when he was put to bed by main force by the apprentice, after repeatedly expressing an uncontrollable desire to pitch his reverend parent out of the second-floor window, and to throttle the apprentice with his own neck-handkerchief.

Weeks had worn on, and the seven-and-sixpenny town-mades had nearly worn out, when the night arrived for the grand dress-ball at which the whole of the five-and-seventy pupils were to meet together for the first time that season, and to take out some portion of their respective four-and-sixpences in lamp-oil and fiddlers. Mr Augustus

Cooper had ordered a new coat for the occasion—a two-pound-tenner from Turnstile. It was his first appearance in public; and after a grand Sicilian shawl-dance by fourteen young ladies in character, he was to open the quadrille department with Miss Bellsmethi herself, with whom he had become quite intimate since his first introduction.

It *was* a night! Everything was admirably arranged. The sandwich-boy took the hats and bonnets at the street-door; there was a turn-up bedstead in the back parlour, on which Miss Billsmethi made tea and coffee for such of the gentlemen as chose to pay for it, and such of the ladies as the gentlemen treated; red port-wine, negus and lemonade were handed round at eighteen pence a head, and, in pursuance of a previous engagement with the public-house at the corner of the street, an extra potboy was laid on for the occasion. In short, nothing could exceed the arrangements, except the company. Such ladies! Such pink silk stockings! Such artificial flowers! Such a number of cabs! No sooner had one cab set down a couple of ladies, than another cab drove up and set down another couple of ladies, and they all knew, not only one another, but the majority of the gentlemen into the bargain, which made it all as pleasant and lively as could be. Signor Billsmethi in black tights, with a large blue bow in his buttonhole, introduced the ladies to such of the gentlemen as were strangers: and the ladies talked away —and laughed they did—it was delightful to see them.

As to the shawl-dance, it was the most exciting thing that ever was beheld; there was such a whisking, and rustling, and fanning, and getting ladies into a tangle with artificial flowers, and then disentangling them again; and as to Mr Augustus Cooper's share in the quadrille, he got through it admirably. He was missing from his partner now and then certainly, and discovered on such occasions to be either dancing with laudable perseverance in another set, or sliding about in perspective, apparently without any definite object; but, generally speaking, they managed to shove him through the figure, until he turned up in the right place. Be this as it may, when he had finished a great many ladies and gentlemen came up and complimented him very much, and said they had never seen a beginner do any thing like it before; and Mr August Cooper was perfectly satisfied with himself, and everybody else into the bargain, and 'stood' considerable quantities of spirits and water, negus, and compounds, for the use and behoof of two or three

Miss Billsmethi betrayed her jealousy by calling the young lady a 'creeter'.

dozen very particular friends, selected from the select circle of five-and-seventy pupils.

Now, whether it was the strength of the compounds, or the beauty of the ladies, or what not, it did so happen that Mr Augustus Cooper encouraged, rather than repelled, the very flattering attentions of a young lady in brown gauze over white calico who had appeared particularly struck with him from the first; and when the encouragements had been prolonged for some time, Miss Billsmethi betrayed her spite and jealousy thereat by calling the young lady in brown gauze a 'creeter', which induced the young lady in brown gauze to retort in certain sentences containing a taunt founded on the payment of four-and-sixpence a quarter, and some indistinct reference to a 'fancy man'; which reference Mr Augustus Cooper, being then and there in a state of considerable bewilderment, expressed his entire concurrence in. Miss Billsmethi, thus renounced, forthwith began screaming in the loudest key of her voice at the rate of fourteen screams a minute; and being unsuccessful, in an onslaught on the eyes and face, first of the lady in gauze and then of Mr Augustus Cooper, called distractedly on the other three-and-seventy pupils to furnish her with oxalic acid for her own private drinking, and the call not being honoured, made another rush at Mr Cooper, and then had her stay-lace cut and was carried off to bed.

Mr Augustus Cooper, not being remarkable for quickness of apprehension, was at a loss to understand what all this meant, till Signor Billsmethi explained it in a most satisfactory manner by stating to the pupils that Mr Augustus Cooper had made and confirmed diverse promises of marriage to his daughter on diverse occasions, and had now basely deserted her; on which the indignation of the pupils became universal and as several chivalrous gentlemen inquired rather pressingly of Mr Augustus Cooper, whether he required anything for his own use, or, in other words, whether he 'wanted anything for himself', he deemed it prudent to make a precipitate retreat.

And the upshot of the matter was, that a lawyer's letter came the next day, and an action was commenced next week; and that Mr Augustus Cooper, after walking twice to the Serpentine for the purpose of drowning himself, and coming twice back without doing it, made a confidant of his mother, who compromised the matter with twenty pounds from the till, which made twenty pounds four shillings and sixpence paid to Signor Billsmethi, exclusive of treats and pumps; and Mr Augustus Cooper went back and lived with his mother, and there he lives to this day; and as he has lost his ambition for society, and never goes into the world, he will never see this account of himself and will never be any the wiser.

ARIADNE ON NAXOS

Iain Finlayson

Theseus was one of the great heroes of Greek legend, and his reputation as a fearless man of action was fully deserved, although—but I am getting ahead of myself. Let us review the facts.

It is said that Theseus was the son of the sea god Poseidon, but Aegeus, the king of Athens, acknowledged Theseus as his son and heir to the throne. At that time a levy of seven youths and seven maidens was sent every nine years from Athens to Crete to be hostages in restitution for the death of Androgeus, son of Minos, the Cretan king. Theseus volunteered to be one of the hostages and sailed with his companions to Crete, where he learned that they were to take part in the royal games as bull dancers.

The Cretans held bulls to be sacred, and at the heart of a great labyrinth lived the Minotaur, half-man, half-bull. He was Asterion, son of Pasiphaë, the Cretan queen. Minos and Pasiphaë had three other children—Glaucus, Phaedra and Ariadne, the eldest. Impressed by the courage of Theseus, Ariadne fell in love with him and helped him, with the aid of a ball of thread, to penetrate the labyrinth and kill the Minotaur. In return, Theseus promised to take her back with him to Athens if they could escape from Crete. Ariadne laid plans and, together with her sister Phaedra (disguised as Glaucus to avert suspicion), en-

183

abled Theseus to rescue his companions and sail away, after scuttling Minos's fleet to delay pursuit.

But Ariadne never reached Athens. She was abandoned by Theseus on the island of Naxos. Some say that Aeolus, the god of the winds, blew Theseus's ship out to sea and he was forced to leave her there. . . .

Theseus continued on his journey with Phaedra. Before leaving Athens he had promised his father that white sails would be hoisted if his ship were returning with the mission safely accomplished, black sails if his plans has miscarried. When Aegeus, watching out for the arrival of his son, saw that the sails were black, he threw himself to his death and Theseus was proclaimed king in his place.

Meanwhile Ariadne, still on Naxos, had learned that the god of wine, Dionysos, had chosen her to be his bride, and that Theseus had been told in a dream that she was promised to the god. They were married and Ariadne was given a crown of seven stars by Dionysos. The stars may be seen to this day in the night sky as a symbol of the love between them and of Ariadne's immortality as a goddess.

And Phaedra? She became the wife of Theseus and stepmother to his son, Hippolytus. She fell in love with her stepson, but when he rejected her love she came to hate him and called upon Theseus to kill the boy. But that's another story.

Well, that is the outline of the tale, the bare bones, you might say. And it has been accepted readily enough down the ages. But recently some ancient letters have been unearthed which cast the events of that far-off time in a rather different light. . . .

Ariadne to Minos, King of Crete

Dear Papa,

I have been abandoned. Theseus has put me ashore on an island and sailed away without a by-your-leave or any word of explanation. I'm afraid you were quite right about him—he is totally unscrupulous and certainly no gentleman, for all that he claims to be a son of Poseidon (which I don't believe for a moment. We all know that his mother, Aethra, never married Aegeus and put out the story as a cover up. She was forever putting on airs). I couldn't be more depressed, and I'm very sorry now for all the trouble. I can still see the sails of Theseus's boat on the horizon. I hope he remembers to change them before he gets to Athens. You know how even the slightest thing upsets Aegeus nowadays. He's liable to do anything.

My head feels funny. Theseus has left me my vanity case and a hand-maiden. Fortunately she is literate and I'm making her take dictation on the back of some boring old scrolls Theseus has kindly left for my entertainment. The girl tells me that I was taken ashore while asleep. Now I am a very light sleeper, anyone will tell you, and I can only think that Theseus put something in my wine at dinner. That would be just like him. Not content with worming his way into my affections in Crete and making me leave my home, my friends and my dear family (not to mention my religious duties as a royal priestess), he has evidently tired of me and cast me away on—well, I don't exactly know where. The girl thinks it's Naxos, wherever that is. I shall explore more fully when I've finished this, but it appears to be uninhabited.

I feel I owe you some explanation. Naturally, mother will think the worst, but I'm sure you will have kept an open mind. Everyone says you are a good judge of character and even you must admit I have been dreadfully wronged. It is very difficult being a princess, you know, and obviously anyone as handsome and as clever as Theseus would be bound to turn anyone's head. He did awfully well in the games, and in the bull dance, leaping over those frightening beasts like a pro-fessional athlete. You said so yourself, and you were very pleased when he rescued your gold ring from the sea. It was very natural that we should get on well, especially as I have been told that I am not unattractive. Goodness knows what I must look like at the moment—a night in the open air is no good for the complexion, and the sun is positively shrivelling me up.

Well, I felt sorry for Theseus, which is understandable, considering he'd been sent to us as a hostage with the other youths and maidens from Athens. And he didn't have to come; he volunteered, you know, which was brave of him. Then when he gave me the jewelled crown he'd found in the sea when he was looking for your ring, I suppose I fell in love with him. He said that if ever he got back to Athens he'd take me with him because he was desperately in love with me. That's what he said then! Of course, it was all a front and he is a philanderer. It was then I thought of *you*, Papa. I have always had the good of Crete at heart, and in my opinion an alliance with Athens seemed a good idea. You, of course, have always been suspicious of the mainland tribes—'provincials', you called them, greedy for our riches and our lands. I admit they are unsophisticated, some of them little short of barbarous, but Theseus spoke very nicely and knew how to behave himself at table. His companions may not have been as fastidious as Cretans are, and their arrogance was entirely inappropriate, considering their artistic and technological achievements are little more than prehistoric, but all in all I was able to overlook these minor matters. You know my generosity and concern for those worse off than myself. Yes, I am softhearted, Papa, and I'm not ashamed to admit it. Crete is, of course, highly civilized, but in my opinion we had reached the point at which we might well have drifted dangerously near decadence within a short time, so I made up my mind to go with Theseus and try to balance our civilization with a little healthy roughness. Naturally, I insisted that we should be married and that I should be Theseus's queen when he succeeded Aegeus.

Well, of course, Theseus saw the sense of this at once, and persuaded me that you would never agree. He made me promise not to tell you and that we should elope. Although I was in love with Theseus, I sincerely considered it my duty to Crete to marry him, and after a little argument I agreed to the secrecy—very reluctantly, as I knew how much it would hurt you personally. Then Theseus said we must also take Asterion with us, and that he needed my help to reach him in the middle of the labyrinth. I did *not* think this necessary, but Theseus can be very forceful with women and finally I agreed to that too. I regret to say I used my magic ball of thread to lead Theseus to Asterion and there was the most frightful row. Asterion, left to himself, is quite harmless and you know how fond I was of him. Well, the long and the short of it is that Theseus came out of the labyrinth (I had been sent back) saying he'd killed the Minotaur. I was *frantic*. Theseus convinced me that I had no option but to go away with him, though I refused point-blank. But he said you'd be angry, and certainly mother would have made my life misery.

We were just about to run off to the ship when suddenly Phaedra appeared and wanted to know what all the noise was about. She listens at doors, you know, and she knew all about what was going on. Apparently, she'd even been egging Theseus on behind my back. She insisted on coming with us, and Theseus made no objection. Of course, I should have been suspicious immediately, but you have often remarked about how trusting and good-natured I am. You know the rest, of course. The scuttling of your ships in the harbour was necessary in case you tried to follow us, and I was much too frightened to say anything to Theseus, who looked very stern, although I noticed Phaedra prattling on nineteen to the dozen and hanging on to his sleeve, constantly bringing herself to his attention in a most undignified manner. I'm glad to say I have more self-respect than my sister, and I resolved to make her behave herself when I was queen. But, of course, I shall never be queen now, and that little cat will have it all. It will turn out badly, that marriage, mark my words.

Dear Papa, I know you will understand. It wasn't my fault, and I am so miserable. It is not very nice here, and I would like to come home. If you don't have any ships left, can you get old Daedalus to invent another of his flying contraptions? He could fly over here and whizz me back to Crete in no time. It would be quite safe, now that we know it is best not to fly too near the sun. Poor Icarus, he was such a nice boy.

Love,

Ariadne

P.S. I'm putting this letter in an empty wineskin to catch the tide. Somebody is bound to pick it up and forward it to you at the palace. There are an awful lot of empty wineskins littered about the beach. I've just noticed. I can't think how they got here. Perhaps this island is inhabited after all. I shall go off in a few moments and try to find some friendly natives.

Theseus, King of Athens, to Minos, King of Crete

Dear Minos,

As you may have heard, I am now King of Athens in succession to my father, Aegeus, who fell off the west corner of the Acropolis just as my ship was about to reach port. Apparently he had got up there to get a better view, and I can only assume that the excitement of my safe arrival home caused him to become over-excited and accidentally lose his footing. I have named the sea the Aegean in his memory. Please ask your cartographers to make a note of that.

No doubt you have had a version of events from Ariadne, but I do not wish to enter into abusive exchanges over the matter. You probably know your daughter a great deal better than I do, and I will say that her conduct towards me was most embarrassing. She has been thoroughly spoilt and her demands were outrageous. It was out of the question for me to take her back with me to Athens as my queen. She was perfectly welcome as a political refugee, of course, but I'm afraid she entirely misconstrued my interest in her. Naturally, I wished to escape and return to my father. Now, no doubt, so does she. The last I saw of her, she was a small figure running to and fro along the beach at Naxos in a most unbecoming fashion, screeching as only she knows how. I'm sure you will have no difficulty remembering her particularly penetrating manner of screaming when she does not get her own way. It is quite unmistakable.

However, I am not so heartless as to abandon a young woman on purpose, however much I might have been tempted. The truth of the matter is that Ariadne was not a good sailor. In response to her constant complaints of seasickness, I was obliged to put in at Naxos so that she could recover. Quite unexpectedly, the wind changed as she was sleeping on the shore and my ship was carried out to sea. Unfortunate, you will agree, but none of my doing. Nobody had made the usual sacrifice to Aeolus, and the god of the winds is more capricious than most. A strong breeze caught the sails and I only reached the ship myself by swimming strongly after it for quite some time. Ariadne, of course, could not be awakened. Considering the amount of wine she is accustomed to drink, I'm not surprised. I left her snoring. I doubt, in any case, if she can swim. However, I'm sure, you have no cause to worry about Ariadne. Naxos is a perfectly nice and popular resort. I am told that the islanders are wholly devoted to religious observances and that they are hospitable to strangers—embarrassingly so, I believe.

Phaedra is still with me and she has been very sensible throughout the voyage. She seems a nice girl, and very affectionate. In fact, we have decided to marry, since she takes a friendly interest in my son,

Hippolytus. She is quite devoted to him, even after a short acquaintance, and I'm sure they will be friends. The boy needs a mother and I have urged him to spend as much time as he can with Phaedra and really get to know her.

Best regards,

Theseus

P.S. I didn't want to kill Asterion, the Minotaur. But he didn't seem to understand and was rather bull-headed about leaving the labyrinth. It really as an accident. Please apologize to your wife, Pasiphaë, for me.

Ariadne to Minos, King of Crete

Dear Papa,

I hope you got my letter three months ago. I am still here, and I have made a lot of wonderful new friends. I was miserable when I last wrote to you, and I spent a few minutes looking out over the sea and feeling sorry for myself. But then I pulled myself together and had the girl do something with my hair. Isn't it amazing how much better one feels after putting on a little make-up and a clean dress? Just as well I did, too, because almost immediately there was a loud commotion in some nearby bushes. I was terrified and thought it could only be a wild beast and hat I'd be instantly *devoured*. I quite gave myself up for dead, but suddenly lots of laughing people appeared, dancing to the sound of musical instruments. It was obviously some sort of very elaborate picnic, and by this time I was feeling peckish (Theseus had *not* thought to leave food or wine). My silly hand-maiden did not think they looked quite right in the head, but I told her not to be silly and leave everything to me.

Some of the women came up and asked me what I was doing on the island, and I'm afraid I lost all control (quite understandably, I think in the circumstances), and burst into tears. I raged against Theseus like a madwoman, calling on Zeus to punish him and swearing to tear him limb from limb. I was quite mad with anger for a moment, but everyone was very kind and gave me a little wine to calm me. They said they had just arrived on the island in a fleet of ships with somebody

I spent a few minutes looking out to sea and feeling sorry for myself.

called Dionysos who was looking for a wife. Then a lot of drunken men appeared twining vine leaves around themselves and squashing grapes everywhere. They were very jolly, like all sailors are after a long voyage, and one has to make allowances for high spirits when they reach land. They offered me some more wine, and of course I couldn't refuse without being impolite. I became quite giggly. I was anxious to meet this Dionysos who is apparently a god. He arrived in a chariot and leaped to the ground. He is very good-looking and I was feeling more cheerful by this time, so we got on like a house on fire. He told me that I was the one he was looking for and that he had appeared in a dream to Theseus and told him to leave me here. Of course, Theseus mentioned nothing to me.

Papa, I'm married! I couldn't be happier. Dionysos is enchanting—full of merriment and jokes, and he makes everyone so happy. He has given me a crown and promises to make me a goddess (which is only right, as I am married to a god). We plan to have lots of children and I really can't feel badly about anything or anyone. I have cursed Theseus, of course, and I can't help that now—there's going to be trouble there, I'm afraid. Phaedra has given herself to an *earthly* crown, but I am beginning to realize there is more to life than that. Dionysos and I are blissfully happy, so it's all turned out for the best. There are constant parties and games, although behind it all is a deeply religious feeling. Some of the rites are perhaps a little unusual, and I hesitate to describe them in detail, but Dionysos says you are very understanding and tolerant as long as you know *why* things happen. He says you will be a judge in Hades, so that's something to look forward to. Isn't it exciting? Kiss Mama for me, and don't worry.

Love,
Ariadne

THE PICTURE OF DORIAN GRAY

Oscar Wilde

When young Dorian Gray sees the marvellous picture that Basil Hallward has painted of him, he exclaims that he would like the picture to grow old while he retains his incredible beauty and youth.

Under the amoral influence of Lord Henry Wooton, Dorian begins to lead a life of unsurpassed debauchery, leading others astray, and his prayer is answered — he retains his youth and the face in the portrait ages and becomes more despicable with every sin that Dorian commits.

It was on the ninth of November, the eve of his own thirty-eighth birthday, as he often remembered afterwards.

He was walking home about eleven o'clock from Lord Henry's, where he had been dining, and was wrapped in heavy furs, as the night was cold and foggy. At the corner of Grosvenor Square and South Audley Street a man passed him in the mist, walking very fast, and with the collar of his grey ulster turned up. He had a bag in his hand. Dorian recognised him. It was Basil Hallward. A strange sense of fear, for which he could not account, came over him. He made no sign of recognition, and went on quickly in the direction of his own house.

But Hallward had seen him. Dorian heard him first stopping on the pavement, and then hurrying after him. In a few moments his hand was on his arm.

'Dorian! What an extraordinary piece of luck! I have been waiting for you in your library ever since nine o'clock. Finally I took pity on your tired servant, and told him to go to bed, as he let me out. I am off to Paris by the midnight train, and I particularly wanted to see you before I left. I thought it was you, or rather your fur coat, as you passed me. But I wasn't quite sure. Didn't you recognise me?'

'In this fog, my dear Basil? Why, I can't even recognise Grosvenor Square. I believe my house is somewhere about here, but I don't feel at all certain about it. I am sorry you are going away, as I have not seen you for ages. But I suppose you will be back soon?'

'No: I am going to be out of England for six months. I intended to take a studio in Paris, and shut myself up until I have finished a great picture I have in my head. However, it wasn't about myself I wanted to talk. Here we are at your door. Let me come in for a moment. I have something to say to you.'

'I shall be charmed. But won't you miss your train?' said Dorian Gray, languidly, as he passed up the steps and opened the door with his latchkey.

The lamplight struggled out through the fog, and Hallward looked at his watch. 'I have heaps of time,' he answered. 'The train doesn't go until twelve-fifteen, and it is only just eleven. In fact, I was on my way to the club to look for you, when I met you. You see, I shan't have any delay about luggage, as I have sent on my heavy things. All I have with me is in this bag, and I can easily get to Victoria in twenty minutes.'

Dorian looked at him and smiled. 'What a way for a fashionable painter to travel! A Gladstone bag, and an ulster! Come in, or the fog will get into the house. And mind you don't talk about anything serious. Nothing is serious nowadays. At least nothing should be.'

Hallward shook his head as he entered, and followed Dorian into the library. There was a bright wood fire blazing in the large open hearth. The lamps were lit, and an open Dutch silver spirit-case stood, with some siphons of soda-water and large cut-glass tumblers, on a little marqueterie table.

'You see your servant made me quite at home, Dorian. He gave me everything I wanted, including your best gold-tipped cigarettes. He is a most hospitable creature. I like him much better than the Frenchman you used to have. What has become of the Frenchman, by the by?'

Dorian shrugged his shoulders. 'I believe he married Lady Radley's maid, and has established her in Paris as an English dressmaker. *Anglomanie* is very fashionable over there now, I hear. It seems silly of the French, doesn't it? But – do you know? – he was not at all a bad servant. I never liked him, but I had nothing to complain about. One often imagines things that are quite absurd. He was really devoted to me, and seemed quite sorry when he went away. Have another brandy-and-soda? Or would you like hock-and-seltzer? I always take hock-and-seltzer myself. There is sure to be some in the next room.'

'Thanks, I won't have anything more,' said the painter, taking his cap and coat off, and throwing them on the bag that he had placed in the corner. 'And now, my dear fellow, I want to speak to you seriously. Don't frown like that. You make it so much more difficult for me.'

'What is it all about?' cried Dorian, in his petulant way, flinging himself down on the sofa. 'I hope it is not about myself. I am tired of myself tonight. I should like to be somebody else.'

'It is about yourself,' answered Hallward, in his grave, deep voice, 'and I must say it to you. I shall only keep you half an hour.'

Dorian sighed, and lit a cigarette. 'Half an hour!' he murmured.

'It is not much to ask of you, Dorian, and it is entirely for your own sake that I am speaking. I think it right that you should know that the most dreadful things are being said against you in London.'

'I don't wish to know anything about them. I love scandals about other people, but scandals about myself don't interest me. They have not got the charm of novelty.'

'They must interest you, Dorian. Every gentleman is interested in his good name. You don't want people to talk of you as something vile and degraded. Of course you have your position, and your wealth, and all that kind of thing. But position and wealth are not everything. Mind you, I don't believe these rumours at all. At least, I can't believe them when I see you. Sin is a thing that writes itself across a man's face. It cannot be concealed. People talk sometimes of secret vices. There are no such things. If a wretched man has a vice, it shows itself in the lines of his mouth, the droop of his eyelids, the moulding of his hands even. Somebody – I won't mention his name, but you know him – came to me last year to have his portrait done. I had never seem him before, and had never heard anything about him at the time, though I have heard a good deal since. He offered an extravagant price. I refused him. There was something in the shape of his fingers that I hated. I know now that I was quite right in what I fancied about him. His life is dreadful. But you, Dorian, with your pure, bright, innocent face, and your marvellous untroubled youth – I can't believe anything against you. And yet I see you very seldom, and you never come down to the studio now, and when I am away from you, and I hear all these hideous things that people are whispering about you, I don't know what to say. Why is it, Dorian, that a man like the Duke of Berwick leaves the room of a club when you enter it? Why is it that so many gentlemen in London will neither go to your house nor invite you to theirs? You used to be a friend of Lord Staveley. I met him at dinner last week. Your name happened to come up in conversation, in connection with the miniatures you have lent to the exhibition at the Dudley. Staveley curled his lip, and said that you might have the most artistic tastes, but that you were a man whom no pure-minded girl should be allowed to know, and whom no chaste woman should sit in the same room with. I reminded him that I was a friend of yours, and asked him what he meant. He told me. He told me right out before everybody. It was horrible! Why is your friendship so fatal to young men? There was that wretched boy in the Guards who committed suicide. You were his great friend. There was Sir Henry Ashton, who had to leave England, with a tarnished name. You and he were inseparable. What about Adrian Singleton, and his dreadful end? What about Lord Kent's only son, and his career? I met his father yesterday in St James's Street. He seemed broken with shame and sorrow. What about the young Duke of Perth? What sort of life has he got now? What gentleman would associate with him?'

'Stop, Basil. You are talking about things of which you know nothing,' said Dorian Gray, biting his lip, and with a note of infinite contempt in his voice. 'You ask me why Berwick leaves a room when I enter it. It is because I know everything about his life, not because he knows anything about mine. With such blood as he has in his veins, how could his record be clean? You ask me about Henry Ashton and young Perth. Did I teach the one his vices, and the other his debauchery? If Kent's silly son takes his wife from the streets what is that to me? If Adrian Singleton writes his friend's name across a bill, am I his keeper? I know how people chatter in England. The middle classes air their moral prejudices over their gross dinner-tables, and whisper about what they call the profligacies of their betters in order to try and pretend that they are in smart society, and on intimate terms with the people they slander. In this country it is enough for a man to have distinction and brains for every common tongue to wag against him. And what sort of lives do these people, who pose as being moral, lead themselves? My dear fellow, you forget that we are in the native land of the hypocrite.'

'Dorian,' cried Hallward, 'that is not the question. England is bad enough, I know, and English society is all wrong. That is the reason why I want you to be fine. You have not been fine. One has a right to judge of a man by the effect he has over his friends. Yours seem to lose all sense of honour, of goodness, of purity. You have filled them with a madness for pleasure. They have gone down into the depths. You led them there. Yes: you led them there, and yet you can smile, as you are smiling now. And there is worse behind. I know you and Harry are inseparable. Surely for that reason, if for none other, you should not have made his sister's name a byword.'

'Take care, Basil. You go too far.'

'I must speak, and you must listen. You shall listen. When you met Lady Gwendolen, not a breath of scandal had ever touched her. Is there a single decent woman in London now who would drive with her in the Park? Why, even her children are not allowed to live with her. Then there are other stories – stories that you have been seen creeping at dawn out of dreadful houses and slinking in disguise into the foulest dens in London. Are they true? Can they be true? When I first heard them I laughed. I hear them now, and they make me shudder. What about your country house, and the life that is led there? Dorian, you don't know what is said about you. I won't tell you that I don't want to preach to you. I remember Harry saying once that every man who turned himself into an amateur curate for the moment always began by saying that, and then proceeded to break his word. I do want to preach to you. I want you to lead such a life as will make the world respect you. I want you to have a clean name and a fair record. I want you to get rid of the dreadful people you associate with. Don't shrug your shoulders like that. Don't be so indifferent. You have a wonderful influence. Let it be for good, not for evil. They say that you corrupt everyone with whom you become intimate, and that it is quite sufficient for you to enter a house, for shame of some kind to follow after. I don't know whether it is so or not. How should I know? But it is said of you. I am told things that it seems impossible to doubt. Lord Gloucester was one of my greatest friends at Oxford. He showed me a letter that his wife had written to him when she was dying alone in her villa at Mentone. Your name was implicated in the most terrible confession I ever read. I told him that it was absurd – that I knew you thoroughly, and that you were incapable of anything of the kind. Know you? I wonder do I know you? Before I could answer that, I should have to see your soul.'

'To see my soul!' muttered Dorian Gray, starting up from the sofa and turning almost white from fear.

'Yes,' answered Hallward, gravely, and with deep-toned sorrow in his voice – 'to see your soul. But only God can do that.'

A bitter laugh of mockery broke from the lips of the younger man. 'You shall see it yourself, tonight!' he cried, seizing a lamp from the table. 'Come: it is your own handiwork. Why shouldn't you look at it? You can tell the world all about it afterwards, if you choose. Nobody would believe you. If they did believe you, they would like me all the better for it. I know the age better than you do, though you will prate about it so tediously. Come, I tell you. You have chattered enough about corruption. Now you shall look on it face to face.'

There was the madness of pride in every word he uttered. He stamped his foot upon the ground in his boyish insolent manner. He felt a terrible joy at the thought that someone else was to share his secret, and that the man who had painted the portrait that was the origin of all his shame was to be burdened for the rest of his life with the hideous memory of what he had done.

'Yes,' he continued, coming closer to him, and looking steadfastly into his stern eyes. 'I shall show you my soul. You shall see the thing that you fancy only God can see.'

Hallward started back. 'This is blasphemy, Dorian!' he cried. 'You must not say things like that. They are horrible, and they don't mean anything.'

'You think so?' He laughed again.

'I know so. As for what I said to you tonight, I said it for your good. You know I have been always a staunch friend to you.'

'Don't touch me. Finish what you have to say.'

A twisted flash of pain shot across the painter's face. He paused for a moment, and a wild feeling of pity came over him. After all, what right had he to pry into the life of Dorian Gray? If he had done a tithe of what was rumoured about him, how much he must have suffered! Then he straightened himself up, and walked over to the fireplace, and stood there, looking at the burning logs with their frostlike ashes and their throbbing cores of flame.

'I am waiting, Basil,' said the young man, in a hard, clear voice.

He turned round. 'What I have to say is this,' he cried. 'You must give me some answer to these horrible charges that are made against you. If you tell me that they are absolutely untrue from beginning to end, I shall believe you. Deny them, Dorian, deny them! Can't you see what I am going through? My God! Don't tell me that you are bad, and corrupt, and shameful.'

Dorian Gray smiled. There was a curl of contempt in his lips. 'Come upstairs, Basil,' he said, quietly. 'I keep a diary of my life from day to day, and it never leaves the room in which it is written. I shall show it to you if you come with me.'

'I shall come with you, Dorian, if you wish it. I see I have missed my train. That makes no matter. I can go tomorrow. But don't ask me to read anything tonight. All I want is a plain answer to my question.'

'That shall be given to you upstairs. I could not give it here. You will not have to read long.'

*   *   *   *

He passed out of the room, and began the ascent, Basil Hallward following close behind. They walked softly, as men do instinctively at night. The lamp cast fantastic shadows on the wall and staircase. A rising wind made some of the windows rattle.

When they reached the top landing, Dorian set the lamp down on the floor, and taking out the key turned it in the lock. 'You insist on knowing, Basil?' he asked, in a low voice.

'Yes.'

'I am delighted,' he answered, smiling. Then he added, somewhat harshly, 'You are the one man in the world who is entitled to know everything about me. You have had more to do with my life than you think': and, taking up the lamp, he opened the door and went in. A cold current of air passed them, and the light shot up for a moment in a flame of murky orange. He shuddered. 'Shut the door behind you,' he whispered, as he placed the lamp on the table.

Hallward glanced round him, with a puzzled expression. The room looked as if it had not been lived in for years. A faded Flemish tapestry, a curtained picture, an old Italian *cassone*, and an almost empty bookcase – that was all that it seemed to contain, besides a chair and a table. As Dorian Gray was lighting a half-burned candle that was standing on the mantelshelf, he saw that the whole place was covered with dust, and that the carpet was in holes. A mouse ran scuffling behind the wainscoting. There was a damp odour of mildew.

'So you think that it is only God who sees the soul, Basil? Draw that curtain back, and you will see mine.'

The voice that spoke was cold and cruel. 'You are mad, Dorian, or playing a part,' muttered Hallward, frowning.

'You won't? Then I must do it myself,' said the young man; and he tore the curtain from its rod and flung it on the ground.

An exclamation of horror broke from the painter's lips as he saw in the dim light the hideous face on the canvas grinning at him. There was something in its expression that filled him with disgust and loathing. Good heavens! It was Dorian Gray's own face that he was looking at! The horror, whatever it was, had not yet entirely spoiled that marvellous beauty. There was still some gold in the thinning hair and some scarlet on the sensual mouth. The sodden eyes had kept something of the loveliness of their blue, the noble curves had not yet completely passed away from chiselled nostrils and from plastic throat. Yes, it was Dorian himself. But who had done it? He seemed to recognise his own brushwork, and the frame was his own design. The idea was monstrous, yet he felt afraid. He seized the lighted candle, and held it to the picture. In the left-hand corner was his own name, traced in long letters of bright vermilion.

It was some foul parody, some infamous, ignoble satire. He had never done that. Still, it was his own picture! He knew it, and he felt as if his blood had changed in a moment from fire to sluggish ice. His own picture! What did it mean? Why had it altered? He turned, and looked at Dorian Gray, with the eyes of a sick man. His mouth twitched, and his parched tongue seemed unable to articulate. He passed his hand across his forehead. It was dank with clammy sweat.

The young man was leaning against the mantelshelf, watching him with that strange expression that one sees on the faces of those who are absorbed in a play when some great artist is acting. There was neither real sorrow in it nor real joy. There was simply the passion of the spectator, with perhaps a flicker of triumph in his eyes. He had taken the flower out of his coat, and was smelling it, or pretending to do so.

'What does this mean?' cried Hallward, at last. His own voice sounded shrill and curious in his ears.

'Years ago, when I was a boy,' said Dorian Gray, crushing the flower in his hand, 'you met me, flattered me, and taught me to be vain of my good looks. One day you introduced me to a friend of yours, who explained to me the wonder of youth, and you finished the portrait of me that revealed to me the wonder of beauty. In a mad moment, that, even now, I don't know whether I regret or not, I made a wish, perhaps you would call it a prayer . . .'

'I remember it! Oh, how well I remember it! No, the thing is impossible! The room is damp. Mildew has got into the canvas. The paints I used had some wretched mineral poison in them. I tell you the thing is impossible.'

'Ah, what is impossible?' murmured the young man, going over to the window, and leaning his forehead against the cold, mist-stained glass.

'You told me you had destroyed it.'

'I was wrong. It has destroyed me.'

'I don't believe it is my picture.'

'Can't you see your ideal in it?' said Dorian, bitterly.

'My ideal, as you call it . . .'

'As you called it.'

'There was nothing evil in it, nothing shameful. You were to me such an ideal as I shall never meet again. This is the face of a satyr.'

'It is the face of my soul.'

'Christ! What a thing I must have worshipped! It has the eyes of a devil.'

'Each of us has Heaven and Hell in him, Basil,' cried Dorian, with a wild gesture of despair.

Hallward turned again to the portrait, and gazed at it. 'My God! If it is true,' he exclaimed, 'and this is what you have done with your life, why, you must be worse even than those who talk against you fancy you to be!' He held the light up again to the canvas, and examined it. The surface seemed to be quite undisturbed, and as he had left it. It was from within, apparently, that the foulness and horror had come. Through some strange quickening of inner life the leprosies of sin were slowly eating the thing away. The rotting of a corpse in a watery grave was not so fearful.

His hand shook, and the candle fell from its socket on the floor, and lay there sputtering. He placed his foot on it and put it out. Then he flung himself into the rickety chair that was standing by the table and buried his face in his hands.

'Good God, Dorian, what a lesson! What an awful lesson!' There was no answer, but he could hear the young man sobbing at the window. 'Pray, Dorian, pray,' he murmured. 'What is it that one was taught to say in one's boyhood? 'Lead us not into temptation. Forgive us our sins. Wash away our iniquities.' Let us say that together. The prayer of your pride has been answered. The prayer of your repentance will be answered also. I worshipped you too much. We are both punished.'

Dorian Gray turned slowly around, and looked at him with tear-dimmed eyes. 'It is too late, Basil,' he faltered.

'It is never too late, Dorian. Let us kneel down and try if we cannot remember a prayer. Isn't there a verse somewhere, "Though your sins be as scarlet, yet I will make them as white as snow"?'

'Those words mean nothing to me now.'

'Hush! Don't say that. You have done enough evil in your life. My God! Don't you see that accursed thing leering at us?'

Dorian Gray glanced at the picture, and suddenly an uncontrollable feeling of hatred for Basil Hallward came over him, as though it had been suggested to him by the image on the canvas, whispered into his ear by those grinning lips. The mad passions of a hunted animal stirred within him, and he loathed the man who was seated at the table, more than in his whole life he had ever loathed anything. He glanced wildly around. Something glimmered on the top of the painted chest that faced him. His eye fell on it. He knew what it was. It was a knife that he had brought up, some days before, to cut a piece of cord, and had forgotten to take away with him. He moved slowly towards it, passing Hallward as he did so. As soon as he got behind him, he seized it, and turned round. Hallward stirred in his chair as if he was going to rise. He rushed at him, and dug the knife into the great vein that is behind the ear, crushing the man's head down on the table, and stabbing again and again.

There was a stifled groan, and the horrible sound of someone choking with blood. Three times the outstretched arms shot up convulsively, waving grotesque stiff-fingered hands in the air. He stabbed him twice more, but the man did not move. Something began to trickle on the floor. He waited for a moment, still pressing the head down. Then he threw the knife on the table, and listened.

He could hear nothing but the drip, drip on the threadbare carpet. He opened the door and went out on the landing. The house was absolutely quiet. No one was about. For a few seconds he stood bending over the balustrade, and peering down into the black seething well of darkness. Then he took out the key and returned to the room, locking himself in as he did so.

The thing was still seated in the chair, straining over the table with bowed head, and humped back, and long fantastic arms. Had it not been for the red jagged tear in the neck, and the clotted black pool that was slowly widening on the table, one would have said that the man was simply asleep.

How quickly it had all been done! He felt strangely calm, and, walking over to the window, opened it, and stepped out on the balcony. The wind had blown the fog away, and the sky was like a monstrous peacock's tail, starred with myriads of golden eyes. He looked down, and saw the policeman going his rounds and flashing the long beam of his lantern on the doors of the silent houses. The crimson spot of a prowling hansom gleamed at the corner, and then vanished. A woman in a fluttering shawl was creeping slowly by the railings, staggering as she went. Now and then she stopped, and peered back. Once, she began to sing in a hoarse voice. The policeman strolled over and said something to her. She stumbled away, laughing. A bitter blast swept across the Square. The gas–lamps flickered, and became blue, and the leafless trees shook their black iron branches to and fro. He shivered, and went back, closing the window behind him.

Having reached the door, he turned the key, and opened it. He did not even glance at the murdered man. He felt that the secret of the whole thing was not to realise the situation. The friend who had painted the

He got behind Basil, seized the knife and turned round

fatal portrait to which all his misery had been due had gone out of his life. That was enough.

Then he remembered the lamp. It was a rather curious one of Moorish workmanship, made of dull silver inlaid with arabesques of burnished steel, and studded with coarse turquoises. Perhaps it might be missed by his servant, and questions would be asked. He hesitated for a moment, then he turned back and took it from the table. He could not help seeing the dead thing. How still it was! How horribly white the long hands looked! It was like a dreadful wax image.

Having locked the door behind him, he crept quietly downstairs. The woodwork creaked, and seemed to cry out as if in pain. He stopped several times, and waited. No: everything was still. It was merely the sound of his own footsteps.

When he reached the library, he saw the bag and coat in the corner. They must be hidden away somewhere. He unlocked a secret press that was in the wainscoting, a press in which he kept his own curious disguises, and put them into it. He could easily burn them afterwards. Then he pulled out his watch. It was twenty minutes to two.

He sat down, and began to think. Every year – every month, almost – men were strangled in England for what he had done. There had been a madness of murder in the air. Some red star had come too close to the earth . . . And yet what evidence was there against him? Basil Hallward had left the house at eleven. No one had seen him come in again. Most of the servants were at Selby Royal. His valet had gone to bed . . . Paris! Yes. It was to Paris that Basil had gone, and by the midnight train, as he had intended. With his curious reserved habits, it would be months before any suspicions would be aroused. Months! Everything could be destroyed long before then.

A sudden thought struck him. He put on his fur coat and hat, and went out into the hall. There he paused, hearing the slow heavy tread of the policeman on the pavement outside, and seeing the flash of the bull's-eye reflected in the window. He waited, and held his breath.

After a few moments he drew back the latch, and slipped out, shutting the door very gently behind him. Then he began ringing the bell. In about five minutes his valet appeared half dressed, and looking very drowsy.

'I am sorry to have had to wake you up, Francis,' he said, stepping in;

'but I had forgotten my latchkey. What time is it?'

'Ten minutes past two, sir,' answered the man, looking at the clock and blinking.

'Ten minutes past two? How horribly late! You must wake me at nine tomorrow. I have some work to do.'

'All right, sir.'

'Did anyone call this evening?'

'Mr Hallward, sir. He stayed here until eleven, and then he went away to catch his train.'

'Oh! I am sorry I didn't see him. Did he leave any message?'

'No, sir, except that he would write to you from Paris, if he did not find you at the club.'

'That will do, Francis. Don't forget to call me at nine tomorrow.'

'No sir.'

The man shambled down the passage in his slippers.

Dorian Gray threw his hat and coat upon the table, and passed into the library. For a quarter of an hour he walked up and down the room biting his lip, and thinking. Then he took down the Blue Book from one of the shelves, and began to turn over the leaves. 'Alan Campbell, 152, Hertford Street, Mayfair.' Yes: that was the man he wanted.

★   ★   ★   ★

Dorian blackmails Alan Campbell into disposing of the body. Unable to live with himself, Campbell commits suicide. Dorian goes to his country house, Selby Royal, and falls in love with a simple country girl. He returns to London to tell Lord Henry this and that he has decided to reform. Lord Henry tells Dorian that it is too late and Dorian leaves Lord Henry's house, having arranged to ride with him in the Park the following morning.

★   ★   ★   ★

It was a lovely night, so warm that he threw his coat over his arm, and did not even put his silk scarf round his throat. As he strolled home, smoking his cigarette, two young men in evening dress passed him. He heard one of them whisper to the other, 'That is Dorian Gray.' He remembered how pleased he used to be when he was pointed out, or stared at, or talked about. He was tired of hearing his own name now. Half the charm of the little village where he had been so often lately was that no one knew who he was. He had often told the girl whom he had lured to love him that he was poor, and she had believed him. He had told her once that he was wicked, and she had laughed at him, and answered that wicked people were always very old and very ugly. What a laugh she had! – just like a thrush singing. And how pretty she had been in her cotton dress and her large hats! She knew nothing, but she had everything that he had lost.

When he reached home, he found his servant waiting up for him. He sent him to bed, and threw himself down on the sofa in the library, and began to think over some of the things that Lord Henry had said to him.

Was it really true that one could never change? He felt a wild longing for the unstained purity of his boyhood – his rose-white boyhood, as Lord Henry had once called it. He knew that he had tarnished himself, filled his mind with corruption, and given horror to his fancy; that he had been an evil influence to others, and had experienced a terrible joy in being so; and that, of the lives that had crossed his own, it had been the fairest and the most full of promise that he had brought to shame. But was it all irretrievable? Was there no hope for him?

Ah! in what a monstrous moment of pride and passion he had prayed that the portrait should bear the burden of his days, and he keep the unsullied splendour of eternal youth! All his failure had been due to that. Better for him that each sin of his life had brought its sure, swift penalty along with it. There was purification in punishment. Not 'Forgive us our sins,' but 'Smite us for our iniquities,' should be the prayer of a man to a most just God.

The curiously carved mirror that Lord Henry had given to him, so many years ago now, was standing on the table, and the white-limbed Cupids laughed round it as of old. He took it up, as he had done on that night of horror, when he had first noted the change in the fatal picture, and with wild, tear-dimmed eyes looked into its polished shield. Once, someone who had terribly loved him had written to him a mad letter, ending with these idolatrous words: 'The world is changed because you are made of ivory and gold. The curves of your lips rewrite history.' The phrases came back to his memory, and he repeated them over and over to himself. Then he loathed his own beauty, and, flinging the mirror on the floor, crushed it into silver splinters beneath his heel. It was his beauty that had ruined him, his beauty and the youth that he had prayed for. But for those two things, his life might have been free from stain. His beauty had been to him but a mask, his youth but a mockery. What was youth at best? A green, an unripe time, a time of shallow moods and sickly thoughts. Why had he worn its livery? Youth had spoiled him.

It was better not to think of the past. Nothing could alter that. It was of himself, and of his own future, that he had to think. James Vane was hidden in a nameless grave in Selby Churchyard. Alan Campbell had shot himself one night in his laboratory, but had not revealed the secret that he had been forced to know. The excitement, such as it was, over Basil Hallward's disappearance would soon pass away. It was already waning. He was perfectly safe there. Nor, indeed, was it the death of Basil Hallward that weighed most upon his mind. It was the living death of his own soul that troubled him. Basil had painted the portrait that had marred his life. He could not forgive him that. It was the portrait that had done everything. Basil had said things to him that were unbearable, and that he had yet borne with patience. The murder had been simply the madness of a moment. As for Alan Campbell, his suicide had been his own act. He had chosen to do it. It was nothing to him.

A new life! That was what he wanted. That was what he was waiting for. Surely he had begun it already. He had spared one innocent thing, at any rate. He would never again tempt innocence. He would be good.

As he thought of Hetty Merton, he began to wonder if the portrait in the locked room had changed. Surely it was not still so horrible as it had been? Perhaps if his life became pure, he would be able to expel every sign of evil passion from the face. Perhaps the signs of evil had already gone away. He would go and look.

He took the lamp from the table and crept upstairs. As he unbarred the door a smile of joy flitted across his strangely young-looking face and lingered for a moment about his lips. Yes, he would be good, and the hideous thing that he had hidden away would no longer be a terror to him. He felt as if the load had been lifted from him already.

He went in quietly, locking the door behind him, as was his custom, and dragged the purple hanging from the portrait. A cry of pain and indignation broke from him. He could see no change save that in the eyes there was a look of cunning, and in the mouth the curved wrinkle of the hypocrite. The thing was still loathsome – more loathsome, if possible, than before – and the scarlet dew that spotted the hand seemed brighter, and more like blood newly spilt. Then he trembled. Had it been merely vanity that had made him do his one good deed? Or the desire for a new sensation, as Lord Henry had hinted, with his mocking laugh? Or that passion to act a part that sometimes makes us do things finer than we are ourselves? Or, perhaps, all these? And why was the red stain larger than it had been? It seemed to have crept like a horrible disease over the wrinkled fingers. There was blood on the painted feet, as though the thing had dripped – blood even on the hand that had not held the knife. Confess? Did it mean that he was to confess? To give himself up, and be put to death? He laughed. He felt that the idea was monstrous. Besides, even if he did confess, who would believe him? There was no trace of the murdered man anywhere. Everything belonging to him had been destroyed. He himself had burned what had been below-stairs. The world would simply say that he was mad. They would shut him up if he persisted in his story . . . Yet it was his duty to confess, to suffer public shame, and to make public atonement. There was a God who called upon men to tell their sins to earth as well as to heaven. Nothing that he could do would cleanse him until he had told his own sin. His sin? He shrugged his shoulders. The death of Basil Hallward seemed very little to him. He was thinking of Hetty Merton. For it was an unjust mirror, this mirror of his soul that he was looking at. Vanity? Curiosity? Hypocrisy? Had there been nothing more in his renunciation than that? There had been something more. At least he thought so. But who could tell? . . . No. There had been nothing more. Through vanity he had spared her. In hypocrisy he had worn the mask of goodness. For curiosity's sake he had tried the denial of self. He recognised that now.

But this murder – was it to dog him all his life? Was he always to be burdened by his past? Was he really to confess? Never. There was only one bit of evidence left against him. The picture itself – that was evidence. He would destroy it. Why had he kept it so long? Once it had given him pleasure to watch it changing and growing old. Of late he had felt no such pleasure. It had kept him awake at night. When he had been away, he had been filled with terror lest other eyes should look upon it. It had brought melancholy across his passions. Its mere memory had marred many moments of joy. It had been like conscience to him. Yes, it had been conscience. He would destroy it.

He looked round, and saw the knife that had stabbed Basil Hallward. He had cleaned it many times, until there was no stain left upon it. It was bright, and glistened. As it had killed the painter, so it would kill the painter's work, and all that that meant. It would kill the past and when that was dead he would be free. It would kill this monstrous soul-life, and, without its hideous warnings, he would be at peace. He seized the thing, and stabbed the picture with it.

There was a cry heard, and a crash. The cry was so horrible in its agony that the frightened servants woke, and crept out of their rooms. Two gentlemen, who were passing in the Square below, stopped, and looked up at the great house. They walked on until they met a policeman, and brought him back. The man rang the bell several times, but there was no answer. Except for a light in one of the top windows, the house was all dark. After a time, he went away and stood in an adjoining portico and watched.

'Whose house is that, constable?' asked the elder of the two gentlemen.

'Mr Dorian Gray's, sir,' answered the policeman.

They looked at each other, as they walked away, and sneered.

Inside, in the servants' part of the house, the half-clad domestics were talking in low whispers to each other. Old Mrs Leaf was crying and wringing her hands. Francis was as pale as death.

After about a quarter of an hour, he got the coachman and one of the footmen and crept upstairs. They knocked, but there was no reply. They called out. Everything was still. Finally, after vainly trying to force the door, they got on the roof, and dropped down on the balcony. The windows yielded easily; their bolts were old.

When they entered they found, hanging upon the wall, a splendid portrait of their master as they had last seen him, in all the wonder of his exquisite youth and beauty. Lying on the floor was a dead man, in evening dress, with a knife in his heart. He was withered, wrinkled, and loathsome of visage. It was not until they had examined the rings that they recognised who it was.

A NORMAL LIFE

Sam Rose

It was the end of the summer that rationing of fruit finally was lifted in England, the first year since the war had begun that people began to feel that normalcy was returning. The young surgeon, Mr Norman, decided Karen must have her operation.

Mr Norman had been seeing Karen at St Bart's Hospital for a year, ever since he came down for the job from Liverpool. Her case had particularly struck and disturbed him from the first. She was nearly fourteen when he met her, gentle and shy, slightly withdrawn in that way most deaf people are; with nevertheless a fawn-like eagerness to reach out, explore, to make normal contacts. She spoke comprehensibly enough, but with a noticeable thickness of tongue that came from never properly hearing the words she was using. She had been born with her hearing deficiency.

Karen was extremely pretty. If she could be animated, if she could be given more confidence by one day having her hearing properly repaired: what a beauty she could be! And now the country was returning to normal, Frank Norman could afford the luxury of turning his attention to cases that were less than emergencies. (Not that normal would ever have the same meaning as it had had before the war.) He had put Karen on the National Health waiting list after her second visit. It still took over a year for her turn to come up. It was that kind of case, the necessity to postpone that kind of operation, that made him think of emigrating to Canada, where life would be easier, where Karen might have been operated on months ago. One had to be extraordinarily ill or extraordinarily lucky to rate immediate treatment. He should have found it bearable after the heavy burden of exhaustion and continuous emergency he had suffered through the war years. And St Bart's was certainly an improvement on the hospital he'd worked in in Liverpool, which still had not been reconstructed after bomb damage. He'd thanked his stars when he got the job; but neither he nor Gail had ever really been happy in London. Since he did not wish to go back, maybe they should move on.

To Karen the war meant what she looked back upon as normal times. She could hardly remember the raids and terror she had experienced at its beginning. For her it meant living with her mother in a country village in Wales, having less than enough money yet plenty of food and friends; and fields to play in all day. Karen had never adjusted to moving (it seemed to her for the first time) to London after the war. Normal times were *before* her father came back from the war—she had no memories of him before that day he appeared at the cottage. He took them 'home', grimly determined to work extra shifts in his factory to provide for them, to make a better life for his family.

Even though half her life had been spent living in London's East End playing in bomb sites, she was unused to this still. Mr Norman assured her she would be able to live a normal life after the operation. She badly wanted that. She knew he did not mean a return to the life in Wales. But the word 'normal' conveyed to her a kind of relief she craved. Though she could not define its details, she knew it meant a good change for her. All she had to do was endure an operation. And Mr Norman, whom she had learned to trust, would perform it.

The operation loomed for Frank Norman in a way none he'd performed before had done. He could not explain why. He would be trying a new technique, it was true; he would be going very deep into the head. But he was confident of his skill. However, Karen might be no better off afterwards. Perhaps the element of risk disturbed him?

'At least she will be no worse off,' Gail told him for comfort. She was getting used to comforting him, to the stresses he brought home, disrupting the ordinary pleasures of life. She had wanted them to visit her sister who had just moved to a flat in Shepherd's Bush to start her first job in London. But it was two nights before the operation and already Frank was what she laughingly called 'in training'.

Gail was going to have a baby, their first. That satisfied her. She felt placid, these days, somehow untroubled by the loneliness their move to London had initially engendered. Grown large with child, satisfied by a long phone call to her sister to check how she was getting on and a call to her mother in Liverpool to report, Gail sat reading Doctor Spock by the light of a standing lamp. Frank was through the arch at their dining room table, his notes and diagrams spread before him, preparing for the operation on Karen Kelly.

'Is it going to be long?' Gail asked.

'Yes. Several hours. I'll have to go deeper than I thought at first. I'm cutting away bone in one ear and replacing it with grafts.' He'd only been working on this kind of case for a short time; it was a major challenge. He wanted, apart from anything else, to succeed for the sake of his career. He was pioneering techniques. They could make many handicapped children like Karen normal—well, almost. As near, as good, as normal. He had already begun writing up the case for publication.

'Are you afraid it might not work?'

'No! No! It's not that—I'm as sure as I ever can be that I'll correct the physical side of things. It's that horrid mother of hers. Damn Mrs Kelly!'

'What's she like?'

'Oh, small—youngish, really—rather pretty; early forties. I always think of her as older. She makes herself dowdy. She makes her daughter dowdy too—and Karen could be so lovely. She does her best to subdue Karen altogether. My examinations make me think that even now, even before the operation, Karen's hearing could be better than it is. The speech therapist agrees with me. It's impossible—that cringeing, hopeless mother. She's some kind of foreigner—I guess she was a refugee before the war from somewhere or other. You should see her, hanging on to incongruous leftovers of some past elegance. She insists on discussing Karen's handicap as if it's some sort of martyrdom for her. She's a disgusting woman and she's used Karen's problem to make that child dependent, far more dependent than is necessary even for a deaf child.'

'I suppose she's Jewish.'

'What?'

'This Mrs Kelly—I suppose she must have been Jewish to get out of Europe like that before the war.'

'No. I don't think so. Her father was a Communist and an intellectual and just saw it wasn't safe any more. Something like that. She wasn't one of the really persecuted, I don't think. She just chose to get out in 1937 when it was lucky her father or someone saw the writing on the wall.'

'I don't understand why she upsets you so much, Frank.'

'Because she should know better—the wretched woman! She should be more . . . more . . . *responsible!*'

'Does it matter? She agreed to the operation. Surely her misgivings are the natural reaction of a mother.'

'What's the point of bothering if a possessive woman like that . . .'. He stopped. He could say no more. He was that exasperated!

'You'll make the girl all right. I know you will. But should you have put her in the children's ward?'

'She'll get closer attention there—there just wouldn't be the proper facilities with the older children for someone as sensitive as she's liable to be in hospital.'

The Sister of the ward asked him the same question next day. Karen, a bit bewildered, stood calmly holding onto a book she had brought for distraction and comfort. Then she was shown her bed, told to change into a hospital nightgown and dressing gown and led off to the examining room by an intern, a young woman, who would give her a physical for tomorrow. The operation was next morning— give the child a chance to settle in first so she wouldn't be too disorientated and scared when she came to afterwards.

Mr Norman was confronted by the Sister again after his rounds but remained adamant. The ward for pre-adolescents was safest for Karen emotionally. He did not want to risk her being upset.

Karen was more fascinated than bewildered by the processes in the hospital. It had been exciting packing her bag to take to the hospital, being allowed to choose things she wanted for her convalescence. She'd never had a bag all to herself before On the rare holidays the family could afford, all their things went into one valise. Her things then came out smelling of her father's talc and his permanent, vague sweatiness. She found she was more aware of his existence when he wasn't at home after that. She didn't so much remember how he looked as a bulk and an aroma. He was rarely home. He laboured at a factory, did lots of overtime, odd shifts. It was, she understood, to meet the extra burden of her needs. But she knew—and was trained to be grateful for it—that all her special needs as a deaf child were met by the National Health. So she wasn't sure why her parents were always so troubled about money. But they had a house fixed up better than most in the neighbourhood. Cleaner; newer furniture; nice curtains and fittings. They even had a telly and a radiogramme in a fancy piece of furniture made entirely of genuine wood. These were not exactly for her. She could not listen to records; the high frequencies caused pain in her ears. And she had trouble understanding most things on the telly, though she sometimes watched it. She had discovered, long ago, that she understood things best through the medium of print—if she could see it written out, put down on a page, it made sense to her; it became real, graspable. If she could see it and it didn't need sound—like the titration experiments at school in chemistry— she comprehended it. Things like telly were for her mother—for Sylvia.

David, her father, was trying to make it up to Sylvia for all the bad in her life. Hounded from Germany to Austria, then to Czechoslovakia, and finally getting away from the continent just in time, just about the time of the Munich Pact, Sylvia had been brought by her family to England at a time when everyone knew there would be a war. Many people—the people they met, at any rate—were suspicious and resentful of refugees. There was something shameful, scandalous, about being a refugee; as if you must be a potential criminal or idiot to be hounded from your homeland. And it was as if the refugees were responsible for the coming war in some inexplicable way.

Adjusting to the alien country had not been easy for Sylvia. She had never lost her sense of fear, the vivid conviction that retribution was a condition of life. Any small gift of luck or cheer would be spoiled, taken away, paid for endlessly. She had grown to believe that in some way she was culpable.

Karen could not articulate this about her mother but she had understood it from earliest childhood, just as she had known always that David's main purpose in life was to make it up to Sylvia. He had met her before the war at a Saturday night dance given at his working-men's club. Karen loved to hear him talk on the rare occasions when he reminisced about that courtship and the period of happiness that followed. David had been entranced by Sylvia's fragility and sadness. It sustained their closeness. And when their first child was born handicapped, David agreed they should have no more and had submitted to a sterilization operation; for surely the next must be more deformed—or an idiot. It was an omen.

Karen became David's ally as soon as she was old enough, his partner in actively making it up to Sylvia, in looking out for Sylvia, because of all her mother had gone through, including Karen's disability. It was the horrid, last bad joke—but they all made the best of it. After the war, when he returned grateful she was still waiting with their child, David worked to provide Sylvia—and Karen—with as safe and comfortable and normal a life as he could. And Karen, guilty for being a constant disruption to their peace, worked for it too.

Going into hospital became an adventure from the start. Away from the family strains and viewpoints it was a break in carefully ordered routines and a rest from responsibility.

Beds were arranged six to a room off long, brightly lit and tiled corridors. There was a common play room at the end of Karen's hallway which all those who were well enough visited and Karen spent most of her day there, in pyjamas and robe, after all the examining was over and they finally made Sylvia go. At first she was a bit insulted, being put in with the younger children; but she was accorded seniority and respect by the youngsters and felt almost the equal of the two therapists who supervized their play. Another team of therapists, a young man and woman, worked with the children who needed more attention. There were very crippled children in wheel chairs too. The room had a restrainedly festive atmosphere.

Someone explained why Karen talked a bit funny and why she sometimes didn't know what you were saying. This made Karen a subject of interest. Also, when the young man acting as special therapist for the crippled children went for a break, he insisted on taking Karen with him for a coffee in the staff canteen. This man's name was David, like her father's. He had red hair and freckles and was as short as she. His teeth were not very good, but he had lovely green eyes and long, long lashes and he was kind to the children, she had noticed. Karen believed that she was in love with him by tea time.

So Karen's day was very exciting. Only when, after dinner, her parents came to visit did she realize she hadn't thought about poor mummy all that time or how lonely mummy must be. Karen made a special effort to focus her attention on mummy now. She was glad of the new book they had brought her—a hardcover novel that grown-ups read—as a treat.

'It'll all be fine tomorrow,' Sylvia insisted. They were sitting alone in the common room. David, Karen's father, had gone to get them drinks. Mummy held Karen's hand. She was trembling slightly and seemed about to cry. 'It will be fine. They simply put you to sleep and when you wake up it will hurt a little, then, perhaps; but you'll—oh, you are so good. I know you will be patient. I. . . .'

Mr Norman came by. He was doing evening rounds. Mrs Kelly turned her head—she was weeping a bit now. The doctor was annoyed about something and he and her mother talked so rapidly that Karen couldn't follow their lips. She heard only the blur of sounds, the hollowness of voice. That frightened her a bit and made her think very hard to keep her self control. Her mother didn't let go her hand that whole time.

Things got a bit better when her father returned with two coffees and a coke. There was more talk Karen couldn't follow. Then her mother and father said farewell. Mummy was struggling not to cry. The nurse had been summoned and took Karen to her bed so quickly she hardly had time to be troubled.

Karen was given some small white pills. She never had any trouble sleeping, but did not protest. She enjoyed the feeling of having to follow hospital rules without thinking. It felt safer than she usually felt. She liked the sensation of falling asleep engendered by the pills. She had been determined to think of her mother. Helping to will Sylvia through her ordeals was a familiar task to Karen's consciousness, as if keeping her thoughts with her mother would give Sylvia the necessary comfort to keep going. But tonight the pills made Karen forget her duties. She forgot that it was not an ordinary night when she might indulge in fantasies, that tonight Sylvia would need special consideration, special help. So before Karen fell asleep she did not think of her mother at all. She thought of the young red-haired David whom she had met in the play room when she'd helped out there all day.

Sylvia was afraid at first that Karen might die. Such things did happen, people died in the simplest operations, she knew. It was always dangerous to administer anaesthetic, she had been told. The anaesthetist could miscalculate.

Sylvia drove herself into a state of despair sitting in the hospital all the morning of Karen's operation.

'Please let me see my child before they take her up. She's asleep. I can't disturb her.'

A kind nurse admitted her to the room in which Karen lay in drugged sleep, but Sylvia was only permitted to stare at her daughter for a few moments. She continued her worried vigil during all the hours they operated, sitting on a chair in the day room.

David had not taken the morning off work but he came after lunch to be with Sylvia and wait for Karen to wake up. The operation took four hours. A nurse told Sylvia that Karen had stopped breathing briefly on the table. Sylvia became terrified. How long? Might there be brain damage? Sylvia was no fool. There might be brain damage if you didn't get oxygen. The nurse reassured her. It had been for only a moment. Karen could have suffered no harm. She was in the recovery room and had already come to briefly. She was asked her name by Mr Norman—a common practice. She had, of course, to read the lips, for her ears were swathed in bandages. But she had replied before falling asleep again, 'Karen Kelly'.

When Karen was brought back to her bed, Sylvia and David were allowed to sit by her. The bed was curtained off for privacy. The bandages reminded David of a nun wearing her wimple.

Karen woke up very late, about ten o'clock that night. She smiled when she saw her parents by her bed. She was then immediately preoccupied with pain and nausea.

The bandages reminded David of a nun wearing her wimple.

'Don't talk, Karen,' Sylvia insisted. 'Rest, rest, *mein kind.*' She took Karen's hand, thinking 'now, truly she cannot hear me' and began to cry. Karen struggled. She pulled her hand back and asked for water. David gave her some from the jug at her bedside. As Karen began to drink she gagged, then vomited. David ran for the nurse, who came with a pan. Another nurse came to give Karen an injection. They did not want her straining to vomit and doing damage to herself after the operation. But Karen retched and heaved for several minutes, though there was no food to throw up. Sylvia grew terrified. The nurses reassured her, once they had calmed Karen. Nausea was common after anaesthesia. One nurse gave Karen an injection to relax her muscles and help her not vomit again; she explained it would also help Karen sleep. Finally the nurses made the Kellys leave.

'She is only one of many to them,' Sylvia mumbled as they left the hospital. She was reluctant to abandon her daughter. 'What do they know? They see only typical reactions. But to me . . . to me . . .'

'To me, too, Sylvia,' David soothed. 'But I have confidence in them and I'm sure they'll treat her very specially. Karen is special. Everyone loves her.'

'She's just another bed to tend to, to them; another problem.'

They were out in the street. David offered to buy Sylvia a meal in a nearby Indian restaurant they knew and they set out for it. Eating out was usually looked upon as an unwarrantable luxury, but tonight Sylvia did not even protest her own cooking was better than any they could buy. It was half past ten. The streets were quite empty, the city quiet and chilly with early-winter night dampness.

Sylvia whispered, 'But I am her mother. And how am I supposed to watch my own child go through all this? Why was it necessary? If I'd known that she'd have to suffer so, like this . . . that we would all have to suffer . . .'

He still tried to comfort her.

But she was not to be stopped. 'I should never, never have agreed to this operation. It probably won't help and we put her through all this. We were mad to agree to it.'

David stopped walking and stared at his wife. 'But what are *you* going through that is so awful? They told us this operation would make our child's hearing nearly normal. We both agreed to it. I agreed too. She'll be able to be like anyone else, go to ordinary schools, have friends like everyone else. Isn't it worth a bit of pain and distress to you? She is the one who is suffering in real, physical pain! She is the one who had to have the operation! How can you? I know you are scared! But how . . .'

Sylvia interrupted, hysterical with anger. 'She is not ordinary! Not like everyone else! She's brighter and gentler and she needs me. She needs *me*! You don't understand. You don't care for her and spend time with her as I do. You want her to be like everyone else with their stupid ways. They get so they don't even care if their mothers live or die. After this what if she doesn't need me again? It's no good— no good! You—the doctor—all of you want to ruin things for me and Karen, ruin it between us. Yes, I'd rather she stayed as she is, was even stone deaf, if it meant she would go on needing me! How can you be so stupid? Can't you see what it means? She'll never need me again as before and it will all be ruined and be no good, no good!'

She was shouting. The few passers-by rushed to avoid them and after an uncomfortable, involuntary stare averted their eyes. Sylvia stood crying and gulping the harsh air.

David was silent.

Sylvia calmed down and noticed he looked sad and angry all at once. Then she realized what she was saying. She wept again, this time more quietly. And this time David embraced her until she was calmer and then they went home in a taxi.

Karen recuperated quickly. She was a notably cheerful patient. She was able to be up and in the play room within a few days, and she saw the young man, David, there; though he seemed less splendid to her, they were still friendly. He offered to come and see her at her home and she said he might, after she was better and the bandages were truly off. Except when they took off the bandages to check the scar tissue, she was surrounded by them and therefore by a silence more profound than she had ever experienced previously. The world was now un- bearably muffled. She also had trouble with her balance for the first weeks and was easily exhausted—so she spent a lot more of the day than she wished in bed and sleeping. Her ears often ached and she had to take many pain killers. Her mother visited twice a day but she seemed distant. She seemed afraid to touch Karen, to be near her.

Sylvia's guilt had become unbearable the first days after her outburst to her husband. She felt humiliated before David and before her child, so intense was her misery. David, sensing her unhappiness, did not refer to their conversation and there was a general silence on the subject.

Mr Norman at last called the Kellys to his office for a meeting. The operation had been more complicated than he'd predicted, he informed them. When he got into the ears the damage was more extensive than expected. They shouldn't hope Karen's hearing would be radically improved.

It was a judgment on her, Sylvia realized. It reinforced her determination to keep silent, to punish herself for being so selfish at Karen's expense, to deny herself the pleasures she had taken in mothering Karen too much.

Karen came home. It was uncomfortable between mother and daughter. Karen's hearing would be no better and Sylvia would get her wish of keeping Karen dependent. There was no longer a risk her child would grow rebellious, insensitive—or grow away from her mother; perhaps she would not even meet boys, go to dances, leave home and marry. Sylvia had wished all this upon Karen. Now she determined fiercely to avoid this fate even if it meant asking Karen to hate her. She would force Karen to be independent for her own good. It was her duty. And so she tried to do less and less for her daughter and Karen became increasingly miserable.

Mr Norman called Sylvia to his office to berate her for not nursing a recuperative child properly. 'Now, of all times, when just what she needs is pampering, you force her to go shopping, to keep up with lessons from the school, even to cook. You send her out on busy streets when she has no hearing and no proper sense of balance. Are you out of your mind, woman? What's come over you?'

Sylvia broke down. She told everything—emphasizing how evil she had been, that her motives had been evil, explaining her efforts to overcome that evil.

Mr Norman was appalled by what had happened. He had not believed this woman capable of noticing what she was doing and so he had never warned her of the dangers or counselled her as, perhaps, he should have. He had held her in too much contempt to believe she was worthy of such attention—for she was incapable of benefitting from it like any ordinary, sane person.

After his first wave of sympathy and horror, however, Mr Norman's hatred for this foolish woman nearly overcame him. His professional discipline, good sense, and good training prevented him from making a scene. Instead he sent for Janet Wells, one of the hospital's psychiatrists. He thus washed his hands of the stupid business. He felt badly enough about bungling the operation and now this stupid woman . . . ! Why had he been so confident he could play God with Karen and change her life? He wanted to forget the whole mess as soon as possible. The idiotic business of this emotionally unstable mother of Karen's was too unbearable! It made the whole business so much worse.

Dr Wells approached Mr Norman in the staff canteen later that afternoon. She thought he might like to know that Mrs Kelly had agreed to see her weekly for a session of out-patient therapy.

'No, Janet, I really don't care to know another thing about what happens to her.'

'But it's your case, doctor.'

'The child—not her dreadful mother.'

'I don't find the mother so dreadful, Frank.'

'She's a type—Possessive Mother—that's all there is to her. Even if the girl's hearing were restored she'd never function as a fully independent human being with that woman about. Her mother would never allow it in a thousand ways a day. She is a totally self-deceived, weak, immature woman. I've seen it over and over but this is a particularly stark case. You're just wasting your time, doctor.'

'Perhaps.'

'I know about women like that. I can tell you a thing or two!'

'I can tell you something too, Frank,' Dr Wells said. She stood up.

Mr Norman smiled at her. Such a pretty woman to be a psychiatrist! 'What's that, my dear?'

'You are an ass.'

Mr Norman took Karen's bandages off a few days later. She sat still in the doctor's office waiting for she knew not what. A moment later she heard an unfamiliar sound. It startled her. She turned round sharply in response to it, for she could not recognize it.

Mr Norman was snapping his fingers behind her head.

Karen let out a cry of surprise and then, like her mother, began to cry.

At last she went over to hug her mother and kiss her.

'Mummy, Mummy,' she said. She could not believe it, quite.

'I know, I know. It's wonderful, just wonderful!'

Mr Norman then settled down to the tedious tests and observations, the most painful of which for Karen involved blowing air into Karen's ear to separate bits of scar tissue that might grow together and close the passage of the ear.

After Karen and her mother were gone, Mr Norman phoned Janet Wells to tell her that the child had, after all, gained a lot in her hearing, it appeared. Not as much as he'd originally hoped, but quite a lot. Sufficient, he supposed, to make some change in her life, however much her mother militated against it.

Dr Wells thanked him rather curtly, he thought.

When she had hung up on Frank Norman, Janet Wells found herself giggling. Frank Norman really was a self-righteous prig! But he was a brilliant surgeon. Mrs Kelly would be coming for therapy again in two days—and bringing Karen too. They had a lot to look forward to. All thanks to Frank Norman. Of all people!

HE FLOATS THROUGH THE AIR

Virginia Newlin

There were four of us guys who had saved the money to buy one, but only three of them, almost grown, playing around their mother. I already knew the one I wanted. The littlest. Grey-brown fur, a long fluffy tail, and curly fingers on his hands and feet. He was playing keep-a-way with a raisin, and when Robert said, 'I have a rabbit cage for mine, Sir,' he stopped tossing it and put his head on one side, looking at Robert with eyes like chocolate smartees, as if he were considering what a rabbit cage might be.

'They can't be kept outdoors. They catch cold easily,' said Mr Woolard.

'But flying squirrels live outdoors in Pennsylvania.'

'These have been raised in captivity. They're delicate, Robert.'

Captivity. I hated that word. My little fellow wasn't going to be in captivity—except from Growltiger, my sister's cat. He would live in my room and be my buddy.

'I'm going to put mine in a box,' said Ted.

'A cage is better,' said Wooly. 'They have sharp squirrel teeth.'

'Do they bite, then?' George asked.

'Not these.' Wooly reached into the cage and picked out my squirrel, put him into George's hand.

'He's soft,' George said.

All of us wanted to hold him, and he was passed around. I could see he didn't like it. I wanted to yell at them, take him away before he got frightened. 'He's afraid. Let's put him back,' I said.

'Could we see him fly, first?' asked Robert.

'They don't really fly, they glide,' said Mr Woolard. 'There's a membrane, running from wrist to foot to base of the tail on each side of a flying squirrel's body, that he stretches out into a kind of parachute. He can glide as far as eighty feet.'

Wooly put him up on his shoulder, where he sat, his little hands folded on his chest, looking at first one of us and then another, exactly like our Headmaster. We all laughed, he was so tiny there, no more than six inches long, I thought, and didn't look a bit impressed by us, as if he were the King of the Lilliputians deciding to make pets out of a posse of Gullivers. Then, all of a sudden, he took off. He spread out his arms and legs and the skin between them and flew through the air, landing on my shoulder. Out of all the guys, he picked me. Maybe even then he knew.

He landed on my shoulder, up against my ear, so soft there. I got a queer feeling down my back, but I laughed with the other guys, only quietly, so I wouldn't scare him. He wasn't scared. He jumped from me to Robert and then to Ted and back to me again and then just sat there. All the guys reached for him, asked if they could have him next.

'Please, Sir. He's the one I want if I get to keep one,' I said. 'I have an old aquarium I can use.'

'How big?' asked Wooly.

I held out my arms to show him the size.

'He seems to have chosen you too, Jeff. You'll have to make a lid for the aquarium, out of screening to let in air, and you, Robert will have to move your rabbit cage indoors and be sure that the mesh is fine enough for such a small animal.

'You, George and Ted, will have to get busy and fix a suitable home if you want one of the squirrels. The first three boys ready will get them. If you're all ready, we'll draw lots. You'll have to bring the homes in for me to see and demonstrate that you understand the proper care of a small animal.'

'Do they have to be caged all the time, Mr Woolard?' asked George.

'Not all the time. They love exercise, and, if you're careful, you can let your squirrels play in your room. You may find he's most playful when you're ready for bed, since flying squirrels are nocturnal, but he'll soon adjust to your habits. There's one thing you must remember, though. Flying squirrels are not like dogs and cats that can safely be left alone in the house.'

I won't keep you caged all the time, but you'll be safe with me, I promised him, as Mr Woolard put him back with the others.

As soon as I got home, I went down in the cellar to make a lid for the aquarium. I used to keep fish in it, but, if they were goldfish, they were forever floating belly-up, and if they were guppies and survived our water, they did what guppies do and I ran out of containers for them. At one time, I had the aquarium and three fish bowls full of guppies sitting on my windowsill. It was too much work, so, when spring came, I set up a guppy stand on the road, sold them off as if they were lemonade, and was glad to forget them.

But I wouldn't forget my squirrel, I promised myself, as I measured the aquarium for a lid, sawed four pieces of wood to the right size, nailed them together into a rectangle, and cut screening to fit. Of course, I didn't do it as fast as it sounds. Even though I'm good at carpentry, I made mistakes.

While I nailed the screening to its wooden frame, I thought of names. Squirrel Nutkin. My mother used to read me that book. And there was Sammy Squirrel, but my squirrel needed his own name. I thought of Fluffy Tail and Bright Eyes and Fly Boy, and then I remembered how much he looked like the Headmaster, so I called him Mr Merryweather. That was a good name. When I looked at the Headmaster, it would make me laugh inside, too.

After the lid was finished, I decided I would make him a little house, so he would have some privacy. That took quite a while. I worked after sports every day, made a little wooden house, with a door and a window he could look out of. Mr Woolard said that squirrels can see colours, so I painted it red. It had a roof but no floor. I put wood shavings and grass thickly on the bottom of the aquarium and set his house on top of that so he'd have a comfortable bed. Then I carried the whole business up to the windowsill in my room until it was time. At the end of the week I would find out if I got him or not.

My mother bought a wheel for him so he could exercise, and Wooly gave us each a list of things that flying squirrels like to eat: apples and raisins and nuts, bird seed, particularly sunflower seed, greens like lettuce or celery leaves and bits of carrot. Hamster food was okay too. I'd forgotten a water bottle. I went to the pet shop and bought one that would fit, and then, on the right day, I took the aquarium to school. Mother would pick me and Mr Merryweather up at four o'clock. If I got him.

I did. Mr Woolard loved his home. 'Good work, Jeff,' he said. And Robert and George got the others, because Ted had nothing to keep one in but a cardboard box. I felt sorry about that and so did Wooly; but then, Ted could have tried harder.

When we got home, I put Mr Merryweather up on my windowsill, close to my desk where I could watch him. He went into his house and stuck his head out the window and then out the door. I gave him some raisins, and he carried them inside one by one. I couldn't tell if he ate them or not, he was so quick about it. I did more watching than homework until supper, and, after supper, I brought him down for the family to meet.

'Where's Growltiger?' I asked Susie, my little sister, as I was carrying him down the stairs.

'On my bed,' she said.

'Well, be sure the door's shut tight.'

Everybody loved him. He jumped from my shoulder to Susie's and then to the curtain and then to Dad. Mother said that she felt left out, and then he jumped from Dad to the curtain to Mother to the mantlepiece, hid behind a candlestick and peered at us.

'He's lovely,' Mom said.

And my Dad sang, 'He floats through the air with the greatest of ease, the daring young man on the flying trapeze.'

Dad is funny. He made that Mr Merryweather's theme song, and I only minded it once.

We were still watching Mr Merryweather play peek-a-boo from behind the candlestick, so we didn't see Growltiger sneak into the room. The first thing we knew was when this big black shape hurtled through the air and landed on the mantel beside Mr

227

Merryweather, who leaped to the floor, the cat after him. Flying squirrels don't move very well on the ground, I could see that and so could Growltiger. I guess he thought he had him, but Mr Merryweather took off again, right from under his nose. Around the room they went, from floor to furniture to windowsill, while we all tried to grab Growltiger and Dad said, 'Damn that cat,' and Susie squealed. For some reason, Mr Merryweather wasn't doing his best flying. I thought the cat would get him, sure. They were both so fast that none of us could lay a hand on them.

Growltiger had Mr Merryweather backed into a corner on top of the bookcase, was switching his tail, waiting to pounce, and Dad was climbing up on a chair to grab him when my flying squirrel made his best flight. He soared through the air and landed on my shoulder, putting his little hands on my neck, close to my ear. I thought I heard a very small chattering, as if he was telling me about his escape. I gave Susie what for, and Growltiger was dumped outdoors.

Actually, after they got to know each other, the cat stopped looking at Mr Merryweather as if he were tabby treat. I tried to keep Growltiger out of my room, as you never know, but sometimes he would come in and climb up on the windowsill, sit beside the aquarium and stare at my squirrel. Mr Merryweather would run into his house and peer out the window at Growltiger. First the window and then the door and then the window again, as if it was a game.

I used to tell the other guys about his games. George said that his squirrel didn't play very much, and Robert's had already died, but Mr Merryweather loved games. When I was doing my homework, I would let him out of his aquarium to play around the room, making sure that the door was closed and that Growltiger wasn't hiding under anything. I would put raisins or bits of cookie or chocolate on my desk, and one of my squirrel's games was to steal them from me when I wasn't looking. Long afterwards, I found a pile of raisins in my closet. It made me feel really bad.

Another place he liked to play was the bathroom. I would take him in with me when I took a shower, make sure to close the toilet and open the closet door so he could play in the towels. He would hide under them, and you could see a tiny head peer at you from the yellow washcloths. Peer at you and then disappear and peer at you from

Mr Merryweather soared about the room while Jeff worked at his desk.

the blue bath-towels instead. When I got into the shower, I would sometimes find him clinging to the top of the curtain out of range of the water and jumping from there to the towel bar. One time he missed and slid down into the tub where he skidded all around trying to get out again. I put him up on the towel rack, where he shook himself and wriggled his little nose at me as if to say that squirrels hate baths more than anything.

Sometimes I'd leave him in the bathroom alone, since he liked it so much. He liked to pop out and surprise people from under the towels, and he liked to leap from the closet shelves to the basin to the shower curtain to the windowsill to the toilet seat. I always made sure it was closed, the window and the door too, and that there was no water in the tub. And I never went to bed leaving him there. Except once.

That once, I had a composition to hand in the next day. I hadn't done it when I should have, so I had to work late that night. Mom and Dad went out after saying, 'Do your homework, Jeff,' and Susie watched television and then went to bed.

I let Mr Merryweather out of the aquarium, but he had much too much energy. While I was working, he was playing around the room, and he kept running across the desk, rustling my papers, crawling under them even, and once carrying off my eraser. The composition was hard enough without him. I was making enough mistakes on my own, so I put him in the bathroom to play. Still I kept messing up, having to start over again, and it was very late when I finished. I guess I staggered to the bathroom, staggered back to my room and fell into bed, not remembering my squirrel at all. I was really tired, but that's no excuse.

Mr Merryweather must have been tired too, because when Mom and Dad came home and Mom started her bath, he didn't scramble out of the towels to greet her. She went back to her bedroom, where Dad was already asleep, and didn't know anything about my squirrel until she came in to take her bath and found him drowned in the tub.

I woke up with her shaking me. 'Mr Merryweather, Mr Merryweather. . . .'

'What . . . what. . . .' And then I remembered where he was.

'Drowned . . . in the bathtub. You forgot him.'

I ran into the bathroom, and he was lying on the bath mat, a heap of tiny wet-fur-covered bones. If his mouth had not been so small, I would have tried the mouth to mouth resuscitation that I'd learned in life-saving, but how do you breathe into a mouth as small as your little fingernail? Maybe I should have tried. ·I should have tried anything, but I just stood there looking at his limp body and saying, 'What happened? What happened?'

'I was running a bath,' Mother said. 'He must have fallen in.'

'Why didn't you save him?'

'I was in my room. . . . Oh, poor little fellow.'

'It's your fault! You didn't watch out for him.'

'I didn't know he was in here. The door wasn't even closed. Oh, Jeff, how could you have left him in the bathroom!'

'You could have thought! Why were you taking a bath so late anyway?' I hated her for it.

'Your poor little pet. Poor Mr Merryweather.' My mother was crying.

I went to my room, carrying him in my hand. He was so little and cold. I took a shirt from my drawer and wrapped him in it, laying him on the roof of his house, thinking, I guess, that if he was warmer and where he liked to be, he might come back to life. Then I got in my bed, trying not to picture how Mr Merryweather must have struggled to climb the sides of the bathtub, and cried into my pillow so my mother wouldn't hear me. But she came into my room and knelt by my bed and put her arm around my shoulders.

'It wasn't your fault, Jeff, or mine or anybody's. It's what happens when wild animals are taken from their habitat and kept as house pets. What you must remember, darling, is that, while Mr Merryweather was living here, you made him happy. That's the most you or anyone could have done.'

Still, I cried myself to sleep.

When Susie found out the next morning, she wouldn't speak to me or go to school. I went, though. I had to hand in that composition, even though I wanted to tear it up. I didn't tell anybody what had happened. I didn't want anybody to know, particularly Mr Woolard, who had congratulated me for being the only guy who had kept his flying squirrel alive.

All during school, I kept hoping that a miracle would have happened, that my little fellow would have come to life again while I was gone, but his body was still where I had left it, wrapped up on the roof of his house. Quite stiff.

I found a box for him and laid his body on some pretty material from Mother's scraps, and I went down in the cellar, got a board and made a marker for his grave. It took me till suppertime to burn in the words with my electric etcher:

'Here lies Mr Merryweather. Loved by all who knew him.'

After supper, we had his funeral. I dug a grave under the crab-apple tree and laid the box in it.

'We must sing a hymn,' Susie said.

'He floats through the air,' Dad suggested, laying his hand on my shoulder.

I was surprised at his bad taste.

'No,' I said. 'Now the Day is Over.'

So we sang, 'Now the day is over; night is falling nigh; shadows of the evening, creep across the sky.'

And Mom said, 'Rest in peace, Mr Merryweather.'

THE MAN WHO KILLED HITLER

Hayden McAllister

The Boeing B-17 Long-Range Bomber showed no navigation lights
as it passed at altitude over Dymchurch on its secret flight toward the
heartland of Germany.

Sentinels attending the shore batteries along Britain's south coast had
been alerted that a lone aircraft would pass overhead at 23.00 hours on
the 15 August. But the B-17 passed so high above them that only a
soft 'humming', like that made by a honey-bee could be discerned.

Inside the pressurized cabin of the modified high-flying 'plane, Pilot
Metcalfe glanced across at his solitary passenger. It was thirty minutes
to midnight. Switching on the internal intercom he spoke tersely into
the microphone. 'Better turn on your oxygen supply Sergeant Weston.
You'll soon be needing it.' Owing to the rarefied upper atmosphere
both men were experiencing difficulty in breathing.

In his headphones Weston heard the crackle of static as the intercom
went dead. He did not bother to reply. He felt very cold and his teeth
were chattering. The B-17 was now flying at 30,000 feet and the
temperature had plunged to *minus* thirty degrees Fahrenheit.

Weston's vision blurred momentarily. Was he on the verge of
blacking out? As he buckled the face mask containing the oxygen inlet
over his mouth he suddenly remembered that he'd forgotten to kiss

Wendy Turnbull goodbye. Well – that was another good reason for returning home safely!

Weston stretched forward to study the control panel. He knew that in a short while the pilot would switch on the AN/APQ-9 blocking-transmitter in an attempt to jam the German radar. The bomber droned on . . . It was ironic to think that the only dangerous object it would be dropping tonight would be – himself!

His left hand fumbled for the value lever which would release the flow of oxygen to his air-starved lungs. He only half accomplished the task and slumped wearily back on his seat. He felt so strange. It was as if he were slipping off the edge of the world.

Anyway, the rest would do him good before they reached the dropping zone . . .

＊　　　＊　　　＊　　　＊

After free-falling nearly a mile, Don Weston pulled the rip-cord of the parachute. It opened with a bone-jolting crack, and he was left swinging like a puppet on a string in mid-air . . . then slowly he began to float down towards enemy territory.

In the distance he could see the black bird-like speck of the B-17 fading into the starry August sky above Berchtesgaden – and that worried him. It meant that *he* would be visible to anyone watching from the ground. His only hope was that here at Untersberg in the mountainous terrain of Upper Bavaria, there wouldn't be too many ferret-eyed Nazis prowling around.

He envied the pilot of the plane. In a few hours the lucky devil would be back home, snug and warm inside a bunk-bed somewhere in Surrey without a care in the world.

The chill wind whistled derisively in Weston's ears and brought his thoughts rudely back to the present. He'd taken on something big this time. The whole might of the Fatherland would soon be set against him and he knew that his chances of getting back to England were virtually nil. Suddenly Weston was pleased that he hadn't married his regular girl Wendy Turnbull. That was one problem out of the way. At least he wouldn't be leaving a widow behind – maybe just a broken heart.

As the dark mass of the wooded valley below rose up to meet him Weston tensed himself. This was the tricky part. If he got stuck thirty feet up a fir tree like a Christmas fairy, it wouldn't look good in his memoirs. He tugged on the cords of one side of his parachute and moved down through the air towards the forest at an angle. The clearing ahead showed itself in the nick of time and he was able to touch down amidst a thin strip of wild corn and then roll forward to break the full impact of the fall. The black silk of the parachute billowed around him and in half a minute he had freed the harness, crushed the whole contraption into a ball and stuffed it down a rabbit hole. Then he loosened the straps attaching the pack to his back, stowed it beneath a clump of decaying bracken and crouched in the shadows – listening.

Like a stone Weston remained until his eyes became accustomed to the post-midnight light, and when at last he'd satisfied himself that his descent from the skies had raised no alarms, he began to check through his equipment.

The luger complete with silencer, snug inside his hip pocket. The throwing knife strapped to his ankle. The dagger at his belt with the hollowed-out handle containing the special fluid.

The strangling wire tucked away in the false heel of the left boot and the poisonous blow-dart in the right heel.

In his pack was the dismantled long-range 'Specialist' rifle with telescopic lens and spare cartridges wrapped in an oilskin cover. One pair of clip-on steel-spiked soles. Two handgrenades. Six pounds of processed survival food consisting of crushed chocolate, oatmeal and raisins. A pencil torch – He stopped! Something had moved. He sensed it. No! It was nothing but a foraging rabbit . . .

All those hours of training on the Sussex Downs had sharpened Weston's senses to perfection. This was what it had all been in aid of – to give him that one chance in a thousand.

Relaxed once more, Weston went back to itemizing the contents of his pack . . . The pencil torch, map section, hip flask, and the capsule containing the cyanide – in case they caught him.

In a rain-proof packet of the pack was the final item. The signal flare. If he should ever get through, a monoplane flying in from neutral Switzerland would look out for the yellow signal rocket on two successive nights. The pick-up point was to be over the frontier in Austria on the shores of a lake six miles outside Saltzburg. *If* he should get through.

If he could signal 'Mission Accomplished' it would mean so much to Wendy Turnbull.

It would also mean that Adolf Hitler would be dead.

*   *   *   *

During the final briefing at Povey Cross, Commander Burgess had shown Weston six enlarged photographs of the area. One print in particular revealed a chalet nestling like an eagle's eyrie on a mountain slope.

'It's called the Berghof,' he heard the commander say. 'Herr Hitler's mountain retreat at Obersalzburg. From it there's a splendid view over Berchtesgaden. In 1938, Neville Chamberlain was most impressed by the scenery. Apparently he could see the glaciers glinting on the Dachstein mountains.'

Burgess lit a pipe as Weston pointed to a mountain which stood facing the Berghof across a valley.

'Could I use this as a reconnaissance point?' he asked.

'The Kehlstein?' frowned Burgess. 'Doubtful. Height 6,000 feet. It's over three miles from the chalet.'

'Out of range of the high-powered rifle then?'

'Exactly! Unless you happen to catch the Fuhrer out strolling.'

Weston shook his head. 'Too unpredictable. I want to nail the Nazi spider in his web . . .'

'Then you'll need to get within 800 yards to make absolutely sure with the "Specialist" rifle', observed Burgess. 'And that is your main problem Sergeant, for the moment Hitler is hit – or missed! – the whole area will be sealed off, and you'll be trapped like a rat in a trap. SS Guards, police, dogs . . . and a few Gestapo thrown in for good measure.'

'I think I can handle any reception committee,' returned Weston quietly, 'But first I'll need to know more of Hitler's movements in and around the Berghof.'

'Very well,' responded Burgess through a blue wreath of pipe smoke. 'Take a good look at the last photograph will you. It's a close-up of the chalet. It shows a grass covered bunker lined with barbed wire fencing. By the side of this runs an asphalt pathway. Hitler often strolls here. Now directly above the path,' Burgess marked the spot with his finger, 'is the Fuhrer's study. It's on the second floor. Notice the balcony . . .'

'Does he use it?'

'Apparently not – but the French windows are large; and occasionally opened – weather permitting. Why not wait until your quarry
appears and then – !!' Burgess broke off. He was sweating.

Weston reflected for a time. When he finally spoke his question
caught the commander off guard.

'You've met Hitler haven't you?

Burgess took off his spectacles before replying. He chose his words
carefully.

'Yes' I met him briefly at the Nurenburg rally in 1936. Strange
character. Can't dress for the life of him. But one glance from those
deep blue eyes and you can sense the magnetic power radiating
from the man. I'd say – and this is off the record – I'd say he started
out with good intentions – then the devil whispered in his ear. He set
a snowball of corruption rolling down the mountain. Now it's
become a black avalanche – and it could snuff out the light of the
world . . .'

'I get the picture,' said Weston.

'Right!' declared Burgess, replacing his spectacles and regaining
his composure. 'From now on you're on 24-hour standby.'

★   ★   ★   ★

Moving at speed, yet with all the stealth of a born hunter, Weston
reached the woods surrounding Obersalzburg in just over three
hours. Once, in the thick bracken he'd almost stumbled on a concealed alarm system. The trip wire had marked the outer perimeter
of the security precautions set up to protect the Fuhrer. From that
moment on Weston kept his eyes skinned for guard – or guard dogs.
He didn't have long to wait.

As he was inching his way forward through the undergrowth he
heard the faint sound of snoring. Slowly, raising his head, Weston
peered in the general direction of the noise. As yet it was only the
vaguest whisper on the wind, but an antelope may well have ignored
it. Weston did not.

He moved like the midnight fox. Probing for safe footholds on the
pine needle carpet. Gently stepping over stray twigs. Nosing forward

toward the source of the sound – all five senses working with the efficiency of radar.

Before he entered the danger zone Weston smeared himself with the scent neutralizing agent contained in the hollow handle of his dagger. As far as a guard dog's sense of smell was concerned – he just didn't exist.

But there was no dog. Instead he saw a uniformed sentry lying, half-propped against the base of a cypress. His greatcoat and a half empty bottle of schnapps at his side. He was as if dead to the world.

Weston crept closer. The only sounds were the steady beat of his own heart rhythm in his ears, the nasal snore of the guard and the thin whine of the breeze in the pine tops.

Weston stole to the far side of the cypress until he became interlocked with the sleeping man's shadow. His fingers slid into the guard's greatcoat pocket. Empty. Weston removed the schnapps and reached down for the coat. The German stirred, scratched at an ear, then continued his contented snoring.

In the other pocket of the greatcoat was a small rectangle of cardboard and printed upon it was a plan of the defence system around the German dictator's den. Weston gazed at it for 20 long seconds, committing every detail to memory. Then he replaced the map, the coat and the schnapps and backed away.

With one rapid check on his compass, the English agent moved to within half a mile of the sleeping Fuhrer.

The German leader was now within rifle range.

*   *   *   *

Fifteen minutes later Weston watched an unsuspecting dog patrol pass within two yards of his temporary hide-out. Then he moved on to select one of the highest evergreens in Obersalzberg.

Unhitching his pack he picked out the steel sole-grips and attached them to his combat boots. After he'd replaced his pack on his shoulders he removed his purpose-built belt from around his waist and once he'd curved it around the base of the tree trunk, he clipped it to his waist and adjusted the tension. Ever so slowly he began to ascend the cleated grey trunk, leaning out at an angle – the steel pitons on his feet biting into the pine wood – the thick leather girdle taking the weight of his body.

The branches were thick and rich with evergreen leaves, but they didn't begin until he'd climbed nearly fifty feet. If a guard or dog should have entered his immediate vicinity, Weston would have had to rely on a whispered prayer.

At last he was able to push aside the thick curtain of pine needles, unfasten the belt and drag himself into the verdant refuge at the top of the tree. As he hauled on the second branch, a wood pigeon's wings exploded in his face as it went careering into space. Weston hung grimly on. A dog barked. Then the night became still once more.

Weston lifted himself into the spread of intertwined branches and a light shower of dead pine needles floated to the floor of the forest eighty feet below. In the vague light he could see something moving beside him. Switching on the pencil torch he saw the young squab of the wood pigeon shifting about in the scattering of twigs the mother bird used as a nest.

Within threequarters of an hour the first glimmer of dawn lit the eastern sky and the sentries could be heard calling out as morning patrols replaced the night watch. At 6.30 a.m. Weston was fastened like a limpet to the pinnacle of the fir tree, and through the detached telescopic sight he observed a house-keeper draw the curtains in the second floor study window of the Berghof. At 7.15 a.m. he saw a half naked Hitler cross to the window in his pyjama trousers. For an instant it looked as if the Fuhrer would step out on the balcony for a breath of fresh air. But a telephone bell jangled, and the German leader was called by his aide to receive a call.

Weston systematically began to assemble the long-range 'Specialist' rifle, while from beneath him came the call of the roosting wood pigeon coo-cooing on the warm breeze.

*   *   *   *

At 10.15 a.m. a German staff car crawled up the thin winding road to the Fuhrer's lair at Obersalzburg. Weston took a sip from his hip flask and idly picked up the telescopic lens. Through it he saw two men climb out of the car and pass through the guard-barrier. The driver remained.

The thick leather girdle took the weight of his body.

Then three men exited from the Berghof. Two of them were generals. They flanked a third man.

All five men exchanged Nazi salutes. Weston grappled with the lens, trying to focus it on the third mans face. Then he saw the clipped moustache and knew it was Adolph Hitler. He wore a brown storm troopers jacket. Black trousers. Jackboots . . .

A sudden wave of inspiration burst upon Weston. Almost feverishly he unhooked the rifle from the shoulder strap, snapping the telescopic sights into place in the same movement.

Already the staff car had begun its slow drive down the narrow precipitous road.

Weston levelled the barrel. The black cross on the optics hovered upon the high ranking officials in the back seat of the Mercedes. Then Weston lowered his aim until the rear wheel entered his circle of vision. The white walled tyre bobbled over a stone. His finger squeezed slowly . . .

There was a dull 'Phut' and a tremendous kick-back against his shoulder. From 500 yards he heard the squealing skidding tyres. There came an eerie silence like when a clock stops ticking in a haunted room.

The staff car nosedived off the precipice, seemed to hang in mid-air and then floundered into the gaping space beyond – the driver still wrestling with the steering wheel.

The sound of splitting branches, buckling metal and an earth shaking 'Keeroomph!' After a count of four the petrol tank exploded like a depth charge.

An alarm bell was ringing from the compound surrounding the Berghof and various running figures converged upon the scene.

Weston unclipped the telescope; unscrewed the still hot barrel from the gun-stock and waited. With luck they would never find the bullet in the burnt-out wreck. He yawned, and decided to stay put till sundown; then sneak over the border into Austria; whence the pick-up point and the yellow signal rocket.

★   ★   ★   ★

By the time the ambulances arrived from Berchtesgaden, guards and officials had formed a tenuous human chain stretching from the roadside down to the deep valley below.

The bodies were brought up one by one. On the first and second stretchers the grey blanket was drawn over the head of the corpses within. Upon the third stretcher Weston could see the unconscious driver.

It seemed like an eternity before the fourth stretcher was borne up the hillside. As it passed by the line of guards Weston could see them doffing their hats and giving the stiff-armed salute. Surely it must mean that Hitler . . . ?

Weston had to be certain. He centred the telescopic lens on the blanket of the stretcher. He seemed to be very near. The bespectacled doctor in the white coat was bending over.

The pine tops swayed in the wind. How his legs ached. He *must* hold his gaze. He *must* make sure.

In his minds-eye the images merged. He became vaguely conscious of a medical blanket around himself also. Suddenly he was very very tired.

*   *   *   *

When Sergeant Don Weston came to in East Grinstead General Hospital, the shadowy figure above his bed told him that he was lucky to be alive . . . Later, Wendy Turnbull sat by his bedside. She looked exactly as he remembered her . . .

Burgess appeared the following afternoon. He explained that the severe lack of oxygen while travelling in the high-flying B-17 may have caused Weston slight brain damage. There would have to be extensive tests. So for six months at least – Adolph Hitler would have to wait.

EXPIATION

E F Benson

Philip Stuart and I, unattached and middle-aged persons, had for the last four or five years been accustomed to spend a month or six weeks together in the summer, taking a furnished house in some part of the country, which by an absence of attractive pursuits, was not likely to be overrun by gregarious holiday-makers. When, as the season for getting out of London draws near, and we scan the advertisement columns which set forth the charms and the cheapness of residences to be let for August, and see the mention of tennis clubs and esplanades and admirable golf links within a stone's throw of the proposed front door, our offended and disgusted eyes instantly wander to the next item.

For the point of a holiday, according to our private heresy, is not to be entertained and occupied and jostled by glad crowds, but to have nothing to do, and no temptation which might lead to any unseasonable activity. London had held employments and diversion enough; we want to be without both. But vicinity to the sea is desirable, because it is easier to do nothing by the sea than anywhere else, and because bathing and basking on the shore cannot be considered an employment but only an apotheosis of loafing. A garden also is a requisite, for that tranquillizes any fidgety notion of going for a walk.

In pursuance of this sensible policy we had this year taken a house on the south coast of Cornwall, for a relaxing climate conduces to laziness. It was too far off for us to make any personal inspection of it, but a perusal of the modestly worded advertisement carried conviction. It was close to the sea; the village Polwithy, outside which it was situated, was remote and, as far as we knew, unknown; it had a garden; and there was attached to it a cook-housekeeper who made for simplification. No mention of golf links or attractive resorts in the neighbourhood defiled the bald and terse specification, and though there was a tennis-court in the garden, there was no clause that bound the tenants to use it. The owner was a Mrs Hearne, who had been living abroad, and our business was transacted with a house agent in Falmouth.

To make our household complete, Philip sent down a parlour-maid and I a housemaid, and after leaving them a day in which to settle in, we followed. There was a six mile drive from the station across high uplands, and at the end a long steady descent into a narrow valley, cloven between the hills, that grew ever more luxuriant in verdure as we descended. Great trees of fuchsia spread up to the eaves of the thatched cottages which stood by the wayside, and a stream, embowered in green thickets, ran babbling through the centre of it. Presently we came to the village, no more than a dozen houses, built of the grey stone of the district, and on a shelf just above it a tiny church with parsonage adjoining. High above us now flamed the gorse-clad slopes of the hills on each side, and now the valley opened out at its lower end, and the still warm air was spiced and renovated by the breeze that drew up it from the sea. Then round a sharp angle of the road we came alongside a stretch of brick wall, and stopped at an iron gate above which flowed a riot of rambler rose.

It seemed hardly credible that it was this of which that terse and laconic advertisement had spoken. I had pictured something of villa-ish kind, yellow bricked, perhaps, with a roof of purplish slate, a sitting-room one side of the entrance, a dining-room the other; with a tiled hall and a pitch-pine staircase, and instead, here was this little gem of an early Georgian manor house, mellow and gracious, with mullioned windows and a roof of stone slabs. In front of it was a paved terrace, below which blossomed a herbaceous border, tangled and tropical, with no inch of earth visible through its luxuriance. Inside, too, was fulfilment of this fair exterior: a broad-balustered staircase led up from the odiously entitled 'lounge hall', which I had pictured as a medley of Benares ware and saddle-bagged sofas, but which proved to be cool, broad, and panelled, with a door opposite that through which we entered, leading on to the farther area of garden at the back.

There was the advertised but innocuous tennis court, bordered on the length of its far side by a steep grass bank, along which was planted a row of limes, once pollarded, but now allowed to develop at will. Thick boughs, some fourteen or fifteen feet from the ground, interlaced with one another, forming an arcaded row; above them, where Nature had been permitted to go her own way, the trees broke into feathered and honey-scented branches. Beyond lay a small orchard climbing upwards, above that the hillside rose more steeply, in broad spaces of short-cropped turf and ablaze with gorse, the Cornish gorse that flowers all the year round, and spreads its sunshine from January to December.

There was time for a stroll through this perfect little domain before dinner, and for a short interview with the housekeeper, a quiet, capable-looking woman, slightly aloof—as is the habit of her race—from strangers and foreigners, for so the Cornish account the English, but who proved herself at the repast that followed to be as capable as she appeared. The evening closed in hot and still, and after dinner we took chairs out on the terrace in front of the house.

'Far the best place we've struck yet,' observed Philip. 'Why did no one say Polwithy before?'

'Because nobody had ever heard of it, luckily,' said I.

'Well, I'm a Polwithian. At least I am in spirit. But how aware Mrs —Mrs Criddle made me feel that I wasn't really.'

Philip's profession, a doctor of obscure nervous diseases, has made him preternaturally acute in the diagnosis of what other people feel, and for some reason, quite undefined, I wanted to know what exactly he meant by this. I was in sympathy with his feeling, but could not analyse it.

'Describe your symptoms,' I said.

'I have. When she came up and talked to us, and hoped we should be comfortable, and told us that she would do her best, she was just gossiping. Probably it was perfectly true gossip. But it wasn't she. However, as that's all that matters, there's no reason why we should probe further.'

'Which means that you have,' I said.

'No; it means that I tried to and couldn't. She gave me an extraordinary sense of her being aware of something which we knew nothing of; of being on a plane which we couldn't imagine. I constantly meet such people; they aren't very rare. I don't mean that there's anything the least uncanny about them, or that they know things that are uncanny. They are simply aloof, as hard to understand as your dog or your cat. She would find us equally aloof if she succeeded in analysing her sensations about us, but like a sensible woman she probably feels not the smallest interest in us. She is there to bake and to boil, and we are there to eat her bakings and appreciate her boilings.'

The subject dropped, and we sat on in the dusk that was rapidly deepening into night. The door into the hall was open at our backs, and a panel of light from the lamps within was cast out to the terrace. Wandering moths, invisible in the darkness, suddenly became manifest as they fluttered into this illumination, and vanished again as they passed out of it. One moment they were there, living things with life and motion of their own, the next they quite disappeared. How inexplicable that would be, I thought, if one did not know from long familiarity, that light of the appropriate sort and strength is needed to make material objects visible.

Philip must have been following precisely the same train of thought, for his voice broke in, carrying it a little further.

'Look at that moth,' he said, 'and even while you look it has gone like a ghost, even as like a ghost it appeared. Light made it visible. And there are other sorts of light, interior psychical light which similarly makes visible the beings which people the darkness of our blindness.'

Just as he spoke I thought for the moment that I heard the tinkle of a telephone bell. It sounded very faintly, and I could not have sworn that I had actually heard it. At the most it gave one staccato little summons and was silent again.

'Is there a telephone in the house?' I asked. 'I haven't noticed one.'

'Yes, by the door into the back garden,' said he. 'Do you want to telephone?'

'No, but I thought I heard it ring. Didn't you?'

He shook his head; then smiled.

'Ah, that was it,' he said.

Certainly now there was the clink of glass, rather bell-like, as the parlour-maid came out of the dining-room with a tray of siphon and decanter, and my reasonable mind was quite content to accept this very probable explanation. But behind that, quite unreasonably, some little obstinate denizen of my consciousness rejected it. It told me that what I had heard was like the moth that came out of darkness and went on into darkness again. . . .

My room was at the back of the house, overlooking the lawn tennis court, and presently I went up to bed. The moon had risen, and the lawn lay in bright illumination, bordered by a strip of dark shadow below the pollarded limes. Somewhere along the hillside an owl was foraging, softly hooting, and presently it swept whitely across the lawn. No sound is so intensely rural, yet none, to my mind, so suggests a signal. But it seemed to signal nothing, and, tired with the long hot journey, and soothed by the deep tranquility of the place, I was soon asleep. But often during the night I woke, though never to more than a dozing dreamy consciousness of where I was, and each time I had the notion that some slight noise had roused me, and each time I found myself listening to hear whether the tinkle of a telephone bell was the cause of my disturbance. There came no repetition of it, and again I slept, and again I woke with drowsy attention for the sound which I felt I expected, but never heard.

Daylight banished these imaginations, but though I must have slept many hours all told, for these wakings had been only brief and partial, I was aware of a certain weariness, as if though my bodily senses had been rested, some part of me had been wakeful and watching all night. This was fanciful enough to disregard, and certainly during the day I forgot it altogether.

Soon after breakfast we went down to the sea, and a short ramble along a shingly shore brought us to a sandy cove framed in promontories of rock that went down into deep water. The most fastidious connoisseur in bathing could have pictured no more ideal scene for his operations, for with hot sand to bask on and rocks to plunge from, and a limpid ocean and a cloudless sky, there was indeed no lacuna in perfection.

All morning we loafed here, swimming and sunning ourselves, and for the afternoon there was the shade of the garden, and a stroll later on up through the orchard and to the gorse-clad hillside. We came back through the churchyard, looked into the church, and coming out, Philip pointed to a tombstone which, from its newness among its dusky and moss-grown companions, easily struck the eye. It recorded, without pious or scriptural reflection, the date of the birth and death of George Hearne; the latter event had taken place close on two years ago, and we were within a week of the exact anniversary. Other tombstones near were monuments to those of the same name, and dated back for a couple of centuries and more.

'Local family,' said I, and strolling on we came to our own gate in the long brick wall. It was opened from inside just as we arrived at it, and there came out a brisk, middle-aged man in clergyman's dress, obviously our vicar.

He very civilly introduced himself.

'I heard that Mrs Hearne's house had been taken, and that the tenants had come,' he said, 'and I ventured to leave my card.'

We performed our part of the ceremony, and in answer to his inquiry professed our satisfaction with our quarters and our neighbourhood.

'That is good news,' said Mr Stephens, 'I hope you will continue to enjoy your holiday. I am Cornish myself, and like all natives think there is no place like Cornwall!'

Philip pointed with his stick towards the churchyard. 'We noticed that the Hearnes are people of the place,' he said. Quite suddenly I found myself understanding what he had meant by the aloofness of the race. Something between reserve and suspicion came into Mr Stephens's face.

'Yes, yes, an old family here,' he said; 'and large landowners. But now some remote cousin—. The house, however, belongs to Mrs Hearne for life.

He stopped, and by that reticence confirmed the impression he had made. In consequence, for there is something in the breast of the most

We met the vicar on our stroll through the churchyard.

incurious, which, when treated with reserve, becomes inquisitive, Philip proceeded to ask a direct question.

'Then I take it that the George Hearne who, as I have just seen, died two years ago, was the husband of Mrs Hearne, from whom we took the house?'

'Yes, he was buried in the churchyard,' said Mr Stephens quickly. Then, for no reason at all, he added:

'Naturally he was buried in the churchyard here.'

Now my impression at that moment was that Mr Stephens had said something he did not mean to say, and had corrected it by saying the same thing again. He went on his way, back to the vicarage, with an amiably expressed desire to do anything that was in his power for us in the way of local information, and we went in through the gate. The post had just arrived; there was the London morning paper and a letter for Philip which cost him two perusals before he folded it up and put it into his pocket. But he made no comment, and presently, as dinner time was near, I went up to my room.

Here in this deep valley, with the great westerly hill towering above us, it was already dark, and the lawn lay beneath a twilight as of deep clear water. Quite idly as I brushed my hair in front of the glass on the table in the window, of which the blinds were not yet drawn, I looked out, and saw that on the bank along which grew the pollarded limes, there was a ladder. It was just a shade odd that it should be there, but the oddity of it was quite accounted for by the supposition that the gardener had had business among the trees in the orchard, and had left it there for the completion of his labours tomorrow. It was just as odd as that, and no odder, just worth a twitch of the imagination to account for it, but now completely accounted for.

I went downstairs, and passing Philip's door heard the swish of ablutions, which implied he was not quite ready, and in the most loafer-like manner I strolled round the corner of the house. The kitchen window which looked onto the tennis court was open, and there was a good smell, I remember, coming from it. And still without thought of the ladder I had just seen, I mounted the slope of the grass onto the tennis court. Just across it was the bank where the pollarded limes grew, but there was no ladder lying there. Of course, the gardener must have remembered he had left it, and had returned to remove it exactly as I came downstairs. There was nothing singular about that, and I could not imagine why the thing interested me at all. But for some inexplicable reason I found myself saying: 'But I did see the ladder just now.'

A bell—no telephone bell, but a welcome harbinger to a hungry man —sounded from inside the house, and I went back onto the terrace, just as Philip got downstairs. At dinner our speech rambled pleasantly over the accomplishments of today, and the prospects of tomorrow, and in due course we came to the consideration of Mr Stephens. We settled that he was an aloof fellow, and then Philip said:

'I wonder why he hastened to tell us that George Hearne was buried in the churchyard, and then added that naturally he was!'

'It's the natural place to be buried in,' said I.

'Quite. That's just why it was hardly worth mentioning.'

I felt then, just momentarily, just vaguely, as if my mind was regarding stray pieces of a jig-saw puzzle. The fancied ringing of the telephone bell last night was one of them, this burial of George Hearne in the churchyard was another, and, even more inexplicably, the ladder I had seen under the trees was a third. Consciously I made nothing whatever out of them, and did not feel the least inclination to devote any ingenuity to so fortuitous a collection of pieces. Why shouldn't I add, for that matter, our morning's bathe, or the gorse on the hillside? But I had the sensation that, though my conscious brain was presently occupied with piquet, and was rapidly growing sleepy with the day of sun and sea, some sort of mole inside it was digging passages and connecting corridors below the soil.

Five eventless days succeeded, there were no more ladders, no more phantom telephone bells, and emphatically no more Mr Stephens. Once or twice we met him in the village street and got from him the curtest salutation possible short of a direct cut. And yet somehow he seemed charged with information, so we lazily concluded, and he made for us a field of imaginative speculation. I remembered that I constructed a highly fanciful romance, which postulated that George Hearne was not dead at all, but that Mr Stephens had murdered some inconvenient blackmailer, whom he had buried with the rites of the church. Or—these romances always broke down under cross-examination from Philip—Mr Stephens himself was George Hearne, who had fled from justice, and was supposed to have died. Or Mrs Hearne was really George Hearne, and our admirable housekeeper was the real Mrs Hearne. From such indications you may judge how the intoxication of the sun had overpowered us.

But there was one explanation of why Mr Stephens had so hastily assured us that George Hearne was buried in the churchyard, which never passed our lips. It was just because Philip and I really believed it to be the true one that we did not mention it. But as if it were some fever or plague, we both knew that we were sickening with it. And then these fanciful romances stopped because we knew that the Real Thing was approaching. There had been faint glimpses of it before, like distant sheet-lightning; now the noise of it, authentic and audible, began to rumble.

There came a day of hot, overclouded weather. We had bathed in the morning, and loafed in the afternoon, but Philip, after tea, had refused to come for our usual ramble, and I set out alone. That morning Mrs Criddle had rather peremptorily told me that a room in the front of the house would prove much cooler for me, for it caught the sea breeze, and though I objected that it would also catch the southerly sun, she had clearly made up her mind that I was to move from the bedroom overlooking the tennis court and the pollarded limes, and there was no resisting so polite yet determined a woman.

When I set out for my ramble after tea, the change had already been effected, and my brain nosed slowly about as I strolled sniffing for her reason; for no self-respecting brain could accept the one she gave. But in this hot, drowsy air I entirely lacked nimbleness, and when I came back, the question had become a mere silly, unanswerable riddle. I returned through the churchyard, and saw that in a couple of days we should arrive at the anniversary of George Hearne's death.

Philip was not on the terrace in front of the house, and I went in at the door of the hall, expecting to find him there or in the back garden. Exactly as I entered my eye told me that there he was, a black silhouette against the glass door at the end of the hall, which was open, and led through into the back garden. He did not turn round at the sound of my entry, but took a step or two in the direction of the far door, still framed in the oblong of it. I glanced at the table where the post lay, found letters both for me and him, and looked up again. There was no one there.

He had hastened his steps, I supposed, but simultaneously I thought how odd it was that he had not taken his letters, if he was in the hall, and that he had not turned when I entered. However, I should find him just round the corner, and with his post and mine in my hand, I went towards the far door. As I approached it I felt a sudden cold stir of air, rather unaccountable, for the day was notably sultry, and went out. He was sitting at the far end of the tennis court.

I went up to him with his letters.

'I thought I saw you just now in the hall,' I said. But I knew already that I had not seen him in the hall.

He looked up quickly.

'And have you only just come in?' he said.

'Yes; this moment. Why?'

'Because half an hour ago I went in to see if the post had come, and thought I saw you in the hall.'

'And what did I do?' I asked.

'You went out onto the terrace. But I didn't find you there.'

There was a short pause as he opened his letters.

'Damned interesting,' he observed. 'Because there's someone here who isn't you or me.'

'Anything else?' I asked.

He laughed, pointing at the row of trees.

'Yes, something too silly for words,' he said. 'Just now I saw a piece of rope dangling from the big branch of that pollarded lime. I saw it quite distinctly. And then there wasn't any rope there at all, any more than there is now.'

* * * *

Philosophers have argued about the strongest emotion known to man. Some say 'love', others 'hate', others 'fear', I am disposed to put 'curiosity' on a level, at least, with these august sensations, just mere, simple inquisitiveness. Certainly at the moment it rivalled fear in my mind, and there was a hint of that.

As he spoke the parlour-maid came out into the garden with a telegram in her hand. She gave it to Philip, who, without a word, scribbled a line on the reply paid form inside it, and handed it back to her.

'Dreadful nuisance,' he said, 'but there's no help for it. A few days ago I got a letter which made me think I might have to go up to town, and this telegram makes it certain. There's an operation possible on a patient of mine, which I hoped might have been avoided, but my locum tenens won't take the responsibility of deciding whether it is necessary or not.'

He looked at his watch.

'I can catch the night train,' he said, 'and I ought to be able to catch the night train back from town tomorrow. I shall be back, that is to say, the day after tomorrow in the morning. There's no help for it. Ha! That telephone of yours will come in useful. I can get a taxi from Falmouth, and needn't start till after dinner.'

He went into the house, and I heard him rattling and tapping at the telephone. Soon he called for Mrs Criddle, and presently came out again.

'We're not on the telephone service,' he said. 'It was cut off a year ago, only they haven't removed the apparatus. But I can get a trap in the village, Mrs Criddle says, and she's sent for it. If I start at once I shall easily be in time. Spicer's packing a bag for me, and I'll take a sandwich.'

He looked sharply towards the pollarded trees.

'Yes, just there,' he said. 'I saw it plainly, and equally plainly. I saw it not. And then there's that telephone of yours.'

I told him now about the ladder I had seen below the tree where he saw the dangling rope.

'Interesting,' he said, 'because it's so silly and unexpected. It is really tragic that I should be called away just now, for it looks as if the— well, the matter were coming out of the darkness into a shaft of light. But I'll be back, I hope, in thirty-six hours. Meantime, do observe very carefully, and whatever you do, don't make a theory. Darwin says somewhere that you can't observe without a theory, but to make a theory is a great danger to an observer. It can't help influencing your imagination; you tend to see or hear what falls in with your hypothesis. So just observe; be as mechanical as a phonograph and a photographic lens.'

Presently the dog-cart arrived and I went down to the gate with him. 'Whatever it is that is coming through, is coming through in bits,' he said. 'You heard a telephone; I saw a rope. We both saw a figure, but not simultaneously nor in the same place. I wish I didn't have to go.'

I found myself sympathizing strongly with this wish, when after dinner I found myself with a solitary evening in front of me, and the pledge to 'observe' binding me. It was not mainly a scientific ardour that prompted this sympathy and the desire for independent combination, but, quite emphatically, fear of what might be coming out of the huge darkness which lies on all sides of human experience. I could no longer fail to connect together the fancied telephone bell, the rope, and the ladder, for what made the chain between them was the figure that both Philip and I had seen. Already my mind was seething with conjectural theory, but I would not let the ferment of it ascend to my surface consciousness; my business was not to aid but rather stifle my imagination.

I occupied myself, therefore, with the ordinary devices of a solitary man, sitting on the terrace, and subsequently coming into the house, for a few spots of rain had began to fall. But though nothing disturbed the outward tranquility of the evening, the quietness administered no opiate to that seething mixture of fear and curiosity that obsessed me. I heard the servants creep bedwards up the back stairs and presently I followed them. Then, forgetting for the moment that my room had been changed, I tried the handle of the door of that which I had previously occupied. It was locked.

Now here, beyond doubt, was the sign of a human agency, and at once I was determined to get into the room. The key, I could see, was not in the door, which must therefore have been locked from outside. I therefore searched the usual cache for keys along the top of the door-frame, found it and entered.

The room was quite empty, the blinds not drawn, and after looking round it I walked across to the window. The moon was up, and, though obscured behind clouds, gave sufficient light to enable me to see objects outside with tolerable distinctness. There was the row of pollarded limes, and then, with a sudden intake of my breath, I saw that a foot or two below one of the boughs there was suspended something whitish and oval which oscillated as it hung there. In the dimness I could see nothing more than that, but now conjecture crashed into my conscious brain. But even as I looked it was gone again; there was nothing there but deep shadow, the trees steadfast in the windless air. Simultaneously I knew that I was not alone in the room.

I turned swiftly about, but my eyes gave no endorsement of that conviction, and yet their evidence that there was no one here except myself failed to shake it. The presence, somewhere close to me, needed no such evidence; it was self-evident though invisible, and I knew that then my forehead was streaming with the abject sweat of terror. Somehow I knew that the presence was that of the figure both Philip and I had seen that evening in the hall, and credit it or not as you will, the fact that it was invisible made it infinitely the more terrible. I knew, too, that though my eyes were blind to it, it had got into closer touch with me; I knew more of its nature now, it had had tragic and awful commerce with evil and despair.

Some sort of catalepsy was on me while it thus obsessed me; presently, minutes afterwards or perhaps mere seconds, the grip and clutch of its power was relaxed, and with shaking knees I crossed the room and went out, and again locked the door. Even as I turned the key I smiled at the futility of that. With my emergence the terror completely passed; I went across the passage leading to my room, got into bed, and was soon asleep. But I had no more need to question myself as to why Mrs Criddle made the change. Another guest, she knew, would come to occupy it as the season arrived when George Hearne died and was buried in the churchyard.

The night passed quietly and then succeeded a day hot and still and sultry beyond belief. The very sea had lost its coolness and vitality, and I came in from my swim tired and enervated instead of refreshed. No breeze stirred; the trees stood motionless as if cast in iron, and from horizon to horizon the sky was overlaid by an ever-thickening pall of cloud. The cohorts of storm and thunder were gathering in the stillness, and all day I felt that power, other than that of these natural forces, was being stored for some imminent manifestation.

As I came near to the house the horror deepened, and after dinner I had a mind to drop into the vicarage, according to Mr Stephens's general invitation, and get through an hour or two with other company than my own. But I delayed till it was past any reasonable time for such an informal visit, and ten o'clock still saw me on the terrace in front of the house. My nerves were all on edge, a stir or step in the house was sufficient to make me turn round in apprehension of seeing I knew not what; but presently it grew still. One lamp burned in the hall behind me; by it stood the candle which would light me to bed.

I went indoors soon after, meaning to go up to bed, then, suddenly ashamed of this craven imbecility of mind, took the fancy to walk round the house for the purpose of convincing myself that all was tranquil and normal, and that my fear, that nameless, indefinable load of my spirit, was but a product of this close thundery night. The tension of the weather could not last much longer; soon the storm must break and the relief come, but it would be something to know that there was nothing more than that. Accordingly I went out again onto the terrace, traversed it and turned the corner of the house where lay the tennis lawn.

Tonight the moon had not yet risen, and the darkness was such that I could barely distinguish the outline of the house, and that of the pollarded limes, but through the glass door that led from this side of the house into the hall, there shone the light of the lamp that stood there. All was absolutely quiet, and half reassured I traversed the lawn, and turned to go back. Just as I came opposite the lit door, I heard a sound very close at hand from under the deep shadow of the   pollarded limes. It was as if some heavy object had fallen with a thump and rebound on the grass, and with it there came the noise of a creaking bough suddenly strained by some weight. Then interpretation came upon me with the unreasoning force of conviction, though in the blackness I could see nothing. But at the sound a horror such as I have never felt laid hold on me. It was scarcely physical at all, it came from some deep-seated region of the soul.

The heavens were rent, a stream of blinding light shot forth, and straight in front of my eyes, a few yards from where I stood, I saw. The noise had been of a ladder thrown down on the grass, and from the bough of the pollarded lime, there was a figure of a man, white-faced against the blackness, oscillating and twisting on the rope that strangled him. Just that I saw before the stillness was torn to atoms by the roar of thunder, and, as from a hose, the rain descended. Once again, even before that first appalling riot had died, the clouds were shredded again by the lightning, and my eyes which had not moved from the place saw only the framed shadow of the trees and their upper branches bowed by the pelting rain. All night the storm raged and bellowed making sleep impossible, and for an hour at least, between the peals of thunder, I heard the ringing of the telephone bell.

★   ★   ★   ★

Next morning Philip returned, to whom I told exactly what is written here, but watch and observe as we might, neither of us, in the three further weeks which we spent at Polwithy, heard or saw anything that could interest the student of the occult. Pleasant lazy days succeeded one another, we bathed and rambled and played piquet of an evening, and incidentally we made friends with the vicar. He was an interesting man, full of curious lore concerning local legends and superstitions, and one night, when in our ripened acquaintanceship he had dined with us, he asked Philip directly whether either of us had experienced anything unusual during our tenancy.

Philip nodded towards me.

'My friend saw most,' he said.

'May I hear it?' asked the vicar.

When I had finished, he was silent awhile.

'I think the—shall we call it explanation?—is yours by right,' he said. 'I will give it to you if you care to hear it.'

Our silence, I suppose, answered him.

'I remember meeting you two on the day after your arrival here,' he said, 'and you inquired about the tombstone in the churchyard erected to the memory of George Hearne. I did not want to say more of him then, for a reason that you will presently know. I told you, I recollect, perhaps rather hurriedly, that it was Mrs Hearne's husband who was buried there. Already, I imagine, you guess that I concealed something. You may even have guessed it at the time.

He did not wait for any confirmation or repudiation of this. Sitting out on the terrace in the deep dusk, his communication was very impersonal. It was just a narrating voice, without identity: an anonymous chronicle.

'George Hearne succeeded to the property here, which is considerable, only two years before his death. He was married shortly after he succeeded. According to any decent standard, his life both before and after his marriage was vile. I think—God forgive me if I wrong him —he made evil his god; he liked evil for its own sake. But out of the middle of the mire of his own soul there sprang a flower: he was devoted to his wife. And he was capable of shame.

'A fortnight before his—his death, she got to know what his life was like, and what he was in himself. I need not tell you about the particular disclosure that came to her knowledge; it is sufficient to say that it was revolting. She was here at the time; he was coming down from London that night. When he arrived he found a note from her saying that she had left him and could never come back. She told him that he must give her opportunity for her to divorce him, and threatened him with exposure if he did not.

'He and I had been friends, and that night he came to me with her letter, acknowledged the justice of it, but asked me to intervene. He said that the only thing that could save him from utter damnation was she, and I believe that there he spoke sincerely. But, speaking as a clergyman, I should not have called him penitent. He did not hate his sin, but only the consequences of it. But it seemed to me that if she came back to him, he might have a chance, and next day I went to her. Nothing that I could say moved her one atom, and after a fruitless day I came back, and told him of the uselessness of my mission.

Now, according to my view, no man who deliberately prefers evil to good just for the sake of wickedness is sane, and this refusal of hers to have anything more to do with him, I fully believe, upset the unstable balance of his soul altogether. There was just his devotion to her which might conceivably have restored it, but she refused—and I can quite understand her refusal—to come near him. If you knew what I know, you could not blame her. But the effect of it on him was portentous and disastrous, and three days afterwards I wrote to her again, saying quite simply that the damnation of his soul would be on her head unless, leaving her personal feelings altogether out of the question, she came back. She got that letter the next evening, and already it was too late.

'That afternoon, two years ago, on the 15th of August, there was washed up in the harbour here a dead body, and that night George

Hearne took a ladder from the fruit-wall in the kitchen garden and hanged himself. He climbed into one of the pollarded limes, tied the rope to a bough, and made a slip-knot at the other end of it. Then he kicked the ladder away.

'Mrs Hearne meantime had received my letter. For a couple of hours she wrestled with her own repugnance and then decided to come to him. She rang him up on the telephone, but the housekeeper here, Mrs Criddle, could only tell her that he had gone out after dinner. She continued ringing him up for a couple of hours, but there was always the same reply.

'Eventually she decided to waste no more time, and motored over from her mother's house where she was staying at the north end of the county. By then the moon had risen, and looking out from his window she saw him.'

He paused.

'There was an inquest,' he said, 'and I could truthfully testify that I believed him to be insane. The verdict of suicide during temporary insanity was brought in, and he was buried in the churchyard. The rope was burned, and the ladder was burned.'

The parlour-maid brought out drinks, and we sat in silence till she had gone again.

'And what about the telephone my friend heard?' asked Philip.

He thought for a moment.

'Don't you think that great emotion like that of Mrs Hearne's may make some sort of record,' he asked, 'so that if the needle of a sensitive temperament comes in contact with it, a reproduction takes place? And it is the same, perhaps, about that poor fellow who hanged himself. One can hardly believe that his spirit is bound to visit and revisit the scene of his follies and his crimes year by year.'

'Year by year?' I asked.

'Apparently. I saw him myself last year, Mrs Criddle did also.'

He got up.

'How can one tell?' he said. 'Expiation, perhaps. Who knows?'

THE HAND

Guy de Maupassant

The whole party had gathered in a circle round Monsieur Bermutier, the magistrate, who was giving his opinion on the mysterious St Cloud affair, an inexplicable crime, which had been distracting Paris for a month. No one could make anything of it. Standing with his back to the fireplace, Monsieur Bermutier was discussing it, marshalling his proofs, analysing theories, but arriving at no conclusion. Some of the ladies had risen from their chairs and had come nearer him. Clustering round him, they kept their eyes on the clean-shaven lips which uttered such weighty words. They shuddered and trembled, thrilled by that strange awe, that eager and insatiable craving for horrors, which haunts the mind of women and tortures them like the pangs of hunger. One of them, paler than the others, ventured to break a sudden silence:

'How ghastly! It has a touch of the supernatural. No one will ever find out the truth about it.'

Monsieur Bermutier turned to her:

'That is likely enough. But as for your word, supernatural, it has no place in this affair. We are confronted with a crime, which was ably conceived and very ably executed. It is wrapped in such profound mystery that we cannot disengage it from the impenetrable circumstances surrounding it. Still, within my own experience, I had once to follow up a case that really appeared to have an element of the supernatural in it. We had eventually to give it up, for lack of means to elucidate it.'

Several ladies exclaimed as with one voice:

'Oh, do tell us about it.'.

With the grave smile appropriate to an investigating magistrate, Monsieur Bermutier resumed:

'At all events pray do not imagine that I myself have for one instant attributed anything of the supernatural to this incident. I believe in normal causes only. It would be much better if we used the word "inexplicable" instead of "supernatural" to express things that we did not understand. In any case, what was striking in the affair I am going to tell you about was not so much the event itself as the circumstances that attended and led up to it. Now to the facts.

'At that time I was investigating magistrate at Ajaccio, a little town of white houses, situated on the edge of a wonderful bay surrounded on all sides by lofty mountains. My principal task there was the investigation of vendettas. Some of these vendettas are sublime, savage, heroic, inconceivably dramatic. In them, one comes across the finest themes of revenge imaginable; hatreds that have endured for centuries, lying for a time in abeyance, but never extinguished; detestable stratagems, assassinations that are mere butchery, others that are almost heroic deeds. For two years I had heard nothing discussed there but the price of blood; nothing but this terrible Corsican tradition, which obliges a man who has been wronged to wreak his revenge upon the man who has wronged him, or upon his descendants or his next-of-kin. Old men, children, distant cousins—I had seen them all slaughtered, and my head was full of tales of vengeance.

'One day I was informed that an Englishman had just taken a lease for several years of a little villa at the far end of the bay. He had brought with him a French manservant, whom he had picked up while passing through Marseilles. It was not long before universal curiosity was excited by this eccentric person, who lived alone and never left his house except to go shooting or fishing. He spoke to no one, never came to the town, and practised for an hour or two every morning with his pistol and carbine. All sorts of legends sprang up about him. He was said to be an exalted personage who had fled his country for political reasons; to this succeeded a theory that he was in hiding because he had committed a horrible crime of which the most shocking details were given.

'In my official capacity, I was anxious to learn something about this man, but my inquiries were fruitless. The name he went by was Sir John Rowell. I had to be satisfied with keeping a close watch upon him, but I never really discovered anything suspicious about him. Nonetheless, the rumours never ceased, and they became so widespread that I determined to make an effort to see this stranger with my own eyes. I therefore took to shooting regularly in the neighbourhood of his property.

'My opportunity was long in arriving, but at length it presented itself in the form of a partridge, which I shot under the Englishman's very nose. My dog brought me the bird, but I took it immediately to Sir John Rowell, and begged him to accept it, at the same time making my apologies for my breach of good manners. He was a red-headed, red-bearded man, very tall and massive, a sort of easy-going, well-mannered Hercules. He had none of the so-called British stiffness, and although his accent came from beyond the Channel, he thanked me warmly for my considerate behaviour. Before a month had elapsed we had conversed five or six times. One evening as I was passing his gate, I caught sight of him smoking his pipe. I greeted him and he invited me to come in and have a glass of beer. I accepted his invitation with alacrity. He received me with all the meticulous English courtesy; and although he made shocking mistakes in grammar he was full of the praises of France and Corsica and professed his affection for these countries. Very cautiously, and under the pretext of a lively interest, I began to question him about his life and his plans for the future. His replies were perfectly frank and he told me that he had travelled much in Africa, India and America.

'"Oh, yes, I have had plenty of adventures," he added, laughing.

'Then I turned the conversation on sport and he gave me the most curious details about shooting hippopotamus, tiger, elephant, and even gorilla.

'"These are all formidable brutes," I said.

'"Why no," he said smiling. "Man is the worst of all."

'He laughed heartily, like a big, genial Englishman.

' " I have done lots of man-hunting, too."

'Then he talked about guns and invited me into his house to look at various makes. His drawing-room was hung with black silk, embroidered with golden flowers that shone like fire on the sombre background. It was Japanese work, he said.

'In the middle of the largest panel, a strange object attracted my attention; it stood out clearly against a square of red velvet. I went up to examine it. It was a hand, the hand of a man. Not a clean, white skeleton hand, but a black, dried-up hand, with yellow nails, bared muscles, and showing old traces of blood, black blood, crusted round the bones, which had been cut clean through as with an axe, about the middle of the forearm. Round the wrist of this unclean object was riveted a powerful chain, which was attached to the wall by a ring strong enough to hold an elephant.

' "What is that?" I asked.

' "That is my worst enemy," replied the Englishman calmly. "He was an American. His hand was chopped off with a sabre. Then it was skinned with sharp flints, and after that it was dried in the sun for a week. It was a good job for me."

'I touched this human relic. The man must have been a Colossus. The fingers were abnormally long and were attached by enormous tendons to which fragments of skin still adhered. It was a terrible sight, this hand, all flayed; it could not but suggest some savage act of vengeance.

' "He must have been a stout fellow," I remarked.

' "Oh yes," replied the Englishman in his gentle tones. "He was strong, but I was stronger. I fixed that chain on his hand to keep it from escaping."

'Thinking that he was joking, I replied:

' "The chain is hardly needed now; the hand can't run away."

'Sir John answered gravely:

' "That hand is always trying to get away. The chain is necessary."

'I cast a rapid, questioning glance at him, wondering whether he was mad or making an unpleasant joke. But this face retained its calm, impenetrable, benevolent expression. I changed the subject and began to admire his guns. I noticed, however that, there were three loaded

Round the wrist of the dried-up hand was riveted a powerful chain.

revolvers lying about on the chairs and tables. Apparently this man lived in constant dread of an attack.

'I went to see him several times, and then my visits ceased. People had become accustomed to his presence and took no further interest in him.

'A whole year passed. One morning towards the end of November, my servant woke me with the news that Sir John Rowell had been murdered during the night. Half an hour later I was in the Englishman's house. With me were the Superintendent of Police and the Captain of gendarmes. Sir John's manservant was weeping at the door of the house; he was distraught and desperate. At first I suspected him. He was, however, innocent. Nor was the murderer ever discovered.

'When I entered the drawing-room, the first thing to strike me was the sight of Sir John's corpse lying flat on its back in the middle of the floor. His waistcoat was torn; one sleeve of his coat was ripped off. There was every indication that a terrible struggle had taken place.

'Death had been caused by strangulation. Sir John's face was black, swollen, and terrifying. It bore an expression of hideous dread. His teeth were clenched on some object. In his neck, which was covered with blood, there were five holes, which might have been made by iron fingers. A doctor arrived. After a prolonged examination of the finger-marks in the flesh, he uttered these strange words:

'"It almost looks as if he has been strangled by a skeleton."

'A shudder passed down my spine, and I cast a glance at the wall, at the spot where I had been wont to see that horrible, flayed hand. The hand was no longer there. The chain had been broken and was hanging loose. I bent down close to the corpse and between his clenched teeth I found one of the fingers of that vanished hand. At the second joint it had been cut, or rather bitten, off by the dead man's teeth. An investigation was held, but without result. No door or window had been forced that night, no cupboard or drawer had been broken into. The watchdogs had not been disturbed. The substance of the servant's evidence can be given briefly. For a month past his master had seemed to have something on his mind. He had received many letters, which he had promptly burnt. Often he would snatch up a horse-whip and in a passion of rage, which suggested insanity, lash furiously at that with-ered hand, which had been riveted to the wall, and had mysteriously vanished at the very hour at which the crime was committed.

'Sir John, said the servant, went late to bed and locked himself carefully in his room. He always had firearms within reach. Often during the night he could be heard speaking in loud tones, as if he were wrangling with someone. On the night in question, however, he had made no sound, and it was only on coming to open the windows the next morn-ing that the servant had discovered the murder. The witness suspected no one.

'I told the magistrates and police officers everything I knew about the deceased, and inquiries were made with scupulous care throughout the whole island, but nothing was ever discovered.

'Well, one night, three months after the murder, I had a frightful nightmare. I thought I saw that hand, that ghastly hand, running like a scorpion or a spider over my curtains and walls. Thrice I awoke, and thrice fell asleep again, and thrice did I see that hideous relic gallop around my room, with its fingers running along like the legs of an insect. The next day the hand itself was brought to me. It had been found in the cemetery on Sir John's tomb. He had been buried there, as no trace of his family was discoverable. The index finger of the hand was missing. Ladies, that is my story. That is all I know about it.'

The ladies were horrified, pale and trembling. One of them protested:

'But the mystery is not solved. There is no explanation. We shall never be able to sleep if you don't tell us what you make of it yourself.'

The magistrate smiled a little grimly:

'Well, ladies, I'm afraid I shall deprive you of your nightmares. My theory is the perfectly simple one that the rightful owner of that hand was not dead at all, and that he came looking for his severed member with the one that was left him. But as for explaining how he managed it, that is beyond me. It was a kind of vendetta.'

Another lady protested:

'No, that can't be the real explanation.'

Still smiling, the narrator rejoined:

'I told you it wouldn't satisfy you.'

ISLAND OF OLD DESIRE

Peter Knight

Whenever I recall the strange island, which is like to be daily for so long as I live, there comes into my mind the picture of my first encounter with Martin Venables.

It was a bitter cold day in February, of the year 1785, when armed with my uncle's letter I climbed through a succession of floors inhabited by attorneys and smelling of old parchment and metal deed boxes, to a topmost set of rooms that looked down upon the City, with near at hand the burial ground of St Dunstan's-in-the-West. Here, an untidy manservant informed me, having relieved me of my letter, that Mr Venables could not see me for a while and that I must please to wait.

Now as I have said the weather was intensely cold, and there was no fire in the outer room in which I found myself. I thought of the little my uncle had told me concerning Mr Venables' projected voyage, a voyage which, it seemed, was to yield my long-awaited chance of going to sea. Well, thought I, if my uncle is right I shall be colder still before many weeks are past. But for the present it occurred to me that I needed an occupation to drive the chill out of my bones while I waited.

Through a closed door I thought I could hear voices engaged in earnest conversation – Mr Venables, I judged, and one other. The talk sounded as though it might go on for some time, and very soon I ceased to pay attention. It was now my hand lighted upon the cricket ball in the pocket of my surtout.

Ours had been a great school for cricket, and though I had left it now, being seventeen, it was my whim that the leathern ball should be my constant companion at all seasons. I missed the regular matches, but a friend had introduced me to a meeting of the famous club of gentlemen who played at Mr Thomas Lord's ground in St Marylebone and I found a game myself whenever I could.

Chiefly it was as a bowler I was ambitious to excel, and this, to my view, called for practice at all times of the year and in as many places as possible. Even in the narrow yard of my uncle's house in St James', where I had lived when not at school since my parents' death, I was by way of being a menace to the servants and the pot plants, striving for hours a day to learn every secret of the vagaries of the ball's behaviour, trying sundry variations of grip on the leather globe, trying experimentally how I might use my fingers on the stitches to give it speed and spin.

And now, awaiting the momentous meeting, with a leaden sky outside and nothing greener to be seen than a dim, distant prospect of the Surrey hills across the river, I fell to tossing my leather charm idly about, while I thought with half my mind.

If you shifted the grip of your fingers a trifle, just so, at the moment you let the ball go . . . the ball dropped with a noisy 'plop' into a basket that was evidently intended for rubbish, and I wondered as I scrabbled for it what the shabby manservant would think if he came back and caught me . . . Martin Venables was verging on sixty, my uncle had said, and had made a fortune from the law. He was adept at various obscure languages and had travelled a good deal besides . . . And now Mr Venables designed to fit out a vessel for a voyage of exploration of which my uncle, though they had been at university together and been fairly friendly ever since, knew nothing save that it was to be in northern waters . . .

I was a tolerably good marksman, I considered, having twice taken three wickets with as many successive balls, a feat that by tradition entitles a fellow to the gift of a new hat from the other side. Perhaps it was rather more speed that I needed, if I could find the trick of it . . . And Mr Venables had a fancy to carry an extra man among his ship's complement, someone in whom a knowledge of seamanship was not needful so much as some qualities beyond those of the common sailor, so that he could keep an intelligible record of the voyage when they came home . . .

It seemed that on my uncle's commendation Mr Venables believed I might meet these conditions. So now I was to meet him; and the great question was: Would he approve me?

I flung the ball again, and was gratified to see it describe a graceful parabola the length of the room and dive into the basket as accurately as a rabbit into its burrow . . .

I had been informed that the vessel was a barquentine, by name the *True Fortune*, of some 300 tons and now lying in the Scottish port of Leith. She would carry a crew of some fifteen, of whom a number had been recruited by Mr Venables himself on the advice of certain ship-owning friends, while the sailing-master he had engaged, one Captain Runacres, was to find the rest.

This much my uncle could tell me. But where was the ship to go, and what was she to do that would require a chronicler, as it seemed was needed? The North Pole, the mysterious North-West Passage round the uttermost tip of the Americas, buried treasure – these were all possibilities on which I speculated in hopeful exhilaration.

At least I should have my long-cherished wish and go to sea; any-thing would be better than the university which I had dreaded, where (unless they played cricket in summer) it would be nothing save lectures and dry books. And in a few minutes now . . .

Suddenly I stood stock still in utter consternation. The ball, which I was carelessly tossing from one hand to the other as one sometimes does with a Christmas apple or orange, had taken an abrupt dive towards the window, and there was a sharp tinkle of broken glass.

My embarrassment was great; but it was some slight consolation that the offending missile – a treasure I valued – dropped back upon the carpet instead of falling outside. The inner door opened as I stooped to pick it up, and a personage who could be none other than my prospective employer came in.

Straightening myself with a mighty red face, I saw that Martin

Venables was a slight, pale man who looked every day of his sixty years, very plainly dressed and, I thought at once, no very likely person to choose the hazards of the northern ocean for a journey in late middle age. He glanced quizzically, with lifted eyebrows, from the cricket ball in my hand to the shattered pane through which the February air blew bitingly.

'I'm prodigious sorry, sir,' I said shame-facedly. 'I am Philip Carn-forth, at your service. It seems a scurvy thing to make a cock-shy of your chamber. But the truth is that having nothing to do' – The effort to explain my childish behaviour made me stammer.

'Say no more, Mr Carnforth,' he interrupted with a smile that impressed me as both genial and gentle. 'I am in hopes we shall find plenty of occupation for you presently' – he said this meaningly, and I saw he had my uncle's letter in his hand – 'and a broken window is soon mended. You will allow me to present you to Captain Joshua Runacres, to whose skill, under God, we are to be beholden for – who knows how long to come?'

He turned to the man who had emerged from the inner chamber at his heels. 'Here, Captain, is Mr Philip Carnforth, who makes havoc with a sphere while we essay only to explore one.'

My heart fairly leapt at his words, for it sounded singularly as though my appointment were decided already. But as Runacres cast his eye over me my spirits fell. It was a shrewd, small, calculating eye, which to my instant view seemed oddly out of accord with the rest of his appearance, which struck me as both crafty and swaggering.

'Indeed, Mr Venables!' said he. 'Is our young friend thinking of putting his ambitions to the test of Northern gales?'

He looked with a suspicion of a smile about his wide, thin mouth over the fine clothes I had put on for the occasion. I was glad to think that at any rate he could find no fault with my physique. But with the quick sensitivity of seventeen years I could have sworn his lean, tanned face held a sneer. I felt a furious regret for the window I had broken like a schoolboy, which was beyond anything I had felt under Mr Venables' scrutiny, and it is from this, our very first meeting, that I date my dislike of the Captain.

'Come, come, Runacres, we shall see, we shall see!' said Mr Venables deprecatingly, his hand on the other's gilt-braided sleeve. 'But you have business, I know. I am glad to have your assurance that all progresses well, and we shall meet later.'

Captain Runacres suffered himself to be piloted to the outer door, which I was not sorry to see close behind him. Then, ushered into the inner room, I faced the queerest interview I could have conceived.

It was a large apartment, with a cheerful fire and well lined with books, most of which I could make out from their bindings to be very old. I found myself, however, paying much less attention to my surroundings than to the man who faced me across a paper-littered table.

Martin Venables asked me first a deal of particulars about myself – what I had wanted to do with my life, whether I had studied geography and in particular ancient history, to which he appeared to attach an odd importance, and what I looked for from a sea life.

'I will wager, now,' said he, regarding me with a quaint lift of his white eyebrows, 'that you have dreams of making a fortune.'

'Yes, I supposed so,' I told him with a smile, and he sighed.

'*Et ego in Arcadia* – or in regions much less idyllic. And after all, I have found at the last . . .'

A strange, far-away look came into his kindly eyes, as though for the present he had forgotten me and the purpose of our meeting, and he fell to talking of himself – how he had become a rich man by his profession but it had brought him no contentment but only taught him, in his childless old age, the hollowness of life.

As his speech grew more earnest and his look more intense, I made out that he cherished some obsession about a sort of earthly paradise where all greed and struggle could be forgotten and a man like himself could find his true heart's desire. He talked like a man with a vision, and more than once he used a singular phrase, '*insula felix*', 'a happy island' – that left me sorely puzzled. I might have thought him a little mad, but to my relief he came back to practical questions and I had the impression he was summing me up shrewdly, and not unfavourably.

The upshot was that at the end of an hour I had agreed terms by which I was to join the *True Fortune* for a cruise of indeterminate duration, my duties being to keep the archives of the expedition as his secretary and to make myself generally as useful as I could. It was not till I was descending the dusty stairs, my cricket ball in my pocket and the broken pane apparently quite forgotten, that I remembered I was no wiser concerning the real object of the voyage than I had been at the beginning.

It was many weeks later, we being then in about the 65th parallel of latitude – I will not be more precise – and among the drifting ice when I came by chance on a clue.

I had elected to stand my watches with the regular crew. It was about four bells in the middle watch, a clear night and fair weather. I was standing betwixt the bulwark and a deckhouse that stood for'ard of the mizzen mast, listening to the weird crepitation of the ice against the forefoot and wondering why the stars shone so much brighter in that frozen air. Suddenly, startling my ear amid the surrounding stillness, I heard a voice.

My watch-mates were all for'ard; the voice came pretty clearly from the deckhouse, which had a little lattice for ventilation above the door, and it sounded like a man quoting from written words:

'The island lifteth herself most comely from the ice, like Queen Cleopatra rising from a couch of silver and pearl. In the midst is a tall hill where is the gold. But beyond lieth a most warm and clement valley, and here, so sweet and perfumed is the air that our men cried out in delight like children upon holiday, and each man – I know not how – felt his heart lifted and his cares and bitterness wafted quite away . . .'

Now Captain Joshua Runacres berthed in the deckhouse; it was his watch below just now, and, as the voice broke off, I thought for a moment that he must have been talking to himself. But instantly after, I caught the sound of another voice, which I recognized as that of Saul Sweeting, the *True Fortune*'s carpenter.

I could not make out what he said, but now came Runacres' voice again. '. . . A true bearing, shipmate, and a landfall soon – maybe tonight or tomorrow.' The voice ended on a laugh; the other said something more. A moment later I was crouching in the shadow of the bulwarks as Saul Sweeting came out of the deckhouse with, I thought, a kind of swagger and strode off for'ard.

I had dodged from sight instinctively, for on the instant I found myself thinking hard. It seemed odd that the Captain should be laughing and sharing confidences at night time in his cabin with a fellow who was really no more than a fo'c'sle hand. But now I recollected that the carpenter was one of the men Runacres himself had brought with him to join the crew, real hang-dog-looking creatures whom I had thought all along contrasted unfavourably with Mr Venables' hearty, good-humoured portion of our complement.

Above all were the words he had been reading. Incomprehensible though they had been, they associated themselves irresistibly with Martin Venables' reference to '*insula felix*'. And here, it seemed, was a landfall we were to sight very shortly! It was evident to me that Runacres and his midnight friend from the fo'c'sle knew more of the goal of our voyage than I did.

Now from the time we had sailed from the port of Leith, I had found my first dislike of the Captain growing on me. It was not that the man was openly uncivil, but he had made his contempt of me as a landlubber quite apparent. He resented me, too, for standing, as he saw it, in a privileged position with Mr Venables.

I suppose my feeling towards the sailing-master formed a fruitful soil for my sudden suspicion to grow on, but the upshot was that, when I joined Mr Venables at breakfast next morning – the master being then on deck – I made haste to tell him what I had overheard.

His immediate response was a singular one. He stared at me with consternation in his look, plainly taken utterly aback and thinking rapidly. Then he started up from the table and, crossing to a little chest that stood laden with books in a corner of the cabin, he unlocked it with a key he took from an inner pocket, rummaged quickly among the contents, and then, stooping down, made a close scrutiny of the lock and the woodwork around it.

'Philip,' said he, turning to me with a small book in his hand, 'I am about to admit you to an old man's confidence – as I perceive, now that I know you better, I might have done some time since. Do you recall that, about the time we were abreast of the Faroes, Master Sweeting, the carpenter, came below here to repair the deadlight upon one of the ports and was left some while to himself? He repaired it to some purpose. My private bureau has been forced and ransacked!'

'What's taken, sir?' I demanded, and he handed me the little book.

'I must assume, from what you said just now, they were anxious for a sight of this volume. Captain Runacres, no doubt, observed it in my chambers in London and guessed its nature, for I will swear I never uttered an incautious word.'

'But what is it, sir?'

'You may see for yourself,' he went on, and his voice shook. 'I ask your pardon for having kept you under a ban with the rest, but an old man is loath to have his secret dreams abraded by the comments and thoughts of the world. There, if I am not grievously mistaken, is the one veritable record of the fabled *insula felix*.

Examining the book, I found it was a mere handful of yellow sheets like the withered leaves of a tree, inscribed in faded, foreign-looking writing but in the English tongue. Almost the first thing my eye lighted on was the passage I had overheard the Captain recite in the deckhouse, word for word. On the last leaf were certain bearings of latitude and longitude.

'You have never heard, I take it,' Venables pursued as I stared, 'of the island called Estotiland which geographers have never been able to place upon the map? Or of Thule the Blessed, or of the Fortunate Island which St Brendan found in the distant sea?' I remembered certain oblique questions he had put to me at our first conference in London and since, as he went on in a voice oddly hushed:

'I have long held that these were no mere fables but fables embodying a truth – that somewhere there lay a land, a real land but happy and benignant beyond the thoughts of worldly men, a land as one might say beyond the world, where all our restlessness might be hushed and all mankind's unutterable dreams and longings through countless aeons of time might find fulfilment in the lightest breath of its air. Well, I believe that I have found it. That manuscript in your hand is a translation of a portion of a ship's log of Carlo Minetti, a gentleman adventurer of Venice who voyaged in Arctic regions in the 15th century. I have failed to find much account of him or of any other record he may have left. This fragment came by chance into my hands in Norway a year ago, and I have sworn since that if God granted me life I should find the place.'

'But Captain Runacres has the bearing, since he spoke of a landfall within a few hours,' said I. He shook his head as I handed him back the book.

'The bearing merely. I did not show him the whole. You will think me an odd enthusiast, Philip, but you observe some mention of gold in that document of old Minetti's. An accursed metal! . . . I have seen what gold can do to men's souls in my time, and believe me, I had rather lose a Golconda than that the island which the ancients cherished like the memory of a lost paradise should become a prize for covetous men to struggle for! But now –' He shrugged.

'It's gold the Captain is thinking of, I'll wager – him and his friends among the crew!' I said with assurance. 'Most likely, if he were to find it, he'd plan to find the money to bring his own expedition to colonize the island for the Bank of England.'

Venables wrung his hands almost like a man in pain saying, 'Yet for me – to walk the world even with empty pockets but with the glory of rediscovering a lost Eden! . . . Ah, heaven, can you conceive what they would make of it, those others?'

He broke off. A shout of 'Land-ho!' had sounded from the deck. Swiftly replacing the log in its locked drawer Venables darted for the companion, I following hard at his heels.

All hands save the man at the wheel had ranged themselves along the starboard bulwarks. For an instant I made sure I saw Runacres in whispered colloquy with Sweeting and one or two others by the main-mast, and I felt more sure than ever that he had brought his recruits aboard for some purpose of his own. Next moment he was swaggering and smirking at Venables' side.

'We have hit our target prettily, it seems,' says he. 'I'm puzzled, though, by the way the ice thins out to landward. We shall be able to sail clear in with this breeze.'

Some five miles off a long shape caught the morning sun, but was strangely wreathed in a vapour that looked oddly like some emanation of its own. Venables' look as he faced the Captain betrayed nothing of what I had revealed, but his eyes were puckered in puzzlement.

'Warm water, and a mist . . .' said he. 'I had not expected this. The island is surely volcanic.'

'Been simmering quietly for a thousand years, must like,' said Runacres. 'Do you design to go ashore immediately, sir?'

And now beneath his accustomed swagger I observed the man was a-twitch with inward excitement, and his little eyes darted for'ard and aft and then towards the island in a way that made me wonder.

'Yes,' Venables replied, 'I think, Captain, that I must claim the honour, with Mr Carnforth here. When you have brought the ship to anchor you will doubtless follow, but for the present you will allow me my whim.'

'And very right and proper, Mr Venables,' said Runacres with a chuckle. 'I will give orders for the gig to be got away.'

As the ship crept nearer through open water I could clearly distinguish the 'tall hill' where Minetti had said the gold was, and lower hills beyond that might be the boundary of the happy valley. It was little I foresaw how brief was to be our acquaintance with the spot that had been the focus of the old lawyer's imaginings, or how cataclysmic was to be its ending.

The Captain had levelled a spyglass at the hill, but he was brisk about his duties as the *True Fortune*, dropping her sails like folded wings, slackened way a hundred yards from a low, grey, rocky coast fringed with shingle on which, as I saw with keen surprise, no ice lay. Even as the anchor plunged, the gig was dropped at the quarter and Martin Venables and I clambered in.

'I'll stand by in the boat,' said Runacres, as he dropped into the sternsheets. 'I shall be at your orders, sir, when you require me,' to which Venables, his eyes ranging the shore eagerly, merely nodded. It was then I noticed, half unconsciously, that the men who rowed us were two of the Captain's own hands. The Captain himself, I noticed also, seemed to be hugging a sort of secret fervour of excitement, and I saw his hands were restless on the gunwales.

I cannot say my first impression of the legendary island was at all that of an earthly paradise, it looked so different from Minetti's description; but there were other matters that powerfully gripped my attention. The strange mist was far thicker than I had expected and had a queer, sulphurous smell. I was baffled, too, by an odd, distant sound like intermittent thunder heard far off. Great clouds of sea birds sped across the heaven above our heads, and I wondered whether it was just our presence that disturbed them or if they were startled by that ominous noise.

Leaving Runacres and the two hands in the gig, Venables and I advanced up an escarpment of loose rock and had soon lost sight of them behind a screen of giant boulders.

'Volcanic,' Venables muttered as if to himself. 'We might expect changes, Philip, after so many centuries. And yet . . . the very heart of a thousand legends!'

He fell silent then, and I did not speak. I could see his hands were trembling, but his eyes as he gazed at the waste of grey, empty stone were as those of a man enchanted, rapt. So he remained for perhaps half an hour, while I tried to conceive what he must be thinking, and wondered more urgently with each moment at the muffled thunder-sounds that at intervals broke the stillness.

Once I heard a sound that could not be thunder but was plainly that of musket shots. They must have come from the ship, and I was still guessing that someone on board had taken a shot at the sea birds when the tinkle of a trodden pebble close behind me made me turn quickly.

Captain Runacres stood there, a venomous grin on his swarthy face and a great knife in his hand.

Mr Venables had swung round also, so that the knife which had been in the act of plunging at his back passed harmlessly over his shoulder. Next instant with a blow of my fist I had struck it from Runacres' grasp.

It is singular how absolute comprehension can spring to a man's mind in a single flash. As the Captain fell back snarling I saw as plainly as if it were written before me that he had never meant Venables to leave the island to which he had piloted him, but that he was to die here, and doubtless myself as well, while the Captain returned to England with a story of our accidental death, to claim the glory and wealth of discovery.

Runacres let the knife lie, but he had a pistol now in his hand, and suddenly it came to me that Venables and I had brought no arms ashore with us. Venables spoke chokingly, like a man awakened abruptly from a dream.

'Is this murder, Captain?' says he, and there seemed no power of sight in his incredulous eyes.

'You fool!' rapped out Runacres, and added an oath. 'Here is your blessed island, and I wish you joy of it, for you will never leave it alive, you or your pampered landlubber here! There are my own men to

Runacres stood grinning venomously, a great knife in his hand.

take me off when I've done with you, ay, and the ship's mine by now – I can trust my lads for that!'

So this was the meaning of the musket shots I had heard; they must have been the signal for both open mutiny and treacherous murder. In the self-same moment I thought of the one thing I could do, weaponless though we were. I had remembered my cricket ball in my pocket.

Runacres had fallen back a few yards among the rocks like a conqueror with all the island at his disposal, and was pointing the pistol at Venables dominatingly from the vantage point of a slight eminence. I measured my distance and hurled the ball like a thunderbolt straight at his grinning head.

My hours of practice did not fail me. The ball struck him full in the forehead, and he clapped his two hands to his head, tottered, fell like a tree, and lay still. I had no time, however, to savour my success, for there came a singular thing to divert my attention.

For a moment the ball had lain where it fell. But now, as I eyed it, I thought it moved again as if by some weird inward power of its own. In another moment I was certain. After another halt the ball was rolling towards me over the rocky floor where we were standing, like a billiard ball on a tilted table.

'Mr Venables! Don't you see?' I shouted, grasping him by the arm as he stood stupefied. 'The island is moving!'

And then it was upon us. There came a succession of rending crashes, and I had a bewildering sensation that the whole island was bursting asunder behind us. Enveloped in a rush of sulphurous mist I saw huge boulders and pieces of rock hurtling through the darkened air. A fragment struck me on the shoulder and Venables' white hair, his wig having fallen off, was thick in an instant with stinking dust.

But it was a larger mass that fell clean upon Captain Runacres' prostrate body and left him flattened and unseemly as a crushed toad. And Venables cast one half-unseeing glance at him before, with my arm supporting him, we were stumbling for the shore with *insula felix* torn by the earthquake's frenzy in our rear.

*   *   *   *

A wave of the Captain's pistol, which I had retrieved, persuaded the frightened fellows in the gig to take us off. Amid a bombardment of fragments, hot and fierce as bombshells, from the rocking land, we regained the barquentine somewhat fearfully, to find muskets and cutlasses out there but all controlled under the keen eye of Mr Harkness, the mate, and Runacres' hands sullenly grouped for'ard like beaten men.

It seemed that mutiny had indeed been raised under the command of Saul Sweeting, but to the credit of English seamen I was glad to find it had been but a half-hearted affair and the loyal hands had got it swiftly under control with little bloodshed. It was a very penitent half-dozen mutineers who now vowed fealty and their willingness to return to their duty under the command of Mr Harkness.

The ship was hastily sailed a mile off shore and there re-anchored, while we watched the awful spectacle of rock and hill and still unexplored land sink bodily, like a vast dying water-beast, below the engulfing sea. Martin Venables, beside me at the bulwark, regarded the last stages of the catastrophe like a man in a trance. But there was a contented light in his dazed eyes as he laid his trembling hand upon my shoulder.

'Thus it goes for ever, Philip – the island, as I conceive, of an aeon of fables. And it is fitting. I have cherished a dream and I have seen it fade – borne down with its legendary beauty by the gross weight of its gold, lest the land of old desire should become a pole of contention for grasping mortals . . .'

He turned to me from the prospect of troubled water and fume and the advancing ice. 'But for you, Philip – ah, youth ever carries its *insula felix* with it, and there are fair territories yet for you to explore.'

BILL BROCK

Henry Williamson

Silence is never of earth or sky—even under the hills when the day and night are balanced in the still air, and blackbirds roosting in the hollies have ceased shrill cries at the passing shadowy owls; when the wintry moon is too wan for shining, and the chalk quarries grow grey in the dusk.

Always there is sound and movement. Worms are pushing out of their galleries, seizing fragments of dead leaves, and drawing them to their holes before roving again for others—always with their tails in the holes, for an instant return; slugs and beetles are abroad in the dewfall; sleepy birds breathing softly through puffed feathers; rabbits lolloping along their runs in the stubble, pausing to nibble the young clover leaves; partridges, their wheezy dimmit-calling over, settling closer in mid-field; mice claws pattering on twigs and leaf-mould; slow sappy pulses of the still trees rising and falling along their cold grey boles. And from the tunnels of the badgers' earth come muffled sounds, and grunts, and the nearer noise of a mouth stretching. Quietness again, while a last leaf falls among the wandering mice, and the edges of black boughs begin to glisten. The wan air of dusk deepens into night, with star points flickering, and the moon lays the pale shadows of trunks and branches. All the while, by the glimmering badgers' earth, a noise is working at the smells of the air, and ears are harkening.

For a hundred and twenty yards along the top of the beech wood the ground was pressed into paths, and heaped in nine places with soil, as though cartloads had been tipped there. Some gleamed white, where tons of chalk had been thrown out. Tree trunks were buried five and six feet deep in the heaps, which were the mine-heads of the badgers' holt. They were always digging to extend their galleries among the roots, and carry their kitchens deeper into the chalk, which was dry.

An owl flew through the wood, alighting on a branch above the main opening. It listened and peered for a minute and a half, hearing the breathing of the badger, but unable to see its head. The moonlight made a blur of the trodden heap before the hole, with its scatter of chalk, and the white-arrowed head in the tunnel's dark opening was part of the blur. The owl flew on to its next perching place, and soon after it had gone the head withdrew, a grunt sounded down the tunnel, followed by the muffled thumping of broad paws.

★   ★   ★   ★

The hole, ragged with broken roots and hanging rootlets, was wider than the badger, yet he came out laboriously, with much scraping and grunting. He did not tread on his pads, but heaved himself along by the blunt black claws of his forepaws against the side of the tunnel. He moved like an immense mole. When his head and shoulders were outside he remained in his awkward position, his sharp nose pointing at the heap of earth. Then putting his nose between his paws he bent his thick neck and turned head over heels. Remaining on his back, he rolled until he had covered the area of the heap. Afterwards he got on his short legs and shook himself.

Every night he rolled like this, in case gins had been tilled there by day to catch him by the paw.

Four other badgers followed the old boar, rolling in the same manner. They followed him down a trodden path among the trees, indistinct in moonlight and shadow, one behind the other, and came to the streamlet at the bottom of the wood, where they drank.

The water was cold. The four smaller badgers lapped steadily, but the old boar drank with many pauses. He stood by the streamlet, lapping and pausing, nearly a minute after the others had gone to their prowling, one along a fox-path which lay straitly down the stubble field, another following up the water by its edge, a third going down the stream, the fourth returning into the wood. Thus they set about their night's work, each badger having its own ways.

The old boar lumbered after the badger in the wood, following by scent. He hastened in his waddling run, being hungry. He was always hungry.

The boar was many years older than the badger he followed. She and the other three had been born in the same farrow seven months before. During the summer her parents had been dug out by the badger-diggers, dropped into canvas bags, taken away, hit on the nose with spades, turned out, and stabbed. The old boar had followed the cubs home one morning, and curled up with them in their kitchen. Since he preferred to sleep warm, with much food inside him, he had remained there. From him the growing cubs had learned, unconsciously, by imitating his tumble, the way to spring gins, which the earth-stopper of the d'Essantville Foxhounds sometimes tilled outside the badger earths. The Hunt wished badgers destroyed, because their deep tunnels gave shelter to hunted foxes, and so spoiled many kills in the open.

Bloody Bill Brock waddled after the young badger among the trees, moving off her trail to gobble a big black slug he smelt two yards away. Then he picked up a couple of worms, rubbed his head against the trunk of a tree, and returned to the trail. He breathed heavily, grunting with exertion.

When he came upon the young badger, she was eating a dead wood-pigeon, one that had been shot in flight, its hard feathers having stopped the lead pellets; but a mile away it had fallen dead of the blow on the breast. The young badger's teeth, which could have bitten through a man's wrist, cracked the bones as though they were straw. Bill Brock, whose jaws were twice the size of her own, tried to pull the food from her mouth, and she let him have the wings and feet. He swallowed the reddish legs with wheezy gulps, while she was finishing the rest of the bird.

The two wandered over ten miles that night. Beside a hawthorn hedge the boar found a rabbit in a wire snare, set by the lime-burner who lived in the quarry beside the Colham road; and although he was hungry the smaller badger, who hurried round from the other side of the quarry when she heard the rabbit's last throttled cries, ate most of it.

The same thing happened with the next large meal he discovered. Thrusting his snout into a leaf-choked hole under a furze bush, the boar blew and sniffed, and then withdrew his snout, and began to dig. Earth, stones, rootlets, all were thrust behind him. At the end of the hole he found a heavy ball of dry leaves. Some of them were holly leaves, but more prickly than ever they had been when guarding the lower branches of their parent trees. Every leaf now bristled with spikes. Bill Brock grunted with pleasure, and rolled the leaf-ball into the open.

Turning it with snout and paws until he had determined, as it were, the axis on which the hedgehog had rolled itself, he then trod on it with a paw, using the paw as a wedge. His weight forced the ball open, and he bit its neck. He dropped it immediately.

When the young badger came she bared her teeth, drew back her tongue—as a horse crops furze—and bit through leaves, spines, and skin; and the hedgehog, which had slept through it all, died in a strange dream.

The young badger ate most of the hedgehog, and all the boar got was some of the skin.

Just before sunrise he followed the young badger into the holt in Rookhurst forest, not exactly famished, but hungry enough. Mice, worms, snails, slugs, pigeons' feet and feathers, dead leaves, hedgehog skin, rabbits' paws and pieces of fur, the core of an apple—poor fare with which to stay strength for the onslaught of seventeen dogs in the open.

*   *   *   *

Already in the barrel room of The Rising Sun, five miles away, the foam of Mr Tinker's second-best ale was rising to the top of the first wicker-covered earthenware jars, and the servant-wench in the kitchen was cutting loaves and cheese into hunks and wedges, for the day's

Bill Brock grunted with pleasure, and rolled the leaf-ball into the open.

sport. Mr Tinker was snoring in bed, the water in his bedroom ewer as yet ungulped—for he had celebrated Christmas in proper style.

At the very moment that Mr Tinker became aware of daylight and an aching head, Bill Brock began to snore. He lay curled on top of two young boar badgers, who were sleeping in the main kitchen when he returned. By his side his young companion was curled, and the four were drowsing off when the fifth badger returned, and, after wiping his pads against a flint to get the mud off them, waddled down the tunnel and scrambled on their backs. Weary grunts greeted him, and then the five settled down, snug and warm, and fell asleep.

★   ★   ★   ★

The annual badger-dig on 'the Day after Christmas Day', as that national holiday was always called by the inhabitants of Colham Old Town, was the biggest of the year. Badgers were always taken, owing to the numbers of labourers who came out to dig—and to get the free beer and food—bringing either pick or shovel or two-bill, and hoping for a large attendance of 'gentry' (a comprehensive term, including, for the occasion, all in brown boots) to swell the collection for diggers at the end of the day's sport.

They began digging at nine o'clock in the morning, after thrusting down slender sticks to discover the direction of the pipe, and encouraging, with horn and voice and patting, a couple of terriers into the tunnel. At one o'clock, the terriers still being underground, they stopped for lunch. For the sportsmen ('Messrs Tinker, Swidge, Potstacker, Corney, Dellbridge, Gammon, Ovey, and Krumm, no tyros at the game,' as the local paper described them) there was whisky. Mr Tinker's headache had gone, after an hour's strenuous digging; it would no doubt return before closing time that night.

At three o'clock in the afternoon—by which time six terriers had been put to ground, four of them creeping back bitten about the shoulders and jaws—Mr Tinker, kneeling at the main breach in the chalk, declared that another ten minutes would do it. He had already identified Bloody Bill Brock by the six-toed pad leading into the tunnel. The Master's teeth (made up by Mr Swidge, the quack dentist) dropped out in his excitement. They all laughed.

'Lucky for me Bloody Bill wasn't nearby!' said Mr Tinker jokingly. 'Well, gentlemen, I've carried the horn for eighteen years, and it looks as though we're going to get the old boar at last.'

He seized a pick from a labourer, and struck at the chalk. Five minutes of work made him wet and breathless, and he stood back, saying: 'To h-ll with that! Here, Jan, take a turn.'

Half an hour later the sportsmen, sitting or standing around and above the miniature quarry, saw a short tail poke out and disappear again.

'The Mullah!' they cried.

'I told you The Mullah'd hold'n,' said Mr Corney, a short man in clothes that looked and smelled as though they had been slept in for weeks. The pawnbroker rapidly brushed his drooping damp moustache with the back of one hand. 'I told you The Mullah'd have'n.'

The Mad Mullah was his terrier.

The tunnel had already been broken in two places, and dim daylight either way barred the escape. Colham Belle held the right entrance, Mad Mullah the left. Mr Tinker edged out of the group, got his badger-tongs, and asked them to stand back.

'As fine a bit of terrier work as I've seen in all the eighteen—yic—years I've carried the—yic—horn,' he announced.

'I'm sure of it,' exclaimed Mr Corney, spitting, or rather squirting tobacco juice and saliva accurately between his boots. 'I told you the Mullah'd have'n.'

The Mad Mullah hastily backed out of the tunnel, as though pushed by a narrow black pointed head, set with a white arrow. The small expressionless eyes glanced about, and the head retired, followed by the terrier, whose tail and hindquarters stuck out of the hole.

'They'm very near. Goo' boy, Mullah!' cried the Master.

'Don't forget Colham Belle,' suggested a voice.

'I'm not forgetting nothing,' replied the Master, shortly.

Mr Corney relit his pipe for the twentieth time, puffing out vast cheekfuls of rank smoke with immense satisfaction.

'Mullah's the boy,' he said. 'I wouldn't part with that dog for something. Noomye! Not if you was to offer me—'

The terrier backed again, and another face poked out. It was twice the size of the first white-arrowed head, and the short hair of the cheeks was grey instead of black. The Master said afterwards that he knew it was Bill, for the badger did what he had never known any other brock do during the eighteen years he had carried the horn—the badger came out to fight.

The sportsmen had been pressed tightly round the cavity. They scrambled back, pushing and pulling in their haste. The Master was unable to open the tongs in time to collar the boar as he waddled between his legs.

'Look out!' yelled Mr Corney. 'The b——'s loose!'

Bill Brock waddled on, the Mad Mullah retreating before him and making sudden rushes forward, but every time the terrier got within snapping distance the arrowed head turned at him and pierced his courage. Then, curiously, when he was about three yards outside the the hole, the boar stopped, opened his mouth as though in a yawn, and gave a prolonged groan. His tail stiffened and trembled. He stood there, with nose pointing to the ground, still except for the shudders that ran along his curved back. The Mad Mullah snarled at the air before him.

'Get the tongs round his neck—quick!' said the Master in a grating voice, as he pushed forward the long iron instrument. 'Quick—yic—get th' tongs round neck.'

Mr Swidge took them.

'Hold on to him tight,' said the Master, in glee, when this had been done easily. 'Hold his head down. Hold'm tight. Don't let'm get away, for God's sake. Gennulmen, I've carried the horn for—yic—eighteen year, and I've never seen a smarter bit of work.'

'The Mullah'd'v 'ad'n without the tongs,' grumbled Mr Corney.

'Not likely!' replied Mr Swidge, the owner of Colham Belle, promptly.

Bill Brock groaned.

★   ★   ★   ★

While Mr Swidge gripped the handles of the tongs with unnecessary strength, the potman called Jan fetched the bag. It was the size of a mail-bag, and the canvas was so stout that no badger teeth could bite through it. Many a badger, curled still in the bottom of that bag, had been bashed on the snout with a spade, and known nothing more.

The Master stooped down and gripped the trembling tail, and, holding his breath, lifted the boar up and dropped him into the bag.

'There,' he said. 'Bliddy William tailed at last!'

Several hands courageously helped to hold open the top of the bag, while peering heads craned over and bumped each other. The top of the bag was twisted, and fastened with cord. With slightly shaking hands the Master unhooked a spring-balance from his belt, where his hunting-knife hung, and hitched the cord to it.

'Two score and two pounds, gentlemen. The biggest brock I've ever dug out in all the eighteen—yic—'

'And yer woudden'v done that wi'out th' Mullah, noomye!' Mr Corney put in, kicking a piece of chalk violently with his boot. 'No other dog'd'v keppim from diggin' away, and I don't care who hears me say it!'

'No one's saying anything dissenting,' declared the Master. 'I think we're all sportsmen here, gentle—yic—'

All agreed to this immediately. Mr Corney muttered something, and looked surly as before.

While the boar lay still in the bag they had drinks all round. Afterwards they opened the bag, thrust in the tongs, encircled his neck with the iron collar, and drew him out. Then, while the Master pressed his weight on the handles so that the boar's chin was fixed on the ground, a young terrier was led forward and urged to attack the head. It whined and growled and snarled, but would not go near the white arrow and the small blinking eyes. Others were brought, and they all refused.

'I'll tell you what, gentlemen,' said the Master, looking over first one shoulder then the other. His voice became low. 'Yic,' he said, beckoning generally with his nose. 'We're all sports here, I think, gentlemen, and this won't go further, I'm sure. I've always tried to show good sport to the field. How about taking the boar down to the cover, and trying the terriers on him loose, a brace at a time?' This was badger-baiting, and illegal.

'Mullah'll 'ave'n, don't you worry,' muttered Mr Corney, looking at the ground and puffing out smoke violently.

The Master looked at the others, and winked.

So the boar was dropped in the bag again, and they took him down to the field. Here they spread out into a circle, holding their dogs on leash. The Master and the huntsman (Jan the potman) untied the bag, dropped it, and ran back. It heaved, and after a while the dreaded head poked out, sniffing the air. Two terriers were released. They ran at the badger, while every leashed dog sprang up and began to howl.

Slowly Bloody Bill Brock waddled out of the bag, and looked about him. When the two terriers were about a foot away he glanced at them, and did not otherwise appear to regard them; but when one of them came near enough to snap, he made a quick turn of his head; and its will broke.

'Try The Mullah,' shouted Mr Corney irritably. Without waiting for permission, he unleashed his terrier, but the dog would not, or could not, get within gripping distance of the boar's head. Mr Corney yelled at it in a bloodthirsty (whisky variety) voice.

★　　★　　★　　★

Bloody Bill Brock walked over the stubble and the clover, while the circle of men moved with him. Whenever he approached the shifting human group he was driven back with shouts and the banging of spades and picks. Up and down the field he walked, his head turning with instant swiftness at any terrier that dashed at him. He walked very slowly. The Master became impatient.

He blew his horn. 'Let every terrier loose!' he shouted, and waved the tongs in a semicircle.

Two of the labourers had brought their lurchers with them— long-legged hairy dogs, of mongrel greyhound strain, used for silent poaching—and these were loosed with the terriers.

'Get back!' yelled the Master, red in the face, to Mr Corney, who was running forward with raised pick. 'Let the terriers tackle him! We're all sports here, not—yic—bliddy rat-catchers!'

The terriers snarled and scrambled and screamed in a tusselling heap around the badger. Four of them—a Parson Jack Russell, two Sealyhams, and a Bedlington—got a grip on each other, and hung on grimly. A long-legged neurotic animal resembling a diminutive elderly sheep, called Trixie, who had been shrieking almost incessantly since the meet in the farmyard that morning, began a fight with one of the lurchers, and the fight spread to their respective owners, when Mr Potstacker kicked the lurcher in the ribs and was himself thumped on the ear by an enraged labourer. Shouts, oaths, drunken laughter, yelps, barks, growls; and in the centre of the confusion walked the old, old badger, opening his jaws slightly and thrusting his head at every snarling dog face. None dared to encounter the bite of the terrible boar.

At last the Master, having told anyone he could get to listen to him what he thought of the whole lot of dogs (he had no terrier of his own), decided to end it. He blew the recall on his horn, and bawled at them, asking if they knew what he was blowing?

One by one the dogs were gripped by their scruffs, and lugged away, collared, and held back on leashes. All became extremely bloodthirsty and leapt up to get at the boar again.

The boar was standing still, shuddering. The Master approached him from behind, and gripped his neck without the least difficulty.

'Keep terriers back! Jan, bring a spade!'

While the huntsman was bringing the spade, the Master said: 'Us'll make sure of ye this time, ye old—!' and with his right hand fumbled round his belt for his hunting knife.

A strange creaking noise was coming from the badger's throat. He gave a prolonged shudder, a feeble groan, and fell on his side. The Master pushed the limp body with his foot, and the head, with its filmy eyes, rolled loosely.

'Darn me if he isn't dead,' said the Master.

When the business of taking the trophies—the sporting term for hacking off head and pads—was done, Mr Tinker, before throwing the trunk to the terriers, thought he would try and find out what had caused the badger's death. He found, among other things, a piece of hedgehog skin with the prickles on it, the feet of a wood pigeon, and the core of an apple, all unchewed and undigested.

'Colic,' he said.

And when he opened the mouth of Bloody Bill Brock, the unconquerable, whose bite all his enemies had feared, he saw the reason of death: for not a tooth was left in the old jaws, but only brown stumps level with the gums.

DICING WITH DEATH

H Rider Haggard

Deep in the rock beneath a gigantic mountain in eastern Africa lay two secret, connecting chambers—the Chamber of the Dead, housing the ancestors of the Kukuana tribe, and the Treasure House of King Solomon, where tons of gold, diamonds and ivory were stored. To this frightening but intriguing place three Britishers had come in search of a lost comrade: Allan Quatermain, the narrator of the following story, Sir Henry Curtis and Captain John Good, of the Royal Navy. Despite warnings from Infadoos, a friendly officer in the Kukuana Army, the three had allowed themselves to be led into the Treasure House by an aged sorceress. Now this treacherous crone had lowered a heavy stone slab, barring the entrance, and they were trapped.

I can give no adequate description of the horrors of the night which followed. Mercifully they were to some extent mitigated by sleep, for even in such a position as ours wearied nature will sometimes assert itself. But I, at any rate, found it impossible to sleep much. Putting aside the terrifying thought of our impending doom—for the bravest man on earth might well quail from such a fate as awaited us, and I never made any pretensions to be brave—the *silence* itself was too great to allow of it.

Reader, you may have lain awake at night and thought the quiet oppressive, but I say with confidence that you can have no idea what a vivid, tangible thing is perfect stillness. On the surface of the earth there is always some sound or motion, and though it may in itself be imperceptible, yet it deadens the sharp edge of absolute silence. But here there was none. We were buried in the bowels of a huge snow-clad peak. Thousands of feet above us the fresh air rushed over the white snow, but no sound of it reached us. We were separated by a long tunnel and five feet of rock even from the awful Chamber of the Dead; and the dead make no noise. The crashing of all the artillery of earth and heaven could not have come to our ears in our living tomb. We were cut off from every echo of the world—we were as men already in the grave.

Then the irony of the situation forced itself upon me. There around us lay treasures enough to pay off a moderate national debt, or to build a fleet of iron-clad ships, and yet we would have bartered them all gladly for the faintest chance of escape. Soon, doubtless, we should be rejoiced to exchange them for a bit of food or a cup of water, and, after that, even for the privilege of a speedy end to our sufferings. Truly wealth, which men spend their lives in acquiring, is a valueless thing at the last.

And so the night wore on.

'Good,' said Sir Henry's voice at last, to the captain, and it sounded awful in the intense stillness, 'how many matches have you in the box?'

'Eight, Curtis.'

'Strike one and let us see the time.'

He did so, and in contrast to the dense darkness the flame nearly blinded us. It was five o'clock by my watch. The beautiful dawn was now blushing on the snow-wreaths far over our heads, and the breeze would be stirring the night mists in the hollows.

'We had better eat something and keep up our strength,' I suggested.

'What is the good of eating?' answered Good; 'the sooner we die and get it over the better.'

'While there is life there is hope,' said Sir Henry.

Accordingly we ate and sipped some water, and another period of time passed. Then Sir Henry suggested that it might be well to get as near the door as possible and yell, on the faint chance of somebody catching a sound outside. Accordingly Good, who, from long practice at sea, has a fine piercing note, groped his way down the passage and set to work. I must say that he made a most diabolical noise. I never heard such yells; but it might have been a mosquito buzzing for all the effect they produced.

After a while he gave it up and came back very thirsty, and had to drink. Then we stopped yelling, as it encroached on the supply of water.

So we sat down once more against the chests of useless diamonds in that dreadful inaction which was one of the hardest circumstances of our fate; and I am bound to say that, for my part, I gave way in despair. Laying my head against Sir Henry's broad shoulder I burst into tears; and I think that I heard Good gulping away on the other side, and swearing hoarsely at himself for doing so.

Ah, how good and brave that great man was! Had we been two frightened children, and he our nurse, he could not have treated us more tenderly. Forgetting his own share of miseries, he did all he could to soothe our broken nerves, telling stories of men who had been in somewhat similar circumstances, and miraculously escaped; and when these failed to cheer us, pointing out how, after all, it was only anticipating an end which must come to us all, that it would soon be over, and that death from exhaustion was a merciful one (which is not true). Then, in a diffident sort of way, as once before I had heard him do, he suggested that we should throw ourselves on the mercy of a higher power, which for my part I did with great vigour.

His is a beautiful character, very quiet, but very strong.

And so somehow the day went as the night had gone, if, indeed, one can use these terms where all was densest night, and when I lit a match to see the time it was seven o'clock.

Once more we ate and drank, and as we did so an idea occurred to me.

'How is it,' said I, 'that the air in this place keeps fresh? It is thick and heavy, but it is perfectly fresh.'

'Great heavens!' said Good, starting up, 'I never thought of that. It can't come through the stone door, for it's air-tight, if ever a door was. It must come from somewhere. If there were no current of air in the place we should have been stifled or poisoned when we first came in. Let us have a look.'

It was wonderful what a change this mere spark of hope wrought in us. In a moment we were all three groping about on our hands and knees, feeling for the slightest indication of a draught.

For an hour or more we went on feeling about, till at last Sir Henry and I gave it up in despair, having been considerably hurt by constantly knocking our heads against tusks, chests, and the sides of the chamber. But Good still persevered, saying, with an approach to cheerfulness, that it was better than doing nothing.

'I say, you fellows,' he said presently, in a constrained sort of voice, 'come here.'

Needless to say we scrambled towards him quickly enough.

'Quatermain, put your hand here where mine is. Now, do you feel anything?'

'I *think* I feel air coming up.'

'Now listen.' He rose and stamped upon the place, and a flame of hope shot up in our hearts. *It rang hollow.*

With trembling hands I lit a match. I had only three left, and we saw that we were in the angle of the far corner of the chamber, a fact that accounted for our not having noticed the hollow sound of the place during our former exhaustive examination. As the match burnt we scrutinized the spot. There was a join in the solid rock floor, and, great heavens! There, let in level with the rock, was a stone ring. We said no word, we were too excited, and our hearts beat too wildly with hope to allow us to speak. Good had a knife, at the back of which was one of those hooks that are made to extract stones from horses' hoofs. He opened it, and scratched round the ring with it. Finally he worked it under, and levered away gently for fear of breaking the hook. The ring began to move. Being of stone it had not rusted fast in all the centuries it had lain there, as would have been the case had it been of iron. Presently it was upright. Then he thrust his hands into it and tugged with all his force, but nothing budged.

'Let me try,' I said impatiently, for the situation of the stone, right in the angle of the corner, was such that it was impossible for two to pull at once. I took hold and strained away, but no results.

Then Sir Henry tried and failed.

Taking the hook again, Good scratched all round the crack where we felt the air coming up.

'Now, Curtis,' he said, 'tackle on, and put your back into it; you are as strong as two. Stop,' and he took off a stout black silk handkerchief, which, true to his habits of neatness, he still wore, and ran it through the ring. 'Quatermain, get Curtis round the middle and pull for dear life when I give the word. *Now.*'

Sir Henry put out all his enormous strength, and Good and I did the same, with such power as nature had given us.

'Heave! heave! It's giving,' gasped Sir Henry; and I heard the muscles of his great back cracking. Suddenly there was a grating sound, then a rush of air, and we were all on our backs on the floor with a heavy flagstone upon the top of us. Sir Henry's strength had done it, and never did muscular power stand a man in better stead.

'Light a match, Quatermain,' he said, as soon as we had picked our-

I heard the muscles of Sir Henry's great back cracking . . .

selves up and got our breath; 'carefully, now.'

I did so, and there before us, heaven be praised! was the *first step of a stone stair.*

'Now what is to be done?' asked Good.

'Follow the stair, of course, and trust to providence.'

'Stop!' said Sir Henry; 'Quatermain, get the bit of biltong [dried meat] and the water that is left; we may want them.'

I went, creeping back to our place by the chests for that purpose, and as I was coming away an idea struck me. We had not thought much of the diamonds for the last twenty-four hours or so; indeed, the very idea of diamonds was nauseous, seeing what they had entailed upon us; but, reflected I, I may as well pocket some in case we ever should get out of this ghastly hole. So I just put my fist into the first chest and filled all the available pockets of my old shooting-coat and trousers, topping up— this was a happy thought—with a few handful of big ones out of the third chest. Also, by an afterthought, I stuffed a basket, which, except for one water-gourd and a little biltong, was empty now, with great quantities of the stones.

'I say, you fellows,' I sang out, 'won't you take some diamonds with you? I've filled my pockets and the basket.'

'Oh, come on, Quatermain, and hang the diamonds!' said Sir Henry. 'I hope that I may never see another.'

As for Good, he made no answer. And curious as it may seem to you, my reader, sitting at home at ease and reflecting on the vast, indeed the immeasurable, wealth which we were thus abandoning, I can assure you that if you had passed some twenty-eight hours with next to nothing to eat and drink in that place, you would not have cared to cumber yourself with diamonds whilst plunging down into the un-known bowels of the earth, in the wild hope of escape from an agoniz-ing death. If from the habits of a lifetime, it had not become a sort of second nature with me never to leave anything worth having behind if there was the slightest chance of my being able to carry it away, I am sure that I should not have bothered to fill my pockets and that basket.

'Come on, Quatermain,' repeated Sir Henry, who was already stand-ing on the first step of the stone stair. 'Steady, I will go first.'

'Mind where you put your feet, there may be some awful hole under-neath,' I answered.

'Much more likely to be another room,' said Sir Henry, while he descended slowly, counting the steps as he went.

When he got to 'fifteen' he stopped. 'Here's the bottom,' he said. 'Thank goodness! I think it's a passage. Follow me down.'

Good went next, and I came last, carrying the basket, and on reaching the bottom lit one of the two remaining matches. By its light we could just see that we were standing in a narrow tunnel, which ran right and left at right angles to the staircase we had descended. Before we could make out any more, the match burnt my fingers and went out. Then arose the delicate question of which way to go. Of course, it was impossible to know what the tunnel was, or where it led to, and yet to turn one way might lead us to safety, and the other to destruction. We were utterly perplexed, till suddenly it struck Good that when I had lit the match the draught of the passage blew the flame to the left.

'Let us go against the draught,' he said; 'air draws inwards, not outwards.'

We took this suggestion, and feeling along the wall with our hands, whilst trying the ground before us at every step, we departed from that accursed treasure chamber on our terrible quest for life. If ever it should be entered again by living man, which I do not think probable, he will find tokens of our visit in the open chests of jewels, the empty lamp, and the white bones of poor Foulata.

When we had groped our way for about a quarter of an hour along the passage, suddenly it took a sharp turn, or else was bisected by another which we followed only in course of time to be led into a third. And so it went on for some hours. We seemed to be in a stone labyrinth which led nowhere. What all these passages are, of course I cannot say, but we thought that they must be the ancient workings of a mine, of which the various shafts and adits travelled hither and thither as the ore led them. This is the only way in which we could account for such a multitude of galleries.

At length we halted, thoroughly worn out with fatigue and with that hope deferred which makes the heart sick, and ate up our poor remaining piece of biltong and drank our last sup of water, for our throats were like lime-kilns. It seemed to us that we had escaped death in the darkness of the treasure chamber only to meet him in the darkness of the tunnels.

As we stood, once more utterly depressed, I thought that I caught a sound, to which I called the attention of the others. It was very faint and very far off, but it *was* a sound, a faint, murmuring sound, for the others heard it too, and no words can describe the blessedness of it after all those house of utter, awful stillness.

'By heaven! It's running water,' said Good. 'Come on.'

Off we started again in the direction from which the faint murmur seemed to come, groping our way as before along the rocky walls. I remember that I laid down the basket full of diamonds, wishing to be rid of its weight, but on second thoughts took it up again. One might as well die rich as poor, I reflected. As we went the sound became more and more audible, till at last it seemed quite loud in the quiet. On, yet on; now we could distinctly make out the unmistakable swirl of rushing water. And yet how could there be running water in the bowels of the earth? Now we were quite near it, and Good, who was leading, swore that he could smell it.

'Go gently, Good,' said Sir Henry, 'we must be close.' *Splash!* and a cry from Good.

He had fallen in.

'Good! Good! Where are you?' we shouted, in terrified distress. To our intense relief an answer came back in a choky voice.

'All right; I've got hold of a rock. Strike a light to show me where you are.'

Hastily I lit the last remaining match. Its faint gleam discovered to us a dark mass of water running at our feet. How wide it was we could not see, but there, some way out, was the dark form of our companion hanging on to a projecting rock.

'Stand clear to catch me,' sung out Good. 'I must swim for it.'

Then we heard a splash, and a great struggle. Another minute and he grabbed at and caught Sir Henry's outstretched hand, and we had pulled him up high and dry into the tunnel.

'My word!' he said, between his gasps, 'that was touch and go. If I hadn't managed to catch that rock, and known how to swim, I should have been done. It runs like a mill-race, and I could feel no bottom.'

We dared not follow the banks of the subterranean river lest we should fall into it again in the darkness. So after Good had rested a while, and we had drunk our fill of the water, which was sweet and fresh, and washed our faces, that needed it sadly, as well as we could, we started from the banks of this African Styx, and began to retrace our steps along the tunnel, Good dripping unpleasantly in front of us. At length we came to another gallery leading to our right.

'We may as well take it,' said Sir Henry wearily; 'all roads are alike here; we can only go on till we drop.'

Slowly, for a long, long while, we stumbled, utterly exhausted, along this new tunnel, Sir Henry now leading the way. Again I thought of abandoning that basket, but did not.

Suddenly he stopped, and we bumped up against him.

'Look!' he whispered, 'is my brain going, or is that light?'

We stared with all our eyes, and there, yes, there, far ahead of us, was a faint, glimmering spot, no larger than a cottage window pane. It was so faint that I doubt if any eyes, except those which, like ours, had for days seen nothing but blackness, could have perceived it at all.

With a gasp of hope we pushed on. In five minutes there was no longer any doubt; it *was* a patch of faint light. A minute more and a breath of real live air was fanning us. On we struggled. All at once the tunnel narrowed, Sir Henry went on his knees. Smaller yet it grew, till it was only the size of a large fox's earth—it was *earth* now, mind you: the rock had ceased.

A squeeze, a struggle, and Sir Henry was out, and so was Good, and so was I, dragging the basket after me; and there above us were the blessed stars, and in our nostrils was the sweet air. Then suddenly something gave, and we were all rolling over and over and over through grass and bushes and soft, wet soil.

The basket caught in something and I stopped. Sitting up I halloed lustily. An answering shout came from just below, where Sir Henry's wild career had been checked by some level ground. I scrambled to him, and found him unhurt, though breathless. Then we looked for Good. A little way off we discovered him also, jammed in a forked root. He was a good deal knocked about, but soon came to himself.

We sat down together, there on the grass, and the revulsion of feeling was so great that really I think we cried with joy. We had escaped from that awful dungeon, which was so near to becoming our grave. Surely some merciful power guided our footsteps to the jackal hole, for that is what it must have been, at the termination of the tunnel. And see, yonder on the mountains the dawn we had never thought to look upon again was blushing rosy red.

Presently the grey light stole down the slopes, and we saw that we were at the bottom, or rather, nearly at the bottom, of the vast pit in front of the entrance to the cave. Doubtless those awful passages, along which we had wandered the lifelong night, had been originally in some way connected with the great diamond mine. As for the subterranean river in the bowels of the mountain, heaven only knows what it is, or whence it flows, or whither it goes. I, for one, have no anxiety to trace its course.

Lighter it grew, and lighter yet. We would see each other now, and such a spectacle as we presented I have never set eyes on before or since. Gaunt-cheeked, hollow-eyed wretches, smeared all over with dust and mud, bruised, bleeding, the long fear of imminent death yet written on our countenances, we were, indeed, a sight to frighten the daylight. And yet it is a solemn fact that Good's eyeglass was still fixed in Good's eye. I doubt whether he had ever taken it out at all. Neither the darkness, nor the plunge in the subterranean river, nor the roll down the slope, had been able to separate Good and his eyeglass.

Presently we rose, fearing that our limbs would stiffen if we stopped there longer, and commenced with slow and painful steps to struggle up the sloping sides of the great pit. For an hour or more we toiled stead-fastly up the blue clay, dragging ourselves on by the help of the roots and grasses with which it was clothed. But now I had no more thought of leaving the basket; indeed, nothing but death should have parted us.

At last it was done, and we stood by the great road.

At the side of the road, a hundred yards off, a fire was burning in front of some huts, and round the fire were figures. We staggered to-wards them, supporting one another, and halting every few paces. Presently one of the figures rose, saw us and fell on to the ground, crying out for fear.

'Infadoos, Infadoos! It is we, thy friends.'

He rose; he ran to us, staring wildly, and still shaking visibly with fear.

'Oh, my lords, my lords, it is indeed you come back from the dead! Come back from the dead!'

And the old warrior flung himself down before us, and clasping Sir Henry's knees, he wept aloud for joy.

THE NIGHTINGALE AND THE ROSE

Oscar Wilde

'She said that she would dance with me if I brought her red roses,' cried the young Student, 'but in all my garden there is no red rose.'

From her nest in the holm-oak tree the Nightingale heard him, and she looked out through the leaves and wondered.

'No red rose in all my garden!' he cried, and his beautiful eyes filled with tears. 'Ah, on what little things does happiness depend! I have read all that the wise men have written, and all the secrets of philosophy are mine,· yet for want of a red rose is my life made wretched.'

'Here at last is a true lover,' said the Nightingale. 'Night after night have I sung of him though I knew him not: night after night have I told his story to the stars and now I see him. His hair is dark as the hyacinth-blossom, and his lips are red as the rose of his desire, but passion has made his face like pale ivory and sorrow has set her seal upon his brow.'

'The Prince gives a ball tomorrow night,' murmured the young Student, 'and my love will be of the company. If I bring her a red rose she will dance with me till dawn. If I bring her a red rose, I shall hold her in my arms, and she will lean her head upon my shoulder and her hand will be clasped in mine. But there is no red rose in my garden, so

I shall sit lonely and she will pass me by. She will have no heed of me, and my heart will break.'

'Here, indeed, is the true lover,' said the Nightingale. 'What I sing of, he suffers: what is joy to me, to him is pain. Surely love is a wonderful thing. It is more precious than emeralds and dearer than fine opals. Pearls and pomegranates cannot buy it, nor is it set forth in the market-place. It may not be purchased of the merchants, nor can it be weighed out in the balance for gold.'

'The musicians will sit in their gallery,' said the young Student, 'and play upon their stringed instruments, and my love will dance to the sound of the harp and the violin. She will dance so lightly that her feet will not touch the floor, and the courtiers in their gay dresses will throng round her. But with me she will not dance, for I have no red rose to give her'; and he flung himself down on the grass, and buried his face in his hands, and wept.

'Why is he weeping?' asked a little Green Lizard, as he ran past him with his tail in the air.

'Why, indeed?' said the Butterfly, who was fluttering about after a sunbeam.

'Why, indeed?' whispered a Daisy to his neighbour, in a soft, low voice.

'He is weeping for a red rose,' said the Nightingale.

'For a red rose?' they cried; 'how very ridiculous!' and the little Lizard, who was something of a cynic, laughed outright.

But the Nightingale understood the secret of the Student's sorrow, and she sat silent in the oak-tree, and thought about the mystery of Love.

Suddenly she spread her brown wings for flight, and soared into the air. She passed through the grove like a shadow and like a shadow she sailed across the garden.

In the centre of the grass-plot was standing a beautiful rose-tree, and when she saw it she flew over to it, and lit upon a spray.

'Give me a red rose,' she cried, 'and I will sing you my sweetest song.'

But the Tree shook its head.

'My roses are white,' it answered; 'as white as the foam of the sea, and whiter than the snow on the mountain. But go to my brother who grows round the old sun-dial, and perhaps he will give you what you want.'

So the Nightingale flew over to the Rose-tree that was growing round the old sun-dial.

'Give me a red rose,' she cried, 'and I will sing you my sweetest song.'

But the Tree shook its head.

'My roses are yellow,' it answered; 'as yellow as the hair of the mermaiden who sits upon an amber throne, and yellower than the daffodil that blooms in the meadow before the mower comes with his scythe. But go to my brother who grows beneath the Student's window, and perhaps he will give you what you want.'

So the Nightingale flew over to the Rose-tree that was growing beneath the Student's window.

'Give me a red rose,' she cried, 'and I will sing you my sweetest song.'

But the Tree shook its head.

'My roses are red,' it answered; 'as red as the feet of the dove, and redder than the great fans of coral that wave and wave in the ocean-cavern. But the winter has chilled my veins, and the frost has nipped my buds, and the storm has broken my branches, and I shall have no roses at all this year.'

'One red rose is all I want,' cried the Nightingale, 'only one red rose! Is there no way by which I can get it?'

'There is a way,' answered the Tree, 'but it is so terrible that I dare not tell it to you.'

'Tell it to me,' said the Nightingale, 'I am not afraid.'

'If you want a red rose,' said the Tree, 'you must build it out of music by moonlight, and stain it with your own heart's-blood. You must sing to me with your breast against a thorn. All night long you must sing to me, and the thorn must pierce your heart, and your life-blood must flow into my veins, and become mine.'

'Death is a great price to pay for a red rose,' cried the Nightingale, 'and Life is very dear to all. It is pleasant to sit in the green wood, and to watch the Sun in his chariot of gold, and the Moon in her chariot of pearl. Sweet is the scent of the hawthorn, and sweet are the bluebells that hide in the valley, and the heather that blows on the hill. Yet Love is better than Life, and what is the heart of a bird compared to the heart of a man?'

So she spread her brown wings for flight, and soared into the air. She swept over the garden like a shadow, and like a shadow she sailed through the grove.

The young Student was still lying on the grass, where she had left him, and the tears were not yet dry in his beautiful eyes.

'Be happy,' cried the Nightingale, 'be happy; you shall have your red rose. I will build it out of music by moonlight, and stain it with my own heart's-blood. All that I ask of you in return is that you will be a true lover, for Love is wiser than Philosophy, though he is wise, and mightier than Power, though he is mighty. Flame-coloured are his wings, and coloured like flame is his body. His lips are sweet as honey, and his breath is like frankincense.'

The Student looked up from the grass, and listened, but he could not understand what the Nightingale was saying to him, for he only knew the things that are written down in books.

But the Oak-tree understood, and felt sad, for he was very fond of the little Nightingale who had built her nest in his branches.

'Sing me one last song,' he whispered; 'I shall feel lonely when you are gone.'

So the Nightingale sang to the Oak-tree, and her voice was like water bubbling from a silver jar.

When she had finished her song, the Student got up, and pulled a note-book and a lead-pencil out of his pocket.

'She has form,' he said to himself, as he walked away through the grove—'that cannot be denied to her; but has she got feeling? I am afraid not. In fact, she is like most artists; she is all style without any sincerity. She would not sacrifice herself for others. She thinks merely of music, and everybody knows that the arts are selfish. Still, it must be admitted that she has some beautiful notes in her voice. What a pity it is that they do not mean anything, or do any practical good!' And he went into his room, and lay down on his little pallet-bed, and began to think of his love; and, after a time, he fell asleep.

And when the moon shone in the heavens the Nightingale flew to the Rose-tree, and set her breast against the thorn. All night long she sang, with her breast against the thorn, and the cold crystal Moon leaned down and listened. All night long she sang, and the thorn went deeper and deeper into her breast, and her life-blood ebbed away from her.

And when the student opened his window he found the beautiful, red rose.

She sang first of the birth of love in the heart of a boy and a girl. And on the topmost spray of the Rose-tree there blossomed a marvellous rose, petal following petal, as song followed song. Pale was it, at first, as the mist that hangs over the river—pale as the feet of the morning, and silver as the wings of the dawn. As the shadow of a rose in a mirror of silver, as the shadow of a rose in a waterpool, so was the rose that blossomed on the topmost spray of the Tree.

But the Tree cried to the Nightingale to press closer against the thorn. 'Press closer, little Nightingale,' cried the Tree, 'or the Day will come before the rose is finished.'

So the Nightingale pressed closer against the thorn, and louder and louder grew her song, for she sang of the birth of passion in the soul of a man and a maid.

And a delicate flush of pink came into the leaves of the rose, like the flush in the face of the bridegroom when he kisses the lips of the bride. But the thorn had not yet reached her heart, so the rose's heart remained white, for only a Nightingale's heart's-blood can crimson the heart of a rose.

And the Tree cried to the Nightingale to press closer against the thorn. 'Press closer, little Nightingale,' cried the Tree, 'or the Day will come before the rose is finished.'

So the Nightingale pressed closer against the thorn, and the thorn touched her heart, and a fierce pang of pain shot through her. Bitter, bitter was the pain, and wilder and wilder grew her song, for she sang of the Love that is perfected by Death, of the Love that dies not in the tomb.

And the marvellous rose became crimson, like the rose of the eastern sky. Crimson was the girdle of petals, and crimson as a ruby was the heart.

But the Nightingale's voice grew fainter, and her little wings began to beat, and a film came over her eyes. Fainter and fainter grew her song, and she felt something choking in her throat.

Then she gave one last burst of music. The white Moon heard it, and she forgot the dawn, and lingered on in the sky. The red rose heard it, and it trembled all over with ecstasy, and opened its petals to the cold morning air. Echo bore it to her purple cavern in the hills, and woke the sleeping shepherds from their dreams. It floated through the reeds of the river, and they carried its message to the sea.

'Look, look!' cried the Tree, 'the rose is finished now'; but the Nightingale made no answer, for she was lying dead in the long grass, with the thorn in her heart.

And at noon the Student opened his window and looked out.

'Why, what a wonderful piece of luck!' he cried; 'here is a red rose! I have never seen any rose like it in all my life. It is so beautiful that I am sure it has a long Latin name'; and he leaned down and plucked it.

Then he put on his hat, and ran up to the Professor's house with the rose in his hand.

The daughter of the Professor was sitting in the door-way winding blue silk on a reel, and her little dog was lying at her feet.

'You said that you would dance with me if I brought you a red rose,' cried the Student. 'Here is the reddest rose in all the world. You will wear it tonight next your heart, and as we dance together it will tell you how I love you.'

But the girl frowned.

'I am afraid it will not go with my dress,' she answered; 'and, besides, the Chamberlain's nephew has sent me some real jewels, and everybody knows that jewels cost far more than flowers.'

'Well, upon my word, you are very ungrateful,' said the Student angrily; and he threw the rose into the street, where it fell into the gutter, and a cart-wheel went over it.

'Ungrateful!' said the girl. 'I tell you what, you are very rude; and, after all, who are you? Only a Student. Why, I don't believe you have even got silver buckles to your shoes as the Chamberlain's nephew has'; and she got up from her chair and went into the house.

'What a silly thing Love is!' said the Student as he walked away. 'It is not half as useful as Logic, for it does not prove anything, and it is always telling one of things that are not going to happen, and making one believe things that are not true. In fact, it is quite unpractical, and, as in this age to be practical is everything, I shall go back to Philosophy and study Metaphysics.'

So he returned to his room and pulled out a great dusty book, and began to read.

THE YELLOW WALL-PAPER

Charlotte Perkins Gilman

It is very seldom that mere ordinary people like John and myself secure ancestral halls for the summer.

A colonial mansion, a hereditary estate, I would say a haunted house, and reach the height of romantic felicity, – but that would be asking too much of fate!

Still I will proudly declare that there is something queer about it.

Else, why should it be let so cheaply? And why have stood so long untenanted?

John laughs at me, of course, but one expects that in marriage.

John is practical in the extreme. He has no patience with faith, an intense horror of superstition, and he scoffs openly at any talk of things not to be felt and seen and put down in figures.

John is a physician, and *perhaps* – (I would not say it to a living soul, of course, but this is dead paper and a great relief to my mind) – *perhaps* that is one reason I do not get well faster.

You see, he does not believe I am sick!

And what can one do?

If a physician of high standing, and one's own husband, assures friends and relatives that there is really nothing the matter with one but temporary nervous depression – a slight hysterical tendency – what is one to do?

My brother is also a physician, and also of high standing, and he says the same thing.

So I take phosphates or phosphites, – whichever it is, – and tonics, and journeys, and air, and exercise, and am absolutely forbidden to 'work' until I am well again.

Personally I disagree with their ideas.

Personally I believe that congenial work, with excitement and change, would do me good.

But what is one to do?

I did write for a while in spite of them; but it *does* exhaust me a good deal – having to be so sly about it, or else meet with heavy opposition.

I sometimes fancy that in my condition if I had less opposition and more society and stimulus – but John says the very worse thing I can do is to think about my condition, and I confess it always makes me feel bad.

So I will let it alone and talk about the house.

The most beautiful place! It is quite alone, standing well back from the road, quite three miles from the village. It makes me think of English places that you read about, for there are hedges, and walls and gates that lock, and lots of separate little houses for the gardeners and people.

There is a *delicious* garden! I never saw such a garden – large and shady, full of box-bordered paths, and lined with long grape-covered arbours with seats under them.

There were greenhouses, too, but they are all broken now.

There was some legal trouble, I believe, something about the heirs and co-heirs; anyhow, the place has been empty for years.

That spoils my ghostliness, I am afraid; but I don't care – there is something strange about the house – I can feel it.

I even said so to John one moonlight evening, but he said what I felt was a draught, and shut the window.

I get unreasonably angry with John sometimes. I'm sure I never used to be so sensitive. I think it is due to this nervous condition.

But John says if I feel so, I shall neglect proper self-control; so I take pains to control myself – before him, at least, and that makes me very tired.

I don't like our room a bit. I wanted one downstairs that opened on the piazza and had roses all over the window, and such pretty, old-fashioned chintz hangings! but John would not hear of it.

He said there was only one window and not room for two beds, and no near room for him if he took another.

He is very careful and loving, and hardly lets me stir without special direction.

I have a schedule prescription for each hour in the day; he takes all care from me, and so I feel basely ungrateful not to value it more.

He said we came here solely on my account, that I was to have perfect rest and all the air I could get. 'Your exercise depends on your strength, my dear,' said he, 'and your food somewhat on your appetite; but air you can absorb all the time.' So we took the nursery, at the top of the house.

It is a big, airy room, the whole floor nearly, with windows that look all ways, and air and sunshine galore. It was nursery first and then playground and gymnasium, I should judge; for the windows are barred for little children, and there are rings and things in the walls.

The paint and paper look as if a boys' school had used it. It is stripped off – the paper – in great patches all around the head of my bed, about as far as I can reach, and in a great place on the other side of the room low down. I never saw a worse paper in my life.

One of those sprawling flamboyant patterns committing every artistic sin.

It is dull enough to confuse the eye in following, pronounced enough to constantly irritate, and provoke study, and when you follow the lame, uncertain curves for a little distance they suddenly commit suicide – plunge off at outrageous angles, destroy themselves in unheard-of contradictions.

The colour is repellent, almost revolting; a smouldering, unclean yellow, strangely faded by the slow-turning sunlight.

It is a dull yet lurid orange in some places, a sickly sulphur tint in others.

No wonder the children hated it! I should hate it myself if I had to live in this room long.

There comes John, and I must put this away – he hates to have me write a word.

We have been here two weeks, and I haven't felt like writing before, since that first day.

I am sitting by the window now, up in this atrocious nursery, and there is nothing to hinder my writing as much as I please, save lack of strength.

John is away all day, and even some nights when his cases are serious.

I am glad my case is not serious!

But these nervous troubles are dreadfully depressing.

John does not know how much I really suffer. He knows there is no *reason* to suffer, and that satisfies him.

Of course it is only nervousness. It does weigh on me so not to do my duty in any way!

I meant to be such a help to John, such a real rest and comfort, and here I am a comparative burden already!

Nobody would believe what an effort it is to do what little I am able – to dress and entertain, and order things.

It is fortunate Mary is so good with the baby. Such a dear baby!

And yet I *cannot* be with him, it makes me so nervous.

I suppose John never was nervous in his life. He laughs at me so about this wall-paper!

At first he meant to repaper the room, but afterwards he said that I was letting it get the better of me, and that nothing was worse for a nervous patient than to give way to such fancies.

He said that after the wall-paper was changed it would be the heavy bedstead, and then the barred windows, and then that gate at the head of the stairs, and so on.

'You know the place is doing you good,' he said, 'and really, dear I don't care to renovate the house just for a three months' rental.'

'Then do let us go downstairs, 'I said, 'there are such pretty rooms there.'

Then he took me in his arms and called me a blessed little goose, and said he would go down the cellar if I wished, and would have it whitewashed into the bargain.

But he is right enough about the beds and windows and things.

It is as airy and comfortable a room as anyone need wish, and of course, I would not be so silly as to make him uncomfortable just for a whim.

I'm really getting quite fond of the big room, all but that horrid paper.

Out of one window I can see the garden, those mysterious

deep-shaded arbours, the riotous old-fashioned flowers, and bushes and gnarly trees.

Out of another I get a lovely view of the bay and a little private wharf belonging to the estate. There is a beautiful shaded lane that runs down there from the house. I always fancy I see people walking in these numerous paths and arbours, but John has cautioned me not to give way to fancy in the least. He says that with my imaginative power and habit of story-making a nervous weakness like mine is sure to lead to all manner of excited fancies, and that I ought to use my will and good sense to check the tendency. So I try.

I think sometimes that if I were only well enough to write a little it would relieve the press of ideas and rest me.

But I find I get pretty tired when I try.

It is so discouraging not to have any advice and companionship about my work. When I get really well John says we will ask Cousin Henry and Julia down for a long visit; but he says he would as soon put fireworks in my pillow-case as to let me have those stimulating people about now.

I wish I could get well faster.

But I must not think about that. This paper looks to me as if it *knew* what a vicious influence it had!

There is a recurrent spot where the pattern lolls like a broken neck and two bulbous eyes stare at you upside-down.

I got positively angry with the impertinence of it and the everlastingness. Up and down and sideways they crawl, and those absurd, unblinking eyes are everywhere. There is one place where two breadths didn't match, and the eyes go all up and down the line, one a little higher than the other.

I never saw so much expression in an inanimate thing before, and we all know how much expression they have!

I used to lie awake as a child and get more entertainment and terror out of the blank walls and plain furniture than most children could find in a toy-store.

I remember what a kindly wink the knobs of our big old bureau used to have, and there was one chair that always seemed like a strong friend.

I used to feel that if any of the other things looked too fierce I could always hop into that chair and be safe.

The furniture in this room is no worse than inharmonious, however, for we had to bring it all from downstairs. I suppose when this was used as a playroom they had to take the nursery things out, and no wonder! I never saw such ravages as the children have made here.

The wall-paper, as I said before, is torn off in spots, and it sticketh closer than a brother – they must have had perseverance as well as hatred.

Then the floor is scratched and gouged and splintered, the plaster itself is dug out here and there, and this great heavy bed, which is all we found in the room, looks as if it had been through the wars.

But I don't mind it a bit – only the paper.

There comes John's sister. Such a dear girl as she is, and so careful of me! I must not let her find me writing.

She is a perfect, an enthusiastic housekeeper, and hopes for no better profession. I verily believe she thinks it is the writing which made me sick!

But I can write when she is out, and see her a long way off from these windows.

There is one that commands the road, a lovely, shaded, winding road, and one that just looks off over the country. A lovely country, too, full of great elms and velvet meadows.

This wall-paper has a kind of sub-pattern in a different shade, a particularly irritating one, for you can only see it in certain lights, and not clearly then.

But in the places where it isn't faded, and where the sun is just so, I can see a strange, provoking, formless sort of figure, that seems to sulk about that silly and conspicuous front design.

There's sister on the stairs!

Well, the Fourth of July is over! The people are all gone and I am tired out. John thought it might do me good to see a little company, so we just had mother and Nellie and the children down for a week.

Of course I didn't do a thing. Jennie sees to everything now.

But it tired me all the same.

John says if I don't pick up faster he shall send me to Weir Mitchell in the fall.

But I don't want to go there at all. I had a friend who was in his hands once, and she says he is just like John and my brother, only more so!

Besides, it is such an undertaking to go so far.

I don't feel as if it was worth while to turn my hand over for anything, and I'm getting dreadfully fretful and querulous.

I cry at nothing, and cry most of the time.

Of course I don't when John is here, or anybody else, but when I am alone.

And I am alone a good deal just now. John is kept in town very often by serious cases, and Jennie is good and lets me alone when I want her to.

So I walk a little in the garden or down that lovely lane, sit on the porch under the roses, and lie down up here a good deal.

I'm getting really fond of the room in spite of the wall-paper. Perhaps *because* of the wall-paper.

It dwells in my mind so!

I lie here on this great immovable bed – it is nailed down, I believe – and follow that pattern about by the hour. It is as good as gymnastics, I assure you. I start, we'll say, at the bottom, down in the corner over there where it has not been touched, and I determine for the thousandth time that I *will* follow that pointless pattern to some sort of a conclusion.

I know a little of the principles of design, and I know this thing was not arranged on any laws of radiation, of alternation, or repetition, or symmetry, or anything else that I ever heard of.

It is repeated, of course, by the breadths, but not otherwise.

Looked at in one way, each breadth stands alone, the bloated curves and flourishes – a kind of 'debased Romanesque' with *delirium tremens* – go waddling up and down in isolated columns of fatuity.

But, on the other hand, they connect diagonally, and the sprawling outlines run off in great slanting waves of optic horror, like a lot of wallowing seaweeds in full chase.

The whole thing goes horizontally, too, at least it seems so, and I exhaust myself in trying to distinguish the order of its going in that direction.

They have used a horizontal breadth for a frieze, and that adds wonderfully to the confusion.

There is one end of the room where it is almost intact, and there, when the cross-lights fade and the low sun shines directly upon it, I can almost fancy radiation, after all – the interminable grotesques seem to form around a common centre and rush off in headlong plunges of equal distraction.

It makes me tired to follow it. I will take a nap, I guess.

I don't know why I should write this.

I don't want to.

I don't feel able.

And I know John would think it absurd. But I *must* say what I feel and think in some way – it is such a relief!

But the effort is getting to be greater than the relief.

Half the time now I am awfully lazy, and lie down ever so much.

John says I mustn't lose my strength, and has me take codliver oil and lots of tonics and things, to say nothing of ale and wine and rare meat.

Dear John! He loves me very dearly, and hates to have me sick. I tried to have a real earnest reasonable talk with him the other day, and tell him how I wished he would let me go and make a visit to Cousin Henry and Julia.

But he said I wasn't able to go, nor able to stand it after I got there; and I did not make out a very good case for myself, for I was crying before I had finished.

It is getting to be a great effort for me to think straight. Just this nervous weakness, I suppose.

And dear John gathered me up in his arms and just carried me upstairs and laid me on the bed, and sat by me and read to me until he tired my head.

He said I was his darling and his comfort and all he had, and that I must take care of myself for his sake, and keep well.

He says no one but myself can help me out of it, that I must use my will and self-control and not let my silly fancies run away with me.

There's one comfort, the baby is well and happy, and does not have to occupy this nursery with the horrid wall-paper.

If we had not used it, that blessed child would have! What a fortunate escape! Why, I wouldn't have a child of mine, an impressionable little thing, live in such a room for worlds.

I never thought of it before, but it is lucky that John kept me here, after all. I can stand it so much easier than a baby, you see.

Of course I never mention it to them any more – I am too wise – but I keep watch of it all the same.

There are things in that paper that nobody knows but me, or ever will.

Behind that outside pattern the dim shapes get clearer every day.

It is always the same shape, only very numerous.

And it is like a woman stooping down and creeping about behind that pattern. I don't like it a bit. I wonder – I begin to think – I wish John would take me away from here!

It is so hard to talk with John about my case, because he is so wise, and because he loves me so.

But I tried it last night.

It was moonlight. The moon shines in all around, just as the sun does.

I hate to see it sometimes, it creeps so slowly, and always comes in by one window or another.

John was asleep and I hated to waken him, so I kept still and watched the moonlight on that undulating wall-paper until I felt creepy.

The faint figure behind seemed to shake the pattern, just as if she wanted to get out.

I got up softly and went to feel and see if the paper *did* move, and when I came back John was awake.

'What is it, little girl?' he said. 'Don't go walking about like that – you'll get cold.'

I thought it was a good time to talk, so I told him that I really was not gaining here, and that I wished he would take me away.

'Why, darling!' said he, 'our lease will be up in three weeks, and I can't see how to leave before.

'The repairs are not done at home, and I cannot possibly leave town just now. Of course if you were in any danger I could and would, but you really are better, dear, whether you can see it or not. I am a doctor, dear, and I know. You are gaining flesh and colour, your appetite is better. I feel really much easier about you.'

'I don't weigh a bit more,' said I, 'nor as much; and my appetite may be better in the evening, when you are here, but it is worse in the morning, when you are away.'

'Bless her little heart!' said he with a big hug; 'she shall be as sick as she pleases. But now let's improve the shining hours by going to sleep, and talk about it in the morning.'

'And you won't go away?' I asked gloomily.

'Why, how can I, dear? It is only three weeks more and then we will take a nice little trip of a few days while Jennie is getting the house ready. Really, dear, you are better!'

'Better in body, perhaps –' I began, and stopped short, for he sat up straight and looked at me with such a stern, reproachful look that I could not say another word.

'My darling,' said he, 'I beg of you, for my sake and for our child's sake, as well as for your own, that you will never for one instant let that idea enter your mind! There is nothing so dangerous, so fascinating, to a temperament like yours. It is a false and foolish fancy. Can you not trust me as a physician when I tell you so?'

So of course I said no more on that score, and we went to sleep before long. He thought I was asleep first, but I wasn't – I lay there for hours trying to decide whether that front pattern and the back pattern really did move together or separately.

On a pattern like this, by daylight, there is a lack of sequence, and a defiance of law, that is a constant irritant to a normal mind.

The colour is hideous enough, and unreliable enough, and infuriating enough, but the pattern is torturing.

You think you have mastered it, but just as you get well under way in following, it turns a back somersault, and there you are. It slaps you in the face, knocks you down, and tramples upon you. It is like a bad dream.

The outside pattern is a florid arabesque, reminding one of a fungus. If you can imagine a toadstool in joints, an interminable string of toadstools, budding and sprouting in endless convolutions – why, that is something like it.

That is, sometimes!

There is one marked peculiarity about this paper, a thing nobody seems to notice but myself, and that is that it changes as the light changes.

When the sun shoots in through the east window – I always watch for that first long, straight ray – it changes so quickly that I never can quite believe it.

That is why I watch it always.

By moonlight – the moon shines in all night when there is a moon – I wouldn't know it was the same paper.

At night in any kind of light, in twilight, candlelight, lamplight, and worst of all by moonlight, it becomes bars! The outside pattern, I mean, and the woman behind it is as plain as can be.

I didn't realise for a long time what the thing was that showed behind – that dim sub-pattern – but now I am quite sure it is a woman.

By daylight she is subdued, quiet. I fancy it is the pattern that keeps her so still. It is so puzzling. It keeps me quiet by the hour.

I lie down ever so much now. John says it is good for me, and to sleep all I can.

Indeed, he started the habit by making me lie down for an hour after each meal.

It is a very bad habit, I am convinced, for, you see, I don't sleep.

And that cultivates deceit, for I don't tell them I'm awake, – oh, no!

The fact is, I am getting a little afraid of John.

He seems very queer sometimes, and even Jennie has an inexplicable look.

It strikes me occasionally, just as a scientific hypothesis, that perhaps it is the paper!

I have watched John when he did not know I was looking, and come into the room suddenly on the most innocent excuses, and I've caught him several times *looking at the paper*! And Jennie too. I caught Jennie with her hand on it once.

She didn't know I was in the room, and when I asked her in a quiet, a very quiet voice, with the most restrained manner possible, what she was doing with the paper she turned around as if she had been caught stealing, and looked quite angry – asked me why I should frighten her so!

Then she said that the paper stained everything it touched, and that she had found yellow smooches on all my clothes and John's, and she wished we would be more careful!

Did not that sound innocent? But I know she was studying that pattern, and I am determined that nobody shall find it out but myself!

*   *   *   *

Life is very much more exciting now than it used to be. You see I have something more to expect, to look forward to, to watch. I really do eat better, and am more quiet than I was.

John is so pleased to see me improve! He laughed a little the other day, and said I seemed to be flourishing in spite of my wall-paper.

I turned it off with a laugh. I had no intention of telling him that it was *because* of the wall-paper – he would make fun of me. He might even want to take me away.

At night the woman behind the paper becomes as plain as can be

I don't want to leave now until I have found it out. There is a week more, and I think that will be enough.

★   ★   ★   ★

I'm feeling ever so much better! I don't sleep much at night, for it is so interesting to watch developments; but I sleep a good deal in the daytime.

In the daytime it is tiresome and perlexing.

There are always new shoots on the fungus, and new shades of yellow all over it. I cannot keep count of them, though I have tried conscientiously.

It is the strangest yellow, that wall-paper! It makes me think of all the yellow things I ever saw – not beautiful ones like buttercups, but old foul, bad yellow things.

But there is something else about that paper – the smell! I noticed it the moment we came into the room, but with so much air and sun it was not bad. Now we have had a week of fog and rain, and whether the windows are open or not the smell is here.

It creeps all over the house.

I find it hovering in the dining-room, skulking in the parlour, hiding in the hall, lying in wait for me on the stairs.

It gets into my hair.

Even when I go to ride, if I turn my head suddenly and surprise it – there is that smell!

Such a peculiar odour, too! I have spent hours in trying to analyse it, to find what it smelled like.

It is not bad – at first, and very gentle, but quite the subtlest, most enduring odour I ever met.

In this damp weather it is awful. I wake up in the night and find it hanging over me.

It used to disturb me at first. I thought seriously of burning the house – to reach the smell.

But now I am used to it. The only thing I can think of that it is like is the *colour* of the paper – a yellow smell!

There is a very funny mark on this wall, low down, near the mopboard. A streak that runs around the room. It goes behind every piece of furniture, except the bed, a long, straight, even *smooch*, as if it had been rubbed over and over.

I wonder how it was done and who did it, and what they did it for. Round and round and round – round and round and round – it makes me dizzy!

★   ★   ★   ★

I really have discovered something at last.

Through watching so much at night, when it changes so, I have finally found out.

The front pattern *does* move – and no wonder! The woman behind shakes it!

Sometimes I think there are a great many women behind, and sometimes only one, and she crawls around fast, and her crawling shakes it all over.

Then in the very bright spots she keeps still, and in the very shady spots she just takes hold of the bars and shakes them hard.

And she is all the time trying to climb through. But nobody could climb through that pattern – it strangles so; I think that is why it has so many heads.

They get through, and then the pattern strangles them off and turns them upside-down, and makes their eyes white!

If those heads were covered or taken off it would not be half so bad.

★   ★   ★   ★

I think that woman gets out in the daytime!

And I'll tell you why – privately – I've seen her!

I can see her out of every one of my windows!

It is the same woman, I know, for she is always creeping, and most women do not creep by daylight.

I see her in that long shaded lane, creeping up and down. I see her in those dark grape arbours, creeping all around the garden.

I see her on that long road under the trees, creeping along, and when a carriage comes she hides under the blackberry vines.

I don't blame her a bit. It must be very humiliating to be caught creeping by daylight!

I always lock the door when I creep by daylight. I can't do it at night, for I know John would suspect something at once.

And John is so queer, now, that I don't want to irritate him. I wish he would take another room! Besides, I don't want anybody to get that woman out at night but myself.

I often wonder if I could see her out of all the windows at once.

But, turn as fast as I can, I can only see out of one at one time.

And though I always see her, she *may* be able to creep faster than I can turn!

I have watched her sometimes away off in the open country, creeping as fast as a cloud shadow in a high wind.

★　　　★　　　★　　　★

If only that top pattern could be gotten off from the under one! I mean to try it, little by little.

I have found out another funny thing, but I shan't tell it this time! It does not do to trust people too much.

There are only two more days to get this paper off, and I believe John is beginning to notice. I don't like the look in his eyes.

And I heard him ask Jennie a lot of professional questions about me. She had a very good report to give.

She said I slept a good deal in the daytime.

John knows I don't sleep very well at night, for all I'm so quiet!

He asked me all sorts of questions, too, and pretended to be very loving and kind.

As if I couldn't see through him!

Still, I don't wonder he acts so, sleeping under this paper for three months.

It only interests me, but I feel sure John and Jennie are secretly affected by it.

Hurrah! This is the last day, but it is enough. John is to stay in town over night, and won't be out until this evening.

Jennie wanted to sleep with me – the sly thing! but I told her I should undoubtedly rest better for a night all alone.

That was clever, for really I wasn't alone a bit! As soon as it was moonlight, and that poor thing began to crawl and shake the pattern, I got up and ran to help her.

I pulled and she shook, I shook and she pulled, and before morning we had peeled off yards of that paper.

A strip about as high as my head and half around the room.

And then when the sun came and that awful pattern began to laugh at me, I declared I would finish it today!

We go away tomorrow, and they are moving all my furniture down again to leave things as they were before.

Jennie looked at the wall in amazement, but I told her merrily that I did it out of pure spite at the vicious thing.

She laughed and said she wouldn't mind doing it herself, but I must not get tired.

How she betrayed herself that time!

But I am here, and no person touches this paper but me – not *alive*!

She tried to get me out of the room – it was too patent! But I said it was so quiet and empty and clean now that I believed I would lie down again and sleep all I could; and not to wake me even for dinner – I would call when I woke.

So now she is gone, and the servants are gone, and the things are gone, and there is nothing left but that great bedstead nailed down, with the canvas mattress we found on it.

We shall sleep downstairs tonight, and take the boat home tomorrow.

I quite enjoy the room, now it is bare again.

How those children did tear about here!

This bedstead is fairly gnawed!

But I must get to work.

I have locked the door and thrown the key down into the front path.

I don't want to go out, and I don't want to have anybody come in, until John comes.

I want to astonish him.

I've got a rope up here that even Jennie did not find. If that woman does get out, and tries to get away, I can tie her!

But I forgot I could not reach far without anything to stand on!

This bed will *not* move!

I tried to lift and push it until I was lame, and then I got so angry I bit off a little piece at one corner – but it hurt my teeth.

Then I peeled off all the paper I could reach standing on the floor. It sticks horribly and the pattern just enjoys it! All those strangled heads and bulbous eyes and waddling fungus growths just shriek with derision!

I am getting angry enough to do something desperate. To jump out of the window would be admirable exercise, but the bars are too strong even to try.

Besides, I wouldn't do it. Of course not. I know well enough that a step like that is improper and might be misconstrued.

I don't like to *look* out of the windows even – there are so many of those creeping women, and they creep so fast.

I wonder if they all come out of that wall-paper, as I did?

But I am securely fastened now by my well-hidden rope – you don't get *me* out in the road there!

I suppose I shall have to get back behind the pattern when it comes night, and that is hard!

It is so pleasant to be out in this great room and creep around as I please!

I don't want to go outside. I won't, even if Jennie asks me to.

For outside you have to creep on the ground, and everything is green instead of yellow.

But here I can creep smoothly on the floor, and my shoulder just fits in that long smooch around the wall, so I cannot lose my way.

Why, there's John at the door!

It is no use, young man, you can't open it!

How he does call and pound!

Now he's crying for an axe.

It would be a shame to break down that beautiful door!

'John, dear!' said I in the gentlest voice, 'the key is down by the front steps, under a plantain leaf!'

That silenced him for a few moments.

Then he said – very quietly indeed, 'Open the door, my darling!'

'I can't, said I. 'The key is down by the front door, under a plantain leaf!'

And then I said it again, several times, very gently and slowly, and said it so often that he had to go and see, and he got it, of course, and came in.

He stopped short by the door.

'What is the matter?' he cried. 'For God's sake, what are you doing?'

I kept on creeping just the same, but I looked at him over my shoulder.

'I've got out at last,' said I, 'in spite of you and Jennie! And I've pulled off most of the paper, so you can't put me back!'

Now why should that man have fainted? But he did, and right across my path by the wall, so that I had to creep over him every time!

PICKING UP
TERRIBLE COMPANY
Amelia B Edwards

I am a Frenchman by birth, and my name is François Thierry. I need not weary you with my early history. Enough that I committed a political offence—that I was sent to the galleys for it—that I am an exile for it to this day. The brand was not abolished in my time. If I chose, I could show you the fiery letters on my shoulder.

I was arrested, tried, and sentened in Paris. I went out of the court with my condemnation ringing in my ears. The rumbling wheels of the prison-van repeated it all the way from Paris to Bicêtre that evening, and all the next day, and the next, and the next, along the weary road from Bicêtre to Toulon. When I look back upon that time, I think I must have been stupefied by the unexpected severity of my sentence; for I remember nothing of the journey, nor of the places where we stopped—nothing but the eternal repetition of 'travaux forcés— travaux forcés—travaux forcés à perpétuité,'[1] over and over and over again. Late in the afternoon of the third day, the van stopped, the door was thrown open, and I was conducted across a stone yard, through a stone corridor, into a huge stone hall, dimly lit from above. Here I was interrogated by a military superintendent, and entered by name in a

[1]'hard labour—hard labour—hard labour for life.'

ponderous ledger bound and clasped with iron, like a book in fetters.

'Number two hundred and seven,' said the superintendent. 'Green.'

They took me into an adjoining room, searched and stripped me, and plunged me into a cold bath. When I came out of the bath, I put on the livery of the galleys—a coarse canvas shirt, trousers of tawny serge, a red serge blouse, and heavy shoes clamped with iron. Last of all, a green woollen cap. On each leg of the trousers, and on the breast and back of the blouse, were printed the fatal letters 'T.F'. On a brass label in the front of the cap were engraved the figures '207'. From that moment I lost my individuality. I was no longer François Thierry. I was number two hundred and seven. The superintendent stood by and looked on.

'Come, be quick,' said he, twirling his long moustache between his thumb and forefinger. 'It grows late, and you must be married before supper.'

'Married!' I repeated.

The superintendent laughed, and lit a cigar, and his laugh was echoed by the guards and jailers.

Down another stone corridor, across another yard, into another gloomy hall, the very counterpart of the last, but filled with squalid figures, noisy with the clank of fetters, and pierced at each end with a circular opening, through which a cannon's mouth showed grimly.

'Bring number two hundred and six,' said the superintendent, 'and call the priest.'

Number two hundred and six came from a farther corner of the hall, dragging a heavy chain, and along with him a blacksmith, bare-armed and leather-aproned.

'Lie down,' said the blacksmith, with an insulting spurn of the foot.

I lay down. A heavy iron ring attached to a chain of eighteen links was then fitted to my ankle, and riveted with a single stroke of the hammer. A second ring next received the disengaged ends of my companion's chain and mine, and was secured in the same manner. The echo of each blow resounded through the vaulted roof like a hollow laugh.

'Good,' said the superintendent, drawing a small red book from his pocket. 'Number two hundred and seven, attend to the prison code. If you attempt to escape without succeeding, you will be bastinadoed[2]. If you succeed in getting beyond the port, and are then taken, you will

---

[2]beaten on the soles of the feet with a stick or baton.

receive three years of double-chaining. As soon as you are missed, three cannon shots will be fired, and alarm flags will be hoisted on every bastion. Signals will be telegraphed to the maritime guards, and to the police of the ten neighbouring districts. A price will be set upon your head. Placards will be posted upon the gates of Toulon, and sent to every town throughout the empire. It will be lawful to fire upon you, if you cannot be captured alive.'

Having read this with grim complacency, the superintendent resumed his cigar, replaced the book in his pocket, and walked away.

All was over now—all the incredulous wonder, the dreamy dullness, the smouldering hope, of the past three days. I was a felon, and (slavery in slavery!) chained to a fellow felon. I looked up, and found his eyes upon me. He was a swart, heavy-browed, sullen-jawed man of about forty; not much taller than myself, but of immensely powerful build.

'So,' said he, 'you're for life, are you? So am I.'

'How do you know I am for life?' I asked, wearily.

'By that.' And he touched my cap roughly with the back of his hand. 'Green, for life. Red, for a term of years. What are you in for?'

'I conspired against the government.'

He shrugged his shoulders contemptuously. 'Devil's mass! Then you're a gentleman-convict, I suppose! Pity you've not a berth to yourselves—we poor hard-labourers hate such fine company.'

'Are there many political prisoners?' I asked, after a moment's pause.

'None, in this department.'

Then, as if detecting my unspoken thought, 'I am no innocent,' he added with an oath. 'This is the fourth time I have been here. Did you ever hear of Gasparo?'

'Gasparo the forger?'

He nodded.

'Who escaped three or four months since, and ——'

'And flung the sentry over the ramparts, just as he was going to give the alarm. I'm the man.'

I had heard of him, as a man who, early in his career, had been sentenced to a long solitary imprisonment in a gloomy cell, and who had come forth from his solitude hardened into an absolute wild beast. I shuddered, and found his evil eye taking vindictive note of me. From that moment he hated me. From that moment I loathed him.

A bell rang, and a detachment of convicts came in from labour. They were immediately searched by the guard, and chained up, two and two, to a wooden platform that reached all down the centre of the hall. Our afternoon meal was then served out, consisting of a mess of beans, an allowance of bread and ship-biscuit, and a measure of thin wine. I drank the wine; but I could eat nothing. Gasparo took what he chose from my untouched allowance, and those who were nearest scrambled for the rest. The supper over, a shrill whistle echoed down the hall, each man took his narrow mattress from under the platform which made our common bedstead, rolled himself in a piece of seaweed matting, and lay down for the night. In less than five minutes, all was profoundly silent. Now and then I heard the blacksmith going round with his hammer, testing the gratings, and trying the locks, in all the corridors. Now and then, the guard stalked past with his musket on his shoulder. Sometimes a convict moaned, or shook his fetters in his sleep. Thus the weary hours went by. My companion slept heavily, and even I lost consciousness at last.

I was sentenced to hard labour. At Toulon the hard labour is of various kinds: such as quarrying, mining, pumping in the docks, loading and unloading vessels, transporting ammunition, and so forth. Gasparo and I were employed with about two hundred other convicts in a quarry a little beyond the port. Day after day, week after week, from seven in the morning until seven at night, the rocks echoed with our blows. At every blow, our chains rang and rebounded on the stony soil. In that fierce climate, terrible tempests and tropical droughts succeed each other throughout the summer and autumn. Often, after toiling for hours under a burning sky, have I gone back to prison and to my pallet, drenched to the skin. Thus the last days of the dreary spring ebbed slowly past; and then the more dreary summer, and then the autumn, came round.

My fellow convict was a Piedmontese. He had been a burglar, a forger, an incendiary. In his last escape he had committed manslaughter. Heaven alone knows how my sufferings were multiplied by that abhorred companionship—how I shrank from the touch of his hand—how I sickened if his breath came over me as we lay side by side at night. I strove to disguise my loathing; but in vain. He knew it as well as I knew it, and he revenged himself upon me by every means that a vindictive nature could devise. That he should tyrannize over me was not wonderful; for his physical strength was gigantic, and he was looked upon as an authorized despot throughout the port; but simple tyranny was the least part of what I had to endure. I had been fastidiously nurtured; he purposely and continually offended my sense of delicacy.

I was unaccustomed to bodily labour; he imposed on me the largest share of our daily work. When I needed rest, he would insist on walking. When my limbs were cramped, he would lie down obstinately and refuse to stir. He delighted to sing blasphemous songs, and relate hideous stories of what he had thought and resolved on in his solitude. He would even twist the chain in ways that would gall me at every step. I was at that time just twenty-two years of age, and had been sickly from boyhood. To retaliate, or to defend myself, would have been alike impossible. To complain to the superintendent would only have been to provoke my tyrant.

There came a day, at length, when his hatred seemed to abate. He allowed me to rest when our hour of repose came round. He abstained from singing the songs I abhorred, and fell into long fits of abstraction. The next morning, shortly after we had begun work, he drew near enough to speak to me in a whisper.

'François, have you a mind to escape?'

I felt the blood rush to my face. I clasped my hands. I could not speak.

'Can you keep a secret?'

'To the death.'

'Listen, then. Tomorrow, a renowned marshal will visit the port. He will inspect the docks, the prisons, the quarries. There will be plenty of cannonading from the forts and the shipping, and if two convicts escape, a volley more or less will attract no attention round about Toulon. Do you understand?'

'You mean that no one will recognize the signals?'

'Not even the sentries at the town gates—not even the guards in the next quarry. Devil's mass! What can be easier than to strike off each other's fetters with the pickaxe when the superintendent is not looking, and the salutes are firing? Will you venture?'

'With my life!'

'A bargain. Shake hands on it.'

I had never touched his hand in fellowship before, and I felt as if my own were blood-stained by the contact. I knew by the sullen fire in his glance that he interpreted my faltering touch aright.

We were roused an hour earlier than usual the following morning, and went through a general inspection in the prison yard. Before going to work, we were served with a double allowance of wine. At one o'clock we heard the first far-off salutes from the ships of war in the harbour. The sound ran through me like a galvanic shock. One by one, the forts took up the signal. It was repeated by the gunboats closer in shore. Discharge followed discharge, all along the batteries on both sides of the port, and the air grew thick with smoke.

'As the first shot is fired yonder,' whispered Gasparo, pointing to the barracks behind the prison, 'strike at the first link of my chain, close to the ankle.'

A rapid suspicion flashed across me.

'If I do, how can I be sure that you will free me afterwards? No, Gasparo; you must deal the first blow.'

'As you please,' he replied, with a laugh.

At the same instant came a flash from the battlements of the barrack close by, and then a thunderous reverberation, multiplied again and again by the rocks around. As the roar burst over our heads I saw him strike and felt the fetters fall. Scarcely had the echo of the first gun died away, when the second was fired. It was now Gasparo's turn to be free. I struck; but less skilfully, and had twice to repeat the blow before breaking the stubborn link. We then went on, apparently, with our work, standing somewhat close together, with the chain huddled up between us. No one had observed us, and no one, at first sight, could have detected what we had done.

At the third shot, a party of officers and gentlemen made their appearance at the bend of the road leading up to the quarry. In an instant, every head was turned in their direction; every felon paused in his work; every guard presented arms. At that moment we flung away our caps and pickaxes, scaled the rugged bit of cliff on which we had been toiling, dropped into the ravine below, and made for the mountain passes that lead into the valley. Encumbered still with the iron anklets to which our chains had been fastened, we could not run very swiftly. To add to our difficulties, the road was uneven, strewn with flints and blocks of fallen granite, and tortuous as the windings of a snake. Suddenly, on turning a sharp angle of projecting cliff, we came upon a little guard-house and a couple of sentries. To retreat was impossible. The soldiers were within a few yards of us. They presented their pieces, and called to us to surrender. Gasparo turned upon me like a wolf at bay.

'Curse you!' said he, dealing me a tremendous blow, 'stay and be taken! I have always hated you!'

I fell as if struck down by a sledge-hammer, and, as I fell, saw him dash one soldier to the ground, dart past the other, heard a shot, and then . . . all became dark, and I knew no more.

When I next opened my eyes, I found myself lying on the floor of a small unfurnished room, dimly lit by a tiny window close against the ceiling. It seemed as if weeks had gone by since I lost consciousness. I had scarcely strength to rise, and, having risen, kept my feet with difficulty. Where my head had lain, the floor was wet with blood. Giddy and perplexed, I leaned against the wall, and tried to think.

In the first place, where was I? Evidently in no part of the prison from which I had escaped. There, all was solid stone and iron grating; here, was only whitewashed wood and plaster. I must be in a chamber of the little guard-house: probably in an upper chamber. Where, then, were the soldiers? Where was Gasparo? Had I strength to clamber up to that window, and if so, in what direction did that window look out? I stole to the door, and found it locked. I listened, breathlessly, but could hear no sound either below or above.

My decision was taken at once. To stay was certain capture; to venture, at all hazards, would make matters no worse. Again I listened, and again all was quiet. I drew myself through the little casement, dropped as gently as I could upon the moist earth, and, crouching against the wall, asked myself what I should do next. To climb the cliff would be to offer myself as a target to the first soldier who saw me. To venture along the ravine would be, perhaps, to encounter Gasparo and his captors face to face. Besides, it was getting dusk, and, under cover of the night, if I could only conceal myself till then, I might yet escape. But where was that concealment to be found? Heaven be thanked for the thought! There was the ditch.

Only two windows looked out upon the garden from the back of the guard-house. From one of those windows I had just now let myself

'Curse you,' he said, dealing me a tremendous blow, 'stay and be taken!'

down, and the other was partly shuttered up. I did not dare, however, openly to cross the garden. I dropped upon my face, and crawled in the furrows between the rows of vegetables, until I came to the ditch. Here, the water rose nearly to my waist, but the banks on either side were considerably higher, and, by stooping, I found that I could walk without bringing my head to the level of the road. I thus followed the course of the ditch for some two or three hundred yards in the direction of Toulon, thinking that my pursuers would be less likely to suspect me of doubling back towards prison than of pushing forward towards the country. Half lying, half crouching under the rank grasses that fringed the bank above, I then watched the gathering shadows.

I suffered an hour to go by before I ventured to move again. By that time it was intensely dark, and had begun to rain heavily. The water in the ditch became a brawling torrent, through which I waded, unheard, past the very windows of the guard-house.

After toiling through the water for a mile or more, I ventured out upon the road again: and so, with the rain and wind beating in my face, and the scattered boulders tripping me up continually, I made my way through the whole length of the winding pass, and came out upon the more open country about midnight. With no other guide than the wind, which was blowing from the north-east, and without even a star to help me, I then struck off to the right, following what seemed to be a rough by-road, lying through a valley. After a while the rain abated, and I discerned the dark outlines of a chain of hills extending all along to the left of the road. These, I concluded, must be the Maures. All was well, so far. I had taken the right direction, and was on the way to Italy.

Excepting to sit down now and then for a few minutes by the way-side, I never paused in my flight the whole night through. Fatigue and want of food prevented me, it is true, from walking very fast; but the love of liberty was strong within me, and, by keeping steadily on, I succeeded in placing about eighteen miles between myself and Toulon. At five o'clock, just as the day began to dawn, I heard a peal of chimes, and found that I was approaching a large town. In order to avoid this town, I was forced to turn back for some distance, and take to the heights. The sun had now risen, and I dared go no farther; so, having pulled some turnips in a field as I went along, I took refuge in a little lonely copse in a hollow among the hills, and there lay all day in safety.

When night again closed in I resumed my journey, keeping always among the mountains, and coming now and then on grand glimpses of moonlit bays, and tranquil islands lying off the shore; now and then, on pastoral hamlets nestled up among the palmy heights; or on promontories overgrown with the cactus and the aloe. I rested all the second day in a ruined shed at the bottom of a deserted sandpit, and, in the evening, feeling that I could no longer sustain life without some fitting nourishment, made my way down towards a tiny fishing village on the coast below. It was quite dark by the time I reached the level ground. I walked boldly past the cottages of the fishermen, meeting only an old woman and a little child on the way, and knocked at the parish priest's door. He opened it himself. I told my story in half-a-dozen words. The good man believed and pitied me. He gave me food and wine, an old handkerchief to wrap about my head, an old coat to replace my convict's jacket, and two or three francs to help me on my way. I parted from him with tears.

I walked all that night again, and all the next, keeping somewhat close upon the coast, and hiding among the cliffs during the daytime. On the fifth morning, having left Antibes behind me during the night's march, I came to the banks of the Var; crossed the torrent about half a mile below the wooden bridge; plunged into the pine-woods on the other side of the frontier; and lay down to rest on Italian ground at last!

Though comparatively safe, I still pursued my journey by the least frequented ways; how I bought a file at the first hamlet to which I came, and freed myself from the iron anklet; how, having lurked about Nice till my hair and beard had grown, I begged my way on to Genoa; how, at Genoa, I hung about the port, earning a scanty livelihood by any chance work that I could get, and so struggled, somehow, through the inclement winter; how, towards the early spring, I worked my passage on board a small trader from Genoa to Fiumicino, touching at all the ports along the coast; and how, coming slowly up the Tiber in a barge laden with oil and wine, I landed one evening in March on the Ripetta quay in Rome. My object had been to get to Rome, and that object was at last attained. In so large a city, and at so great a distance from the scene of my imprisonment, I was personally safe. I might hope to turn my talents and education to account. I might even find friends among the strangers who would flock there to the Easter festivals. Full of hope, therefore, I sought a humble lodging in the neighbourhood of the quay, gave up a day or two to the enjoyment of my liberty and of the sights of Rome, and then set myself to find regular employment.

Regular employment, or, indeed, employment of any kind, was not, however, so easily to be obtained. It was a season of distress. Day by day, my hopes faded and my prospects darkened. Day by day, the little money I had scraped together on the passage melted away. I had thought to obtain a clerkship, or a secretaryship, or a situation in some public library. Before three weeks were over, I would gladly have swept a studio. At length there came a day when I saw nothing before me but starvation—when my last bajocco was expended, when my landlord shut the door in my face, and I knew not where to turn for a meal or a shelter. All that afternoon, I wandered hopelessly about the streets. It was Good Friday, of all days in the year. The churches were hung with black; the bells were tolling; the thoroughfares were crowded with people in mourning. I went into the little church of Santa Martina. They were chanting the Miserere, probably with no great skill, but with a pathos that seemed to open up all the sources of my despair.

Outcast that I was, I slept that night under a dark arch near the theatre of Marcellus. The morning dawned upon a glorious day, and I crept out, shivering, into the sunshine. Once I asked for alms, and was repulsed. I followed mechanically in the stream of carriages and foot passengers, and found myself in the midst of the crowd that ebbs and flows continually about St Peter's during Easter week. Stupefied and weary, I turned aside into the vestibule of the Sagrestia, and cowered down in the shelter of a doorway. Two gentlemen were reading a printed paper wafered against a pillar close by.

'Good heavens!' said one to the other, 'that a man should risk his neck for a few pauls!'

'Ay, and with the knowledge that out of eighty workmen, six or eight are dashed to pieces every time,' added his companion.

'Shocking! Why, that's an average of ten per cent!'

'No less. It's a desperate service.'

'But a fine sight,' said the first speaker, philosophically; and with this they walked away.

I sprang to my feet and read the placard with avidity. It was headed 'Illumination of Saint Peter's', and announced that, eighty workmen being required for the lighting of the dome and cupola, and three hundred for the cornices, pillars, colonnade, and so forth, the amministratore was empowered, etc. etc. In conclusion, it stated that every workman employed on the dome and cupola should receive in payment a dinner and twenty-four pauls, the wages of the rest being less than a third of that sum.

A desperate service, it was true; but I was a desperate man. After all, I could but die, and I might as well die after a good dinner as from starvation. I went at once to the *amministratore*, was entered in his list, received a couple of pauls as earnest of the contract, and engaged to present myself punctually at eleven o'clock on the following morning. That evening I supped at a street stall, and, for a few bajocchi, obtained leave to sleep on some straw in a loft over a stable at the back of the Via del Arco.

At eleven o'clock on the morning of Easter Sunday, 16 April, I found myself, accordingly, in the midst of a crowd of poor fellows, most of whom, I dare say, were as wretched as myself, waiting at the door of the administrator's office. The piazza in front of the cathedral was like a moving mosaic of life and colour. The sun was shining, the fountains were playing, the flags were flying over St Angelo. It was a glorious sight; but I saw it for only a few moments. As the clocks struck the hour, the folding doors were thrown open, and we passed, in a crowd, into a hall, where two long tables were laid for our accommodation. A couple of sentinels stood at the door; an usher marshalled us, standing, round the tables; and a priest read grace.

As he began to read, a strange sensation came upon me. I felt impelled to look across to the opposite table, and there . . . yes, by heaven! there I saw Gasparo.

He was looking full at me, but his eyes dropped on meeting mine. I saw him turn lividly white. The recollection of all he had made me suffer, and of the dastardly blow that he had dealt me on the day of our flight, overpowered for the moment even my surprise at seeing him in this place. Oh that I might live to meet him yet, under the free sky, where no priest was praying, and no guards were by!

The grace over, we sat down and fell to. Not even anger had power to blunt the edge of my appetite just then. I ate like a famished wolf, and so did most of the others. We were allowed no wine, and the doors were locked upon us, that we might not procure any elsewhere. It was a wise regulation, considering the task we had to perform; but it made us none the less noisy. In certain circumstances, danger intoxicates like wine; and on this Easter Sunday, we eighty *sanpietrini*, any one of whom might have his brains dashed about the leads before supper-time, ate, talked, jested, and laughed, with a wild gaiety that had in it something appalling.

The dinner lasted long, and when no one seemed disposed to eat more, the tables were cleared. Most of the men threw themselves on the floor and benches, and went to sleep; Gasparo among the number. Seeing this, I could refrain no longer. I went over, and stirred him roughly with my foot.

'Gasparo! You know me?'

He looked up, sullenly.

'Devil's mass! I thought you were at Toulon.'

'It is not your fault that I am not at Toulon! Listen to me. If you and I survive this night, you shall answer to me for your treachery!'

He glared at me from under his deep brows, and, without replying, turned over on his face again, as if to sleep.

'There's an accursed fellow!' said one of the others, with a significant shrug, as I came away.

'Do you know anything of him?' I asked, eagerly.

'Cospetto! I know nothing of him; but that solitude is said to have made him a wolf.'

I could learn no more, so I also stretched myself upon the floor, as far as possible from my enemy, and fell profoundly asleep.

At seven, the guards roused those who still slept, and served each man with a small mug of thin wine. We were then formed into a double file, marched round by the back of the cathedral, and conducted up an inclined plane to the roof below the dome. From this point, a long series of staircases and winding passages carried us up between the double walls of the dome; and, at different stages in the ascent, a certain number of us were detached and posted ready for work. I was detached about halfway up, and I saw Gasparo going higher still.

When we were all posted, the superintendents came round and gave us our instructions. At a given signal, every man was to pass out through the loophole or window before which he was placed, and seat himself astride upon a narrow shelf of wood hanging to a strong rope just below. This rope came through the window, was wound round a roller, and secured from within. At the next signal, a lighted torch would be put into his right hand, and he was to grasp the rope firmly with his left. At the third signal the rope was to be unwound from within by an assistant placed there for the purpose, he was to be allowed to slide rapidly down, over the curve of the dome, and, while thus sliding, was to apply his torch to every lamp he passed in his downward progress.

Having received these instructions, we waited, each man at his window, until the first signal should be given.

It was fast getting dark, and the silver illumination had been lit since seven. All the great ribs of the dome, as far as I could see; all the cornices and friezes of the façade below; all the columns and parapets of the great colonnade surrounding the piazza four hundred feet below, were traced out in lines of paper lanterns, the light from which, subdued by the paper, gleamed with a silvery fire which had a magical and wondrous look. Between and among these *lanternoni* were placed, at different intervals all over the cathedral on the side facing the piazza, iron cups called *padelle*, ready filled with tallow and turpentine. To light those on the dome and cupola was the perilous task of the *sanpietrini*; when they were all lit the golden illumination would be effected.

A few moments of intense suspense elapsed. At every second the evening grew darker, the *lanternoni* burned brighter, the surging hum of thousands in the piazza and streets below rose louder to our ears. I felt the quickening breath of the assistant at my shoulder—I could almost hear the beating of my heart. Suddenly, like the passing of an electric current, the first signal flew from lip to lip. I got out, and crossed my legs firmly round the board; with the second signal I seized the blazing torch; with the third, I felt myself launched, and, lighting every cup as I glided past, saw all the mountainous dome above and below me spring into lines of leaping flame. The clock was now striking eight, and when the last stroke sounded the whole cathedral was glowing in outlines of fire. A roar, like the roar of a great ocean, rose up from the multitude below, and seemed to shake the very dome against which I was clinging. I could even see the light upon the gazing faces, the crowd upon the bridge of St Angelo, and the boats swarming along the Tiber.

Having dropped safely to the full length of my rope, and lit my allotted share of lamps, I was now sitting in secure enjoyment of this amazing scene. All at once I felt the rope vibrate. I looked up, saw a man clinging by one hand to the iron rod supporting the *padelle*, and with the other . . . Merciful heaven! It was the Piedmontese firing the rope above me with his torch!

I had no time for thought—I acted upon instinct. It was done in one fearful moment. I clambered up like a cat, dashed my torch full in the solitary felon's face, and grasped the rope an inch or two above the spot where it was burning! Blinded and baffled, he uttered a terrible cry, and dropped like a stone. Through all the roar of the living ocean below I could hear the dull crash with which he came down upon the leaded roof—resounding through all the years that have gone by since that night, I hear it now!

I had scarcely drawn breath when I found myself being hauled up. The assistance came not a moment too soon, for I was sick and giddy with horror, and fainted as soon as I was safe in the corridor.

The next day I waited on the *amministratore*, and told him all that had happened. My statement was corroborated by the vacant rope from which Gasparo had descended and the burnt fragment by which I had been drawn up. The *amministratore* repeated my story to a prelate high in office; and while none, even of the *sanpietrini*, suspected that my enemy had come by his death in any unusual manner, the truth was whispered from palace to palace until it reached the Vatican. I received much sympathy, and such financial assistance as enabled me to confront the future without fear.

THE MELANCHOLY HUSSAR

Thomas Hardy

Here stretch the downs, high and breezy and green, absolutely unchanged since those eventful days. A plough has never disturbed the turf, and the sod that was uppermost then is uppermost now. Here stood the camp; here are distinct traces of the banks thrown up for the horses of the cavalry, and spots where the midden-heaps lay are still to be observed. At night, when I walk across the lonely place, it is impossible to avoid hearing, amid the scourings of the wind over the grass-bents and thistles, the old trumpet and bugle calls, the rattle of the halters; to help seeing rows of spectral tents and the *impedimenta* of the soldiery. From within the canvases come guttural syllables of foreign tongues, and broken songs of the fatherland; for they were mainly regiments of the King's German Legion that slept round the tent-poles hereabout at that time.

It was nearly ninety years ago. The British uniform of the period, with its immense epaulettes, queer cocked-hat, breeches, gaiters, ponderous cartridge-box, buckled shoes, and what not, would look strange and barbarous now. Ideas have changed; invention has followed invention. Soldiers were monumental objects then. A divinity still hedged kings here and there; and war was considered a glorious thing.

Secluded old manor-houses and hamlets lie in the ravines and hollows among these hills, where a stranger had hardly ever been seen till the King chose to take the baths yearly at the sea-side watering-place a few miles to the south; as a consequence of which battalions descended in a cloud upon the open country around. Is it necessary to add that the echoes of many characteristic tales, dating from that picturesque time, still linger about here in more or less fragmentary form, to be caught by the attentive ear? Some of them I have repeated; most of them I have forgotten; one I have never repeated, and assuredly can never forget.

Phyllis told me the story with her own lips. She was then an old lady of seventy-five, and her auditor a lad of fifteen. She enjoyed silence as to her share in the incident, till she should be 'dead, buried, and forgotten.' Her life was prolonged twelve years after the day of her narration, and she has now been dead nearly twenty. The oblivion which in her modesty and humility she courted for herself has only partially fallen on her, with the unfortunate result of inflicting an injustice upon her memory; since such fragments of her story as got abroad at the time, and have been kept alive ever since, are precisely those which are most unfavourable to her character.

It all began with the arrival of the York Hussars, one of the foreign regiments above alluded to. Before that day scarcely a soul had been seen near her father's house for weeks. When a noise like the brushing skirt of a visitor was heard on the doorstep, it proved to be a scudding leaf; when a carriage seemed to be nearing the door, it was her father grinding his sickle on the stone in the garden for his favourite relaxation of trimming the box-tree borders to the plots. A sound like luggage thrown down from the coach was a gun far away at sea; and what looked like a tall man by the gate at dusk was a yew bush cut into a quaint and attenuated shape. There is no such solitude in country places now as there was in those old days.

Yet all the while King George and his court were at his favourite sea-side resort, not more than five miles off.

The daughter's seclusion was great, but beyond the seclusion of the girl lay the seclusion of the father. If her social condition was twilight, his was darkness. Yet he enjoyed his darkness, while her twilight depressed her. Dr Grove had been a professional man whose taste for lonely meditation over metaphysical questions had diminished his practice till it no longer paid him to keep it going; after which he had relinquished it and hired at a nominal rent the small, dilapidated, half farm half manor-house of this obscure inland nook, to make a sufficiency of an income which in a town would have been inadequate for their maintenance. He stayed in his garden the greater part of the day, growing more and more irritable with the lapse of time, and the increasing perceptions that he had wasted his life in the pursuit of illusions. He saw his friends less and less frequently. Phyllis became so shy that if she met a stranger anywhere in her short rambles she felt ashamed at his gaze, walked awkwardly, and blushed to her shoulders.

Yet Phyllis was discovered even here by an admirer, and her hand most unexpectedly asked in marriage.

The King, as aforesaid, was at the neighbouring town, where he had taken up his abode at Gloucester Lodge; and his presence in the town naturally brought many country people thither. Among these idlers—many of whom professed to have connections and interests with the Court—was one Humphrey Gould, a bachelor; a personage neither young nor old; neither good-looking nor positively plain. Too steady-going to be 'a buck' (as fast and unmarried men were then called), he was an approximately fashionable man of a mild type. This bachelor of thirty found his way to the village on the down: beheld Phyllis; made her father's acquaintance in order to make hers; and by some means or other she sufficiently inflamed his heart to lead him in that direction almost daily; till he became engaged to marry her.

As he was of an old local family, some of whose members were held in respect in the county, Phyllis, in bringing him to her feet, had accomplished what was considered a brilliant move from one in her constrained position. How she had done it was not quite known to Phyllis herself. In those days unequal marriages were regarded rather as a violation of the laws of nature than as a mere infringement of convention, the more modern view, and hence when Phyllis, of the watering-place *bourgeosie,* was chosen by such a gentlemanly fellow, it was as if she were going to be taken to heaven, though perhaps the uninformed would have seen no great difference in the respective positions of the pair, the said Gould being as poor as a crow.

This pecuniary condition was his excuse—probably a true one—for postponing their union, and as the winter drew nearer, and the King departed for the season, Mr Humphrey Gould set out for Bath, promising to return to Phyllis in a few weeks. The winter arrived, the date of his promise passed, yet Gould postponed his coming, on the ground that he could not very easily leave his father in the city of their sojourn, the elder having no other relative near him. Phyllis, though lonely in the extreme, was content. The man who had asked her in marriage was a desirable husband for her in many ways; her father highly approved of his suit; but this neglect of her was awkward, if not painful, for Phyllis. Love him in the true sense of the word she assured me she never did, but she had a genuine regard for him; admired a certain methodical and dogged way in which he sometimes took his pleasure; valued his knowledge of what the Court was doing, had done, or was about to do; and she was not without a feeling of pride that he had chosen her when he might have exercised a more ambitious choice.

But he did not come; and the spring developed. His letters were regular though formal; and it is not to be wondered that the uncertainty of her position, linked with the fact that there was not much passion in her thoughts of Humphrey, bred an indescribable dreariness in the heart of Phyllis Grove. The spring was soon summer, and the summer brought the King; but still no Humphrey Gould. All this while the engagement by letter was maintained intact.

At this point of time a golden radiance flashed in upon the lives of people here, and charged all youthful thought with emotional interest. This radiance was the aforesaid York Hussars.

★   ★   ★   ★

The present generation has probably but a very dim notion of the celebrated York Hussars of ninety years ago. They were one of the regiments of the King's German Legion, and (though they somewhat degenerated later on) their brilliant uniform, their splendid horses, and above all, their foreign air and mustachios (rare appendages then), drew crowds of admirers of both sexes wherever they went. These with other regiments had come to encamp on the downs and pastures, because of the presence of King George in the neighbouring town.

The spot was high and airy, and the view extensive, commanding Portland—the Isle of Slingers—in front, and reaching to St Aldhelm's Head eastward, and almost to the Start on the west.

Phyllis, though not precisely a girl of the village, was as interested as any of them in this military investment. Her father's home stood somewhat apart, and on the highest point of ground to which the lane ascended, so that it was almost level with the top of the church tower in the lower part of the parish. Immediately from the outside of the garden-wall the grass spread away to a great distance, and it was crossed by a path which came close to the wall. Ever since her childhood it had been Phyllis's pleasure to clamber up this fence and sit on the top—a feat not so difficult as it may seem, the walls in this district being built of rubble, without mortar, so that there were plenty of crevices for small toes.

She was sitting up here one day, listlessly surveying the pasture without, when her attention was arrested by a solitary figure walking along the path. It was one of the renowned German Hussars, and he moved onward with his eyes on the ground, and with the manner of one who wished to escape company. His head would probably have been bent like his eyes but for his stiff neck-gear. On nearer view she perceived that his face was marked with deep sadness. Without observing her, he advanced by the footpath till it brought him almost immediately under the wall.

Phyllis was much surprised to see a fine, tall soldier in such a mood as this. Her theory of the military, and of the York Hussars in particular (derived entirely from hearsay, for she had never talked to a soldier in her life), was that their hearts were as gay as their accoutrements.

At this moment the Hussar lifted his eyes and noticed her on her perch, the white muslin neckerchief which covered her shoulders and neck where left bare by her low gown, and her white raiment in general, showing conspicuously in the bright sunlight of this summer day. He blushed a little at the suddenness of the encounter, and without halting a moment from his pace passed on.

All that day the foreigner's face haunted Phyllis; its aspect was so striking, so handsome, and his eyes were so blue, and sad, and abstracted. It was perhaps only natural that on some following day at the same hour she should look over that wall again, and wait till he had passed a second time. On this occasion he was reading a letter, and at the sight of her his manner was that of one who had half expected or hoped to discover her. He almost stopped, smiled, and made a courteous salute. The end of the meeting was that they exchanged a few words. She asked him what he was reading, and he readily informed her that he was re-perusing letters from his mother in Germany; he did not get them often, he said, and was forced to read the old ones a great many times. This was all that passed at the present interview, but others of the same kind followed.

Phyllis used to say that his English, though not good, was quite intelligible to her, so that their acquaintance was never hindered by difficulties of speech. Whenever the subject became too delicate, subtle, or tender, for such words of English as were at his command, the eyes no doubt helped out the tongue, and—though this was later on—the lips helped out the eyes. In short this acquaintance, unguardedly made, and rash enough on her part, developed and ripened. Like Desdemona, she pitied him, and learnt his history.

His name was Matthäus Tina, and Saarbrück his native town, where his mother was still living. His age was twenty-two, and he had already risen to the grade of corporal, though he had not long been in the army. Phyllis used to assert that no such refined or well-educated young man could have been found in the ranks of the purely English regiments, some of these foreign soldiers having rather the graceful manner and presence of our native officers than of our rank and file.

She by degrees learnt from her foreign friend a circumstance about himself and his comrades which Phyllis would least have expected of the York Hussars. So far from being as gay as its uniform, the regiment was pervaded by a dreadful melancholy, a chronic home-sickness, which depressed many of the men to such an extent that they could hardly attend to their drill. The worst sufferers were the younger soldiers who had not been over here long. They hated England and English life; they took no interest whatever in King George and his island kingdom, and they only wished to be out of it and never to see it any more. Their bodies were here, but their hearts and minds were always far away in their dear fatherland, of which—brave men and stoical as they were in many ways—they would speak with tears in their eyes. One of the worst of the sufferers from this home-woe, as he called it in his own tongue, was Matthäus Tina, whose dreamy musing nature felt the gloom of exile still more intensely from the fact that he had left a lonely mother at home with nobody to cheer her.

Though Phyllis, touched by all this, and interested in his history, did not disdain her soldier's acquaintance, she declined (according to her own account, at least) to permit the young man to overstep the line of mere friendship for a long while—as long, indeed, as she considered herself likely to become the possession of another; though it is probable that she had lost her heart to Matthäus before she was herself aware. The stone wall of necessity made anything like intimacy difficult; and he had never ventured to come, or to ask to come, inside the garden, so that all their conversation had been overtly conducted across this boundary.

★ ★ ★ ★

But news reached the village from a friend of Phyllis's father concerning Mr Humphrey Gould, her remarkably cool and patient betrothed. This gentleman had been heard to say in Bath that he considered his overtures to Miss Phyllis Grove to have reached only the stage of a half-understanding; and in view of his enforced absence on his father's account, who was too great an invalid now to attend to his affairs, he thought it best that there should be no definite promise as yet on either side. He was not sure, indeed, that he might not cast his eyes elsewhere.

This account—though only a piece of hearsay, and as such entitled to no absolute credit—tallied so well with the infrequency of his letters and their lack of warmth, that Phyllis did not doubt its truth for one moment; and from that hour she felt herself free to bestow her heart as she should choose. Not so her father; he declared the whole story to be a fabrication. He had known Mr Gould's family from his boyhood; and if there was one proverb which expressed the matrimonial aspect of that family well, it was 'Love me little, love me long'. Humphrey was an honourable man, who would not think of treating his engagement so lightly. 'Do you wait in patience,' he said; 'all will be right enough in time.'

From these words Phyllis at first imagined that her father was in correspondence with Mr Gould; and her heart sank within her; for in spite of her original intentions she had been relieved to hear that her engagement had come to nothing. But she presently learnt that her father had heard no more of Humphrey Gould than she herself had done; while he would not write and address her affianced directly on the subject, lest it should be deemed an imputation on that bachelor's honour.

'You want an excuse for encouraging one or other of those foreign fellows to flatter you with his unmeaning attentions,' her father exclaimed, his mood having of late been a very unkind one towards her. 'I see more than I say.' Don't you ever set foot outside that garden-fence without my permission. If you want to see the camp I'll take you myself some Sunday afternoon.'

Phyllis had not the smallest intention of disobeying him in her actions, but she assumed herself to be independent with respect to her feelings. She no longer checked her fancy for the Hussar, though she was far from regarding him as her lover in the serious sense in which an Englishman might have been regarded as such. The young foreign soldier was almost an ideal being to her, with none of the appurtenances of an ordinary house-dweller; one who had descended she knew not whence, and would disappear she knew not whither; the subject of a fascinating dream—no more.

They met continually now—mostly at dusk—during the brief interval between the going down of the sun and the minute at which the last trumpet-call summoned him to his tent. Perhaps her manner had become less restrained latterly; at any rate that of the Hussar was so; he had grown more tender every day, and at parting after these hurried interviews she reached down her hand from the top of the wall that he might press it. One evening he held it such a while that she exclaimed, 'The wall is white, and somebody in the field may see your shape against it!'

He lingered so long that night that it was with the greatest difficulty that he could run across the intervening stretch of ground and enter the camp in time. On the next occasion of his awaiting her she did not appear in her usual place at the usual hour. His disappointment was unspeakably keen; he remained staring bleakly at the spot, like a man in a trance. The trumpets and tattoo sounded, and still he did not go.

She had been delayed purely by an accident. When she arrived she was anxious because of the lateness of the hour, having heard as well as he the sounds denoting the closing of the camp. She implored him to leave immediately.

'No,' he said gloomily. 'I shall not go in yet—the moment you come—I have thought of your coming all day.'

'But you may be disgraced at being after time?'

'I don't mind that. I should have disappeared from the world some time ago if it had not been for two persons—my beloved, here, and my mother in Saarbrück. I hate the army. I care more for a minute of your company than for all the promotion in the world.

Thus he stayed and talked to her, and told her interesting details of his native place, and incidents of his childhood, till she was in a simmer of distress at his recklessness in remaining. It was only because she insisted on bidding him goodnight and leaving the wall that he returned to his quarters.

The next time that she saw him he was without the stripes that had adorned his sleeve. He had been broken to the level of private for his lateness that night; and as Phyllis considered herself to be the cause of his disgrace her sorrow was great. But the position was now reversed; it was his turn to cheer her.

'Don't grieve, meine Liebliche!' he said. 'I have got a remedy for whatever comes. First, even supposing I regain my stripes, would your father allow you to marry a non-commissioned officer in the York Hussars?.

She flushed. This practical step had not been in her mind in relation to such an unrealistic person as he was; and a moment's reflection was enough for it. 'My father would not—certainly would not,' she answered unflinchingly. 'It cannot be thought of! My dear friend, please do forget me. I fear I am ruining you and your prospects!'

'Not at all!' said he. 'You are giving this country of yours just sufficient interest to me to make me care to keep alive in it. If my dear land were here also, and my old parent, with you, I could be happy as I am, and would do my best as a soldier. But it is not so. And now listen. This is my plan. That you go with me to my own country, and be my wife there, and live there with my mother and me. I am not a Hanoverian, as you know, though I entered the army as such; my country is by the Saar, and is at peace with France, and if I were once in it I should be free.'

'But how to get there?' she asked. Phyllis had been rather amazed than shocked at his proposition. Her position in her father's house was growing irksome and painful in the extreme; his parental affection seemed to be quite dried up. She was not a native of the village, like all the joyous girls around her; and in some way Matthäus Tina had infected her with his own passionate longing for his country, and mother, and home.

'But how?' she repeated, finding that he did not answer. 'Will you buy your discharge?'

'Ah, no,' he said. 'That's impossible in these times. No; I came here against my will; why should I not escape? Now is the time, as we shall soon be striking camp, and I might see you no more. This is my scheme. I will ask you to meet me on the highway two miles off, on some calm night next week that may be appointed. There will be nothing unbecoming in it, or to cause you shame; you will not fly alone with me, for I will bring with me my devoted young friend Christoph, an Alsatian, who has lately joined the regiment, and who has agreed to assist in this enterprise. We shall have come from yonder harbour, where we shall have examined the boats, and found one suited to our purpose. Christoph has already a chart of the Channel, and we will then go to the harbour, and at midnight cut the boat from her moorings, and row away round the point out of sight; and by the next morning we are on the coast of France, near Cherbourg. The rest is easy, for I have saved money for the land journey, and can get a change of clothes. I will write to my mother, who will meet us on the way.'

He added details in reply to her inquiries, which left no doubt in Phyllis's mind of the feasibility of the undertaking. But its magnitude almost appalled her; and it is questionable if she would ever have gone further in the wild adventure if, on entering the house that night, her father had not accosted her in the most significant terms.

'How about the York Hussars?' he said.

'They are still at the camp; but they are soon going away, I believe.'

'It is useless for you to attempt to cloak your actions in that way. You have been meeting one of those fellows; you have been seen walking with him—foreign barbarians, not much better than the French themselves! I have made up my mind—don't speak a word till I have done, please!—I have made up my mind that you shall stay here no longer while they are on the spot. You shall go to your aunt's.'

It was useless for her to protest that she had never taken a walk with any soldier or man under the sun except himself. Her protestations were feeble, too, for though he was literally correct in his assertion, he was virtually only half in error.

The house of her father's sister was a prison to Phyllis. She had quite recently undergone experience of its gloom; and when her father went on to direct her to pack what would be necessary for her to take, her heart died within her. In after years she never attempted to excuse her conduct during this week of agitation; but the result of her self-communing was that she decided to join in the scheme of her lover and his friend, and fly to the country which he had coloured with such lovely hues in her imagination. She always said that the one feature of his proposal which overcame her hesitation was the obvious purity and straight-forwardness of his intentions. He showed himself to be so virtuous and kind; he treated her with a respect to which she had never before been accustomed; and she was braced to the obvious risks of the voyage by her confidence in him.

★   ★   ★   ★

It was on a soft, dark evening of the following week that they engaged in the adventure. Tina was to meet her at a point in the highway at which the lane to the village branched off. Christoph was to go ahead of them to the harbour where the boat lay, row it round the Nothe—or Look-out as it was called in those days—and pick them up on the other side of the promontory, which they were to reach by crossing the harbour-bridge, and climbing over the Look-out hill.

As soon as her father had ascended to his room she left the house, and, bundle in hand, proceeded at a trot along the lane. At such an

She left the house and proceeded along the lane.

hour not a soul was afoot anywhere in the village, and she reached the junction of the lane with the highway unobserved. Here she took up her position in the obscurity formed by the angle of a fence, whence she could discern everyone who approached along the turnpike-road, without being herself seen.

She had not remained thus waiting for her lover longer than a minute—though from the tension of her nerves the lapse of even that short time was trying—when, instead of the expected footsteps, the stage-coach could be heard descending the hill. She knew that Tina would not show himself till the road was clear, and waited impatiently for the coach to pass. Nearing the corner where she was it slackened speed, and, instead of going by as usual, drew up within a few yards of her. A passenger alighted, and she heard his voice. It was Humphrey Gould's.

He had brought a friend with him, and luggage. The luggage was deposited on the grass, and the coach went on its route to the royal watering-place.

'I wonder where that young man is with the horse and trap?' said her former admirer to his companion. 'I hope we shan't have to wait here long. I told him half-past nine o'clock precisely.'

'Have you got her present safe?'

'Phyllis's? Oh, yes. It is in this trunk. I hope it will please her.'

'Of course it will. What woman would not be pleased with such a handsome peace-offering?'

'Well—she deserves it. I've treated her rather badly. But she has been in my mind these last two days much more than I should care to confess to everybody. Ah, well; I'll say no more about that. It cannot be that she is so bad as they make out. I am quite sure that a girl of her good wit would know better than to get entangled with any of those Hanoverian soldiers. I won't believe it of her, and there's an end on't.'

More words in the same strain were casually dropped as the two men waited; words which revealed to her, as by a sudden illumination, the enormity of her conduct. The conversation was at length cut off by the arrival of the man with the vehicle. The luggage was placed in it, and they mounted, and were driven on in the direction from which she had just come.

Phyllis was so conscience-stricken that she was at first inclined to follow them; but a moment's reflection led her to feel that it would only be bare justice to Matthäus to wait till he arrived, and explain candidly that she had changed her mind—difficult as the struggle would be when she stood face to face with him. She bitterly reproached herself for having believed reports which represented Humphrey Gould as false to his engagement, when, from what she now heard from his own lips, she gathered that he had been living full of trust in her. But she knew well enough who had won her love. Without him her life seemed a dreary prospect, yet the more she looked at his proposal the more she feared to accept it—so wild as it was, so vague, so venturesome. She had promised Humphrey Gould, and it was only his assumed faithlessness which had led her to treat that promise as nought. His solicitude in bringing her these gifts touched her; her promise must be kept, and esteem must take the place of love. She would preserve her self-respect. She would stay at home, and marry him, and suffer.

Phyllis had thus braced herself to an exceptional fortitude when, a few minutes later, the outline of Matthäus Tina appeared behind a field-gate, over which he lightly leapt as she stepped forward. There was no evading it, he pressed her to his breast.

'It is the first and last time!' she wildly thought as she stood encircled by his arms.

How Phyllis got through the terrible ordeal of that night she could never clearly recollect. She always attributed her success in carrying out her resolve to her lover's honour, for as soon as she declared to him in feeble words that she had changed her mind, and felt that she could not, dared not, fly with him, he forbore to urge her, grieved as he was at her decision. Unscrupulous pressure on his part, seeing how romantically she had become attached to him, would no doubt have turned the balance in his favour. But he did nothing to tempt her unduly or unfairly.

On her side, fearing for his safety, she begged him to remain. This, he declared, could not be. 'I cannot break faith with my friend,' said he. Had he stood alone he would have abandoned his plan. But Christoph, with the boat and compass and chart, was waiting on the shore; the tide would soon turn; his mother had been warned of his coming; so he must.

Many precious minutes were lost while he tarried, unable to tear himself away, Phyllis held to her resolve, though it cost her many a bitter pang. At last they parted, and he went down the hill. Before his footsteps had quite died away she felt a desire to behold at least his outline once more, and running noiselessly after him regained view of his diminishing figure. For one moment she was sufficiently excited to be on the point of rushing forward and linking her fate with his. But she could not. The courage which at the critical instant failed Cleopatra of Egypt could scarcely be expected of Phyllis Grove.

A dark shape, similar to his own, joined him in the highway. It was Christoph, his friend. She could see no more; they had hastened on in the direction of the town and harbour, four miles ahead. With a feeling akin to despair she turned and slowly pursued her way homeward.

Tattoo sounded in the camp; but there was no camp for her now. It was as dead as the camp of the Assyrians after the passage of the Destroying Angel.

She noiselessly entered the house, seeing nobody, and went to bed. Grief, which kept her awake at first, ultimately wrapped her in a heavy sleep. The next morning her father met her at the foot of the stairs.

'Mr Gould is come!' he said triumphantly.

Humphrey was staying at the inn, and had already called to inquire for her. He had brought her a present of a very handsome looking-glass in a frame of *repoussé* silverwork, which her father held in his hand. He had promised to call again in the course of an hour, to ask Phyllis to walk with him.

Pretty mirrors were rarer in country-houses at that day than they are now, and the one before her won Phyllis's admiration. She looked into it, saw how heavy her eyes were, and endeavoured to brighten them. She was in that wretched state of mind which leads a woman to move mechanically onward in what she conceives to be her allotted path. Mr Humphrey Gould had, in his undemonstrative way, been adhering all along to the old understanding; it was for her to do the same, and to say not a word of her own lapse. She put on her bonnet and tippet, and when he arrived at the hour named she was at the door awaiting him.

Phyllis thanked him for his beautiful gift; but the talking was soon entirely on Humphrey's side as they walked along. He told her of the latest movements of the world of fashion—a subject which she willingly discussed to the exclusion of anything more personal—and his measured language helped to still her disquieted heart and brain. Had not her own sadness been what it was she must have observed his embarrassment. At last he abruptly changed the subject.

'I am glad you are pleased with my little present,' he said. 'The truth is that I brought it to propitiate 'ee, and to get you to help me out of a mighty difficulty.'

It was inconceivable to Phyllis that this independent bachelor—whom she admired in some respects—could have a difficulty.

'Phyllis—I'll tell you my secret at once; for I have a monstrous secret to confide before I can ask your counsel. The case is, then, that I am married: yes, I have privately married a dear young belle; and if you knew her, and I hope you will, you would say everything in her praise. But she is not quite the one that my father would have chosen for me—you know the paternal ideas as well as I—and I have kept it secret. There will be a terrible noise, no doubt; but I think that with your help I may get over it. If you would only do me this good turn—when I have told my father, I mean—say that you never could have married me, you know, or something of that sort—'pon my life it will help to smooth the way vastly. I am so anxious to win him round to my point of view, and not to cause any estrangement.'

What Phyllis replied she scarcely knew, or how she counselled him as to his unexpected situation. Yet the relief that his announcement brought her was perceptible. To have confided her trouble in return was what her aching heart longed to do; and had Humphrey been a woman she would instantly have poured out her tale. But to him she feared to confess; and there was a real reason for silence, till a sufficient time had elapsed to allow her lover and his comrade to get out of harm's way.

As soon as she reached home again she sought a solitary place, and spent the time in half regretting that she had not gone away, and in dreaming over the meeting with Matthäus Tina from their beginning to their end. In his own country, amongst his own countrywomen, he would possibly soon forget her, even to her very name.

Her listlessness was such that she did not go out of the house for several days. There came a morning which broke in fog and mist, behind which the dawn could be discerned in greenish grey; and the outlines of the tents, and the rows of horses at the ropes. The smoke from the canteen fires drooped heavily.

The spot at the bottom of her garden, where she had been accustomed to climb the wall to meet Matthäus, was the only inch of English ground in which she took any interest; and in spite of the disagreeable haze prevailing she walked out there till she reached the well-known corner. Every blade of grass was weighted with little liquid globes, and slugs and snails had crept out upon the plots. She could hear the faint noises from the camp, and in the other direction the trot of farmers on the road to the town, for it was market-day. She observed that her frequent visits to this corner had quite trodden down the grass in the angle of the wall, and left marks of garden soil on the stepping-stones by which she had mounted to look over the top. Seldom having gone there till dusk, she had not considered that her traces might be visible by day. Perhaps it was these which had revealed her trysts to her father.

While she paused in melancholy regard, she fancied that the customary sounds from the tents were changing their character. Indifferent as Phyllis was to camp doings now, she mounted by the steps to the old place. What she beheld at first awed and perplexed her; then she stood rigid, her fingers hooked to the wall, her eyes staring out of her head, and her face as if hardened to stone.

A firing-party of twenty-four men stood ready with levelled carbines. The commanding officer, who had his sword drawn, waved it through some cuts of the sword-exercise till he reached the downward stroke, whereat the firing party discharged their volley. The two victims fell, one upon his face across his coffin, the other backwards.

As the volley resounded there arose a shriek from the wall of Dr Grove's garden, and someone fell down inside; but nobody among the spectators without noticed at the time. The two executed Hussars were Matthäus Tina and his friend Christoph. The soldiers on guard placed the bodies in the coffins almost instantly; but the colonel of the regiment, an Englishman, rode up and exclaimed in a stern voice: 'Turn them out—as an example to the men!'

The coffins were lifted endwise, and the dead Germans flung out upon their faces on the grass. Then all the regiments wheeled in sections, and marched past the spot in slow time. When the survey was over the corpses were again coffined, and borne away.

Meanwhile Dr Grove, attracted by the noise of the volley, had rushed out into his garden, where he saw his wretched daughter lying motionless against the wall. She was taken indoors, but it was long before she recovered consciousness; and for weeks they despaired of her reason.

It transpired that the luckless deserters from the York Hussars had cut the boat from her moorings in the adjacent harbour, according to their plan, and, with two other comrades, who were smarting under ill-treatment from their colonel, had sailed in safety across the Channel. But mistaking their bearings they steered into Jersey, thinking that island the French coast. Here they were perceived to be deserters, and delivered up to the authorities. Matthäus and Christoph interceded for the other two at the court-martial, saying that it was entirely by the former's representations that these were induced to go. Their sentence was accordingly commuted to flogging, the death punishment being reserved for their leaders.

The visitor to the well-known old Georgian watering-place, who may care to ramble to the neighbouring village under the hills, and examine the register of burials, will there find two entries in these words.

Matth: Tina (Corpl.) in His Majesty's Regmt. of York Hussars, and Shot for Desertion, was Buried June 30th, 1801, aged 22 years. Born in the town of Saarbruk, Germany.

Christoph Bless, belonging to His Majesty's Regmt. of York Hussars, who was Shot for Desertion, was Buried June 30th, 1801, aged 22 years. Born at Lothaargen, Alsatia.

Their graves were dug at the back of the little church, near the wall. There is no memorial to mark the spot, but Phyllis pointed it out to me. While she lived she used to keep their mounds neat; but now they are overgrown with nettles, and sunk nearly flat. The older villagers, however, who know of the episode from their parents, still recollect the place where the soldiers lie. Phyllis lies near.

THE RESCUE
OF LORNA DOONE

R D Blackmore

*John Ridd had first seen Lorna Doone when as a boy he was returning
home from Blundell's School; one of the Doones was carrying the
little girl flung across his saddlebow. The Doones were a band of fierce
and hated outlaws living in Glen Doone, and it was they who had
murdered John's father. John, bent on revenge, finds his way into the
Doone valley, and there meets Lorna. They continue to see each
other secretly as they grow up and fall in love. When Lorna tells John
one day that she is to be starved until she consents to marry Carver
Doone, he decides the time has come to take her away from her captors.*

To my great delight, I found the weather, not often friendly to lovers,
and lately seeming so hostile, had in the most important matter done
me a signal service. For when I had promised to take my love from the
power of those wretches, the only way of escape apparent lay through
the main Doone-gate. For though I might climb the cliffs myself,
especially with the snow to aid me, I durst not try to fetch Lorna up
them, even if she were not half-starved, as well as partly frozen; and
as for Gwenny's door, as we called it (that is to say, the little entrance
from the wooded hollow), it was snowed up long ago to the level of
the hills around. Therefore I was at my wit's end, how to get them out;
the passage by the Doone-gate being long, and dark, and difficult, and
leading to such a weary circuit among the snowy moors and hills.

But now, being homeward-bound by the shortest possible track, I
slipped along between the bonfire and the boundary cliffs, where I
found a caved way of snow behind a sort of avalanche: so that if the
Doones had been keeping watch (which they were not doing, but
revelling) they could scarcely have discovered me. And when I came
to my old ascent, where I had often scaled the cliff and made across the

mountains, it struck me that I would just have a look at my first and painful entrance, to wit, the water-slide. I never for a moment imagined that this could help me now; for I never had dared to descend it, even in the finest weather; still I had a curiosity to know what my old friend was like, with so much snow upon him. But, to my very great surprise, there was scarcely any snow there at all, though plenty curling high over head from the cliff, like bolsters over it. Probably the sweeping of the north-east wind up the narrow chasm had kept the showers from blocking it, although the water had no power under the bitter grip of frost. All my water-slide was now less a slide than a path of ice; furrowed where the waters ran over fluted ridges; seamed where wind had tossed and combed them, even while congealing; and crossed with little steps wherever the freezing torrent lingered. And here and there the ice was fibred with the trail of sludge-weed, slanting from the side, and matted, so as to make resting-place.

Lo, it was easy track and channel, as if for the very purpose made, down which I could guide my sledge, with Lorna sitting in it. There were only two things to be feared; one, lest the rolls of snow above should fall in and bury us; the other lest we should rush too fast, and so be carried headlong into the black whirlpool at the bottom, the middle of which was still unfrozen, and looking more horrible by the contrast. Against this danger I made provision by fixing a stout bar across; but of the other we must take our chance, and trust ourselves to providence.

I hastened home at my utmost speed, and told my mother for God's sake to keep the house up till my return, and to have plenty of fire blazing, and plenty of water boiling, and food enough hot for a dozen people, and the best bed aired with the warming-pan. Dear mother smiled softly at my excitement, though her own was not much less, I am sure, and enhanced by sore anxiety. Then I gave very strict directions to Annie, and praised her a little, and kissed her; and I even endeavoured to flatter Eliza, lest she should be disagreeable.

After this I took some brandy, both within and about me; the former because I had sharp work to do; and the latter in fear of whatever might happen, in such great cold, to my comrades. Also I carried some other provisions, grieving much at their coldness; and then I went to the upper linhay, and took our new light pony-sled, which had been made almost as much for pleasure as for business; though God only knows how our girls could have found any pleasure in bumping along so. On the snow, however, it ran as sweetly as if it had been made for it; yet I durst not take the pony with it; in the first place, because his hoofs would break through the ever-shifting surface of the light and piling snow; and secondly, because those ponies, coming from the forest, have a dreadful trick of neighing, and most of all in frosty weather.

Therefore I girded my own body with a dozen turns of hay-rope, twisting both the ends in under at the bottom of my breast, and winding the hay on the skew a little, that the hemp thong might not slip between, and so cut me in the drawing. I put a good piece of spare rope in the sled, and the cross-seat with the back to it, which was stuffed with our own wool, as well as two or three fur coats: and then just as I was starting, out came Annie, in spite of the cold, panting for fear of missing me, and with nothing on her head, but a lanthorn in one hand.

'Oh, John, here is the most wonderful thing! Mother has never shown it before; and I can't think how she could make up her mind. She had gotten it in a great well of a cupboard, with camphor, and spirits, and lavender. Lizzie says it is a most magnificent sealskin cloak, worth fifty pounds, or a farthing.'

'At any rate it is soft and warm,' said I, very calmly flinging it into the bottom of the sled. 'Tell mother I will put it over Lorna's feet.'

'Lorna's feet! Oh, you great fool,' cried Annie, for the first time reviling me; 'over her shoulders; and be proud, you very stupid John.'

'It is not good enough for her feet,' I answered, with strong emphasis; 'but don't tell mother I said so, Annie. Only thank her very kindly.'

With that I drew my traces hard, and set my ashen staff into the snow, and struck out with my best foot foremost (the best one at snowshoes, I mean), and the sled came after me as lightly as a dog might follow; and Annie with the lanthorn seemed to be left behind and waiting, like a pretty lamp-post.

The full moon rose as bright behind me as a patin of pure silver, casting on the snow long shadows of the few things left above, burned rock, and shaggy foreland, and the labouring trees. In the great white desolation, distance was a mocking vision: hills looked nigh, and valleys far; when hills were far and valleys nigh. And the misty breath of frost, piercing through the ribs of rock, striking to the pith of trees, creeping to the heart of man, lay along the hollow places, like a serpent sloughing.

Even as my own gaunt shadow (travestied as if I were the moonlight's daddy-long-legs) went before me down the slope; even I, the shadow's master, who had tried in vain to cough, when coughing brought good liquorice, felt a pressure on my bosom, and a husking in my throat.

However, I went on quietly, and at a very tidy speed; being only too thankful that the snow had ceased, and no wind as yet arisen. And from the ring of low white vapour girding all the verge of sky, and from the rosy blue above, and the shafts of starlight set upon a quivering bow, as well as from the moon itself and the light behind it, having learned the signs of frost from its bitter twinges, I knew that we should have a night as keen as ever England felt. Nevertheless, I had work enough to keep me warm if I managed it. The question was, could I contrive to save my darling from it?

Daring not to risk my sled by any fall from the valley-cliffs, I dragged it very carefully up the steep incline of ice, through the narrow chasm, and so to the very brink and verge where first I had seen my Lorna, in the fishing days of boyhood. As then I had a trident fork, for sticking of the loaches, so now I had a strong ash stake, to lay across from rock to rock, and break the speed of descending. With this I moored the sled quite safe, at the very lip of the chasm, where all was now substantial ice, green and black in the moonlight; and then I set off up the valley, skirting along one side of it.

The stack-fire still was burning strongly, but with more of heat than blaze; and many of the younger Doones were playing on the verge of it, the children making rings of fire, and their mothers watching them. All the grave and reverend warriors, having heard of rheumatism, were inside of log and stone, in the two lowest houses, with enough of candles burning to make our list of sheep come short.

All these I passed, without the smallest risk of difficulty, walking up the channel of drift which I spoke of once before. And then I crossed, with more care, and to the door of Lorna's house, and made the sign, and listened, after taking my snow-shoes off.

But no one came, as I expected, neither could I espy a light. And I seemed to hear a faint low sound, like the moaning of the snow-wind. Then I knocked again more loudly, with a knocking at my heart; and receiving no answer, set all my power at once against the door. In a moment it flew inwards, and I glided along the passage with my feet still slippery. There in Lorna's room I saw, by the moonlight flowing in, a sight which drove me beyond sense.

Lorna was behind a chair, crouching in the corner, with her hands up, and a crucifix, or something that looked like it. In the middle of the room lay Gwenny Carfax, stupid, yet with one hand clutching the ankle of a struggling man. Another man stood above my Lorna, trying to draw the chair away. In a moment I had him round the waist, and he went out of the window with a mighty crash of glass; luckily for him that window had no bars like some of them. Then I took the other man by the neck; and he could not plead for mercy. I bore him out of the house as lightly as I would bear a baby, yet squeezing his throat a little more than I fain would do to an infant. By the bright moonlight I saw that I carried Marwood de Whichehalse. For his father's sake I spared him, and because he had been my schoolfellow: but with every muscle of my body strung with indignation, I cast him, like a skittle, from me into a snowdrift, which closed over him. Then I looked for the other fellow, tossed through Lorna's window; and found him lying stunned and bleeding, neither able to groan yet. Charleworth Doone, if his gushing blood did not much mislead me.

It was no time to linger now: I fastened my shoes in a moment, and caught up my own darling with her head upon my shoulder, where she whispered faintly; and telling Gwenny to follow me, or else I would come back for her, if she could not walk the snow, I ran the whole distance to my sled, caring not who might follow me. Then by the time I had set up Lorna, beautiful and smiling, with the sealskin cloak all over her, sturdy Gwenny came along, having trudged in the track of my snow-shoes, although with two bags on her back. I set her in beside her mistress, to support her, and keep warm; and then with one look back at the glen, which had been so long my home of heart, I hung behind the sled, and launched it down the steep and dangerous way.

Though the cliffs were black above us, and the road unseen in front, and a great white grave of snow might at a single word come down, Lorna was as calm and happy as an infant in its bed. She knew that I was with her; and when I told her not to speak, she touched my hand in silence. Gwenny was in a much greater fright, having never seen such a thing before, neither knowing what it is to yield to pure love's confidence. I could hardly keep her quiet, without making a noise myself.

I cast him, like a skittle, into a snowdrift . . .

With my staff from rock to rock, and my weight thrown backward, I broke the sled's too rapid way, and brought my grown love safely out, by the self-same road which first had led me to her girlish fancy, and my boyish slavery.

Unpursued, yet looking back as if some one must be after us, we skirted round the black whirling pool, and gained the meadows beyond it. Here there was hard collar work, the track being all uphill and rough; and Gwenny wanted to jump out, to lighten the sled and to push behind. But I would not hear of it; because it was now so deadly cold, and I feared that Lorna might get frozen, without having Gwenny to keep her warm. And after all, it was the sweetest labour I had ever known in all my life, to be sure that I was pulling Lorna, and pulling her to our own farmhouse.

Gwenny's nose was touched with frost, before we had gone much further, because she would not keep it quiet and snug beneath the seal-skin. And here I had to stop in the moonlight (which was very dangerous) and rub it with a clove of snow, as Eliza had taught me; and Gwenny scolding all the time, as if myself had frozen it. Lorna was now so far oppressed with all the troubles of the evening, and the joy that followed them, as well as by the piercing cold and difficulty of breathing, that she lay quite motionless, like fairest wax in the moonlight—when we stole a glance at her, beneath the dark folds of the cloak; and I thought that she was falling into the heavy snow-sleep, whence there is no awaking.

Therefore I drew my traces tight, and set my whole strength to the business; and we slipped along at a merry pace, although with many joltings, which must have sent my darling out into the cold snow-drifts, but for the short strong arm of Gwenny. And so in about an hour's time, in spite of many hindrances, we came home to the old courtyard, and all the dogs saluted us. My heart was quivering, and my cheeks as hot as the Doones' bonfire, with wondering both what Lorna would think of our farmyard, and what my mother would think of her. Upon the former subject my anxiety was wasted, for Lorna neither saw a thing, nor even opened her heavy eyes. And as to what mother would think of her, she was certain not to think at all, until she had cried over her.

And so indeed it came to pass. Even at this length of time, I can hardly tell it, although so bright before my mind, because it moves my heart so. The sled was at the open door, with only Lorna in it: for Gwenny Carfax had jumped out, and hung back in the clearing, giving any reason rather than the only true one—that she would not be intruding. At the door were all our people; first of course Betty Muxworthy, teaching me how to draw the sled, as if she had been born in it, and flourishing with a great broom, wherever a speck of snow lay. Then dear Annie, and old Molly (who was very quiet, and counted almost for nobody), and behind them mother, looking as if she wanted to come first, but doubted how the manners lay. In the distance Lizzie stood, fearful of encouraging, but unable to keep out of it.

Betty was going to poke her broom right in under the sealskin cloak, where Lorna lay unconscious, and where her precious breath hung frozen, like a silver cobweb; but I caught up Betty's broom, and flung it clean away over the corn chamber; and then I put the others by, and fetched my mother forward.

'You shall see her first,' I said; 'is she not your daughter? Hold the light there, Annie.'

Dear mother's hands were quick and trembling, as she opened the shining folds; and there she saw my Lorna sleeping, with her black hair all dishevelled, and she bent and kissed her forehead, and only said, 'God bless her, John!' And then she was taken with violent weeping, and I was forced to hold her.

'Us may tich of her now, I rackon,' said Betty in her most jealous way: 'Annie, tak her by the head, and I'll tak her by the toesen. No taime to stand here like girt gawks. Don'ee tak on zo, missus. Ther be vainer vish in the zea—Lor, but her be a booty!'

With this, they carried her into the house, Betty chattering all the while, and going on now about Lorna's hands, and the others crowding round her, so that I thought I was not wanted among so many women, and should only get the worst of it, and perhaps do harm to my darling. Therefore I went and brought Gwenny in, and gave her a potful of bacon and peas, and an iron spoon to eat it with, which she did right heartily.

Then I asked her how she could have been such a fool as to let those two vile fellows enter the house where Lorna was; and she accounted for it so naturally, that I could only blame myself. For my agreement had been to give one loud knock (if you happen to remember) and after that two little knocks. Well, these two drunken rogues had come; and one, being very drunk indeed, had given a great thump; and then nothing more to do with it; and the other, being three-quarters drunk, had followed his leader (as one might say) but feebly, and making two of it. Whereupon up jumped Lorna, and declared that her John was there.

All this Gwenny told me shortly, between the whiles of eating, and even while she licked the spoon: and then there came a message for me, that my love was sensible, and was seeking all around for me. Then I told Gwenny to hold her tongue (whatever she did, among us), and not to trust to women's words; and she told me they all were liars, as she had found out long ago; and the only thing to believe in was an honest man, when found. Thereupon I could have kissed her, as a sort of tribute, liking to be appreciated; yet the peas upon her lips made me think about it; and thought is fatal to action. So I went to see my dear.

That sight I shall not forget; till my dying head falls back, and my breast can lift no more. I know not whether I were then more blessed, or harrowed by it. For in the settle was my Lorna, propped with pillows round her, and her clear hands spread sometimes to the blazing fireplace. In her eyes no knowledge was of any thing around her, neither in her neck the sense of leaning towards any thing. Only both her lovely hands were entreating something, to spare her or to love her; and the lines of supplication quivered in her sad white face.

'All go away except my mother,' I said very quietly, but so that I would be obeyed; and everybody knew it. Then mother came to me alone; and she said, 'The frost is in her brain: I have heard of this before, John.' 'Mother, I will have it out,' was all that I could answer her; 'leave her to me altogether: only you sit there and watch.' For I felt that Lorna knew me, and no other soul but me; and that if not interfered with, she would soon come home to me. Therefore I sat gently by her, leaving nature, as it were, to her own good time and will. And presently the glance that watched me, as at distance and in doubt, began to flutter and to brighten, and to deepen into kindness, then to beam with trust and love, and then with gathering tears to falter, and in shame to turn away. But the small entreating hands found their way, as if by instinct, to my great protecting palms; and trembled there, and rested there.

For a little while we lingered thus, neither wishing to move away, neither caring to look beyond the presence of the other; both alike so full of hope, and comfort, and true happiness; if only the world would let us be. And then a little sob disturbed us, and mother tried to make believe that she was only coughing. But Lorna, guessing who she was, jumped up so very rashly that she almost set her frock on fire from the great ash-log; and away she ran to the old oak chair, where mother was by the clock-case pretending to be knitting, and she took the work from mother's hands, and laid them both upon her head, kneeling humbly, and looking up.

'God bless you, my fair mistress!' said mother, bending nearer, and then as Lorna's gaze prevailed, 'God bless you, my sweet child!'

And so she went to mother's heart, by the very nearest road, even as she had come to mine; I mean the road of pity, smoothed by grace, and youth, and gentleness.

THE CENTURION'S ESCAPE

Anonymous

'How cursedly hot it is,' muttered the Centurion Septimius to his lieutenant, grave old Lepidus, as he lay half stripped in the shade of his tent, longing for the northern wind.

And he might well say so. The place was Syene, the time the month of August, and the almost vertical sun was pouring down his rays with a fierceness such as the Roman officer had never felt before.

Septimius and his cohort had been marched up to Syene to hold in check the inhabitants of the neighbourhood, who, servile in general, and little caring then as now who was their master, provided the taxes were not too heavy, had been stirred up by the priests to a state of most unwonted agitation, in consequence of some insult offered by the Roman soldiery to the sacred animals of the district.

The palm trees were standing motionless, not a breath stirring their long hanging branches; the broad, swollen Nile was glittering like molten metal as he rolled majestically to the sea. In the background the steep sandy ridges and black crags were baking in the sun, and the only sound that broke the silence was the roar of the distant cataract.

'Curse these Egyptians and their gods,' muttered poor Septimius.

'Hush, hush, Septimius,' answered Lepidus, his second-in-command, 'you shouldn't ventilate those free-thinking opinions of yours so openly. Whatever you *think*, keep a check on your tongue, for the old priesthood is jealous and powerful even yet, and strange stories are told of their secret doings.'

'A fig for the priesthood!' quoth Septimius. 'What care I for Apis or Osiris either? I am a Roman citizen and a Roman soldier. I fear no man but my superior officer, and I know no god but the Emperor.'

'Mark my words,' was the reply. 'Antony was a greater man than you, Septimius, and *he* bowed the knee to Apis and Osiris too; why, they say he was consecrated himself, and stood high in the priestly ranks, and yet he crouched like a beaten hound to old Petamon, the priest of Isis, and obeyed his very nod. I have heard strange things of that Petamon; men say he knew the old Egyptian secrets, and could raise the very dead from their long sleep to answer him. And his grandson and successor is a mightier enchanter than his sire. It was he that stirred up these poor Egyptian slaves almost to rebellion not ten days ago, because one of the legionaries broke the head of a dirty ape that he caught stealing the stores. They say he is at Philae just now concocting some new plot; so, my good fellow, keep your eyes open and your mouth shut—if you can.'

Septimius laughed, half good-naturedly, half contemptuously; and, humming a stave of Horace, turned in to take a nap, while Lepidus went round the sentries to see that none was sleeping at his post.

It was evening, the sun had set some half-hour before; and the sky, after melting through all the hues of the rainbow, had merged in one delicious violet, in which the pure clear moon and the planet Venus were shining with a glorious light such as they never attain in duller climes. Septimius, shaking off his drowsiness, left his tent to saunter through the village and see how his troops were faring.

The beauty and stillness of the night tempted him to extend his ramble. The outskirts of the town were soon passed, the few dogs he met shrank cowering from before his tall form and the clank of his good sword at his side, and in a few moments he was alone in the desert. He had more than once followed the same track towards the now silent quarries, where the old Egyptians once hewed those blocks of granite which are a wonder to all succeeding ages. It was the same scene, yet how different! When he had marched over the ground once before at the head of his legionaries to check an incursion of one of the marauding desert tribes, the sky seemed brass, the earth iron, the sun was blazing overhead like a ball of molten metal, and scorching all colour and life out of the landscape; the heat, reflected from the black basalt and red syenite rocks, had beaten on his armour almost beyond endurance, while his stout soldiers could barely struggle on through the heavy sand, sighing and groaning for one drop of water where none was to be had.

How different it was now; the moon, hanging low in the heavens, threw the long black shadows of the craggy rocks over the silvered sand; and the air was deliciously cool and fresh after the extreme heat of the day.

So he wandered on till he reached a huge boulder, on which some old Pharaoh, now forgotten, had carved the record of his marches and victories.

Suddenly from behind the boulder an old man advanced to him, and bowing low, with the cringing servility to which the lower classes of the Egyptians had been reduced by long ages of tyranny, prostrated himself at the feet of the Centurion, and in broken Greek craved a hearing.

'My lord Centurion,' said the beggar, 'I have followed your steps for days in the hope of obtaining a hearing. My tongue is Greek, but my heart is true. You have heard of the Egyptian priesthood and their wiles; not long ago one of your nation, a Centurion like yourself, fell into their hands, and they hold him captive in the neighbourhood. If you would deliver him come here tomorrow night, and come alone; I will tell you then what must be done, but I cannot now—meanwhile farewell.'

And before the Centurion could utter a word he had vanished behind the rocks.

'By Castor and Pollux,' muttered Septimius, 'was ever a decent fellow—not that I am a particularly decent fellow—in such a fix before? It may be a trap set for me; yet surely they dare not touch a soldier of the Emperor's—a Centurion too,' he said. 'Ay, poor Claudius vanished a month ago; they said it was a crocodile, but none saw it—yes, it must be Claudius; go I will, let Lepidus say what he likes. But wait, if I tell Lepidus he will have my steps dogged, or some such nonsense. I'll keep my own counsel; I'll go, and go alone.' With a brisk step he turned on his heel and made his way back to his quarters.

The beggar stood behind the rock, his keen black eyes glittering with the light of triumph; his long white beard fell off, and the rags dropped from his shoulders as he joined his companion, who was lying hidden behind the rock. He drew himself up to his full stature, and his haughty step and proud port marked Petamon, the son of Osorkon, and grandson of Petamon, the High Priest of Isis at Philae.

'Hey, Sheshonk,' he laughed to his subordinate, with a snort of scorn, 'I have baited the trap for my eagle right daintily, and the noble bird shall have his wings clipped 'ere long. He mocks the divine Apis, does he, and blasphemes the Ape of Thoth!'

'Well done, Petamon,' quoth Sheshonk, the assistant priest, whose low forehead, heavy brow, and sensual lips were in strange contrast to his companion's face. 'What a pity there is nobody here to listen to you, and that such eloquence should be thrown away upon me, who knows, as well as you do yourself, if the truth were told, that Apis is only a bull after all, and Thoth's ape is a very dirty troublesome ape;

at least the one I had charge of at Hermopolis was.'

'Peace, fool,' replied Petamon, with an angry glare of his eye. The beasts are but beasts, that *I* know as well as you; but the beast is only the type of the divinity, whom the vulgar may not know. Enough.'

The rest of their conversation was lost in the distance as they slowly wended their way to the south.

Next day Septimius was somewhat thoughtful; he retired early to his tent on the pretence of weariness, and when all was still he stole out of the town as before. The hour was the same, but how different this night was from the last. A tornado had been blowing from the south all day, raising the sand in huge clouds, which obscured everything and nearly choked man and beast with a fine, penetrating dust. Even now the air was hot and depressing, the sand felt heavy under foot, and the Centurion's heart was so full of foreboding that more than once he had almost turned back.

At last he reached the granite boulder, and, crouching in its shade as

The four mysterious phantoms raised the litter and bore it across the sands.

before, sat the beggar. He rose as the Centurion approached, and beckoned him silently to proceed. Somewhat puzzled, Septimius obeyed and followed in silence, plodding wearily through the deep sand. At last the beggar turned.

'Sir Centurion,' he said, 'the night is hot and the way heavy; let me ease you of your sword'; and before Septimius could argue or resist, his nimble hands had unstrapped the belt and slung the sword over his own shoulder. 'What men you Romans are!' he continued, slightly raising his voice as they passed along a narrow track between high rocks on either side. 'You fear nothing in heaven or on earth. I verily believe you would make beef-steaks of the divine Apis'; and he halted full in the way and seemed absolutely to grow before the Centurion's eyes, he loomed so large and majestic in the moonlight, while his eyes glared like blazing coals with hatred and revenge.

The Centurion recoiled, and at the same moment two from each side, four strange white figures, each with the head of a hawk, surmounted by the disc of the sun, glided forth and laid hands on him. Septimius struggled like a snared lion, but it was of no avail; he threatened them with the wrath of the Emperor, and they answered with a low mocking laugh. He made one furious rush at the former beggar who had betrayed him, and clutched him by the robe. Petamon quietly threw the sword far away over the sand and crossed his arms, while his ghostly allies advanced to the rescue. In another moment the prisoner was torn away, but not before he had rent off a fragment of the priest's robes, which fell upon the sand. His good sword was gone far beyond his reach, and after a few frantic plunges he was bound hand and foot and lashed to a rude litter which was brought from behind the rock. The four mysterious phantoms silently raised the litter and bore it swiftly across the sands, while Petamon, with a vigour remarkable in one so far advanced in years, led the way.

They had advanced along the sandy tract for some distance when suddenly the eye of Septimius, who could just raise his head and look forward by straining painfully against his bonds, caught the glimmer of the moonlight on the water, and before him rose perhaps the most unearthly, most beautiful scene that can meet the eyes of man.

Ruined as it now is, with its broken columns and shattered piers, marked at every turn by the hand of the destroyer, Philae, and Philae by moonlight, is wondrously lovely; what must it have been then?

In the midst of a quiet lagoon lay the Sacred Island, enclosed by hills, on whose rugged sides the black basalt rocks were piled in the most magnificent confusion—a green spot in the midst of a desert of stone—and, amid the grove of palms upon its shore, rose the roofs of temples and the tops of huge pyramidal gateways, while the solemn moonlight poured over all. A boat, manned by four more of the strange hawk-headed beings, was anchored at the shore. Silently the priest embarked, silently Septimius was lifted on board, silently the rowers bent to their oars, and in a few minutes they were passing along under the massy wall which rises sheer out of the water on the western side.

Suddenly the boat stopped and the priest struck the wall thrice, repeating each time, 'In the name of Him who sleeps at Philae.' Silently a portion of the apparently massy wall swung back and disclosed a narrow stair, up which they carried the Centurion; and by a side door entered the outer court. Before them rose the huge gateway, on each of whose towers was carved the giant semblance of a conqueror grasping with his left hand a group of captives by the hair, while he lifts the right to strike the death-blow. They hurried on through the great Hall of Pillars up a narrow stair, and, opening a small aperture, more like a window than a door, thrust in the Centurion, and left him, bound hand and foot, to his own reflections.

Next morning Lepidus was early astir, and, after going his rounds, entered the tent of Septimius. It was empty, the bed had not been slept on, and there were no signs whatever of the tenant. 'Mad boy,' muttered Lepidus; 'off on some frolic as usual. I must hush it up, or Septimius, great though his family interest be, will get but a rough welcome from the General on our return.'

Noonday and evening came and went, and still Septimius was absent; and next morning, Lepidus, blaming himself much for having delayed so long, gave the alarm that the Centurion had vanished or been spirited away, and instituted a regular inquiry. Little information could be elicited. One of the sentries had noticed Septimius wandering away towards the desert, but he was too much accustomed to his officer's little vagaries to take much note of the fact.

Towards evening one of the sergeants craved an audience with him, and when they were alone together produced the Centurion's sword and a piece of a heavy golden fringe. He had struck into the desert, come upon a spot where there were evident marks of a struggle, and picked up the sword and torn fringe lying on the ground. Sergeant and officer looked at each other, and the same fear clouded the faces of both.

'Petamon is at Philae?' inquired Lepidus.

'He is, sir.'

'Then may Jove the Preserver help the poor boy, for he will need all his help. I see it now: his foolish scoffs at the gods have reached the ears of the crafty priest, who has hated us Romans bitterly for long, and he has kidnapped the lad. We may be too late to save him not too late for revenge. Muster the men at once and let us to Philae—quick!'

In half an hour the cohort were tramping through the sand under the still moonlight, and an hour more brought them to the banks of the quiet river. There was no boat, and they had to halt till morning broke.

At sunrise a boat was brought from the neighbouring village, and Lepidus, embarking with a portion of his troop, was rowed over to the Sacred Island. He landed at a flight of steps on the northern side, and mounting them, halted for an instant, giving the quick imperative, 'In the name of the Emperor.' Ere many minutes elapsed a band of priests, headed by Petamon himself, appeared at the great gateway, and the Centurion, advancing, briefly demanded to speak with their High Priest.

Petamon, with the rising sun flashing on his leopard-skin cloak and the golden fringe of his girdle, with his head and beard close-shaven, in his pure linen garments and papyrus sandals, stepped forward.

'I am Petamon, the grandson of Petamon, High Priest of Isis. Roman soldier, speak on.'

'I seek——' commenced Lepidus; but he stopped abruptly. His eye had caught the glitter of the golden fringe, and he saw that at one side a piece had been torn away. He sprung forward like a tiger and grasped the priest's throat. 'Petamon, Priest of Isis, I arrest you on the charge of kidnapping a Roman citizen. In the name of Caesar Domitian; soldiers, secure him!'

Priests and soldiers stood for a moment transfixed with amazement while Lepidus slowly released his grasp on the priest's throat, and they stood face to face till the Roman almost flinched before the fierce glare of the Egyptian's eye. The other priests began to press forward with threatening gestures; they outnumbered the Romans three times, and, though the strength and discipline of the latter would doubtless have proved victorious in the end, might have offered a stout resistance; but Petamon motioned them back. 'Fear not, children,' he said, speaking in the Greek tongue, so that both parties might understand him, 'the gods can protect their own, and you, Sir Roman, that have laid hands on the servant of Isis, tremble!' He walked forward and surrendered himself to two of the soldiers.

'Rather him than me,' muttered Sheshonk. 'The gods are all very well to fool the people with, but I doubt if Isis herself will save him under the Roman rods.'

Petamon raised his eyes and met those of Sheshonk. A few words in the Egyptian tongue and a few secret signals passed between them, and Sheshonk, with a deep reverence, retired into the temple and disappeared.

The soldiers were despatched to search the island, and poor Septimius heard them several times pass the very door of his prison, but his gaolers had had time to thrust a gag into his mouth, so he could give no alarm. He lay there sick at heart, for he was stiff and weary, and even his cheerful spirits felt nearly broken.

The search was fruitless, as Lepidus had fully expected; and he commanded Petamon again to be brought before him. 'Sir Priest,' he said, 'I seek Septimius the Centurion, who is or was in your hands; unless he is restored before tomorrow's sun sinks in the west you die the death.'

'It is well,' said the priest, while the mock submission of his attitude was belied by the sinister fire of his eye; 'the gods can protect their own.'

Towards evening Petamon requested an audience of Lepidus, and when they were again together addressed him with more civility than he had hitherto condescended to use. He explained that it was the practice that the High Priest should, at certain seasons, sleep in the sacred recesses of the temple, and have the decrees of the goddess revealed to him in visions; he humbly craved permission to perform this sacred duty, as it might be for the last time. Lepidus mused for a moment and then gave orders that the priest, chained between two soldiers, should have leave to sleep where he would.

The night closed in; the shrine of the goddess was illuminated; and the blaze of a hundred lamps flashed on the rich colours and quaint designs on the walls of the shrine. One picture especially, behind the altar, attracted the eye of Lepidus. It represented King Ptolemy trampling down an enemy, while Isis stood by his side, with her hand raised in blessing, and Osiris held out a huge blue falchion as if to bid him complete his task. Before the altar stood Sheshonk burning incense, while Petamon, chained between his guards, bowed for a time in prayer. By midnight the ceremony was over; Petamon, chained to a soldier on each side, lay down before the altar; the lights, all but one, were extinguished; the great door of the sacred chamber was closed. Lepidus lay down across it with his drawn sword in his hand, and, wearied with anxiety and care, soon fell fast asleep.

The sun was rising when he awoke, and, hastily rising, gave orders to change the guard upon the prisoner, and himself entered the chamber to see that the fetters were properly secured. The lamp was burning dimly, and there lay the two soldiers: but where was the prisoner? He was gone—utterly gone. The fetters were there, but Petamon had vanished. Half mad with vexation, Lepidus gave one of his soldiers an angry kick; the man neither stirred nor groaned; he snatched up the lamp and threw its rays upon the soldier's face. It was white and still, and a small stream of blood, which had flowed from a wound over the heart, told too plain a tale. It was the same with the other; the soldiers' last battle was fought, and they had gone to their long home.

Terrified and perplexed beyond measure Lepidus rushed out into the court, and hastily roused the cohort. It was some minutes ere he could get them to comprehend what had happened; and even then men followed him most unwillingly as he snatched up a torch and hurried back. To his amazement the corpses of the soldiers were gone, and in their place lay two rams, newly slaughtered and bound with palm ropes; the fetters had also vanished. He raised his eyes and now noticed what he had not seen before—the picture of Osiris and Isis was behind the altar still, but the blade of the falchion of the god was dyed red, and dripping with newly-shed gore. Shuddering and horror-stricken he left the chamber, followed by the soldiers; and, as he passed out of the temple, met Sheshonk in his priestly robes going in to perform the morning services.

A panic seized the soldiery, in which Lepidus more than half concurred. They were men, they said; why fight against the gods? In half an hour they had left Philae and were marching through the desert to Syene, with drooping heads and weary steps, under the already scorching sun.

Terrified though he was at this awful tragedy, Lepidus was too honest and true to abandon the quest. The soldiers positively refused to assist further in the search, and he was left almost to his own resources. After much thought he published a proclamation in Egyptian and Greek offering a thousand pieces of gold for the Centurion, if alive; five hundred for the conviction of his murderers, if dead; and five hundred more for the head of the priest Petamon; and threatening the last penalty of the law on all men detaining the Roman a prisoner or sheltering his murderers.

His hopes were faint, but he could do no more; and having despatched a full report of the whole case to the Roman General at Alexandria, he waited, impatiently enough, his heart sickened with alternate hopes and fears.

During the next few days he was much disturbed by the sentiments of disaffection which he heard being muttered among the soldiers. Like all ignorant men they were superstitious, the events which had occurred at Philae had produced a deep impression on their minds, and they murmured almost openly at Lepidus for having taken them to such a fearful place, and even now for halting in so ill-omened a neighbourhood.

This feeling was much increased by an old beggar-man who constantly haunted the camp. He had attracted the attention of the soldiers by some ordinary tricks of magic, and was constantly telling fortunes and reciting prophecies, all foreboding evil to the cohort if it stayed in the neighbourhood; and, indeed, foretelling the speedy and utter downfall of Roman power.

Much grieved and perplexed, Lepidus ordered the beggar to be brought before him, and when he came taxed him with attempting to incite the soldiers to mutiny, and sternly reminded him that the punishment for such an attempt was death. The old man listened quietly and calmly, crossing his arms and fixing his glittering eye, which seemed strangely familiar to Lepidus, on the Roman officer.

After a pause he spoke—'My lord,' and again the tone struck Lepidus as strangely familiar to his ear, 'I serve the gods, and you the Emperor: let us both serve our masters truly. You would have news of Septimius the Centurion? It may be that the gods will permit you to see a vision: shall it be so?'

A slight curl of contempt was on the Roman's lips as he answered: 'You know the proclamation. I am prepared to fulfil its terms.'

The old man shook himself like an awakening lion, and again the gesture struck Lepidus as familiar.

'I seek not gold,' he said; 'give me your attention, and keep the gold for those that need it.'

'It is well,' said Lepidus. 'Proceed.'

A small stove was burning in the tent; the old man cast upon the charcoal some drugs that raised a dense smoke and filled the tent with a heavy perfumed smell.

'Look!' said the old man, pointing to the smoke; and retiring behind Lepidus he crouched upon the ground.

A circle of light formed itself clearly and well defined among the smoke, and in its midst Lepidus suddenly saw the image of the bull Apis, as he had seen him once before at Memphis, with all his gorgeous scarlet and gold trappings, and the golden disc between his horns. A moment, and the image suddenly grew smaller and smaller, and vanished from the eyes of the wondering Roman.

Again the circle of light formed and he saw Osiris seated on his judgment throne, and the human soul being tried before him. There was the child Horus seated on a lotus flower, with his finger at his lips. There was the dog of the infernal regions, panting to devour the wicked; and there was the Ape of Thoth, watching the turn of the balance. Again the vision faded.

'These are our gods,' said the beggar. 'Now behold thine own.'

The circle formed again, and he saw the Emperor Domitian, his features bloated with intemperance, revelling among the degenerate senators and trembling patricians. The soldier sighed and the vision faded again.

Again the circle formed, and this time he saw the Centurion Septimius sitting at his tent door, as when we first saw him, and, stranger still, he saw himself in converse with him.

But suddenly, whether it was the perfumes or the excitement that overcame him he never knew, but the circle of light, the old man, the tent spun round and round, and he sank fainting to the ground.

When he awoke from his swoon the stove was burnt out, the old man was gone, and he hardly knew whether he had been dreaming or not. He felt dull and heavy and could scarcely rise. His servant entered with a light. He glanced at his finger, on which he wore his signet-ring, with which all important despatches must be sealed, and which marked their authenticity—it was gone. He felt in his bosom for the secret orders which the General had entrusted to him rather than to the headlong Septimius—they were gone too. His head still swum round; he could not think; he fell upon his bed, and sank into a heavy sleep.

We must now return to Philae—on the fifth day after Lepidus so hurriedly left it.

Septimius was still alive. A scanty allowance of bread and water was daily furnished him and his bonds had been somewhat loosed, but he had not seen the light of day since his capture, and his heart sank within him in hopeless despondency.

The news of Lepidus's proclamation had just reached the island of Philae. It was the turn of Sheshonk to officiate at the altar of Isis, and, while the incense was burning, he stood for a few moments wrapped in deep thought, then proceeded briskly about his accustomed duties.

The evening closed, the night was half spent, and Petamon, who had been away all day, had not returned, when Sheshonk stole silently up the stair with a bundle under his arm, and, touching the spring, entered the dungeon of Septimius. The weary-worn Centurion inquired in a languid voice who it was.

'A friend,' whispered Sheshonk. 'Hush, Sir Centurion, and hearken. Lepidus, your second in command, has offered a thousand pieces of gold for your safe return; do you confirm the offer?'

'Ay, and add a thousand to it,' answered the Centurion. 'I have an old father in Rome who values his son at that sum ten times fold, spendthrift youngster though he be.'

'Good,' said the priest. 'Petamon seeks your life, and in a few days will take it; you cannot be worse than you are, therefore you can lose nothing by trusting me—will you do so?'

'I will,' said the Centurion.

A knife was drawn gently across the cords which bound him, and he stretched his limbs here and there with a delicious sense of recovered freedom. Cautiously the priest struck a light with flint and steel and lighted a small lantern, after which he produced from his bundle a pair of huge hawks' heads, surmounted by the disc of the sun, with great glass eyes, and a pair of white disguises, such as the original captors of Septimius had worn. The Centurion eyed them with an amused smile, and muttering to himself, 'so much for the hawk demons,' proceeded to array himself in the disguise, while Sheshonk did the same. This accomplished, the priest opened the door and they cautiously descended the stairs. They met a young priest, but at a whispered word from Sheshonk he bowed and passed them by. They entered a small chamber on the west side; the priest touched a mark on the floor, and a trap-door opened at their feet, showing a long dark stair. Down this they slowly made their way, the priest stopping for a moment to draw a heavy bolt on the under side of the trap-door to impede pursuit.

After some time the Centurion heard a rushing of water above him, the passage grew damper and damper, and the priest in a whisper explained that they were passing under the bed of the river. In a little while they again ascended a high flight of steps, another trap-door opened at the touch of Sheshonk, and they emerged in a small temple on the Island of Snem, now called Biggeh. The priest silently opened the door, and they stole out. The fresh breeze was blowing from the north, and Septimius, raising for a moment the choking weight of the hawk's head, let the air play about his temples, and then, at a warning sign from his companion, replaced the mask.

The moon had set and the night was almost dark. Cautiously picking their steps they crossed the island, and found at the other side a small skiff lying at anchor, and two swarthy Nubian rowers in attendance; a few words passed between them and Sheshonk.

'We must wait,' he said, 'till the day breaks; they dare not pass the cataract by night. Sleep if you can, and I will watch.'

Septimius was too glad of the permission; he had slept but ill in his dungeon, and, taking off the heavy mask, he buried his head in his garments and fell fast asleep.

In a few hours the morning broke, and ere the sun was risen Sheshonk and Septimius were on board the boat. The rowers pulled stoutly at their oars, and they soon neared the cataract, whose roar became louder as they advanced. Before them lay a stretch of the river, fenced in on either hand with desolate rocky hills; here, there, everywhere, in the course of the stream jutted out the heads of cruel black rocks, round which the water foamed and raced like the stream of a mill-dam. On sped the boat. The Centurion shut his eyes and held his breath; the current caught them; they were hurried helplessly along for a moment, stern foremost, and were on the point of being dashed upon a rock, when a dextrous stroke of one of the oars righted them: a rush—a tumult of waters—dashing spray and the roar of the current for a moment, then the boat floated again in calm water and the danger was past.

In a few moments they reached the Roman encampment. The Nubians, at a word from Sheshonk, pulled away up the stream, while the two hawk-headed ones hurried through the camp, to the no small wonderment of several drowsy sentries.

Lepidus was just awakening with the weary disheartened feelings of one who dreads impending misfortune, when the flap of his tent-door was thrown back, and the sleepy officer fancied he must still be dreaming when he saw a hawk-headed phantom rush into the room.

It was no phantom, as he found to his cost, for it hugged him close in its arms, while its huge beak left a dint on his face that he bore till his dying day, and a voice—the voice of Septimius—issued forth, hollow sounding, from the depths of the mask:

'Dear, dear, old Lepidus. I never thought to see your sulky face again.'

There was little time for greeting and congratulations, Sheshonk was urgent on them to complete their work, and ere long the legionaries, their fears dispelled by the reappearance of the young Centurion, hastened again across the desert to Philae, burning so hotly to wipe out the insult that had been offered to the Roman name that they never felt the sun.

Several boats were lying at the shore, and while Lepidus with the main body of the men made for the stairs upon the northern side, Septimius and a few chosen followers, under the guidance of Sheshonk, crept along under the western wall in a small boat and reached the secret door. It opened, obedient to the touch of the priest, and silently they mounted the stair—they met the other party in the great Hall of Columns; the island seemed deserted—no living thing was to be seen.

Sheshonk's eye twinkled. 'Five hundred golden pieces for Petamon's head!'

'Ay, and five hundred more,' said Septimius.

The priest beckoned them on. They entered the sacred chamber where Petamon had kept his vigil on that memorable night, and Lepidus half shuddered as he looked round at the familiar paintings on the wall. The altar was prepared and the fire burning on it. The priest advanced and set his foot heavily on one side of the step in front. Suddenly altar and step, solid though they seemed, rolled away noiselessly to one side, disclosing a dark passage beneath. In a moment the Romans leapt down, Lepidus hastily lighting a torch at the altar fire as they did so. The passage led them to a small room in the thickness of the wall, and throwing in the light of his torch, he saw the arms and accoutrements of the two murdered soldiers, and the fetters that had bound Petamon lying in a corner. Here the passage apparently terminated abruptly, but the priest raised a stone in the roof with his hand, and they crept up through the narrow aperture thus opened. A strongly barred wooden door was on their left. They shot back the bolts and the door opened, revealing a small cell hewn out of one solid stone, with no aperture save the door for the admission of air; the light of day has never penetrated these gloomy recesses. The cell was untenanted, but a heap of human bones at one corner told of the uses to which it had been applied.

Shuddering they closed the door, and upon Sheshonk touching another spring, a square aperture opened, through which they glided, serpentwise, into another of the sacred chambers, and gladly hailed the light of day as it glimmered faintly through the door.

They searched the whole temple, but in vain; secret chambers they found more than one; even the dungeon of Septimius was opened, but nothing was discovered, and even the bloodhound sagacity of Sheshonk seemed for a moment at fault.

But his eye soon brightened, and muttering to himself 'five hundred pieces of gold,' he led them through the court under the high painted pillars, and opening a door in one of the sides of the pyramidal gateway, proceeded up a long narrow stair. Suddenly a rustle of garments was heard above them, and they caught sight of the robes of Petamon, his leopard-skin cloak and his golden fringe, as he fled before them. The two Romans dashed after him like greyhounds on a hare, but as they reached the top of the staircase Septimius stumbled and fell, and so checked the pursuit for an instant. In a moment he recovered himself, but in that instant Petamon, casting back on his pursuers a glance of baffled hatred, sprang from the tower, and in another moment lay, dashed upon the pavement of the hall, a shapeless mass, while his blood and brains were splashed over the gay painting of the pillars.

The soldiers and Sheshonk, horror-struck, hastened down, and were standing beside the body—Lepidus had just recovered from the finger of the priest the signet-ring that he had lost, and was in the act of drawing the roll of secret orders from his bosom—Sheshonk had raised his head-dress and was wiping the perspiration from his brow,

A sharp dagger was hurled with unerring aim . . .

when suddenly, from aloft—it almost seemed from heaven—a sharp dagger was hurled with unerring aim. It cleft the bald skull of the traitor, and he fell, with scarcely a groan, on the top of Petamon's corpse.

The Romans looked up: no one was to be seen. With a party of soldiers they searched the huge gateway towers, but without a guide such a quest was hopeless, and they never traced the hand from which the dagger came.

Their main object was accomplished. Petamon was dead, and with him expired all chances of a revolutionary outbreak. Sheshonk was dead too; but, as Lepidus said, that saved the good gold pieces.

The same evening they returned to Syene, and next day the camp was broken up, and the cohort embarked on the river and floated down to rejoin the garrison at Memphis.

REMORSELESS REVENGE

Guy Boothby

To use that expressive South Sea phrase, I have had the misfortune to be 'on the beach' in a variety of places in my time. There are people who say that it is worse to be stranded in Trafalgar Square than, shall we say, Honolulu or Rangoon. Be that as it may, the worst time I ever had was that of which I am now going to tell you. I had crossed the Pacific from San Francisco before the mast on an American mail boat, had left her in Hong Kong, and had made my way down to Singapore on a collier. As matters did not look very bright there, I signed aboard a Dutch boat for Batavia, intending to work my way on to Australia. It was in Batavia, however, that the real trouble began. As soon as I arrived I fell ill, and the little money I had managed to scrape together melted like snow before the mid-day sun. What to do I knew not – I was on my beam ends. I had nothing to sell, even if there were anyone to buy, and horrible visions of Dutch gaols began to obtrude themselves upon me.

It was on the night of the 23rd of December, such a night as I'll be bound they were not having in the old country. There was not a cloud in the sky, and the stars shone like the lamps along the Thames Embankment when you look at them from Waterloo Bridge. I was smoking in the brick-paved verandah of the hotel and wondering how I was going to pay the bill, when a man entered the gates of the hotel and walked across the garden and along the verandah toward where I was seated. I noticed that he was very tall, very broad-shouldered, and that he carried himself like a man who liked his own way and generally managed to get it.

'I wonder who he can be?' I said to myself, and half expected that he would pass me and proceed in the direction of the manager's office. My astonishment may be imagined, therefore, when he picked up a chair from beside the wall and seated himself at my side.

'Good evening,' he said, as calmly as you might address a friend on the top of a 'bus.

'Good evening,' I replied in the same tone.

'Frank Riddington is your name, I believe?' he continued, still with the same composure.

'I believe so', I answered, 'but I don't know how you became aware of it.'

'That's neither here nor there,' he answered; 'putting other matters aside for the moment, let me give you some news.'

He paused for a moment and puffed meditatively at his cigar.

'I don't know whether you're aware that there's an amiable plot on hand in this hotel to kick you into the street in the morning,' he went on. 'The proprietor seems to think it unlikely that you will be able to settle your account.'

'And, by Jove, he is not far wrong,' I replied. 'It's Christmas time, I know, and I am probably in bed and dreaming. You're undoubtedly the fairy godmother sent to help me out of my difficulty.'

He laughed – a short, sharp laugh.

'How do you propose to do it?'

'By putting a piece of business in your way. I want your assistance, and if you will give it me I am prepared to hand you sufficient money not only to settle your bill, but to leave a bit over. What's more, you can leave Batavia, if you like.'

'Provided the business of which you speak is satisfactory,' I replied, 'you can call it settled. What am I to do?'

He took several long puffs at his cigar.

'You have heard of General Van der Vaal?'

'The man who, until lately, has been commanding the Dutch forces up in Achin?'

'The same. He arrived in Batavia three days ago. His house is situated on the King's Plain, three-quaters of a mile or so from here.'

'Well, what about him?'

Leaning a little towards me, and sinking his voice, he continued:

'I want General Van der Vaal – badly – and tonight!'

For a moment I had doubts as to his sanity.

'I'm afraid I haven't grasped the situation,' I said. 'Do I understand that you are going to abduct General Van der Vaal?'

'Exactly!' he replied. 'I am going to deport him from the island. You need not ask why, at this stage of the proceedings. I shouldn't have brought you into the matter at all, but that my mate fell ill, and I had to find a substitute.'

'You haven't told me your name yet,' I replied.

'It slipped my memory,' he answered. 'But you are welcome to it now. I am Captain Berringer!'

You may imagine my surprise. Here I was sitting talking face to face with the notorious Captain Berringer, whose doings were known from Rangoon to Vladivostock – from Nagasaki to Sourabaya. He and his brother – of whom, by the way, nothing had been heard for some time past – had been more than suspected of flagrant acts of piracy. They were well known to the Dutch as pearl stealers in prohibited waters. The Russians had threatened to hang them for seal-stealing in Behring Straits, while the French had some charges against them in Tonkin that would ensure them a considerable sojourn there should they appear in that neighbourhood again.

'Well, what do you say to my proposal?' he asked. 'It will be as easy to accomplish as it will be for them to turn you into the street in the morning.'

I knew this well enough, but I saw that if he happened to fail I should, in all probability, be even worse off than before.

'Where's your vessel,' I asked, feeling sure that he had one near at hand.

'Dodging about off the coast,' he said. 'We'll pick her up before daylight.'

'And you'll take me with you?'

'That's as you please,' he answered.

'I'll come right enough. Batavia will be too hot for me after tonight. But first you must hand over the money. I must settle with that little beast of a proprietor tonight.'

'I like your honesty,' he said, with a sneer. 'Under the circumstances it is so easy to run away without paying.'

'Captain Berringer,' said I, 'whatever I may be now, I was once a gentleman.'

A quarter-of-an-hour later the bill was paid, and I had made my arrangements to meet my employer outside the Harmonic Club punctually at midnight. I am not going to say that I was not nervous, for it would not be the truth. Van der Vaal's reputation was a cruel one, and if he got the upper hand of us we should be likely to receive but scant mercy. Punctually to the minute I reached the rendezvous, where I found the captain awaiting me. Then we set off in the direction of the King's Plain, as you may suppose keeping well in the shadow of the trees. We had not walked very far before Berringer placed a revolver into my hand, which I slipped into my pocket.

'Let's hope we shan't have to use them,' he said; 'but there's nothing like being prepared.'

By the time we had climbed the wall and were approaching the house, still keeping in the shadow of the trees, I was beginning to think I had had enough of the adventure, but it was too late to draw back, even had the Captain permitted such a thing.

Suddenly the Captain laid his hand on my arm.

'His room is at the end on this side,' he whispered. 'He sleeps with his window open, and his bed is in the furthest corner. His lamp is still burning, but let us hope that he is asleep. If he gives the alarm we're done for.'

I won't deny that I was too frightened to answer him. My fear, however, did not prevent me from following him into the clump of trees near the steps that led to the verandah. Here we slipped off our boots, made our preparations, and then tiptoed with the utmost care across the path, up the steps, and in the direction of the General's room. That he was a strict disciplinarian we were aware, and that, in consequence, we knew that his watchman was likely to be a watchman in the real sense of the word.

The heavy breathing that came from the further corner of the room told us that the man we wanted was fast asleep. A faint light, from a wick which floated in a bowl of coconut oil, illuminated the room, and

He slipped a revolver into my hand

showed us a large bed of the Dutch pattern, closely veiled with mosquito curtains. Towards this we made our way. On it, stretched out at full length, was the figure of a man. I lifted the netting while the Captain prepared for the struggle. A moment later he leapt upon his victim, seized him by the throat and pinioned him. A gag was quickly thrust into his mouth, whilst I took hold of his wrists. In less time than it takes to tell he was bound hand and foot, unable either to resist or to summon help.

'Bundle up some of his clothes,' whispered Berringer, pointing to some garments on a chair. 'Then pick up his heels, while I'll take his shoulders. But not a sound as you love your life.'

In less than ten minutes we had carried him across the grounds, had lifted him over the wall, where we found a native cart waiting for us, and had stowed him and ourselves away in it.

'Now for Tanjong Prick,' said the Captain. 'We must be out of the islands before daybreak.'

At a prearranged spot some four or five miles from the port we pulled up beneath a small tope of palms.

'Are you still bent upon accompanying me?' asked the Captain, as we lifted the inanimate General from the cart and placed him on the ground.

'More than ever,' I replied. 'Java shall see me no more.'

Berringer consulted his watch, and found the time to be exactly half-past two. A second later a shrill whistle reached us from the beach.

'That's the boat,' said Berringer. 'Now let's carry him down to her.'

We accordingly set off in the direction indicated. It was not, however, until we were alongside a smart-looking brig, and I was clambering aboard, that I felt in any way easy in my mind.

'Pick him up and bring him aft to the cuddy,' said the skipper to two of the hands, indicating the prostrate General. Then turning to the second mate, who was standing by, he added: 'Make sail, and let's get out of this. Follow me, Mr Riddington.'

I accompanied him along the deck, and from it into the cuddy, the two sailors and their heavy burden preceding us. Once there the wretched man's bonds were loosed. They had been tight enough, goodness knows, for when we released him he was so weak that he could not stand, but sank down on one of the seats beside the table, and buried his face in his hands.

'What does this mean?' he asked at last, looking up at us with a pitiable assumption of dignity. 'Why have you brought me here?'

'That's easily told,' said the Captain. 'Last Christmas you were commanding in Achin. Do you remember an Englishman named Bernard Watson who threw in his lot with them?'

'I hanged him on Christmas Day,' said the other, with a touch of his old spirit.

'Exactly,' said Berringer. 'And that's why you're here tonight. He was my brother. We will cry "quits" when I hang you on the yard-arm on Christmas morning.'

'Good heavens, Captain!' I cried, 'you're surely not going to do this?'

'I am,' he answered, with a firmness there was no mistaking. The idea was too horrible to contemplate. I tried to convince myself that, had I known what the end would be, I should have taken no part in it.

A cabin had already been prepared for the General, and to it he was forthwith conducted. The door having been closed and locked upon him, the Captain and I were left alone together. I implored him to reconsider his decision.

'I never reconsider my decisions,' he answered. 'The man shall hang at sunrise the day after tomorrow. He hanged my brother in cold blood, and I'll do the same for him. That's enough. Now I must go and look at my mate, he's being ailing this week past. If you want food the steward will bring it to you, and if you want a bunk – well, you can help yourself.'

With that he turned on his heel, and left me.

Here I was in a nice position. To all intents and purposes I had aided and abetted a murder, and if any of Berringer's crew should care to turn Queen's evidence I should find myself in the dock, a convicted murderer. In vain I set my wits to work to try to find some scheme which might save the wretched man and myself. I could discover none, however.

All the next day we sailed on, heading for the Northern Australian Coast, so it seemed to me. I met the Captain at meals, and upon the deck, but he appeared morose and sullen, gave his orders in peremptory jerks, and never once, so far as I heard, alluded to the unhappy man below. I attempted to broach the subject to the mate, in the hope that he might take the same view of it as I did, but I soon found that my advances in that quarter were not likely to be favourably received. The crew, as I soon discovered, were Kanakas, with two exceptions, and devoted to their Captain. I was quite certain that they would do nothing but what he wished. Such a Christmas Eve I sincerely trust I may never spend again.

Late in the afternoon I bearded the Captain in his cabin, and once more endeavoured to indú.:ce him to think well before committing such an act. Ten minutes later I was back in the cuddy, a wiser and sadder man. From that moment I resigned myself to the inevitable.

At half-past six that evening the Captain and I dined together in solitary state. Afterwards I went on deck. It was a beautiful moonlight night, with scarcely enough wind to fill the canvas. The sea was as smooth as glass, with a long train of phosphorous light in our wake. I had seen nothing of the skipper since eight bells. At about ten o'clock, however, and just as I was thinking of turning in, he emerged from the companion. A few strides brought him to my side.

'A fine night, Riddington,' he said, in a strange, hard voice, very unlike his usual tone.

'A very fine night,' I answered.

'Riddington,' he began again, with sudden vehemence, 'do you believe in ghosts?'

'I have never thought much about the matter,' I answered. 'Why do you ask?'

'Because I've seen a ghost tonight,' he replied. The ghost of my brother Bernard, who was hanged by that man locked in the cabin below, exactly a year ago, at daybreak. Don't make any mistake about what I'm saying. You can feel my pulse, if you like, and you will find it beating as steady as ever it has done in my life. I haven't touched a drop of liquor today, and I honestly believe I'm as sane a man as there is in the world. Yet I tell you that, not a quarter of an hour ago, my brother stood beside me in my cabin.'

Not knowing what answer to make, I held my tongue for the moment. At last I spoke.

'Did he say anything?' I inquired.

'He told me that I should not be permitted to execute my vengeance on Van der Vaal! It was to be left to him to deal with him. But I've passed my word, and I'll not depart from it. Ghost or no ghost, he hangs at sunrise.'

So saying, he turned and walked away from me, and went below.

I am not going to pretend that I slept that night. Of one thing I am quite certain, and that is that the Captain did not leave his cabin all night. Half an hour before daybreak, however, he came to my cabin.

'Come on deck,' he said. 'The time is up.'

I followed him, to find all the ghastly preparations complete. Once more I pleaded for mercy with all the strength at my command, and once more I failed to move him. Even the vision he had declared he had seen seemed now to be forgotten.

'Bring him on deck,' he said at last, turning to the mate and handing him the key of the cabin as he spoke. The other disappeared, and I, unable to control myself, went to the side of the vessel and looked down at the still water below. The brig was scarcely moving. Presently I heard the noise of feet in the companion, and turning, with a white face, no doubt, I saw the mate and two of the hands emerge from the hatchway. They approached the Captain, who seemed not to see them. To the amazement of everyone, he was looking straight before him across the poop, with an expression of indescribable terror on his face. Then, with a crash, he lost his balance and fell forward upon the deck. We ran to his assistance, but were too late. He was dead.

Who shall say what he had seen in that terrible half-minute? The mate and I looked at each other in stupefied bewilderment. I was the first to find my voice.

'The General?'

'Dead,' the other replied. 'He died as we entered the cabin to fetch him out. God help me – you never saw such a sight! It looked as if he were fighting with someone whom we could not see, and was being slowly strangled.'

I waited to hear no more, but turned and walked aft. I am not a superstitious man, but I felt that the Captain's brother had been right after all, when he had said that he would take the matter of revenge into his own hands.

THE HIGHER PRAGMATISM

O Henry

Where to go for wisdom has become a question of serious import. The ancients are discredited; Plato is boiler-plate; Aristotle is tottering; Marcus Aurelius is reeling; AEsop has been copyrighted by Indiana; Solomon is too solemn; you couldn't get anything out of Epictetus with a pick.

The ant, which for many years served as a model of intelligence and industry in the school-readers, has been proven to be a doddering idiot and a waster of time and effort. The owl to-day is hooted at. Chautauqua conventions have abandoned culture and adopted diabolo. Greybeards give glowing testimonials to the vendors of patent hair-restorers. There are typographical errors in the almanacs published by the daily newspapers. College professors have become——

But there shall be no personalities.

To sit in classes, to delve into the encyclopedia or the past-performances page, will not make us wise. As the poet says, 'Knowledge comes, but wisdom lingers.' Wisdom is dew, which, while we know it not, soaks into us, refreshes us, and makes us grow. Knowledge is a strong stream of water turned on us through a hose. It disturbs our roots.

Then, let us rather gather wisdom. But how to do so requires knowledge. If we know a thing, we know it; but very often we are not wise to it that we are wise, and——

But let's go on with the story.

Once upon a time I found a ten-cent magazine lying on a bench in a little city park. Anyhow, that was the amount he asked me for when I sat on the bench next to him. He was a musty, dingy, and tattered magazine, with some queer stories bound in him, I was sure. He turned out to be a scrap-book.

'I am a newspaper reporter,' I said to him, to try him. 'I have been detailed to write up some of the experiences of the unfortunate ones who spend their evenings in this park. May I ask you to what you attribute your downfall in——'

I was interrupted by a laugh from my purchase—a laugh so rusty and unpractised that I was sure it had been his first for many a day.

'Oh, no, no,' said he. 'You ain't a reporter. Reporters don't talk that way. They pretend to be one of us, and say they've just got in on the blind baggage from St. Louis. I can tell a reporter on sight. Us park bums get to be fine judges of human nature. We sit here all day and watch the people go by. I can size up anybody who walks past my bench in a way that would surprise you.'

'Well,' I said, 'go on and tell me. How do you size me up?'

'I should say,' said the student of human nature with unpardonable hesitation, 'that you was, say, in the contracting business—or maybe worked in a store—or was a sign-painter. You stopped in the park to finish your cigar, and thought you'd get a little free monologue out of me. Still, you might be a plasterer or a lawyer—it's getting kind of dark, you see. And your wife won't let you smoke at home.'

I frowned gloomily.

'But, judging again,' went on the reader of men, 'I'd say you ain't got a wife.'

'No,' said I, rising restlessly. 'No, no, no, I ain't. But I *will* have, by the arrows of Cupid! That is, if——'

My voice must have trailed away and muffled itself in uncertainty and despair.

'I see you have a story yourself,' said the dusty vagrant—impudently, it seemed to me. 'Suppose you take your dime back and spin your yarn for me. I'm interested myself in the ups and downs of unfortunate ones who spend their evenings in the park.'

Somehow, that amused me. I looked at the frowsy derelict with more interest. I did have a story. Why not tell it to him? I had told none of my friends. I had always been a reserved and bottled-up man. It was psychical timidity or sensitiveness—perhaps both. And I smiled to myself in wonder when I felt an impulse to confide in this stranger and vagabond.

'Jack,' said I.

'Mack,' said he.

'Mack,' said I, 'I'll tell you.'

'Do you want the dime back in advance?' said he.

I handed him a dollar.

'The dime,' said I, 'was the price of listening to *your* story.'

'Right on the point of the jaw,' said he. 'Go on.'

And then, incredible as it may seem to the lovers in the world who confide their sorrows only to the night wind and the gibbous moon, I laid bare my secret to that wreck of all things that you would have supposed to be in sympathy with love.

I told him of the days and weeks and months that I had spent in adoring Mildred Telfair. I spoke of my despair, my grievous days and wakeful nights, my dwindling hopes and distress of mind. I even pictured to this night-prowler her beauty and dignity, the great sway she had in society, and the magnificence of her life as the elder daughter of an ancient race whose pride overbalanced the dollars of the city's millionaires.

'Why don't you cop the lady out?' asked Mack, bringing me down to earth and dialect again.

I explained to him that my worth was so small, my income so minute, and my fears so large that I hadn't the courage to speak to her of my worship. I told him that in her presence I could only blush and stammer, and that she looked upon me with a wonderful, maddening smile of amusement.

'She kind of moves in the professional class, don't she?' asked Mack.

'The Telfair family——' I began, haughtily.

'I mean professional beauty,' said my hearer.

'She is greatly and widely admired,' I answered, cautiously.

'Any sisters?'

'One.'

'You know any more girls?'

'Why, several,' I answered. 'And a few others.'

'Say,' said Mack, 'tell me one thing—can you hand out the dope to other girls? Can you chin 'em and make matinée eyes at 'em and squeeze 'em? You know what I mean. You're just shy when it comes to this particular dame—the professional beauty—ain't that right?'

'In a way you have outlined the situation with approximate truth,' I admitted.

'I thought so,' said Mack grimly. 'Now that reminds me of my own case. I'll tell you about it.'

I was indignant, but concealed it. What was this loafer's case or anybody's case compared with mine? Besides, I had given him a dollar and ten cents.

'Feel my muscle,' said my companion, suddenly flexing his biceps. I did so mechanically. The fellows in gymns are always asking you to do that. His arm was as hard as cast-iron.

'Four years ago,' said Mack. 'I could lick any man in New York outside the professional ring. Your case and mine is just the same. I come from the West Side—between Thirteenth and Fourteenth—and I won't give the number on the door. I was a scrapper when I was ten, and when I was twenty no amateur in the city could stand up four rounds with me. 'S a fact. You know Bill McCarty? No? He managed the smokers for some of them swell clubs. Well, I knocked out everything Bill brought up before me. I was a middle-weight, but could train down to a welter when necessary. I boxed all over the West Side at bouts and benefits and private entertainments, and was never put out once.

'But, say, the first time I put my foot in the ring with a professional I was no more than a canned lobster. I dunno how it was—I seemed to lose heart. I guess I got too much imagination. There was a formality and publicness about it that kind of weakened my nerve. I never won a fight in the ring. Light-weights and all kinds of scrubs used to sign up with my manager and then walk up and tap me on the wrist and see me fall. The minute I seen the crowd and a lot of gents in evening clothes down in front, and seen a professional come inside the ropes, I got weak as ginger-ale.

'Of course, it wasn't long till I couldn't get no backers, and I didn't have any more chances to fight a professional—or many amateurs, either. But lemme tell you—I was as good as most men inside the ring or out. It was just that dumb, dead feeling I had when I was up against a regular that always done me up.

'Well, sir, after I had got out of the business, I got a mighty grouch on. I used to go round town licking private citizens and all kinds of unprofessionals just to please myself. I'd lick cops in dark streets and car-conductors and cab-drivers and draymen whenever I could start a row with 'em. It didn't make any difference how big they were, or how much science they had, I got away with 'em. If I'd only just have had the confidence in the ring that I had beating up the best men outside of it, I'd be wearing black pearls and heliotrope silk socks to-day.

'One evening I was walking along near the Bowery, thinking about things, when along comes a slumming-party. About six or seven they was, all in swallowtails, and these silk hats that don't shine. One of the gang kind of shoves me off the sidewalk. I hadn't had a scrap in three days, and I just says, "Delight-ed!" and hits him back of the ear.

'Well, we had it. That Johnnie put up as decent a little fight as you'd want to see in the moving pictures. It was on a side street, and no cops around. The other guy had a lot of science, but it only took me about six minutes to lay him out.

'Some of the swallowtails dragged him up against some steps and began to fan him. Another one of 'em comes over to me and says:

'"Young man, do you know what you've done?"

'"Oh, beat it," says I. "I've done nothing but a little punching-bag work. Take Freddy back to Yale and tell him to quit studying sociology on the wrong side of the sidewalk."

'"My good fellow," says he, "I don't know who you are, but I'd like to. You've knocked out Reddy Burns, the champion middle-weight of the world! He came to New York yesterday, to try to get a match on with Jim Jeffries. If you——"

'But when I come out of my faint I was laying on the floor in a drug-store saturated with aromatic spirits of ammonia. If I'd known that was Reddy Burns, I'd have got down in the gutter and crawled past him instead of handing him one like I did. Why, if I'd ever been in a ring and seen him climbing over the ropes I'd have been all to the salvolatile.

'So that's what imagination does,' concluded Mack. 'And as I said, your case and mine is simultaneous. You'll never win out. You can't go up against the professionals. I tell you, it's a park bench for yours in this romance business.'

Mack, the pessimist, laughed harshly.

'I'm afraid I don't see the parallel,' I said coldly. 'I have only a very slight acquaintance with the prize ring.'

The derelict touched my sleeve with his forefinger, for emphasis, as he explained his parable.

'Every man,' said he, with some dignity, 'has got his lamps on something that looks good to him. With you, it's this dame that you're afraid to say your say to. With me, it was to win out in the ring. Well, you'll lose just like I did.'

'Why do you think I shall lose?' I asked warmly.

''Cause,' said he, 'you're afraid to go in the ring. You dassen't stand up before a professional. Your case and mine is just the same. You're a amateur! and that means that you'd better keep outside of the ropes.'

'Well, I must be going,' I said, rising and looking with elaborate care at my watch.

When I was twenty feet away the park-bencher called to me.

'Much obliged for the dollar,' he said. 'And for the dime. But you'll never get 'er. You're in the amateur class.'

'Serves you right,' I said to myself, 'for hob-nobbing with a tramp. His impudence!'

But, as I walked, his words seemed to repeat themselves over and over again in my brain. I think I even grew angry at the man.

'I'll show him!' I finally said, aloud. 'I'll show him that I can fight Reddy Burns, too—even knowing who he is.'

I hurried to a telephone-booth and rang up the Telfair residence.

A soft, sweet voice answered. Didn't I know that voice? My hand holding the receiver shook.

'Is that *you*?' said I, employing the foolish words that form the vocabulary of every talker through the telephone.

'Yes, this is I,' came back the answer in the low, clear-cut tones that are an inheritance of the Telfairs. 'Who is it, please?'

'It's me,' said I, less ungrammatically than egotistically. 'It's me, and I've got a few things that I want to say to you right now and immediately and straight to the point.'

'*Dear* me,' said the voice. 'Oh, it's you, Mr. Arden!'

I wondered if any accent on the first word was intended. Mildred was fine at saying things that you had to study out afterwards.

'Yes,' said I, 'I hope so. And now to come down to brass tacks.' I thought that rather a vernacularism, if there is such a word, as soon as I had said it; but I didn't stop to apologize. 'You know, of course, that I love you, and that I have been in that idiotic state for a long time. I don't want any more foolishness about it—that is, I mean I want an answer from you right now. Will you marry me or not? Hold the wire, please. Keep out, Central. Hello, hello! Will you, or will you *not*?'

That was just the uppercut for Reddy Burns's chin. The answer came back:

'Why, Phil, dear, of course I will! I didn't know that you—that is, you never said—oh, come up to the house, please—I can't say what I want to over the 'phone. But please come up to the house, won't you?'

Would I?

I rang the bell of the Telfair house violently. Some sort of a human came to the door and shooed me into the drawing-room.

'Oh, well,' said I to myself, looking at the ceiling, 'anyone can learn from anyone. That was a pretty good philosophy of Mack's, anyhow. He didn't take advantage of his experience, but I get the benefit of it. If you want to get into the professional class—

I stopped thinking then. Someone was coming down the stairs. My knees began to shake. I knew then how Mack had felt when a professional began to climb over the ropes. I looked around foolishly for a door or a window by which I might escape. If it had been any other girl approaching, I mightn't have——

But just then the door opened, and Bess, Mildred's younger sister, came in. I'd never seen her look so much like a glorified angel. She walked straight up to me, and—and——

I'd never noticed before what wonderful eyes and hair she had.

'Phil,' she said, in the Telfair, sweet, thrilling tones, 'why didn't you tell me about it before? I thought it was sister you wanted all the time!'

I suppose Mack and I always will be hopeless amateurs. But, as the thing has turned out in my case, I'm mighty glad of it.

I'd never seen her look so much like a glorified angel.

ACCESSORY BEFORE THE FACT

Algernon Blackwood

At the moorland crossroads Martin stood examining the signpost for several minutes in some bewilderment. The names on the four arms were not what he expected, distances were not given, and his map, he concluded with impatience, must be hopelessly out of date. Spreading it against the post, he stooped to study it more closely. The wind blew the corners flapping against his face. The small print was almost indecipherable in the fading light. It appeared, however—as well as he could make out—that two miles back he must have taken the wrong turning.

He remembered that turning. The path had looked inviting; he had hesitated a moment, then followed it, caught by the usual lure of walkers that it 'might prove a short cut'. The short-cut snare is old as human nature. For some minutes he studied the signpost and the map alternately. Dusk was falling, and his knapsack had grown heavy. He could not make the two guides tally, however, and a feeling of uncertainty crept over his mind. He felt oddly baffled, frustrated. His thought grew thick. Decision was most difficult. 'I'm muddled,' he thought; 'I must be tired,' as at length he chose the most likely arm. 'Sooner or later it will bring me to an inn, though not the one I intended.' He accepted his walker's luck, and started briskly. The arm read 'Over Litacy Hill' in small, fine letters that danced and shifted every time he looked at them; but the name was not discoverable on the map. It was, however, inviting like the short cut. A similar impulse again directed his choice. Only this time it seemed more insistent, almost urgent.

And he became aware, then, of the exceeding loneliness of the country about him. The road for a hundred yards went straight, then curved like a white river running into space; the deep blue-green of heather lined the banks, spreading upwards through the twilight; and occasional small pines stood solitary here and there, all unexplained. The curious adjective, having made its appearance, haunted him. So many things that afternoon were similarly unexplained: the short cut, the darkened map, the names on the signpost, his own erratic impulses, and the growing strange confusion that crept upon his spirit. The entire countryside needed explanation, though perhaps 'interpretation' was the truer word. Those little lonely trees had made him see it. Why had he lost his way so easily? Why did he suffer vague impressions to influence his directions? Why was he *here*—exactly here? And why did he go now 'over Litacy Hill'?

Then, by a green field that shone like a thought of daylight amid the darkness of the moor, he saw a figure lying in the grass. It was a blot upon the landscape, a mere huddled patch of dirty rags, yet with a certain horrid picturesqueness too; and his mind—though his German was of the schoolroom order—at once picked out the German equivalents as against the English. *Lump* and *Lumpen* flashed across his brain most oddly. They seemed in that moment right, and so expressive, almost like onomatopoeic words, if that were possible of sight. Neither 'rags' nor 'rascal' would have fitted what he saw. The adequate description was in German.

Here was a clue tossed up by the part of him that did not reason. But it seems he missed it. And the next minute the tramp rose to a sitting posture and asked the time of evening. In German he asked it. And Martin, answering without a second's hesitation, gave it, also in German, '*halb sieben*'—half-past six. The instinctive guess was accurate. A glance at his watch when he looked a moment later proved it. He heard the man say, with the covert insolence of tramps, 'T'ank you;

much opliged.' For Martin had not shown his watch—another intuition subconsciously obeyed.

He quickened his pace along that lonely road, a curious jumble of thoughts and feelings surging through him. He had somehow known the question would come, and come in German. Yet it flustered and dismayed him. Another thing had also flustered and dismayed him. He had expected it in the same queer fashion: it was right. For when the ragged brown thing rose to ask the question, a part of it remained lying on the grass—another brown, dirty thing. There were two tramps. And he saw both faces clearly. Behind the untidy beards, and below the old slouch hats, he caught the look of unpleasant, clever faces that watched him closely while he passed. The eyes followed him. For a second he looked straight into those eyes, so that he could not fail to know them. And he understood, quite horridly, that both faces were too sleek, refined, and cunning for those of ordinary tramps. The men were not really tramps at all. They were disguised.

'How covertly they watched me!' was his thought, as he hurried along the darkening road, aware in dead earnestness now of the loneliness and desolation of the moorland all about him.

Uneasy and distressed, he increased his pace. Midway in thinking what an unnecessarily clanking noise his nailed boots made upon the hard white road, there came upon him with a rush together the company of these things that haunted him as 'unexplained'. They brought a single definite message: that all this business was not really meant for him at all, and hence his confusion and bewilderment; that he had intruded into some one else's scenery, and was trespassing upon another's map of life. By some wrong *inner* turning he had interpolated his person into a group of foreign forces which operated in the little world of someone else. Unwittingly, somewhere, he had crossed the threshold, and now was fairly in—a trespasser, an eavesdropper, a Peeping Tom. He was listening, peeping; overhearing things he had no right to know, because they were intended for another. Like a ship at sea he was intercepting wireless messages he could not properly interpret, because his receiver was not accurately tuned to their reception. And more—these messages were warnings!

Then fear dropped upon him like the night. He was caught in a net of delicate, deep forces he could not manage, knowing neither their origin nor purpose. He had walked into some huge psychic trap elaborately planned and baited, yet calculated for another man than himself. Something had lured him in, something in the landscape, the time of day, his mood. Owing to some undiscovered weakness in himself he had been easily caught. His fear slipped easily into terror.

What happened next occurred with such speed and concentration that it all seemed crammed into a moment. At once and in a heap it happened. It was quite inevitable. Down the white road to meet him a man came swaying from side to side in drunkenness quite obviously feigned—a tramp; and while Martin made room for him to pass, the lurch changed in a second to attack, and the fellow was upon him. The blow was sudden and terrific, yet even while it fell Martin was aware that behind him rushed a second man, who caught his legs from under him and bore him with a thud and crash to the ground. Blows rained then; he saw a gleam of something shining; a sudden deadly nausea plunged him into utter weakness where resistance was impossible. Something of fire entered his throat, and from his mouth poured a thick sweet thing that choked him. The world sank far away into darkness . . . Yet through all the horror and confusion ran the trail of two clear thoughts: he realized that the first tramp had sneaked at a fast double through the heather and so come down to meet him; and that something heavy was torn from the fastenings that clipped it tight and close beneath his clothes against his body . . .

Abruptly then the darkness lifted, passed utterly away. He found himself peering into the map against the signpost. The wind was flapping the corners against his cheek, and he was poring over names that now he saw quite clear. Upon the arms of the signpost above were those he had expected to find, and the map recorded them quite faithfully. All was accurate again and as it should be. He read the name of the village he had meant to make—it was plainly visible in the dusk, two miles the distance given. Bewildered, shaken, unable to think of anything, he stuffed the map into his pocket unfolded, and hurried forward like a man who has just awakened from an awful dream that had compressed into a single second all the detailed misery of some prolonged, oppressive nightmare.

He broke into a steady trot that soon became a run; the perspiration poured from him; his legs felt weak, and his breath was difficult to manage. He was only conscious of the overpowering desire to get away as fast as possible from the signpost at the crossroads where the dreadful vision had flashed upon him. For Martin, accountant on a holiday, had never dreamed of any world of psychic possibilities. The entire thing was torture. It was worse than a 'cooked' balance of the books that some conspiracy of clerks and directors proved at his innocent door. He raced as though the countryside ran crying at his heels. And always still ran with him the incredible conviction that none of this was really meant for himself at all. He had overheard the secrets of another. He had taken the warning for another unto himself, and so altered its direction. He had thereby prevented its right delivery. It all shocked him beyond words. It dislocated the machinery of his just and accurate soul. The warning was intended for another, who could not—would not—now receive it.

The physical exertion, however, brought at length a more comfortable reaction and some measure of composure. With the lights in sight, he slowed down and entered the village at a reasonable pace. The inn was reached, a bedroom inspected and engaged, and supper ordered with the solid comfort of a large Bass to satisfy an unholy thirst and complete the restoration of balance. The unusual sensations largely passed away, and the odd feeling that anything in his simple, wholesome world required explanation was no longer present. Still with a vague uneasiness about him, though actual fear quite gone, he went into the bar to smoke an after-supper pipe and chat with the locals, as his pleasure was upon a holiday, and so saw two mean leaning upon the counter at the far end with their backs towards him. He saw their faces instantly in the glass, and the pipe nearly slipped from between his teeth. Clean-shaven, sleek, clever faces—and he caught a word or two as they talked over their drinks—German words. Well dressed they were, both men, with nothing about them calling for particular attention; they might have been two tourists holiday-making like himself in tweeds and walking-boots. And they presently paid for their drinks and went out. He never saw them face to face at all; but the sweat broke out afresh all over him, a feverish rush of heat and ice together ran about his body; beyond question he recognized the two tramps, this time not disguised—not *yet* disguised.

He remained in his corner without moving, puffing violently at

He saw their faces instantly in the glass, and his pipe nearly slipped . . .

an extinguished pipe, gripped helplessly by the return of that first vile terror. It came again to him with an absolute clarity of certainty that it was not with himself they had to do, these men, and, further, that he had no right in the world to interfere. He had no right to interfere; it would be immoral . . . even if the opportunity came. And the opportunity, he felt, would come. He had been an eavesdropper, and had come upon private information of a secret kind that he had no right to make use of, even that good might come—even to save life. He sat on in his corner, terrified and silent, waiting for the thing that should happen next.

But night came without explanation. Nothing happened. He slept soundly. There was no other guest at the inn but an elderly man, apparently a tourist like himself. He wore gold-rimmed glasses, and in the morning Martin overheard him asking the landlord what direction he should take for Litacy Hill. His teeth began then to chatter and a weakness came into his knees. 'You turn to the left at the crossroads,' Martin broke in before the landlord could reply. 'You'll see the signpost about two miles from here, and after that it's a matter of four miles

411

more.' How in the world did he know, flashed horribly through him. 'I'm going that way myself,' he was saying next. 'I'll go with you for a bit—if you don't mind!' The words came out impulsively and ill-considered; of their own accord they came. For his own direction was exactly opposite. *He did not want the man to go alone.* The stranger, however, easily evaded his offer of companionship. He thanked him with the remark that he was starting later in the day . . . They were standing, all three, beside the horse-trough, in front of the inn, when at that very moment a tramp, slouching along the road, looked up and asked the time of day. And it was the man with the gold-rimmed glasses who told him.

'T'ank you; much opliged,' the tramp replied, passing on with his slow, slouching gait, while the landlord, a talkative fellow, proceeded to remark upon the number of Germans that lived in England and were ready to swell the Teutonic invasion which *he*, for his part, deemed imminent.

But Martin heard it not. Before he had gone a mile upon his way he went into the woods to fight his conscience all alone. His feebleness, his cowardice, were surely criminal. Real anguish tortured him. A dozen times he decided to go back upon his steps, and a dozen times the singular authority that whispered he had no right to interfere prevented him. How could he act upon knowledge gained by eavesdropping? How interfere in the private business of another's hidden life merely because he had overheard, as at the telephone, its secret dangers? Some inner confusion prevented straight thinking altogether. The stranger would merely think him mad. He had no 'fact' to go upon. He smothered a hundred impulses . . . and finally went on his way with a shaking, troubled heart.

The last two days of his holiday were ruined by doubts and questions and alarms—all justified later when he read of the murder of a tourist upon Litacy Hill. The man wore gold-rimmed glasses, and carried in a belt about his person a large sum of money. His throat was cut. And the police were hard upon the trail of a mysterious pair of tramps, said to be—Germans.

ORDEAL

Angus Macdonald

On 6th November, 1942 the Ellerman liner City of Cairo, *five days out of Cape Town was torpedoed by a German U-boat. Many of the passengers and crew were either killed or went down with the ship. A few were lucky enough to take to the lifeboats. One of them was Quartermaster Angus Macdonald. This is his story.*

I was a quartermaster and had charge of No. 4 lifeboat. After seeing everything in order there and the boat lowered, I went over to the starboard side of the ship to where my mate, quartermaster Bob Ironside, was having difficulty in lowering his boat. I climbed inside the boat to clear a rope fouling the lowering gear, and was standing in the boat pushing it clear of the ship's side as it was being lowered, when a second torpedo exploded right underneath and blew the boat to bits. I remember a great flash, and then felt myself flying through space, then going down and down. When I came to I was floating in the water, and could see all sorts of wreckage around me in the dark. I could not get the light on my life-jacket to work, so I swam towards the largest bit of wreckage I could see in the darkness. This turned out to be No. 1 lifeboat and it was nearly submerged, it having been damaged by the second explosion. There were a few people clinging to the gunwale, which was down to water-level, and other people were sitting inside the flooded boat.

I climbed on board, and had a good look around to see if the boat was badly damaged. Some of the gear had floated away, and what was left was in a tangled mess. There were a few lascars, several women and children, and two European male passengers in the boat, and I explained to them that if some of them would go overboard and hang on to the gunwale or the wreckage near us for a few minutes we could bale out the boat and make it seaworthy. The women who were there acted immediately. They climbed outboard and, supported by the life-jackets every one was wearing, held on to an empty tank that was floating near by. I felt very proud of these women and children. One woman (whose name, if I remember rightly, was Lady Tibbs) had three children, and the four of them were the first to swim to the tank. One young woman was left in the boat with two babies in her arms.

We men then started to bale out the water. It was a long and arduous task, as just when we had the gunwale a few inches clear, the light swell running would roll in and swamp the boat again. Eventually we managed to bale out the boat, and then we started to pick up survivors who were floating on rafts or just swimming. As we worked we could see the *City of Cairo* still afloat, but well down in the water, until we heard someone say, 'There she goes.' We watched her go down, stern first, her bow away up in the air, and then she went down and disappeared. There was no show of emotion, and we were all quiet. I expect the others, like myself, were wondering what would happen to us.

We picked up more survivors as the night wore on, and by the first light of dawn the boat was full. There were still people on the rafts we could see with the daylight, and in the distance were other lifeboats. We rowed around picking up more people, among them Mr Sydney Britt, the chief officer, and quartermaster Bob Ironside, who was in No. 3 boat with me when the second torpedo struck. Bob's back had been injured, and one of his hands had been cut rather badly. We picked up others, then rowed to the other boats to see what decision had been made about our future. Mr Britt had, naturally, taken over command of our boat, and now he had a conference with Captain Rogerson, who was in another boat. They decided we would make for the nearest land, the island of St Helena, lying five hundred miles due north. We transferred people from boat to boat so that families could be together. Mr Britt suggested that, as our boat was in a bad way, with many leaks and a damaged rudder, and at least half its water-supply lost, all the children should shift to a dry boat and a few adults take their places in our boat.

When everything was settled we set sail and started on our long voyage. Our boat was now overcrowded with fifty-four persons on board – twenty-three Europeans, including three women, and thirty-one lascars. There was not enough room for everyone to sit down, so we had to take turns having a rest. The two worst injured had to lie down flat, so we made a place in the bows for Miss Taggart, a ship's stewardess, and cleared a space aft for my mate, quartermaster Bob Ironside. We did not know exactly what was wrong with Bob's back. We had a doctor in the boat, Dr Taskar, but he was in a dazed condition and not able to attend to the injured, so we bandaged them up as best we could with the first-aid materials on hand. The youngest person among us, Mrs Diana Jarman, one of the ship's passengers, and only about twenty years of age, was a great help with the first-aid. She could never do enough, either in attending to the sick and injured, boat work, or even actually handling the craft. She showed up some of the men in the boat, who seemed to lose heart from the beginning.

Once we were properly under way Mr Britt spoke to us all. He explained all the difficulties that lay ahead, and asked every one to pull their weight in everything to do with managing the boat, such as rowing during calm periods and keeping a look-out at night. He also explained that as we had lost nearly half our drinking water we must start right away on short rations. We could get two tablespoonfuls a day per person, one in the morning and one in the evening. He told us there were no passengers in a lifeboat, and every one would have to take turns baling as the boat was leaking very badly.

Before noon on that first day we saw our first sharks. They were enormous, and as they glided backward and forward under the boat it seemed they would hit and capsize us. They just skimmed the boat each time they passed, and they were never to leave us all the time we were in the boat.

The first night was quiet and the weather was fine, but we didn't get much rest. A good proportion of us had to remain standing for long periods, and now and then someone would fall over in their sleep. I was in the fore-part of the boat attending to the sails and the running gear, helped by Robert Watts from Reading, whom we called 'Tiny' because he was a big man. He didn't know much about seamanship, as he was an aeronautical engineer, but he said to me that first day, 'If you want anything done at any time just explain the job to me and I'll do it.' His help was very welcome as we did not have many of the crew available for the jobs that needed to be done. From the very beginning the lascars refused to help in any way, and just lay in the bottom of the boat, sometimes in over a foot of water.

On the second day the wind increased, and we made good speed. Sometimes the boats were close together and at other times almost out of sight of each other. Our boat seemed to sail faster than the others, so Mr Britt had the idea that we might go ahead on our own. If we could sail faster than the others, and as we were leaking so badly, we should go ahead and when we got to St Helena we could send help to the others. Mr Britt had a talk with Captain Rogerson when our boats were close, and the captain said that if the mate thought that was the best plan then go ahead. So we carried on on our own.

During the hours of darkness the wind rose stronger, and, as we could see the running gear was not in the best of condition, we hove to. As it got still worse, we had to put out a sea anchor to take turns at the steering-oar to hold the boat into the seas. We had a bad night, and two or three times sea broke over the heavily laden boat and soaked us all to the skin. It was during the night that we noticed Dr Taskar was failing mentally. Every now and then he shouted, 'Boy, bring me coffee,' or, 'Boy, another beer.' He had a rip in his trousers, and in the crowded boat during the night he cut a large piece out of the trousers of the ship's storekeeper, Frank Stobbart. I noticed the doctor with the knife and a piece of cloth in his hand. He was trying to fit the cloth over his own trousers. I pacified him and took his knife, a small silver knife with a whisky advertisement on the side. I had the same knife all through the years I was a prisoner in Germany, and only lost it after the war while serving in another Ellerman liner.

At noon on the third day the wind abated, and we set sails again and went on. We had lost sight of the other boats now and were on our own. We all expected to see a rescue ship or plane at any time, but nothing turned up. On the evening of the fourth day the doctor got worse, and rambled in his speech. He kept asking for water, and once Mr Britt gave him an extra ration, although there was not much to spare. During the night the doctor slumped over beside me, and I knew he was dead. That was the first death in the boat. We cast the body overboard at dawn while Mr Britt read a short prayer. We all felt gloomy after this first burial, and wondered who would be next.

Later in the day I crawled over to have a yarn with my mate Bob, and he said, 'Do you think we have a chance, Angus?' I said, 'Everything will be all right, Bob. We are bound to be picked up.' Bob hadn't long been married, and he was anxious about his wife and little baby in Aberdeen. He couldn't sit up, and I was afraid his back was broken or badly damaged.

Day and night the lascars kept praying to Allah, and repeating 'Pani, sahib, pani, sahib,' and they would never understand that the water was precious and had to be rationed out. On the sixth morning we found three of them dead in the bottom of the boat. The old engine-room serang read a prayer for them, and Tiny and I pushed them overboard, as the lascars never would help to bury their dead. The only two natives who helped us at any time were the old serang, a proper gentleman, and a fireman from Zanzibar, and they couldn't do enough to help.

We were getting flat calms for long periods, and we lowered the sails and used the oars. We didn't make much headway, but the work helped to keep our minds and bodies occupied. I know that doing these necessary tasks helped to keep me physically fit and able to stand up to the ordeal that lay ahead. There were a few Europeans who never gave a helping hand, and I noticed that they were the first to fail mentally. They died in the first two weeks.

I was worried about Miss Taggart's sores, as they had now festered and we had nothing to dress them with except salt water. With her lying in the same position all the time her back was a mass of sores. Tiny knew more about first-aid than the rest of us, and with the aid of old life-jackets he padded her up a bit. But on the seventh night she died and slipped down from her position in the bows. As she fell she got tangled up with another passenger, a Mr Ball from Calcutta, and when we got things straightened out they were both dead. A few more lascars died during the same night, and we had to bury them all at daybreak. The sharks were there in shoals that morning, and the water was churned up as they glided backward and forward near the bodies. Things were now getting worse on board, and a good few of the people sat all day with their heads on their chests doing and saying nothing. I talked to one young engineer, and told him to pull himself together as he was young and healthy and to take a lesson from Diana, who was always cheerful and bright. She had told us, 'Please don't call me Mrs Jarman; just call me Diana.' The young engineer did pull himself back to normal but within two days he dropped back and gave up hope and died. As we buried the bodies the boat gradually became lighter and the worst leaks rose above the water-line, so there was not so much water to bale out, although we had still to bale day and night.

Our own ship's stewardess, Annie Crouch, died on the tenth day. She had been failing mentally and physically for a time, and persisted in sitting in the bottom of the boat. We shifted her to drier places, but she always slid back. Her feet and legs had swollen enormously. Her death left only one woman among us, Diana. She was still active and full of life, and she spent most of her time at the tiller. Mr Britt was beginning to show signs of mental strain, and often mumbled to himself. If I asked him a question he would answer in a dazed sort of way. I worried about him a lot, for he was always a gentleman, and every one thought the world of him. On the twelfth day he was unable to sit up or talk, so we laid him down alongside Bob Ironside, who was also failing fast. Bob called me over one day, and asked me if I thought there was still a chance. I said certainly there was, and urged him not to give up hope as he would soon be home. He said, 'I can't hang on much longer, Angus. When I die, will you take off my ring and send it home if you ever get back?' There were only a few able-bodied men left among the Europeans now, and Tiny Watts, my right-hand man, died on the fourteenth morning. He hadn't complained at any time, and I was surprised when I found him dead. We buried seven bodies that morning: five lascars, Tiny, and Frank Stobbart. It took a long time to get them overboard, and I had to lie down and rest during the operation.

On the fifteenth morning at dawn both Mr Britt and Bob were dead, also three other Europeans and a few lascars. A few more lascars died during the day. One of the firemen said that if he couldn't get extra water he would jump overboard, and later in the day he jumped over the stern. He had forgotten to take off his life-jacket, and as we were now too weak to turn the boat round to save him, the sharks got him before he could drown. The remaining survivors voted that I should take over command. On looking through Mr Britt's papers I could see the estimated distances for each day up to about the tenth day, but after that there were only scrawls and scribbles. When I checked up on the water I found we had enough only for a few days, so I suggested cutting down the issue to one tablespoonful a day. There were plenty of biscuits and malted-milk tablets, but without water to moisten the mouth the biscuits only went into a powder and fell out of the corner of the mouth again. Those people with false teeth had still more trouble as the malted-milk tablets went into a doughy mess and stuck to their teeth.

The boat was now much drier, and there was not so much baling to do as we rode higher in the water and most of the leaks were above the surface. The movement, however, was not so steady as when we were heavier laden, but about the middle of the seventeenth night the boat appeared to become very steady again. I heard Diana cry out. 'We're full of water,' and I jumped up and found the boat half-full of water. I could see the plug-hole glittering like a blue light, and I started looking for the plug. I put a spare one in place, and a few of us baled out the water. There were two people lying near the plug-hole, and they seemed to take no interest in what was happening. About an hour later I discovered the plug gone again and water entering the boat. I put the plug back, and this time I lay down with an eye on watch. Sure enough, in less than half an hour I saw a hand over the plug pulling it out. I grasped the hand and found it belonged to a young European. He was not in his right mind, although he knew what he was doing. When I asked him why he tried to sink the boat he said, 'I'm going to die, so we might as well go together.' I shifted him to the fore part of the boat, and we others took turns in keeping an eye on him, but he managed to destroy all the contents of the first-aid box and throw them over the side. He died the next day, with seven or eight lascars, and a banker from Edinburgh, a Mr Crichton. Mr Crichton had a patent waistcoat fitted with small pockets, and the valuables we found there we put with rings and other things in Diana's handbag. Among Mr Crichton's possessions were the three wise monkeys in jade and a silver brandy flask that was empty.

At the end of the third week there were only eight of us left alive in the boat: the old engine-room serang, the fireman from Zanzibar, myself, Diana, Jack Edmead, the steward, Joe Green from Wigan, Jack Oakie from Birmingham, and a friend of his, Jack Little. Two of them had been engineers working on the new Howrah bridge at Calcutta.

There was still no rain, we had not had a single shower since we started our boat voyage, and the water was nearly finished. Only a few drops were left on the bottom of the tank. About the middle of the fourth week

I was lying down dozing in the middle of the night when the boat started to rattle and shake. I jumped up, thinking we had grounded on an island. Then I discovered a large fish had jumped into the boat and was thrashing about wildly. I grabbed an axe that was lying handy, and hit the fish a few hard cracks. The axe bounded off it like rubber, and it was a while before I made any impression, but when it did quieten down I tied a piece of rope round the tail and hung the fish on the mast. It took me all my time to lift the fish, as it was about three feet long and quite heavy. I lay down again, and at daybreak examined the fish closer. It was a dog-fish. During the struggle with it I had gashed a finger against its teeth, and as we now had no bandages or medicine all I could do was wash the cut in sea water before I proceeded to cut up the fish. I had heard and read about people drinking blood, and I thought that I could get some blood from the carcase for drinking. I had a tough job cutting up the fish with my knife, and only managed to get a few teaspoonsful of dirty, reddish-black blood. I cut the liver and heart out, and sliced some of the flesh off. By this time all hands were awake, although every one was feeling weak. I gave the first spoonful of blood to Diana to taste, but she spat it out and said it was horrible. I tried every one with a taste, but nobody could swallow the vile stuff. I tried it myself, but couldn't get it down. It seemed to swell the tongue. We tried eating the fish, but that was also a failure. I chewed and chewed at my piece, but couldn't swallow any and eventually spat it into the sea.

The day following my encounter with the big dog-fish my hand and arm swelled up, and Diana said I had blood-poisoning. The following day it was much worse, and throbbed painfully. I asked Diana if she could do anything for it, as we had no medical supplies left. She advised me to let the hand drag in the water, and later in the day she squeezed the sore, and all sorts of matter came out. I then put my hand back in the water, and that seemed to draw out more poison. At intervals Diana squeezed the arm from the shoulder downward, and gradually got rid of the swelling, although the sore didn't heal for months, and the scar remains to this day.

There was no water left now, and Jack Oakie, Jack Little, and the Zanzibar fireman all died during the one night. It took the remainder of us nearly a whole day to lift them from the bottom of the boat and roll them overboard. The serang was now unconscious and Joe Green was rambling in his speech. There were a few low clouds drifting over us, but no sign of rain, and I had lost count of the days. I had written up Mr. Britt's log-book to the end of the fourth week, but after that day and night seemed to be all the same. Diana had the sickness that nearly every one in turn had suffered: a sore throat and a thick yellow phlegm oozing from the mouth. I think it was due to us lying in the dampness all the time and never getting properly dry. The sails were now down and spread across the boat as I was too feeble to do anything in the way of running the boat. Against all advice, I often threw small quantities of sea water down my throat, and it didn't seem to make me any worse, although I never overdid it.

One night Joe Green would not lie in the bottom of the boat in comfort, but lay on the after end in an uncomfortable position. When I tried to get him to lie down with us he said, 'I won't last out the night, and if I lie down there you will never be able to lift me up and get me over the side.' The next morning he was dead. So was the serang. Two grand old men, though of different races. There were only three of us left now. Jack Edmead was pretty bad now, and Diana still had the sore throat. But we managed to get the bodies over the side. The serang by this time was very thin and wasted, and if he had been any heavier we would not have managed to get him over.

By this time we were only drifting about on the ocean. I had put the jib up a couple of times, but discovered we drifted in circles, so I took it down again. One day I had a very clear dream as I lay there in the bottom of the boat. I dreamed that the three of us were walking up the pierhead at Liverpool, and the dream was so clear that I really believed it would happen. I told Diana and Jack about the dream, and said I was sure we would be picked up. There wasn't a drop of water in the boat now, and the three of us just lay there dreaming of water in all sorts of ways. Sometimes it was about a stream that ran past our house when I was a child, another time I would be holding a hose and spraying water all round, but it was always about water. Jack was getting worse, and was laid out in the stern, while Diana was forward where it was drier. Sick as she was, she always used to smile and say, 'We still have a chance if we could only get some rain.'

Then one night rain came. I was lying down half asleep when I felt the rain falling on my face. I jumped up shouting, 'Rain, rain', but Jack wasn't able to get up and help me. Diana was in a pretty bad condition, but she managed to crawl along and help me spread the main sail to catch the water. It was a short sharp shower and didn't last long, but we collected a few pints in the sail and odd corners of the boat. We didn't waste a drop, and after pouring it carefully into the tank we sucked the raindrops from the woodwork and everywhere possible. Diana had trouble swallowing anything as her throat was swollen and raw, but I mixed some pemmican with water, and we had a few spoonfuls each. The water was very bitter as the sail had been soaked in salt water for weeks, but it tasted good to us. We all felt better after our drink, and I sat down in the well of the boat that day and poured can after can of sea water over myself, and gave Diana a bit of a wash. She was in good spirits now, although she could only speak in whispers. She told me about her home in the South of England: I think she said it was Windsor, on the Thames. She was very fond of horses and tennis and other sports, and she said, 'You must come and visit us when we get home,' which showed that like myself she had a firm conviction that we would get picked up.

The three days after the rain were uneventful. Diana was a bit better, but Jack was in a bad way, and lying down in the stern end. On the third day I had another shower-bath sitting down in the boat, as it had livened me up a lot the last time. Afterwards I set the jib and tried to handle the main sail, but couldn't make it, so I spread the sail and used it as a bed. I had the best sleep in weeks. In the early hours of the morning Diana shook me, and said excitedly, 'Can you hear a plane?' I listened, and heard what sounded like a plane in the distance, so I dashed aft and grabbed one of the red flares and tried to light it. It didn't go off, so I struck one of the lifeboat matches. It ignited at once, and I held it up as high as I could, and immediately a voice shouted, 'All right, put that light out.' It was still dark, but on looking in the direction of the voice we could see the dim outline of a ship, and hear the sound of her diesel engines. The same voice shouted, 'Can you come alongside?' God knows how we managed, but manage it we did. Even Jack found enough strength to give a hand, and with Diana at the tiller he and I rowed the boat alongside the ship. A line was thrown to us, and I made it fast. A pilot ladder was dropped, and two men came down to help us on board. They tied a rope round Diana, and with the help of others on the ship hauled her on board. I climbed up unaided, and the men helped Jack. The

I held the lifeboat match up as high as I could.

first thing I asked for was a drink, and we sat on a hatch waiting to see what would happen. We thought we were on a Swedish ship at first, but I saw a Dutch flag painted across the hatch. Then I heard a couple of men talking, and I knew then we were on a German ship, as I had a slight knowledge of the language. I told the other two, and Diana said , 'It doesn't matter what nationality it is as long as it is a ship.'

A man came to us soon and asked us to go with him and meet the captain. Two of the crew helped Diana and Jack, and we were taken amidships to the doctor's room, where a couch had been prepared for Diana. The captain arrived, and asked us about our trip in the boat and inquired how long we had been in it. I told him our ship had been torpedoed on the 6th of November, and that I had lost count of the days. He said this was the 12th of December, and that we were on board the German ship *Rhakotis*, and we should be well looked after. I remembered the bag of valuables in the boat, and told the captain where Diana's bag was. The bag was found and passed up, and given into the captain's charge. It was probably lost when the ship was sunk three weeks later. The lifeboat was stripped and sunk before the ship got under way again.

We were given cups of coffee, but were told that the doctor's orders were for us not to drink much at a time, and only eat or drink what he ordered. Diana was lying on the doctor's couch, and when the three of us were left alone for a while she bounced up and down on the springs and said, 'This is better than lying in that wet boat.' Later Jack and I were given a hot bath by a medical attendant, and my hand was bandaged, as it was still festering. We were taken aft to a cabin, and Diana was left in the doctor's room. The crew had orders not to bother us and to leave us on our own, as we had to rest as much as possible. When I looked at myself in the mirror I didn't recognise myself with a red beard and haggard appearance. There didn't seem to be any flesh left on my body, only a bag of bones. Jack looked even worse with his black beard and hollow cheeks.

We had been given some tablets and injected, and were now told to go to bed. Before I did so I asked one of the crew to fetch me a bottle of water. Although this was against the doctor's orders the man did so, and I hid the bottle under my pillow. Then I asked another man to bring me a bottle of water, and in this way I collected a few bottles and I drank the lot. Jack was already asleep when I turned in after drinking the water, and

I turned in on the bunk above him. We slept for hours and when I awoke I found I had soaked the bedding. Later I discovered I had soaked Jack's bed too. He was still asleep. I wakened him and apologised, but he only laughed. The steward brought us coffee at 7 am and when I told him about my bladder weakness he didn't seem annoyed, but took the bedclothes away to be changed. It was over a year before I was able to hold any liquid for more than an hour or so.

We were well looked after and well fed on the German ship, and from the first day I walked round the decks as I liked. Jack was confined to bed for a few days. We were not allowed to visit Diana, but the captain came aft and gave us any news concerning her. She couldn't swallow any food, and was being fed by injections. When we had been five days on the ship the doctor and the captain came along to our cabin, and I could see they were worried. The captain did the talking, and said that as the English girl still hadn't been able to eat, and couldn't go on living on injections, the doctor wanted to operate on her throat and clear the inflammation. But first of all he wanted our permission. I had never liked the doctor and had discovered he was disliked by nearly everyone on board, but still, he was the doctor, and should know more about what was good for Diana than I could. So I told the captain that if the doctor thought it was necessary to operate he had my permission as I wanted to see Diana well again. Jack said almost the same, and the captain asked if we would like to see her. We jumped at the chance, and went with the doctor. She seemed quite happy, and looked well, except for being thin. Here hair had been washed and set, and she said she was being well looked after. We never mentioned the operation to her, but noticed she could still talk only in whispers.

That evening at seven o'clock the captain came to us, and I could see that something was wrong. He said, 'I have bad news for you. The English girl has died. Will you follow me, please?' We went along, neither of us able to say a word. We were taken to the doctor's room where she lay with a bandage round her throat. You would never know she was dead, she looked so peaceful. The doctor spoke, and said in broken English that the operation was a success, but the girl's heart was not strong enough to stand the anaesthetic. I couldn't speak, and turned away broken-hearted. Jack and I went aft again, and I turned in to my bunk and lay crying like a baby nearly all night. It was the first time I had broken down and cried, and I think Jack was the same. The funeral was the next day, and when the time came we went along to the foredeck where the ship's crew were all lined up wearing uniform and the body was in a coffin covered by the Union Jack. The captain made a speech in German, and then spoke in English for our benefit. There were tears in the eyes of many of the Germans, as they had all taken an interest in the English girl. The ship was stopped, and after the captain had said a prayer the coffin slid slowly down a slipway into the sea. It had been weighted, and sank slowly. The crew stood to attention bareheaded until the coffin disappeared. It was an impressive scene, and a gallant end to a brave and noble girl. We had been through so much together, and I knew I would never forget her.

THE MASQUE OF THE RED DEATH

Edgar Allan Poe

The 'Red Death' had long devastated the country. No pestilence had ever been so fatal, or so hideous. Blood was its Avatar and its seal – the redness and horror of blood. There were sharp pains, and sudden dizziness, and then profuse bleeding at the pores, with dissolution. The scarlet stains upon the body and especially upon the face of the victim, were the pest ban which shut him out from the aid and from the sympathy of his fellow-men. And the whole seizure, progress, and termination of the disease, were the incidents of half an hour.

But the Prince Prospero was happy and dauntless and sagacious. When his dominions were half-depopulated, he summoned to his presence a thousand hale and light-hearted friends from among the knights and dames of his court, and with these retired to the deep seclusion of one of his castellated abbeys. This was an extensive and magnificent structure, the creation of the prince's own eccentric yet august taste. A strong and lofty wall girdled it in. This wall had gates of iron. The courtiers, having entered, brought furnaces and massy hammers and welded the bolts. They resolved to leave means neither of ingress nor egress to the sudden impulses of despair or of frenzy from within. The abbey was amply provisioned. With such precautions the courtiers might bid defiance to contagion. The external world could take care of itself. In the meantime it was folly to grieve, or to think. The prince had provided all the appliances of pleasure. There were buffoons, there were improvisatori, there were ballet-dancers, there were musicians, there was Beauty, there was wine. All these and security were within. Without was the 'Red Death'.

It was toward the close of the fifth or sixth month of his seclusion, and while the pestilence raged most furiously abroad, that the Prince Prospero entertained his thousand friends at a masked ball of the most unusual magnificence.

It was a voluptuous scene, that masquerade. But first let me tell of the rooms in which it was held. These were seven – an imperial suite. In many palaces, however, such suites form a long and straight vista, while the folding doors slide back nearly to the walls on either hand, so that the view of the whole extent is scarcely impeded. Here the case was very different, as might have been expected from the duke's love of the *bizarre*. The apartments were so irregularly disposed that the vision embraced but little more than one at a time. There was a sharp turn at every twenty or thirty yards, and at each turn a novel effect. To the right and left, in the middle of each wall, a tall and narrow Gothic window looked out upon a closed corridor which pursued the windings of the suite. These windows were of stained glass whose colour varied in accordance with the prevailing hue of the decorations of the chamber into which it opened. That at the eastern extremity was hung, for example, in blue – and vividly blue were its windows. The second chamber was purple in its ornaments and tapestries, and here the panes were purple. The third was green throughout, and so were the casements. The fourth was furnished and lighted with orange – the fifth with white – the sixth with violet. The seventh apartment was closely shrouded in black velvet tapestries that hung all over the ceiling and down the walls, falling in heavy folds upon a carpet of the same material and hue. But in this chamber only, the colour of the windows failed to correspond with the decorations. The panes here were scarlet – a deep blood colour. Now, in no one of the seven apartments was there any lamp or candelabrum, amid the profusion of golden ornaments that lay scattered to and fro or depended from the roof. There was no light of any kind emanating from lamp or candle within the suite of chambers. But in the corridors that followed the suite there stood, opposite to each window, a heavy tripod, bearing a brazier of fire, that projected its rays through the tinted glass and so glaringly illumined the room. And thus were produced a multitude of gaudy and fantastic appearances. But in the western or black chamber the effect of the firelight that streamed upon the dark hangings through the blood-tinted panes was ghastly in the extreme, and produced so wild a look upon the countenances of those who entered that there were few of the company bold enough to set foot within its precincts at all.

It was in this apartment, also, that there stood against the western wall, a gigantic clock of ebony. Its pendulum swung to and fro with a dull, heavy, monotonous clang; and when the minute-hand made the circuit of the face, and the hour was to be stricken, there came from the brazen lungs of the clock a sound which was clear and loud and deep and exceedingly musical, but of so peculiar a note and emphasis that, at each lapse of an hour, the musicians of the orchestra were constrained to pause, momentarily, in their performance, to harken to the sound; and thus the waltzers perforce ceased their evolutions; and there was a brief disconcert of the whole gay company; and, while the chimes of the clock yet rang, it was observed that the giddiest grew pale, and the more aged and sedate passed their hands over their brows as if in confused reverie or meditation. But when the echoes had fully ceased, a light laughter at once pervaded the assembly; the musicians looked at each other and smiled as if at their own nervousness and folly, and made whispering vows, each to the other, that the next chiming of the clock should produce in them no similar emotion; and then, after the lapse of sixty minutes (which embrace three thousand and six hundred seconds of the Time that flies), there came yet another chiming of the clock, and then were the same disconcert and tremulousness and meditation as before.

But, in spite of these things, it was a gay and magnificent revel. The tastes of the duke were peculiar. He had a fine eye for colours and effects. He disregarded the *decora* of mere fashion. His plans were bold and fiery, and his conceptions glowed with barbaric lustre. There are some who would have thought him mad. His followers felt that he was not. It was necessary to hear and see and touch him to be *sure* that he was not.

He had directed, in great part, the movable embellishments of the seven chambers, upon occasion of this great *fête*; and it was his own guiding taste which had given character to the masqueraders. Be sure

429

they were grotesque. There were much glare and glitter and piquancy and phantasm – much of what has been since seen in *Hernani*. There were arabesque figures with unsuited limbs and appointments. There were delirious fancies such as the madman fashions. There were much of the beautiful, much of the wanton, much of the *bizarre*, something of the terrible, and not a little of that which might have excited disgust. To and fro in the seven chambers there stalked, in fact, a multitude of dreams. And these – the dreams – writhed in and about, taking hue from the rooms, and causing the wild music of the orchestra to seem as the echo of their steps. And, anon, there strikes the ebony clock which stands in the hall of the velvet. And then, for a moment, all is still, and all is silent save the voice of the clock. The dreams are stiff-frozen as they stand. But the echoes of the chime die away – they have endured but an instant – and a light, half-subdued laughter floats after them as they depart. And now again the music swells, and the dreams live, and writhe to and fro more merrily than ever, taking hue from the many-tinted windows through which stream the rays from the tripods. But to the chamber which lies most westwardly of the seven there are now none of the maskers who venture; for the night is waning away; and there flows a ruddier light through the blood-coloured panes; and the blackness of the sable drapery appals; and to him whose foot falls upon the sable carpet, there comes from the near clock of ebony a muffled peal more solemnly emphatic than any which reaches *their* ears who indulged in the more remote gaieties of the other apartments.

But these other apartments were densely crowded, and in them beat feverishly the heart of life. And the revel went whirlingly on, until at length there commenced the sounding of midnight upon the clock. And then the music ceased, as I have told; and the evolutions of the waltzers were quieted; and there was an uneasy cessation of all things as before. But now there were twelve strokes to be sounded by the bell of the clock; and thus it happened, perhaps, that more of thought crept, with more of time, into the meditations of the thoughtful among those who revelled. And thus too, it happened, perhaps, that before the last echoes of the last chime had utterly sunk into silence, there were many individuals in the crowd who had found leisure to become aware of the presence of a masked figure which had arrested the attention of no single individual before. And the rumour of this new presence having spread itself whis-

The tall, gaunt figure was shrouded from head to foot

peringly around, there arose at length from the whole company a buzz, or murmur, expressive of disapprobation and surprise – then, finally, of terror, of horror, and of disgust.

In an assembly of phantasms such as I have painted, it may well be supposed that no ordinary appearance could have excited such sensation. In truth the masquerade licence of the night was nearly unlimited; but the figure in question had out-Heroded Herod, and gone beyond the bounds of even the prince's indefinite decorum. There are chords in the hearts of the most reckless which cannot be touched without emotion. Even with the utterly lost, to whom life and death are equally jests, there are matters of which no jest can be made. The whole company, indeed, seemed now deeply to feel that in the costume and bearing of the stranger neither wit nor propriety existed. The figure was tall and gaunt, and shrouded from head to foot in the habiliments of the grave. The mask which concealed the visage was made so nearly to resemble the countenance of a stiffened corpse that the closest scrutiny must have had difficulty in detecting the cheat. And yet all this might have been endured, if not approved, by the mad revellers around. But the mummer had gone so far as to assume the type of the Red Death. His vesture was dabbled in *blood* – and his broad brow, with all the features of the face, was besprinkled with the scarlet horror.

When the eyes of Prince Prospero fell upon this spectral image (which, with a slow and solemn movement, as if more fully to sustain its *rôle*, stalked to and fro among the waltzers) he was seen to be convulsed in the first moment with a strong shudder either of terror or distaste; but, in the next, his brow reddened with rage.

'Who dares,' – he demanded hoarsely of the courtiers who stood near him – 'who dares insult us with this blasphemous mockery? Seize him and unmask him – that we may know whom we have to hang, at sunrise, from the battlements!'

It was in the eastern or blue chamber in which stood the Prince Prospero as he uttered these words. They rang throughout the seven rooms loudly and clearly, for the prince was a bold and robust man, and the music had become hushed at the waving of his hand.

It was in the blue room where stood the prince, with a group of pale courtiers by his side. At first, as he spoke, there was a slight rushing movement of this group in the direction of the intruder, who at the moment was also near at hand, and now, with deliberate and stately step, made closer approach to the speaker. But from a certain nameless awe with which the mad assumptions of the mummer had inspired the whole party, there were found none who put forth hand to seize him; so that, unimpeded, he passed within a yard of the prince's person; and while the vast assembly, as if with one impulse, shrank from the centres of the rooms to the walls, he made his way uninterruptedly, but with the same solemn and measured step which had distinguished him from the first, through the blue chamber to the purple – through the purple to the green – through the green to the orange – through this again to the white – and even thence to the violet, ere a decided movement had been made to arrest him. It was then, however, that the Prince Prospero, maddening with rage and the shame of his own momentary cowardice, rushed hurriedly through the six chambers, while none followed him on account of a deadly terror that had seized upon all. He bore aloft a drawn dagger, and had approached, in rapid impetuosity, to within three or four feet of the retreating figure, when the latter, having attained the extremity of the velvet apartment, turned suddenly and confronted his pursuer. There was a sharp cry – and the dagger dropped gleaming upon the sable carpet, upon which, instantly afterward, fell prostrate in death the Prince Prospero. Then, summoning the wild courage of despair, a throng of the revellers at once threw themselves into the black apartment, and, seizing the mummer, whose tall figure stood erect and motionless within the shadow of the ebony clock, gasped in unutterable horror at finding the grave cerements and corpse-like mask, which they handled with so violent a rudeness, untenanted by any tangible form.

And now was acknowledged the presence of the Red Death. He had come like a thief in the night. And one by one dropped the revellers in the blood-bedewed halls of their revel, and died each in the despairing posture of his fall. And the life of the ebony clock went out with that of the last of the gay. And the flames of the tripods expired. And darkness and Decay and the Red Death held illimitable dominion over all.

DANIEL WITH GUITAR

Anthea Courtenay

Daniel left, as he had arrived, in a flurry of noise and laughter, and after he'd gone the house seemed very quiet. Miranda didn't feel like being with the others. She went up to the little guest-room at the top of the house which over the last few weeks had become her room. It was small and rather bare, but from the window she could gaze out at the long, barely perceptible line where the sky merged into the waters of the Channel, and dream, uninterrupted by anyone asking her what she was doing or making her feel she should be doing something else.

Here there was none of the clutter of her room at home—no dolls, posters, books, paintings, constantly around her to remind her of the rather unsatisfactory person she was. It was as if its very bareness had given her the space to be someone new, and she had been, oh, she had, in this house, in this family; she had felt herself flowering; she had been accepted, liked, she had begun to like herself.

And now?

She went to the mirror and looked at the face there. It was different from the face she'd brought with her, but she wasn't certain where the difference lay. It was still squarish, with a nose she considered too long; it was tanned, of course, and her light brown hair was nicely streaked blonde by the sun. But the brown eyes that stared back at her seemed to be conveying a message she couldn't understand; she held their gaze for a long time, wondering who? who? until she became afraid and had to stop.

On the dressing-table lay the pile of photographs Daniel had given her yesterday. Take as many as you want, he'd said; he'd get them reprinted in Paris. They'd exchanged addresses at the same time, but he wouldn't write, she thought, not now. Somehow, she'd spoiled things. Something inside her had crept up and crept up and had not allowed her to go on being happy. And now he'd gone, and there was no way of mending it.

She sat down on the bed and laid the photographs out beside her, ordering them like a game of patience. There it all lay, the summer that had begun so magically: the white house on the cliff top, looking as if at any moment it might float away; Monsieur and Madame Barbier, grey-haired and plumpish, both; the three girls ('My three graces', Madame Barbier called them, and they were in fact like sisters out of a story, Antoinette the good one, Geneviève the beautiful one, and Marie-José the lively one). And Miranda herself—many, many pictures of Miranda, no one had ever photographed her so often—on the beach, in the garden, looking starled from the depths of an armchair (no, but why had she chosen *that* one?), Miranda giggling with Marie-José, Miranda on that trip they'd made to Rouen, standing by the statue of Joan of Arc (whom *she*, Daniel informed her, had burned), and Miranda with Daniel, taken by Marie-José, laughing, happy-looking. Her mother would be pleased. 'You always look so miserable in photographs,' she used to say, '*do* cheer up.'

Happy. She'd been happy before he arrived; so much of the time at home and at school she seemed to be all wrong; dreamy, clumsy, she was like one of those puzzles you get in Christmas stockings, constantly shifting and tilting and tugging at herself to try and fit in with what other people wanted of her. And here, despite being packed off to this strange French family like an unwanted parcel while her mother went to America to write travel articles—here, almost as soon as she'd walked through the front door, it was as if all the pieces had slotted neatly and smoothly into place. The house and its inhabitants seemed in some way charmed, magical; together they transformed Miranda effortlessly into the person she wanted so badly to be.

When Marie-José explained to her that their nineteen-year-old cousin was coming to stay ('He is very amusing, very funny!'), Miranda felt something inside her shrink. Boys, like tennis and maths and saying the right thing, were something she wasn't good at. And from the viewpoint of her not quite fifteen years, someone of nineteen was a man, almost. It didn't occur to her beforehand that Daniel would be magic too.

The day after his arrival, they had gone to the beach below the house— Antoinette, Marie-José, Daniel and Miranda. Up till now it had usually been just herself and Marie-José; Geneviève had a job, and Antoinette, who was engaged, sewed her trousseau and helped in the house. Four of them made the little beach unusually crowded and lively.

He wasn't good-looking, Miranda decided, watching Daniel as he stood on his hands in the sand. He had a big, rather toothy smile; with his hair plastered down from swimming his head looked too small; his body was longish but very muscular. She was glad he wasn't good-looking. But he was very amusing, very funny. Supper last night had been eaten in a veritable hailstorm of jokes and stories and imitations, most of which Miranda had been unable to follow; afterwards they'd sat out in the garden and Daniel had played his guitar and they'd all sung; and his smile had included Miranda and she'd stopped shrinking.

As he came down from his handstand the girls applauded and he looked pleased. He began telling them something, talking very fast— 'Slowly!' commanded Marie-José in French. 'Speak more slowly, so Miranda can understand.'

'It's all right,' murmured Miranda, but Daniel complied. They had established the evening before that her stumbling French was a great deal better than his two or three words of English. Very slowly, and with exaggerated mime gestures, he explained that he had taken up judo—'Le judo—yes?' Look how strong his neck muscles were! He invited Miranda to try to strangle him. Miranda laughed and shook her head. Marie-José put on an evil expression and crept up behind him and attacked, and very gently, in slow motion, Daniel flung her to the ground where they grappled, sandily. Miranda envied them, like brother and sister, not afraid to touch each other. He must think her a fool, a baby.

Antoinette slightly po-faced, looked at her watch and reminded them

As she hesitated over her choice, Daniel came up beside her.

that they had to do some shopping before lunch. Lunch in the Barbier household was always a three-course affair, starting with home-made soup from a large tureen; and lunch was never late.

As she fastened her smock over her bikini, Miranda heard Daniel saying something about her to Marie-José. She didn't know if she was meant to hear and pretended not to, but Marie-José said in English, 'Do you hear, Miranda? Daniel thinks you are very pretty.'

And instead of mumbling, 'No, I'm not, 'Miranda found herself curtseying to Daniel and saying, 'Merci, Monsieur!', as if she were used to compliments.

There was a small argument going on between Antoinette and Marie-José. Marie-José wanted to go shopping on her own, and Miranda knew why. Marie-José had told her confidentially that she was in love with a boy called Alain; at seventeen her parents thought her too young to get engaged and they didn't approve of Alain. When she went to the village on her own or with Miranda, Marie-José would disappear into the post office to telephone him, emerging at length flushed and very talkative. Miranda found these secret phone calls highly romantic, and was flattered to be told about them. Now Antoinette was insisting on coming too. Marie-José put her tongue out at her behind her back, and they all four went to the village.

Miranda enjoyed shopping, which was a ritual with the Barbier household, just as meals were. Every cut of meat, every tomato, was pondered over, considered, criticized and discussed and discussed before a purchase could be made, and once the transaction was complete, the price paid was written in beside the item on the shopping list. Miranda wondered what Madame Barbier would have made of her mother's flying visits to the frozen foods section of the supermarket. The orderliness, the care with which everything here was carried out were a constant delight to her.

When they reached the village she went to buy some postcards while the sisters were in the butcher's. As she hesitated over her choice, David came up beside her.

Are you choosing a card for your boyfriend?' he asked, and Miranda nodded demurely. She picked three cards—here, she had learned, there was even an art in buying postcards. 'Never,' Marie-José had instructed her, 'take cards from the front of the rack—they are all dirty, look. Always take them from the *back*.'

Daniel seemed to take it for granted that they would walk back to the house together, and Miranda felt too shy to object that they perhaps ought to wait for the others. As they climbed the hill he asked, what was the name of her boyfriend?

'Henry,' she replied, without too much thought. She did in fact know a boy called Henry, the son of some neighbours—for which reason her mother and his seemed to think they should be friends. He was a very serious boy with spectacles; his voice had not properly broken, and he and Miranda never found anything to talk about.

'Henry!' repeated Daniel. 'Hen-ree!' What sort of a name was that?

'Henri,' Miranda translated helpfully.

'Hen-ree!' Daniel didn't believe her— she didn't, she couldn't truly have a friend called Henry!

'Yes, I do,' she said, nearly convincing herself.

'C'est vrai, ce petit mensonge-là?' said Daniel.

Miranda tried to work this out. 'Vrai' meant true, but what was 'mensonge'? 'Oui, c'est vrai!'

'Alors,' said Daniel, triumphantly, she was lying!

Miranda remembered that a 'mensonge' was a lie. So, what he'd said was, 'Is that lie true?' And when she said yes, it meant it was true she'd been lying. For a moment she wanted to burst into tears with sheer frustration. Then she decided to laugh.

Henry was very handsome and very nice, she told Daniel, cocking her head in a way she'd never tried before.

And Miranda loved him passionately? Daniel pursued, rolling his eyes, and Miranda got the giggles, partly at his face, and partly at the idea of anyone loving Henry passionately. When they reached the house she was laughing so much she had to run up to her room to tidy her face, as well as her hair.

Looking in the mirror she saw that she *was* pretty. She cocked her head at her reflection. 'Merci, Monsieur!' she said, and flung herself on her bed, so full of laughter she had to cling to it in case she should float away out of the window.

A few days later there was a fête in a nearby village. Miranda hadn't quite grasped what was being celebrated, but they were to dress up for it. They went down in the evening in two cars; the square was lit up; there was a band, and dancing. Daniel and Monsieur Barbier and Antoinette's fiancé danced with the girls in turn; Madame preferred to watch. Some of the village boys wanted to dance with the girls too, but Monsieur said no—though when Marie-José pointed out that one girl was always left out he allowed a particularly polite young man to dance with Geneviève. She was wearing a white dress, and the young man took his handkerchief from his pocket and held it between his right hand and her dress, so that the white fabric would not be stained.

Miranda danced with Monsieur Barbier, who was slow and heavy, and Antoinette's fiancé, who held her at arm's length, and Daniel, ah, Daniel, who whirled and twirled like a demon, swinging her round, under his arm and round and about so her skirt swung and spun and her feet seemed to know by themselves what to do, and she was happy and dizzy and breathless.

There were incomprehensible noises from a loudspeaker, and the dancing stopped. Into the black starry sky new stars burst, fireworks, soaring and cascading, turning the upturned faces pink and green and silver, while weightless diamonds sank and died in the air. Miranda and Daniel had been dancing together when the music stopped, and were a little way away from the others. As they stood, he put his arm round her waist. It was extraordinary. For though they had touched while dancing, nothing had happened then like the tingle that went through her now, from head to toes, as if he and she completed an electric circuit. And, still with his arm round her waist, he dropped on her hair the lightest of kisses.

On the journey home Madame said how nice it was of that young man to protect Geneviève's dress with his handkerchief, and how pretty all the girls had looked dancing. And in the darkness of the back of the car, Miranda's small hand was enclosed in Daniel's large one, and she knew that she could never be happier than this, because any more and she would explode, sending a shower of sparks in her wake.

There were swims and walks, and car trips to see châteaux and churches and relations. When no one was looking Daniel held Miranda's hand, or dropped butterfly kisses swiftly on the back of her neck, her ear, her cheek. He teased her, he joked with her, he told her she had pretty eyes. He took her photograph wherever they went. 'C'est vrai, ce petit mensonge-là?' he asked her at least once a day, and she never worked out a suitable reply, but stamped her foot at him and pretended to be angry. And had she heard from Henry? Henry didn't write to her, Henry was unfaithful! And Miranda knew perfectly well that he knew perfectly well that she had no boyfriend called Henry.

Only Marie-José knew of their flirtation, and she didn't comment, but clearly approved. Miranda wanted no one to know, and yet at the same time hoped people would notice that there was something different about her—for it must show, surely, it must shine around her like an aura, that she was in love.

It didn't seem to matter that they were never alone. Daniel danced around her, dazzling her; there was no time to wonder what was coming next, or pause to want more than she had.

The weather became overcast, not suitable for swimming. Monsieur Barbier let Daniel take Miranda and Marie-José out in his car for a drive in the countryside. Marie-José made one of her phone calls first, and they went a long way to a town on the coast, where they met Marie-José's Alain. He was better-looking than Daniel, but Miranda didn't like him. They all had coffee, and then Daniel and she walked to the seashore.

They walked among rocks and pebbles, not talking much, picking up shells. Miranda liked the mistiness and emptiness of the sea and sky; it was like a moonscape; they could be anywhere, on another planet, at the beginning of time. Daniel put his arm round her shoulders. She was happy and sad all at once.

He wasn't in a teasing mood today. He told her he would be going back to Paris soon; he hated Paris in August, but he had to catch up with some studies. He didn't say that he wished she could come too; he didn't say he would write.

He asked her about her life at home; she felt bad telling him she'd never known her father, which always made her feel there was something wrong with her. Daniel's parents were divorced, he told her; he had a stepfather he got on well with. That made her feel better. It must be nice, though, to have a stepfather you liked. It was the first time she and Daniel had had a serious conversation.

When they went back to the car Marie-José was sitting in it alone. She looked odd; Miranda thought her eyes were swollen; and when Daniel began to tease her she snapped back at him fiercely. He said, 'Oh, là, là!', shaking his hand as if it had been stung.

'You won't say to my mother—that I met Alain?'

Miranda was hurt that she should feel it necessary to ask.

It was Sunday, and the family had gone to Mass, except Daniel who had conveniently overslept—he'd told Miranda he didn't believe in all that nonsense. Miranda curled up in an armchair in the *salon,* struggling with a French novel she'd picked up at random from the shelves. It was a thriller, full of slang, and she couldn't concentrate on it anyway; pictures and thoughts kept flitting in front of the pages, distracting her. She felt listless that morning. The weather had been gloomy for some days. Ever since the meeting with Alain, Marie-José had been moody, less friendly; two nights ago Antoinette and Geneviève had had an argument that became quite acrimonious and their father had shouted at them both. Miranda was waiting for someone to be cross with her.

Only Daniel was the same, and Daniel was going soon. The hand-holding, the butterfly kisses, the teasing flirtation continued, but underneath she was anxious. She tried not to be; she tried to hold on to the enchantment of it all, but it seemed to be slipping through her fingers, and she could not see why or how or what she could do about it.

Suddenly, Daniel was in the room. She hadn't heard him coming. He had his camera, and as she looked up he snapped her startled face, click, click, walking up to her. She felt his tallness in a new way from the low armchair, and suddenly felt shy.

All alone? he asked. What was she reading?

He kneeled down besdie her, his face level with hers, looked at the book, pretended to be shocked. Nice English girls shouldn't be reading books like that.

She couldn't understand it anyway, Miranda said.

'C'est vrai, ce petit mensonge-là?'

He leaned forward and kissed her on the lips. She jumped as if he had hit her. He looked startled himself. He leaned forward again, but she began to giggle, trying to get up from the chair. He put his arms, one each side of her, against the back of the chair, imprisoning her, laughing. She pushed against him; he was as solid as a tree trunk.

Don't push my chest, he said—how would she like it if he pushed hers?

He was laughing, he was only playing, and she went on struggling, giggling, it was a game, a brother-and-sister game like the ones he played with Marie-José, but she knew she must stop laughing soon or she would start crying—oh, stop, stop, stop!

He did stop, and knelt back on the floor, looking at her. Then he put his tongue out at her and said she wasn't nice.

He wasn't nice, she said.

For a moment they were both at a loss.

Then he decided that yes, she was nice, and he took her hands and pulled her out of the chair. 'Très gentille,' he said, 'très douce,' and stroked back her tousled hair.

They heard the car coming up the drive and sprang apart. Miranda rearranged herself in the chair with her book and Daniel wandered out into the garden, whistling.

That evening everyone was a bit mad. Antoinette had a sore throat, and her mother had painted it with some blue stuff. Antoinette, who was usually so grown-up, so almost middle-aged, kept sticking her blue tongue out, saying 'La lune est bleue!' and everyone got the giggles.

When she went to bed that night Miranda felt a bit sick. She told herself it was from the laughing, but underneath there was something else. One minute she was drifting dizzily to sleep and the next, her eyes were wide open.

'But I'm not in love with him!' she heard herself think. And she felt sick again, as if she'd done something terribly wrong, though she hadn't, she knew she hadn't. Nor had Daniel, nothing bad at all. He was nice, he was kind, he wouldn't do anything bad. But there was something that was not right, it was too late, a window had opened in her heart and the bird of love had flown away, leaving the doomy sick feeling pressing down on her stomach.

Next day was still gloomy. Madame sent them off on another expedition, Marie-José, Daniel and Miranda, to look at another château. Once on the coach, Daniel took her hand. She couldn't bear it, she took her hand away. Daniel became very silent. Miranda wished she hadn't withdrawn her hand, but later, as they entered the courtyard of the château, he put his arm round her shoulders and again she had to move away, went and studied the postcard racks at the gate.

Marie-José came up beside her. 'Daniel is very upset!' she said. 'What has happened? You have hurt his feelings.'

Miranda took four cards at random.

'What is wrong? Did he offend you?'

Miranda shook her head dumbly. It was impossible to explain when she didn't understand herself. She had been in love with him; now she didn't want him to touch her. She couldn't say so.

She glanced at Daniel's closed face. Had she really hurt his feelings? It hadn't even occurred to her that she could. She didn't know what to do, what to say. But she hated him looking so upset. Gently, she slipped her hand into his, and he looked at her with a quick, open smile. And Miranda felt powerful and false and a whole lot of other things, all at once.

Let's see your cards, he said. When she took them out, she realized that she had forgotten to take them from the back of the rack. Marie-José had been right. They were all dog-eared. She could have cried.

For the two days after that until Daniel left, they both pretended things were the same. They were not alone together again. Daniel maintained his flow of high spirits and jokes, but, guiltily, Miranda almost looked forward to his going.

On the last evening he got out his guitar and they all sat round, joining in some of the songs and listening to Daniel sing others. One was a folksong about a faithless shepherdess, with a sad little refrain; as it ended, in spite of everyone being there, Daniel looked right at Miranda, a look that seemed to her to be fulll of reproach and sadness. She wanted to hug him. And now it was too late.

She turned over the remaining photographs. There were several of Daniel. No, he wasn't good-looking. But it was a nice face. Ah, yes, here was the one she had taken herself quite early on: Daniel playing his guitar, the sea behind him; absorbed in his music-making his face was turned away slightly, his dark hair flopping over his eyes. She was proud of that photograph.

As she stared at it in a large tear rolled down her cheek and dropped on to the bedspread, followed shortly by another. And another. That look he'd given her last night. . . . But she hadn't known, she hadn't really thought. . . . It had all been a game, and he'd been the one who'd led it, the one in command. All the time, underneath her happiness, a small voice she hadn't quite been aware of had been telling her, he's only playing, he's not really interested in you, how could he be, when he's so attractive and you're so ordinary, so dull, so young?

But supposing the voice had been wrong?

Once again, her jumbled feelings tilted and slid and slotted into place, and the pattern was not what she'd thought it was.

She wiped her eyes and set on one side the photograph of Daniel playing his guitar. That was the one she would put in her dressing-table mirror at school. She would tell the others casually about this super French guy, Daniel, she'd been going around with all summer. And they'd be surprised, and would see that there as something different about her, and envy her.

FRANKENSTEIN

Mary Shelley

Frankenstein . . . a name that strikes a sudden chill. Frankenstein . . . probably thought of as the most famous and terrifying 'monster' in all literature. Yet this was not the name of the monster, but that of the fictional scientist who created him. And the creator of both was a young, delicate girl.

She was Mary, wife of Percy Bysshe Shelley, one of Britain's great poets. She and her husband were spending the summer of 1816 in Switzerland, where one of their friends and neighbours was the equally famous Lord Byron. It proved to be a wet and miserable summer and the friends were constantly kept indoors. Finally, almost as a piece of fun, Byron suggested that each of them write a ghost story.

This was not to prove difficult for Shelley and Byron, both accomplished writers, but for the young Mary it was far from easy. One evening, however, she sat quietly, listening while her husband and Lord Byron discussed the writings of a scientist who had suggested that a corpse could be given back life. As she later wrote: 'Night waned upon this talk; and even the witching hour had gone by before we retired to rest. When I placed my head on my pillow, I did not sleep. I saw—with shut eyes, but acute mental vision—I saw the pale student of unhallowed arts kneeling beside the thing he had put together. I saw the hideous phantasm of a man stretched out, and then, on the working of some powerful engine, show signs of life, and stir with an uneasy, half vital motion.'

And so, almost as if in a dream, the fantastic and mysterious story of Frankenstein was born . . .

The story begins with letters from Captain Walton to his sister in England. His ship lay becalmed, nearly enclosed in ice, when he and his men saw a strange sight. 'We perceived a low carriage, fixed on a sledge and drawn by dogs, pass on towards the north, at the distance of half a mile. A being which had the shape of a man, but apparently of gigantic stature, sat in the sledge and guided the dogs. We watched the rapid progress of the traveller with our telescopes, until he was lost among the distant inequalities of the ice.'

The following morning the captain went on deck and found some of his men talking to someone. By the side of the ship was a sledge which had drifted towards the vessel during the night on a large piece of ice. Only one dog remained alive, but there was a human being within it, whom the sailors were persuading to come aboard the ship. The man was not, as the other traveller had seemed to be, a savage inhabitant of some undiscovered island, but a European. When Captain Walton looked over the side of his ship the stranger addressed him in English, although with a foreign accent. 'Before I come on board your vessel, will you have the kindness to inform me whither you are bound?'

The captain was amazed at such a question. The stranger's limbs were nearly frozen and his body thin from fatigue and suffering. He had never seen a man in so wretched a condition. When told that the ship was on a voyage of discovery to the North Pole, the stranger seemed satisfied and allowed himself to be carried on board.

The stranger spoke little but once, when the ship's lieutenant asked him why he had come so far upon the ice in so strange a vehicle, and he replied, gloomily, 'To seek one who fled from me.'

'And did the man whom you pursued travel in the same fashion?'

'Yes.'

'Then I fancy we have seen him; for the day before we picked you up, we saw some dogs drawing a sledge, with a man in it, across the ice.'

This news seemed to rouse the stranger and, with rest and good food, his health steadily improved. He and the captain became friends and finally he decided to tell him the whole, terrible story . . .

His name was Frankenstein and had been born in Geneva. For a while he had been an only child and then his parents, who had always wanted a daughter, adopted Elizabeth—'my more than sister, the beautiful and adored companion of all my occupations and pleasures.'

After a while the young Frankenstein had to go to college. Here he was greatly influenced by a Professor Waldman, who quickly saw in

447

his young pupil a student of genius. After a while he took him into his laboratory and explained to him the uses of various machines. He told his pupil what he should procure, promising him the use of his own equipment when he had advanced enough not to spoil the mechanism of his machines. He then gave him a list of books to read and, grateful for the professor's interest, young Frankenstein left the laboratory.

But that visit had decided his future destiny.

He worked hard at the university for two years and made some discoveries in the improvement of some chemical instruments, which procured him both esteem and admiration among those around him. One of the phenomena which had particularly attracted his attention was the structure of the human frame and, indeed, any animal endowed with life. He decided that to examine the causes of life, one must first understand death. He studied anatomy but it was not sufficient; he also had to observe the natural decay and corruption of the human body. He began to spend days and nights in vaults and charnel-houses.

He paused, examining and analysing all the facts that occurred during the change from life to death, and from death to life, until from the midst of darkness a sudden light broke in on him—a light so brilliant and wondrous, yet so simple, that he became dizzy with the immensity of his findings. At the same time he was surprised that among so many men of genius who had directed their inquiries towards the same science, he alone should be the one to discover so astonishing a secret.

Frankenstein's ideals were of the highest, and he had long decided to use his new-found secret for the good of mankind. He had discovered himself capable of giving life to lifeless matter, but the effort of preparing a frame for the reception of this life, with all its intricacies of fibres, muscles and veins, was obviously to be one of incredible difficulty and labour. But after much thought he decided to go ahead with the task—to create a human being. As the minuteness of its parts would slow his work, he resolved to make a being of gigantic stature. He would create a human being of some eight feet in height and proportionately large.

That decided, he began to collect the necessary materials.

He collected bones from charnel-houses and disturbed the tremendous secrets of the human frame. In a solitary chamber, or rather cell, at the top of his house, and separated from all other rooms by a gallery and staircase, he kept his experiment to himself. The dissecting room and the slaughter-house furnished many of his materials, yet his own nature often turned with loathing from his occupation. Still, urged on by an eagerness which increased as the work went on, he found himself nearing completion.

After a year and more it was finished at last. It was a dreary night in November when, with an anxiety that almost amounted to agony, he collected the instruments of life about him that he might infuse a spark of being into the lifeless thing that lay before him. It was already one o'clock in the morning, the rain pattered dismally against the panes, and his candle was almost burnt out when, by the glimmer of the half-extinguished light, he saw the dull yellow eye of the creature open. It breathed hard, and a convulsive motion began to move its limbs.

As he told Captain Walton: 'How can I describe my emotions at this catastrophe, or how delineate the wretch whom with such infinite pains and care I had endeavoured to form? His limbs were in proportion and I had selected his features as beautiful. Beautiful! Great God! His yellow skin scarcely covered the work of muscles and arteries beneath; his hair was of a lustrous black, and flowing; his teeth of a pearly whiteness; but these luxuriances only formed a more horrid contrast with his watery eyes that seemed almost of the same colour as the dun-white sockets in which they were set, his shrivelled complexion and straight black lips.

'I had worked hard for nearly two years, for the sole purpose of infusing life into an inanimate body. For this I had deprived myself of rest and health. I had desired it with an ardour that far exceeded moderation. But now that I had finished, the beauty of the dream vanished and breathless horror and disgust filled my heart. Unable to endure the aspect of the being I had created, I rushed out of the room and continued a long time traversing my bedchamber, unable to compose my mind to sleep.

'I threw myself on the bed in my clothes, endeavouring to seek a few moments of forgetfulness. But it was in vain. I slept, indeed, but I was disturbed by the wildest dreams. I thought I saw Elizabeth, in the bloom of health, walking in the streets of Ingolstadt. Delighted and surprised, I embraced her, but as I imprinted the first kiss on her lips they became livid with the hue of death, her features appeared to change,

He saw the dull yellow eye of the creature open . . .

and I thought that I held the corpse of my dead mother in my arms; a shroud enveloped her form and I saw the grave-worms crawling in the folds of the flannel. I started from my sleep with horror; a cold dew covered my forehead, my teeth chattered, and every limb became convulsed, when, by the dim and yellow light of the moon, as it forced its way through the window shutters, I beheld the wretch—the miserable monster whom I had created.

'He held up the curtain of the bed and his eyes, if eyes they may be called, were fixed on me. His jaws opened, and he muttered some inarticulate sounds, while a grin wrinkled his cheeks. He might have spoken, but I did not hear. One hand was stretched out, seemingly to detain me, but I escaped and rushed downstairs. I took refuge in the courtyard belonging to the house which I inhabited; there I remained during the rest of the night, catching and fearing every sound as if it were to announce the approach of the demoniacal corpse to which I had so miserably given life.

'Oh! no mortal could support the horror of that countenance. A mummy again endowed with animation could not be so hideous as that wretch. I had gazed on him while unfinished; he was ugly then, but when those muscles and joints were rendered capable of motion, it became a thing such as even Dante could not have conceived.'

When morning came at last, Frankenstein did not dare return to his apartment, but hurried into the street, although drenched by rain which poured from a black and comfortless sky. At last he came to an inn, where he was greeted by an old friend, Henry Clerval. They chatted for a while and then Frankenstein asked, 'Tell me how you left my father, brothers and Elizabeth?'

'Very well and very happy, only a little uneasy that they hear from you so seldom. But my dear Frankenstein,' the friend went on, gazing full in the other's face, 'I did not before remark how very ill you appear; so thin and pale. You look as if you had been watching for several nights.'

'You have guessed right. I have lately been so deeply engaged in one occupation that I have not allowed myself sufficient rest, as you see. But I hope that all these employments are now at an end, and that I am at length free.'

Accompanied by his friend, Frankenstein made his way back to his apartment. He dreaded to look at his monster, but feared even more that Clerval should see him. He asked him to remain at the bottom of the stairs for a few minutes and then paused at the door of the room, his hand on the handle. He then forcibly threw the door open, expecting to see the monster on the other side. But there was no one there; his room was freed from its hideous guest.

He invited Clerval to breakfast but behaved in such a strange manner that his friend was finally glad to go. He felt ill and began a nervous fever that confined him to his room for several months. Had it not been for the unremitting attentions of his friend he would surely have died. The form of the monster he had created was always before his eyes, and he raved incessantly about him.

It was spring when he finally recovered and soon became something of his old, cheerful self. He wrote to his beloved Elizabeth, telling her of his return to complete health, and then went back to the university and to his studies.

He went on holiday in May with Henry Clerval and returned feeling perfectly restored. But a letter that awaited him quickly dashed his spirits. It was from his father, telling him that his younger brother William had been murdered! When it was learned that the young boy was missing, a search was made and Elizabeth insisted on looking at the corpse when it was found and carried home. She entered the room where it lay, hastily examined the neck of the victim and then exclaimed, 'O God! I have murdered my darling child!'

She explained that she had been teased by the boy, who asked her for permission to wear a very valuable miniature that had belonged to his mother. Elizabeth finally allowed him to do so the previous evening, and when the body was found the miniature was missing. The girl was convinced that he had been murdered for this jewel.

Frankenstein hurried home to Geneva to try and console his father and Elizabeth. When he arrived in the environs of the city the gates were shut and he had to spend the night in a village nearby. Heavy with his sadness he went for a walk, and decided to visit the spot where William had been murdered. A sudden storm broke over the countryside, yet he walked on, ignoring the rain that beat about him. He stood for a while to watch the tempest and, clasping his hands and exclaimed aloud, 'William, dear angel! This is thy funeral, this is thy dirge!'

As he spoke he saw in the gloom a figure which stole from a clump of trees nearby. He stood, gazing intently. He could not be mistaken. A flash of lightning revealed its shape—its gigantic stature; and the deformity of its aspect, more hideous than belongs to humanity, told him at once that it was the filthy demon to whom he had given life. What was the monster doing there? Could he be, and Frankenstein shuddered at the thought, the murderer of his brother? At once he was convinced of the truth of the thought and he was forced to lean against a tree for support. Nothing in human shape could have destroyed that fair child. *He*, the monster, was the murderer! There could be no doubt about it.

Almost two years had passed since the night on which he had given him life. Was this his first crime? Wet, cold and miserable, Frankenstein spent the rest of the night in the open, realizing that he had turned loose into the world a wretch who delighted in carnage and misery.

He returned to a confused house. To his surprise, a young girl called Justine had confessed to the crime. This seemed impossible, yet on the morning on which the murder of the boy had been discovered, Justine had been taken ill and confined to her bed. One of the servants had happened to examine the clothes she had been wearing on the night of the murder and had discovered the miniature in one of her pockets. On being charged with the fact, the poor girl confirmed suspicion by her extreme confusion of manner.

Both Frankenstein and Elizabeth spoke up on behalf of the girl, but to no avail. She was put to death for murder and Frankenstein, who was sure he was guilty of the death of both, sat sorrowfully by their graves. They were, he was sure, the first hapless victims to his unhallowed arts.

Hoping to forget, for a while at least, something of his terrible feelings of guilt, Frankenstein went off on his own, wandering through the countryside in the neighbourhood of Mont Blanc. Then, once again, he saw the horrific figure of the monster he had created. He tried to escape but finally was forced to listen to the other's story. He learned how the monster he had created had slowly discovered the elementary things of life—of the warmth of fire, the pleasures of natural food, the protection given against snow and rain by the simplest cottage. But he learned, too, that his monster, which had started out with good feelings towards everyone, slowly became despondent, then angry, when all who saw him ran away as if they had seen the devil himself.

He turned on Frankenstein. 'Hateful day when I received life! Accursed creator! Why did you form a monster so hideous that even *you* turned from me in disgust. God, in pity, made man beautiful and alluring, after his own image, but my form is a filthy type of yours, more horrid even from the very resemblance. Satan has his companions, fellow-devils, to admire and encourage him; but I am solitary and abhorred.'

He continued his sad story until he came to the part which caused Frankenstein to hang on his every word. He said that he had just awakened from sleep when he was disturbed by the approach of a beautiful child, who came running towards his resting place. As he passed he seized the boy and tried to assure him that he meant him no harm.

But the boy struggled violently. 'Let me go. Monster! Ugly wretch! You want to eat me and tear me to pieces. Let me go, or I will tell my papa!'

'Boy, you will never see your father again; you must come with me.'

'Hideous monster, let me go! My papa is Monsieur Frankenstein. He will punish you. You will not keep me.'

'Frankenstein! You belong to my enemy—to him towards whom I have sworn eternal revenge. You shall be my first victim,' and the other listened with horror as the monster described how he had grasped the boy's neck and so killed him.

But he went on. 'As I fixed my eyes on the child I saw something glittering on his breast. I took it. It was a portrait of a most lovely woman.'

He then went on to explain to the horrified Frankenstein how he had left the dead boy and entered a barn nearby, where he saw a young girl asleep. Delighted with her beauty, he bent over her and placed the portrait in a fold of her dress. Then, as she moved in her sleep, he fled.

Finally, he said, 'You must create a female for me. This you alone can do; and I demand it of you as a right which you must not refuse.'

Although Frankenstein at first refused to do this, he finally agreed when the monster promised to take his new mate and fly far from the habitations of man, dwelling where only the beasts of the field would be their companions.

It was a long time before Frankenstein could bring himself to begin this new task. He found that he could not compose a female without again devoting several months to profound study. He learned of an English philosopher who had much knowledge on this subject, and decided to visit England. It was also agreed that he would marry Elizabeth on his return. His travelling companion was his old friend Henry Clerval. Together they visited London and many other cities in England, then arrived in Scotland, for Frankenstein had decided to complete his labours in some obscure nook of the northern highlands. Leaving Clerval in Perth, he found a small hut on one of the most remote of the Orkneys, and began work, at every moment expecting to look up and see the terrible face of his monster staring at him.

This was to happen. He had almost completed a female counterpart when, on looking up, he saw by the light of the moon the demon at the window, a ghastly grin wrinkling his lips as he watched the other at work. He had followed him on his travels, hiding in caves or taking refuge on wide and deserted heaths. Now he had come to mark the other's progress. It was too much! With a sense of madness at the thought of creating another such monster, Frankenstein tore to pieces the creature on which he had been working. The monster saw him, and with a howl of devilish despair and revenge, moved away from the hut.

Later that night, Frankenstein heard the creaking of his door. Next he heard a voice say, from the darkness, 'You have destroyed the work which you began; what is it that you intend? Do you dare to break your promise? I have endured toil and misery. I left Switzerland with you; I have followed you everywhere. I have endured incalculable fatigue and cold and hunger. Do you dare destroy my hopes?'

'Begone! I *do* break my promise. Never will I create another like yourself, equal in deformity and wickedness.'

They argued bitterly for a while then the monster, seeing that the other's mind was firmly fixed, left at last. Before he went, however, he uttered a chilling threat: *'I will be with you on your wedding night!'*

Frankenstein left the island, after hiding the remains of his half-finished creature, and went on board a little skiff. A storm blew up and when he was able to reach land, he was immediately arrested. A handsome young man had been found on the beach; he had apparently been strangled, for there was no sign of any violence, except the mark of

The monster seemed to jeer as he pointed to the corpse of the girl.

fingers on his neck. A woman came forward who swore that she had
seen a boat, with a single man in it, an hour before the discovery of the
body; and her evidence was supported by another.

Frankenstein entered the room where the corpse lay. As he looked at
it he was parched with horror for there, before him, lay the lifeless body
of his friend, Henry Clerval. The human frame could no longer support
the agonies that he endured and he was carried out of the room in strong
convulsions. A fever succeeded this. He lay for two months on the
point of death and his ravings were terrible to hear, as he often felt he,
too, was being strangled, and cried out aloud with agony and terror.
He stayed in prison for a while but it was finally proved that he was
on Orkney at the hour the body of his friend had been discovered, and
he was released.

He travelled home with his father, looking forward to being re-
united with Elizabeth, whom he was soon to marry. Their meeting
was a joyful one and soon afterwards the pair were united in marriage.
Their plan was to spend their honeymoon at a villa she owned on the
shores of Lake Como and, saying goodbye to the guests, they set sail for

Evian, where they were to stay the night. As Frankenstein stepped ashore he suddenly felt those cares and fears revive which were soon to cling to him forever.

They reached a small inn, and whilst Elizabeth went to their room, he walked up and down the passages of the house, carefully looking into every corner that might afford a hiding place for his enemy. But there was no trace of him and he began to feel more at ease. Then, suddenly, there came a shrill and dreadful scream. It came from the room into which Elizabeth had retired. For a moment he seemed paralysed then, as the scream was repeated, he rushed into the room. There, before him, thrown across the bed, her head hanging down, her pale and distorted features half covered by her hair, lay the lifeless body of his new wife.

For a moment he stared at the terrible sight; the next he fell senseless to the ground. When he recovered he found himself surrounded by the people of the inn, but their horror seemed to him a mockery. He ran back to the room and saw Elizabeth, who had been moved to a new posture, her head on her arm, as if she but slept. But as he bent forward to take her cold body in his arms, he saw the murderous mark of the fiend's grasp was on her neck.

While he still held her in the agony of despair, he happened to look up. The window shutters had been thrown back and he saw at the open window the hideous and abhorred figure. A grin was on the face of the monster, he seemed to jeer as with his finger he pointed towards the corpse of the young girl. Frankenstein rushed to the window, drew a pistol from his breast, and fired. But the other eluded him, leaped from his place and, running with the swiftness of lightning, plunged into the lake.

A search was begun immediately, but without success. The monster had scored again. The death of William, the execution of Justine, the murder of Clerval and, now, the death of his beloved wife. Then, as the horror slowly sunk in, Frankenstein had a further terrible thought. Even at that moment his father might be writhing in the monster's grasp or his other brother, Ernest, might be dead at his feet. There was no time to lose.

He raced home to find that his father and Ernest were still alive—although the former sank under the terrible tidings he bore.

After a period of utter misery, Frankenstein formed in his heart a resolution to pursue his creature to its death. And so his wanderings began. Revenge and guilt kept him alive; he dared not die and leave his enemy in being. The chase followed the windings of the Rhône, went along the shores of the blue Mediterranean; he followed him by ship from the Black Sea to the wilds of Russia.

As he pursued his journey to the north, the snows thickened and the cold increased in a degree almost too severe to support. Yet still Frankenstein hunted the monster he had created. He procured a sledge and dogs, and covered the snows with tremendous speed. He now found that he was gaining on his quarry. Reaching a small hamlet by the sea he learned from the terrified inhabitants that a gigantic monster had arrived the night before. He had carried off their store of winter food and, placing it on a sledge, had harnessed some dogs and then continued his journey across the sea in a direction that led nowhere.

Exchanging his land-sledge for one better fashioned for the frozen ocean, and purchasing a large stock of provisions, Frankenstein went after him. It was during this chase that the monster, and then the scientist himself, had been sighted by the men of Captain Walton's ship.

Almost as soon as Frankenstein had finished his long and terrible story, the ice had become such that it was necessary that the ship was to give up her mission and return to England. Hearing this, Frankenstein said, 'Do so if you will, but I will not go with you. You may give up your purpose, but mine is assigned to me by heaven, and I dare not.'

Yet for a time the scientist was obviously too weak to leave the ship. The captain, who had become his close friend, spent many hours talking to him and doing his best to cheer him, whilst the ship's cook and surgeon brought him nourishing broths. Yet he gradually weakened until the sad moment when Captain Walton saw that the scientist was dead. Grieving in his cabin, he suddenly heard strange sounds coming from the dead man's cabin. He entered it and saw a form, gigantic in stature, yet uncouth and distorted in its proportions. When he heard the captain enter he stopped uttering his sounds of grief and sprang towards the window. The captain had never seen a vision as horrible as the creature's face, one of such loathsome and appalling hideousness. Yet without realizing what he did, Captain Walton called on him to stay.

The monster paused, looking on the other with wonder. Then, turning back towards the lifeless form of his creator he seemed to forget the other's presence, and every feature and gesture seemed moved by the wildest rage of some uncontrollable passion.

'That is also my victim!' he shouted. 'In his murder my crimes are consummated. Oh, Frankenstein! Generous and self-devoted being! What does it avail that I now ask thee to pardon me? I, who destroyed thee by destroying all thou lovest. Alas! He is cold; he cannot answer me.

'It is true that I am a wretch. I have murdered the lovely and the helpless. I have strangled the innocent as they slept, and grasped to death by the throat one who never injured me or any other living thing. I have devoted my creator, the finest of all that is worthy of love and admiration among men, to misery. I have pursued him to ruin. There he lies, white and cold in death. You hate me, but your abhorrence cannot equal that with which I regard myself. I look on these hands which executed the deed. I think on the heart in which the imagination of it was conceived, and long for the moment when these hands will meet my eyes, when that imagination will haunt my thoughts no more.'

He turned to stare at the captain. 'I shall quit your vessel on the ice-raft which brought me hither, and shall seek the most northern extremity of the globe. I shall die. He is dead who called me into being; and when I shall be no more, the very remembrance of us both will speedily vanish. Then my spirit will sleep in peace. Farewell!'

He sprung from the cabin window as he ended, landing on the ice-raft which lay close to the ship. As the captain and crew watched, the monster was soon borne away by the waves to be lost in darkness and distance, never to be seen again.

THE ISLAND

Shelagh Macdonald

When the silhouette came at last, strained through heat-mist, she was ashamed because she was not sure if in fact it was the island.

She leaned into the wind and said nothing, staring for a clue.

Is that it, Mum? she heard from the girl at her shoulder. Is it?

That's it, she replied. But added: I think so. It must be.

Don't you remember?

It must be.

She had expected certainty, even if her eye had forgotten. Intuitively, unquestionably, she would know. But how alike all the islands looked, on their sections of the horizon. Perhaps it would have been easier on a clearer day, instead of this bright haziness which blanked out detail and painted shapes in blurred slate.

The steamer was due to arrive in about an hour; was that island too near, too far? She had forgotten how to judge. And yet that must be it.

Yes, she said, it is. And smacked her palm on the rail.

Honestly, Mum. Fancy not knowing.

She was as irritated with herself as her daughter was surprised. Fancy not knowing. And irritated with her daughter for expecting it of her. As if she had given the impression, somehow, that nothing could make her forget this place. An impression, she saw, she must indeed have given, over the years, in tiny references to a story never told.

It *is* twenty-two years ago, she defended herself. She knew she was sharp because her daughter did not see, and could not possibly see what she had not been told—that she was being presented with the gift of her own youth: the chance of it, if she wanted.

That was when she was seventeen: that was her youth, to her mind. A year older than her daughter was now. She looked at the girl under her sun-shielding hand, and remembered herself. Her parents, not knowing, or refusing to know, how much a woman she knew herself to be. Her own impatience, her rages, which only confirmed in their minds what they believed so surely, so stubbornly—that she was still a child.

Now, looking at her daughter, she recognized in herself some of the concern they must have felt. But she was glad, thankful, that she did not have that other selfish, maternal thing—envious, restricting—which they had called protectiveness. Rather, she would hand her daughter that freedom which she, and he, had not had. And there would be no envy.

Let her daughter feel as she had felt: she would find joy in witnessing it. The sensation could still rush through her, if she let herself think of it, and did so now while she watched the island's grey bulk. A complex thing in her mind and body, and she had never since experienced it in the same way.

Easy to say that it was because it had been the first falling in love. Easy to say she had been only an adolescent, devastated at her own sensations. Easy to say that everyone goes through such a stage. But she could look back, with those very devastating sensations lingering, and say in truth: it was never again like that. She almost wished it might have been, so that she might have looked back with a tolerant shrug at herself, and that month would have faded completely. She would have made a greater success of her marriage, she must suppose.

She had, though, loved her husband, her daughter's father. Loved him and wanted him—five years after the spring of this island, when she had been sure she would never now want to marry anyone. Five years in which she had fallen in love a few times, or had briefly believed so, and tipped herself out again without regret.

He was a good man, and loving, considerate. Of course she loved him—she would be a fool not to, with him loving her so much. She felt safe with him, and content. Not the same feeling she remembered, but she told herself she was no longer waiting for that. This would perhaps be a more solid and reliable thing. That it had not proved so was not through any failing of her husband's; more because, as time went on and they grew used to each other, she had given less than she might, because she still felt that old loss far more than she had let herself believe. And eventually she had been rewarded by her husband's drifting away.

She knew the pain of that was no more than the pain of public failure and dented pride, and jealousy. Not the deep, cruel mourning of real loss. She had found it easy enough to save her public face—with one of her typical wisecracks, meant to indicate she was bravely hiding the truth. In fact she was simply hiding another lie.

The lie, she later saw, was that beneath the pain she was relieved. Perhaps, she began to admit, she had unconsciously driven him away to someone else, for her freedom. Freedom not so much from him, but from something she had never, or so she felt, quite lived up to: a structure they had made together and within which she, very occasionally, felt suddenly and sharply fraudulent. She the talented wife and hostess, he the successful businessman, their clever, pretty daughter, the good taste of their house. The ideal marriage. Exactly what others wanted to see, for their own needs. And both recognized that in an obscure way (she now believed) they had not admitted to themselves that anything was lacking. It was only when her husband fell in love with someone else, and in misery acknowledged what she had already guessed, that they confronted the truth at all—and then only fearfully.

She had probably been more childish, stubbornly resisting what was true, over that than she had been at seventeen on this island, now emerging gently from the haze. She recognized, too, that in marrying she had submitted to conventions, and selfishly. Perhaps she had never really intended, or wanted, to contribute as much as she wanted to be given. It was true that she had decided to marry shortly after she had learned (from her well-meaning mother, who had been back again to this part of the world, being newly widowed and herself, perhaps, in search of something lost) that he, a year before, on this island, had married the girl to whom he had been promised since childhood. She had known, of course, that it might be so by now. Nevertheless, to hear it was a finality—brutally cutting that fine, stretched gossamer thread of hope.

So it was four years after that spring on the island that he married. An old promise, to be kept honourably. She had never seen the girl, who, that crucial month, was away with relatives in the capital. He had spoken of her pleasantly, affectionately. As if he were luckier than some. But that was in their first conversion, before they knew (or before he knew) what was happening.

The steamer pushed steadily nearer to the shore. She could just make out the scrubby greenish growth on the rocky hillsides, the distant shining white of a few perched houses, far from any village, so that one was bound to wonder who lived there and what they did. She was suddenly nervous. Stupid: nobody here would remember her. From one month's visit, twenty-two years ago? And he was no longer here. Her mother's report had made that very clear. He and his new wife had left the island, left the country, and probably gone to America or Australia, as so many young men did, looking for decent work and money. How extraordinary. He, also, somewhere, was twenty-two years older, and probably a parent.

It was his arms that she had noticed first. How laughable. How could she say to anyone (were she ever to tell the story) that she had fallen in love with his arms?

It was in the café by the harbour's edge, where the quayside lay quiet, the fishing boats calm and waiting. The light over the mountainside was pure pearl, or opal—she had not been able to find the right word, but was, anyway, astounded by its beauty. And the water, luminous pale, with the reflections as smooth as the boats themselves: a miracle of peace, sinking through her skin, into her bones and her lungs, where she absorbed it, and marvelled. And this in spite of her parents sitting there, and her mother being indecisive about where they would eat, and her father saying nothing, but sighing and taking a larger gulp of his drink, a movement her mother watched with pointed grimness, and made him sigh again. For once, it did not touch her, their bitter friction; she could have almost giggled openly when her mother, looking still at his drink, said: Well, anyway, we're not going to have those damned stuffed tomatoes again.

The white houses on the hill had turned blue and lavender, then rose and grey, and were all that mattered. Until, distracted by a voice or a movement at a nearby table, she glanced sideways and saw his arms.

She did not look beyond the arms—or what she could see of them, which was from elbows to fingertips—because she simply did not dare. Or did not dare to be seen looking, either by the owner of the arms or by her parents. She could not have explained adequately, either then or now, why her attention was so caught, unless it was a heightened awareness of beauty—and that sounded silly enough.

You're grinning, said her daughter, nudging beside her at the rail. What for?

Oh, something.

What?

Somebody's arms, she said, and still grinned. I was thinking about arms.

Being in them, you mean, or just the look of them? Her daughter was amused too.

Both, she said. And mind your own business.

Anyone I know?

She turned to her daughter, and saw how very like herself she was. Apart from the nose, which on the girl was straighter and neater, she had looked like that. No, she said, nobody you know. But I'd be delighted if you met someone like him.

Come on. Tell me more.

No.

Pah, said the girl, but shrugged and accepted. Either because she thought she could find out sometime, if necessary, or because she really wasn't interested.

The arms were long, but not slender, except at the wrists. In fact, the wrists were surprisingly slim, after the broad muscular forearm. Brown. Not sun-blackened, but nicely roasted. Dark hair, bleached a little at the ends.

The mountainside light was not keeping her attention altogether now. She kept glancing back at these arms, and inwardly laughing at herself, so casually glancing, and even changing the position of her chair slightly to make it easier, so that her mother said: Aren't you comfortable dear? with irritation. She had not replied, being too absorbed by the way these arms mysteriously thrilled her. And the hands, broad, but the fingers long. Beautiful hands. (She had told him so, eventually. He had laughed, and stared at his hands, not believing her, not sure if she was making fun.)

Then there was a movement which showed her he was leaving; a scraping of chairs on the stones. He and his friends stood. It was a natural thing, following the arms' movement in an idle way, to look upwards and find their owner. She expected to hear her mother ask her why she was staring, for stare was precisely what she did.

It was not that he was stunningly handsome. Nobody would say so. She was, though, intensely conscious of certain aspects of him, so that the whole—for her, at any rate—was exceptional. She felt, rather than saw, his tallness, and the broad slope of his shoulders as he turned from the table, resting a hand lightly on a friend's back; she could feel that hand. She saw, and felt, something exquisitely innocent about his eyes and the bridge of his nose, in profile. This moved her, though she could not have said exactly how; she knew she could so easily reach out to him just then. She shocked herself. And, furtively, glanced at her mother, as if she might guess.

Her mother was saying: We haven't really got time for another drink. Her father smiled, blandly determined, and said: We're on holiday, we've got all the time in the world. And turned to her, saying: Haven't we dear? So she grinned in support, and he said: See? And her mother breathed out, and hardened her face as she looked away, towards the water, setting herself apart.

She saw all that, and herself turned her head away. And found that he, turning also, was looking at her.

It was a moment she could recall only as complete internal chaos. Although, at the same time, she felt a vague pride in her outward calm. They looked, that was all. How foolish, she told herself, to make so much of it. And yet she felt that something had been exchanged.

Then he was walking away, and she watched him go. It was then that her mother said: Why are you staring? She replied: Am I? in a tone that showed she didn't care, so that her mother glanced at her oddly. She did not want to be with them. She was, abruptly, crazily excited, and hardly knew how to conceal it. A million blossoms burst under her still, cool skin. She might run to the edge of the harbour and swim out into the warm silk of water, warm silk all over her body. Or rush into the hillsides and snatch fruit from the dark leaves, and gobble it barbarically, the juice all over her face and hands. She felt ludicrously happy, and reckless. Anything might happen, and she would let it.

But when she drifted along by the fishing boats next morning, her slow and pointless movements superbly hiding (or at any rate that was her intention) the awful anxiety with which she sought him, the courage of fantasy had left her. So that, when she did see him, leaning there on the frondy tree growing out of the sand, discussing something in another man's newspaper, she felt only panic. She changed her direction abruptly so that she would not pass too near. And then was infuriated at herself, and kicked at the sand like a kid.

She heard her daughter say beside her: Of course. It's just dawned on me.

She turned and found the girl not looking at her, but at the approaching island. Rocks were clear now; layers of rough stone, flung there millions of years before by some vast violence. The steamer slid along parallel with the shore. It was probably less than half an hour to the harbour.

What's dawned on you?

This place. And you. The way you've always mentioned it, but not really let on why it was so important, and you'd never say more if I asked.

She was laughing, this girl, looking mischievous. A blank look was the only answer to give.

Oh yes, her daughter laughed. *I* know. I bet this was where you met your very first love. (The way she said it, it might have been in lurid quotation marks.) And you've been indulging in romantic dreams about it ever since.

She had a maddening sense of blushing. And she was angry, underneath; not at the guess, but the flippancy.

It's all right, her daughter smirked. You don't have to tell me. But I'm pleased I guessed. And she had moved away, staring across the boat at a group of young people laughing.

It was difficult to remember how it was that she had decided to sit at the café and order some fruit juice. But she did sit, and sip, and gaze at boats and people, but never quite at him. Nor could she remember him approaching the table. Nevertheless, there he was, and saying hello, and something about it being his father's café (she noted his English was very good) and he'd seen her there yesterday, and was she having a good holiday? She thought: He's picking me up. But none of the guards went up. She felt bold. Let him pick her up.

He was sitting, and talking. She listened, mostly, and the thought seeped in: He isn't picking me up, after all. He was the model of friendly hospitality. So much, she mocked herself, for me thinking there was something exchanged; so much for my fantasy. She swirled her fruit juice in her glass, saying yes please when he asked if she would like more, and hearing him talk about the island. She looked at his hands, and his arms, but rarely at his eyes; she was afraid of that. He was at college in the capital, and sometimes now (he was saying) the island's traditions struck him as old-fashioned and strange; still, he could recognize their value. Had she been to the festival in the next village, just last week? No, of course not, this was only her fourth day. He described the festival and other customs and traditions. It led naturally to his telling her of his betrothal (he used that old-fashioned world), since he was fourteen. He was fortunate, he said; she was pretty, and a good girl. In two years, when he had finished at college, they would marry. (He hadn't though, had he? It had been four years. Had he waited? Hoped his girl would release him from his promise if she heard the rumours?)

He was talking about his family's lands, and her family's lands, the marriage being welcome to them all. Her own cool voice came in, remarking that it might have been a business transaction, not a wedding. And he said: Well, it is in a way. But that doesn't mean it is without affection. He changed the subject. They talked for a long time. And even though her mood of last night was now scattered, she could acknowledge: We think alike. We are naturally friends. When they parted she was both joyful to have found him and desolate at a loss.

But he sought her out. In spite of what he had told her. He mustn't, she was thinking; but was of course glad. Her father said: I think that young man has taken a liking to you. Her mother merely watched.

She thought: He's picking me up. But none of her guards went up.

He caught her up on the beach, and they walked. He was on the path by the hotel when she came back from an early swim, and they breakfasted together there in the sun. He took her to another village, where the little church was celebrating a saint's day. They talked, talked. And laughed; they made each other laugh. He caught lobsters, and brought them to the place where she was eating with her parents one evening, insisting that they share with him.

She knew, as days went on, that he wanted to see her just as much as she wanted to see him. Their hours were caught up together, and they sought to be alone, if only for minutes. Often she marvelled that she did not seize his hand, or his arm. Sometimes it was as if the air dazzled around them. She also noticed hostility growing in the women of the village. She mentioned it; he looked disturbed, but said it was nothing, ignore them.

She could not remember how it was arranged that they had dinner together alone. Only that they were in an ill-lit corner, facing each other. She could not remember eating. She could not remember (perhaps because of the village wine) how their conversation developed; only, it seemed, that they had suddenly both confessed how they felt, and were staring at each other with a kind of fear, but smiling. Again she felt as on the first evening, her skin cool and unmoved, but a deep trembling within. She was not sure who reached out first, but thought it was probably herself, for loving him had made her bold, and besides she sensed his fear was the greater, because this was forbidden, and he had a promise to break. When her hand reached his, however, he did grasp it. She was certain then that they had their lives to spend together; and so was he. He was admitting that he had not allowed himself to believe what was happening, but knew it had been there from that evening, while she sat with her parents, and all he could see of her was a third of her face and her hair hanging, so. I was trying to talk myself out of it, he said, when I told you of my betrothal. Yes, she said, I know that now.

She did not know where they walked. Only that there was no moon, but stars in frightening millions. And a breeze touching her skin, and a gentleness in the cool moist grass, and the world afire for them both.

So it was for days. She did not remember how many, only that they were committed to one another, and rightly, and joy was stupefying.

So that when everything collapsed, the shock was the more terrible. The ferocity of opposition was appalling. They were found out by the village. Or, rather, the village knew, and told the families. A village girl's name and honour was at stake. The brothers, the father, the mother were united in what seemed to be a murderous anger. Disbelief protected her a little—which was all that could protect her, for her parents were of no use. She was a little girl, unable to make a sound judgement. Her mother withdrew in fear and disgust from her passionate feelings. For a foreigner. But most of all was humiliated and embarrassed at the fuss.

And finally, unbearably, the island, the families, the traditions won. She could hate him, accusing him, an educated man, of being unable to oppose an archaic set of conventions he could not possibly believe in. But I do believe, in a way, he said. Or I respect their belief. Intolerably, he took all the blame: for seeking her out, pursuing her, letting her know how he felt. No, she said, I did as much, and I'm not sorry. I cannot be sorry that I love you. And I am not sorry, he said, that I love you. Only I am grieving now and I cannot see an end to that. She protested still; she fought. But still she had to admire his strength, and the way he accepted the burden of honour. In the end, in glimpses, she could almost understand.

Her mother told her, the day they left (earlier than planned), that she was behaving hysterically. Probably she was. There was a row: heaven knew how it began. She remembered her parents' faces, and no warmth. And holding his face in her mind—despairing, guilty, haunted. And his hands, as she touched them. Her very centre had been torn out; the pain was enough to make her crazy. Her father had hated that, the lack of control. Her mother, flashing irritation at him, demanded she put on a calm face for the departure. She had looked at their antagonism: for each other, for her passion. She cried: Don't expect me to be like you. I can't be you.

The words, forgotten twenty-two years, smacked back at her now as the steamer entered the harbour, and she saw again, but as if for the first time, the white stillness of the village, which had grown and changed, and the frondy trees, now mature. She felt her daughter stir beside her. We're here, Mum. You never said it was so beautiful.

It is beautiful, she agreed.

They watched the preparations for the boat to slip alongside the quay, and she put an arm round her daughter's shoulders. She said: I've got a confession to make. The girl's eyebrows rose a little. She went on: I nearly did to you what I once hated my mother for, and even if my reasons were different, it amounts to the same.

What on earth do you mean? asked the girl.

She looked at the village, and acknowledged how it had changed and how it was also the same; and, at last, she accepted. She answered: Wanting you to be me. Or like me. Or trying to live something again through you. Something like that. Instead of admitting that I was looking for something myself, I was afraid and hoped you'd find it. Does that make sense?

Not in the least, her daughter laughed. But I think you've got a story to tell me.

SPECTRE LOVERS

Sheridan le Fanu

There lived some fifteen years since, in a small and ruinous house little better than a hovel, an old woman who was reported to have considerably exceeded her eightieth year, and who rejoiced in the name of Alice, or popularly, Ally Moran. Her society was not much courted, for she was neither rich, nor, as the reader may suppose, beautiful. In addition to a lean cur and a cat she had one human companion, her grandson, Peter Brien, whom, with laudable good nature, she had supported from the period of his orphanage down to that of my story which finds him in his twentieth year.

Peter was a good-natured slob of a fellow, much more addicted to wrestling, dancing, and love-making than to hard work, and fonder of whisky punch than good advice. His grandmother had a high opinion of his accomplishments, which indeed was but natural, and also of his genius, for Peter had of late years begun to apply his mind to politics; and as it was plain that he had a mortal hatred of honest labour, his grandmother predicted, like a true fortune-teller, that he was born to marry an heiress, and Peter himself (who had no mind to forego his freedom even on such terms) that he was destined to find a pot of gold.

Upon one point both agreed, that being unfitted by the peculiar bias of his genius for work, he was to acquire the immense fortune to which his merits entitled him by means of a pure run of good luck. This solution of Peter's future had the double effect of reconciling both himself and his grandmother to his idle courses, and also of maintaining that even flow of hilarious spirits which made him everywhere welcome, and which was in truth the natural result of his consciousness of approaching affluence.

It happened one night that Peter had enjoyed himself to a very late hour with two or three choice spirits near Palmerstown. They had talked politics and love, sung songs, and told stories, and, above all, had swallowed, in the chastened disguise of punch, at least a pint of good whisky, every man.

It was considerably past one o'clock when Peter bid his companions good-bye, with a sigh and a hiccough, and lighting his pipe set forth on his solitary homeward way.

The bridge of Chapelizod was pretty nearly the midway point of his night march, and from one cause or another his progress was rather slow, and it was past two o'clock by the time he found himself leaning over its old battlements, and looking up the river, over whose winding current and wooded banks the soft moonlight was falling.

The cold breeze that blew lightly down the stream was grateful to him. It cooled his throbbing head, and he drank it in at his hot lips. The scene, too, had, without his being well sensible of it, a secret fascination. The village was sunk in the profoundest slumber, not a mortal stirring, not a sound afloat, a soft haze covered it all, and the fairy moonlight hovered over the entire landscape.

In a state between rumination and rapture, Peter continued to lean over the battlements of the old bridge, and as he did so he saw, or fancied he saw, emerging one after another along the river-bank in the little gardens and enclosures in the rear of the street of Chapelizod, the queerest little white-washed huts and cabins he had ever seen there before. They had not been there that evening when he passed the bridge on the way to his merry tryst. But the most remarkable thing about it was the odd way in which these quaint little cabins showed themselves.

First he saw one or two of them just with the corner of his eye, and when he looked full at them, strange to say, they faded away and disappeared. Then another and another came in view, but all in the same coy way, just appearing and gone again before he could well fix his gaze upon them; in a little while, however, they began to bear a fuller gaze, and he found, as it seemed to himself, that he was able to by an effort of attention to fix the vision for a longer and a longer time, and when they waxed faint and nearly vanished he had the power of recalling them into light and substance, until at last their vacillating indistinctness became less and less, and they assumed a permanent place in the moonlit landscape.

'Be the hokey,' said Peter, lost in amazement, and dropping his pipe into the river unconsciously, 'them is the quarist bits iv mud cabins I ever seen, growing up like musharoons in the dew of an evening, and poppin' up here and down again there, and up again in another place, like so many white rabbits in a warren; and there they stand at last as firm and fast as if they were there from the deluge; bedad it's enough to make a man a'most believe in the fairies.'

This latter was a large concession from Peter, who was a bit of a freethinker, and spoke contemptuously in his ordinary conversation of that class of agencies.

Having treated himself to a long last stare at these mysterious fabrics, Peter prepared to pursue his homeward way; having crossed the bridge and passed the mill, he arrived at the corner of the main street of the little town, and casting a careless look up the Dublin road, his eye was arrested by a most unexpected spectacle.

There was no other than a column of foot-soldiers, marching with perfect regularity towards the village, and headed by an officer on horseback. They were at the far side of the turnpike, which was closed; but much to his perplexity he perceived that they marched on through it without appearing to sustain the least check from that barrier.

On they came at a slow march; and what was most singular in the matter was, that they were drawing several cannons along with them; some held ropes, others spoked the wheels, and others again marched in front of the guns and behind them, with muskets shouldered, giving a stately character of parade and regularity to this, as it seemed to Peter, most unmilitary procedure.

It was owing either to some temporary defect in Peter's vision, or to some illusion attendant upon mist and moonlight, or perhaps to some other cause, that the whole procession had a certain waving and vapoury character which perplexed and tasked his eyes not a little. It was like the pictured pageant of a phantasmagoria reflected upon smoke. It was as if every breath disturbed it; sometimes it was blurred, sometimes obliterated; now here, now there. Sometimes, while the upper part was quite distinct, the legs of the column would nearly fade away or vanish outright, and then again they would come out into clear relief, marching on with measured tread, while the cocked hats and shoulders grew, as it were, transparent, and all but disappeared.

Notwithstanding these strange optical fluctuations, however, the column continued steadily to advance. Peter crossed the street from the corner near the old bridge, running on tip-toe, and with his body stopped to avoid observation, and took up a position upon the raised footpath in the shadow of the houses, where, as the soldiers kept the middle of the road, he calculated that he might, himself undetected, see them distinctly enough as they passed.

'What the div——, what on airth,' he muttered, checking the irreligious ejaculation with which he was about to start, for certain queer misgivings were hovering about his heart, notwithstanding the artificial courage of the whisky bottle. 'What on airth is the manin' of all this? Is it the French that's landed at last to give us a hand and help us in airnest to this blessed repale? If it is not them, I simply ask who the div——, I mane who on airth are they, for such sogers as them I never seen before in my born days?'

By this time the foremost of them were quite near, and truth to say they were the queerest soldiers he had ever seen in the course of his life. They wore long gaiters and leather breeches, three-cornered hats bound with silver lace, long blue coats with scarlet facings and linings, which latter were sewn by a fastening which held together the two opposite corners of the skirt behind; and in front the breasts were in like manner connected at a single point, where and below which they sloped back, disclosing a long-flapped waistcoat of snowy whiteness; they had very large, long cross-belts, and wore enormous pouches of white leather hung extraordinarily low, and on each of which a little silver star was glittering.

But what struck him as most grotesque and outlandish in their costume was their extraordinary display of shirt-frill in front, and of ruffle about their wrists, and the stranger manner in which their hair was frizzled out and powdered under their hats, and clubbed up into great rolls behind. But one of the party was mounted. He rode a tall white horse, with high action and arching neck; he had a snow-white feather in this three-cornered hat, and his coat was shimmering all over with a profusion of silver lace. From these circumstances Peter concluded that he must be the commander of the detachment, and examined him attentively as he passed. He was a slight, tall man, whose legs did not half fill his leather breeches, and he appeared to be at the wrong side of sixty. He had a shrunken, weather-beaten, mulberry-coloured face, carried a large black patch over one eye, and turned neither to the right nor to the left, but rode on at the head of his men, with a grim, military inflexibility.

The countenances of these soldiers, officers as well as men, seemed all full of trouble, and, so to speak, scared and wild. He watched in vain for a single contented or comely face. They had, one and all, a melancholy and hang-dog look; and as they passed by, Peter fancied that the air grew cold.

He had seated himself upon a stone bench, from which, staring with all his might, he gazed upon the grotesque and noiseless procession as it filed by him. Noiseless it was; he could neither hear the jingle of accoutrements, the tread of feet, nor the rumble of the wheels; and when the old colonel turned his horse a little, and made as though he were giving the word of command, and a trumpeter, with a swollen blue nose and white feather fringe round his hat, who was walking beside him, turned about and put his bugle to his lips, still Peter heard nothing, although it was plain the sound had reached the soldiers, for they instantly changed their front to three abreast.

'Botheration!' muttered Peter, 'is it deaf I'm growing?'

But that could not be, for he heard the sighing of the breeze and the rush of the neighbouring Liffey plain enough.

'Well,' said he, in the same cautious key, 'by the piper, this bangs Banagher fairly! It's either the French Army that's in it, come to take the town iv Chapelizod by surprise, an' makin' no noise for feard iv wakenin' the inhabitants; or else it's—it's—what it's—somethin' else. But, tundher-an-ouns, what's gone wrong wid Fitzpatrick's shop across the way?'

The brown dingy stone building at the opposite side of the street looked newer and cleaner than he had been used to see it; the front door of it stood open, and a sentry in the same grotesque uniform, with shouldered musket, was pacing noiselessly to and fro before it. At the angle of this building, in like manner, a wide gate (of which Peter had no recollection whatever) stood open, before which, also, a similar sentry was gliding and into this gateway the whole column gradually passed, and Peter finally lost sight of it.

'I'm not asleep; I'm not dhramin',' said he, rubbing his eyes, and stamping slightly on the pavement, to assure himself that he was wide awake. 'It is a quare business, whatever it is; an' it's not alone that, but everything about the town looks strange to me. There's Tresham's house new painted, bedad, an' them flowers in the windies! An' Delaney's house, too, that had not a whole pane of glass in it this morning, and scarce a slate on the roof of it! It is not possible it's that it's dhrunk I am. Sure there's the big tree, and not a leaf of it changed since I passed, and the stars overhead, all right. I don't think it is in my eyes it is.'

And so looking about him, and every moment finding or fancying new food for wonder, he walked along the pavement, intending, without further delay, to make his way home.

But his adventures for the night were not concluded. He had nearly reached the angle of the short lane that leads up to the church, when for the first time he perceived that an officer, in the uniform he had just seen, was walking before, only a few yards in advance of him.

The officer was walking along at an easy, swinging gait, and carried his sword under his arm, and was looking down on the pavement with an air of reverie.

In the very fact that he seemed unconscious of Peter's presence, and disposed to keep his reflection to himself, there was something reassuring. Besides, the reader must please to remember that our hero had a sufficient quantity of good punch before his adventure commenced, and was thus fortified against those qualms and terrors under which, in a more reasonable state of mind, he might not impossibly have sunk.

The idea of the French invasion revived in full power in Peter's fuddled imagination, as he pursued the nonchalant swagger of the officer.

'Be the powers iv Molly Kelly, I'll ax him what it is,' said Peter, with a sudden accession of rashness. 'He may tell me or not, as he plases, but he can't be offinded, anyhow.'

With this reflection having inspired himself, Peter cleared his voice and begun:

'Captain!' said he, 'I ax your pardon, an' maybe you'd be so con-descindin' to my ignorance as to tell me, if it's plasin' to yer honour, whether your honour is not a Frenchman, if it's plasin' to you.'

This he asked, not thinking that, had it been as he suspected, not one word of his question in all probability would have been intelligible to the person he addressed. He was, however, understood, for the officer answered him in English, at the same time slackening his pace and moving a little to the side of the pathway, as if to invite his interrogator to take his place beside him.

'No; I am an Irishman,' he answered.

'I humbly thank your honour,' said Peter, drawing nearer—for the affability and the nativity of the officer encouraged him—'but maybe your honour is in the sarvice of the King of France?'

'I serve the same king as you do,' he answered, with a sorrowful sig-nificance which Peter did not comprehend at the time; and, interrogat-ing in turn, he asked, 'But what calls you forth at this hour of the day?'

'The day, your honour!—the night, you mane.'

'It was always our way to turn night into day, and we keep to it still,' remarked the soldier. 'But no matter, come up here to my house; I have a job for you, if you wish to earn some money easily. I live here.'

As he said this, he beckoned authoritatively to Peter, who followed almost mechanically at his heels, and they turned up a little lane near the old Roman Catholic chapel, at the end of which stood, in Peter's time, the ruins of a tall, stone-built house.

Like everything else in the town, it had suffered a metamorphosis. The stained and ragged walls were now erect, perfect, and covered with pebble-dash; window-panes glittered coldly in every window; the green hall-door had a bright knocker on it. Peter did not know whether to believe his previous or his present impressions: seeing is believing, and Peter could not dispute the reality of the scene. All the records of his memory seemed but the images of a tipsy dream. In a trance of astonishment and perplexity, therefore, he submitted himself to the chances of his adventure.

The door opened, the officer beckoned with a melancholy air of authority to Peter, and entered. Our hero followed him into a sort of hall, which was very dark, but he was guided by the steps of the soldier, and, in silence, they ascended the stairs. The moonlight, which shone in at the lobbies, showed an old, dark wainscoting, and a heavy, oak banister. They passed by closed doors at different landing-places, but all was dark and silent as, indeed, became that late hour of the night.

Now they ascended to the topmost floor. The captain paused for a minute at the nearest door, and, with a heavy groan, pushing it open, entered the room. Peter remained at the threshold. A slight female form in a sort of loose, white robe, and with a great deal of dark hair hanging loosely about her, was standing in the middle of the floor with her back towards them.

The soldier stopped short before he reached her, and said, in a voice of great anguish, 'Still the same, sweet bird—sweet bird! Still the same.' Whereupon, she turned suddenly, and threw her arms about the neck of the officer, with a gesture of fondness and despair, and her frame was agitated as if by a burst of sobs. He held her close to his breast in silence; and honest Peter felt a strange terror creep over him, as he witnessed these mysterious sorrows and endearments.

'Tonight, tonight—and then ten years more—ten long years— another ten years.'

The officer and the lady seemed to speak these words together; her voice mingled with his in a musical and fearful wail, like a distant summer wind, in the dead hour of night wandering through ruins. Then he heard the officer say, alone in a voice of anguish:

'Upon me be it all, for ever, sweet birdie, upon me.'

And again they seemed to mourn together in the same soft and desolate wail, like sounds of grief heard from a great distance.

Peter was thrilled with horror, but he was also under a strange fascination, and an intense and dreadful curiosity held him fast.

The moon was shining obliquely into the room, and through the window Peter saw the familiar slopes of the Park, sleeping mistily under its shimmer. He could also see the furniture of the room with tolerable distinctness—the old balloon-backed chairs, a four-post bed in a sort of recess, and a rack against the wall, from which hung some military clothes and accoutrements; and the sight of all these homely objects reassured him somewhat and he could not help feeling unspeakably curious to see the face of the girl whose long hair was streaming over the officer's epaulet.

Peter, accordingly, coughed, at first slightly, and afterward more loudly, to recall her from her reverie of grief, and, apparently, he succeeded; for she turned round, as did her companion, and both, standing hand in hand, gazed upon him fixedly. He thought he had never seen such large, strange eyes in all his life; and their gaze seemed to chill the very air around him, and arrest the pulses of his heart. An eternity of misery and remorse was in the shadowy faces that looked upon him.

If Peter had taken less whisky by a single thimbleful, it is probable that he would have lost heart altogether before these figures, which seemed every moment to assume a more marked and fearful, though hardly definable, contrast to ordinary human shapes.

'What is it you want with me?' he stammered.

'To bring my lost treasure to the churchyard,' replied the lady, in a silvery voice of more than mortal désolation.

The word 'treasure' revived the resolution of Peter, although a cold sweat was covering him, and his hair was bristling with horror; he believed, however, that he was on the brink of fortune, if he could but command nerve to brave the interview to its close.

'And where,' he gasped, 'is it hid—where will I find it?'

They both pointed to the sill of the window, through which the moon was shining at the far end of the room, and the soldier said:

'Under that stone.'

Peter drew a long breath, and wiped the cold dew from his face, preparatory to passing to the window, where he expected to secure the reward of his protracted errors. But looking steadfastly at the window, he saw the faint image of a new-born child sitting upon the sill in the moonlight, with its little arms stretched toward him, and a smile so heavenly as he never beheld before.

At sight of this, strange to say, his heart entirely failed him, he looked on the figures that stood near, and beheld them gazing on the infantine form with a smile so guilty and distorted, that he felt as if he were entering alive among the scenery of hell, and, shuddering, he cried in an irrepressible agony of horror:

'I'll have nothing to say with you, and nothing to do with you; I

He saw the faint image of a new-born child.

don't know what yez are or what yez want iv me, but let me go this
minute, every one of yez, in the name of God.'

With these words there came a strange rumbling and sighing about
Peter's ears; he lost sight of everything, and felt that peculiar and not
unpleasant sensation of falling softly, that sometimes supervenes in
sleep, ending in a dull shock. After that he had neither dream nor consciousness till he wakened, chill and stiff, stretched between two piles
of old rubbish, among the black and roofless walls of the ruined house.
We need hardly mention that the village had put on its wonted air of
neglect and decay, or that Peter looked around him in vain for traces
of those novelties which had so puzzled and distracted him upon the
previous night.

'Ay, ay,' said his grandmother, removing her pipe, as he ended his
description of the view from the bridge, 'sure enough I remember
myself, when I was a slip of a girl, these little white cabins among the
gardens by the river-side. The artillery sogers that was married, or had
not room in the barracks, used to be in them, but they're all gone long
ago.'

'The Lord be merciful to us!' she resumed, when he had described
the military procession, 'it's often I seen the regiment marchin' into
the town, just as you saw it last night, acushla. Oh, voch, but it makes
my heart sore to think iv them days; they were pleasant times, sure
enough; but is not it terrible, avick, to think it's what it was the ghost
of the rigiment you seen? The Lord betune us an' harm, for it was
nothing else, as sure as I'm sittin' here.'

When he mentioned the peculiar figure of the old officer who rode
at the head of the regiment:

'That,' said the old crone, dogmatically, 'was ould Colonel Grim-
shaw, the Lord preserve us! He's buried in the churchard iv Chapelizod,
and well I remember him, when I was a young thing, an' a cross ould
floggin' fellow he was wid the men, an' a devil's boy among the girls—
rest his soul!'

'Amen!' said Peter; 'it's often I read his tombstone myself; but he's
a long time dead.'

'Sure, I tell you he died when I was no more nor a slip iv a girl—the
Lord betune us and harm!'

'I'm afeard it is what I'm not long for this world myself, afther seeing such a sight as that,' said Peter fearfully.

'Nonsense, avourneen,' retorted his grandmother, indignantly, though she had herself misgivings on the subject; 'sure there was Phil Doolan, the ferryman, that seen black Ann Scanlan in his own boat, and what harm ever kem of it?'

Peter proceeded with his narrative, but when he came to the description of the house, in which his adventure had had so sinister a conclusion, the old woman was at fault.

'I know the house and the ould walls well, an' I can remember the time there was a roof on it, and the doors an' windows in it, but it had a bad name about being haunted, but by who, or for what, I forget intirely.'

'Did you ever hear was there gold or silver there?' he inquired.

'No, no, avick, don't be thinking about the likes; take a fool's advice, and never go next or near them ugly black walls again the longest day you have to live; an' I'd take my davy, it's what it's the same word the priest himself I'd be afther sayin' to you if you wor to ax his raverence consarnin' it, for it's plain to be seen it was nothing good you seen there, and there's neither luck nor grace about it.'

Peter's adventure made no little noise in the neighbourhood, as the reader may well suppose; and a few evenings after it, being on an errand to old Major Vandeleur, who lived in a snug old-fashioned house, close by the river, under a perfect bower of ancient trees, he was called on to relate the story in the parlour.

The Major was, as I have said, an old man; he was small, lean, and upright, with a mahogany complexion, and a wooden inflexibility of face; he was a man, besides, of few words, and if he was old, it follows plainly that his mother was older still. Nobody could guess or tell how old, but it was admitted that her own generation had long passed away, and that she had not a competitor left. She had French blood in her veins, and although she did not retain her charms quite so well as Ninon de l'Enclos, she was in full possession of all her mental activity, and talked quite enough for herself and the Major.

'So, Peter,' she said, 'you have seen the dear old Royal Irish again in the streets of Chapelizod. Make him a tumbler of punch, Frank; and Peter, sit down, and while you take it let us have the story.'

Peter accordingly, seated near the door, with a tumbler of the nectarian stimulant steaming beside him, proceeded with marvellous courage, considering they had no light but the uncertain glare of the fire, to relate with minute particularity his awful adventure. The old lady listened at first with a smile of good-natured incredulity; her cross-examination touching the drinking-bout at Palmerstown had been teasing, but as the narrative proceeded she became attentive, and at length absorbed, and once or twice she uttered ejaculations of pity or awe. When it was over, the old lady looked with a somewhat sad and stern abstraction on the table, patting her cat assiduously meanwhile, and then suddenly looking upon her son, the Major, she said:

'Frank, as sure as I live, he has seen the wicked Captain Devereux.'

The major uttered an inarticulate expression of wonder.

'The house was precisely that he had described. I have told you the story often, as I heard it from your dear grandmother, about the poor young lady he ruined, and the dreadful suspicion about the little baby. She, poor thing, died in that house heartbroken, and you know he was shot shortly after in a duel.'

This was the only light that Peter ever received respecting his adventure. It was supposed, however, that he still clung to the hope that treasure of some sort was hidden about the old house, for he was often seen lurking about its walls, and at last his fate overtook him, poor fellow, in the pursuit; for climbing near the summit one day, his holding gave way, and he fell upon the hard uneven ground, fracturing a leg and a rib, and after a short interval died; he, like the other heroes of these true tales, lies buried in the little churchyard of Chapelizod.

THE SMALL WOMAN

Michael Hardwick

Only the sound of harsh, ragged breathing and the buzz of flies could be heard in the Chinese prison compound. The sun beat down on the heads of the convicts as they cringed against a wall, staring in silence at the scene before them. On the ground lay several men, their heads and bodies horribly gashed. Over them stood their attacker. A blood-stained axe was in his hand. His eyes glittered with a dangerous light, as he watched the small English woman who confronted him.

Slowly, deliberately, she began to move towards him, hand out-stretched.

'Give me the axe,' she said quietly.

The man frowned. 'Give me the axe,' she repeated, her voice firmer.

There was a gasp from the watching convicts as they saw the man move suddenly—then stop, and meekly hold the axe out to her.

The small woman siezed it. From their place of safety, the prison authorities watched her order the convicts to line up and return quietly to their quarters. They obeyed. She was a 'foreign devil', a European missionary whom they distrusted, but nobody else had been brave enough to go into that compound. Her courage that day earned her much 'face'. She was in need of it.

Gladys Aylward had dreamed of China ever since her childhood in the London suburb of Edmonton. She knew that she wanted to spend her life as a missionary, teaching the Chinese people about Christ and his Church. When she left school she had to go into domestic service as a parlour-maid, but as she grew older her ambition strengthened. Eventually, she enrolled as a student in the China Inland Mission School in London.

After three months she was told that her work was not good enough. It was doubted that she would ever be able to speak Chinese. Besides, she was too old for missionary work abroad. She was twenty-six.

Gladys was deeply disappointed. But she had a strong and determined spirit. She decided that she would make her own way to China. She returned to domestic service and began to save for the journey. The cheapest and quickest route at that time was by train, across Europe and Russia on the Trans-Siberian Railway to Tientsin. The fare was £47. 10s.

She must have seemed an eccentric to the booking clerk at the travel agency when she told him that she wanted to reserve a ticket. He pointed out that Russia and China were at war, and that the Trans-Siberian Railway ran right through the battle zone—if it still ran at all at its eastern end. Gladys was undeterred. The clerk shrugged his shoulders, accepted her three pounds deposit and made the reservation. During the following months she paid regular instalments towards her ticket, worked hard at Bible study, and taught herself to preach by standing on a box at Speakers' Corner, Hyde Park, addressing the crowd always gathered there on Sundays. Few bothered to listen, but it was good practice.

Her perseverance was rewarded. She learned of a missionary in China, an old lady named Jeannie Lawson, who was looking for a younger woman to assist her. Gladys wrote to her at once, and was accepted.

On 18 October 1930, she left London on the first stage of the long and often difficult journey across half the world. Because of the Eastern war, Gladys found herself stranded in Vladivostok. She had little money left and the Russian authorities were on the point of forcing her to work in a factory when she found a friendly young Japanese captain who offered her a free lift to Japan in his ship. It was a roundabout route to China, but she was helped along by missionaries and put aboard another ship which took her to her original destination, Tientsin.

The journey was not over yet, though. Mrs Lawson's mission was in a town in the northern province of Shansi, a wild, mountainous area difficult to cross and swarming with bandits. To avoid attracting their attention, Gladys abandoned her European clothes and travelled as a Chinese, in quilted jacket and trousers. It took her a month—by train, bus, and finally mule—to reach the high-walled town of Yangcheng.

The mission was very small and there were few converts. The people of the town were superstitious and unfriendly and treated the 'foreign devils' with open dislike. Soon after her arrival Gladys saw a man publicly beheaded in the town square. She realized that everything was going to be far harder than she had ever imagined, but she was determined to succeed and began teaching herself the local dialect.

To attract more converts to the mission, she and Mrs Lawson opened a small inn to cater for the men who led the endless mule trains across the mountains. They called it The Inn of Eight Happinesses. After their guests had been fed it became the custom for them to sit around the fire listening to stories from the Bible. The inn began to be a success, and some of the muleteers became Christian converts.

But it was not to last long. Mrs Lawson died after a bad fall, and Gladys was left to carry on alone. Funds were running out. Then, just as things seemed very bleak, help arrived in the unlikely guise of the Mandarin, or chief official, of Yangcheng. The Central Chinese Government had recently banned the ancient custom of binding the feet of baby girls in order to stunt the growth—small feet are considered beautiful by the Chinese. The Mandarin required a 'Foot Inspector' to travel around the villages to see that the new law was obeyed. He wished the appointment to be held by a woman with normal feet, to set an example.

Gladys Aylward became the Mandarin's official Foot Inspector. She combined her tours of inspection with Bible story telling, as she had at The Inn of Eight Happinesses. Before long there was a growing band of Christian converts attending the mission in Yangcheng. The town authorities regarded this with suspicion. When one of the convicts in the local prison went berserk with an axe, and the soldiers refused to tackle him, the authorities decided to test Gladys. After all, had she not often said that her God protected from harm those who loved him?

Following her success in the prison incident, Gladys decided to work on behalf of the convicts. She was able to secure better living conditions for them. The Governor's friend, a Christian convert, was allowed to preach to them. The grateful convicts gave Gladys a name —Ai-weh-deh, meaning The Virtuous One. She was a foreign devil no longer.

It was through her work as Foot Inspector that she adopted the first of her five children. On one of her tours a woman offered to sell her a small child, a girl, and therefore useless to the woman's family. Gladys was outraged that such traffic was allowed to flourish unchecked. The child was obviously starving. The only thing she could do was to accept the offer. She bought the little girl and named her Ninepence—the price she had cost.

In 1936, when she had been in China six years, Gladys Aylward became a Chinese citizen. Two years later she found herself in the horror of the Japanese invasion.

With Japanese troops gradually occupying the province of Shansi, and treating the people with barbaric cruelty, Yangcheng received its first warning of their approach when planes bombed and machine-gunned the town. Gladys took some of the women and children into the hills for safety. When she returned, it was to a town of the dead. Everyone who had not fled had been massacred. Gladys helped to organize the burials, then left to start a makeshift hospital at a town on the other side of the mountains. On one of her return trips to Yang-cheng she had the proud satisfaction of learning that her erstwhile employer, the Mandarin, wished to become a Christian.

Life was very rough during this period. The Japanese were every-where, killing, destroying, looting, maiming. They attacked the mission at Tsehchow where Gladys was organizing the care of orphaned and refugee children, and beat her up badly when she tried to defend some of the girls from the soldiers. Another time her life was saved from bullets by the quilted jacket which had long since become her habitual wear.

'Do not wish me out of this or in any way seek to get me out,' she wrote to her family in England; 'for I will not be got out while this trial is on. These are my people; God has given them to me, and I will live or die with them for Him and His Glory.'

With her small band of converts she survived terrible acts of carnage, and time after time she organized relief work in towns that had suffered at the enemy's hands. After one raid she was forced to shelter for three weeks in a mountain cave. Her work inevitably brought her to the notice of the Japanese. A price was put on her head—one hundred dollars for 'The Small Woman known as Ai-weh-deh'.

Gladys knew that her time was up in Shansi Province. With the children in her care—almost one hundred of them—she decided to set out for a camp for refugee orphans, far away across the mountains and beyond the great Yellow River. It was a daunting mission, but some of her children were in their teens and would be able to help to look after the little ones. She believed they could make it.

In March 1940 they set out. During the first stage of their journey they were helped by Chinese Nationalist soldiers, but there came a time when they were alone on the mountains—cold, hungry and exhausted. After twelve days they reached the wide, fast-flowing Yellow River. Luckily, they found more soliders willing to ferry them across. But because all traffic on the river was prohibited by the local authorities, Gladys found herself under arrest when she reached the opposite bank. There were several uncomfortable, uncertain hours before she was allowed to continue the journey.

For four days she and the children were able to travel by train. When a bridge was blown up, destroying the track, they had to start walking again. Many of them had no shoes. Sharp stones cut through the rags tied around their feet, so the older children took it in turns to carry the little ones. To keep up their spirits, Gladys encouraged them to sing as they walked, and for hours on end the sound of their voices marked the slow progress through the mountains. After four more days they reached the plain, and were able to get a ride on a coal train.

It was now April. The month-long journey was over, and the children were safe. But the strain and utter exhaustion had proved too much for their leader. She collapsed and was seriously ill for some time. On her recovery she settled with her five adopted children in the westerly province of Chengtu, where she taught English. When the children had grown up she worked in a leper colony.

Gladys Aylward returned to England in 1950, after twenty years. The results of her wartime injuries required hospital treatment of a kind not then available in China.

She spent her last years in England, dying in 1970. Few people had heard of her in her native country, and Gladys saw no reason why she should be singled out for attention. After all, she had only done her duty. 'Nothing very exciting happened,' she replied, when first asked about her long years in China.

A MIDNIGHT BRIDAL

Halliwell Sutcliffe

Maurice St Quain rode out from Edinburgh town—rode as a man rides on whom the world's cares sit lightly. Seen by the light of the moon, the stars, the oil lamps that creaked fretfully the length of the Canongate, he showed a square, big-headed, well-knit fellow; and his clothes were London-made.

'Damme, what a night!' he muttered as the keen wind blew through him and about. 'For an east wind and a raw air, commend me to this same capital of Scotland.'

He rode far out from the smoky lamps of the town, and was nearing a small and lonesome loch that lay on the left hand of his road, when a figure, bent and cloaked, stepped out into the moonlit road. A hand was laid upon his bridle, and at the moment a wild blast of wind swept back the cloak, revealing a woman's face—old, worn and wrinkled beyond belief. For a full moment she stood there, saying no word, but looking at his face, his wearing-gear, the appointments of his horse. Nor did he break the silence; this figure, coming from the dreary night, seemed rather a spirit's than a woman's, and time and place alike combined to overlay the man's undoubted courage.

'Aye, the Lord is guid,' murmured the old woman at last. 'Didna I pray for sic a callant to come riding by the loch-side?'

'What is it, mother?' asked St Quain, finding his voice again.

'I sent up many a prayer, an' ye have come.'

St Quain laughed—laughed as the Scots themselves are wont to do, with hardship and a sound of dryness in the throat. ' 'Tis the first time, to my knowledge, that I have come in answer to any woman's prayer, unless she chanced to be young and buxom. Come, mother, can I serve you? And if so, how? For time is pressing with me.'

'An' isna time pressing wi' the bonnie bairn—the bit lassie I nursed on my ain knee? There's a tryst for ye the nicht, an' ye'll no fail to keep it.'

'A tryst? Why, yes; but how should you know of it?'

Again she eyed him for awhile in silence; then, 'The hour is no just one for yon kind o' love,' said she. 'There's death will be the grooms-man if ye winna come wi' me.'

Maurice St Quain began to shiver, what with the wind that chilled his body and this queer speech that chilled his soul.

'What would you?' he said.

'Ye maun let me hold your bridle an' guide ye to the muckle house above the loch'—pointing a shrivelled finger, as she spoke, across the moonlit lake. 'Ye maun ask naething as to aething, for there's little time, I'm thinking if the lassie's to be kept from out a bridal shroud.'

Slowly it was borne in upon him that there was a life to be saved—a young girl's life. Not all the night wind could frost his chivalry; not all the love trysts in the world could turn him from a clear errand of mercy such as this.

'I'll go with you,' he said.

The woman clutched his bridle, muttered a blessing, so it seemed, and strode off along a grass-grown bridle-track with the step of one who had fewer years to carry. Down by the loch-side they went, with a mist of spray in their faces; up the further side of the steep they journeyed, and in at a rude gateway. The moon shone fair upon a rugged, loose-built house, and from an upper chamber came the light of many candles.

'Get ye doon,' murmured the old nurse. 'I'll lead your beastie to the stable, if ye'll bide a wee.'

He waited, as if under orders from his superior officer; and the wind shrilled about the walls; and the waters of the loch went lapping, lapping up the reedy beach.

'Com wi' me,' the same voice murmured at his ear, while yet he was in the midst of wonder and of vague affright.

He followed her across the courtyard, and up a flight of steps, and into a great hall. And now, for the first time, he ventured to draw breath. Without, there was the wind, the moonlight and the witchery; within all seemed to have a usual air about it—the air of a house whose master is well-found in this world's goods. A manservant was putting logs upon the great fire on the hearth-place; a hound, long-nosed, long-bodied, dozed beside the blaze; the very nurse herself, who had shown as some weird creature of the night, grew to the likeness of a woman as she doffed her cloak. She crossed to the board that held the middle of the floor, and poured a goblet of wine, and brought it to the strangely bidden guest.

'And, aye, she's bonnie,' she murmured, with a sort of hard encouragement. 'Ye needna look as if 'twere pain to save the lassie's life.'

St Quain gulped down his wine, and felt the red of it go tingling through him. The old nurse watched him curiously, and something like a smile was on her face as she noted once again the big comeliness, the air of consequence, that hung about this Englishman.

'My lady waits ye, and the meenister,' she said.

He could make nothing of it. Who was my lady? And the minister—surely he would not be there unless the maid were on the point of death; and if she were so near the end, what service could a stranger render her? The house, moreover, did not seem like one that entertained old death as visitor; for serving-men, with careless faces, free from any trace of woe, were moving in and out of the grim hall, making ready against supper-time. Again, what did it mean, he asked himself.

'Perchance there is a supper party,' he said, with sudden inspiration, 'and a guest has failed you?'

The old nurse was plucking at his sleeve impatiently. 'There'll be one guest o' the twa come into hall the nicht,' she muttered. 'One o' the twa —and the other's death, I'm telling ye.'

He followed her, with quickened breath. They mounted a broad stair of oak, and crossed a landing hung round about with trophies of the case and battlefield.

The nurse flung open a door on the right hand, and St Quain found himself in a well-lit parlour. A spinet stood at the far end, and round the hearth was grouped a company of three. The first, a lean greybeard, habited in black, was talking to a stately matron; the third member of the group sat on the other side of the hearth, and twined and untwined her white fingers restlessly.

All the gallantry in Maurice St Quain, all the tenderness and passion, came headlong to the front as he looked at that third figure. There was witchery in the pale face; he had known no other like her, though he had wandered through many countries with an eye wide open for such matters.

'My prayer went bonnily, my lady,' the old nurse said. 'I met him on the road doon by the loch, an', tho' he's Southron, he's no that ill to look at.'

My lady checked her. 'Your errand here must seem a strange one, sir,' she said. 'It will seem stranger when you hear the nature of it.'

He scarcely heard her; for his glance was on the lassie seated at the far side of the hearth, and he was thinking how gladly he would have journeyed half through England to win a sight of her.

'Your name, sir, is——?' went on my lady.

'St Quain, at your service.'

'A gentleman of quality, if I mistake not?'

'Nephew to Lord St Quain,' he answered drily.

'Then, sir, I must ask your patience while I tell you how it comes that we entertain a guest so unexpected—and so welcome,' she added, with a cold politeness that was almost insolence.

'We are the Lockerbies of Loch,' went on my lady, with the air of one who has said enough to compel both homage and surprise.

St Quain, indeed, felt no little surprise, for the Lockerbies were famed for their poverty, their pride, and the beauty of their women. He understood now my lady's bearing, and resented it not at all; for no Lockerbie that he had heard or read of had thought to find his equal.

'I am honoured by any summons from Lady Lockerbie,' he said.

My lady glanced shrewdly at him; it seemed she liked his quick address, and liked the fashion of his face and figure.

'There is a curse upon our house,' she went on, with a note of fear beneath her coldness.

'I have heard of it.'

'Who has not? You know the danger, then, that overhangs our daughters?'

In a flash he saw the meaning of it all, and his first sense was one of wonder that an old superstition could die so hard. Was it not the year of grace 1750? And could it be that four folk gathered here together—one a minister, the others women of pluck and sense—were following this Jack-o'-Lanthorn legend with implicit faith? He caught the minister's eye, and the man of prayer began to shift his feet uneasily.

'Such matters are idle; they are snares of Belial,' he said; 'yet the curse has never failed through three long centuries.'

'Legend and history bear out your tale, sir,' said St Quain, and he paused in doubt.

The pause was broken by a sudden, eager cry from the lassie who was the head and fount of all this trouble.

'It is idle, sir,' she said, with a swift glance at St Quain. 'Scots lassies do not die of legends, and so I tell them.'

Yet under her gaiety, too, there was a note of fear. And under her gaiety, likewise, there was a something that told St Quain the truth he hungered for. Mystery or no—hasty wedlock or no—it was plain that in her denial of the need there was a confession that he had already found some place in her regard.

My lady came and laid a hand on the girl's shoulder; and all her pride was gone. 'Janet,' she said tenderly, 'I have but you, and the curse is stronger than we are.'

'But, mother, you are asking'—the colour swept across her face and left it pale again—'you are asking this gentleman to—to give his life for mine.'

'What folly, child!'

'He will be bound to me—to me, whom he did not know a half-hour since. What will his life be worth to him afterwards?'

It was St Quain who spoke now. 'My life will be worth little to me if I lose you,' he said.

And the old nurse, standing in the shadows, rubbed her lean hands together. Southron or no, he spoke as women like to hear a lover speak.

There was an awkward silence, broken on the sudden by a deep whirr from the eight-day clock that stood beside the hearth. All turned to the dial-face; all listened while the ten strokes were struck, sonorous and deliberate. The girl herself began to tremble, for the legends of her race were strong on her, and two more hours might see her wedded to a grimmer bridegroom than St Quain.

'Haste ye, haste ye,' crooned the old nurse. 'It's gey ill to play wi' time as ye are doing.'

The minister was grey of face, and now and then he muttered a prayer. And then there came a wailing from without, as if in answer to the deep voice of the clock—a wailing that drifted round the courtyard, and down the slope, and across the lapping waters of the loch.

'Cannot ye hear?' the old nurse cried.

'It is the wind—the wind, woman,' said the minister fretfully.

'Oh, an' it's the wind, say ye? Well, I've heard it twice in a long life, an' I dinna like its voice.' She looked at her young mistress, 'For the love of heaven, dearie, save yoursel',' she said.

St Quain could scarce remember afterwards what chanced. He was aware of wind and rain against the window panes, of the loud ticking of the clock, of Janet's hand in his. He recalled vaguely that the minister had talked and prayed above them, and that his heart beat high as he named the girl his wife. But what he did remember in after years was the great sob of relief that came from Lady Lockerbie; it was plain that she looked on her daughter as one returned almost from the grave.

When next he felt himself awake, Lady Lockerbie's voice was in his ears, and the pride that was almost insult had come back to it.

'We owe you more of explanation than we have given,' she said, taking him aside. 'Why, you will ask, knowing as we did the danger that hunger over us, why did we leave all to the last moment?'

St Quain's air was full of quiet gaiety. 'I ask for no explanation,' he said. 'I have won your daughter, and I count it the happiest evening of my life.'

'Yet you will wonder by and by, and I must tell you. My daughter was to have been married this morning to an old lover of hers; everything was in readiness, and he—he was killed in a duel yesternight. The news reached us at daybreak, and we have spent the day in fear so horrible that you could not credit it.'

'There was a fate in it,' said St Quain—and, indeed, he felt as much; 'and if I bring your daughter one-half the happiness I have won——'

'Our pride must suffer,' put in my lady; 'the Lockerbies have never yet needed to go abroad in search of an alliance—to seek it in the public road. I fear, sir, your thoughts of us must be something of the strangest.'

Plain as was my lady's attitude—of gratitude all chilled by Scottish pride—her daughter's was different altogether. Half-shy she was, not knowing how this trim-built gallant felt toward her; but the pressure of her hand upon his arm was friendly, warm, confiding almost.

'I shall love wild nights henceforward,' he whispered in her ear. 'The wind and the rain have brought me—you!'

It seemed that she had suffered from deep feeling long repressed; for on the sudden she looked him in the face, and let a dangerous light come into her grey eyes. 'I was to have married Bruce of Muirtown,' she murmured, 'and, oh, how I hated him. Better have died, I think, than go through life with him.'

They were in the hall by this time, and the minister was bowing Lady Lockerbie into her chair.

'Why should such a destiny as ours hang over us?' the girl murmured. The fear, suspense and shame that she had undergone lay heavy still upon her, and she shivered as she spoke.

'The legend says, if I remember rightly, it was because some long-dead Lockerbie did bitter wrong to his neighbour's daughter.'

'You know our story well, it seems.'

'I have lived much in Scotland, and its tales are dear to me.'

'Yet where is the justice of it? All this was centuries ago, and I——'

'And you have pride and all the other legacies to bear. He did grievous wrong to this girl, did he not—your ancestor? And she drowned herself upon her eighteenth birthday; and the mother came to him as he sat in the hall, and cursed him, saying that no maid of his should pass her eighteenth year.'

She nodded gravely, and turned to shudder at the wind-beats that rocked the very walls. 'And we have escaped—all but two of our race—by making maidens wives before they reached the fatal age.'

Lady Lockerbie frowned at them from her seat at the table-head. 'Mr St Quain,' she said, in measured tones, 'I must offer you a lodging for the night. Tomorrow, if it suits you, I should wish you to ride into England, to warn your friends of this alliance, and to make all preparations for a second marriage in due form.'

St Quain laughed outright. The wine and the witchery and the sweetness of it all had got into his blood. 'I ask for no second marriage,' he said. 'Happiness is happiness—and I have found it here tonight.'

Lady Lockerbie looked coldly at her son-in-law.

'I think,' she said, 'that happiness has very little to do with this matter. We are an old race, sir—indeed, you come of an old race yourself, so far as England goes—and I should wish to treat with your father as to settlements, and——'

St Quain felt a dull pain at his heart. He had loved his father well. 'My father died,' he said gravely, 'four years ago—at Culloden.'

Had he unsheathed his sword at the supper-table, the effect of this quiet speech could not have been more dire.

'Died at Culloden?' echoed Lady Lockerbie, clutching the table with restless fingers. 'On which side, sir, did he fight?'

'Why, for the King.'

'The King? Which King—our own Stuart, or the Usurper?'

'For King George. We have been loyal subjects always.'

The minister began to mutter vaguely to himself. He knew not what might follow this rash confession of St Quain's.

'*Loyalty*, sir?' cried my lady, in a voice of bitter scorn. 'We Lockerbies do not play with words, as you would seem to do. I lost my husband at Culloden—and your father fought against him, so it seems.'

'I can but regret,' said St Quain slowly. 'Yet it would be a poor thing, surely, for the children to cherish enmity because the fathers were brave men and fought for different causes.'

'It takes all rights from you, so far as my daughter is concerned.'

St Quain felt the girl on his right hand move closer to him, with a sort of instinctive denial.

'You have saved her life, sir,' went on my lady, in the same cold, even tones; 'you have done us a service, and we thank you for it—but you must never have speech or sight of her again.'

It was St Quain's turn now. He rose to his full height, and Janet, looking up at him, could not keep back that glow of pride and tenderness which had swept over her at his first coming.

'Lady Lockerbie,' he said, 'I have won my wife, and I shall take her home with me as soon as she has made her preparations. I care little for King George or Charlie Stuart—but I love *her* as I never thought that a man could love a woman.'

'You do not understand,' put in my lady. 'Culloden was worse than Flodden even; the memory of it is with us day and night. We *hate* you English folk.'

'Janet,' said St Quain, and he laughed as he turned to the girl—'Janet, what say you? Granted I was unhappy in my English birth—and, faith, I had little choice about the matter!—are you willing to fare out with me and trust to my sword-arm and my honour?'

The Lockerbie pride took diverse forms, and my lady had no exclusive share in it. The girl rose, too, and put a warm hand into her lover's. 'I will go with you,' she said, 'and—I shall go fearlessly.'

Again there was a troubled silence, broken this time by a loud rattling at the door.

'The wind, my lady,' murmured the grey minister, who seemed more uneasy than the rest.

'Open, open!' came a shout from the other side of the door.

'God help us, 'tis Bruce's voice!' murmured Lady Lockerbie. 'Bruce —and we thought him dead!'

'The nicht is full of the wee bit ghosties,' murmured the old nurse, standing behind her lady's chair. 'He, too, I'm thinking, couldna rest quiet i' his quiet bed, while the English-born stepped into his dead shoon.'

Again the girl moved nearer to St Quain, and slipped her hand into his own under cover of the board. 'It is Bruce's voice,' she whispered. 'Bruce of Muirtown, and I fear him so!'

'Fear him, with me beside you?'

'Yes, for he has loved me since I was a child. Oh, he's not bad, not bad at all! But he is fierce, and I do not love him, and—and I would this trouble had not been brought on you.'

St Quain's heart leaped high. Her last thought was for him, despite her own dread of Bruce; the pressure of her hand was sure and wifely.

'See, child,' he whispered, 'do you love me? May I act as if you were my wife in truth as well as in the letter?'

The pressure of her hand alone replied; and then the sound of knocking at the door grew louder, unmistakable. The old nurse went to open, and let in a storm of wind and rain that half-blinded those within. And when at last their eyes grew clearer, they saw a big fellow, with blue eyes and rain-wet hair of yellow, standing, like a storm-sprite, his eyes fixed upon my lady's daughter.

'I feared to be too late,' he cried. 'It wants but an hour to midnight, and——'

He paused, and clutched his heart as if in pain. And now they noticed that his left arm was bandaged, and that a kerchief was wrapped about his brow.

'They—they said that you were dead,' my lady stammered. 'Say, Bruce of Muirtown, is't your ghost?'

'My ghost?' he echoed. 'Nay, but 'twas like to be. I was wounded, and fell into a sort of trance through loss of blood; and when I woke there was a voice that called to me—your voice, Janet—and I rode out through the storm.'

A sudden pity fell upon them. His eyes dwelt hungrily upon the girl, and it was clear that only love had given him strength to ride so far.

'She is married already,' whispered my lady.

He looked more like a fiend than any fleshly man, as he paused to understand his misery. 'Married? To whom?' he thundered.

St Quain bowed quietly. 'To me, sir, an hour gone,' he said.

Bruce of Muirtown began to mutter like a man deranged; then asked the minister if this were true.

'They are fast as the Kirk can make them,' said the grey man of peace.

Again there was a silence; then Bruce laughed harshly, and lifted a glass from the table, and flung the contents full in his rival's face.

'We'll fight upon it, sir, and she shall be a widow before tomorrow breaks.'

St Quain felt a rush of shame come over him—shame, not for his wine-stained face, but for the weakness of this man who had challenged him to combat.

'I regret, sir,' he stammered, wiping his cheeks and brow, 'that you are only strong enough to offer insult—not to atone for it.'

Bruce of Muirtown turned his hungry eyes away—turned them from the lass he worshipped, and let them rest upon St Quain.

'I am recovered,' he said, with a heaviness of voice that belied him; 'I will fight you in the meadows by the loch tonight.'

'Nay, for I refuse,' St Quain answered quietly. 'I do not fight with wounded men.'

Bruce lifted a wine glass from the table and flung the contents in his rival's face.

Janet, for her part, wondered at his self-command; for already she had grown to love him, and no love-ridden woman doubts her lover's courage. But Lady Lockerbie was of different mould, and her voice was cold as the raving wind without when she turned toward St Quain.

'In Scotland, sir, *men* answer insult with the sword,' she said.

St Quain drew back, with something near to horror. For the first time he understood this woman—understood the depth of her prejudice and her pride. She had been glad to save her daughter's life; she was more glad to think that Bruce of Muirtown had returned to cut the bridal-knot with one sharp stroke of his sword.

And yet the man was weak through loss of blood and long riding under rough skies. How could he fight with him?

' 'Tis not the first time we have daunted Englishmen,' said Bruce, with a mocking laugh. 'See how he pales beneath the wine-stains—and all because he sees a hand go down toward a sword-hilt.'

St Quain was mortal, though brave and tender-hearted. 'You fasten a quarrel on me,' he said. 'Well and good—but these ladies should know nothing of it.'

'Ay, ay, they should, seeing that one of them is my promised wife. And, gad, sir,' he added, in a white heat of passion, 'if you dally further, I'll thrash you in their presence.'

St Quain could do no more. He lifted his wife's hand and kissed it; he bowed, as a courtier might have done, to Lady Lockerbie.

'I am ready, sir, and the moon is full tonight,' he said.

The black-robed minister stepped forward. 'Gentlemen, gentlemen——' he began.

'It is too late,' said Bruce of Muirtown.

'Too late,' echoed St Quain, turning, as he left the hall, to find his wife's eyes fixed on his, with a tenderness in them beyond belief.

'Yet think, sir,' said the minister, his hand on St Quain's arm. 'A duel is at all times a godless enterprise; but when your adversary is sick——'

'True,' said St Quain quietly. 'In England we do not fight with such as Mr Bruce here, but it seems that in Scotland the matter shows far otherwise.'

'In Scotland men fight for a right cause, whether they be sick or well,' said Lady Lockerbie sharply.

St Quain bowed low to her. He was beginning to understand how pride—Scottish pride—may oust all womanhood.

'You will fight?' said Bruce of Muirtown eagerly, as he gulped down a measure of red wine.

'You leave me no option, sir,' answered St Quain.

Together they went out into the windy night, he and the man whose left arm carried bandages; and even now, amid the stress of weather and of feeling, he wondered that the prospect of sword-play could be so bracing to a wounded man.

'There will be none to watch us,' muttered Bruce. 'The minister is pledged to peace, and we can scarcely ask the women-folk to act as seconds.'

'Where is the ground?' said St Quain shortly.

'Rather, what is your weapon? You are the challenged party.'

'Swords,' said the other, after a scarce perceptible pause.

The clouds had left the moon by this time, and the wind was dying into fitful moans and gusts as they went out into the grim courtyard and forward to the meadow-lands beyond. From time to time Bruce halted in his walk, but always recovered and went forward with an air so hard and desperate that St Quain felt chilled and awestruck. He could love and hate, this thwarted lover, and spared himself as little, so it seemed, as he spared man or woman when his heart was set upon a matter.

They marked their ground, and once again St Quain drew back.

'You are ill, sir, and I am ashamed,' he said. 'Will you not wait awhile, and send your friend to me in proper form?'

'And let you snatch *my wife* from me? I think not, sir. Either you fight me now, or I have you kicked into the high road by the serving-men.'

St Quain drew his sword. 'I am ready,' he said, in a voice as hard as Bruce's own.

His enemy's attack was overwhelming at the first; Bruce, it was plain, distrusted his own staying-power, and his onslaught, like himself, was rash, impetuous, regardless of all laws. St Quain, recovering after the first surprise, played a quiet, watchful blade; he made no effort of any sort to thrust, but parried each wild stroke with a studied ease that brought the other's blood to fever pitch.

Time after time Bruce strove to beat the other down; and then a mist came before his eyes; and after that he felt his sword go up, and up, and up, toward the grey moon, and a heaviness, as of death, came over him.

He awoke to find St Quain bending over him—bending over him with a strange, almost womanish, solicitude.

'You fought—you fought well, sir,' murmured Bruce.

But shame was strong upon St Quain. True, he had striven to avoid the combat; yet it was terrible to fight, as he had done, with one so weak.

'Can you stand?' he said. 'If so, I'll help you to the house; your bandages have slipped, and the blood is trickling.'

'Where did you prick me?' said Bruce of Muirtown faintly.

'Prick you? Nowhere. I robbed you of your sword, and then you fell into a swoon. I am English, sir, but I am not the coward you would wish.'

Bruce rose stiffly from the wet, moon-bright grass, and passed a hand across his brow. 'I played the bully awhile since,' he stammered;

'I raved and swore, and challenged you to fight; but them—God help me, I had lost a wife.'

St Quain would listen to no more. He linked his arm in Bruce's. 'And I have gained one,' he said softly. 'Surely, sir, you will grant feelings to us English, though we're of a different race.'

Dizzy as he was, sick of heart and brain and fortune, Bruce could not but warm to the manliness, the straightforward wish to give and take which marked his rival's manner. It was his turn now to feel shame; and, in love or war, in pride or shame, it had never been his way to do anything by halves.

'St Quain,' he said, stammering even as he spoke for weakness' sake, 'you are a man—and I regret that insult more than any other deed of my wild life.'

'Then quit regrets, for I have forgotten all. Good God, does not Janet make a good excuse for any folly!'

They had reached the door by this time, and Bruce of Muirtown leaned a heavy hand upon his arm.

'And the girl,' he muttered. 'Will she go with you, do you think?'

'Yes, though her mother says she shall not.'

'And why?'

'I named Culloden in her hearing, and she learned that my father had fought upon the English side.'

Despite his weakness, despite his old sense of loss and his new sense of repentance, Bruce laughed aloud. 'Even for a Scot, she dwells too much upon Culloden,' he said. 'You had better have robbed her plate-chest than mention what you did. The serving-folk are of a like mind, too; you'll have trouble, if you wish to take your bride.'

'I'll take her, if all Scotland says I shall not.'

Like most wildings, Bruce of Muirtown had a heart. He had shown it once tonight, when he could find room for honest admiration of a rival—a rival who had robbed him of a mistress, and who had given him back a forfeit life.

'St Quain,' he said, still standing on the wind side of the oaken door, 'I'll play no dog-in-the-manger part. She's yours, and you shall win her yet.'

They passed into the hall, where Lady Lockerbie was seated alone in front of the great fire. She looked up eagerly as they came in, and her face was white as Bruce's own, soon as she saw them standing there—St Quain in health, his adversary leaning heavily on his arm.

'You—you are hurt, Bruce,' she stammered.

'No,' he said, 'except so far as I was hurt before. Mr St Quain has worsted me, and given me my life. I hope that he will count me his friend henceforward.'

My lady rose. There was a sort of madness in her face—the madness of long hatred indulged in overmuch. She seemed to gain in stature and in coldness.

'His father fought against my husband,' she said. 'He is English; he can be nothing to any Lockerbie.'

'He chances to be husband to a Lockerbie,' put in St Quain drily, 'and he means to claim his right.'

Taller yet she seemed to grow, and her grey eyes deepened, and her voice, no longer cold, was full of passion.

'My daughter is in safety, sir. She would have followed you, to interrupt this duel which has ended so unhappily; but I prevented it.'

'I will find her,' said St Quain doggedly, 'if I spend a twelve-month in the search.'

'And I will help you,' put in Bruce of Muirtown.

My lady looked from one to the other. 'What is this talk of friendliness, Bruce? This stranger has robbed you—robbed you.'

'Nay, it is I who would have robbed him; and I, no less than Janet, owe my life to him.'

Obeying a sudden impulse, Bruce took my lady to one side and talked to her. St Quain could hear nothing of what passed; but he guessed that his own cause was being pleaded by one who had so lately wished to kill him. And by and by Lady Lockerbie returned, and held her hand out with some show of warmth.

'I cannot pretend to welcome the match,' she said, 'but I am old, and weary, and I cannot but see that lives may well be ruined. Will you—will you treat her well?'

Her voice broke at the last; and St Quain saw down into the tenderness that lay beneath her pride.

'I will treat her well,' he answered huskily.

My lady turned to a manservant who stood by the door. 'Prepare the bridal chamber,' she said.

And St Quain looked out upon the loch, the moonlight, and the peaceful sky. And only the whimpering wind was left to recall the storm that had brought a wife to him.

BETTER LET
BLAME'WELL ALONE

Mark Twain

Huckleberry Finn is living with the Widow Douglas, who has custody of him, and is slowly adapting to a life of schoolwork and regular habits. However, his drunken father reappears and is granted custody of the boy by a new judge. Huck makes his escape, and stages it so that it seems he has been murdered. On Jackson Island in the Mississippi he meets Jim, the Widow Douglas's Negro, who has run away because he thinks the widow's sister is about to sell him. They link their fortunes, and continue together down the Mississippi.

It must 'a' been close on to one o'clock when we got below the island at last, and the raft did seem to go mighty slowly. If a boat was to come along we was going to take to the canoe and break for the Illinois shore; and it was well a boat didn't come, for we hadn't ever thought to put the gun in the canoe, or a fishing line, or anything to eat. We was in ruther too much of a sweat to think of so many things. It warn't good judgment to put *everything* on the raft.

If the men went to the island I just expect they found the campfire I built, and watched it all night for Jim to come. Anyways, they stayed away from us, and if my building the fire never fooled them it warn't no fault of mine. I played it as low-down on them as I could.

When the first streak of day began to show we tied up to a towhead in a bend on the Illinois side, and hacked off cottonwood branches with the hatchet, and covered up the raft with them so she looked like there had been a cave-in in the bank there. A towhead is a sand-bar that has cottonwoods on it as thick as harrow teeth.

We had mountains on the Missouri shore and heavy timber on the Illinois side, and the channel was down the Missouri shore at that place, so we warn't afraid of anybody running across us. We laid there all day, and watched the rafts and steamboats spin down the Missouri shore, and up-bound steamboats fight the big river in the middle. I told Jim all about the time I had jabbering with that woman; and Jim said she was a smart one, and if she was to start after us herself *she* wouldn't set down and watch a campfire—no, sir, she'd fetch a dog. Well, I said, why couldn't she tell her husband to fetch a dog? Jim said he bet she did think of it by the time the men was ready to start, and he believed they must 'a' gone uptown to get a dog and so they lost all that time, or else we wouldn't be here on a towhead sixteen or seventeen mile below the village—no, indeedy, we would be in that same town again. So I said I didn't care what was the reason they didn't get us as long as they didn't.

When it was beginning to come on dark we poked our heads out of the cottonwood thicket, and looked up and down and across; nothing in sight; so Jim took up some of the top planks of the raft and built a snug wigwam to get under in blazing weather and rainy, and to keep the things dry. Jim made a floor for the wigwam, and raised it a foot or more above the level of the raft, so now the blankets and all the traps was out of reach of steamboat waves. Right in the middle of the wigwam we made a layer of dirt about five or six inches deep with a frame around it for to hold it to its place; this was to build a fire on in sloppy weather or chilly; the wigwam would keep it from being seen. We made an extra steering oar, too, because one of the others might get broke on a snag or something. We fixed up a short forked stick to hang the old lantern on, because we must always light the lantern whenever we see a steamboat coming downstream, to keep from getting run over; but we wouldn't have to light it for upstream boats unless we see we was in what they call a 'crossing'; for the river was pretty high yet, very low banks being still a little under water; so upbound boats didn't always run the channel, but hunted easy water.

This second night we run between seven and eight hours, with a current that was making over four mile an hour. We catched fish and talked, and we took a swim now and then to keep off sleepiness. It was kind of solemn, drifting down the big, still river, laying on our backs looking up at the stars, and we didn't ever feel like talking loud, and it warn't often that we laughed—only a little kind of a low chuckle.

We had mighty good weather as a general thing, and nothing ever happened to us at all—that night, nor the next, nor the next.

Every night we passed towns, some of them away up on black hillsides nothing but just a shiny bed of lights; not a house could you see. The fifth night we passed St Louis, and it was like the whole world lit up. In St Petersburg they used to say there was twenty or thirty thousand people in St Louis, but I never believed it till I see that wonderful spread of lights at two o'clock that still night. There warn't a sound there; everybody was asleep.

Every night now I used to slip ashore toward ten o'clock at some little village, and buy ten or fifteen cents' worth of meal or bacon or other stuff to eat; and sometimes I lifted a chicken that warn't roosting comfortable, and took him along. Pap always said take a chicken when you get a chance, because if you don't want him yourself you can easy find somebody that does, and a good deed ain't ever forgot. I never see Pap when he didn't want the chicken himself, but that is what he used to say, anyway.

Mornings before daylight I slipped into cornfields and borrowed a watermelon, or a mushmelon, or a punkin, or some new corn, or things of that kind. Pap always said it warn't no harm to borrow things if you was meaning to pay them back sometime; but the widow said it warn't anything but a soft name for stealing, and no decent body would do it. Jim said he reckoned the widow was partly right and Pap was partly right; so the best way would be for us to pick out two or three things from the list and say we wouldn't borrow them any more—then he reckoned it wouldn't be no harm to borrow the others. So we talked it over all one night, drifting along down the river, trying to make up our minds whether to drop the water-melons, or the cantaloups, or the musk-melons, or what. But toward daylight we got it all settled satisfactory, and concluded to drop crab-apples and p'simmons. We warn't feeling just right before that, but it was all comfortable now. I was glad the way it come out, too, because crab-apples ain't ever good and the p'simmons wouldn't be ripe for two or three months yet.

We shot a waterfowl now and then that got up too early in the morning or didn't go to bed early enough in the evening. Take it all round, we lived pretty high.

The fifth night below St Louis we had a big storm after midnight, with a power of thunder and lightning, and the rain poured down in a solid sheet. We stayed in the wigwam and let the raft take care of itself. When the lightning glared out we could see a big straight river ahead, and high, rocky bluffs on both sides. By and by says I, 'Hel-*lo*, Jim, looky yonder!' It was a steamboat that had killed herself on a rock. We was drifting straight down for her. The lightning showed her very distinct. She was leaning over, with part of her upper deck above water, and you could see every little chimbly guy clean and clear, and a chair by the big bell, with an old slouch hat hanging on the back of it, when the flashes come.

Well, it being away in the night and stormy, and all so mysterious-like, I felt just the way any other boy would 'a' felt when I seen that wreck laying there so mournful and lonesome in the middle of the river. I wanted to get aboard of her and slink around a little, and see what there was there. So I says:

'Le's land on her, Jim.'

But Jim was dead against it at first. He says:

'I doan' want to go fool'n' 'long er no wrack. We's doin' blame' well, en we better let blame' well alone, as de good book says. Like as not dey's a watchman on dat wrack.'

'Watchman your grandmother,' I says; 'there ain't nothing to watch but the texas and the pilothouse; and do you reckon anybody's going to resk his life for a texas and a pilothouse such a night as this, when it's likely to break up and wash off down the river any minute?' Jim couldn't say nothing to that, so he didn't try. 'And besides,' I says, 'we might borrow something worth having out of the captain's stateroom. See-gars, *I* bet you—and cost five cents apiece, solid cash. Steamboat captains is always rich, and get sixty dollars a month, and *they* don't care a cent what a thing costs, you know, long as they want it. Stick a candle in your pocket; I can't rest, Jim, till we give her a rummaging. Do you reckon Tom Sawyer would ever go by this thing? Not for pie, he wouldn't. He'd call it an adventure—that's what he'd call it; and he'd land on that wreck if it was his last act. And wouldn't he throw style into it?—wouldn't he spread himself, nor nothing? Why, you'd think it was Christopher C'lumbus discovering Kingdom Come. I wish Tom Sawyer *was* here.'

Jim he grumbled a little, but give in. He said we mustn't talk any more than we could help, and then talk mighty low. The lightning showed us the wreck again just in time, and we fetched the starboard derrick, and made fast there.

The deck was high out here. We went sneaking down the slope of it to labboard, in the dark, towards the texas, feeling our way slow with our feet, and spreading our hands out to fend off the guys, for it was so dark we couldn't see no sign of them. Pretty soon we struck the forward end of the skylight, and clumb on to it; and the next step fetched us in front of the captain's door, which was open, and by Jimminy, away down through the texas hall we see a light! and all in the same second we seem to hear low voices in yonder!

Jim whispered and said he was feeling powerful sick, and told me to come along. I says, all right, and was going to start for the raft; but just then I heard a voice wail out and say:

'Oh, please don't, boys; I swear I won't ever tell!'

Another voice said, pretty loud:

'It's a lie, Jim Turner. You've acted this way before. You always want more'n your share of the truck, and you've always got it, too, because you've swore 't if you didn't you'd tell. But this time you've said it jest one time too many. You're the meanest, treacherousest hound in this country.'

By this time Jim was gone for the raft. I was just a-biling with curiosity; and I says to myself, Tom Sawyer wouldn't back out now, and so I won't either; I'm a-going to see what's going on here. So I dropped on my hands and knees in the little passage, and crept aft in the dark till there warn't but one stateroom betwixt me and the cross hall of the texas. Then in there I see a man stretched on the floor and tied hand and foot, and two men standing over him, and one of them had a dim lantern in his hand, and the other one had a pistol. This one kept pointing the pistol at the man's head on the floor, and saying:

'I'd *like* to! And I orter, too—a mean skunk!'

The man on the floor would shrivel up and say, 'Oh, please don't, Bill; I hain't ever goin' to tell.'

And every time he said that the man with the lantern would laugh and say:

''Deed you *ain't!* You never said no truer thing 'n that, you bet you.' And once he said: 'Hear him beg! and yit if we hadn't got the best of

'In there I see a man stretched on the floor tied, hand and foot, and two men standing over him.'

him and tied him he'd 'a' killed us both. And what *for?* Jist for noth'n'. Jist because we stood on our *rights*—that's what for. But I lay you ain't a-goin' to threaten nobody any more, Jim Turner. Put *up* that pistol, Bill.'

Bill says:

'I don't want to, Jake Packard. I'm for killin' him—and didn't he kill old Hatfield jist the same way—and don't he deserve it?'

'But I don't *want* him killed, and I've got my reasons for it.'

'Bless yo' heart for them words, Jake Packard! I'll never forget you long's I live!' says the man on the floor, sort of blubbering.

Packard didn't take no notice of that, but hung up his lantern on a nail and started toward where I was, there in the dark, and motioned Bill to come. I crawfished as fast as I could about two yards, but the boat slanted so that I couldn't make very good time; so to keep from getting run over and catched I crawled into a stateroom on the upper side. The man came a-pawing along in the dark, and when Packard got to my stateroom, he says:

'Here—come in here.'

And in he come, and Bill after him. But before they got in I was up in the upper berth, cornered, and sorry I come. Then they stood there, with their hands on the ledge of the berth, and talked. I couldn't see them, but I could tell where they was by the whisky they'd been having. I was glad I didn't drink whisky; but it would't made much difference anyway, because most of the time they couldn't 'a' treed me because I didn't breathe. I was too scared. And, besides, a body *couldn't* breathe and hear such talk. They talked low and earnest. Bill wanted to kill Turner. He says:

'He's said he'll tell, and he will. If we was to give both our shares to him *now* it wouldn't make no difference after the row and the way we've served him. Shore's you're born, he'll turn state's evidence; now you hear *me*. I'm for putting him out of his troubles.'

'So'm I,' says Packard, very quiet.

'Blame it, I'd sorter begun to think you wasn't. Well, then, that's all right. Le's go and do it.'

'Hold on a minute; I hain't had my say yit. You listen to me. Shooting's good, but there's quieter ways if the things *got* to be done. But what *I* say is this: it ain't good sense to go court'n' around after a halter if you can git at what you're up to in some way that's jist as good and at the same time don't bring you into no resks. Ain't that so?'

'You bet it is. But how you goin' to manage it this time?'

'Well, my idea is this: we'll rustle around and gather up whatever pickin's we've overlooked in the staterooms, and shove for shore and hide the truck. Then we'll wait. Now I say it ain't a-goin' to be more'n two hours befo' this wrack breaks up and washes off down the river. See? He'll be drownded, and won't have nobody to blame for it but his own self. I reckon that's a considerable sight better 'n killin' of him. I'm unfavourable to killin' a man as long as you can git aroun' it; it ain't good sense, it ain't good morals. Ain't I right?'

'Yes, I reck'n you are. But s'pose she *don't* break up and wash off?'

'Well, we can wait the two hours anyway and see, can't we?'

'All right, then; come along.'

So they started, and I lit out, all in a cold sweat, and scrambled forward. It was dark as pitch there; but I said, in a kind of a coarse whisper, 'Jim!' and he answered up, right at my elbow, with a sort of a moan, and I says:

'Quick, Jim, it ain't no time for fooling around and moaning; there's a gang of murderers in yonder, and if we don't hunt up their boat and set her drifting down the river so these fellows can't get away from the wreck there's one of 'em going to be in a bad fix. But if we find their boat we can put *all* of 'em in a bad fix—for the sheriff'll get 'em. Quick —hurry! I'll hunt the labboard side, you hunt the stabboard. You start at the raft, and——'

'Oh, my lordy, lordy! *Raf'*? Dey ain' no raf' no mo'; she done broke loose en gone!—en here we is!'

Well, I catched my breath and 'most fainted. Shut up on a wreck with such a gang as that! But it warn't no time to be sentimentering. We'd *got* to find that boat now—had to have it for ourselves. So we went a-quaking and shaking down the stabboard side, and slow work it was, too—seemed a week before we got to the stern. No sign of a boat. Jim said he didn't believe he could go any farther—so scared he hadn't hardly any strength left, he said. But I said, come on, if we get left on this wreck we are in a fix, sure. So on we prowled again. We struck for the stern of the texas, and found it, and then scrabbled along forwards on the skylight, hanging on from shutter to shutter, for the edge of the skylight was in the water. When we got pretty close to the cross-hall door there was the skiff, sure enough! I could just barely see her. I felt ever so thankful. In another second I would 'a' been aboard of her, but just then the door opened. One of the men stuck his head out only about a couple of foot from me, and I thought I was gone; but he jerked it in again, and says:

'Heave that blame lantern out o' sight, Bill!'

He flung a bag of something into the boat, and then got in himself and set down. It was Packard. Then Bill *he* come out and got in. Packard says, in a low voice:

'All ready—shove off!'

I couldn't hardly hang on to the shutters, I was so weak. But Bill says:

'Hold on—'d you go through him?'

'No. Didn't you?'

'No. So he's got his share o' the cash yet.'

'Well, then, come along; no use to take truck and leave money.'

'Say, won't he suspicion what we're up to?'

'Maybe he won't. But we got to have it anyway. Come along.'

So they got out and went in.

The door slammed to because it was on the careened side; and in a half second I was in the boat, and Jim come tumbling after me. I out with my knife and cut the rope, and away we went!

We didn't touch an oar, and we didn't speak nor whisper, nor hardly even breathe. We went gliding swift along, dead silent, past the tip of the paddlebox, and past the sterm; then in a second or two more we was a hundred yards below the wreck, and the darkness soaked her up, every last sign of her, and we was safe, and knowed it.

When we was three or four hundred yards downstream we see the lantern show like a little spark at the texas door for a second, and we knowed by that that the rascals had missed their boat, and was beginning to understand that they was in just as much trouble now as Jim Turner was.

Then Jim manned the oars, and we took out after our raft. Now was the first time that I begun to worry about the men—I reckon I hadn't had time to before. I begun to think how dreadful it was, even for murderers, to be in such a fix. I says to myself, there ain't no telling but I might come to be a murderer myself yet, and then how would I like it? So says I to Jim:

'The first light we see we'll land a hundred yards below it or above it, in a place where it's a good hiding place for you and the skiff, and then I'll go and fix up some kind of a yarn, and get somebody to go for that gang and get them out of their scrape, so they can be hung when their time comes.'

THE MODEL MILLIONAIRE

Oscar Wilde

Unless one is wealthy there is no use in being a charming fellow. Romance is the privilege of the rich, not the profession of the unemployed. The poor should be practical and prosaic. It is better to have a permanent income than to be fascinating. These are the great truths of modern life which Hughie Erskine never realized. Poor Hughie! Intellectually, we must admit, he was not of much importance. He never said a brilliant or even an ill-natured thing in his life. But then he was wonderfully good-looking, with his crisp, brown hair, his clear-cut profile, and his grey eyes. He was as popular with men as he was with women, and he had every accomplishment except that of making money. His father had bequeathed him his cavalry sword and a *History of the Peninsular War* in fifteen volumes. Hughie hung the first over his looking-glass, put the second on a shelf between *Ruff's Guide* and *Bailey's Magazine,* and lived on two hundred a year that an old aunt allowed him. He had tried everything. He had gone on the Stock Exchange for six months; but what was a butterfly to do among bulls and bears? He had been a tea-merchant for a little longer, but had soon tired of souchong. Then he had tried selling dry sherry but the sherry was a little too dry. Ultimately he became nothing, a delightful, ineffectual young man with a perfect profile and no profession.

To make matters worse, he was in love. The girl he loved was Laura Merton, the daughter of a retired Colonel who had lost his temper and his digestion in India, and had never found either of them again. Laura adored him, and he was ready to kiss her shoe-strings. They were the handsomest couple in London, and had not a penny-piece between them. The Colonel was very fond of Hughie, but would not hear of any engagement.

'Come to me, my boy, when you have got ten thousand pounds of your own, and we will see about it,' he used to say; and Hughie looked very glum in those days, and had to go to Laura for consolation.

One morning, as he was on his way to Holland Park, where the Mertons lived, he dropped in to see a great friend of his, Alan Trevor. Trevor was a painter. Indeed, few people escape that nowadays. But he was also an artist, and artists are rather rare. Personally he was a strange rough fellow, with a freckled face and a red, ragged beard. However, when he took up the brush he was a real master, and his pictures were eagerly sought after. He had been very much attracted by Hughie at first, it must be acknowledged, entirely on account of his personal charm. 'The only people a painter should know,' he used to say, 'are people who are *bête* and beautiful, people who are an artistic pleasure to look at and an intellectual repose to talk to. Men who are dandies and women who are darlings rule the world, at least they should do so.' However, after he got to know Hughie better, he liked him quite as much for his bright, buoyant spirits and his generous, reckless nature, and had given him the permanent *entrée* to his studio.

When Hughie came in he found Trevor putting the finishing touches to a wonderful life-size picture of a beggar-man. The beggar himself was standing on a raised platform in a corner of the studio. He was a wizened old man, with a face like wrinkled parchment, and a most piteous expression. Over his shoulder was flung a coarse brown cloak, all tears and tatters; his thick boots were patched and cobbled, and with one hand he leant on a rough stick, while with the other he held out his battered hat for alms.

'What an amazing model!' whispered Hughie, as he shook hands with his friend.

'An amazing model?' shouted Trevor at the top of his voice; 'I should think so! Such beggars as he are not to be met with every day.

The beggar was standing on a raised platform in a corner of the room.

A *trouvaille, mon cher*; a living Velasquez! My stars! what an etching Rembrandt would have made of him!'

'Poor old chap!' said Hughie, 'how miserable he looks! But I suppose, to you painters, his face is his fortune?'

'Certainly,' replied Trevor, 'you don't want a beggar to look happy, do you?'

'How much does a model get for sitting?' asked Hughie, as he found himself a comfortable seat on a divan.

'A shilling an hour.'

'And how much do you get for your picture, Alan?'

'Oh, for this I get two thousand!'

'Pounds?'

'Guineas. Painters, poets, and physicians always get guineas.'

'Well, I think the model should have a percentage,' cried Hughie, laughing; 'they work quite as hard as you do.'

'Nonsense, nonsense! Why, look at the trouble of laying on the paint alone, and standing all day long at one's easel! It's all very well, Hughie, for you to talk, but I assure you that there are moments when Art almost attains to the dignity of manual labour. But you mustn't chatter; I'm very busy. Smoke a cigarette, and keep quiet.'

After some time the servant came in, and told Trevor that the frame-maker wanted to speak to him.

'Don't run away, Hughie,' he said, as he went out, 'I will be back in a moment.'

The old beggar man took advantage of Trevor's absence to rest for a moment on a wooden bench that was behind him. He looked so forlorn and wretched that Hughie could not help pitying him, and felt in his pockets to see what money he had. All he could find was a sovereign and some coppers. 'Poor old fellow,' he thought to himself, 'he wants it more than I do, but it means no hansoms for a fortnight'; and he walked across the studio and slipped the sovereign into the beggar's hand.

The old man started, and a faint smile flitted across his withered lips. 'Thank you, sir,' he said, 'thank you.'

Then Trevor arrived, and Hughie took his leave, blushing a little at what he had done. He spent the day with Laura, got a charming scolding for his extravagance, and had to walk home.

That night he strolled into the Palette Club about eleven o'clock, and found Trevor sitting by himself in the smoking-room drinking hock and seltzer.

'Well, Alan, did you get the picture finished all right?' he said, as he lit his cigarette.

'Finished and framed, my boy!' answered Trevor; 'and, by the by, you have made a conquest. That old model you saw is quite devoted to you. I had to tell him all about you—who you are, where you live. What your income is, what prospects you have—'

'My dear Alan,' cried Hughie, 'I shall probably find him waiting for me when I go home. But, of course, you are only joking. Poor old wretch! I wish I could do something for him. I think it is dreadful that anyone should be so miserable. I have got heaps of old clothes at home—do you think he would care for any of them? Why, his rags were falling to bits.'

'But he looks splendid in them,' said Trevor. 'I wouldn't paint him in a frock coat for anything. What you call rags I call romance. What seems poverty to you is picturesqueness to me. However, I'll tell him of your offer.'

'Alan,' said Hughie seriously, 'you painters are a heartless lot.'

'An artist's heart is his head,' replied Trevor; 'and besides, our business is to realize the world as we see it, not to reform it as we know it. *A chacun son métier*. And now tell me how Laura is. The old model was quite interested in her.'

'You don't mean to say you talked to him about her?' said Hughie.

'Certainly I did. He knows all about the relentless Colonel, the lovely Laura, and the ten thousand pounds.'

'You told that old beggar all my private affairs?' cried Hughie, looking very red and angry.

'My dear boy,' said Trevor, smiling, 'that old beggar, as you call him, is one of the richest men in Europe. He could buy all London to-morrow without overdrawing his account. He has a house in every capital, dines off gold plate, and can prevent Russia going to war when he chooses.'

'What on earth do you mean?' exclaimed Hughie.

'What I say,' said Trevor. 'The old man you saw today in the studio was Baron Hausberg. He is a great friend of mine, buys all my pictures and that sort of thing, and gave me a commission a month ago to paint him as a beggar. *Que voulez-vous? La fantaise d'un millionnaire!* And I must say he made a magnificent figure in his rags, or perhaps I should say in my rags; they are an old suit I got in Spain.'

'Baron Hausberg!' cried Hughie. 'Good heavens! I gave him a sovereign!' and he sank into an arm-chair the picture of dismay.

'Gave him a sovereign!' shouted Trevor, and he burst into a roar of laughter. 'My dear boy, you'll never see it again. *Son affaire c'est l'argent des autres.*'

'I think you might have told me, Alan,' said Hughie sulkily, 'and not have let me make such a fool of myself.'

'Well, to begin with, Hughie,' said Trevor, 'it never entered my mind that you went about distributing alms in that reckless way. I can understand your kissing a pretty model, but your giving a sovereign to an ugly one—by Jove, no! Besides, the fact is that I really was not at home today to anyone; and when you came in I didn't know whether Hausberg would like his name mentioned. You know he wasn't in full dress.'

'What a duffer he must think me!' said Hughie.

'Not at all. He was in the highest spirits after you left; kept chuckling to himself and rubbing his old wrinkled hands together. I couldn't make out why he was so interested to know all about you; but I see it all now. He'll invest your sovereign for you, Hughie, pay you the interest every six months, and have a capital story to tell after dinner.'

'I am an unlucky devil,' growled Hughie. 'The best thing I can do is to go to bed; and, my dear Alan, you mustn't tell anyone. I shouldn't dare show my face in the Row.'

'Nonsense! It reflects the highest credit on your philanthropic spirit, Hughie. And don't run away. Have another cigarette, and you can talk about Laura as much as you like.'

However, Hughie wouldn't stop, but walked home, feeling very unhappy, and leaving Alan Trevor in fits of laughter.

The next morning, as he was at breakfast, the servant brought him up a card on which was written, 'Monsieur Gustave Naudin, *de la part de* M. le Baron Hausberg'.

'I suppose he has come for an apology,' said Hughie to himself; and he told the servant to show the visitor up.

An old gentleman with gold spectacles and grey hair came into the room, and said, in a slight French accent, 'Have I the honour of addressing Monsieur Erskine?'

Hughie bowed.

'I have come from Baron Hausberg,' he continued. 'The Baron—'

'I beg, sir, that you will offer him my sincerest apologies,' stammered Hughie.

'The Baron,' said the old gentleman with a smile, 'has commissioned me to bring you this letter'; and he extended a sealed envelope.

On the outside was written, 'A wedding present to Hugh Erskine and Laura Merton, from an old beggar,' and inside was a cheque for ten thousand pounds.

When they were married Alan Trevor was the best man, and the Baron made a speech at the wedding breakfast.

'Millionaire models,' remarked Alan, 'are rare enough; but, by Jove, model millionaires are rarer still!'

THE SIRE DE MALETROIT'S DOOR

Robert Louis Stevenson

It was September, 1429; the weather had fallen sharp; a flighty piping wind, laden with showers, beat about the township; and the dead leaves ran riot along the streets. Here and there a window was already lighted up; and the noise of men-at-arms making merry over supper within, came forth in fits and was swallowed up and carried away by the wind. The night fell swiftly; the flag of England, fluttering on the spire-top, grew ever fainter and fainter against the flying clouds— a black speck like a swallow in the tumultuous, leaden chaos of the sky. As the night fell the wind rose and began to hoot under archways and roar amid the tree-tops in the valley below the town.

Denis de Beaulieu walked fast and was soon knocking at his friend's door; but though he promised himself to stay only a little while and make an early return, his welcome was so pleasant, and he found so much to delay him, that it was already long past midnight before he said good-bye upon the threshold. The wind had fallen again in the meanwhile; the night was as black as the grave; not a star, nor a glimmer of moonshine, slipped through the canopy of cloud. Denis was ill-acquainted with the intricate lanes of Château Landon; even by daylight he had found some trouble in picking his way; and in this absolute darkness he soon lost it altogether. He was certain of one thing only—to keep mounting the hill; for his friend's house lay at the lower end, or tail of Château Landon, while the inn was up at the head, under the great church spire. With this clue to go upon he stumbled and groped forward, now breathing more freely in open places where there was a good slice of sky overhead, now feeling along the wall in stifling closes. It is an eerie and mysterious position to be thus submerged in opaque blackness in an almost unknown town. The silence is terrifying in its possibilities. The touch of cold window bars to the exploring hand startles the man like the touch of a toad; the inequalities of the pavement shake his heart into his mouth; a piece of denser darkness threatens an ambuscade or a chasm in the pathway; and where the air is brighter, the houses put on strange and bewildering appearances, as if to lead him farther from his way. For Denis, who had to regain his inn without attracting notice, there was real danger as well as mere discomfort in the walk; and he went warily and boldly at once, and at every corner paused to make an observation.

He had been for some time threading a lane so narrow that he could touch a wall with either hand, when it began to open out and go sharply downward. Plainly this lay no longer in the direction of his inn; but the hope of a little more light tempted him forward to reconnoitre. The lane ended in a terrace with a bartisan wall, which gave an outlook between high houses, as out of an embrasure, into the valley lying dark and formless several hundred feet below. Denis looked down, and could discern a few tree-tops waving and a single speck of brightness where the river ran across a weir. The weather was clearing up, and the sky had lightened, so as to show the outline of the heavier clouds and the dark margin of the hills. By the uncertain glimmer, the house on his left hand should be a place of some pretensions; it was surmounted by several pinnacles and turret-tops; the round stern of a chapel, with a fringe of flying buttresses, projected boldly from the main block; and the door was sheltered under a deep porch carved with figures and overhung by two long gargoyles. The windows of the chapel gleamed through their intricate tracery with a light as of many tapers, and threw out the buttresses and the peaked roof in a more intense blackness against the sky. It was plainly the hotel of some great family of the neighbourhood; and as it reminded Denis of a town house of his own at Bourges, he stood for some time gazing up at it and mentally gauging the skill of the architects and the consideration of the two families.

There seemed to be no issue to the terrace but the lane by which he had reached it; he could only retrace his steps, but he had gained some notion of his whereabouts, and hoped by this means to hit the main thoroughfare and speedily regain the inn. He was reckoning without that chapter of accidents which was to make this night memorable above all others in his career; for he had not gone back above a hundred yards before he saw a light coming to meet him, and heard loud voices speaking together in the echoing of the lane. It was a party of men-at-arms going the night round with torches. Denis assured himself that they had all been making free with the wine-bowl, and were in no mood to be particular about safe-conducts or the niceties of chivalrous war. It was as like as not that they would kill him like a dog and leave him where he fell. The situation was inspiriting but nervous. Their own torches would conceal him from sight, he reflected; and he hoped that they would drown the noise of his footsteps with their own empty voices. If he were but fleet and silent, he might evade their notice altogether.

Unfortunately, as he turned to beat a retreat, his foot rolled upon a pebble; he fell against the wall with an ejaculation, and his sword rang loudly on the stones. Two or three voices demanded who went there—some in French, some in English; but Denis made no reply, and ran the faster down the lane. Once upon the terrace, he paused to look back. They still kept calling after him, and just then began to double the pace in pursuit, with a considerable clank of armour, and great tossing of the torchlight to and fro in the narrow jaws of the passage.

Denis cast a look around and darted into the porch. There he might escape observation, or—if that were too much to expect—was in a capital posture whether for parley or defence. So thinking, he drew his sword and tried to set his back against the door. To his surprise, it yielded behind his weight; and though he turned in a moment, continued to swing back on oiled and noiseless hinges, until it stood wide open on a black interior. When things fall out opportunely for the person concerned, he is not apt to be critical about the how or why, his own immediate personal convenience seeming a sufficient reason for the strangest oddities and revolutions in our sublunary things; and so Denis, without a moment's hesitation, stepped within and partly closed the door behind him to conceal his place of refuge. Nothing was further from his thoughts than to close it altogether; but for some inexplicable reason—perhaps by a spring or a weight—the ponderous mass of oak whipped itself out of his fingers and clanked to.

The round, at that very moment, debouched upon the terrace and proceeded to summon him with shouts and curses. He heard them ferreting in the dark corners, the stock of a lance even rattled along the outer surface of the door behind which he stood; but these gentlemen were in too high a humour to be long delayed and soon made off down a corkscrew pathway which had escaped Denis's observation, and passed out of sight and hearing along the battlements of the town.

Denis breathed again. He gave them a few minutes' grace for fear of accidents, and then groped about for some means of opening the door and slipping forth again. The inner surface was quite smooth, not a handle, not a moulding, not a projection of any sort. He got his finger-nails round the edges and pulled, but the mass was immovable. He shook it, it was as firm as a rock. Denis de Beaulieu frowned and gave vent to a little noiseless whistle? What ailed the door? he wondered. Why was it open? How came it to shut so easily and so effectually after him? There was something obscure and underhand about all this, that was little to the young man's fancy. It looked like a snare; and yet who would suppose a snare in such a quiet by-street and in a house of so prosperous and even noble an exterior? And yet—snare or no snare, intentionally or unintentionally—here he was, prettily trapped; and for the life of him he could see no way out of it again. The darkness began to weigh upon him. He gave ear; all was silent without, but within and close by he seemed to catch a faint sighing, a faint sobbing rustle, a little stealthy creak—as though many persons were at his side, holding themselves quite still, and governing even their respiration with the extreme of slyness. The idea went to his vitals with a shock, and he faced about suddenly as if to defend his life. Then, for the first time, he became aware of a light about the level of his eyes and at some distance in the interior of the house—a vertical thread of light, widening towards the bottom, such as might escape between two wings of arras over a doorway. To see anything was a relief to Denis; it was like a piece of solid ground to a man labouring in a morass; his mind seized upon it with avidity; and he stood staring at it and trying to piece together some logical conception of his surroundings. Plainly there was a flight of steps ascending from his own level to that of this illuminated doorway; and indeed he thought he could make out another thread of light, as fine as a needle and as faint as phosphorescence, which might very well be reflected along the polished wood of a handrail. Since he had begun to suspect that he was not alone, his heart had continued to beat with smothering violence, and an intolerable desire for action of any sort had possessed itself of his spirit. He was in deadly peril, he believed. What could be more natural than to mount the staircase, lift the curtain, and confront his difficulty at once? At least he would be dealing with something tangible; at least he would be no longer in the dark. He stepped slowly forward with outstretched hand, until his foot struck the bottom step; then he rapidly scaled the stairs, stood for a moment to compose his expression, lifted the arras and went in.

He found himself in a large apartment of polished stone. There were three doors; one on each of three sides; all similarly curtained with tapestry. The fourth side was occupied by two large windows and a great stone chimney-piece, carved with the arms of the Malétroits. Denis recognised the bearings, and was gratified to find himself in such good hands. The room was strongly illuminated; but it contained little furniture except a heavy table and a chair or two, the hearth was innocent of fire, and the pavement was but sparsely strewn with rushes clearly many days old.

On a high chair beside the chimney, and directly facing Denis as he entered, sat a little old gentleman in a fur tippet. He sat with his legs crossed and his hands folded, and a cup of spiced wine stood by his elbow on a bracket on the wall. His countenance had a strongly masculine cast; not properly human, but such as we see in the bull, the goat, or the domestic boar; something equivocal and wheedling, something greedy, brutal, and dangerous. The upper lip was inordinately full, as though swollen by a blow or a toothache; and the smile, the peaked eyebrows, and the small, strong eyes were quaintly and almost comically evil in expression. Beautiful white hair hung straight all round his head, like a saint's, and fell in a single curl upon the tippet. His beard and moustache were the pink of venerable sweetness. Age, probably in consequence of inordinate precautions, had left no mark upon his hands; and the Malétroit hand was famous. It would be difficult to imagine anything at once so fleshy and so delicate in design; the taper, sensual fingers were like those of one of Leonardo's women; the fork of the thumb made a dimpled protuberance when closed; the nails were perfectly shaped, and of a dead, surprising whiteness. It rendered his aspect tenfold more redoubtable, that a man with hands like these should keep them devoutly folded in his lap like a virgin martyr—that a man with so intense and startling an expression of face should sit patiently on his seat and contemplate people with an unwinking stare, like a god, or a god's statue. His quiescence seemed ironical and treacherous, it fitted so poorly with his looks.

Such was Alain, Sire de Malétroit.

Denis and he looked silently at each other for a second or two.

'Pray step in,' said the Sire de Malétroit. 'I have been expecting you all the evening.'

He had not arisen, but he accompanied his words with a smile and a slight but courteous inclination of the head. Partly from the smile, partly from the strange musical murmur with which the Sire prefaced his observation, Denis felt a strong shudder of disgust go through his marrow. And what with disgust and honest confusion of mind, he could scarcely get words together in reply.

'I fear,' he said, 'that this is a double accident. I am not the person you suppose me. It seems you were looking for a visit; but for my part, nothing was further from my thoughts—nothing could be more contrary to my wishes—than this intrusion.'

'Well, well,' replied the old gentleman indulgently, 'here you are, which is the main point. Seat yourself, my friend, and put yourself entirely at your ease. We shall arrange our little affairs presently.'

Denis perceived that the matter was still complicated with some misconception, and he hastened to continue his explanations.

'Your door . . .' he began.

'About my door?' asked the other, raising his peaked eyebrows. 'A little piece of ingenuity.' And he shrugged his shoulders. 'A hospitable fancy! By your own account, you were not desirous of making my acquaintance. We old people look for such reluctance now and then;

and when it touches our honour, we cast about until we find some way of overcoming it. You arrive uninvited, but believe me, very welcome.'

'You persist in error, sir,' said Denis. 'There can be no question between you and me. I am a stranger in this countryside. My name is Denis, damoiseau de Beaulieu. If you see me in your house, it is only——'

'My young friend,' interrupted the other, 'you will permit me to have my own ideas on that subject. They probably differ from yours at the present moment,' he added, with a leer, 'but time will show which of us is in the right.'

Denis was convinced he had to do with a lunatic. He seated himself with a shrug, content to wait the upshot; and a pause ensued, during which he thought he could distinguish a hurried gabbling as of prayer from behind the arras immediately opposite him. Sometimes there seemed to be but one person engaged, sometimes two; and the vehemence of the voice, low as it was, seemed to indicate either great haste or an agony of spirit. It occurred to him that this piece of tapestry covered the entrance to the chapel he had noticed from without.

The old gentleman meanwhile surveyed Denis from head to foot with a smile, and from time to time emitted little noises like a bird or a mouse, which seemed to indicate a high degree of satisfaction. This state of matters became rapidly insupportable; and Denis to put an end to it, remarked politely that the wind had gone down.

The old gentleman fell into a fit of silent laughter, so prolonged and violent that he became quite red in the face. Denis got upon his feet at once, and put on his hat with a flourish.

'Sir', he said, 'if you are in your wits, you have affronted me grossly. If you are out of them, I flatter myself I can find better employment for my brains than to talk with lunatics. My conscience is clear; you have made a fool of me from the first moment; you have refused to hear my explanations; and now there is no power under God will make me stay here any longer; and if I cannot make my way out in a more decent fashion, I will hack your door in pieces with my sword.'

The Sire de Malétroit raised his right hand and wagged it at Denis with the fore and little fingers extended.

'My dear nephew,' he said, 'sit down.'

'Nephew!' retorted Denis, 'you lie in your throat;' and he snapped his fingers in his face.

'Sit down, you rogue!' cried the old gentleman, in a sudden harsh voice, like the barking of a dog. 'Do you fancy,' he went on, 'that when I had made my little contrivance for the door I had stopped short with that? If you prefer to be bound hand and foot till your bones ache, rise and try to go away. If you choose to remain a free young buck, agreeably conversing with an old gentleman—why, sit where you are in peace, and God be with you.'

'Do you mean I am a prisoner?' demanded Denis.

'I state the facts,' replied the other. 'I would rather leave the conclusion to yourself.'

Denis sat down again. Externally he managed to keep pretty calm; but within, he was now boiling with anger, now chilled with apprehension. He no longer felt convinced that he was dealing with a madman. And if the old gentleman was sane, what, in God's name, had he to look for? What absurd or tragical adventure had befallen him? What countenance was he to assume?

While he was thus unpleasantly reflecting, the arras that overhung the chapel door was raised, and a tall priest in his robes came forth and, giving a long, keen stare at Denis, said something in an undertone to Sire de Malétroit.

'She is in a better frame of spirit?' asked the latter.

'She is more resigned, messire,' replied the priest.

'Now the Lord help her, she is hard to please!' sneered the old gentleman. 'A likely stripling—not ill-born—and of her own choosing, too? Why, what more would the jade have?'

'The situation is not usual for a young damsel,' said the other, 'and somewhat trying to her blushes.'

'She should have thought of that before she began the dance. It was none of my choosing. God knows that: but since she is in it, by our Lady, she shall carry it to the end.' And then addressing Denis, 'Monsieur de Beaulieu,' he asked, 'may I present you to my niece? She has been waiting your arrival, I may say, with even greater impatience than myself.'

Denis had resigned himself with a good grace—all he desired

was to know the worst of it as speedily as possible; so he rose at once, and bowed in acquiescence. The Sire de Malétroit followed his example and limped, with the assistance of the chaplain's arm, towards the chapel door. The priest pulled aside the arras, and all three entered. The building had considerable architectural pretensions. A light groining sprang from six stout columns, and hung down in two rich pendants from the centre of the vault. The place terminated behind the altar in a round end, embossed and honeycombed with a superfluity of ornament in relief, and pierced by many little windows shaped like stars, trefoils, or wheels. These windows were imperfectly glazed, so that the night air circulated freely in the chapel. The tapers, of which there must have been half a hundred burning on the altar, were unmercifully blown about; and the light went through many different phases of brilliancy and semi-eclipse. On the steps in front of the altar knelt a young girl richly attired as a bride. A chill settled over Denis as he observed her costume; he fought with desperate energy against the conclusion that was thrust upon his mind; it could not—it should not—be as he feared.

'Blanche,' said the Sire, in his most flute-like tones, 'I have brought a friend to see you, my little girl; turn round and give him your pretty hand. It is good to be devout; but it is necessary to be polite, my niece.'

The girl rose to her feet and turned towards the newcomers. She moved all of a piece; and shame and exhaustion were expressed in every line of her fresh young body; and she held her head down and kept her eyes upon the pavement, as she came slowly forward. In the course of her advance, her eyes fell upon Denis de Beaulieu's feet— feet of which he was justly vain, be it remarked, and wore in the most elegant accoutrement even while travelling. She paused—started, as if his yellow boots had conveyed some shocking meaning—and glanced suddenly up into the wearer's countenance. Their eyes met; shame gave place to horror and terror in her looks; the blood left her lips; with a piercing scream she covered her face with her hands and sank upon the chapel floor.

'That is not the man!' she cried. 'My uncle, that is not the man!'

The Sire de Malétroit chirped agreeably. 'Of course not,' he said; 'I expected as much. It was so unfortunate you could not remember his name.'

'Indeed,' she cried, 'indeed, I have never seen this person till this

With a piercing scream she sank upon the chapel floor.

moment—I have never so much as set eyes upon him—I never wish to see him again. Sir,' she said, turning to Denis, 'if you are a gentleman, you will bear me out. Have I ever seen you—have you ever seen me—before this accursed hour?'

'To speak for myself, I have never had that pleasure,' answered the young man. 'This is the first time, messire, that I have met with your engaging niece.'

The old gentleman shrugged his shoulders.

'I am distressed to hear it,' he said. 'But it is never too late to begin. I had little more acquaintance with my own late lady ere I married her; which proves,' he added with a grimace, 'that these impromptu marriages may often produce an excellent understanding in the long run. As the bridegroom is to have a voice in the matter, I will give him two hours to make up for lost time before we proceed with the ceremony.' And he turned towards the door, followed by the clergyman.

The girl was on her feet in a moment. 'My uncle, you cannot be in earnest,' she said. 'I declare before God I will stab myself rather than be forced on that young man. The heart rises at it; God forbids such marriages; you dishonour your white hair. Oh, my uncle, pity me! There is not a woman in all the world but would prefer death to such a nuptial. Is it possible,' she added, faltering, 'is it possible that you do not believe me—that you still think this'—and she pointed at Denis with a tremor of anger and contempt—'that you still think *this* to be the man?'

'Frankly,' said the old gentleman, pausing on the threshold, 'I do. But let me explain to you once for all, Blanche de Malétroit, my way of thinking about this affair. When you took it into your head to dishonour my family and the name that I have borne, in peace and war, for more than three-score years, you forfeited, not only the right to question my designs, but that of looking me in the face. If your father had been alive, he would have spat on you and turned you out of doors. His was the hand of iron. You may bless your God you have only to deal with the hand of velvet, mademoiselle. It was my duty to get you married without delay. Out of pure goodwill, I have tried to find your own gallant for you. And I believe I have succeeded. But before God and all the holy angels, Blanche de Malétroit, if I have not,

I care not one jackstraw. So let me recommend you to be polite to our young friend; for upon my word, your next groom may be less appetising.'

And with that he went out, with the chaplain at his heels; and the arras fell behind the pair.

The girl turned upon Denis with flashing eyes.

'And what, sir,' she demanded, 'may be the meaning of all this?'

'God knows,' returned Denis gloomily. 'I am a prisoner in this house, which seems full of mad people. More I know not; and nothing do I understand.'

'And pray how came you here? she asked.

He told her as briefly as he could. 'For the rest,' he added, 'perhaps you will follow my example, and tell me the answer to all these riddles, and what, in God's name, is like to be the end of it.'

She stood silent for a little, and he could see her lips tremble and her tearless eyes burn with a feverish lustre. Then she pressed her forehead in both hands.

'Alas, how my head aches!' she said wearily—'to say nothing of my poor heart! But it is due to you to know my story, unmaidenly as it must seem. I am called Blanche de Malétroit; I have been without father or mother for—oh! for as long as I can recollect, and indeed I have been most unhappy all my life. Three months ago a young captain began to stand near me every day in church. I could see that I pleased him; I am much to blame, but I was so glad that any one should love me; and when he passed me a letter, I took it home with me and read it with great pleasure. Since that time he has written many. He was so anxious to speak with me, poor fellow! and kept asking me to leave the door open some evening that we might have two words upon the stair. For he knew how much my uncle trusted me.' She gave something like a sob at that, and it was a moment before she could go on. 'My uncle is a hard man, but he is very shrewd,' she said at last. 'He has performed many feats in war, and was a great person at court, and much trusted by Queen Isabeau in old days. How he came to suspect me I cannot tell; but it is hard to keep anything from his knowledge; and this morning, as we came from mass, he took my hand in his, forced it open, and read my little billet, walking by my side all the while. When he had finished, he gave it back to me with great politeness. It contained another request to have the door left open; and this has been the ruin of us all. My uncle kept me strictly in my room until evening, and then ordered me to dress myself as you see me—a hard mockery for a young girl, do you not think so? I suppose, when he could not prevail with me to tell him the young captain's name, he must have laid a trap for him; into which, alas! you have fallen in the anger of God. I looked for much confusion; for how could I tell whether he was willing to take me for his wife on these sharp terms? He might have been trifling with me from the first; or I might have made myself too cheap in his eyes. But truly I had not looked for such a shameful punishment as this! I could not think that God would let a girl be so disgraced before a young man. And now I have told you all; and I can scarcely hope that you will not despise me.'

Denis made her a respectful inclination.

'Madam,' he said, 'you have honoured me by your confidence. It remains for me to prove that I am not unworthy of the honour. Is Messire de Malétroit at hand?'

'I believe he is writing in the salle without,' she answered.

'May I lead you thither, madam?' asked Denis, offering his hand with his most courtly bearing.

She accepted it; and the pair passed out of the chapel, Blanche in a very drooping and shamefast condition, but Denis strutting and ruffling in the consciousness of a mission, and the boyish certainty of accomplishing it with honour.

The Sire de Malétroit rose to meet them with an ironical obeisance.

'Sir,' said Denis, with the grandest possible air, 'I believe I am to have some say in the matter of this marriage; and let me tell you at once, I will be no party to forcing the inclination of this young lady. Had it been freely offered to me, I should have been proud to accept her hand, for I perceive she is as good as she is beautiful; but as things are, I have now the honour, messire, of refusing.'

Blanche looked at him with gratitude in her eyes; but the old gentleman only smiled and smiled, until his smile grew positively sickening to Denis.

'I am afraid,' he said, 'Monsieur de Beaulieu, that you do not perfectly understand the choice I have to offer you. Follow me, I beseech you, to this window.' And he led the way to one of the large windows which stood open on the night. 'You observe,' he went on, 'there is an iron ring in the upper masonry, and reeved through that, a very efficacious rope. Now, mark my words; if you should find your disinclination to my niece's person insurmountable, I shall have you hanged out of this window before sunrise. I shall only proceed to such an extremity with the greatest regret, you may believe me. For it is not at all your death that I desire, but my niece's establishment in life. At the same time, it must come to that if you prove obstinate. Your family, Monsieur de Beaulieu, is very well in its way; but if you sprang from Charlemagne, you should not refuse the hand of a Malétroit with impunity—not if she had been as common as the Paris road—not if she were as hideous as the gargoyle over my door. Neither my niece nor you, nor my own private feelings, move me at all in this matter. The honour of my house has been compromised; I believe you to be the guilty person; at least you are now in the secret; and you can hardly wonder if I request you to wipe out the stain. If you will not, your blood be on your own head! It will be no great satisfaction to me to have your interesting relics kicking their heels in the breeze below my windows; but half a loaf is better than no bread, and if I cannot cure the dishonour, I shall at least stop the scandal.'

There was a pause.

'I believe there are other ways of settling such imbroglios among gentlemen,' said Denis. 'You wear a sword, and I hear you have used it with distinction.'

The Sire de Malétroit made a signal to the chaplain, who crossed the room with long silent strides and raised the arras over the third of the three doors. It was only a moment before he let it fall again; but Denis had time to see a dusky passage full of armed men.

'When I was a little younger, I should have been delighted to honour you, Monsieur de Beaulieu,' said Sire Alain; 'but I am now too old. Faithful retainers are the sinews of age, and I must employ the strength I have. This is one of the hardest things to swallow as a man grows up in years; but with a little patience, even this becomes habitual. You and the lady seem to prefer the salle for what remains of your two hours; and as I have no desire to cross your preference, I shall resign it to your use with all the pleasure in the world. No haste!' he added, holding up his hand, as he saw a dangerous look come into Denis de Beaulieu's face. 'If your mind revolts against hanging, it will be time enough two hours hence to throw yourself out of the window or upon the pikes of my retainers. Two hours of life are always two hours. A great many things may turn up in even as little a while as that. And, besides, if I understand her appearance, my niece has still something to say to you. You will not disfigure your last hours by a want of politeness to a lady?'

Denis looked at Blanche, and she made him an imploring gesture.

It is likely that the old gentleman was hugely pleased at this symptom of an understanding; for he smiled on both, and added sweetly: 'If you will give me your word of honour, Monsieur de Beaulieu, to await my return at the end of the two hours before attempting anything desperate, I shall withdraw my retainers, and let you speak in greater privacy with mademoiselle.'

Denis again glanced at the girl, who seemed to beseech him to agree.

'I give you my word of honour,' he said.

Messire de Malétroit bowed, and proceeded to limp about the apartment, clearing his throat the while with that odd musical chirp which had already grown so irritating in the ears of Denis de Beaulieu. He first possessed himself of some papers which lay upon the table; then he went to the mouth of the passage and appeared to give an order to the men behind the arras; and lastly he hobbled out through the door by which Denis had come in, turning upon the threshold to address a last smiling bow to the young couple, and followed by the chaplain with a hand-lamp.

No sooner were they alone than Blanche advanced towards Denis with her hands extended. Her face was flushed and excited, and her eyes shone with tears.

'You shall not die!' she cried, 'you shall marry me after all.'

'You seem to think, madam,' replied Denis, 'that I stand much in fear of death.'

'Oh, no, no,' she said, 'I seee you are no poltroon. It is for my own sake—I could not bear to have you slain for such a scruple.'

'I am afraid,' returned Denis, 'that you underrate the difficulty, madam. What you may be too generous to refuse, I may be too proud to accept. In a moment of noble feeling towards me, you forgot what you perhaps owe to others.'

He had the decency to keep his eyes upon the floor as he said this, and after he had finished, so as not to spy upon her confusion. She stood silent for a moment, then walked suddenly away, and falling on her uncle's chair, fairly burst out sobbing. Denis was in the acme of embarrassment. He looked round, as if to seek for inspiration, and seeing a stool, plumped down upon it for something to do. There he sat, playing with the guard of his rapier, and wishing himself dead a thousand times over, and buried in the nastiest kitchen-heap in France. His eyes wandered round the apartment, but found nothing to arrest them. There were such wide spaces between the furniture, the light fell so badly and cheerlessly over all, the dark outside air looked in so coldly through the windows, that he thought he had never seen a church so vast, nor a tomb so melancholy. The regular sobs of Blanche de Malétroit measured out the time like the ticking of a clock. He read the device upon the shield over and over again, until his eyes became obscured; he stared into shadowy corners until he imagined they were swarming with horrible animals; and every now and again he awoke with a start, to remember that his last two hours were running, and death was on the march.

Oftener and oftener, as the time went on, did his glance settle on the girl herself. Her face was bowed forward and covered with her hands, and she was shaken at intervals by the convulsive hiccup of grief. Even thus she was not an unpleasant object to dwell upon, so plump and yet so fine, with a warm brown skin, and the most beautiful hair, Denis thought, in the whole world of womankind. Her hands were like her uncle's; but they were more in place at the end of her young arms, and looked infinitely soft and caressing. He remembered how her blue eyes had shone upon him, full of anger, pity, and innocence. And the more he dwelt on her perfections, the uglier death looked, and the more deeply was he smitten with penitence at her continued tears. Now he felt that no man could have the courage to leave a world which contained so beautiful a creature; and now he would have given forty minutes of his last hour to have unsaid his cruel speech.

Suddenly a hoarse and ragged peal of cockcrow rose to their ears from the dark valley below the windows. And this chattering noise in the silence of all around was like a light in a dark place, and shook them both out of their reflections.

'Alas, can I do nothing to help you?' she said, looking up.

'Madam,' replied Denis, with a fine irrelevancy, 'if I have said anything to wound you, believe me, it was for your own sake and not for mine.'

She thanked him with a tearful look.

'I feel your position cruelly,' he went on. 'The world has been bitter hard on you. Your uncle is a disgrace to mankind. Believe me, madam, there is no young gentleman in all France but would be glad of my opportunity to die in doing you a momentary service.'

'I know already that you can be very brave and generous,' she answered. 'What I *want* to know is whether I can serve you—now or afterwards,' she added, with a quaver.

'Most certainly,' he answered, with a smile. 'Let me sit beside you as if I were a friend, instead of a foolish intruder; try to forget how awkwardly we are placed to one another; make my last moments go pleasantly; and you will do me the chief service possible.'

'You are very gallant,' she added, with a yet deeper sadness . . . 'very gallant . . . and it somehow pains me. But draw nearer, if you please; and if you find anything to say to me, you will at least make certain of a very friendly listener. Ah! Monsieur de Beaulieu,' she broke forth—'ah! Monsieur de Beaulieu, how can I look you in the face?' And she fell to weeping again with a renewed effusion.

'Madam,' said Denis, taking her hand in both of his, 'reflect on the little time I have before me, and the great bitterness into which I am cast by the sight of your distress. Spare me, in my last moments, the spectacle of what I cannot cure even with the sacrifice of my life.'

'I am very selfish,' answered Blanche. 'I will be braver, Monsieur de Beaulieu, for your sake. But think if I can do you no kindness in the future—if you have no friends to whom I could carry your adieux. Charge me as heavily as you can; every burden will lighten, by so little, the invaluable gratitude I owe you. Put it in my power to do something more for you than weep.'

'My mother is married again, and has a young family to care for. My brother Guichard will inherit my fiefs; and if I am not in error, that will content him amply for my death. Life is a little vapour that passeth away, as we are told by those in holy orders. When a man is in a fair way and sees all life open in front of him, he seems to himself to make a very important figure in the world. His horse whinnies to him; the trumpets blow and the girls look out of window as he rides into town before his company; he receives many assurances of trust and regard—sometimes by express in a letter—sometimes face to face, with persons of great consequence falling on his neck. It is not wonderful if his head is turned for a time. But once he is dead, were he as brave as Hercules or as wise as Solomon, he is soon forgotten. It is not ten years since my father fell, with many other knights around him, in a very fierce encounter, and I do not think that any one of them, nor so much as the name of the fight, is now remembered. No, no, madam, the nearer you come to it, you see that death is a dark and dusty corner, where a man gets into his tomb and has the door shut after him till the Judgment Day. I have few friends just now, and once I am dead I shall have none.'

'Ah, Monsieur de Beaulieu!' she exclaimed, 'you forget Blanche de Malétroit.'

'You have a sweet nature, madam, and you are pleased to estimate a little service far beyond its worth.'

'It is not that,' she answered. 'You mistake me if you think I am so easily touched by my own concerns. I say so, because you are the noblest man I have ever met; because I recognise in you a spirit that would have made even a common person famous in the land.'

'And yet here I die in a mouse-trap—with no more noise about it than my own squeaking,' answered he.

A look of pain crossed her face, and she was silent for a little while. Then a light came into her eyes, and with a smile she spoke again.

'I cannot have my champion think meanly of himself. Any one who gives his life for another will be met in Paradise by all the heralds and angels of the Lord God. And you have no such cause to hang your head. For . . . pray, do you think me beautiful?' she asked, with a deep flush.

'Indeed, madam, I do,' he said.

'I am glad of that,' she answered heartily. 'Do you think there are many men in France who have been asked in marriage by a beautiful maiden—with her own lips—and who have refused her to her face? I know you men would half despise such a triumph; but, believe me, we women know more of what is precious in love. There is nothing that should set a person higher in his own esteem; and we women would prize nothing more dearly.'

'You are very good,' he said; 'but you cannot make me forget that I was asked in pity and not for love.'

'I am not so sure of that,' she replied, holding down her head. 'Hear me to an end, Monsieur de Beaulieu. I know how you must despise me; I feel you are right to do so; I am too poor a creature to occupy one thought of your mind, although, alas! you must die for me this morning. But when I asked you to marry me, indeed, and indeed, it was because I respected and admired you, and loved you with my whole soul, from the very moment that you took my part against my uncle. If you had seen yourself, and how noble you looked, you would pity rather than despise me. And now,' she went on, hurriedly checking him with her hand, 'although I have laid aside all reserve and told you so much, remember that I know your sentiments towards me already. I would not, believe me, being nobly born, weary you with importunities into consent. I too have a pride of my own: and I declare before the holy mother of God, if you should now go back from your word already given, I would no more marry you than I would marry my uncle's groom.'

Denis smiled a little bitterly.

'It is a small love,' he said, 'that shies at a little pride.'

She made no answer, although she probably had her own thoughts.

'Come hither to the window,' he said, with a sigh. 'Here is the dawn.'

And indeed the dawn was already beginning. The hollow of the sky was full of essential daylight, colourless and clean; and the valley underneath was flooded with a grey reflection. A few thin vapours clung in the coves of the forest or lay along the winding course of the river. The scene disengaged a surprising effect of stillness, which was hardly interrupted when the cocks began once more to crow among the steadings. Perhaps the same fellow who had made so horrid a clangour in the darkness not half an hour before, now sent up the merriest cheer to greet the coming day. A little wind went bustling and eddying among the tree-tops underneath the windows. And still the daylight kept flooding insensibly out of the cast, which was soon to grow incandescent and cast up that red-hot cannon-ball, the rising sun.

Denis looked out over all this with a bit of a shiver. He had taken her hand, and retained it in his almost unconsciously.

'Has the day begun already?' she said; and then, illogically enough: 'the night has been so long! Alas! what shall we say to my uncle when he returns?'

'What you will,' said Denis, and he pressed her fingers in his.

She was silent.

'Blanche,' he said, with a swift, uncertain, passionate utterance, 'you have seen whether I fear death. You must know well enough that I would as gladly leap out of that window into the empty air as lay a finger on you without your free and full consent. But if you care for me at all do not let me lose my life in a misapprehension; for I love you better than the whole world; and though I will die for you blithely, it would be like all the joys of Paradise to live on and spend my life in your service.'

As he stopped speaking, a bell began to ring loudly in the interior of the house; and a clatter of armour in the corridor showed that the retainers were returning to their post, and the two hours were at an end.

'After all that you have heard?' she whispered, leaning towards him with her lips and eyes.

'I have heard nothing,' he replied.

'The captain's name was Florimond de Champdivers,' she said in his ear.

'I did not hear it,' he answered, taking her supple body in his arms and covering her wet face with kisses.

A melodious chirping was audible behind, followed by a beautiful chuckle, and the voice of Messire de Malétroit wished his new nephew a good morning.

DEATH'S HEAD

Gordon Roddick

As Tommy and Les—used to the bush their entire lives—usually snored all night without interruption, the Englishman picked up his blanket, skirted the tangled heap of dogs that lay in front of the fire, and chose himself a patch of ground beneath a big white gum tree. With his already battered hat, he smacked the dust off his jeans and shirt, took off his spurs, scooped out a small hollow in the hard red earth to accommodate his hip bones, wrapped his blanket loosely round him and flopped down on to the ground.

This was the moment of the day that he really savoured. All days were hard and today had been no exception. After eleven or twelve hours in the saddle he was pleased to get off his horse, fill his belly and roll up in his blanket. It had been three weeks since he had slept in a bed; now they were only twenty miles from their destination and this promised to be his last night under the stars. With the bonus they would get tomorrow for bringing the cattle in on schedule, and the money he had already saved, he could afford to leave Queensland and divert himself in Sydney for a while. After which he was due to return to England to take over the management of his father's farm. As these thoughts ran through his mind he smiled, in the fading light, with the confidence of a man, who, even at the age of twenty-three, knows what he is doing.

He rolled over on to his back and watched the flickering spasms of the dying fire. He drank in the still night, its peace more underlined than disturbed by the harmonic snoring of dogs and men. He was thinking idly about a hot bath and clean clothes when suddenly he saw it, silhouetted darkly somewhere between him and the fire: a thin swaying band of death, a snake.

He should have moved, rolled away, but he was paralysed by its hypnotic menace. In the half-light he could not estimate clearly the distance between them, but he was sure it could not be more than three feet. He watched, with mingled fascination and terror, the liquid, almost gentle rhythm as the creature swung in its ghastly dance, forked tongue flickering in unison with the flames. It dropped its head and he could no longer see it. He thought it had glided off, but his sigh of relief was cut to a strangled gasp as he felt it slipping over his feet and, worse still, moving firmly but leisurely towards his head, with a strong ripple of muscle. His whole body, caught in fear and revulsion, froze as the snake moved relentlessly upward, and he could hardly contain the hysterical scream that rose in his throat as the forked tongue tickled feather-like over his face.

The snake turned, coil after coil, and slithered under his blanket; when he opened his eyes it was to see the tail give a final derisive flick as it vanished under cover. Now he could feel it surging over the lower half of his body, and he prayed meaninglessly, frantically, 'God, no, no! God, oh God!' Then abruptly all movement ceased and he was aware that it had settled down in the hollow between his knees.

At first, the shock stupefied him. It was as if he had been hurled from a comfortable dream into an awakening so terrible that both his mind and his body utterly rejected it. In the crazy half-world of whirling, incoherent thought that followed, he almost managed to persuade himself that it *was* some kind of nightmare—until his returning wits, and the cold touch of the scaly body against his knees, forced him to accept the horrifying reality. Then, like a man coming round from an anaesthetic, he tried desperately to pull himself together, to adjust to the reality, to cut it down to size. To think.

He tried to hazard a guess at how long he had been lying there: was

His whole body froze as the snake moved relentlessly upward.

it minutes or hours? He decided at last that it was probably about half an hour. They had turned in at eleven o'clock, and now it must be at least half-past eleven. That meant another seven hours before sun-up. Could he keep still that long?

Already he was growing conscious of his body. Small aches were becoming manifest in several isolated regions, in his buttocks and thighs, in his midriff, and on the points of his shoulder-blades. The only parts of his body that he could move with any degree of safety were his head and his neck. How long would it be, he wondered, before these small aches grew into a massive pain too intense to be endured? How long before his limbs grew numb—before he cried out in pain and terror? And what would happen if he had an attack of cramp? Could he control the spasms?

He began to be conscious of every undulation in the ground beneath him. Each hollow was an abyss threatening to swallow him up, each hump a mountain boring into his back, and, to add to his discomfort, he had started to sweat. He thought vaguely of his mother. *Only horses sweat, dear; gentlemen perspire.* He started to cry silently in an orgy of

545

self-pity until the sobs almost shook his body. Then he remembered that, if he moved so much as a muscle, he would almost certainly die; so his weeping ceased abruptly.

The snake moved briefly, convulsively. He thought for a moment that it might emerge and leave him, but no, it settled again, nestling more firmly against the heat of his body. How could he escape? He considered and dismissed the idea of a sudden violent leap; the creature would almost certainly nail him before they parted company. Then how? He turned his head to look at Tommy and Les snoring peacefully twenty yards away. He did not dare shout out to them. The noise might rouse the snake, or it might be disturbed by the vibrations of his voice. He tried a loud whisper but fear had dried the saliva in his mouth and the only sound he could make was a frustrated croak. His vocal chords simply refused to function.

He kept on trying until he was exhausted, then just lay there. Poised in a hinterland between death and life, he thought of his home and his childhood, but irrationally and incoherently. For a time he relapsed into a near coma, then crept back to a painful reality in which he alternated between passive resignation and almost suicidal despair. He even contemplated ending his ordeal by moving, but directly the thought took shape he realized how much he wanted to live . . .

He began to search the sky for any hint of a let up in darkness, any faint sign that dawn would in the end stab its way over the horizon. He kept his ears alert to every variation of tone in the snoring of Tommy and Les, reminding himself that one or other of them must eventually wake up. But night seemed never-ending and by now he had lost all count of time. His body became an angry fire of blood unable to flow, of knotted muscles unable to relax. He had not known he could stand so much unrelenting pain. His legs had become so numb that he prayed he might not move them involuntarily.

Then one of the dogs moved, whimpering in its sleep. He wondered if it was his dog, and a new wave of terror swept over him. Suppose his blue cattle bitch woke up before Tommy or Les? Then, as she did every morning, she would come charging across to leap all over him and wash away his morning torpor. If that happened, he would indeed be finished. Why had he not listened to Les when he had warned him not to treat her like a 'bloody English lapdog'? The night breeze danced over his face and mocked silently at his impotence.

The hours dragged interminably on, with death's messenger lying in comfortable repose between his knees. Whyever had this happened to him? Why not to one of the others? Was it an act of God, or was it a natural biological occurrence? When would the snake leave? It might just have killed, then sought a warm place to digest its victim. So it would probably emerge when the sun rose, to bask in its heat. The night seemed longer than the whole of his life, and he relived every detail of it as, moment by moment, the hours crawled by.

At last all hope seeped out of him and he lay like a discarded doll, his unseeing eyes staring blankly into the limbs of the tree above him. Then slowly, unbelievably, he realized that he could see the branches and leaves a little more clearly. He turned his head and his eyes greedily drank in the line of the horizon: yes, it was true, the first slow beginnings of dawn were there. With the dawn came fresh hope that buoyed up inside him and threatened to burst out in a whoop of joy. Then he remembered his dog and looked anxiously over to where she lay curled up among the others. She showed no signs of stirring.

The night fled slowly, reluctantly, in the face of the day, but, with its receding, he turned his mind back to living. He started to moisten his lips and tongue with what little saliva he had left, and turned his head once more towards the two sleeping men. He whispered to them as loudly as he dared, hoarsely, desperately praying that one of them should waken, but neither moved. Every second brought more light flooding through the bush, and he gave up trying to call the others for fear of rousing the dogs.

The sun rolled just clear of the horizon, and as the morning light washed away the shadows before his eyes the whole landscape lay revealed in stark clarity. Then, suddenly, he was sure he felt the snake move again. Was it just another false alarm? But no, the movement was more definite this time. His terror reached a climax as he felt it uncoil and, with a long liquid thrust, weave its way once more towards his head. He closed his eyes so tight that it hurt them as the snake's endless length brushed past his cheek; then with a whip it was gone.

He rolled over, gave a strangled croak which woke the others. The undammed blood in his body ran riot, and the pain cut off sharply his incoherent babble of words. But, just before unconsciousness enshrouded him, he heard Les guffaw in the distance. 'Bloomin' pommy's gone raving mad or had a nightmare. Shouting something about snakes, wasn't he? Can't stand up to the sun—that's what's the matter with him.'

THE OLD STAGE-COACH

Washington Irvine

Washington Irving, a famous American writer and historian, once spent a Christmas in England, and his account of a ride in an old stage-coach is a reminder of how important horses were to the travellers in the nineteenth century. Travelling by stage-coach was often a test of endurance: the pace was slow—little more than ten miles an hour—and poor roads often made the journey a very uncomfortable one. Sometimes, on hills or over rough ground, coachman and passengers would have to plod alongside the struggling horses. But, for the most part, horses were well cared for and rested at scheduled stops.

In the course of a December tour in Yorkshire, I rode for a long distance in one of the public coaches, on the day preceding Christmas. The coach was crowded, both inside and out, with passengers who, by their talk, seemed to be principally bound to the mansions of relations or friends, to eat the Christmas dinner. It was loaded also with hampers of game, and baskets and boxes of delicacies; and hares hung dangling their long ears about the coachman's box, presents from distant friends for the impending feast.

I had three fine rosy-cheeked schoolboys for my fellow-passengers inside, full of the buxom health and manly spirit which I have observed in the children of this country. They were returning home for the holidays in high glee, and promising themselves a world of enjoyment. It was delightful to hear the gigantic plans of the little rogues, and the impracticable feats they were to perform during their six weeks' emancipation from the abhorred captivity of book, birch and pedagogue.

They were full of anticipations of the meeting with the family and household, down to the very cat and dog; and of the joy they were to give their little sisters by the presents with which their pockets were crammed. But the meeting to which they seemed to look forward with the greatest impatience was with Bantam, which I found to be a pony, and according to their talk, possessed of more virtues than any steed since the days of Bucephalus. How he could trot! How he could run! And then such leaps as he would take—there was not a hedge in the whole country that he could not clear.

They were under the particular guardianship of the coachman, to whom, whenever an opportunity presented, they addressed a host of questions, and pronounced him one of the best fellows in the world.

Indeed, I could not but notice the more than ordinary air of bustle and importance of the coachman, who wore his hat a little on one side, and had a large bunch of Christmas greens stuck in the buttonhole of his coat. He is always a personage full of mighty care and business, but he is particularly so during this season, having so many commissions to execute in consequence of the great interchange of presents.

And here, perhaps, it may not be unacceptable to my untravelled readers to have a sketch that may serve as a general representation of this very numerous and important class of functionaries, who have a dress, a manner, a language, an air, peculiar to themselves, and prevalent throughout the fraternity; so that, wherever an English stage-coachman may be seen, he cannot be mistaken for one of any other craft or mystery.

He has commonly a broad, full face, curiously mottled with red, as if the blood had been forced by hard feeding into every vessel of the skin. He is swelled into jolly dimensions by frequent consumptions of malt liquors, and his bulk is still further increased by a multiplicity of coats, in which he is buried like a cauliflower, the upper one reaching to his heels. He wears a broad-brimmed, low-crowned hat; a huge roll of coloured handkerchief about his neck, knowingly knotted and tucked in at the bosom; and has in summertime a large bouquet of flowers in his buttonhole—the present, most probably, of some enamoured country lass.

His waistcoat is commonly of some bright colour, striped, and his smallclothes extend far below the knees, to meet a pair of jockey-boots which reach about halfway up his legs. All this costume is maintained with much precision; he has a pride in having his clothes of excellent

Here the coachman is surrounded by those nameless hangers-on that infest inns.

materials. And, notwithstanding the seeming grossness of his appearance, there is still discernible that neatness and propriety of person which is almost inherent in an Englishman.

He enjoys great consequence and consideration along the road; he has frequent conferences with the village housewives, who look upon him as a man of great trust and dependence, and he seems to have a good understanding with every bright-eyed country lass. The moment he arrives where the horses are to be changed, he throws down the reins with something of an air and abandons the cattle to the care of the ostler; his duty being merely to drive from one stage to another.

When off the box his hands are thrust into the pockets of his great coat, and he rolls about the inn yard with an air of the most absolute lordliness. Here he is generally surrounded by an admiring throng of ostlers, stableboys, shoe-blacks and those nameless hangers-on that infest inns and taverns, and run errands, and do all kinds of odd jobs, for the privilege of battening on the drippings of the kitchen and the leakage of the tap-room. These all look up to him as to an oracle; treasure up his cant phrases; echo his opinions about horses and other topics of jockey lore; and above all, endeavour to imitate his air and carriage. Every ragamuffin that has a coat to his back thrusts his hands in the pockets, rolls in his gait, talks slang, and is an embryo 'coachey'.

Perhaps it might be owing to the pleasing serenity that reigned in my own mind, that I fancied I saw cheerfulness in every countenance throughout the journey. A stage-coach, however, carries animation always with it, and puts the world in motion as it whirls along. The horn, sounded at the entrance of a village, produces a general bustle. Some hasten forth to meet friends, some with bundles and bandboxes to secure places, and in the hurry of the moment can hardly take leave of the group that accompanies them.

In the meantime the coachman has a world of small commissions to execute. Sometimes he delivers a hare or pheasant; sometimes he jerks a small parcel or newspaper to the door of a public-house. And sometimes, with knowing leer and words of sly import, he hands to some half-blushing, half-laughing housemaid, an odd-shaped *billet-doux* from some rustic admirer.

As the coach rattles through the village, everyone runs to the window, and you have glances on every side of fresh country faces and blooming, giggling girls. At the corners are assembled groups of village idlers and wise men, who take their stations there for the important purpose of seeing company pass.

But the sagest knot is generally at the blacksmith's, to whom the passing of the coach is an event fruitful of much speculation. The smith, with the horse's heel in his lap, pauses as the vehicle whirls by; the cyclops round the anvil suspend their ringing hammers, and suffer the iron to grow cool. And the sooty spectre in brown paper cap, labouring at the bellows, leans on the handle for a moment, and permits the asthmatic engine to heave a long-drawn sigh while he glares through the murky smoke and sulphureous gleams of the smithy.

Perhaps the impending holiday might have given a more than usual animation to the country, for it seemed to me as if everybody was in good looks and good spirits. Game, poultry and other luxuries of the table were in brisk circulation in the villages; the grocers', butchers', and fruiterers' shops were thronged with customers. The housewives were stirring briskly about, putting their dwellings in order; and the glossy branches of holly, with their bright red berries, began to appear at the leaded windows.

The scene brought to mind an old writer's account of Christmas preparations:

'Now capons and hens, besides turkeys, geese, and ducks, with beef and mutton—must all die—for in twelve days a multitude of people will not be fed with a little. Now plums and spice, sugar and honey, square it among pies and broth. Now or never must music be in tube, for the youth must dance and sing to get them a heat, while the aged sit by the fire. The country maid leaves half her market, and must be sent again, if she forgets a pack of cards on Christmas Eve. Great is the contention of holly and ivy, whether master or dame wears the breeches. Dice and cards benefit the butler; and if the cook do not lack wit, he will sweetly lick his fingers.'

I was roused from this fit of luxurious meditation by a shout from my little travelling companions. They had been looking out of the coach windows for the last few miles, recognizing every tree and cottage as they approached home, and now there was a general burst of joy—'There's John! and there's old Carlo! and there's Bantam!' cried the happy little rogues, clapping their hands.

At the end of the lane there was an old sober-looking servant in livery, waiting for them. He was accompanied by a superannuated pointer, and by the redoubtable Bantam, a little old rat of a pony, with a shaggy mane and long rusty tail, who stood dozing quietly by the roadside, little dreaming of the bustling times that awaited him.

I was pleased to see the fondness with which the little fellows leaped about the steady old footman, and hugged the pointer, who wriggled his whole body for joy. But Bantam was the great object of interest! All wanted to mount at once, and it was with some difficulty that John arranged that they should ride by turns, and the eldest should ride first.

Off they set at last, one on the pony, with the dog bounding and barking before him, and the others holding John's hands; both talking at once, and over-powering him with questions about home, and with school anecdotes. I looked after them with a feeling in which I do not know whether pleasure or melancholy predominated. For I was reminded of those days when, like them, I had known neither care nor sorrow, and a holiday was the summit of earthly joy.

We stopped a few moments afterwards to water the horses, and on resuming our route, a turn of the road brought us in sight of a neat country seat. I could just distinguish the forms of a lady and two young girls in the portico, and I saw my little comrades, with Bantam, Carlo, and old John, trooping along the carriage road. I leaned out of the coach window in the hopes of witnessing the happy meeting, but a grove of trees shut it from my sight.

In the evening we reached a village where I had determined to pass the night. As we drove into the great gateway of the inn, I saw on one side the light of a rousing kitchen fire beaming through a window.

I entered, and admired for the hundredth time, that picture of convenience, neatness, and broad, honest enjoyment, the kitchen of an English inn. It was of spacious dimensions, hung round with copper and tin vessels highly polished, and decorated here and there with a Christmas green. Hams, tongues, and flitches of bacon were suspended from the ceiling; a smoke-jack made its ceaseless clanking beside the fireplace, and a clock ticked in one corner. A well-scoured deal table extended along one side of the kitchen, with a cold round of beef and other hearty provisions upon it, over which two foaming tankards of ale seemed to be mounting guard.

Travellers of inferior order were preparing to attack this stout repast, while others sat smoking and gossiping over their ale on two high-backed oaken settles beside the fire. Trim housemaids were hurrying backwards and forwards under the directions of a fresh bustling landlady, but still seizing an occasional moment to exchange a flippant word, and have a rallying laugh with the group round the fire . . .

I had not been long at the inn when a post-chaise drove up to the door. A young gentleman stepped out, and by the light of the lamps, I caught a glimpse of a countenance which I thought I knew. I moved forward to get a nearer view, when his eye caught mine. I was not mistaken: it was Frank Bracebridge, a sprightly good-humoured young fellow with whom I had once travelled on the continent.

Our meeting was extremely cordial, for the countenance of an old fellow-traveller always brings up the recollection of a thousand pleasant scenes, odd adventures and excellent jokes. To discuss all these in a transient interview at an inn was impossible, and finding that I was not pressed for time, and was merely making a tour of observation, he insisted that I should give him a day or two at his father's country seat, to which he was going to pass the holidays, and which lay at a few miles' distance.

'It is better than eating a solitary Christmas dinner at an inn,' said he, 'and I can assure you of a hearty welcome in something of the old-fashioned style.'

His reasoning was cogent, and I must confess the preparation I had seen for universal festivity and social enjoyment had made me feel a little impatient of my loneliness. I closed, therefore, at once, with his invitation. The chaise drove up to the door, and in a few moments I was on my way to the family mansion of the Bracebridges.

ROMEO AND JULIET

Charles Lamb

The two chief families in Verona were the rich Capulets and the Montagues. There had been an old quarrel between these families, which was grown to such a height, and so deadly was the enmity between them, that it extended to the remotest kindred, to the followers and retainers of both sides, insomuch that a servant of the house of Montague could not meet a servant of the house of Capulet, nor a Capulet encounter with a Montague by chance, but fierce words and sometimes bloodshed ensued; and frequent were the brawls from such accidental meetings, which disturbed the happy quiet of Verona's streets.

Old Lord Capulet made a great supper, to which many fair ladies and many noble guests were invited. All the admired beauties of Verona were present, and all comers were made welcome if they were not of the house of Montague. At this feast of Capulets, Rosaline, beloved of Romeo, son to the old Lord Montague, was present; and though it was dangerous for a Montague to be seen in this assembly, yet Benvolio, a friend of Romeo, persuaded the young lord to go to this assembly in the disguise of a mask, that he might see his Rosaline, and seeing her, compare her with some choice beauties of Verona, who (he said) would make him think his swan a crow. Romeo had small faith in Benvolio's words; nevertheless, for the love of Rosaline, he was persuaded to go. For Romeo was a sincere and passionate lover, and one that lost his sleep for love, and fled society to be alone, thinking on Rosaline, who disdained him, and never requited his love, with the least show of courtesy or affection; and Benvolio wished to cure his friend of this love by showing him diversity of ladies and company. To this feast of Capulets then young Romeo with Benvolio and their friend Mercutio went masked. Old Capulet bid them welcome, and told them that ladies who had their toes unplagued with corns would dance with them. And the old man was light hearted and merry, and said that he had worn a mask when he was young, and could have told a whispering tale in a fair lady's ear. And they fell to dancing, and Romeo was suddenly struck with the exceeding beauty of a lady who danced there, who seemed to him to teach the torches to burn bright, and her beauty to show by night like a rich jewel worn by a blackamoor; beauty too rich for use, too dear for earth! like a snowy dove trooping with crows (he said), so richly did her beauty and perfections shine above the ladies her companions. While he uttered these praises, he was overheard by Tybalt, a nephew of Lord Capulet, who knew him by his voice to be Romeo. And this Tybalt, being of a fiery and passionate temper, could not endure that a Montague should come under cover of a mask, to fleer and scorn at their solemnities. And he stormed and raged exceedingly, and would have struck young Romeo dead. But his uncle, the old Lord Capulet, would not suffer him to do any injury at that time, both out of respect to his guests, and because Romeo had borne himself like a gentleman, and all tongues in Verona bragged of him to be a virtuous and well-governed youth. Tybalt, forced to be patient against his will, restrained himself, but swore that this vile Montague should at another time dearly pay for his intrusion.

The dancing being done, Romeo watched the place where the lady stood; and under favour of his masking habit, which might seem to excuse in part the liberty, he presumed in the gentlest manner to take her by the hand, calling it a shrine, which if he profaned by touching it, he was a blushing pilgrim, and would kiss it for atonement. 'Good pilgrim,' answered the lady, 'your devotion shows by far too mannerly and too courtly: saints have hands, which pilgrims may touch, but kiss not.'—'Have not saints lips, and pilgrims too?' said Romeo. 'Ay,' said the lady, 'lips which they must use in prayer.'—'O then, my dear saint,' said Romeo, 'hear my prayer, and grant it, lest I despair.' In such like allusions and loving conceits they were engaged, when the lady was called away to her mother. And Romeo, inquiring who her mother was, discovered that the lady whose peerless beauty he was so much struck with was young Juliet, daughter and heir to the Lord Capulet, the great enemy of the Montagues; and that he had unknowingly engaged his heart to his foe. This troubled him, but it could not dissuade him from loving. As little rest had Juliet, when she found that the gentleman that she had been talking with was Romeo and a Montague, for she had been suddenly smit with the same hasty and inconsiderate passion for Romeo, which he had conceived for her; and a prodigious birth of love it seemed to her, that she must love her enemy, and that her affections should settle there, where family considerations should induce her chiefly to hate.

It being midnight, Romeo with his companions departed; but they soon missed him, for, unable to stay away from the house where he had left his heart, he leaped the wall of an orchard which was at the back of Juliet's house. Here he had not been long, ruminating on his new love, when Juliet appeared above at a window, through which her exceeding beauty seemed to break like the light of the sun in the east; and the moon, which shone in the orchard with a faint light, appeared to Romeo as if sick and pale with grief at the superior lustre of his new sun. And she, leaning her cheek upon her hand, he passionately wished himself a glove upon that hand, that he might touch her cheek. She all this while thinking herself alone, fetched a deep sigh, and exclaimed, 'Ah me!' Romeo, enraptured to hear her speak, said softly, and unheard by her, 'O speak again, bright angel, for such you appear, being over my head, like a winged messenger from heaven whom mortals fall back to gaze upon.' She, unconscious of being overheard, and full of the new passion which that night's adventure had given birth to, called upon her lover by name (whom she supposed absent): 'O Romeo, Romeo!' said she, 'wherefore art thou Romeo? Deny thy father, and refuse thy name, for my sake; or if thou wilt not, be but my sworn love, and I no longer will be a Capulet.' Romeo, having this encouragement, would fain have spoken, but he was desirous of hearing more; and the lady continued her passionate discourse with herself (as she thought), still chiding Romeo for being Romeo and a Montague, and wishing him some other name, or that he would put away that hated name, and for that name which was no part of himself, he should take all herself. At this loving word Romeo could no longer refrain, but taking up the dialogue as if her words had been addressed to him personally, and not merely in fancy, he bade her call him Love, or by whatever other name she pleased, for he was no longer Romeo, if that name was displeasing to her. Juliet, alarmed to hear a man's voice in the garden, did not at first know who it was, that by favour of the night and darkness had thus stumbled upon the discovery of her secret; but when he spoke again, though her ears had not yet drunk a hundred words of that tongue's uttering, yet so nice is a lover's hearing, that she immediately knew him to be young Romeo, and she expostulated with him on the danger to which he had exposed himself by climbing the orchard walls, for if any of her kinsmen should find him there, it would be death to him, being a Montague. 'Alack,' said Romeo, 'there is more peril in your eye, than in twenty of their swords. Do you but look kind upon me, lady, and I am proof against their enmity. Better my life should be ended by their hate, than that hated life should be prolonged, to live without your love.'—'How came you into this place,' said Juliet, 'and by whose direction?'—'Love directed me,' answered Romeo: 'I am no pilot, yet wert thou as far apart from me, as that vast shore which is washed with the farthest sea, I should venture for such merchandise.' A crimson blush came over Juliet's face, yet unseen by Romeo by reason of the night, when she reflected upon the discovery which she had made, yet not meaning to make it, of her love to Romeo. She would fain have recalled her words, but that was impossible: fain would she have stood upon form, and have kept her lover at a distance, as the custom of discreet ladies is, to frown and be perverse, and give their suitors harsh denials at first; to stand off, and affect a coyness or indifference, where they most love, that their lovers may not think them too lightly or too easily won; for the difficulty of attainment increases the value of the object. But there was no room in her case for denials, or puttings off, or any of the customary arts of delay and protracted courtship. Romeo had heard from her own tongue, when she did not dream that he was near her, a confession of her love. So with an honest frankness, which the novelty of her situation excused, she confirmed the truth of what he had before heard, and addressing him by the name of *fair Montague* (love can sweeten a sour name), she begged him not to impute her easy yielding to levity or an unworthy mind, but that he must lay the fault of it (if it were a fault) upon the accident of the night which had so strangely discovered her thoughts. And she added, that though her behaviour to him might not be sufficiently prudent, measured by the custom of her sex, yet that she would prove more true than many whose prudence was dissembling, and their modesty artificial cunning.

Romeo was beginning to call the heavens to witness, that nothing was farther from his thoughts than to impute a shadow of dishonour to such an honoured lady, when she stopped him, begging him not to swear; for although she joyed in him, yet she had no joy of that night's contract: it was too rash, too unadvised, too sudden. But he being urgent with her to exchange a vow of love with him that night, she said that she had already had given him hers before he requested it; meaning, when he overheard her confession; but she will retract what she then bestowed, for the pleasure of giving it again, for her bounty was as infinite as the sea, and her love as deep. From this loving conference she was called away by her nurse, who slept with her, and thought it time for her to be in bed, for it was near to daybreak; but hastily returning, she said three or four words more to Romeo, the purport of which was, that if his love was indeed honourable, and his purpose marriage, she would send a messenger to him tomorrow, to appoint a time for their marriage, when she would lay all her fortunes at his feet, and follow him as her lord through the world. While they were settling this point, Juliet was repeatedly called for by her nurse, and went in and returned, and went and returned again, for she seemed as jealous of Romeo going from her, as a young girl of her bird, which she will let hop a little from her hand, and pluck it back with a silken thread; and Romeo was as loath to part as she; for the sweetest music to lovers is the sound of each other's tongues at night. But at last they parted, wishing mutually sweet sleep and rest for that night.

The day was breaking when they parted, and Romeo, who was too full of thoughts of his mistress and that blessed meeting to allow him to sleep, instead of going home, bent his course to a monastery hard by, to find Friar Lawrence. The good friar was already up at his devotions, but seeing young Romeo abroad so early, he conjectured rightly that he had not been abed that night, but that some distemper of youthful affection had kept him waking.

He was right in imputing the cause of Romeo's wakefulness to love, but he made a wrong guess at the object, for he thought that his love for Rosaline had kept him waking. But when Romeo revealed his new passion for Juliet, and requested the assistance of the friar to marry them that day, the holy man lifted up his eyes and hands in a sort of wonder at the sudden change in Romeo's affections, for he had been privy to all Romeo's love for Rosaline, and his many complaints of her disdain: and he said, that young men's love lay not truly in their hearts, but in their eyes. But Romeo replying, that he himself had often chidden him for doting on Rosaline, who could not love him again, whereas Juliet both loved and was beloved by him, the friar assented in some measure to his reasons; and thinking that a matrimonial alliance between young Juliet and Romeo might happily be the means of making up the long breach between the Capulets and the Montagues; which no one more lamented than this good friar, who was a friend to both the families and had often interposed his mediation to make up the quarrel without effect; partly moved by policy, and partly by his fondness for young Romeo, to whom he could deny nothing, the old man consented to join their hands in marriage.

Now was Romeo blessed indeed, and Juliet, who knew his intent from a messenger which she had despatched according to promise, did not fail to be early at the cell of Friar Lawrence, where their hands were joined in holy marriage; the good friar praying the heavens to smile upon that act, and in the union of this young Montague and young Capulet to bury the old strife and long dissensions of their families.

The ceremony being over, Juliet hastened home, where she stayed impatient for the coming night, at which time Romeo promised to come and meet her in the orchard, where they had met the night before; and the time between seemed as tedious to her, as the night before some great festival seems to an impatient child, that has got new finery which it may not put on till the morning.

The good friar prayed that heaven smiled upon the union.

That same day, about noon, Romeo's friends, Benvolio and Mercutio, walking through the streets of Verona, were met by a party of the Capulets with the impetuous Tybalt at their head. This was the same angry Tybalt who would have fought with Romeo at old lord Capulet's feast. He, seeing Mercutio, accused him bluntly of associating with Romeo, a Montague. Mercutio, who had as much fire and youthful blood in him as Tybalt, replied to this accusation with some sharpness; and in spite of all Benvolio could say to moderate their wrath, a quarrel was beginning, when Romeo himself passing that way, the fierce Tybalt turned from Mercutio to Romeo, and gave him the disgraceful appellation of villain. Romeo wished to avoid a quarrel with Tybalt above all men, because he was the kinsman of Juliet, and much beloved by her; besides, this young Montague had never thoroughly entered into the family quarrel, being by nature wise and gentle, and the name of a Capulet, which was his dear lady's name, was now rather a charm to allay resentment, than a watchword to excite fury. So he tried to reason with Tybalt, whom he saluted mildly by the name of *good Capulet*, as if he, though a Montague, had some secret pleasure in uttering that name: but Tybalt, who hated all Montagues as he hated hell, would hear no reason, but drew his weapon; and Mercutio, who knew not of Romeo's secret motive for desiring peace with Tybalt, but looked upon his present forbearance as a sort of calm dishonourable submission, with many disdainful words provoked Tybalt to the prosecution of his first quarrel with him; and Tybalt and Mercutio fought, till Mercutio fell, receiving his death's wound while Romeo and Benvolio were vainly endeavouring to part the combatants. Mercutio being dead, Romeo kept his temper no longer, but returned the scornful appellation of villain Tybalt had given him; and they fought till Tybalt was slain by Romeo. This deadly broil falling out in the midst of Verona at noonday, the news of it quickly brought a crowd of citizens to the spot, and among them the old Lords Capulet and Montague, with their wives; and soon after arrived the prince himself, who being related to Mercutio, whom Tybalt had slain, and having had the peace of his government often disturbed by these brawls of Montagues and Capulets, came determined to put the law in strictest force against those who should be found to be offenders. Benvolio, who had been eye-witness to the fray, was commanded by the prince to relate the origin of it; which he did, keeping as near the truth as he could without injury to Romeo, softening and excusing the part which his friends took in it. Lady Capulet, whose extreme grief for the loss of her kinsman Tybalt made her keep no bounds in her revenge, exhorted the prince to do strict justice upon his murderer, and to pay no attention to Benvolio's representation, who, being Romeo's friend and a Montague, spoke partially. Thus she pleaded against her new son-in-law, but she knew not as yet that he was her son-in-law and Juliet's husband. On the other hand was to be seen Lady Montague pleading for her child's life, and arguing with some justice that Romeo had done nothing worthy of punishment in taking the life of Tybalt, which was already forfeited to the law by his having slain Mercutio. The prince, unmoved by the passionate exclamations of these women, on a careful examination of the facts, pronounced his sentence, and by that sentence Romeo was banished from Verona.

Heavy news to young Juliet, who had been but a few hours a bride, and now by this decree seemed everlastingly divorced! When the tidings reached her, she at first gave way to rage against Romeo, who had slain her dear cousin: she called him a beautiful tyrant, a fiend angelical, a ravenous dove, a lamb with a wolf's nature, a serpent-heart hid with a flowering face, and other like contradictory names, which denoted the struggles in her mind between her love and her resentment: but in the end love got the mastery, and the tears which she shed for grief that Romeo had slain her cousin, turned to drops of joy that her husband lived whom Tybalt would have slain. Then came fresh tears, and they were altogether of grief for Romeo's banishment. That word was more terrible to her than the death of many Tybalts.

Romeo, after the fray, had taken refuge in Friar Lawrence's cell, where he was first made acquainted with the prince's sentence, which seemed to him far more terrible than death. To him it appeared there was no world out of Verona's walls, no living out of the sight of Juliet. Heaven was there where Juliet lived, and all beyond was purgatory, torture, hell. The good friar would have applied the consolation of philosophy to his griefs: but this frantic young man would hear of none, but like a madman he tore his hair, and threw himself all along upon the ground, as he said, to take the measure of his grave. From this unseemly state he was roused by a message from his dear lady, which a little revived him; and then the friar took the advantage to expostulate with him on the unmanly weakness which he had shown. He had slain Tybalt, but would he also slay himself, slay his dear lady, who lived but in his life? The noble form of man, he said, was but in a shape of wax, when it wanted the courage which should keep it firm. The law had been lenient to him, that instead of death, which he had incurred, had pronounced by the prince's mouth only banishment. He had slain Tybalt, but Tybalt would have slain him: there was a sort of happiness in that. Juliet was alive, and (beyond all hope) had become his dear wife; therein he was most happy. All these blessings, as the friar made them out to be, did Romeo put from him like a sullen misbehaved wench. And the friar bade him beware, for such as despaired (he said) died miserable. Then, when Romeo was a little calmed, he counselled him that he should go that night and secretly take his leave of Juliet, and thence proceed straightways to Mantua, at which place he should sojourn, till the friar found fit occasion to publish his marriage, which might be a joyful means of reconciling their families; and then he did not doubt but the prince would be moved to pardon him, and he would return with twenty times more joy than he went forth with grief. Romeo was convinced by these wise counsels of the friar, and took his leave to go and seek his lady, proposing to stay with her that night, and by day-break pursue his journey alone to Mantua; to which place the good friar promised to send him letters from time to time, acquainting him with the state of affairs at home.

That night Romeo passed with his dear wife, gaining secret admission to her chamber, from the orchard in which he had heard her confession of love the night before. That had been a night of unmixed joy and rapture; but the pleasures of this night, and the delight which these lovers took in each other's society, were sadly allayed with the prospect of parting, and the fatal adventures of the past day. The unwelcome daybreak seemed to come too soon, and when Juliet heard the morning song of the lark she would have persuaded herself that it was the nightingale, which sings by night; but it was too truly the lark which sang, and a discordant and unpleasing note it seemed to her; and the streaks of day in the east too certainly pointed out that it was time for these lovers to part. Romeo took his leave of his dear wife with a heavy heart, promising to write to her from Mantua every hour in the day; and when he had descended from her chamber-window, as he stood below her on the ground, in that sad foreboding state of mind in which she was, he appeared to her eyes as one dead in the bottom of a tomb. Romeo's mind misgave him in like manner: but now he was forced hastily to depart, for it was death for him to be found within the walls of Verona after daybreak.

This was but the beginning of the tragedy of this pair of star-crossed lovers. Romeo had not been gone many days, before the old Lord Capulet proposed a match for Juliet. The husband he had chosen for her, not dreaming that she was married already, was count Paris, a gallant, young, and noble gentleman, no unworthy suitor to the young Juliet, if she had never seen Romeo.

The terrified Juliet was in a sad perplexity at her father's offer. She pleaded her youth unsuitable to marriage, the recent death of Tybalt, which had left her spirits too weak to meet a husband with any face of joy, and how indecorous it would show for the family of the Capulets to be celebrating a nuptial feast, when his funeral solemnities were hardly over: she pleaded every reason against the match, but the true one, namely, that she was married already. But lord Capulet was deaf to all her excuses, and in a peremptory manner ordered her to get ready, for by the following Thursday she should be married to Paris: and having found her a husband, rich, young, and noble, such as the proudest maid in Verona might joyfully accept, he could not bear that out of an affected coyness, as he construed her denial, she should oppose obstacles to her own good fortune.

In this extremity Juliet applied to the friendly friar, always her counsellor in distress, and he asking her if she had resolution to undertake a desperate remedy, and she answering that she would go into the grave alive rather than marry Paris, her own dear husband living; he directed her to go home, and appear merry, and give her consent to marry Paris, according to her father's desire, and on the next night, which was the night before the marriage, to drink off the contents of a phial which he then gave her, the effect of which would be that for two-and-forty hours after drinking it she should appear cold and lifeless; and when the bridegroom came to fetch her in the morning, he would find her to appearance dead; that then she would be borne, as the manner in that country was, uncovered on a bier, to be buried in the family vault; that if she could put off womanish fear, and consent to this terrible trial, in forty-two hours after swallowing the liquid (such was its certain operation) she would be sure to awake, as from a dream; and before she should awake, he would let her husband know their drift, and he should come in the night, and bear her thence to Mantua. Love, and the dread of marrying Paris, gave young Juliet strength to undertake this horrible adventure; and she took the phial of the friar, promising to observe his directions.

Going from the monastery, she met the young count Paris, and modestly dissembling, promised to become his bride. This was joyful news to the lord Capulet and his wife. It seemed to put youth into the old man; and Juliet, who had displeased him exceedingly, by her refusal of the count, was his darling again, now she promised to be obedient. All things in the house were in a bustle against the approaching nuptials. No cost was spared to prepare such festival rejoicings as Verona had never before witnessed.

On the Wednesday night Juliet drank off the potion. She had many misgivings lest the friar, to avoid the blame which might be imputed to him for marrying her to Romeo, had given her poison; but then he was always known for a holy man: then lest she should awake before the time that Romeo was to come for her; whether the terror of the place, a vault full of dead Capulets' bones, and where Tybalt, all bloody, lay festering in his shroud, would not be enough to drive her distracted: again she thought of all the stories she had heard of spirits haunting the places where their bodies bestowed. But then her love for Romeo, and her aversion for Paris returned, and she desperately swallowed the draught, and became insensible.

When young Paris came early in the morning with music to awaken his bride, instead of a living Juliet, her chamber presented the dreary spectacle of a lifeless corpse. What death to his hopes! What confusion then reigned through the whole house! Poor Paris lamenting his bride, whom most detestable death had beguiled him of, had divorced from him even before their hands were joined. But still more piteous it was to hear the mournings of the old Lord and Lady Capulet, who having but this one, one poor loving child to rejoice and solace in, cruel death had snatched her from their sight, just as these careful parents were on the point of seeing her advanced (as they thought) by a promising and advantageous match. Now all things that were ordained for the festival were turned from their properties to do the office of a black funeral. The wedding cheer served for a sad burial feast, the bridal hymns were changed for sullen dirges, the sprightly instruments to melancholy bells, and the flowers that should have been strewed in the bride's path, now served but to strew her corse. Now, instead of a priest to marry her, a priest was needed to bury her; and she was borne to church indeed, not to augment the cheerful hopes of the living, but to swell the dreary numbers of the dead.

Bad news, which always travels faster than good, now brought the dismal story of his Juliet's death to Romeo, at Mantua, before the messenger could arrive, who was sent from Friar Lawrence to apprise him that these were mock funerals only, and but the shadow and representation of death, and that his dear lady lay in the tomb but for a short while, expecting when Romeo would come to release her from that dreary mansion. Just before, Romeo had been unusually joyful and light-hearted. He had dreamed in the night that he was dead (a strange dream, that gave a dead man leave to think), and that his lady came and found him dead, and breathed such life with kisses in his lips, that he revived, and was an emperor! And now that a messenger came from Verona, he thought surely it was to confirm some good news which his dreams had presaged. But when the contrary to this flattering vision appeared, and that it was his lady who was dead in truth, whom he could not revive by any kisses, he ordered horses to be got ready, for he determined that night to visit Verona, and to see his lady in her tomb. And as mischief is swift to enter into the thoughts of desperate men, he called to mind a poor apothecary, whose shop in Mantua he had lately passed, and from the beggarly appearance of the man, who seemed famished, and the wretched show in his show of empty boxes ranged on dirty shelves, and other tokens of extreme wretchedness, he had said at the time (perhaps having some misgivings that his own disastrous life might haply meet with a conclusion so desperate), 'If a man were to need poison, which by the law of Mantua it is death to sell, here lives a poor wretch who would sell it him.' These words of his now came into his mind, and he sought out the apothecary, who after some pretended scruples, Romeo offering him gold, which his poverty could not resist, sold him a poison, which, if he swallowed, he told him, if he had the strength of twenty men, would quickly despatch him.

With this poison he set out for Verona, to have a sight of his dear lady in her tomb, meaning, when he had satisfied his sight, to swallow the poison, and be buried by her side. He reached Verona at midnight, and found the churchyard, in the midst of which was situated the ancient tomb of the Capulets. He had provided a light, and a spade, and wrenching iron, and was proceeding to break open the monument, when he was interrupted by a voice, which by the name of *vile Montague,* bade him desist from his unlawful business. It was the young Count Paris, who had come to the tomb of Juliet at that unseasonable time of night, to strew flowers and to weep over the grave of her that should have been his bride. He knew not what an interest Romeo had in the dead, but knowing him to be a Montague, and (as he supposed) a sworn foe to all the Capulets, he judged that he was come by night to do some villanous shame to the dead bodies; therefore in an angry tone he bade him desist; and as a criminal, condemned by the laws of Verona to die if he were found within the walls of the city, he would have apprehended him. Romeo urged Paris to leave him, and warned him by the fate of Tybalt, who lay buried there, not to provoke his anger, or draw down another sin upon his head, by forcing him to kill him. But the count in scorn refused his warning, and laid hands on him as a felon, which Romeo resisting, they fought, and Paris fell. When Romeo, by the help of a light, came to see who it was that he had slain, that it was Paris, who (he learned in his way from Mantua) should have married Juliet, he took the dead youth by the hand, as one whom misfortune had made a companion, and said that he would bury him in a triumphant grave, meaning in Juliet's grave, which he now opened: and there lay his lady, as one whom death had no power upon to change a feature or complexion, in her matchless beauty; or as if Death were amorous, and the lean abhorred monster kept her there for his delight; for she lay yet fresh and blooming, as she had fallen to sleep when she swallowed that benumbing potion; and near her lay Tybalt in his bloody shroud, whom Romeo seeing, begged pardon of his lifeless corse, and for Juliet's sake called him *cousin,* and said that he was about to do him a favour by putting his enemy to death. Here Romeo took his last leave of his lady's lips, kissing them; and here he shook the burden of his cross stars from his weary body, swallowing that poison which the apothecary had sold him, whose operation was fatal and real, not like that dissembling potion which Juliet had swallowed, the effect of which was now nearly expiring, and she about to awake to complain that Romeo had not kept his time, or that he had come too soon.

For now the hour was arrived at which the friar had promised that she should awake; and he, having learned that his letters which he had sent to Mantua, by some unlucky detention of the messenger, had never reached Romeo, came himself, provided with a pickaxe and lantern, to deliver the lady from her confinement; but he was surprised to find a light already burning in the Capulets' monument, and to see swords and blood near it, and Romeo and Paris lying breathless by the monument.

Before he could entertain a conjecture, to imagine how these fatal accidents had fallen out, Juliet awoke out of her trance, and seeing the friar near her, she remembered the place where she was, and the occasion of her being there, and asked for Romeo, but the friar, hearing a noise, bade her come out of that place of death, and of unnatural sleep, for a greater power than they could contradict had thwarted their intents; and being frightened by the noise of people coming, he fled: but when Juliet saw the cup closed in her true love's hands, she guessed that poison had been the cause of his end, and she would have swallowed the dregs if any had been left, and she kissed his still warm lips to try if any poison yet did hang upon them; then hearing a nearer noise of people coming, she quickly unsheathed a dagger which she wore, and stabbing herself, died by her true Romeo's side.

The watch by this time had come up to the place. A page belonging to count Paris, who had witnessed the fight between his master and Romeo, had given the alarm, which had spread among the citizens, who went up and down the streets of Verona confusedly exclaiming, A Paris! a Romeo! a Juliet! as the rumour had imperfectly reached them, till the uproar brought Lord Montague and Lord Capulet out of their beds, with the prince, to inquire into the causes of the disturbance. The friar had been apprehended by some of the watch, coming from the churchyard, trembling, sighing, and weeping, in a suspicious manner. A great multitude being assembled at the Capulets' monument, the friar was demanded by the prince to deliver what he knew of these strange and disastrous accidents.

And there, in the presence of the old Lords Montague and Capulet, he faithfully related the story of their children's fatal love, the part he took in promoting their marriage, in the hope that in that union to end the long quarrels between their families: how Romeo, there dead, was husband to Juliet; and Juliet, there dead, was Romeo's faithful wife; how before he could find a fit opportunity to divulge their marriage, another match was projected for Juliet, who, to avoid the crime of a second marriage, swallowed the sleeping draught (as he advised), and all thought her dead; how meantime he wrote to Romeo, to come and take her thence when the force of the potion should cease, and by what unfortunate miscarriage of the messenger the letters never reached Romeo: further than this the friar could not follow the story, nor knew more than that coming himself, to deliver Juliet from that place of death, he found the count Paris and Romeo slain. The remainder of the transactions was supplied by the narration of the page who had seen Paris and Romeo fight, and by the servant who came with Romeo from Verona, to whom this faithful lover had given letters to be delivered to his father in the event of his death, which made good the friar's words, confessing his marriage with Juliet, imploring the forgiveness of his parents, acknowledging the buying of the poison of the poor apothecary, and his intent in coming to the monument, to die, and lie with Juliet. All these circumstances agreed together to clear the friar from any hand he could be supposed to have in these complicated slaughters, further than as the unintended consequences of his own well meant, yet too artificial and subtle contrivances.

And the prince, turning to these old lords, Montague and Capulet, rebuked them for their brutal and irrational enmities, and showed them what a scourge Heaven had laid upon such offences, that it had found means even through the love of their children to punish their unnatural hate. And these old rivals, no longer enemies, agreed to bury their long strife in their children's graves; and Lord Capulet requested Lord Montague to give him his hand, calling him by the name of brother, as if in acknowledgement of the union of their families, by the marriage of the young Capulet and Montague; and saying that Lord Montague's hand (in token of reconcilement) was all he demanded for his daughter's jointure: but Lord Montague said he would give him more, for he would raise her a statue of pure gold, that while Verona kept its name, no figure should be so esteemed for its richness and workmanship as that of the true and faithful Juliet. And Lord Capulet in return said that he would raise another statue to Romeo. So did these poor old lords, when it was too late, strive to outgo each other in mutual courtesies: while so deadly had been their rage and enmity in past times, that nothing but the fearful overthrow of their children (poor sacrifices to their quarrels and dissensions) could remove the rooted hates and jealousies of the noble families.

THE SIGNALMAN

Charles Dickens

'Halloa! Below there!'

When he heard a voice thus calling to him, he was standing at the door of his box, with a flag in his hand, furled round its short pole. One would have thought, considering the nature of the ground, that he could not have doubted from what quarter the voice came; but instead of looking up to where I stood on the top of the steep cutting nearly over his head, he turned himself about, and looked down the line. There was something remarkable in his manner of doing so, though I could not have said for my life what. But I know it was remarkable enough to attract my notice, even though his figure was foreshortened and shadowed, down in the deep trench, and mine was high above him, so steeped in the glow of an angry sunset that I had shaded my eyes with my hand before I saw him at all.

'Halloa! Below!'

From looking down the line, he turned himself about again, and, raising his eyes, saw my figure high above him.

'Is there any path by which I can come down and speak to you?'

He looked up at me without replying, and I looked down at him without pressing him too soon with a repetition of my idle question. Just then there came a vague vibration in the earth and air, quickly changing into a violent pulsation, and an oncoming rush that caused me to start back, as though it had force to draw me down. When such vapour as rose to my height from this rapid train had passed me, and was skimming away over the landscape, I looked down again, and saw him refurling the flag he had shown while the train went by.

I repeated my inquiry. After a pause, during which he seemed to regard me with fixed attention, he motioned with his rolled-up flag towards a point on my level, some two or three hundred yards distant. I called down to him, 'All right!' and made for that point. There, by dint of looking closely about me, I found a rough zigzag descending path notched out, which I followed.

The cutting was extremely deep and unusually precipitate. It was made through a clammy stone that became oozier and wetter as I went down. For these reasons, I found the way long enough to give me time to recall a singular air of reluctance or compulsion with which he had pointed out the path.

When I came down low enough upon the zigzag descent to see him again, I saw that he was standing between the rails on the way by which the train had lately passed, in an attitude as if he were waiting for me to appear. He had his left hand at his chin, and that left elbow rested on his right hand, crossed over his breast. His attitude was one of such expectation and watchfulness that I stopped a moment, wondering at it.

I resumed my downward way, and stepping out upon the level of the railroad, and drawing nearer to him, saw that he was a dark sallow man, with a dark beard and rather heavy eyebrows. His post was in as solitary and dismal a place as ever I saw. On either side, a dripping-wet wall of jagged stone, excluding all view but a strip of sky; the perspective one way only a crooked prolongation of this great dungeon; the shorter perspective in the other direction terminating in a gloomy red light, and the gloomier entrance to a black tunnel, in whose massive architecture there was a barbarous, depressing and forbidding air. So little sunlight ever found its way to this spot that it had an earthy, deadly smell; and so much cold wind rushed through it that it struck chill to me, as if I had left the natural world.

Before he stirred, I was near enough to him to have touched him.

Not even then removing his eyes from mine, he stepped back one step, and lifted his hand.

This was a lonesome post to occupy (I said), and it had riveted my attention when I looked down from up yonder. A visitor was a rarity, I should suppose; not an unwelcome rarity, I hoped? In me, he merely saw a man who had been shut up within narrow limits all his life, and who, being at last set free, had a newly-awakened interest in these great works. To such purpose I spoke to him; but I am far from sure of the terms I used; for, besides that I am not happy in opening any conversation, there was something in the man that daunted me.

He directed a most curious look towards the red light near the tunnel's mouth, and looked all about it, as if something were missing from it, and then looked at me.

That light was part of his charge? Was it not?

He answered in a low voice, 'Don't you know it is?'

The monstrous thought came into my mind, as I perused the fixed eyes and the saturnine face, that this was a spirit, not a man. I have speculated since, whether there may have been infection in his mind.

In my turn I stepped back. But in making the action, I detected in his eyes some latent fear of me. This put the monstrous thought to flight.

'You look at me,' I said, forcing a smile, 'as if you had a dread of me.'

'I was doubtful,' he returned, 'whether I had seen you before.'

'Where?'

He pointed to the red light he had looked at.

'There?' I said.

Intently watchful of me, he replied (but without sound), 'Yes.'

'My good fellow, what should I do there? However, be that as it may, I never was there, you may swear.'

'I think I may,' he rejoined. 'Yes; I am sure I may.'

His manner cleared, like my own. He replied to my remarks with readiness, and in well-chosen words. Had he much to do there? Yes; that was to say, he had enough responsibility to bear; but exactness and watchfulness were what was required of him, and of actual work— manual labour—he had next to none. To change that signal, to trim those lights, and to turn this iron handle now and then, was all he had to under that head.

Regarding those many long and lonely hours of which I seemed to make so much, he could only say that the routine of his life had shaped itself into that form, and he had grown used to it. He had taught himself a language down here—if only to know it by sight, and to have formed his own crude ideas of its pronunciation, could be called learning it. He had also worked at fractions and decimals, and tried a little algebra; but he was, and had been as a boy, a poor hand at figures. Was it necessary for him when on duty always to remain in that channel of damp air, and could he never rise into the sunshine from between those high stone walls? Why, that depended upon times and circumstances. Under some conditions there would be less upon the line than under others, and the same held good as to certain hours of the day and night. In bright weather, he did choose occasions for getting a little above those lower shadows; but, being at all times liable to be called by his electric bell, and at such times listening for it with redoubled anxiety, the relief was less than I would suppose.

He took me into his box, where there was a fire, a desk for an official book in which he had to make certain entries, a telegraphic instrument with its dial, face, and needles, and the little bell of which he had spoken. On my trusting that he would excuse the remark that he had been well educated, and (I hoped I might say without offence) perhaps educated above that station, he observed that instances of slight incongruity in such wise would rarely be found wanting among large bodies of men; that he had heard it was so in workhouses, in the police force, even in that last desperate resource, the army; and that he knew it was so, more or less, in any great railway staff. He had been, when young (if I could believe it, sitting in that hut—he scarcely could), a student of natural philosophy, and had attended lectures; but he had run wild, misused his opportunities, gone down, and never risen again. He had no complaint to offer about that. He had made his bed, and he lay upon it. It was far too late to make another.

All that I have here condensed he said in a quiet manner, with his grave dark regards divided between me and the fire. He threw in the word 'sir' from time to time, and especially when he referred to his youth—as though to request me to understand that he claimed to be nothing but what I found him. He was several times interrupted by the little bell, and had to read off messages and send replies. Once he had to stand without the door, and display a flag as a train passed, and make some verbal communication to the driver. In the discharge of his duties, I observed him to be remarkably exact and vigilant, breaking off his discourse at a syllable, and remaining silent until what he had to do was done.

In a word, I should have set this man down as one of the safest of men to be employed in that capacity, but for the circumstance that while he was speaking to me he twice broke off with a fallen colour, turned his face towards the little bell when it did *not* ring, opened the door of the hut (which was kept shut to exclude the unhealthy damp), and looked out towards the red light near the mouth of the tunnel. On both of those occasions he came back to the fire with the inexplicable air upon him which I had remarked, without being able to define, when we were so far asunder.

Said I, when I rose to leave him, 'You almost make me think that I have met with a contented man.'

(I am afraid I must acknowledge that I said it to lead him on.)

'I believe I used to be so,' he rejoined, in the low voice in which he had first spoken; 'but I am troubled, sir, I am troubled.'

He would have recalled the words if he could. He had said them, however, and I took them up quickly.

'With what? What is your trouble?'

'It is very difficult to impart, sir. It is very, very difficult to speak of. If ever you make me another visit, I will try to tell you.'

'But I expressly intend to make you another visit. Say, when shall it be?'

'I go off early in the morning, and I shall be on again at ten tomorrow night, sir.'

'I will come at eleven.'

He thanked me, and went out at the door with me. 'I'll show my white light, sir,' he said in his peculiar low voice, 'till you have found the way up. When you have found it, don't call out! And when you are at the top, don't call out!'

His manner seemed to make the place strike colder to me, but I said no more than 'Very well.'

'And when you come down tomorrow night, don't call out! Let me ask you a parting question. What made you cry, "Halloa! Below there!" tonight?'

'Heaven knows,' said I, 'I cried something to that effect——'

'Not to that effect, sir. Those were the very words. I know them well.'

'Admit those were the very words. I said them, no doubt, because I saw you below.'

'For no other reason?'

'What other reason could I possibly have?'

'You have no feeling that they were conveyed to you in any supernatural way?'

'No.'

He wished me good-night, and held up his light. I walked by the side of the down line of rails (with a very disagreeable sensation of a train coming behind me) until I found the path. It was easier to mount than to descend, and I got back to my inn without any adventure.

Punctual to my appointment, I placed my foot on the first notch of the zigzag next night as the distant clocks were striking eleven. He was waiting for me at the bottom, with his white light on. 'I have not called out,' I said, when we came close together; 'may I speak now?' 'By all means, sir.' 'Good-night, then, and here's my hand.' 'Good-night, sir, and here's mine.' With that we walked side by side to his box, entered it, closed the door, and sat down by the fire.

'I have made up my mind, sir,' he began bending forward as soon as we were seated, and speaking in a tone but a little above a whisper, 'that you shall not have to ask me twice what troubles me. I took you for someone else yesterday evening. That troubles me.'

'That mistake?'

'No. That someone else.'

'Who is it?'

'I don't know.'

'Like me?'

'I don't know. I never saw the face. The left arm is across the face, and the right arm is waved—violently waved. This way.'

I followed his action with my eyes, and it was the action of an arm gesticulating, with the utmost passion and vehemence, 'For God's sake, clear the way!'

'One moonlit night,' said the man, 'I was sitting here, when I heard a voice cry, "Halloa! Below there!" I started up, looked from that door, and saw this someone else standing by the red light near the tunnel, waving as I just now showed you. The voice seemed hoarse with shouting, and it cried, "Look out! Look out!" And then again, "Halloa! Below there! Look out!" I caught up my lamp, turned it on red, and ran towards the figure, calling, "What's wrong? What has happened? Where?" It stood just outside the blackness of the tunnel. I advanced so close upon it that I wondered at its keeping the sleeve across its eyes. I ran right up at it, and had my hand stretched out to pull the sleeve away, when it was gone.'

'Into the tunnel?' said I.

'No. I ran on into the tunnel, five hundred yards. I stopped, and held my lamp above my head, and saw the figures of the measured distance, and saw the wet stains stealing down the walls and trickling through the arch. I ran out again faster than I had run in (for I had a mortal abhorrence of the place upon me), and I looked all round the red light with my own red light, and I went up the iron ladder to the gallery atop of it, and I came down again, and ran back here. I telegraphed both ways, "An alarm has been given. Is anything wrong?" The answer came back, both ways, "All well".'

Resisting the slow touch of a frozen finger tracing out my spine, I showed him how that this figure must be a deception of his sense of sight; and how that figures, originating in disease of the delicate nerves that minister to the functions of the eye, were known to have often troubled patients, some of whom had become conscious of the nature of their affliction, and had even proved it by experiments upon themselves. 'As to an imaginary cry,' said I, 'do but listen for a moment to the wind in this unnatural valley while we speak so low, and to the wild harp it makes of the telegraph wires.'

That was all very well, he returned, after we had sat listening for a while, and he ought to know something of the wind and the wires—he who so often passed long winter nights there, alone and watching. But he would beg to remark that he had not finished.

I asked his pardon, and he slowly added these words, touching my arm: 'Within six hours after the appearance, the memorable accident on this line happened, and within ten hours the dead and wounded were brought along the tunnel over the spot where the figure had stood.'

A disagreeable shudder crept over me, but I did my best against it. It was not to be denied, I rejoined, that this was a remarkable coincidence, calculated deeply to impress his mind. But it was unquestionable that remarkable coincidences did continually occur, and they must be taken into account in dealing with such a subject. Though to be sure I must admit, I added (for I thought I saw that he was going to bring the objection to bear upon me), men of common sense did not allow much for coincidences in making the ordinary calculations of life.

He again begged to remark that he had not finished.

I again begged his pardon for being betrayed into interruptions.

'This,' he said, again laying his hand upon my arm, and glancing over his shoulder with hollow eyes, 'was just a year ago. Six or seven months passed, and I had recovered from the surprise and shock, when one morning, as the day was breaking, I, standing at the door, looked towards the red light, and saw the spectre again.' He stopped, with a fixed look at me.

'Did it cry out?'

'No. It was silent.'

'Did it wave its arm?'

'No. It leaned against the shaft of the light with both hands before the face. Like this.'

Once more I followed his action with my eyes. It was an action of mourning. I have seen such an attitude on stone figures on tombs.

'Did you go up to it?'

'I came in and sat down, partly to collect my thoughts, partly because it had turned me faint. When I went to the door again, daylight was above me, and the ghost was gone.'

'But nothing followed? Nothing came of this?'

He touched me on the arm with his forefinger twice or thrice, giving a ghastly nod each time.

'That very day, as a train came out of the tunnel, I noticed, at a carriage window on my side, what looked like a confusion of hands and heads, and something waved. I saw it just in time to signal the driver "Stop!" He shut off, and put his brake on, but the train drifted past here a hundred and fifty yards or more. I ran after it, and, as I went along, heard terrible screams and cries. A beautiful young lady had died instantaneously in one of the compartments, and was brought in here, and

'He touched me on the arm twice or thrice, giving a ghastly nod each time.'

laid down on this floor between us.'

Involuntarily I pushed my chair back, as I looked from the boards at which he pointed to himself.

'True, sir. True. Precisely as it happened, so I tell it you.'

I could think of nothing to say, to any purpose, and my mouth was very dry. The wind and the wires took up the story with a long lamenting wail.

He resumed, 'Now, sir, mark this, and judge how my mind is troubled. The spectre came back a week ago. Ever since, it has been there, now and again, by fits and starts.'

'At the light?'

'At the danger-light.'

'What does it seem to do?'

He repeated, if possible with increased passion and vehemence, that former gesticulation of 'For God's sake, clear the way!'

Then he went on. 'I have no peace or rest for it. It calls to me, for many minutes together, in an agonized manner, "Below there! Look out! Look out!" It stands waving to me. It rings my little bell——'

I caught at that. 'Did it ring your bell yesterday evening when I was here, and you went to the door?'

'Twice.'

'Why, see,' said I, 'how your imagination misleads you. My eyes were on the bell, and my ears were open to the bell, and if I am a living man, it did *not* ring at those times. No, nor at any other time, except when it was rung in the natural course of physical things by the station communicating with you.'

He shook his head. 'I have never made a mistake as to that yet, sir. I have never confused the spectre's ring with the man's. The ghost's ring is a strange vibration in the bell that it derives from nothing else, and I have not asserted that the bell stirs to the eye. I don't wonder that you failed to hear it. But *I* heard it.'

'And did the spectre seem to be there when you looked out?'

'It *was* there.'

'Both times?'

He repeated firmly: 'Both times.'

'Will you come to the door with me, and look for it now?'

He bit his lower lip as though he were somewhat unwilling, but arose. I opened the door, and stood on the step, while he stood in the doorway. There was the danger-light. There was the dismal mouth of the tunnel. There were the high, wet stone walls of the cutting. There were the stars above them.

'Do you see it?' I asked him, taking particular note of his face. His eyes were prominent and strained, but not very much more so, perhaps, than my own had been when I had directed them earnestly towards the same spot.

'No,' he answered. 'It is not there.'

'Agreed,' said I.

We went in again, shut the door, and resumed our seats. I was thinking how best to improve this advantage, if it might be called one, when he took up the conversation in such a matter-of-course way, so assuming that there could be no serious question of fact between us, that I felt myself placed in the weakest of positions.

'By this time you will fully understand, sir,' he said, 'that what troubles me so dreadfully is the question: what does the spectre mean?'

I was not sure, I told him, that I did not fully understand.

'What is its warning against?' he said, ruminating, with his eyes on the fire, and only by times turning them on me. 'What is the danger? Where is the danger? There is danger overhanging somewhere on the line. Some dreadful calamity will happen. It is not to be doubted this third time, after what has gone before. But surely this is a cruel haunting of *me*. What can I do?'

He pulled out his handkerchief, and wiped the drops from his heated forehead.

'If I telegraph danger on either side of me, or on both, I can give no reason for it,' he went on, wiping the palms of his hands. 'I should get into trouble and do no good. They would think I was mad. This is the way it would work: Message: "Danger! Take care!" Answer: "What Danger? Where?" Message: "Don't know. But for God's sake, take care!" They would displace me. What else could they do?'

His pain of mind was most pitiable to see. It was the mental torture of a conscientious man, oppressed beyond endurance by an unintelligible responsibility involving life.

'When it first stood under the danger-light,' he went on, putting his dark hair back from his head, and drawing his hands outward across and across his temples in an extremity of feverish distress, 'why not tell me where that accident was to happen—if it must happen? Why not tell me how it could be averted—if it could have been averted? When on its second coming it hid its face, why not tell me, instead, "She is going to die. Let them keep her at home"? If it came, on those two occasions, only to show me that its warnings were true, and so to prepare me for the third, why not warn me plainly now? And I, Lord help me! A mere poor signalman on this solitary station! Why not go to somebody with credit to be believed, and power to act?'

When I saw him in this state, I saw that for the poor man's sake, as well as for the public safety, what I had to do for the time was to compose his mind. Therefore, setting aside all question of reality or unreality between us, I represented to him that whoever thoroughly discharged his duty must do well, and that at least it was his comfort that he understood his duty, though he did not understand these confounding appearances. In this effort I succeeded far better than in the attempt to reason him out of his conviction. He became calm; the occupations incidental to his post as the night advanced began to make larger demands on his attention: and I left him at two in the morning. I had offered to stay through the night, but he would not hear of it.

That I more than once looked back at the red light as I ascended the pathway, that I did not like the red light, and that I should have slept but poorly if my bed had been under it, I see no reason to conceal. Nor did I like the two sequences of the accident and the dead girl. I see no reason to conceal that either.

But what ran most in my thoughts was the consideration how ought I to act, having become the recipient of this disclosure? I had proved the man to be intelligent, vigilant, painstaking, and exact; but how long might he remain so, in his state of mind? Though in a subordinate position, still he held a most important trust, and would I (for instance) like to stake my own life on the chances of his continuing to execute it with precision?

Unable to overcome a feeling that there would be something treacherous in my communicating what he had told me to his superiors in the company, without first being plain with himself and proposing a middle course to him, I ultimately resolved to offer to accompany him (otherwise keeping his secret for the present) to the wisest medical practitioner we could hear of in those parts, and to take his opinion. A change in his time of duty would come round next night, he had apprised me, and he would be off an hour or two after sunrise, and on again soon after sunset. I had appointed to return accordingly.

Next evening was a lovely evening, and I walked out early to enjoy it. The sun was not yet quite down when I traversed the field-path near the top of the deep cutting. I would extend my walk for an hour, I said to myself, half an hour on and half an hour back, and it would then be time to go to my signalman's box.

Before pursuing my stroll, I stepped to the brink, and mechanically looked down, from the point from which I had first seen him. I cannot describe the thrill that seized upon me, when, close at the mouth of the tunnel, I saw the appearance of a man, with his left sleeve across his eyes, passionately waving his right arm.

The nameless horror that oppressed me passed in a moment, for in a moment I saw that this appearance of a man was a man indeed, and that there was a little group of other men standing at a short distance, to whom he seemed to be rehearsing the gesture he made. The danger-light was not yet lit. Against its shaft a little low hut entirely new to me had been made of some wooden supports and tarpaulin. It looked no bigger than a bed.

With an irresistible sense that something was wrong—with a flashing self-reproachful fear that fatal mischief had come of my leaving the man there, and causing no one to be sent to overlook or correct what he did—I descended the notched path with all the speed I could make.

'What is the matter?' I asked the men.

'Signalman killed this morning, sir.'

'Not the man belonging to that box?'

'Yes, sir.'

'Not the man I know?'

'You will recognize him, sir, if you knew him,' said the man who spoke for the others, solemnly uncovering his own head, and raising an end of the tarpaulin, 'for his face is quite composed.'

'Oh, how did this happen, how did this happen?' I asked, turning from one to another as the hut closed in again.

'He was cut down by an engine, sir. No man in England knew his work better. But somehow he was not clear of the outer rail. It was just at broad day. He had struck the light, and had the lamp in his hand. As the engine came out of the tunnel, his back was towards her, and she cut him down. That man drove her, and was showing how it happened. Show the gentleman, Tom.'

The man, who wore a rough dark dress, stepped back to his former place at the mouth of the tunnel.

'Coming round the curve in the tunnel, sir,' he said, 'I saw him at the end, like as if I saw him down a perspective-glass. There was no time to check speed, and I knew him to be very careful. As he didn't seem to take heed of the whistle, I shut if off when we were running down upon him, and called to him as loud as I could call.'

'What did you say?'

'I said, "Below there! Look out! Look out! For God's sake, clear the way!"'

I started.

'Ah! it was a dreadful time, sir. I never left off calling to him. I put this arm before my eyes not to see, and I waved this arm to the last; but it was no use.'

Without prolonging the narrative to dwell on any one of its curious circumstances more than on any other, I may, in closing it, point out the coincidence that the warning of the engine-driver included, not only the words which the unfortunate signalman had repeated to me as haunting him, but also the words which I myself—not he—had attached, and that only in my own mind, to the gesticulation he had imitated.

THE BOY ON THE HILL

Brian Hayles

The rectory, its outline dark against a violet sky, settled into the habitual peace of a summer evening. It was the time that the rector and his wife loved most, when the scent of honeysuckle hung on the air and the stillness outside was accentuated by the steady ticking of the grandfather clock in the hall.

Constance, their niece, was upstairs. She could manage to pretend involvement in the affairs of the house during the day, but the evenings worked on her withdrawn and solitary nature to provoke such sadness that she shrank from the company of others. In her own room she had to contend with no anxious glances, no well-intentioned inquiries. The kindness of her aunt and uncle, of which her parents' weekly letters from India gently and insistently reminded her, did nothing to alleviate her loneliness. Her refuge was the world she created for herself beyond their reach.

She opened the window of her room and leant on the window sill, looking out on to the dim rose garden. By the wall at the end of the garden silver birches rustled gently, obscuring the brow of the hill which rose beyond the grounds of the rectory. She remained there, for a long time, until she could no longer sense the sill beneath her arms, until the view was no longer framed by the window. . . .

Breathless, Constance stood quite still. Her first feeling of strangeness had slipped away and she was calm again. She was on a hill, alone, and it was late summer; although she had never been there before, she felt she knew the place immediately. She recognized the close-cropped slopes that rose so cleanly from the combe below and, at the crest, the cluster of tall trees looming against the burnished sky. Not even a breath of wind touched her soft dark curls; the grass beneath her was un-crushed by the motion of her feet, yet there was a vibrance in the air that suggested, like perfume, a pleasure to come. She turned away from the trees, whose shade was mildly threatening by contrast with the sunlight, and looked across the sweep of the hill.

A movement caught her eye. About a hundred yards away a figure appeared above the contour of the slope. It stood for a moment, then stooped out of sight again. She experienced a slight shock; she had been so sure that she was alone in this bare landscape. But, driven on by curiosity, she walked slowly towards the spot where she thought she had seen the figure. There was nothing to guide her—no sound, no further movement. As she climbed a small rise to get her bearings, she stopped suddenly. Just below her, his back to her, a boy was kneeling on the ground, his concentration fixed on something before him.

Constance paused, aware that her presence was an intrusion. She watched as the boy reached for a clasp knife which was lying beside him and scored several marks on the turf. She craned to see what he had carved but was unable to make it out. Cautiously she advanced, until she was standing beside him. He did not look up.

Her attention was drawn first to his hands. The wrists were thin and the fingers long and delicate, suited more to musicianship, she thought, than the rugged labour he was engaged in. She gazed at his face, partly hidden by the lank hair which fell across it. His skin was pale, almost luminous, and his fine features had a somewhat harsh set to them, as though contorted by the intensity of his efforts. She guessed that he was about a year older than she was, perhaps seventeen, and he was evidently a scholar, to judge by some battered leatherbound books which lay in a heap on the ground nearby.

The boy seemed quite unconscious of her scrutiny. He got up, moved to a new position and knelt again. Constance followed him, a little uncertainly. The moment for a conventional greeting had passed and she could not think of a suitable opening. At last he raised his eyes to hers. They were dark, deep-set in the pale face. He held her gaze, and in his expression there was a hint of arrogance, of mockery.

'Why have you come?' he asked.

The boy's abrupt question revealed a hostility which Constance felt was undeserved. She was silent, anxiously seeking the correct answer—for she sensed that he was testing her response and that there was only one which would be acceptable. Defeated, she turned away in acknowledgement that she had trespassed. Loneliness, she knew, establishes its own boundaries. As she walked slowly back up to the rise, she was startled by his voice:

'You may watch if you wish.'

It was not an invitation, more a challenge. She stood for a moment, considering. The hill lay tranquil in the sunshine. A buzzard glided overhead, drawing lazy spirals in the cloudless sky. She looked back at the boy, who was standing now, with a look on his face which was part defiance, part appeal. She retraced her steps.

They stood together in silence, examining the boy's work. He had stripped small pieces of turf from an area about ten yards square. Some of the strips formed right angles; others, curves and disconnected segments, appeared to have been carved in a random fashion.

'What is it?' she asked.

He hesitated, perhaps to gauge the sincerity of her interest, then he stepped across on to a bare fragment of chalk and gestured to her to follow him. He took another step, placing his foot carefully to avoid trampling on the edges of the turf. He turned right, then left, then right again, clearly guided by some principle which she could not understand.

'Now do you see?'

She slowly shook her head. He picked up the knife and walked away from her. Kneeling down, he began to carve the turf with the same fierce concentration as before. His face, which had relaxed briefly, hardened again, and he seemed to shrink into himself, to withdraw from her so suddenly, so completely, that she felt herself dismissed. This time, though, she was not intimidated. She picked her way over the cut turf and stood on the slope a little way behind him, so that she could watch his progress without disturbing him.

He worked quickly and with precision, stopping only to check one patch of chalk against another or to pace out the distance between certain points. As she followed his movements with her eyes, she was suddenly aware that the bare strips of chalk were beginning to form a kind of broken pattern and that the apparent eccentricity of his design was deliberate. It was an exercise in illogic, a complicated and meticulously planned confusion.

She ran down the slope to tell him that she now understood, but halted as he looked up.

'It is clear now?'

She nodded, hoping that she had earned a fuller explanation. He bent over his work without a word, but after a few strokes with the knife she stopped. He sat back and motioned to her to step clear of the chalk mosaic. Rising to his feet, he surveyed the area critically, then picked up his knife and snapped it shut.

'But it's not nearly finished,' Constance said. 'You can't leave it like that. There's so much more to—'

He cut her short. 'I've finished what I needed to do today.'

She looked down, disappointed. 'Will you go on with it tomorrow?' she asked. 'May I . . . come back tomorrow?'

'If you wish. You may watch if you wish.'

He turned from her, gathered up his books and strode away.

As Constance climbed the hill next morning, the quiet excitement she felt was tempered with anxiety. She was eager to find the boy there again but afraid that she might not be welcome. She had recognized in him all the signs of profound loneliness which she knew so well in herself: the caution which adopted the defence of haughtiness, the formality which signalled distrust, the self-sufficiency which deflected pity. Her reappearance might stretch his tolerance too far.

She stood on the rise. There was no one there. A light breeze stirred among the long grasses by her feet. A cloud hid the sun momentarily, shading the patchwork of turf and chalk in front of her, incomplete and abandoned now. Constance struggled to reason away the desolation that swept over her. Compelled to do something to show that she had kept her word in case he ever came back to this spot, she stooped to pick up a stone to use as a tool and walked to the patch on which he had been working. From her vantage point she had noticed that the last strip of chalk he had bared was too short to fit the design dictated by the other pieces, and she knelt now to scrape away a few more inches of turf.

'You must not touch it—please!' His voice was harsh and urgent. She turned to see him standing behind her, his hands clenched. She jumped up in consternation.

'I'm sorry, I didn't mean . . . I wasn't going to do anything more than . . . .' She was mortified, unable to offer any excuse. She saw that what she had done was unpardonable. Her clumsy attempt to improve on his work was a breach of trust, an assault. But he said nothing more. He bent to see what she had been doing, then took out his knife and opened it. He crouched over the piece of turf and neatened the edges where she had cut it. Slowly he extended the cuts and exposed the chalk beneath, lengthening the strip to match the others.

'I think that will do,' he said. He paused. 'Don't you?'

She was forgiven. The boy was too proud to acknowledge his error or her motive in trying to rectify it, but she understood that her participation was accepted. Shaking slightly with relief, she knelt on the grass near him, leaving him to work on in silence.

Eventually he sat back on his heels and glanced at her. She took this as a sign that she could speak and asked, tentatively, 'Why a maze? Why here?'

He smiled, not at her but to himself, as he tested the blade of the knife on his thumb. He did not answer.

'I know,' she suggested, 'you are trying to create a puzzle without a solution. But who is going to find it? Hardly anyone comes to this spot. We haven't seen anyone else here.'

He shook his head slightly. 'A maze *is* a solution,' he said. 'The confusion is illusory. Though you can't see it at first, the path which leads you to the centre is there all along. The confusion lies not in the maze but in the belief that its pattern is bewildering.'

'But you are designing it to be bewildering,' Constance interrupted with a laugh.

He corrected her quickly: 'My intention is to clarify, not to confuse. My design has simply assumed a disguise.'

'A disguise?'

'The appearance of randomness. But the maze is not random: it is a question which contains its own answer.'

Constance frowned. 'But if you know the answer, what is the purpose of the disguise?'

The boy's eyes rested on her briefly, then turned to follow the slope of the hill up to the clump of trees at its crest. 'It is an experiment,' he said, 'to test an idea I had. Whatever plans you make, however carefully you shape the future in your mind, chance always intervenes. The patterns you see suddenly shatter into slivers of chaos. There is only one defence against disappointment and confusion: to accept that randomness is the sole certainty—to imitate its strange designs and deceive chance itself.' He looked back at her. 'Do you understand?'

Constance could not hide her perplexity. 'No, I'm afraid I don't.'

'No.' He shrugged. 'It is not important.'

Abruptly he resumed his work, and his expression discouraged further talk. Constance felt once again that she had failed him. Her interest was not enough: she could not keep pace with his mind. She left him and wandered up the hill towards the trees. At the top she sat down, her back against an ancient stump. The sound of the wind among the leaves above her was soothing, and the shade was a relief after the glare of the hillside. She could just make out the solitary figure of the boy, and she leant back, comforted by the knowledge that he was still there. Once he stood, scanning the hill, and she raised her hand. After a moment's hesitation he waved back.

When she returned to the maze she noticed with surprise that its perimeter was now complete and that more than half of the interior was marked out in strips. She watched him as he progressed towards the centre; then she turned and walked slowly to the point where he had started cutting the turf the day before.

Very carefully she made her way along the narrow white paths, aiming for the area on which he was working. She was so preoccupied that she did not see the boy look up, not did she observe the faint glimmer of a smile which transformed his face.

'You won't manage it,' he called out, but his tone was gentle, no longer peremptory.

Eventually he sat back and glanced at her.

'I'm nearly there,' she retorted.

'But I know you can't reach me—unless you cheat.'

She stood, poised, searching for a route. Then she nodded. 'You're quite right,' she conceded.

'Of course.' But he held out his hand to her, to indicate that she was permitted to waive the rules for the last few yards. She reached out shyly, half-afraid that he was mocking her. He took her hand and held it while she regained her balance.

'But do you promise there *will* be a solution when it is complete?' she asked, smiling up at him.

He gazed at her, with an expression in his eyes that she could not interpret. 'There will be a solution,' he said softly.

Constance was detained the next morning by the arrival of visitors at the rectory, and it was noon by the time she climbed the rise above the maze. As she looked down on it, she laughed out loud in sheer pleasure. The bare strips of chalk gleamed below her in the sun, a complete and perfect pattern. He had finished it for her.

She saw that it would be an injustice to work out the path she should take from her position on the rise, so she closed her eyes and walked forward until she stood at the entrance to the maze. She rejected the route she had taken the day before and chose a different one. It was no more successful. She turned back and tried again. After several attempts she was still on the edge of the maze and she paused, bemused and partially blinded by the dazzling white of the chalk. She went on, halted, retraced her steps, selected another path, moved forward a few paces, halted again. Gradually she eliminated path after path. Resolutely resisting the temptation to look ahead beyond her feet, she glanced back and was astonished to find that she had made progress. She was now half-way to the centre. She pressed on, impatient with herself for being so slow. But cheating was out of the question.

And then, as she recalled his words, something about outwitting chance, she began to ignore the paths which presented themselves as obvious choices and chose instead those that appeared to lead backwards or sideways. Now progress was a little faster, although she quickly realized that the boy had anticipated her reaction, and that the maze made its own rules at every turn and broke them as consistently. The little white paths taunted her, now leading her on innocently, now blocking her advance, encouraging then betraying her trust.

At least, sensing that she must by now be nearing the centre, she allowed herself to look up. She discovered that although she was not quite at the opening to the central square, the path she was on had no further junctions. She had only to walk forward a pace or two and she had solved the puzzle. She smiled to herself. She was sure that she was being watched with approval; surer still when she arrived at the centre and found his knife, sunk to its shaft in the turf.

When Constance came down to breakfast next morning there was a lightness in her mood that transformed the atmosphere of the rectory for her. During the past weeks its rooms had seemed cold and forbidding; now only the gilding of soft morning sunlight caught her eye, not the shadows. She entered the breakfast-room with none of her usual hesitancy and kissed her aunt and uncle with unaccustomed warmth. Aunt Mildred acknowledged her with an absent-minded smile, but her glance rested on the young face a fraction longer than normal; the sadness that had lingered over Constance appeared to have lifted at last.

Breakfast was usually a silent meal, as the rector dedicated that part of the morning to the newspaper; but Constance could not prevent herself from telling them of the curious dream, as vivid now as it was when she first woke up. She recounted it in great detail, and they heard her out, at first indulgently and then more attentively as they observed with relief how animated the girl was. She blossomed under their attention, hardly aware that her uncle was watching her with marked interest as she talked. His wife put her own construction on his look; she willed him not to quell the girl's enthusiasm, however wildly romantic the dream might seem. But he made no comment, and Constance ended her account with a smile they had longed to see for weeks. She excused herself and left the room through the french windows which led on to the rose garden.

The rector's eyes followed her thoughtfully.

'Thank you, Edgar,' said his wife. 'You didn't tell Constance that the dream was fanciful nonsense, which must have been what you were thinking. That was kind.'

'I had no such idea in mind,' he answered. 'The puzzling thing is that I know the place she described very well—but I believe, as she said herself, that she has never been there. It is St Catherine's Hill, outside Winchester. I used to spend time up there myself when I was a boy. . . .' His voice trailed away, perhaps a little nostalgically, Mildred thought with surprise. Her husband's references to his school days at Winchester College were infrequent and his reminiscences always wry: he did not recall those years with pleasure.

'My dear, now you're being fanciful,' she said, 'one hill is much like another—'. But she stopped, uneasy at the glance he gave her. He was troubled and that was rare indeed. Her hand reached out and touched his. 'What is it, Edgar?'

He paused before replying. 'There is a legend,' he said at length. 'About a hundred years ago a Winchester boy is said to have been kept back at the College throughout one summer as a punishment. He was not allowed to see his family and all companionship with boys of his own age was forbidden. The boy spent the summer up on St Catherine's Hill alone . . . cutting a miniature maze in the turf.'

At first Mildred was silent. Then she responded, non-committal and safe: 'A strange coincidence—we must tell Constance the story.'

'I think not.' The rector rose and stood at the window watching his niece as she strolled among the roses, pretty but fragile in summer frock and straw bonnet. Images of his own childhood trembled on the fringe of memory, and his face, usually gentle and kindly, tautened with purpose. 'No, I think not,' he repeated, half to himself. 'We will leave Constance her dream. In it she solved one of the problems posed by the maze, and that is enough; she need never know that the boy faced another . . . and found his own solution.'

'Edgar, what can you mean?' his wife asked, leaving the table and crossing the room to him. She slipped her arm through his affectionately, and together they watched Constance stoop to cut some roses and place them in the basket she was carrying over her arm.

'There is a little more to the legend, my dear,' the rector answered quietly. 'When the boy had achieved his aim, when the last strip of turf had been carved and the maze was complete . . . he hanged himself from one of the beech trees at the top of the hill.'

HAPPINESS

Guy de Maupassant

It was tea-time, just before the lights were brought in. The sky was all rosy with sunset and shimmering with gold dust. The villa looked down upon the Mediterranean, which lay without ripple or quiver, like a vast sheet of burnished metal, smooth and shining in the fading daylight. The irregular outline of the distant mountains on the right stood out black against the pale purple background of the western sky.

The conversation turned on love, that old familiar topic, and remarks that had been made many times before were being offered once again. The gentle melancholy of the twilight diffused a languorous charm and created an atmosphere of tender emotion. The word 'love', constantly reiterated, now in a man's virile voice, now in a woman's delicate tones, seemed to dominate the little drawing-room, hovering like a bird, brooding like a spirit.

'Is it possible to remain faithful to one love year after year?'

Some said yes, some said no. Distinctions were made, limits defined, and instances cited. The minds of all, men and woman alike, were surging with a host of disturbing memories, which trembled on their lips, but which they dared not utter. Their emotion expressed itself in the deep and ardent interest with which they discussed this commonplace, yet sovereign, passion, this tender and mysterious bond between two beings.

Suddenly someone, with his eyes on the distant prospect, exclaimed:

'Oh, look over there. What can it be?'

On the sky-line, a great blurred mass of grey was rising out of the sea. The ladies sprang to their feet and gazed in surprise at this startling thing that they had never seen before.

'It is Corsica,' someone explained. 'It is visible two or three times a year in certain exceptional atmospheric conditions. When the air is perfectly clear the mists of water vapour, which usually veil the horizon, are lifted.'

The ridges of the mountains could be faintly discerned, and some thought that they could make out even the snow on the peaks.

This sudden apparition of a phantom world, emerging from the sea, produced on those who witnessed it a disquieting impression, a feeling of uneasiness, almost of consternation.

An old gentleman, hitherto silent, exclaimed:

'That very island which has risen from the waters as if in response to our conversation, reminds me of a curious experience. It was there that I came upon a wonderful instance of faithful love, a love that was incredibly happy. This is the story:

'Five years ago I paid a visit to Corsica. Although visible now and then, like today, from the coast of France, less is known of that wild island than of America, and it seems almost more remote. Picture to yourselves a world still in a state of chaos, a raging sea of mountains, intersected by narrow gorges with rushing torrents. Instead of plains, there are vast, rolling sweeps of granite and gigantic undulations of the earth, overgrown with bush and great forests of chestnut trees and pines. It is a virgin country, desolate, uncultivated, in spite of an occasional village planted like a heap of rocks on a mountain top. There is no agriculture, industry, or art. You never come upon a scrap of wood-carving or sculpture, or any relic, showing in the Corsicans of old a taste, whether primitive or cultured, for graceful and beautiful things. It is this that strikes you most forcibly in that superb but austere country, its hereditary indifference to that striving after exquisite forms, which we call Art. In Italy, every palace is not only full of masterpieces, but is itself a masterpiece; in Italy, marble, wood, bronze, iron, metals, stone, all testify to the genius of man, and even the humblest relics of antiquity, that lie about in old houses, reveal this divine passion for beauty. Italy is to all of us a beloved and sacred land, because it displays convincingly the energy, grandeur, power and triumph of creative intelligence.

'And opposite her shores lies wild Corsica, just as she was in her earliest days. There a man leads his own life in his rude cottage, indifferent to everything that does not directly concern himself or his family quarrels. And he still retains the defects and qualities of primitive races. Passionate, vindictive, frankly bloodthirsty, he is at the same time hospitable, generous, faithful, ingenuous. He opens his door to the stranger and repays the most trifling act of kindness with loyal friendship.

'For a whole month I had been wandering all over this magnificent island, and I had a feeling of having reached the end of the world. There were no inns, no taverns, no roads. Mule tracks lead up to hamlets that cling to the mountain sides and look down upon winding cañons, from whose depths rises of an evening the deep, muffled roar of torrents. The wanderer knocks at the door of a house and asks for a night's hospitality. He takes his place at his host's frugal board, sleeps beneath his humble roof, and the next day the master of the house escorts his guest to the outskirts of the village, where they shake hands and part.

'One evening, after a ten hours' tramp, I reached a little solitary dwelling at the upper end of a valley, which, a mile lower, fell away abruptly to the sea. It was a ravine of intense dreariness, walled in by bleak mountains, rising steeply on either side, and covered with bush, fallen rocks, and lofty trees. Near the hut there were some vines and a small garden, and at a little distance, some tall chestnut trees. It was enough to support life, and indeed amounted to a fortune on that poverty-stricken island.

'I was met by an old woman of severe aspect and unusual cleanliness. Her husband rose from a straw-bottomed chair, bowed to me, and then resumed his seat without a word.

'"Pray excuse him," said his wife. "He is deaf. He is eighty-two."

'To my surprise, she spoke French like a Frenchwoman.

'"You are not a native of Corsica?" I asked.

'Never mind about him,' she continued, 'he can't hear us.'

'"No, we are from the mainland, but we have lived here for fifty years."

'A wave òf horror and dismay swept over me at the thought of those fifty years spent in that gloomy cranny, so far from towns and places where men live. An old shepherd entered, and we all sat down to supper, which consisted of a single course, thick broth containing potatoes, bacon, and cabbages all cooked together. When the short meal was over I took a seat before the door. I was weighed down by the melancholy aspect of that forbidding landscape and by that feeling of depression which at times overtakes the traveller on a dismal evening in dreary surroundings, a foreboding that the end of everything, the end of existence, the end of the world, is at hand. Suddenly the appalling wretchedness of life is borne in upon us; the isolation of each one of us; the hollowness of everything, the black loneliness of the heart, which is lulled and deceived by its own imaginings to the brink of the grave.

'Presently the old woman rejoined me, and with the curiosity which lingers even in the serenest soul, she began to question me.

'"So you come from France?"

'"Yes, I am on a pleasure trip."

'"I suppose you live in Paris."

'"No, my home is Nancy."

'At this she seemed to be seized by some violent emotion, and yet I cannot explain how it was that I saw, or rather felt, her agitation.

'"Your home is Nancy?" she repeated slowly.

'Her husband appeared in the doorway, with the impassive air that deaf people have.

'"Never mind about him," she continued, "he cannot hear us." After a pause she resumed:

'"Then you know people at Nancy?"

'"Yes, nearly everyone."

'"Do you know the Saint-Allaizes?"

'"Very well indeed. They were friends of my father's."

'"What is your name?"

'I told her. She looked at me searchingly. Then, in the low voice of one conjuring up the past:

'"Yes, yes, I remember perfectly. And what has become of the Brisemares?"

'"They are all dead."

'"Ah! And did you know the Sirmonts?"

'"Yes, the last of them is a General now."

'She was quivering with excitement, with pain, with mingled emotions, strong, sacred, impossible to describe, with a strange yearning to break the silence, to utter all the secrets hitherto locked away in her heart, to speak about those people, whose very names shook her to the soul.

'"Henri de Sirmont. Yes, I know," she exclaimed. "He is my brother."

'I glanced at her in amazement. Suddenly I remembered.

'Long ago there had been a terrible scandal among the Lorraine aristocracy. Suzanne de Sirmont, a beautiful and wealthy girl, had eloped with a non-commissioned officer in the Hussar regiment commanded by her father. The son of a peasant, but for all that a fine figure in his blue pelisse, this common soldier had captivated his Colonel's daughter. No doubt she had had opportunities of seeking him, admiring him, and falling in love with him, as she watched the squadrons trooping past. But how had she contrived to speak to him? How had they managed to meet and come to an understanding? How had she ventured to convey to him that she loved him? No one ever knew.

'No suspicion had been aroused. At the end of the soldier's term of service they disappeared together one night. A search was made for them, but without result. Nothing was ever heard of them again and the family looked upon her as dead.

'And now I had found her in this desolate valley.

'"I remember perfectly," I said at last. "You are Mademoiselle Suzanne."

'She nodded. Tears welled from her eyes. Then, with a glance towards the old man, who was standing motionless on the threshold of his hut:

'"And that is my husband."

'Then I realized that she still loved him, that she still beheld him with eyes that had not lost their illusion.

'"I trust that you have been happy?" I ventured.

'In a voice straight from the heart she answered:

'"Yes, very happy. He has made me very happy. I have never regretted anything."

'I gazed at her in sympathetic surprise, marvelling at the power of love. This well-bred, wealthy girl had followed that humble peasant, and had stooped to his level. She had submitted to an existence destitute of all the graces, luxuries, and refinements of life. She had conformed to his simple ways. And she still loved him. She had become a peasant woman, in bonnet and cotton gown. She sat on a straw-bottomed chair at a wooden table, and supped on a broth of cabbages, potatoes, and bacon, served in an earthenware dish. All night she lay on a palliasse by his side. She had never had a thought for anything but her lover. And she regretted nothing, neither jewels, silks and satins, luxuries, cushioned chairs, the warmth and perfume of tapestried rooms, nor downy couches so grateful to weary limbs. He was her one desire. As long as he was there she asked no more of life.

'A mere girl, she had sacrificed her whole future, the world, and those who had brought her up and loved her. All alone with him, she had come to this wild ravine. And he had been all in all to her. He had satisfied her heart's desires, its dreams, its endless longings, its undying hopes. He had filled her whole life with bliss from beginning to end. She could not possibly have been happier.

'I lay awake all night, listening to the old soldier's stertorous breathing, as he slept on his pallet by the side of her who had followed him to the ends of the earth, and I pondered on their strange, yet simple story; their happiness, so perfect, yet founded on so little.

'At sunrise I shook hands with the old couple and bade them farewell.'

★   ★   ★   ★   ★

The speaker was silent.

'You may say what you please,' one of the women exclaimed,' her ideals were paltry. Her wants and desires were absurdly primitive. She was just a fool.'

'What did that matter?' replied another woman pensively. 'She was happy.'

On the horizon, Corsica was vanishing in the gloom of night, sinking slowly back into the sea, as if its vast shadowy form had manifested itself for no other purpose than to tell its tale of those two simple lovers who had found a refuge on its shores.

LOVE OF LIFE

Jack London

They limped painfully down the bank, and once the foremost of the two men staggered among the rough-strewn rocks. They were tired and weak, and their faces had the drawn expression of patience which comes of hardship long endured. They were heavily burdened with blanket packs which were strapped to their shoulders. Head straps, passing across the forehead, helped support these packs. Each man carried a rifle. They walked in a stooped posture, the shoulders well forward, the head still farther forward, the eyes bent upon the ground.

'I wish we had just about two of them cartridges that's layin' in that cache of ourn,' said the second man.

His voice was utterly and drearily expressionless. He spoke without enthusiasm; and the first man, limping into the milky stream that foamed over the rocks, vouchsafed no reply.

The other man followed at his heels. They did not remove their footgear, though the water was icy cold—so cold that their ankles ached and their feet went numb. In places the water dashed against their knees, and both men staggered for footing.

The man who followed slipped on a smooth boulder, nearly fell, but recovered himself with a violent effort, at the same time uttering a sharp exclamation of pain. He seemed faint and dizzy and put out his free hand while he reeled, as though seeking support against the air. When he had steadied himself he stepped forward, but reeled again and nearly fell. Then he stood still and looked at the other man, who had never turned his head.

The man stood still for fully a minute, as though debating with himself. Then he called out:

'I say, Bill, I've sprained my ankle.'

Bill staggered on through the milky water. He did not look around. The man watched him go, and though his face was expressionless as ever, his eyes were like the eyes of a wounded deer.

The other man limped up the farther bank and continued straight on without looking back. The man in the stream watched him. His lips trembled a little, so that the rough thatch of brown hair which covered them was visibly agitated. His tongue even strayed out to moisten them.

'Bill!' he cried out.

It was the pleading cry of a strong man in distress, but Bill's head did not turn. The man watched him go, limping grotesquely and lurching forward with stammering gait up the slow slope towards the soft skyline of the low-lying hill. He watched him go till he passed over the crest and disappeared. Then he turned his gaze and slowly took in the circle of the world that remained to him now that Bill was gone.

Near the horizon the sun was smouldering dimly, almost obscured by formless mists and vapours, which gave an impression of mass and density without outline or tangibility. The man pulled out his watch, the while resting his weight on one leg. It was four o'clock, and as the season was near the last of July or first of August—he did not know the precise date within a week or two—he knew that the sun roughly marked the north-west. He looked to the south and knew that somewhere beyond those bleak hills lay the Great Bear Lake; also he knew that in that direction the Arctic Circle cut its forbidding way across the Canadian Barrens. This stream in which he stood was a feeder to the Coppermine River, which in turn flowed north and emptied into Coronation Gulf and the Arctic Ocean. He had never been there, but he had seen it, once, on a Hudson's Bay Company chart.

Again his gaze completed the circle of the world about him. It was not a heartening spectacle. Everywhere was soft sky line. The hills were all low-lying. There were no trees, no shrubs, no grasses—naught but a tremendous and terrible desolation that sent fear swiftly dawning into his eyes.

'Bill!' he whispered, once and twice. 'Bill!'

He cowered in the midst of the milky water, as though the vastness were pressing in upon him with overwhelming force, brutally crushing him with its complacent awfulness. He began to shake as with an ague fit, till the gun fell from his hand with a splash. This served to rouse him. He fought with his fear and pulled himself together, groping in the water and recovering the weapon. He hitched his pack farther over on his left shoulder, so as to take a portion of its weight from off the injured ankle. Then he proceeded, slowly and carefully, wincing with pain, to the bank.

He did not stop. With a desperation that was madness, unmindful of the pain, he hurried up the slope to the crest of the hill over which his comrade had disappeared—more grotesque and comical by far than that limping, jerking comrade. But at the crest he saw a shallow valley, empty of life. He fought his fear again, overcame it, hitched the pack still farther over on his left shoulder, and lurched on down the slope.

The bottom of the valley was soggy with water, which the thick moss held, spongelike, close to the surface. This water squirted out from under his feet at every step, and each time he lifted a foot the action culminated in a sucking sound as the wet moss reluctantly released its grip. He picked his way from muskeg to muskeg, and followed the other man's footsteps along and across the rocky ledges which thrust like islets through the sea of moss.

Though alone, he was not lost. Farther on, he knew, he would come to where dead spruce and fir, very small and wizened, bordered the shore of a little lake, the *titchin-nichilie*, in the tongue of the country, the 'land of little sticks'. And into that lake flowed a small stream, the water of which was not milky. There was rush grass on that stream—this he remembered well—but no timber, and he would follow it till its first trickle ceased at a divide. He would cross this divide to the first trickle of another stream, flowing to the west, which he would follow until it emptied into the river Dease, and here he would find a cache under an upturned canoe and piled over with many rocks. And in this cache would be ammunition for his empty gun, fishhooks and lines, a small net—all the utilities for the killing and snaring of food. Also he would find flour—not much—a piece of bacon, and some beans.

Bill would be waiting for him there, and they would paddle away south down the Dease to the Great Bear Lake. And south across the lake they would go, ever south, till they gained the Mackenzie. And south, still south, they would go, while the winter raced vainly after them, and the ice formed in the eddies, and the days grew chill and crisp, south to some warm Hudson's Bay Company post, where timber grew tall and generous and there was grub without end.

These were the thoughts of the man as he strove onward. But hard as he strove with his body, he strove equally hard with his mind, trying to think that Bill had not deserted him, that Bill would surely wait for him at the cache. He was compelled to think this thought, or else there would not be any use to strive, and he would have lain down and died. And as the dim ball of the sun sank slowly into the northwest he covered every inch—and many times—of his and Bill's flight south before the downcoming winter. And he conned the grub of the cache and the grub of the Hudson's Bay Company post over and over again. He had not eaten for two days; for a far longer time he had not had all he wanted to eat. Often he stooped and picked pale muskeg berries, put them into his mouth, and chewed and swallowed them. A muskeg berry is a bit of seed enclosed in a bit of water. In the mouth the water melts away and the seed chews sharp and bitter. The man knew there was no nourishment in the berries, but he chewed them patiently with a hope greater than knowledge and defying experience.

At nine o'clock he stubbed his toe on a rocky ledge, and from sheer weariness and weakness staggered and fell. He lay for some time, without movement, on his side. Then he slipped out of the pack straps and clumsily dragged himself into a sitting posture. It was not yet dark, and in the lingering twilight he groped about among the rocks for shreds of dry moss. When he had gathered a heap he built a fire—a smouldering, smudgy fire—and put a tin pot of water on to boil.

He unwrapped his pack and the first thing he did was to count his matches. There were sixty-seven. He counted them three times to make sure. He divided them into several portions, wrapping them in oil paper, disposing of one bunch in his empty tobacco pouch, of another bunch in the inside band of his battered hat, of a third bunch under his shirt on the chest. This accomplished, a panic came upon him, and he unwrapped them all and counted them again. There were still sixty-seven.

He dried his wet footgear by the fire. The moccasins were in soggy shreds. The blanket socks were worn through in places, and his feet were raw and bleeding. His ankle was throbbing, and he gave it an examination. It had swollen to the size of his knee. He tore a long strip from one of his two blankets and bound the ankle tightly. He tore other strips and bound them about his feet to serve for both moccasins and socks. Then he drank the pot of water, steaming hot, wound his watch, and crawled between his blankets.

He slept like a dead man. The brief darkness around midnight came and went. The sun arose in the north-east—at least the day dawned in that quarter, for the sun was hidden by grey clouds.

At six o'clock he awoke, quietly lying on his back. He gazed straight up into the grey sky and knew that he was hungry. As he rolled over on his elbow he was startled by a loud snort, and saw a bull caribou regarding him with alert curiosity. The animal was not more than fifty feet away, and instantly into the man's mind leaped the vision and the savour of a caribou steak sizzling and frying over a fire. Mechanically he reached for the empty gun, drew a bead, and pulled the trigger. The bull snorted and leaped away, his hoofs rattling and clattering as he fled across the ledges.

The man cursed and flung the empty gun from him. He groaned aloud as he started to drag himself to his feet. It was a slow and arduous task. His joints were like rusty hinges. They worked harshly in their sockets, with much friction, and each bending or unbending was accomplished only through a sheer exertion of will. When he finally gained his feet, another minute or so was consumed in straightening up, so that he could stand erect as a man should stand.

He crawled up a small knoll and surveyed the prospect. There were no trees, no bushes, nothing but a grey sea of moss scarcely diversified

Mechanically he reached for the empty gun.

by grey rocks, grey lakelets, and grey streamlets. The sky was grey. There was no sun nor hint of sun. He had no idea of north, and he had forgotten the way he had come to this spot the night before. But he was not lost. He knew that. Soon he would come to the land of the little sticks. He felt that it lay off to the left somewhere, not far—possibly just over the next low hill.

He went back to put his pack into shape for travelling. He assured himself of the existence of his three separate parcels of matches, though he did not stop to count them. But he did linger, debating, over a squat moose-hide sack. It was not large. He could hide it under his two hands. He knew that it weighed fifteen pounds—as much as all the rest of the pack—and it worried him. He finally set it to one side and proceeded to roll the pack. He paused to gaze at the squat moose-hide sack. He picked it up hastily with a defiant glance about him, as though the desolation were trying to rob him of it; and when he rose to his feet to stagger on into the day, it was included in the pack on his back.

He bore away to his left, stopping now and again to eat muskeg berries. His ankle had stiffened, his limp was more pronounced, but the pain of it was as nothing compared with the pain of his stomach. The hunger pangs were sharp. They gnawed and gnawed until he could not keep his mind steady on the course he must pursue to gain the land of the little sticks. The muskeg berries did not allay this gnawing, while they made his tongue and the roof of his mouth sore with their irritating bite.

He came upon a valley where rock ptarmigan rose on whirring wings from the ledges and muskegs. *Ker—ker—ker* was the cry they made. He threw stones at them but could not hit them. He placed his pack on the ground and stalked them as a cat stalks a sparrow. The sharp rocks cut through his pants legs till his knees left a trail of blood; but the hurt was lost in the hurt of his hunger. He squirmed over the wet moss, saturating his clothes and chilling his body; but he was not aware of it, so great was his fever for food. And always the ptarmigan rose, whirring, before him, till their *ker—ker—ker* became a mock to him, and he cursed them and cried aloud at them with their own cry.

Once he crawled upon one that must have been asleep. He did

not see it till it shot up in his face from its rocky nook. He made a clutch as startled as was the rise of the ptarmigan, and there remained in his hand three tail feathers. As he watched its flight he hated it, as though it had done him some terrible wrong. Then he returned and shouldered his pack.

As the day wore along he came into valleys or swales where game was more plentiful. A band of caribou passed by, twenty and odd animals, tantalizingly within rifle range. He felt a wild desire to run after them, a certitude that he could run them down. A black fox came towards him, carrying a ptarmigan in his mouth. The man shouted. It was a fearful cry, but the fox, leaping away in fright, did not drop the ptarmigan.

Late in the afternoon he followed a stream, milky with lime, which ran through sparse patches of rush grass. Grasping these rushes firmly near the root, he pulled up what resembled a young onion sprout no larger than a shingle nail. It was tender, and his teeth sank into it with a crunch that promised deliciously of food. But its fibres were tough. It was composed of stringy filaments saturated with water, like the berries, and devoid of nourishment. He threw off his pack and went into the rush grass on hands and knees, crunching and munching, like some bovine creature.

He was very weary and often wished to rest—to lie down and sleep; but he was continually driven on, not so much by his desire to gain the land of little sticks as by his hunger. He searched little ponds for frogs and dug up the earth with his nails for worms, though he knew in spite that neither frogs nor worms existed so far north.

He looked into every pool of water vainly, until, as the long twilight came on, he discovered a solitary fish, the size of a minnow, in such a pool. He plunged his arm in up to the shoulder, but it eluded him. He reached for it with both hands and stirred up the milky mud at the bottom. In his excitement he fell in, wetting himself to the waist. Then the water was too muddy to admit of his seeing the fish, and he was compelled to wait until the sediment had settled.

The pursuit was renewed, till the water was again muddied. But he could not wait. He unstrapped the tin bucket and began to bail the pool. He bailed wildly at first, splashing himself and flinging the water so short a distance that it ran back into the pool. He worked more carefully, striving to be cool, though his heart was pounding against his chest and his hands were trembling. At the end of half an hour the pool was nearly dry. Not a cupful of water remained. And there was no fish. He found a hidden crevice among the stones through which it had escaped to the adjoining and larger pool—a pool which he could not empty in a night and a day. Had he known of the crevice, he could have closed it with a rock at the beginning and the fish would have been his.

Thus he thought, and crumpled up and sank down upon the wet earth. At first he cried softly to himself, then he cried loudly to the pitiless desolation that ringed him around; and for a long time after he was shaken by great dry sobs.

He built a fire and warmed himself by drinking quarts of hot water, and made camp on a rocky ledge in the same fashion he had the night before. The last thing he did was to see that his matches were dry and to wind his watch. The blankets were wet and clammy. His ankle pulsed with pain. But he knew only that he was hungry, and through his restless sleep he dreamed of feasts and banquets and of food served and spread in all imaginable ways.

He awoke chilled and sick. There was no sun. The grey of earth and sky had become deeper, more profound. A raw wind was blowing, and the first flurries of snow were whitening the hilltops. The air about him thickened and grew white while he made a fire and boiled more water. It was wet snow, half rain, and the flakes were large and soggy. At first they melted as soon as they came in contact with the earth, but ever more fell, covering the ground, putting out the fire, spoiling his supply of moss fuel.

This was a signal for him to strap on his pack and stumble onward, he knew not where. He was not concerned with the land of little sticks, nor with Bill and the cache under the upturned canoe by the river Dease. He was mastered by the verb *to eat*. He was hunger-mad. He took no heed of the course he pursued, so long as that course led him through the swale bottoms. He felt his way through the wet snow to the watery muskeg berries, and went by feel as he pulled up the rush grass by the roots. But it was tasteless stuff and did not satisfy. He found a weed that tasted sour and he ate all he could find of it, which was not much, for it was a creeping growth, easily hidden under the several inches of snow.

He had no fire that night, nor hot water, and crawled under his blanket to sleep the broken hunger sleep. The snow turned into a cold rain. He awakened many times to feel it falling on his upturned face. Day came—a grey day and no sun. It had ceased raining. The keenness of his hunger had departed. Sensibility, as far as concerned the yearning for food, had been exhausted. There was a dull, heavy ache in his stomach, but it did not bother him so much. He was more rational, and once more he was chiefly interested in the land of little sticks and the cache by the river Dease.

He ripped the remnant of one of his blankets into strips and bound his bleeding feet. Also he recinched the injured ankle and prepared himself for a day of travel. When he came to his pack he paused long over the squat moose-hide sack, but in the end it went with him.

The snow had melted under the rain, and only the hilltops showed white. The sun came out, and he succeeded in locating the points of the compass, though he knew now that he was lost. Perhaps, in his previous days' wanderings, he had edged away too far to the left. He now bore off to the right to counteract the possible deviation from his true course.

Though the hunger pangs were no longer so exquisite, he realized that he was weak. He was compelled to pause for frequent rests, when he attacked the muskeg berries and rush-grass patches. His tongue felt dry and large, as though covered with a fine hairy growth, and it tasted bitter in his mouth. His heart gave him a great deal of trouble. When he had travelled a few minutes it would begin a remorseless thump, thump, thump, and then leap up and away in a painful flutter of beats that choked him and made him go faint and dizzy.

In the middle of the day he found two minnows in a large pool. It was impossible to bail it, but he was calmer now and managed to catch them in his tin bucket. They were no longer than his little finger, but he was not particularly hungry. The dull ache in his stomach had been growing duller and fainter. It seemed almost that his stomach was dozing. He ate the fish raw, masticating with painstaking care, for the eating was an act of pure reason. While he had no desire to eat, he knew that he must eat to live.

In the evening he caught three more minnows, eating two and saving the third for breakfast. The sun had dried stray shreds of moss, and he was able to warm himself with hot water. He had not covered more than ten miles that day; and the next day, travelling whenever his heart permitted him, he covered no more than five miles. But his stomach did not give him the slightest uneasiness. It had gone to sleep. He was in a strange country, too, and the caribou were growing more plentiful, also the wolves. Often their yelps drifted across the desolation, and once he saw three of them slinking away before his path.

Another night; and in the morning, being more rational, he untied the leather string that fastened the squat moose-hide sack. From its open mouth poured a yellow stream of coarse gold dust and nuggets. He roughly divided the gold in halves, caching one half on a prominent ledge, wrapped in a piece of blanket, and returning the other half to the sack. He also began to use strips of the one remaining blanket for his feet. He still clung to his gun, for there were cartridges in that cache by the river Dease.

This was a day of fog, and this day hunger awoke in him again. He was very weak and was afflicted with a giddiness which at times blinded him. It was no uncommon thing now for him to stumble and fall; and stumbling once, he fell squarely into a ptarmigan nest. There were four newly hatched chicks, a day old—little specks of pulsating life no more than a mouthful; and he ate them ravenously, thrusting them alive into his mouth and crunching them like eggshells between his teeth. The mother ptarmigan beat about him with great outcry. He used his gun as a club with which to knock her over, but she dodged out of reach. He threw stones at her and with one chance shot broke a wing. Then she fluttered away, running, trailing the broken wing, with him in pursuit.

The little chicks had no more than whetted his appetite. He hopped and bobbed clumsily along on his injured ankle, throwing stones and screaming hoarsely at times; at other times hopping and bobbing silently along, picking himself up grimly and patiently when he fell, or rubbing his eyes with his hand when the giddiness threatened to overpower him.

The chase led him across swampy ground in the bottom of the valley, and he came upon footprints in the soggy moss. They were not his own—he could see that. They must be Bill's. But he could not stop, for the mother ptarmigan was running on. He would catch her first, then he would return and investigate.

He exhausted the mother ptarmigan; but he exhausted himself. She lay panting on her side. He lay panting on his side, a dozen feet away, unable to crawl to her. And as he recovered she recovered, fluttering out of reach as his hungry hand went out to her. The chase was resumed. Night settled down and she escaped. He stumbled from weakness and pitched head foremost on his face, cutting his cheek, his pack upon his back. He did not move for a long while; then he rolled over on his side, wound his watch, and lay there until morning.

Another day of fog. Half of his last blanket had gone into foot-wrappings. He failed to pick up Bill's trail. It did not matter. His hunger was driving him too compellingly—only—only he wondered if Bill, too, were lost. By midday the irk of his pack became too oppressive. Again he divided the gold, this time merely spilling half of it on the ground. In the afternoon he threw the rest of it away, there remaining to him only the half blanket, the tin bucket, and the rifle.

A hallucination began to trouble him. He felt confident that one cartridge remained to him. It was in the chamber of the rifle and he had overlooked it. On the other hand, he knew all the time that the chamber was empty. But the hallucination persisted. He fought it off for hours, then threw his rifle open and was confronted with emptiness. The disappointment was as bitter as though he had really expected to find the cartridge.

He plodded on for half an hour, when the hallucination arose again. Again he fought it, and still it persisted, till for very relief he opened his rifle to unconvince himself. At times his mind wandered farther afield, and he plodded on, a mere automaton, strange conceits and whimsicalities gnawing at his brain like worms. But these excursions out of the real were of brief duration, for ever the pangs of the hunger bite called him back. He was jerked back abruptly once from such an excursion by a sight that caused him nearly to faint. He reeled and swayed, doddering like a drunken man to keep from falling. Before him stood a horse. A horse! He could not believe his eyes. A thick mist was in them, intershot with sparkling points of light. He rubbed his eyes savagely to clear his vision, and beheld not a horse but a great brown bear. The animal was studying him with bellicose curiosity.

The man had brought his gun halfway to his shoulder before he realized. He lowered it and drew his hunting knife from its beaded sheath at his hip. Before him was meat and life. He ran his thumb along the edge of his knife. It was sharp. The point was sharp. He would fling himself upon the bear and kill it. But his heart began its warning thump, thump, thump. Then followed the wild upward leap and tattoo of flutters, the pressing as of an iron band about his forehead, the creeping of the dizziness into his brain.

His desperate courage was evicted by a great surge of fear. In his weakness, what if the animal attacked him? He drew himself up to his most imposing stature, gripping the knife and staring hard at the bear. The bear advanced clumsily a couple of steps, reared up, and gave vent to a tentative growl. If the man ran, he would run after him; but the man did not run. He was animated now with the courage of fear. He, too, growled, savagely, terribly, voicing the fear that is to life germane and that lies twisted about life's deepest roots.

The bear edged away to one side, growling menacingly, himself appalled by this mysterious creature that appeared upright and un-afraid. But the man did not move. He stood like a statue till the danger was past, when he yielded to a fit of trembling and sank down into the wet moss.

He pulled himself together and went on, afraid now in a new way. It was not the fear that he should die passively from lack of food, but that he should be destroyed violently before starvation had exhausted the last particle of the endeavour in him that made towards surviving. There were the wolves. Back and forth across the desolation drifted their howls, weaving the very air into a fabric of menace that was so tangible that he found himself, arms in the air, pressing it back from him as it might be the walls of a wind-blown tent.

Now and again the wolves, in packs of two and three, crossed his path. But they sheered clear of him. They were not in sufficient num-bers, and besides, they were hunting the caribou, which did not battle, while this strange creature that walked erect might scratch and bite.

In the late afternoon he came upon scattered bones where the wolves had made a kill. The debris had been a caribou calf an hour before, squawking and running and very much alive. He contemplated the bones, clean-picked and polished, pink with the cell life in them which had not yet died. Could it possibly be that he might be that ere the day was done! Such was life, eh? A vain and fleeting thing. It was only life that pained. There was no hurt in death. To die was to sleep. It meant cessation, rest. Then why was he not content to die?

But he did not moralize long. He was squatting in the moss, a bone in his mouth, sucking at the shreds of life that still dyed it faintly pink. The sweet meaty taste, thin and elusive almost as a memory, maddened him. He closed his jaws on the bones and crunched. Sometimes it was the bone that broke, sometimes his teeth. Then he crushed the bones between rocks, pounding them to a pulp, and swallowed them. He pounded his fingers, too, in his haste, and yet found a moment in which to feel surprise at the fact that his fingers did not hurt much when caught under the descending rock.

Came frightful days of snow and rain. He did not know when he made camp, when he broke camp. He travelled in the night as much as in the day. He rested wherever he fell, crawled on whenever the dying life in him flickered up and burned less dimly. He, as a man, no longer strove. It was the life in him, unwilling to die, that drove him on. He did not suffer. His nerves had become blunted, numb, while his mind was filled with weird visions and delicious dreams.

But ever he sucked and chewed on the crushed bones of the caribou calf, the least remnants of which he had gathered up and carried with him. He crossed no more hills or divides, but automatically followed a large stream which flowed through a wide and shallow valley. He did not see this stream nor this valley. He saw nothing save visions. Soul and body walked or crawled side by side, yet apart, so slender was the thread that bound them.

He awoke in his right mind, lying on his back on a rocky ledge. The sun was shining bright and warm. Afar off he heard the squawking of caribou calves. He was aware of vague memories of rain and wind and snow, but whether he had been beaten by the storm for two days or two weeks he did not know.

For some time he lay without movement, the genial sunshine pouring upon him and saturating his miserable body with its warmth. A fine day, he thought. Perhaps he could manage to locate himself. By a painful effort he rolled over on his side. Below him flowed a wide and sluggish river. Its unfamiliarity puzzled him. Slowly he followed it with his eyes, winding in wide sweeps among the bleak, bare hills, bleaker and barer and lower-lying than any hills he had yet encountered. Slowly, deliberately, without excitement or more than the most casual interest, he followed the course of the strange stream towards the sky line and saw it emptying into a bright and shining sea. He was still unexcited. Most unusual, he thought, a vision or a mirage—more likely a vision, a trick of his disordered mind. He was confirmed in this by sight of a ship lying at anchor in the midst of the shining sea. He closed his eyes for a while, then opened them. Strange how the vision persisted! Yet not strange. He knew there were no seas or ships in the heart of the barren lands, just as he had known there was no cartridge in the empty rifle.

He heard a snuffle behind him—a half-choking gasp or cough. Very slowly, because of his exceeding weakness and stiffness, he rolled over on his other side. He could see nothing near at hand, but he waited patiently. Again came the snuffle and cough, and outlined between two jagged rocks not a score of feet away he made out the grey head of a wolf. The sharp ears were not pricked so sharply as he had seen them on other wolves; the eyes were bleared and bloodshot, the head seemed to droop limply and forlornly. The animal blinked continually in the sunshine. It seemed sick. As he looked it snuffled and coughed again.

This, at least, was real, he thought, and turned on the other side so that he might see the reality of the world which had been veiled from him before by the vision. But the sea still shone in the distance and the ship was plainly discernible. Was it reality after all? He closed his eyes for a long while and thought, and then it came to him. He had been making north by east, away from the Dease Divide and into the Coppermine Valley. This wide and sluggish river was the Coppermine. That shining sea was the Arctic Ocean. That ship was a whaler, strayed east, far east, from the mouth of the Mackenzie, and it was lying at anchor in Coronation Gulf. He remembered the

Hudson's Bay Company chart he had seen long ago, and it was all clear and reasonable to him.

He sat up and turned his attention to immediate affairs. He had worn through the blanket wrappings, and his feet were shapeless lumps of raw meat. His last blanket was gone. Rifle and knife were both missing. He had lost his hat somewhere, with the bunch of matches in the band, but the matches against his chest were safe and dry inside the tobacco pouch and oil paper. He looked at his watch. It marked eleven o'clock and was still running. Evidently he had kept it wound.

He was calm and collected. Though extremely· weak, he had no sensation of pain. He was not hungry. The thought of food was not even pleasant to him, and whatever he did was done by his reason alone. He ripped off his pants legs to the knees and bound them about his feet. Somehow he had succeeded in retaining the tin bucket. He would have some hot water before he began what he foresaw was to be a terrible journey to the ship.

His movements were slow. He shook as with a palsy. When he started to collect dry moss he found he could not rise to his feet. He tried again and again, then contented himself with crawling about on hands and knees. Once he crawled near to the sick wolf. The animal dragged itself reluctantly out of his way, licking its chops with a tongue which seemed hardly to have the strength to curl. The man noticed that the tongue was not the customary healthy red. It was a yellowish brown and seemed coated with a rough and half-dry mucus.

After he had drunk a quart of hot water the man found he was able to stand, and even to walk as well as a dying man might be supposed to walk. Every minute or so he was compelled to rest. His steps were feeble and uncertain, just as the wolf's that trailed him were feeble and uncertain; and that night, when the shining sea was blotted out by blackness, he knew he was nearer to it by no more than four miles.

Throughout the night he heard the cough of the sick wolf, and now and then the squawking of the caribou calves. There was life all around him, but it was strong life, very much alive and well, and he knew the sick wolf clung to the sick man's trail in the hope that the man would die first. In the morning, on opening his eyes, he beheld it regarding him with a wistful and hungry stare. It stood crouched, with tail between its legs, like a miserable and woebegone dog. It shivered in the chill morning wind and grinned dispiritedly when the man spoke to it in a voice that achieved no more than a hoarse whisper.

The sun rose brightly, and all morning the man tottered and fell towards the ship on the shining sea. The weather was perfect. It was the brief Indian summer of the high latitudes. It might last a week. Tomorrow or the next day it might be gone.

In the afternoon the man came upon a trail. It was of another man, who did not walk, but who dragged himself on all fours. The man thought it might be Bill; but he thought in a dull, uninterested way. He had no curiosity. In fact sensation and emotion had left him. He was no longer susceptible to pain. Stomach and nerves had gone to sleep. Yet the life that was in him drove him on. He was very weary, but it refused to die. It was because it refused to die that he still ate muskeg berries and minnows, drank his hot water, and kept a wary eye on the sick wolf.

He followed the trail of the other man who dragged himself along, and soon came to the end of it—a few fresh-picked bones where the soggy moss was marked by the foot pads of many wolves. He saw a squat moose-hide sack, mate to his own, which had been torn by sharp teeth. He picked it up, though its weight was almost too much for his feeble fingers. Bill had carried it to the last. Ha-ha! He would have the laugh on Bill. He would survive and carry it to the ship in the shining sea. His mirth was hoarse and ghastly, like a raven's croak, and the sick wolf joined him, howling lugubriously. The man ceased suddenly. How could he have the laugh on Bill if that were Bill; if those bones, so pinky-white and clean, were Bill?

He turned away. Well, Bill had deserted him; but he would not take the gold, nor would he suck Bill's bones. Bill would have, though, had it been the other way around, he mused as he staggered on.

He came to a pool of water. Stooping over in quest of minnows, he jerked his head back as though he had been stung. He had caught sight of his reflected face. So horrible was it that sensibility awoke long enough to be shocked. There were three minnows in the pool, which was too large to drain; and after several ineffectual attempts to catch them in the tin bucket he forbore. He was afraid, because of his great weakness, that he might fall in and drown. It was for this reason that he did not trust himself to the river astride one of the many drift logs which lined its sandspits.

That day he decreased the distance between him and the ship by three miles; the next day by two—for he was crawling now as Bill had crawled; and the end of the fifth day found the ship still seven miles away and him unable to make even a mile a day. Still the Indian summer held on, and he continued to crawl and faint, turn and turn about; and ever the sick wolf coughed and wheezed at his heels. His knees had become raw meat like his feet, and though he padded them with the shirt from his back it was a red track he left behind him on the moss and stones. Once, glancing back, he saw the wolf licking hungrily his bleeding trail, and he saw sharply what his own end might be—unless—unless he could get the wolf. Then began as grim a tragedy of existence as was ever played—a sick man that crawled, a sick wolf that limped, two creatures dragging their dying carcasses across the desolation and hunting each other's lives.

Had it been a well wolf, it would not have mattered so much to the man; but the thought of going to feed the maw of that loathsome and all but dead thing was repugnant to him. He was finicky. His mind had begun to wander again and to be perplexed by hallucinations, while his lucid intervals grew rarer and shorter.

He was awakened once from a faint by a wheeze close in his ear. The wolf leaped lamely back, losing its footing and falling in its weakness. It was ludicrous, but he was not amused. Nor was he even afraid. He was too far gone for that. But his mind was for the moment clear, and he lay and considered. The ship was no more than four miles away. He could see it quite distinctly when he rubbed the mists out of his eyes, and he could see the white sail of a small boat cutting the water of the shining sea. But he could never crawl those four miles. He knew that, and was very calm in the knowledge. He knew that he could not crawl half a mile. And yet he wanted to live. It was unreasonable that he should die after all he had undergone. Fate asked too much of him. And, dying, he declined to die. It was stark madness, perhaps, but in the very grip of death he defied death and refused to die.

He closed his eyes and composed himself with infinite precaution. He steeled himself to keep above the suffocating languor that lapped like a rising tide through all the wells of his being. It was very like a sea, this deadly languor that rose and rose and drowned his consciousness bit by bit. Sometimes he was all but submerged, swimming through oblivion with a faltering stroke; and again, by some strange alchemy of soul, he would find another shred of will and strike out more strongly.

Without movement he lay on his back, and he could hear, slowly drawing near and nearer, the wheezing intake and output of the sick wolf's breath. It drew closer, ever closer, through an infinitude of time, and he did not move. It was at his ear. The harsh dry tongue grated like sandpaper against his cheek. His hands shot out—or at least he willed them to shoot out. The fingers were curved like talons, but they closed on empty air. Swiftness and certitude require strength, and the man had not this strength.

The patience of the wolf was terrible. The man's patience was no less terrible. For half a day he lay motionless, fighting off unconsciousness and waiting for the thing that was to feed upon him and upon which he wished to feed. Sometimes the languid sea rose over him and he dreamed long dreams; but ever through it all, waking and dreaming, he waited for the wheezing breath and the harsh caress of the tongue.

He did not hear the breath, and he slipped slowly from some dream to the feel of the tongue along his hand. He waited. The fangs pressed softly; the pressure increased; the wolf was exerting its last strength in an effort to sink teeth in the food for which it had waited long. But the man had waited long, and the lacerated hand closed on the jaw. Slowly, while the wolf struggled feebly and the hand clutched feebly, the other hand crept across to a grip. Five minutes later the whole weight of the man's body was on top of the wolf. The hands had not sufficient strength to choke the wolf, but the face of the man was pressed close to the throat of the wolf and the mouth of the man was full of hair. Later the man rolled over on his back and slept.

*   *   *   *

There were some members of a scientific expedition on the whale ship

Bedford. From the deck they remarked a strange object on the shore. It was moving down the beach towards the water. They were unable to classify it, and, being scientific men, they climbed into the whaleboat alongside and went ashore to see. And they saw something that was alive but which could hardly be called a man. It was blind, unconscious. It squirmed along the ground like some monstrous worm. Most of its efforts were ineffectual, but it was persistent, and it writhed and twisted and went ahead perhaps a score of feet an hour.

★　　★　　★　　★

Three weeks afterwards the man lay in a bunk on the whale ship *Bedford,* and with tears streaming down his wasted cheeks told who he was and what he had undergone. He also babbled incoherently of his mother, of sunny southern California, and a home among the orange groves and flowers.

The days were not many after that when he sat at table with the scientific men and ship's officers. He gloated over the spectacle of so much food, watching it anxiously as it went into the mouths of others. With the disappearance of each mouthful an expression of deep regret came into his eyes. He was quite sane, yet he hated those men at mealtime. He was haunted by a fear that the food would not last. He inquired of the cook, the cabin boy, the captain, concerning the food stores. They reassured him countless times; but he could not believe them, and pried cunningly about the lazaret to see with his own eyes.

It was noticed that the man was getting fat. He grew stouter with each day. The scientific men shook their heads and theorized. They limited the man at his meals, but still his girth increased and he swelled prodigiously under his shirt.

The sailors grinned. They knew. And when the scientific men set a watch on the man they knew. They saw him slouch for'ard after breakfast, and, like a mendicant, with outstretched palm, accost a sailor. The sailor grinned and passed him a fragment of sea biscuit. He clutched it avariciously, looked at it as a miser looks at gold, and thrust it into his shirt bosom. Similar were the donations from other grinning sailors.

The scientific men were discreet. They let him alone. But they

privily examined his bunk. It was lined with hardtack; the mattress was
stuffed with hardtack; every nook and cranny was filled with hardtack.
Yet he was sane. He was taking precautions against another possible
famine—that was all. He would recover from it, the scientific men
said; and he did, ere the *Bedford's* anchor rumbled down in San
Francisco Bay.

WAR GAMES

Keith Miles

War dominated the life of Terry Heggotty from the very start. On the night that he was born behind thick, black curtains in an upstairs room, a stray German bomb fell on the house next door and brought it crashing to the ground. The Heggotty dwelling was shaken to its foundations and all its windows were blown out by the blast. Falling plaster from walls and ceiling made the job of the midwife more difficult and the terrified young mother screamed when the electric light bulb exploded above her head. But the baby was delivered safely and came into the world with an amazing eagerness.

'It's a boy, Mrs Heggotty.'

'What?' The mother was distraught with fear.

'It's a boy. A fine, healthy boy.'

The midwife did not have to administer the traditional slap of the baby's bare rump. Right on cue, Terry Heggotty yelled his first welcome to a war-torn city.

'It's a boy,' smiled his mother, dopily, and then she drifted off to sleep.

The air raid was now over and anxious voices could be heard outside as wardens assessed the damage to the house next door. There was a harsh grating noise as shovels began to dig the neighbours out of their shelter. Terry seemed almost to understand what had happened and he added his own cries of defiance at the bombers now heading back towards the Channel.

Photographers came the next morning and the bombed house was given stark fame on the front page of the *South Wales Echo*. The paper also carried a photograph of a tiny child, scarcely twenty-four hours old, wrapped in a blanket but waving his infant fist at the camera. The caption was to be prophetic—MIRACULOUS ESCAPE.

Throughout that year enemy aircraft continued to oppress the people of Cardiff and to send them, at periodic intervals, scuttling to their cellars or their air raid shelters. The main target for the bomber squadrons was the Dowlais, the huge steelworks which stood on East Moors and which was working at full stretch to help the British war effort. Since the Dowlais was less than a mile from Terry's house, his ears grew accustomed very quickly to the menacing drone of German aircraft and to the screech of the sirens.

'Let me take him, Ann.'

'I can manage, Dad.' She was bundling the child into his crib before lifting it up and rushing out of the house.

'Give it to me. It's too heavy for you.'

Tom Heggotty was her father-in-law, a strong, kind, wiry little man who was doing all that he could to help the young mother through testing times. He reached for the crib but his daughter-in-law would not surrender it. As the sirens reached a more strident and insistent note, she hurried down the path of the small garden until she got to the steps at the top of the shelter. Black sky suddenly lit up with dramatic effect as bombs scored marginal hits nearby. Ann was so startled that she missed her footing and pitched head first down the steps onto the hard stone floor. She was knocked senseless at once and the crib almost split in two with the impact.

'Dear God!' cried Tom, going first to the baby.

But Terry Heggotty was in no need of help. As the crib had struck the floor, he had been catapulted clear to make a soft landing on an old carpet that had been put down in one corner. The boy was excited but not alarmed by what had happened and he lay there gurgling happily, kicking his legs in the air. Had he been thrown another six inches further, his head would have been smashed against

the damp red brick. It was another miraculous escape and his grandfather could not believe it.

'Come here, boy!'

He hugged the child to his chest then remembered the inert
woman behind him. Terry looked on with a kind of amused curiosity
as his grandfather tried to revive his mother. Her first words,
inevitably, showed concern for the baby.

'Where's Terry? How's Terry?'

'He's fine, girl. It'll take more than a nose-dive down a few steps
to upset our Terry. He's fine.'

The months passed and both war and child grew older together.
Terry learned to speak and found that he liked the sound of words
such as 'gun', 'bomb', 'tank', and 'sub'. As soon as his tongue would
let him, he talked about soldiers and hand-grenades and the barrage
balloon in nearby Splott Park. By the time he had reached his second
birthday, he was quite seasoned in the vocabulary of battle and was
already playing his own uncertain war games in the street.

The pattern of the war had changed now and the blitz was a
thing of the past. With the allied forces on the offensive, there was
little sign of large bomber squadrons over Cardiff and the citizens
were enjoying better nights. There was still a kind of suppressed
panic in people's faces but there was a feeling that the real crisis
on the home front had been weathered and that there would not be
many more nasty accidents on the steps of air raid shelters. Newspapers
tried to keep morale high by praising every advance by the Allies
and by playing down the losses that had been sustained. Wirelesses all
over the nation offered crackling reassurances with their daily
propaganda.

Like many other Cardiffians, Tom Heggotty put his faith in the skill
of the American soldier.

'The Yanks'll show 'em!'

'Gor anythin' for me, Grandad?'

'You watch, son. Ole Jerry won't know what hit him. Just wait till
the Yanks really get going.'

'Wor did they give you today?'

While the old man was expecting deliverance at the hands of the
Americans, the boy was ready to settle for a good deal less. His

grandfather was a docker and he often came home from work with proof of the generosity of American sailors. That very morning, indeed, while helping to unload a US cargo vessel in the Alexandra Dock, Tom had been given three packets of chewing gum by friendly crew members. In a city that suffered the horrors of sweets rationing, chewing gum was like gold dust.

'Thanks, Grandad! Thass great!'

'The Yanks always give something.'

'Don't chew that stuff now, Terry,' warned his mother, uselessly, as the first piece of gum was slipped into his mouth. 'It'll put you off your tea.'

The boy's jaws moved rhythmically and he turned his attention to higher things. As always, war obsessed him.

'Do the Yanks kill lots of Germans?'

'Oh yes, Terry,' grinned Tom. 'They eat 'em for breakfast.'

'Tell me, Grandad.'

The old man spoke with passion on the subject and his grandson's imagination was fired. The lad was still well short of his fourth birthday yet he was already committed to the idea of one day joining the US army so that he could lead a battalion of gum-chewing heroes to some decisive victory.

Ann Heggotty was not at all happy at the way that her son talked about the war all the time but she could do nothing to stop it. A weak and wasted woman, she needed all her strength simply to get through those pinched days. Tom kept advising her to go to the doctor's for a tonic of some sorts, but she could not afford it so she managed without. She just hoped that she would feel better soon. With her husband abroad with the army, she felt that she had to press on and bring up the child as best she could. Even if he presented special problems.

'Where is he, Dad?' Her voice was anxious.

'I thought he was with you in the scullery, Ann.'

'I thought he was with you.'

'No, I haven't seen him since he went out the garden.'

It was a Sunday afternoon and a boy of three had vanished into thin air. They searched the house from top to bottom but there was no trace of him. Terry was in the habit of locking himself into some of the cupboards in order to effect an escape from them but a search of these yielded no results either. Worry became fear and fear turned to hysteria. Ann was trembling.

'Where can he be, Dad? Where on earth can he be?'

'Take it easy, woman. He'll turn up.'

'But *where*?'

'Let's take a look in the street.'

As they opened the front door and stepped out onto the pavement, they were given an immediate clue as to the whereabouts of Terry Heggotty. A cluster of people stood there, staring up at something with helpless amazement. Ann followed the direction of their gaze, then almost fainted when she saw him. Terry was in the bombed house. He had somehow clambered over the garden wall, made his way up the remains of the staircase next door, crawled on past the exposed peeling wallpaper, and climbed up the chimney breast by means of some jagged footholds. He was now clinging to the chimney itself, twenty-five feet above the ground.

'Don't move,' gulped Tom. 'For heaven's sake, don't move.'

'Hello, Grandad,' called the boy, unruffled.

'Stay there,' urged his grandfather, then he despatched one of the bystanders to fetch a ladder.

'It's a job for the Fire Brigade,' opined one woman.

'Or an ambulance,' decided her morbid friend.

Ann was speechless with terror. Her son had only to release his grasp and he would fall to certain death amid the rubble below. There seemed no way that he could escape. What made it more unbearable was the fact that Terry was treating the whole thing as some sort of game. He kept saying something about being an American soldier escaping from a concentration camp.

The ladder was brought and Tom propped it gingerly up against the other side of the chimney, vaguely hoping that he could climb to the top and somehow reach round to grasp the boy. He began to ascend the rings, calling out softly to his grandson.

'Stay right where you are. I'm coming. Stay right there.'

The audience down below had almost trebled in size and it included many of Terry's friends. They were enormously impressed and yelled out words of encouragement before being silenced by grim adults. Terry responded to all this with a wave and his mother felt faint again.

'No! Don't budge from there!' ordered his grandfather.

'Hang on, Terry,' she breathed.

'I'm nearly there,' promised Tom, reaching what had once been a slate roof. 'I'll get you down.'

Terry Heggotty looked quite offended by the suggestion. He did not need any assistance. It was an insult even to suggest it. He was a highly trained member of the US Armed Forces and he knew how to cope with any emergency. He would prove it.

'No! Don't budge from there!' ordered his grandfather.

'Terry!' shrieked his mother.

But the boy ignored them both. With a reckless disregard of his safety, he started to feel his way along the chimney until he found a proper purchase for his feet. Then he lowered himself inch by inch down the vestigial chimney breast, dislodging a half-brick and a lot of dust as he did so.

'He'll fall,' noted the morbid woman.

'Go on, Terry,' laughed a friend in his exhilaration.

'Stop him, someone,' gasped the hapless mother.

Terry kept on coming and another brick fell to its doom. It did not disturb him in the least and his progress, though slow, continued. For a moment it almost looked as if he would gain the first floor of the house without any setback. Then his foot slipped. In a flash he fell from his precarious position on a brick face and landed on the rotting remains of a floor joist that was jutting out at right angles to the wall. The joist sagged, then gave way, but not before it had broken the first part of his fall. Terry was now sent hurtling down on to a pile of bricks in what had once been the living room of the house. A dozen hands came up to help him up but he shrugged them away and stood up with a grin. He was bruised and filthy but otherwise unhurt.

'Wor you doin' up there, Grandad?' he asked, waving up at the old man on the ladder. 'I can ger down easy, see?'

Ann Heggotty was not sure whether to embrace or scold him and so she did both at the same time. The neighbours discussed what they had seen and shook their heads in astonishment. It was his third miraculous escape. Clearly, Terry Heggotty led a charmed life.

The legend of Terry grew quickly in that area of the city and he became something of a celebrity. His friends all insisted on playing games that involved escapes and each time he managed to get away. He was tied up, locked away, even rolled up in a tarpaulin but nothing could hold Terry Heggotty. He celebrated his fifth birthday by tempting fate once more. Before the stunned gaze of his family and friends, he threw a stone at the baker's horse, causing the animal to bolt forward. As it headed straight for him, he threw himself to the ground so that both hooves and wheels passed over him without touching him. The applause he drew from his admirers more than made up for the clout his was given by the baker.

'Thar was fantastic, Terry.' It was his best friend, Glyn Griffiths.

'You've seen nothin' yet.'

'A wild 'orse and you escapes. Fantastic!'

'I can escape from anythin'!' boasted the adventurer.

'Yeah, I know,' conceded Glyn, eyes glowing with pride. 'I know.'

The war came to an end and a pall seemed to lift from the city. Cardiff had been a drab, beleaguered city of old men, dark-eyed women and confused children. Suddenly it was fully alive again, bedecked with flags and bunting and all the paraphernalia of victory. Large messages of welcome were painted on the walls and streets and families who had not seen a father for five years all gathered at the railway station for the first batch of returning soldiers.

'My Dad was a Desert Rat,' said Glyn, knowledgeably, as he was jostled by the crowd.

'Thass nor as good as my Dad,' countered Terry. 'My Dad escaped from 'itler's gas chambers.'

The boys, like hundreds of others present on that occasion, turned ordinary men into conquering heroes and were ready to worship them by the time the train finally arrived. Reunions were tearful and ecstatic and the whole platform seemed to be swarming with khaki. One by one families drifted away to homes that now had fathers.

'Where's *my* Dad?' asked Terry.

'Maybe he wasn't on this train,' suggested his grandfather.

'He should have been,' reminded Ann. 'Eddie's in the same regiment as Ron Griffiths. And Ron was on the train.'

'Yeah. I saw Glyn's Dad. He was no Desert Rat. *My* Dad's better than Glyn's Dad. My Dad is a master of escape.' Certainty deserted him and he became a lost and frightened child. 'Where is he, Mam?'

'Uh, would it be Mrs Heggotty, by any chance?'

The man was wearing the uniform of a lieutenant and he seemed to have some information about Corporal Edward Heggotty. He broke the news to a stricken wife and a numb father in the privacy of the Station Master's office. Terry was left outside in the care of a uniformed sergeant. It transpired that Eddie Heggotty was a casualty of peacetime. After surviving five years of war, he had returned to his native soil only to be killed in an unfortunate accident in the docks at Dover. The shunting had not been scheduled to take place when it did. It was a source of regret to all concerned that there had been no time to contact the family sooner.

Tom Heggotty, musing on the irony of it all, took the grieving widow home. One arm stayed around the shoulders of a puzzled boy. Unlike his son, Eddie Heggotty did not bear a charmed life.

★　　★　　★　　★

'Show 'im your gun, Dad.'

'Terry's seen it twice,' smiled Ron Griffiths, indulgently.

'Aw go on, Dad,' insisted Glyn. 'Lerrim see it again.'

'Please,' added Terry.

'All right.' The demobbed soldier took the gun out from his kit bag. It was a Luger pistol, filched from the belt of a dead German. 'Here, Terry.'

The boy handled the weapon with a fond care, raised it and disposed of ten more Germans with pin-point accuracy. Glyn Griffiths was a true friend. Since Terry had no father, Glyn was keen to share his own with him. Terry was touched by this and yet he felt somehow that he was better off than Glyn. Ron Griffiths could never compare as a father with the figure of Eddie Heggotty. Terry's imagination provided him with a paragon. A boy who had been told nothing about a crushed body beneath a railway wagon devised a story about a thrilling escape bid from the very heart of Hitler's empire. His father, leader of that daring band, had let the others get away first before being shot to death.

'My Dad was one of the best escapers of the war.'

'I knows, Terry.' Glyn believed his friend implicitly.

'He gor away from Rommel when he was captured in the desert.'

'Cor!'

'He always gor away in the end.'

'They should have given him the VC.' Glyn's tone was reverential.
'They did,' bragged Terry, until hard fact caused him to modify
the lie. 'Well—almost.'

It was curious. With a real father at home, Glyn Griffiths grew
into a shy, nervous boy who could never shake off the hold which his
friend had over him. Terry, on the other hand, became self-confident
to the point of arrogance and was much bigger and sturdier than the
spindly Glyn. Their reliance on each other was total. Glyn needed
someone to look up to and idolize, while Terry required someone
who would offer complete obedience. Other boys might join in their
games but it was always the friendship between these two that was
paramount.

The war informed all that Terry Heggotty did. Every game had to
have an element of escape in it and he always had to emerge as the
hero. Glyn was dragged into all kinds of dangers so that his friend could
prove his superiority. He was terrified at some of the risks he was
called upon to take but he was even more afraid of disobeying his
master. Years passed; the games became more and more sophisticated;
Terry yearned for greater challenges.

'You carn, Terry!' For once, Glyn was opposing a plan.

'*Who* carn!' Defiance made his face shine.

'Worrabout the police, like?'

'They'll never catch us.'

'They'd catch me,' admitted the smaller boy, miserably. '*You'd* ger
away with it. I wouldn't.'

'Chicken!'

'Please, Ter.'

'Chicken!'

Glyn Griffiths eventually bowed to the pressure and went along
with the plan. It made his mind cloud over. Terry had announced that
the National Museum of Wales, a superb, neo-Classical building of
white stone in the civic centre, was the headquarters of the Nazi regime.
Two prisoners had to be held there before finding their way back to
freedom under the cover of darkness. All that Glyn could think about
were the hazards. The Museum was full of hawk-eyed little men in
uniform and it only made it worse when he was told that these
attendants were really members of the Gestapo. Full of dread, he went

into the building with his friend. He saw none of the thousands of exhibits that they passed.

'Less go 'ome, Ter.'

'We gorru *escape.*'

Glyn could do nothing but follow orders and these—he should have had more faith—were carefully designed to achieve a certain objective. Shortly before closing time, the boys slipped into one of the lavatories and hid there until the attendants had made their rounds. When the Museum was completely locked and guarded by its hyper-sensitive alarm system, the escape was put into operation. It involved a journey through a ventilation duct, a balancing act along the coping on a part of the roof and a perilous descent down a drainpipe.

'We done it, Ter,' laughed Glyn, shaking with relief. 'We done it.'

'Dead easy.'

The ten-year-old boy had brought off his greatest feat yet.

Glyn's dependence on his friend was now more complete than ever and it worried his parents. There was a manic quality about Terry Heggotty that they distrusted. Glyn did not heed their warnings, however, and the friendship intensified. It excited a lot of envy among other boys and, inevitably, a measure of contempt.

'Liar!'

'We did, Jacko. 'oness!' Glyn turned to his friend. 'Tell 'em, Ter.'

'We did,' shrugged Terry.

'Liar!'

Jacko Armstrong was a tall, sneering boy with a hare-lip. He was two years older than Terry and could not cope with the idea that the latter was in some way braver and better. Jacko's companion, Derek Evans, was equally sceptical when he heard the story about the escape from the Gestapo at the National Museum of Wales. Argument led to blows and blows led to a challenge. Terry was not big enough to fight and beat the two of them but he did know a way to demonstrate his superiority. It involved yet another escape.

'Then we all meets 'ere and tells where we been. Okay?'

'Okay,' accepted Jacko.

'Suits me,' agreed Derek.

'Terry will win,' Glyn piped up, and he collected a reflex cuff from Jacko.

Terry's game was simple. Each of the four boys was a prisoner inside some kind of stockade. His task was to warn his army colleagues by displaying a flag—they each took a scarf—at the highest point they could reach. The boy whose flag fluttered the highest and who had taken the most risks to put it there would be deemed to be the champion. All four of them set out to become the master escaper.

Jacko Armstrong knew at once where he would go. After cycling to Splott Park, he shinned up the ironwork of the bandstand and tied his flag to the ornate pinnacle. Nobody would get higher than that. Derek Evans opted for a set of rugby posts and climbed almost to the top of one of the uprights before leaving his mark. Glyn Griffiths could not compete with either of these. Without the support and encouragement of Terry, he lost all confidence and simply climbed up the nearest lamp post. His scarf would earn the sniggers of Jacko and Derek but he did not mind. He knew that Terry would be supreme.

'Useless!'

'Oh. S'all I could think of, Ter.'

'Flippin' lamp post!' Terry was disgusted by Glyn's lack of courage. 'Follow me. I'll show you.'

With his audience trotting at his heels, Terry set off to show the world and two sneering older boys his true mettle. They went over Beresford Road Bridge and on down to the Royal Oak Hotel. Only when they swung into Newport Road and quickened their pace did Glyn have the slightest idea where they might be going. When he was at length confronted with the enormity of it all, he gaped. Terry, as ever, had set himself something very special.

'Be careful, Ter!'

'Shurrup!'

'But all them volts.'

Terry dismissed his friend's qualms with a wave. He was a boy with a charmed life and nothing could hurt him. After glancing around to make sure that nobody could see him, he padded through the long grass and tackled the first stage of his climb. Thick iron railings stood eight feet out of the ground but he was up and over them in seconds. Without pausing he ran to the second stage of his climb, drawing a gasp of pain from Glyn. The pylon was a tower of metal surmounted by twisted cables that were humming with evil power. Terry Heggotty was going to thread his way past the cables so that he could tie his scarf to the very apex of the pylon. It was an act that would attest his supremacy once and for all and humble two older lads.

'Steady, Ter,' murmured Glyn, watching him rise higher and higher.

A wave from his friend made Glyn feel much better. Terry could and would do it. He was being disloyal in fearing that there could be any slip. A boy who could escape German bombs, a fall down the steps of an air raid shelter and a drop onto a pile of rubble in Railway Street could certainly scale a pylon in the grounds of the power station.

'Go on, Ter. You can do it.'

Glyn began to laugh with pride. Terry had outwitted the Gestapo at the Museum and pulled off dozens of similar escapes. This latest feat was simplicity itself to a person of his rare talents.

'Show 'em, Terry. Show 'em.'

His laughter became almost hysterical as he imagined the looks on the faces of the others when they learned what had happened. Then the laughter stopped. Glyn froze. High above him, moving with the authority and bravery of one who knows exactly what he wants to do in a testing situation, Terry Heggotty had drawn level with the cables. Assured that nothing could harm him, he brushed against one of them as he went past and there was an ominous flash.

'No, Terry! Don't!'

Glyn's warning came too late. The body fell to the ground with a thud and lay there, stiff and tormented.

It was a long time before Glyn could move, but he knew instinctively what he had to do. He had to follow Terry's lead just once more. It took effort and concentration and nerve, but he was spurred on by the memory of a friendship. Fifteen minutes later, Terry's scarf was flying at the very top of the pylon.

No one had witnessed the tragedy. No one was there to see Glyn's slow and painful descent. But as the boy, shaking violently, reached the ground again and bent to take a last look at the anguished face of his friend, he was dimly aware that this had been their greatest escape. He had been released from the tyranny of his own fears—and Terry had escaped forever from war games and all that they had meant.

HOW DO I LOVE THEE?

Janet Sachs

How do I love thee? Let me count the ways.
I love thee to the depth and breadth and height
My soul can reach . . .
I love thee freely, as men strive for Right;
I love thee purely, as they turn from Praise.
I love thee with a passion put to use
In my old griefs, and with my childhood's faith.
. . . I love thee with the breath,
Smiles, tears, of all my life—and if God choose,
I shall but love thee better after death.

This great avowal of love is one of the most beautiful in the English language. It was written by Elizabeth Barrett whose love for the poet Robert Browning could not have been more bravely expressed than in this her most famous sonnet.

No less beautiful is their love story—a story of passion, tenderness and the utmost devotion under the most trying of circumstances. Theirs is a story in which two poets fall in love long after both had reconciled themselves to a life without love, a story of the awakening of love; a fairy tale of 'Sleeping Beauty' come true. For who could have imagined that Elizabeth, an invalid suffering from consumption, unwilling to move from her dark, airless, high-up room, would be discovered by a handsome younger man—a poet too—who would fall deeply in love with her and bring her out into the light and warmth again? Robert, in fact, restored her to life, when she had resigned herself to death.

How could they have met, when Elizabeth allowed very few people to visit and particularly shunned strangers? And why did Browning, who vowed he had made up his mind to 'the impossibility of loving any woman', fall so passionately for a woman older than himself and confined to a sick bed? Their romance seems like a Victorian novel of thwarted love, but it was lived and breathed for almost two years before they were married.

Who was the sleeping princess, Elizabeth Barrett? And how did she come to be shut up in her dark impenetrable tower? At the time of her meeting with Robert, she was a well-known and greatly admired poetess, certainly more famous than her poet-suitor. She was the eldest of a family of eleven children, whose father's wealth came from plantations in Jamaica. From the age of twelve, she had had a classical education, studying Greek, Latin and French with her brother, Edward (affectionately known as 'Bro'). She had begun reading at the age four and by twelve was enjoying the philosophers, Hume and Locke. She was also composing poems. Her verse was first published anonymously in the *New Monthly Magazine* in 1821 when the author was only fifteen.

The Barrett family lived on a lovely estate in Herefordshire called Hope End. Elizabeth's childhood was a happy and, surprisingly enough, a healthy one. But as well as being highly gifted, she was extraordinarily sensitive and idealistic. She set herself very high standards and her imperfections coupled with her hypersensitivity threw her into fits of depression and self-pity, which were exaggerated by the tyranny of her father and her own illness.

Elizabeth first became ill in 1821. Her sisters seemed to suffer the same kind of attack in the same year, but much less severely. All the girls recovered, but Elizabeth had further and longer-lasting attacks for the rest of her life. She at first believed the illness to be the result of an injury to her spine, but it seems clear later on that in fact she was suffering from tuberculosis.

Elizabeth loved her father, but found his harshness difficult to deal with. He was a man of very strict religious Nonconformist principles which tempered every aspect of his life, particularly in the absolute obedience he demanded of his children. Elizabeth wrote, 'The principle of passive filial obedience is held—drawn (and quartered) from Scripture. He sees the law and gospel on his side.' He was strongly convinced of the correctness of his views on children's behaviour and would brook no argument. In any case he was not a man to discuss things with anyone, not even his wife who was rarely informed of her husband's plans for the family. And yet he was not without humour, for Elizabeth wrote of 'his elastic spirit and merry laugh.'

He was possessive of his children to such an extent that he could not tolerate their falling in love and getting married. In the end, Elizabeth had to rebel against him, if she was to be happy with Robert Browning. (Much later, her brother, Alfred, was to do the same.) Perhaps it was worse for Elizabeth as her father believed her to be 'the purest woman he ever knew'. The others had given cause for offence. Henrietta (who Elizabeth described as the sister who liked polkas!) was suspected of an "attachment" and, in horror, Elizabeth recalled what happened:

'I hear how her knees were made to ring upon the floor, now! She was carried out of the room in strong hysterics, and I, who rose up to follow her, though I was quite well at that time and suffered only by sympathy, fell flat on my face in a fainting fit.'

Mr Barrett obviously terrified his children. This fear affected them in different ways—one of the younger boys had a speech impediment, Arabel turned to religion and never married, looking after her father until his death. With Elizabeth fear preyed on her nervous disposition and made recovery difficult. She came to use her illness as a protective cloak: all the conflict she felt in the face of her father's stern will she must have suppressed, believing she was too ill to fight him anyway. The death of Mrs Barrett, when Elizabeth was 22 and, soon afterwards, financial problems on the estates caused the widower to draw into himself, never showing a flicker of emotion to the world, becoming more unbending and remote.

The Barretts moved from Herefordshire to Sidmouth and there Elizabeth's health improved immensely. But after three years they moved to London to be nearer Mr Barrett's business, and soon afterwards took up the address Elizabeth made famous: 50 Wimpole Street.

In London, Elizabeth became a little more adventurous in going out to meet her literary peers. But going out was a trial for her. She describes meeting the poet Wordsworth: 'I trembled both in my soul and body. But he was very kind, and sat near me and talked to me as long as he was in the room.' It was during this period that she began to be recognized as a literary figure. In 1835 she published her first volume of poetry under her own name rather than anonymously, and was acclaimed as one of the most promising of a new generation of poets.

Unfortunately a few months later, Elizabeth's health deteriorated to such a degree that her doctor strongly advised her moving to sunnier climes. Reluctantly Mr Barrett arranged for Elizabeth to go to Torquay in Devon, accompanied by her favourite brother, Bro, and other members of the family. When she arrived in Torquay she wrote to a friend that she 'felt grief in the air' but there was no way of her anticipating what tragedy was to befall her in the warm clean air of that seaside resort.

At first Elizabeth seemed to improve for she went out boating every day. But then she suffered a relapse and the boating had to stop. Her doctor prescribed opium to calm her and she spent all her time in her sick room until, when she was well enough to come downstairs again, she feared going among people once more. She wrote to her sister Arabel, 'I did most emphatically abominate . . . going downstairs yesterday. The change from a four-month-long imprisonment, where from habitude I had grown to like the air and the silence, was quite sure to be felt unpleasantly . . .' Her desire for the solitude of her sick room and the shunning of company—even those close to her—had now become a habit.

The first of the blows dealt her in Torquay came with the death of her young doctor. She became seriously ill. Six months later she was sufficiently recovered to resume a more active life, but the news of her brother Sam's death in Jamaica sent her back to the sick room. But the tragedy that was to set the seal on her confined existence took place three months later.

Her brother Bro had always been closest to Elizabeth. When her father ordered him back to Wimpole Street, Elizabeth pleaded for him to stay with her in Torquay, and there he stayed. He became involved with a lady whom he wanted to marry and in an attempt to rid him of financial dependence on their father, Elizabeth wanted to make over part of her income to Bro. This was greeted by a bitter tirade from the tyrannical Mr Barrett. In the midst of this family dissension, tragedy struck. Bro went boating and was caught up in a storm and his boat capsized. For three days Elizabeth and her sisters waited for news of him, but when his body was finally washed up on shore Elizabeth had already succumbed to the most serious of her illnesses. She had fits of delirium during which she saw visions of 'long dark spectral trains' and 'staring infantine faces'. She could not think or concentrate, neither could she find relief in tears, her grief was so deep. She longed for death. In some strange way she believed herself responsible for his death as he had remained in Torquay on her account. She blamed herself for giving into her own desires and decided that she should henceforth not wish anything but submit to what others thought was best.

When she was well enough to travel, she left Torquay—a name which along with Bro she never mentioned again—and started her long, lonely life in her dark room. Her only constant companion was her little spaniel, Flush, which her friend, Miss Mitford, had sent for her company when Elizabeth was in Torquay. She wrote to a friend, 'My castle-building is at end! A great change has passed both upon my inward and outward life . . . One stroke ended my youth.' She had loved Bro 'best in the world beyond comparison and rivalship'. From that time until Robert Browning entered her life, she began striving to love her father best of all. He had blamed her once for entreating him to let Bro stay in Torquay. Instead he spoke to her 'kindly and gently' and visited her every evening to pray with her and she anticipated seeing him with delight. Apart from the occasional visits of two other close friends and her family, Elizabeth led an isolated life. She seldom ventured from her room and dedicated herself to correspondence and her poetry. 'All the life and strength which are in me, seem to have passed into my poetry,' she wrote.

Thus the scene was set for the arrival of the prince. But what kind of a man is it who casts himself in the role of 'awakening' such a princess? By the time Robert Browning met Elizabeth, he had never been in love (although he was already 33) and was strongly inclined to bachelorhood. This was not helped by dependence on his father for an income.

His life up to that point had been happy enough. His childhood had been spent pleasantly under the protection of his loving parents and he was particularly close to his mother. By 24 his poetry had been acclaimed by a small group of esteemed literary figures including Wordsworth, who toasted his health on one occasion. He had travelled to Russia and twice to Italy. He had flirted, although not very successfully, with the theatre. A society lady described him as 'slim and dark, and very handsome; and—may I hint it—just a trifle of a dandy, addicted to lemon-coloured kid gloves and such things . . . But full of ambition, eager for success, eager for fame . . .' In short, he was gregarious and full of life and energy, the opposite of Elizabeth.

He was also a great admirer of the poetry of Elizabeth Barrett. And thus he came to write her a letter dated 10 January 1845: 'I love your verses with all my heart, dear Miss Barrett—and this is no off-hand complimentary letter that I shall write.'

Miss Barrett was astounded that a poet whose genius she herself had admired for many years should write so encouraging a letter, and replied in kind. Thus their correspondence began.

Elizabeth in her reply to Browning asked that he 'tell me of such fault as rise to the surface and strike you as important in my poems'. And at a later date Browning was to write in appreciation of her understanding response to his work, 'You do not understand what a new feeling it is for me to have someone who is to like my verses or I shall not ever like them after!'

It was not surprising that a strong friendship began immediately. Their sympathetic appreciation and understanding of each other's poetry forged a bond—and a strong one it would prove to be.

And as if this alone was not enough, Elizabeth and Robert shared similar religious beliefs and a view of the affairs of the world that embraced the particular brand of liberalism peculiar to the Victorians. Also Elizabeth looked forward to learning from her new friend about all those aspects of life which her seclusion prevented her from experiencing—literary acquaintances, the theatre, painting and music (Browning played the piano and organ).

Before long Robert was requesting permission to come and see her. Elizabeth demurred. In fact she longed to meet him, but was afraid that he would be disappointed in her. He insisted as gently as he could and finally, several letters later, she agreed. Her anxiety however prompted her to warn him that he had seen the best of her already—in her poetry: 'I have lived most and been most happy in it, and so it has all my colours; the rest of me is nothing but a root, fit for the ground and the dark.'

Robert was not deterred and Tuesday, 20 May 1845, was arranged for their meeting. Poor Elizabeth was so nervous that at the last minute she changed the time from two to three o'clock. But she need not have worried. Browning stayed one-and-a-half hours, and later that evening wrote her the most concerned note hoping that he had not tried her or disturbed her by speaking too loud and that he had not stayed too long. Her frailty and sensitivity must have touched him. She had been described earlier by Miss Mitford, one of her close friends, as 'of a slight, delicate figure, with a shower of dark curls falling on either side of a most expressive face, large tender eyes fringed by dark eyelashes', and such a description may well have accorded with Browning's idea of her.

Elizabeth was strangely haunted by his presence after his departure. The next day she remarked to her father, 'It is most extraordinary how the idea of Mr Browning does beset me—I suppose it is not being used to seeing strangers, in some degrees—but it haunts me . . . it is a persecution.' And to Miss Mitford she commented that she 'liked him much. Younger looking that I had expected . . . with natural and not ungraceful manners.' But she could not understand why Browning should be attracted to her and imagined that it was 'a mere poet's fancy . . . an illusion of a confusion between the woman and the poetry.'

Browning was a little too hasty. Four days after this meeting he wrote her a wild love letter. Elizabeth was startled into replying that he was not to say such things again 'but *forget at once*, and *for ever, having said at all*, (otherwise) *I must not . . . I will not see you again.*'

Like most men whose pride has been wounded, Browning back-pedalled fast and rather ungallantly declared that she had misunderstood him. Elizabeth apologized, and Browning then proceeded to woo her at a slower, gentler pace.

The effect of his weekly visits and their almost daily correspondence was to cheer and enliven the invalid. At every opportunity Robert encouraged her to go out and enjoy the warmer weather—'Do pray make fresh endeavours to profit by this partial respite of the weather!' Elizabeth was not so keen—sunshine, she said, 'makes my head ache a little, while it comes in at the window, and makes most other people gayer.'

Nonetheless in July she went up Wimpole Street to the gates of Regent's Park, and by September she was making two trips round the inner ring of the park without feeling unduly tired. Her attempts were enthusiastically congratulated by her suitor, who was particularly delighted when she declared to 'living more in the outer life for the last few months than I have done for years before.'

The improvement in Elizabeth's health, in her doctor's opinion, made it possible for her to travel. He recommended her wintering in Pisa with a brother and sister to take care of her. Robert, who had often discussed his love for Italy with her, naturally planned to be there. The whole idea seemed to combine a variety of good things. Over the summer Robert had been cautiously approaching the subject of his love for Elizabeth and on 13 September he dared to write what was uppermost in his mind: 'I *know*, if one may know anything, that to make (my) life yours and increase it by union with yours, would render me *supremely happy*, as I said, and say, and feel.'

Elizabeth's reply reminded him of the barrier that God had put between them—her ill-health. True to the style of fated Victorian romance, she urged him, 'And so if you are wise and would be happy . . . you must leave me—these thoughts of me, I mean . . . But we may be friends always.'

The winter in Pisa had still not been decided upon. While all the brothers and sisters were in favour, Mr Barrett remained resolutely silent, until Elizabeth could no longer endure it. She broached the subject herself, making it quite clear that by remaining in England she would be endangering her health, but that she would stay if he would not give his assent. Her father was angry that she had phrased the question in such a way and replied, as she wrote to Browning, 'I had better do what I liked:—for his part, he washed his hands of me altogether.'

Unfortunately Elizabeth could not go alone to Pisa, and any act of rebellion on her part would involve her sister and brother. This she felt was unfair. Besides which, she wrote to Browning, 'My spirits sink altogether at the thought of leaving England so—'. A few weeks later her brother George 'in great indignation, pressed the question fully; but all was in vain.'

An enormous rift had occurred between Elizabeth and her father. He believed her self-indulgent in pressing to go to Italy. For Elizabeth, the incident and its outcome were a revelation. 'The bitterest "fact" of all is, that I had believed Papa to have loved me more than he obviously does.' Disappointment in her father's love led her to appreciate more the nature of Browning's love. She wrote to him, 'You have touched me more profoundly than I thought even *you* could have touched me— my heart was full when you came here today. Henceforward I am yours for everything but to do you harm.'

At last an understanding had been reached. Browning declared his love once more: 'I love you because I *love* you.' Elizabeth responded to this with, 'The first moment in which I seemed to admit to myself in a flash of lightening the *possibility* of your affection for me being more than dreamwork . . .was *that* when you intimated . . . that you cared for me not for a reason but because you cared for me.'

Elizabeth had been won, but what was to be the next move? Her father would never approve the match. There would be no 'getting over' him, she wrote to Browning—'You might as well think to sweep off a third of the stars of Heaven with the motion of your eyelashes.' Robert did not fully appreciate Mr Barrett's unreasonableness. He wanted to behave like the honourable Victorian gentleman he was and inform Mr Barrett of his intentions. Elizabeth, who knew better, would have none of this. She recalled a conversation held in jest with her sister Arabel. ' "If a prince of Eldorado should come, with a pedigree of lineal descent from some signory in the moon in one hand, and a ticket of good behaviour from the nearest Independent chapel in the other"—?'

' "Why even *then*," said my sister Arabel, "it would not do." '

Browning acquiesced for he didn't want Elizabeth to suffer any retribution for his actions. At the same time he realized that Elizabeth, who was unused to action, was going to find it difficult to act upon her feelings. His anxiety on this count caused him several migraine headaches, but fortunately the winter brought no relapses in Elizabeth's health.

By the beginning of the New Year, Browning was urging her to plan ahead for 'this living without you is too tormenting now'. Poor Browning, however, had to be patient a good deal longer. To his suggestion that they marry and go to live in Italy, she gave a hesitant reply: 'If in the time of fine weather, I am not ill . . . then . . . not now . . . you shall decide, and your decision shall be duty and desire to me.' Robert urged her to keep herself well, to excercise by going up and down the stairs, for he was worried that the winter confinement would weaken her will power, as well as sap her physical strength.

In the midst of spring, Elizabeth bought herself a fashionable bonnet and began to take drives in Regents Park accompanied by Arabel and Flush. Not only that but she began to take walks as well. 'We stopped the carriage and got out and walked, and I put both my feet on the grass . . . which was the strangest feeling . . . and gathered this laburnum for you.' This took place almost a year after the lovers' first meeting, so the improvement in her physical strength was impressive.

One obstacle lying in the path to marriage was the question of money—a problem which Elizabeth had to deal with tactfully as it was on *her* independent income (inherited from her uncle) that they would come to live. 'It is not of the least importance . . .' she said, whether the sixpence we live by, came most from you or from me.' But this was a sore point with Browning, and a month or so later he was urging her to make over her fortune to her brothers and sisters and suggesting that he enter the diplomatic service.

Elizabeth pointed out that her frailty and the nature of her illness made it imperative that they have money to fall back on, and that in any case she wanted him to concentrate on developing his poetic genius. Finally Browning agreed, saying, 'I have only to be thankful that you are not dependent on my exertions—which I could not be sure of—particularly with this uncertain head of mine.' (Elizabeth's income came to £360 per annum, a greater sum than Robert's father earned and a princely sum for Italy, where they planned to live.)

So spring rolled into summer and while Elizabeth became stronger, Robert's headaches increased—not surprisingly. For Elizabeth, though committed to the ideas of marriage and going to Italy, was being dilatory as usual. 'I am going to ask you a question, dearest of mine,' she wrote. 'I want to know whether . . . you see it to be wise and better for me to go to Italy with Miss Bayley . . . leaving other thoughts for another year.' Robert's response was quick. 'Every day that passes before *that day* is one the more of hardly endurable anxiety and irritation, to say the least.'

Browning had informed his parents and sister, Sarianna, of his plans and naturally wanted Elizabeth to meet his family. He suggested that she receive Sarianna, but Elizabeth was anxious that she would be judged not good enough for Browning. Browning then suggested she confide her secret to mutual friends, but once again Elizabeth baulked. So the secrecy remained.

More difficult was trying to avoid arousing the suspicion of Mr Barrett, and in this the sisters, who knew something of the matter, played their part. The situation became more dangerous however, when relatives, the Hedleys, came to stay on the occasion of Arabella Hedley's wedding. Marriage was in the air and Aunt Hedley watched Elizabeth's visitors with interest. 'I have not seen Ba all day,' she said to Mr Barrett, '—and when I went to her room, to my astonishment a gentleman was sitting there.' Arabel said it was only Mr Browning. The aunt was not to be put off. 'And Ba bowed her head as if she meant to signify to me that I was not to come in.' Henrietta quickly brushed her insinuation aside. 'Oh *that* must have been a mistake of yours, perhaps she meant just the contrary.' It seemed however that there was no need to pull the wool over Mr Barrett's eyes—he appeared to see nothing. 'You should have gone in and seen the *poet*,' was all he replied.

The brothers were not so easily fooled. One day in August, Stormie (Charles) asked Arabel outright, 'Is it true that there is an engagement between Mr Browning and Ba?' Taken unawares she managed to reply, 'You had better ask them if you want to know. What nonsense, Storm.' 'Well,' he resumed, 'I'll ask Ba when I go upstairs.' George overheard this conversation with a grave look on his face, but fortunately, Stormie never asked Elizabeth the question.

After this incident Browning suggested visiting her less frequently to avert suspicion. At the same time he wanted to start planning the details of the departure. Would she not rather go by sea than rail, he asked, informing her of the sailing dates of the steamers. In subsequent letters he urged the importance of choosing an early date for travelling. Elizabeth, although vowing she would keep her promise of marriage and leave England 'at any time you choose', would not agree to a day. Long-suffering Browning retired to bed, ill from the strain.

At the same time as he took to his bed, an incident took place which prevented Elizabeth from concentrating on her and Robert's plans for a few days. Flush, her constant companion, was snatched by a band of dog thieves when Elizabeth and Arabel were out shopping. They returned home drearily without the little spaniel while Arabel tried to comfort her sister by saying that Flush could easily be recovered for a ransom of ten pounds at most. Her brother, Henry, made enquiries. The next day one of the thieves came to Wimpole Street to tell them that Flush was safe in Whitechapel and they were going to have a meeting to decide what the ransom would be. Elizabeth wrote 'The worst is poor Flush's fright and suffering,' and then went on to explain to her ailing lover that even though it was wrong to give in to thieves, 'I can't run any risk and bargain and haggle'—a lady in the neighbourhood had had 'her dog's head sent to her in a parcel.'

Mr Taylor, the gang leader, returned that night to ask for six guineas but Mr Barrett refused to allow Henry to pay. When Elizabeth discovered this in the morning, she was extremely upset and tried to persuade Henry to go to Whitechapel with the money. But Henry was afraid of his father and would not. So Elizabeth taking courage in both hands, accompanied by Wilson, her maid, took the cab to Mr Taylor's house. He was not in, but his wife, 'an immense feminine bandit', assured her that her husband was on his way to Wimpole Street. Elizabeth did an about turn and made her way home.

Not long afterwards the thief arrived and while plans to return the dog were in progress, another brother, Alfred, happened to see Mr Taylor in the passage, and angrily called him 'a swindler and a liar and a thief'. Mr Taylor left the house swearing they would never see Flush again.

Elizabeth was distraught. The idea of receiving Flush's poor head in a parcel was becoming closer to reality every minute. Having shouted at Alfred for his tactlessness, she tried to rush out of the house to go and save her pet, but her brothers and sisters prevented her—she was quite mad, and it was dusk already. Finally her brother, Septimus, said he

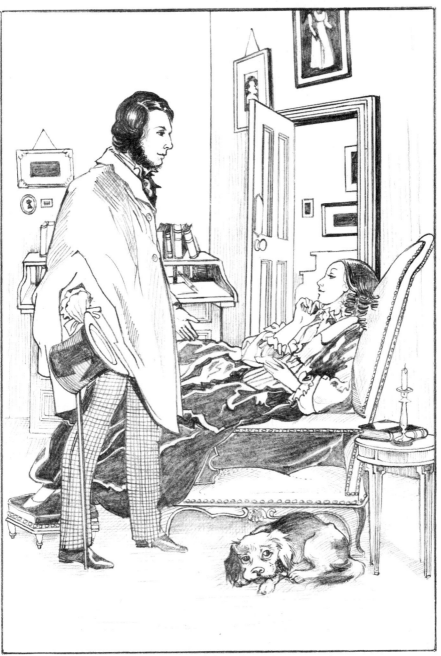

'*We must be married directly and go to Italy.*'

would go. At eight o'clock the little spaniel arrived back home looking much thinner and proceeded to drink three full cups of water.

It was only a few days after Flush's return that a new and serious problem presented itself. Mr Barrett sent George into the country to look for a house to move to while 50 Wimpole Street was cleaned and repaired—and Mr Barrett's authority would allow no questions about which date they were likely to go. When Elizabeth broke the news to Robert his reaction was swift—'We must be *married directly* and go to Italy. I will go for a licence today and we can be married on Saturday.' This happened on a Wednesday.

On Saturday morning, 12 September, Elizabeth and Wilson took a cab to St Marylebone Parish Church, where Browning and his cousin were waiting. The bride arrived looking 'more dead than alive'.

They had agreed that Robert should not visit her after the marriage.

Elizabeth could hardly grasp what had happened. Her everyday existence was continuing as it always had done, she could not wear her wedding ring as tangible proof that she was married. 'I sit in a dream, when left to myself. I cannot believe, or understand,' she admitted to her new husband.

They then took to discussing their marriage announcement in the papers and plans for the journey to Italy. Elizabeth had to complete her hardest task, that of writing to her family. 'I am paralysed when I think of having to write such words as—"Papa I am married; I hope you will not be too displeased."' She decided to ask her brother George to intercede with her father on her behalf. In her last letter to Browning she wrote 'It is dreadful . . . dreadful . . . to have to give pain here by a voluntary act—for the first time in my life.'

On Saturday afternoon under pretence of going for a drive, Elizabeth, Wilson and Flush left 50 Wimpole Street to meet Browning, and then the four of them travelled to Southampton to suffer a 'miserable' all-night passage across the Channel.

Elizabeth and Robert went on to spend fifteen happy years of married life. Unfortunately George did not react to the elopement with sympathy and it was several years before brother and sister were reconciled. It was left to Henrietta to break the news to her father. Mr Barrett threatened to disinherit Elizabeth (a threat which he carried out) and refused ever to see her again.

THE FUGITIVE

Maxwell Gray

The day was hot and fiercely bright. The town was full of life. Gay carriages were bearing ladies in light summer bravery to garden parties, afternoon dances on board ships, and other revels; bands were playing on piers; vessels of every kind, some gay with flags, dotted the Solent and the calm blue harbour; colours had been trooped on the common, troops had marched past the convicts; the sweet chimes of St Thomas' had rung a wedding peal; the great guns had thundered out royal salutes to the royal yacht as she bore the sovereign over to the green Wight—there was such a rush and stir of life as quite bewildered Everard, and made to the sharpest contrast to his grey and dreary prison life. To see these freest of free creatures, the street boys, sauntering or springing at will along the hot streets, or, casting off their dirty rags, flinging themselves into the fresh salt sea and revelling there like young Tritons, or, balanced on rails, criticizing the passing troops, was maddening.

The day grew hotter, but pick and barrow had to be plied without respite, though the sweat poured from hot brows, and one man dropped. Everard saw that it was sunstroke, and not malingering, as the warder was inclined to think, and by his earnest representations got the poor creature proper treatment. The brassy sky grew lurid purple, and heavy growls of thunder came rumbling from the distance;

some large drops of rain fell scantily, and then suddenly the sky opened from horizon to horizon and let down a sheet of vivid flame. Darkness followed, and a roar as of all the artillery at Portsmouth firing and all its magazines exploding at once.

'Now or never,' thought Everard, and, dropping his barrow at the end of his plank, he leaped straight ahead down into a waste patch, over which he sprang to the road. He ran for life and liberty with a speed he did not know himself capable of, straight on, blindly aiming at the shore, tearing off his cap and jacket and flinging them wildly in different directions, as he went through the dark curtain of straight rushing rain.

The warders, bewildered by the awful roar of the thunder, blinded by the fierce, quick dazzle of the lightning and the blackness of the all-concealing rain, did not at first miss him. It was only when he leaped the palisade bounding the road, and showed through the rain curtain a bare-headed, fugitive figure, that the grim guardian caught sight of him. Had he possessed the nerve to walk quietly out through the gate, he might have got off unobserved under cover of the storm.

Quick as thought, the warder, on seeing him, lifted his piece to his shoulder and fired. He was a good marksman, and his face lighted up with satisfaction as he hit his flying quarry, in spite of the bad light and confusing storm.

Everard felt a sharp, hot sting in the thigh, but ran on, his course marked with blood, which the friendly storm quickly washed away. The darkness became intenser, the lightning more blinding, the downrush of rain heavier, and the crashing of the thunder more deafening. Nevertheless, the alarm was given, and the pursuers were soon in full chase.

Down the now deserted highroad dashed the fugitive, every faculty he possessed concentrated on flight. With the blind instinct of the hunted, he rushed at the first turning, through a gate, up some steps, along to the bastion which rose behind the powder magazines. He darted along some pleasant green walk under the massy elms, till he reached the first sentry box, in which stood the sentry, a stalwart Highlander, sheltering from the storm.

Instead of firing on him, as the desperate fugitive expected, the man stepped swiftly aside, and the panting runner, divining his friendly purpose, ran into the box.

The soldier swiftly resumed his station.

The soldier swiftly resumed his station, and stood looking out with an immovable face as before, while the hunted convict, in the darkness in the narrow space at his side, stood face inward, close pressed to the wooden wall, soaked to the skin, and panting in hard gasps that were almost groans, yet sufficiently master of himself to press a wad of folded trouser on the bleeding wound which proved to be only a flesh graze, but which might ruin the friendly Scot by its damning stains on the floor of the box.

'Quiet's the word,' said the hospitable sentry, and nothing more.

Some minutes passed. Everard's breathing became less laboured, and his reflections more agonized; the thunder peals grew less tremendous, while the rain became heavier. The pursuers had lost sight of their prey in the road before he reached the gate, and had been thrown off the scent, while still sending searchers in all directions. Two of these turned up through the gate, and one explored all the nooks and crannies of the crescent-shaped space walled by the bastion which sheltered the powder magazines, while the other examined the path itself, and interrogated the sentry.

'Past the Garrison Chapel, towards High Street; out of my range,' he said coolly; and the pursuer, calling his comrade, flew with him along the bastion, not stopping to enquire of the other sentries. 'Gone away,' observed the Highlander to his quivering guest, who had feared lest his light-coloured dress might betray him behind the sentry, whose plaid and kilt and feather bonnet filled up all of the opening not darkened by his tall figure. 'Off the scent. What next, mate?'

'Heaven knows! I only hope I may not ruin you. If I get off, I will not forget you. My friends are well off, and I am—'

'Henry Everard. Seen you often with your gang—recognized at once.'

'Good heavens!' cried Everard, not seeing his host's handsome face, but feeling a vague stir of memory at his voice; 'who are you?'

'Private Walker, 179th Highlanders. Was Balfour of Christ Church.'

'Balfour? What! come to this? What did we not expect of you?'

'Wear a better coat than yours. Manby rough on you—hard lines. Do anything for you.'

'You always were a good-hearted fellow. And I was innocent,

Balfour; I had not the faintest grudge against the poor fellow. But how did you come to this? You took honours.'

'Governor poor—large family—small allowance at Cambridge—debts. Always liked the service—enlisted—Hussar regiment—jolly life—saw service—full sergeant—time expired. Sent into Reserve—not allowed to re-enlist—name of Smith. Tried civil life—down on my luck again—deserted from Reserve—re-enlisted in Highlander—name of Walker—enlisted fraudulent—liable to imprisonment—foreign service soon—all right. Now for you.'

Everard had to confess that he did not in the least know what to do next, unless he could hide till the darkness rendered his dress unobservable. The moment he was seen he would be recognized anywhere as a convict. Various schemes were revolved between them as rapidly as possible, for it was essential that Everard should leave the sentry box for a better hiding place before the rapid diminishing of the storm should once more open the bastion to observers.

The massive foliage of the elms hard by might have hidden a regiment, and Balfour had observed that the branches attracted no suspicion on the part of the pursuers, and, as the forking of the boughs did not begin till many feet off the ground, and the broad, smooth trunk offered not the smallest foothold, it was impossible for a man to climb into them unassisted.

But the sentry remembered that a stout rope had been flung aside there by some gunners busy cleaning the cannon on the bastion that day. If Everard could find this, and fling it over a bough, he might hoist himself up. If he could not find it, the soldier offered to come and lend him his shoulder—an action that might attract attention even in the darkness of the storm, since that part of the bastion was commanded by many windows, and that would, if discovered, bring certain ruin upon both men.

Everard darted swiftly from the box, and groped about in the wet grass till he found the rope. This, in the still blinding rain, he threw over the lowest stout branch, keeping one end, and fearful lest the other would not descend within reach. After a couple of casts, however, he succeeded in bringing the second end, in which he had fastened a stone, within easy reach, and grasping both, and planting his feet against the broad bole, slippery with wet, managed to struggle up with moderate speed. He was halfway up, and pausing a moment to steady himself and look round, saw to his infinite horror that he was exactly opposite to, and in full view and firing range of, the sentry on the opposite end of the bastion, which was roughly crescent-shaped.

Outlined as he was. and almost stationary against the tree trunk, he presented the easiest target for a moderate range shot. The man was in no hurry for his easy prey, he lifted his musket slowly, while Everard paused, transfixed with horror. The sentry seemed as if waiting for him to rise into a still better position for a shot. Everard slipped down, expecting to hear a ball sing over his head, if not into his body; but there was no report, and he stood irresolute a moment, seeking where to fly.

A signal of warning and haste from Balfour made him once more grasp his rope in desperation, and climb through the peril of the sentry's aim. A flash of lightning showed him his foe standing as before, with his musket planted firmly in front of him; he was supporting himself placidly with both hands clasped upon it, and his head bent slightly down, almost as if he had fallen asleep at his post.

But Everard knew that the most careless sentries do not fall asleep in the process of aiming at fugitive prisoners, and he pressed on till he reached the first fork, where he rested, wondering why no shot had been fired. The fact was, the rain was beating straight into the man's face, and he had much ado to see a yard before him, and had raised his musket merely to see if the breech was properly shielded from the wet. Everard, however, hoisting up his rope, climbed higher into his green fortress, expecting nothing less than to have it soon riddled in all directions by a fusillade from below. To his surprise he heard Balfour's signal of safety, and gladly responded to it; for they had framed a little code of signals before parting.

It was comparative luxury to the weary, wounded man to sit astride a branch, with his back against the trunk, and the foot of the wounded limb supported upon a lower bough, and he gave a deep sigh of relief, and reflected that he was at last, after all those dreary years of bondage, free. Balfour could do nothing till he was off guard, which would happen in another half-hour. Nothing could be done during the next sentry's guard, because it would be impossible to get at him and see how far he could be trusted; but if any subsequent sentry proved manageable, and if Balfour could get a pass for the night, he might bring him some sort of clothing, and then, under favourable circumstances, he might get off. And then?

The storm abated, the last, low mutterings of thunder died away in the distance, the rain ceased, and the evening sun shone out with golden clearness. Some of the long, slanting beams pierced the green roof of his airy prison, and fell hopefully upon the fugitive's face. He heard the sentry's measured tread below, and then the change of guard; the hum of the town, and the noises from the vessels at anchor came, mingled with distant bugle calls, to his lonely tower. The light faded, the sun went down in glory, the gun on the bastion fired the sunset, the parish church chimed half-past eight, the sounds from sea and shore came more distinct on the quieting night air, and he heard the band of a Highland regiment begin its skirl of pipes on the Clarence pier. It was probably Balfour's regiment.

Poor Balfour! He fell to thinking of his unfortunate lot, much as he had to occupy his thoughts with regard to his own immediate safety.

★   ★   ★   ★

The air was chill after sunset. Everard, motionless on his airy perch, bareheaded, and in his shirt sleeves, was wet to the skin, and shivered with a double chill after the heat of his hard labour in the sultry afternoon. His wound ached till he began to fear it might lame him, and his hunger waxed keener as the night deepened and the cold increased. The stars came out and looked at him with their friendly, quieting gaze. He could see the sparkle of lights in the water and in the town; he could make out the lights of the admiral's signal station on his housetop above the dockyard.

Which man-of-war was Keppel's, he wondered, knowing nothing even of the outside world that was so near him. The chimes of the parish church told him the hours, and he knew when the guard would be relieved.

It was a weary night; its minutes lagged by leaden paced. He thought their long procession would never end; and yet there was a strange, delicious enchantment in the feeling that he had at last broken the bars of that iron prison, with its terrible bondage of unending routine and drudgery. The thick foliage of the elm still held the wet, which every passing breath of the night wind shook on the grass below in a miniature shower. The moon rose and wandered in pale majesty across the sweet blue sky—such a free, broad night sky as had not blessed his eyes for years and years; its beams hung his green fortress roof with pearls and trembling diamonds, falling ever and anon to the earth. Sentinel after sentinel came on guard below, but there was no friendly signal from beneath. He had descended to the lowest bough to catch the lightest sound. The watch was passing; the early dawn would shine on the next watch, and, if help did not come before the sunrise, he would have to wait till the following night, wet, starved, suffering as he was. But no; there is the welcome signal at last.

Quickly he gave the answering signal; and, bending down in the darkness, heard the following sentence above the sound of the sentinel's backward and forward steps: 'Sentry blind and deaf—sneak off to right. Catch.'

Something flew up to him in the dark, and, after two misses, he caught it; and then, rising to where a rift in the foliage let in a shaft of rays from the waning moon, unfastened his bundle, which was roughly tied with string.

A battered hat, very large, so that it would hide the close-cropped head; a boatman's thick blue jersey; and a pair of wide trousers, worn and stained, with a belt to fasten them; also some second-hand boots,— such was the simple but sufficient wardrobe which Balfour had purchased with his slender means, and brought him at deadly risk.

Everard was able to discard every rag of the tell-tale prison garb, stamped all over as it was with the broad arrow, and securing the dangerous garments to a branch of the tree, invested himself in the contents of the bundle—an occupation that took so long, owing to the inconvenience of his lofty dressing room, that the eastern sky was brightening and the friendly sentinel's watch almost expired by the time he was ready to descend from his perch, which he did noiselessly and apparently unobserved by the sentry.

Then, slowly and painfully,—for his limbs were cramped and chilled, and his wound ached,—he glided behind the dark boles till he reached the steps, and, descending them, found to his dismay that the gate was locked.

There is almost always some small but vitally important hitch in the best-laid human plans, and the hitch in Balfour's arrangement was that he forgot the nightly locking of the gate leading onto the bastion. He had approached the tree from the other side, passing the sentries, being challenged by them and giving the word in reply.

Everard knew the bastion, and had had many a pleasant stroll there in old days, when stopping with his father when in port, and he knew well that his only course was now to climb the gate, which he could not do without noise, and which was in no case an easy feat, the plain board of which the gate was made being high and the top thickly studded with those dreadful crooked nails, which look like alphabets gone wrong, and do dreadful damage to both hands and clothing.

Fortunately, the moon had set, the sun was not yet risen, and the darkness favoured him—a darkness which every moment threatened to dissipate. He struggled up with as little sound as possible, with set teeth and a beating heart, lacerating his hands cruelly. Then, having gained the top—not without some rents in his scanty clothing— he grasped the nail-studded ridge and sprang down. Alas! not to the ground, for one of the crooked nails caught in the back part of the wide trousers, and, with a rending of cloth and a knocking of his feet against the boards, he found himself arrested midway, and suspended by the waist against the gate, like a mole on a keeper's paling.

Had he been caught in front, he might have raised himself and somehow torn himself free; but being hooked thus in the rear, he was almost helpless, and his slightest effort to free himself brought the heels of his boots knocking loudly against the gate as if to obtain admittance, which was the last thing he wanted. Meantime the minutes flew on, the darkness was breaking fast; before long the sun would rise and disclose him hung thus helplessly on his nail to the earliest passer-by, who would probably be a policeman.

A beautiful faint flush of red rose suddenly shot up over the eastern sky, and the brown shadows lessened around him. He heard footsteps echoing through the dewy stillness, and struggled with blind desperation. The rose red turned deep glowing orange, objects became more and more distinct before him, the street lamps sickened, a soft orange ray shot straight from the sea across the common, through the leaves of the tree shadowing the gate, onto the fugitive's cheek. At the same instant he heard the boom of the sunrise guns; it was day.

The footsteps approached nearer and nearer; on the bastion he heard the change of watch. He felt that all was lost, and yet, in his mental tension, his chief consciousness was of the awful beauty of the dawn, the dewy quiet and freshness brooding over the great town, and—strange contrast!—the grotesque absurdity of his situation. He heard the lively twitter of the birds waking in the trees, and admired the soft radiance of the ruddy beams on the sleeping town; and then something gave way and he found himself full length on the pavement.

The echoing footsteps had as yet brought no figure round the corner, and Everard welcomed the hard salute of the paving stones as the first greeting of freedom, and, quickly picking himself up, he fell into the slow, slouching walks he had observed in tramps, and moved on, adjusting his discoloured garments as best he might. The footsteps proved indeed to be those of a policeman, whose eyes were dazzled with the level sunbeam which he faced, and who gave him a dissatisfied but not suspicious glance and passed on.

Everard drew a deep breath, and limped on, trying to disguise the lameness of the wounded limb, which he feared might betray him, and thrust his torn hands into the pockets of the trousers which had so nearly ruined him. His surprise and joy were great on touching with his left hand a substance which proved to be bread and cheese, which he instantly devoured, and with his right a few pence, and, what moved him to tears of gratitude for Balfour's thankful kindness, a short, brier-wood pipe, well seasoned, and doubtless the good fellow's own, a screw of cheap tobacco and some matches. He had not touched tobacco for nine years.

A drinking fountain supplied him with the draught of water which his fevered throat and parched lips craved; it also enabled him to wash off some of the blood and dirt from his torn hand. And then, dragging his stiff and wounded limb slowly along, and eating his stale bread and cheese in the sweet sunshine, he made his morning orisons in the dewy quiet of the yet unawakened town, and felt a glow of intense gratitude, which increased as the food and water strengthened him, and exercise warmed his chill and stiffened frame.

He was glad to see the houses open one by one, and the streets begin to fill; he thought he should attract less attention among numbers. He passed groups of free labourers, hurrying to the dockyards to work, and it gave him an eerie shudder to think that some of them, whose faces he knew, might recognize him. His terror increased when he saw a light on a workman's face—a face he knew well, for the man had slipped over the side of the dock one morning, and was in imminent danger of being jammed by some floating timber, when Everard had promptly sprung after him, regardless of prison discipline, and held him up, for he could not swim, till a rope was brought, and the two men were hauled out, bruised, but otherwise uninjured.

The man stopped; Everard went straight on, not appearing to see him, and, after a few seconds, to his dismay, heard footsteps running after him. He dared not quicken his pace, lest he should attract attention, but the food he was eating stuck in his throat, and his face paled. His pursuer gained his side, and, seizing his hand, pressed some pence into it, saying, in a low tone, 'Mum's the word, mate! All the ready I've got. Simon Jones, 80 King Street, for help. Better not stop.'

Then he turned and resumed his road, telling his companions something about a chum of his down in his luck, and Everard slouched on with a lightened heart and increased gratitude for the pence. He had now nearly two shillings in his pockets, and when he had lighted Balfour's brierwood, he felt like a king. The last time he handled a coin was when he gave pence to a blind man, sitting by the police station at Oldport, just before his arrest. He bought needle and thread to repair the tremendous fissure in the unlucky garments which had played him so ill a trick, and in two hours' time found himself well clear of the town and suburbs. Presently he found a shed used for sheltering cattle, but now empty. This he entered, and, having with some difficulty drawn the chief rents in his clothes together, washed his wound in a trough placed for some cattle to drink from, and bandaged that and the worst hurts in his hand with the handkerchief in which the bread and cheese was wrapped, lay down on some litter behind a turnip-cutting machine, and in a moment was fast asleep, utterly oblivious of prisons, wounds, and hunger.

A ROYAL ROMANCE

Sarah Tooley

When Queen Victoria announced to her Prime Minister that she had resolved to marry, Lord Melbourne replied, with paternal solicitude: 'Your Majesty will be much more comfortable, for a woman cannot stand alone for any time, in whatever position she may be.'

This was in the autumn of 1839, and the previous six months had probably been to the young Queen the most unhappy which she had ever experienced, owing to the strifes and jealousies of the two great political parties in the country. The atmosphere of reserve in which Her Majesty was compelled to live was very unnatural for a young girl, and oppressive to one of her open, candid disposition. Often she must have longed for the companionship of one with whom she could be herself, unrestricted by regal considerations. The happy change which her marriage wrought in her isolated position is thus expressed by the Queen: 'We must all have trials and vexations; but if one's *home is happy*, then the rest is comparatively nothing . . . My happiness at home, the love of my husband, his kindness, his advice, his support, and his company make up for all.'

There were many suitors for the hand of the fair occupant of the greatest throne in the world, among them the Prince of Orange; and it is a curious coincidence that a former Prince of Orange came a-wooing to the Princess Charlotte. After a period of indecision, that royal lady dismissed her suitor peremptorily, not, however, without going to the window to take a last look at him as he mounted his horse, which caused the ladies-in-waiting to think that the Princess was about to relent; but when, after gazing intently at his retreating figure, clad in a scarlet uniform surmounted by a hat with nodding green plumes, she exclaimed, 'How like a radish he looks!' it was felt that his fate was finally settled. There are not any stories about Queen Victoria either receiving or dismissing suitors, the proposals for her hand being made officially and rejected in the same manner. The one love episode of her life was with her cousin, Prince Albert, second son of the reigning Duke of Saxe-Coburg-Gotha, and all the world knows of its happy fulfilment.

When a small boy, Prince Albert was often promised by his nurse, as a reward for good behaviour, that he should marry his cousin, the Princess Victoria. Such a union had been designed by fond relatives when the children were yet in their cradles, and became the darling hope of Grandmamma of Coburg and Uncle Leopold, and was favoured by the Queen's mother, the Duchess of Kent, though it was by no means popular with King William IV and the royal dukes. A visit was paid by Prince Albert to the Duchess of Kent, at Kensington Palace, in 1836, and he then made a favourable impression upon the Princess Victoria. The cousins rode, sang, played, danced, and walked together, and enjoyed each other's society after the usual manner of a youth and maiden at the impressionable age of seventeen. We have heard of little love tokens exchanged, but it is not generally known that a ring—a small enamel with a tiny diamond in the centre—was given by the Prince to his pretty cousin during this visit. This early gift from her lover has always been worn by the Queen, together with her engagement-ring, a beautiful emerald serpent, above her wedding-ring, which, we believe, has never been taken off since her wedding-day. One of her ladies tells the story that, when a sculptor was modelling Her Majesty's hand, she was in an agony lest the ring should come off with the plaster, which she would have regarded as a bad omen.

After the return of the Prince to Germany, letters occasionally passed between him and the Princess Victoria; but after her accession to the throne even these cousinly epistles ceased. In reply to the wish expressed by her Uncle Leopold that a formal betrothal with Prince Albert should take place, the young Queen said that she wished the affair to be considered broken off, and that for four years she could not think of marriage. Not that her feelings towards the Prince had really changed, for Her Majesty says that, 'from her girlhood, she had never thought of marrying anyone else.' It was the Prince's youth which stood in the way. Girl though she was, the Queen had plenty of sound common sense, and she shrewdly suspected that, though the people were romantically loyal to a young maiden, their lawful sovereign, they might not be very enthusiastic about a consort who was only a youth of eighteen. Moreover, the Queen had her part to learn, for she had determined to be a ruling monarch, and it seemed better that she should be unfettered by new ties during her apprentice-ship in statecraft. In short, Her Majesty found queenhood enough for the present, without the addition of wifehood and motherhood.

But when, in after years, she realised the burden of a crown, and the value of the wise head beside her own, and the comfort of a loving husband's help, she greatly regretted that her marriage had not taken place earlier, and with characteristic candour Her Majesty has expressed the indignation which she feels against herself at having kept the Prince waiting. The excuse which the Queen makes is that the sudden change from the secluded life at Kensington to the independence of her position as Queen Regnant, at the age of eighteen, put all ideas of marriage out of her mind. 'A worse school for a young girl,' she adds, 'or one more detrimental to all natural feelings and affections, cannot well be imagined, than the position of a queen at eighteen, without experience and without a husband to guide and support her. This the Queen can state from painful experience, and she thanks God that none of her dear daughters are exposed to such danger.'

Her Majesty was beginning to find that standing alone was not a very pleasant thing, and when, in the autumn of 1839, Prince Albert, accompanied by his brother, Prince Ernest, paid a visit to Windsor Castle, her views about marrying underwent a change. The Prince was now greatly improved by foreign travel, and had developed into a strikingly handsome man, with graceful, winning manners. A graphic sketch of Prince Albert at this period was written by an

English gentleman resident at Gotha: 'His Serene Highness Prince Albert is a fine young man; his complexion is clear; his eyes greyish blue, exceedingly expressive; his features are regular, the forehead expanding nobly, and giving the notion of intellectual power. His hair is brown, parted on the side of the head in the modern fashion. He wears mustachios, which add much to the manliness of his countenance, and he has also whiskers. He is exceedingly erect in his person, and is said to excel in all the martial exercises of the military profession, and to be exceedingly *au fait* in the more elegant exercises of the drawing-room, the saloon, and the ball-room.' He was three months younger than the Queen, having been born August 1819, at Rosenau, the summer residence of his father, the reigning Duke of Saxe-Coburg-Gotha. An unhappy estrangement took place between his parents when he was a little fellow of five, and he never again saw the beautiful mother whom he was said to resemble, and for whose memory he entertained the deepest affection. She died murmuring the names 'Ernest!' 'Albert!'—the two boys, whom in her last moments she longed to clasp in her arms. The young Princes were carefully trained by their father, and watched with loving solicitude by their two grandmothers. Prince Albert pursued his studies at the University of Bonn, and became an accomplished student in literature and the fine arts. He was thoughtful, reserved, and dignified beyond his years, and a veritable Galahad in all the moral virtues; it seemed to everyone that he was just the man to make the young Queen happy.

When the Prince came to Windsor in 1839, he was undoubtedly a little touched in his dignity, and had resolved to tell the Queen, like a man, that he was not going to be played with; she must make up her mind to a formal betrothal or consider the affair at an end. His mind, however, was soon set at rest. 'On the second day after our arrival,' he wrote home to a college friend, 'the most friendly demonstrations were directed towards me, and two days later I was secretly called to a private audience, in which the Queen offered me her hand and heart. I think,' he adds, 'that I shall be very happy, for Victoria possesses all the qualities which make a home happy, and seems to be attached to me with her whole heart.'

Her Majesty's superior rank made it imperative that the proposal of marriage should come from her, and it is variously reported how she made it. There is a story that she tentatively asked the Prince such leading questions as, 'How did he like England?' 'Would he like to make it his home?' But the Prince says that the Queen declared her feeling for him in a 'genuine outburst of love and affection,' with which he was 'quite enchanted and carried away.' The proposal was made on the morning of 15 October 1839. The Prince had been out hunting early with his brother, and immediately after his return the Queen summoned him to her boudoir and made the interesting communication. The happiness of the young pair seems to have been beyond expression, and we find both of them writing ecstatic letters to their near relations; the Queen dwelling upon the great sacrifice which the Prince was making in leaving his country to share her life, and he in his turn feeling all unworthy of the love which was shown him. Uncle Leopold and the worthy Baron Stockmar were delighted at the news, and both the Duchess of Kent and Lord Melbourne were pleased also. Beyond these and a favoured few the engagement was not made known until after Prince Albert had returned home.

For a whole month the lovers courted in secret. The Queen took her first holiday from Lord Melbourne's political instructions, and enjoyed a merry time, galloping about the Park in the day with the handsome Prince at her side, and having delightful little dances and festivities in the evening. She reviewed the troops in the Home Park, dressed in her Windsor uniform and cap, and mounted on her old charger 'Leopold,' having the Prince in his green uniform of the Coburg troops on her right hand. It rained and was piercingly cold, but what did that matter when 'dearest Albert' settled her cape 'so comfortably' for her?

The gay, happy time came to an end all too soon. The Prince and his brother returned home, and the Queen, according to the gossip of the time, gave herself up to a sweet melancholy, and would sing only German songs; and in sympathy with the royal lovers young ladies warbled 'I caught her tear at parting', which became the popular song of the day. The royal lovers corresponded daily, and the miscarriage of one of the letters was the occasion of an amusing incident. The Queen was sitting one morning at Windsor Castle in conversation with Lord Melbourne, when word was brought that a young man had called demanding to see the Queen on private business. Her Majesty of course declined to see the stranger; but finding that he would not go away unheard, Lord Melbourne went to inquire what he wanted. He refused to say at first, but, further pressed, admitted that he had a packet which he must place in no one's hands but those of the Queen. Finally he was brought to the royal presence, and drawing forth from his breast a mysterious package he delivered it to Her Majesty, who on opening it found that it was a letter from Prince Albert, which had been omitted by mistake from the royal letter-bag, and which the postal authorities had sent by special messenger. The young man received a suitable reward, and was commended for his fidelity to his trust.

In the midst of her new-found happiness the Queen had important business to perform; first the Privy Council was summoned, and she declared to these solemn old gentlemen, some eighty in number, that it was her intention to marry Prince Albert of Saxe-Coburg and Gotha. The reading of the formal declaration only occupied a few minutes, and Her Majesty says that she was very nervous, and saw nothing save Lord Melbourne looking at her with tears in his eyes, and upon her wrist the medallion of her 'beloved Albert', which seemed to give her courage. Next came a more trying ordeal still, the announcement of her approaching marriage in a speech from the throne, in the House of Lords. She did it with the utmost dignity, and in those clear musical tones so peculiar to her. Both were doubtless 'nervous occasions', but the Queen confided to the Duchess of Gloucester that neither of them was half so trying as 'having to propose to Albert'. The troubles were not as yet over, and it seemed that the course of true love was not in this case to run smooth. There was heated discussion both in and out of Parliament regarding the allowance to be given to the Prince. The original proposal of £50,000 a year was voted down to £30,000, and the discussion concerning it was in the worst possible taste; when Mr Hume told Lord John Russell that he 'must know the danger of setting a young man down in London with so much money in his pockets', the House, instead of calling him to order, roared with laughter. Then came the matter of the Prince's precedency. The Queen wished a clause put in the Naturalization Bill to the effect that her husband was to take rank in the country next to herself, but the royal Dukes, her uncles, objected to this, and Parliament dropped the clause, upon which the Queen asserted her royal prerogative that it was her will and pleasure that the Prince should 'enjoy place, pre-eminence, and precedence next to Her Majesty'. This settled the question within British dominions; but the refusal of Parliament to pass the Precedency Clause left it optional with foreign courts to give the Prince the same royal status as his wife, and in after years caused the Queen great annoyance when visiting continental sovereigns. The Queen's sentiments were very creditable to her womanly feelings, and we do not wonder that she was highly indignant at the action of Parliament, for was not the Prince to be regarded, not only as the Queen's husband, but as the father of our kings to be? The nation practically insulted itself when it refused him royal status.

With manly independence Prince Albert refused all the titles which his future wife might have conferred upon him, and never displayed the least resentment at the recent squabbles over his income and precedence. 'While I possess your love,' he wrote to the Queen, 'they cannot make me unhappy.'

The Queen's wedding was a grand and beautiful pageant. It took place on 10 February 1840, in the Royal Chapel of St James, before an assembly second only in magnificence to that which had witnessed her coronation in Westminster Abbey. The Royal bride was pale, but looked very sweet in her magnificent bridal robe of Honiton lace over white satin trimmed with the time-honoured orange blossoms. The train was of white satin trimmed with the same flowers, and borne by two pages of honour. Her veil was comparatively short, being only one yard and a half square, and was worn flowing back from the wreath over her shoulders, leaving her face uncovered. She wore a necklace and earrings of diamonds, and the armlet of the Garter. The satin for the dress was manufactured at Spitalfields, and the Honiton lace was made by two hundred poor lace-workers in the village of Beer, near to Honiton, the Queen sending Miss Bidney from London to superintend the work. The joy of these poor women at being employed, expressly by the Queen's command, to make her bridal lace was unbounded; they could not sufficiently express their gratitude. When the lace was completed, the pattern was destroyed.

The wedding took place from Buckingham Palace at noon. Previously royal marriages had been celebrated in an evening, but it was the wish of the Queen to conform to the same rule as her subjects, and she was also desirous of giving them an opportunity to see the procession as it passed to the Chapel Royal. First down the grand staircase of the Palace came the bridegroom, looking very handsome in his uniform with the collar of the Garter, surmounted by two white rosettes, carrying a Prayer Book bound in green velvet in his hand. He was accompanied by his father, the Duke of Saxe-Coburg and his brother, Prince Ernest, and as he passed to his carriage was saluted by the household with the same honours given to royal personages. When he entered the chapel, the organ played 'See the Conquering Hero Comes'. He was the man who among all the princes of Europe had secured Victoria, Queen of England, for his bride. After an interval Her Majesty the Queen, escorted by her Lord Chamberlain, came sweeping slowly down the grand staircase in her snowy satin and lace, graciously acknowledging the obeisances made and looking very lovely. It was observed that for this occasion she had laid aside her crown, and only a wreath of orange blossoms rested upon her brow. She was accompanied by Her Royal Highness the Duchess of Kent, wearing a white satin dress embroidered in silver, and by the Duchess of Sutherland, Mistress of the Robes, who wore a superb dress of pink moiré, embroidered in sea-weed and shell pattern. At the Chapel Royal twelve bridesmaids, young and fair, dressed in white, with wreaths of pale roses, were ready to attend her to the altar. She was given away by her uncle of Sussex, of whom a wag of the time said, 'The Duke of Sussex is always ready to give away what does not belong to him.'

The marriage service was conducted according to the rubric of the Church of England, the Archbishop having dutifully waited upon Her Majesty beforehand, to know if the promise to 'obey' was to be omitted, but she replied that she wished 'to be married as a woman, not as a Queen.' When Prince Albert solemnly repeated the words, 'With all my wordly goods I thee endow,' it was observed by some that the bride gave him an arch smile. He took the wedding-ring from his own finger to hand it to the Archbishop, and when it was placed upon the Queen's slender finger volleys of cannon mingled with the pealing and the clanging of the marriage bells. Unfortunately 'Queen's weather', which has since become proverbial, did not prevail; but the

The marriage ceremony was conducted by the Archbishop at noon.

rain did not damp the loyalty of the people, and the streets were thronged with cheering multitudes to greet the young Queen and the husband of her choice. As Prince Albert led his wife from the altar he held her hand in a position which prominently displayed the wedding-ring. It is said that the Queen's look of confidence and comfort at the Prince as they walked away together as man and wife was very pleasing to see. It was such a new thing for her to have an equal companion, friend, and husband, a young heart against which she could rest her own. Few bridegrooms show to advantage at the wedding ceremony; but the quiet dignity and stately simplicity of bearing shown by the Prince filled everyone with admiration. After the marriage register had been signed in the royal attestation book, placed upon a golden table, the wedding party returned to Buckingham Palace to a *déjeuner*. The great feature of the table was the gigantic wedding cake—three hundred pounds in weight, three yards in circumference, and fourteen inches in depth, which took four men to carry it. The ornamentation was superb. On the top was Britannia blessing the royal couple, and amongst other figures was a cupid writing in a volume spread upon his knees, '10th February, 1840.'

The brief honeymoon of three days was spent at Royal Windsor, where the Prince was seen driving his wife about, *tête-à-tête* in a pony phaeton. The day after her marriage the Queen wrote to Baron Stockmar, 'There cannot exist a purer, dearer, nobler being in the world than the Prince.' Happy Queen! that in the years which followed she never had occasion to modify her young bride's enthusiasm. A Royal Idyll had indeed begun such as this country had never looked upon before.

TEMPEST

Charles Dickens

Of all Dickens's books David Copperfield *was the author's own favourite. As a child David had become friendly with the family of his faithful nurse Peggotty, and one of his happiest recollections was of the time he had spent with them in the upturned boat at Yarmouth that was their home. Mr Peggotty, Peggotty's brother, was an honest and good fisherman who had brought up his niece Emily and nephew Ham. Emily and Ham were engaged to be married when David introduced Steerforth, a dashing friend whom he had known at school.*

The result is disaster: Emily abandons the unfortunate Ham and goes abroad with Steerforth, only to be deserted by him in due course; and Mr Peggotty devotes his life to finding his niece. Emily eventually returns, and Mr Peggotty decides that they should both emigrate. Ham has meantime given a message to David for Emily, and this is on David's mind as this chapter, which is the book's climax, opens. It describes the deaths of both Ham and Steerforth.

I now approach an event in my life so indelible, so awful, so bound by an infinite variety of ties to all that has preceded it, in these pages, that, from the beginning of my narrative, I have seen it growing larger and larger as I advanced, like a great tower in a plain, and throwing its forecast shadow even on the incidents of my childish days.

For years after it occurred, I dreamed of it often. I have started up so vividly impressed by it, that its fury has yet seemed raging in my quiet room, in the still night. I dream of it sometimes, though at lengthened and uncertain intervals, to this hour. I have an association between it and a stormy wind, or the lightest mention of a sea-shore, as strong as any of which my mind is conscious. As plainly as I behold what happened, I will try to write it down. I do not recall it, but see it done; for it happens again before me.

The time drawing on rapidly for the sailing of the emigrant ship, my good old nurse (almost broken-hearted for me, when we first met) came up to London. I was constantly with her, and her brother, and the Micawbers (they being very much together); but Emily I never saw.

One evening, when the time was close at hand, I was alone with Peggotty and her brother. Our conversation turned on Ham. She described to us how tenderly he had taken leave of her and how manfully and quietly he had borne himself. Most of all, of late, when she believed he was most tried. It was a subject of which the affectionate creature never tired; and our interest in hearing the many examples which she, who was so much with him, had to relate, was equal to hers in relating them.

My aunt and I were at that time vacating the two cottages at Highgate; I intending to go abroad, and she to return to her house at Dover. We had a temporary lodging in Covent Garden. As I walked home to it, after this evening's conversation, reflecting on what had passed between Ham and myself when I was last at Yarmouth, I wavered in the original purpose I had formed, of leaving a letter for Emily when I should take leave of her uncle on board the ship, and thought it would be better to write to her now. She might desire, I thought, after receiving my communication, to send some parting word by me to her unhappy lover. I ought to give her the opportunity.

I therefore sat down in my room, before going to bed, and wrote to her. I told her that I had seen him, and that he had requested me to tell her what I have already written in its place in these sheets. I faithfully repeated it. I had no need to enlarge upon it, if I had had the right. Its deep fidelity and goodness were not to be adorned by me or any man. I left it out, to be sent round in the morning; with a line to Mr Peggotty, requesting him to give it to her; and went to bed at daybreak.

I was weaker than I knew then; and, not falling asleep until the sun was up, lay late, and unrefreshed, next day. I was roused by the silent presence of my aunt at my bedside. I felt it in my sleep, as I suppose we all do feel such things.

'Trot, my dear,' she said, when I opened my eyes, 'I couldn't make up my mind to disturb you. Mr Peggotty is here; shall he come up?'

I replied yes, and he soon appeared.

'Mas'r Davy,' he said, when we had shaken hands, 'I giv Em'ly your letter, sir, and she writ this heer; and begged of me fur to ask you to read it, and if you see no hurt in't, to be so kind as take charge on't.'

'Have you read it?' said I.

He nodded sorrowfully. I opened it, and read as follows:

'I have got your message. Oh, what can I write, to thank you for your good and blessed kindness to me!

I have put the words close to my heart. I shall keep them till I die. They are sharp thorns, but they are such comfort. I have prayed over them, oh, I have prayed so much. When I find what you are, and what uncle is, I think what God must be, and can cry to Him.

Good-bye for ever. Now, my dear friend, good-bye for ever in this world. In another world, if I am forgiven, I may wake a child and come to you. All thanks and blessings. Farewell, evermore!'

This, blotted with tears, was the letter.

'May I tell her as you doen't see no hurt in't, and as you'll be so kind as take charge on't, Mas'r Davy?' said Mr Peggotty when I had read it.

'Unquestionably,' said I—'but I am thinking——'

'Yes, Mas'r Davy?'

'I am thinking,' said I, 'that I'll go down again to Yarmouth. There's time, and to spare, for me to go and come back before the ship sails. My mind is constantly running on him, in his solitude; to put this letter of her writing in his hand at this time, and to enable you to tell her, in the moment of parting, that he has got it, will be a kindness to both of them. I solemnly accepted his commission, dear good fellow, and cannot discharge it too completely. The journey is nothing to me. I am restless, and shall be better in motion. I'll go down tonight.'

Though he anxiously endeavoured to dissuade me, I saw that he was of my mind; and this, if I had required to be confirmed in my intention, would have had the effect. He went round to the coach-office at my request, and took the box-seat for me on the mail. In the evening I started, by that conveyance, down the road I had travelled under so many changes of fortune.

'Don't you think that,' I asked the coachman, in the first stage out of London, 'a very remarkable sky? I don't remember to have seen one like it.'

'Nor I—not equal to it,' he replied. 'That's wind, sir. There'll be mischief done at sea, I expect, before long.'

It was a murky confusion—here and there blotted with a colour like the colour of the smoke from damp fuel—of flying clouds tossed up into most remarkable heaps, suggesting greater heights in the clouds than there were depths below them to the bottom of the deepest hollows in the earth, through which the wild moon seemed to plunge headlong, as if, in a dread disturbance of the laws of nature, she had lost her way and were frightened. There had been a wind all day; and it was rising then, with an extraordinary great sound. In another hour it had much increased, and the sky was more overcast, and it blew hard.

But as the night advanced, the clouds closing in and densely over-spreading the whole sky, then very dark, it came on to blow, harder and harder. It still increased, until our horses could scarcely face the wind. Many times, in the dark part of the night (it was then late in September, when the nights were not short), the leaders turned about, or came to a dead stop; and we were often in serious apprehension that the coach would be blown over. Sweeping gusts of rain came up before this storm, like showers of steel; and, at those times, when there was any shelter of trees or lee walls to be got, we were fain to stop, in a sheer impossibility of continuing the struggle.

When the day broke, it blew harder and harder. I had been in Yarmouth when the seamen said it blew great guns, but I have never known the like of this, or anything approaching it. We came to Ipswich—very late, having had to fight every inch of ground since we were ten miles out of London—and found a cluster of people in the market-place, who had risen from their beds in the night, fearful of falling chimneys. Some of these, congregating about the inn-yard while we changed horses, told us of great sheets of lead having been ripped off a high church-tower, and flung into a by-street, which they then blocked up. Others had to tell of country people, coming in from neighbouring villages, who had seen great trees lying torn out of the earth, and whole ricks scattered about the roads and fields. Still, there was no abatement in the storm, but it blew harder.

As we struggled on, nearer and nearer to the sea, from which this mighty wind was blowing dead on shore, its force became more and more terrific. Long before we saw the sea, its spray was on our lips, and showered salt rain upon us. The water was out, over miles and miles of the flat country adjacent to Yarmouth; and every sheet and puddle lashed its banks, and had its stress of little breakers setting heavily towards us. When we came within sight of the sea, the waves on the horizon, caught at intervals above the rolling abyss, were like glimpses of another shore with towers and buildings. When at last we got into the town, the people came out to their doors, all aslant, and with streaming hair, making a wonder of the mail that had come through such a night.

I put up at the old inn, and went down to look at the sea; staggering along the street, which was strewn with sand and seaweed, and with flying blotches of foam; afraid of falling slates and tiles; and holding by people I met, at angry corners. Coming near the beach, I saw not only the boatmen but half the people of the town, lurking behind buildings; some, now and then braving the fury of the storm to look away to sea, and blown sheer out of their course in trying to get zigzag back.

Joining these groups, I found bewailing women whose husbands were away in herring or oyster boats, which there was too much reason to think might have foundered before they could run in anywhere for safety. Grizzled old sailors were among the people, shaking their heads as they looked from water to sky, and muttering to one another; shipowners, excited and uneasy; children, huddling together, and peering into old faces; even stout mariners, disturbed and anxious, levelling their glasses at the sea from behind places of shelter, as if they were surveying an enemy.

The tremendous sea itself, when I could find sufficient pause to look at it, in the agitation of the blinding wind, the flying stones and sand, and the awful noise, confounded me. As the high watery walls came rolling in, and, at their highest, tumbled into surf, they looked as if the least would engulf the town. As the receding wave swept back with a hoarse roar, it seemed to scoop out deep caves in the beach, as if its purpose was to undermine the earth. When some white-headed billows thundered on, and dashed themselves to pieces before they reached the land, every fragment of the late whole seemed possessed by the full might of its wrath, rushing to be gathered to the composition of another monster. Undulating hills were changed to valleys, undulating valleys (with a solitary storm-bird sometimes skimming through them) were lifted up to hills; masses of water shivered and shook the beach with a booming sound; every shape tumultuously rolled on, as soon as made, to change its shape and place, and beat another shape and place away; the ideal shore on the horizon, with its towers and buildings, rose and fell; the clouds flew fast and thick; I seemed to see a rending and up-heaving of all nature.

Not finding Ham among the people whom this memorable wind—for it is still remembered down there as the greatest ever known to blow upon that coast—had brought together, I made my way to his house. It was shut; and as no one answered to my knocking, I went, by back ways and by-lanes, to the yard where he worked. I learned, there, that he had gone to Lowestoft, to meet some sudden exigency of ship-repairing in which his skill was required; but that he would be back tomorrow morning, in good time.

I went back to the inn; and when I had washed and dressed, and tried to sleep, but in vain, it was five o'clock in the afternoon. I had not sat five minutes by the coffee-room fire, when the waiter coming to stir it, as an excuse for talking, told me that two colliers had gone down, with all hands, a few miles away; and that some other ships had been seen labouring hard in The Roads, and trying, in great distress, to keep off shore. Mercy on them, and on all poor sailors, said he, if we had another night like the last!

I was very much depressed in spirits; very solitary; and felt an un-easiness in Ham's not being there, disproportionate to the occasion. I was seriously affected, without knowing how much, by late events; and my long exposure to the fierce wind had confused me. There was that jumble in my thoughts and recollections, that I had lost the clear arrangement of time and distance. Thus, if I had gone out into the town, I should not have been surprised, I think, to encounter someone who I knew must be then in London. So to speak, there was in these respects a curious inattention in my mind. Yet it was busy, too, with all the re-membrances the place naturally awakened; and they were particularly distinct and vivid.

In this state, the waiter's dismal intelligence about the ships immedi-ately connected itself, without any effort of my volition, with my un-easiness about Ham. I was persuaded that I had an apprehension of his returning from Lowestoft by sea, and being lost. This grew so strong with me that I resolved to go back to the yard before I took my dinner, and ask the boat-builder if he thought his attempting to return by sea at all likely? If he gave me the least reason to think so, I would go over to Lowestoft and prevent it by bringing him with me.

I hastily ordered my dinner, and went back to the yard. I was none too soon; for the boat-builder, with a lantern in his hand, was locking the yard-gate. He quite laughed when I asked him the question, and said there was no fear; no man in his senses, or out of them, would put off in such a gale of wind, least of all Ham Peggotty, who had been born to sea-faring.

So sensible of this, beforehand, that I had really felt ashamed of doing what I was nevertheless impelled to do, I went back to the inn. If such a wind could rise, I think it was rising. The howl and roar, the rattling of the doors and windows, the rumbling in the chimneys, the apparent rocking of the very house that sheltered me, and the prodigious tumult of the sea, were more fearful than in the morning. But there was now a great darkness besides; and that invested the storm with new terrors, real and fanciful.

I could not eat, I could not sit still, I could not continue steadfast to anything. Something within me, faintly answering to the storm without, tossed up the depth of my memory, and made a tumult in them. Yet, in all the hurry of my thoughts, wild running with the thundering sea—the storm, and my uneasiness regarding Ham, were always in the foreground.

My dinner went away almost untasted, and I tried to refresh myself with a glass or two of wine. In vain. I fell into a dull slumber before the fire, without losing my consciousness, either of the uproar out of doors, or of the place in which I was. Both became overshadowed by a new and indefinable horror; and when I awoke—or rather when I shook off the lethargy that bound me in my chair—my whole frame thrilled with objectless and unintelligible fear.

I walked to and fro, tried to read an old gazetteer, listened to the awful noises: looked at faces, scenes, and figures in the fire. At length, the steady ticking of the undisturbed clock on the wall tormented me to that degree that I resolved to go to bed.

It was reassuring, on such a night, to be told that some of the inn-servants had agreed together to sit up until morning. I went to bed, exceedingly weary and heavy; but, on my lying down, all such sensations vanished, as if by magic, and I was broad awake.

For hours I lay there, listening to the wind and water: imagining, now, that I heard shrieks out at sea; now, that I distinctly heard the firing of signal guns; and now, the fall of houses in the town. I got up, several times, and looked out; but could see nothing, except the reflection in the window-panes of the faint candle I had left burning, and of my own haggard face looking in at me from the black void.

At length, my restlessness attained to such a pitch that I hurried on my clothes, and went downstairs. In the large kitchen, where I dimly saw bacon and ropes of onions hanging from the beams, the watchers were clustered together, in various attitudes, about a table, purposely moved away from the great chimney, and brought near the door. A pretty girl, who had her ears stopped with her apron, and her eyes upon the door, screamed when I appeared, supposing me to be a spirit; but the others had more presence of mind, and were glad of an addition to their company. One man, referring to the topic they had been discussing, asked me whether I thought the souls of the collier-crews who had gone down, were out in the storm?

I remained there, I dare say, two hours. Once, I opened the yard-gate, and looked into the empty street. The sand, the seaweed, and the flakes of foam were driving by; and I was obliged to call for assistance before I could shut the gate again, and make it fast against the wind.

There was a dark gloom in my solitary chamber, when I at length returned to it; but I was tired now, and, getting into bed again, fell—off a tower and down a precipice—into the depths of sleep. I have an impression that for a long time, though I dreamed of being elsewhere and in a variety of scenes, it was always blowing in my dream. At length, I lost that feeble hold upon reality, and was engaged with two dear friends, but who they were I don't know, at the siege of some town in a roar of cannonading.

The thunder of the cannon was so loud and incessant, that I could not hear something I much desired to hear, until I made a great exertion and awoke. It was broad day—eight or nine o'clock; the storm raging, in lieu of the batteries; and someone knocking and calling at my door.

'What is the matter?' I cried.

'A wreck! Close by!'

I sprang out of bed, and asked, 'What wreck?'

'A schooner, from Spain or Portugal, laden with fruit and wine.

Make haste, sir, if you want to see her! It's thought, down on the beach, she'll go to pieces every moment.'

The excited voice went clamouring along the staircase; and I wrapped myself in my clothes as quickly as I could, and ran into the street.

Numbers of people were there before me, all running in one direction, to the beach. I ran the same way, outstripping a good many, and soon came facing the wild sea.

The wind might by this time have lulled a little, though not more sensibly than if the cannonading I had dreamed of, had been diminished by the silencing of half-a-dozen guns out of hundreds. But the sea, having upon it the additional agitation of the whole night, was infinitely more terrific than when I had seen it last. Every appearance it had then presented, bore the expression of being *swelled*; and the height to which the breakers rose, and, looking over one another, bore one another down, and rolled in, in interminable hosts, was most appalling.

In the difficulty of hearing anything but wind and waves, and in the crowd, and the unspeakable confusion, and my first breathless efforts to stand against the weather, I was so confused that I looked out to sea for the wreck, and saw nothing but the foaming heads of the great waves. A half-dressed boatman, standing next to me, pointed with his bare arm (a tattooed arrow on it, pointing in the same direction) to the left. Then, O great heaven, I saw it, close in upon us!

One mast was broken short off, six or eight feet from the deck, and lay over the side, entangled in a maze of sail and rigging; and all that ruin, as the ship rolled and beat—which she did without a moment's pause, and with a violence quite inconceivable—beat the side as if it would stave it in. Some efforts were even then being made to cut this portion of the wreck away; for, as the ship, which was broadside on, turned towards us in her rolling, I plainly descried her people at work with axes, especially one active figure with long curling hair, conspicuous among the rest. But, a great cry, which was audible even above the wind and water, rose from the shore at this moment; the sea, sweeping over the rolling wreck, made a clean breach, and carried men, spars, casks, planks, bulwarks, heaps of such toys, into the boiling surge.

The second mast was yet standing, with the rags of a rent sail, and a wild confusion of broken cordage flapping to and fro. The ship had struck once, the same boatman hoarsely said in my ear, and then lifted in and struck again. I understood him to add that she was parting amidships, and I could readily suppose so, for the rolling and beating were too tremendous for any human work to suffer long. As he spoke, there was another great cry of pity from the beach; four men arose with the wreck out of the deep, clinging to the rigging of the remaining mast; uppermost the active figure with the curling hair.

There was a bell on board; and as the ship rolled and dashed, like a desperate creature driven mad, now showing us the whole sweep of her deck, as she turned on her beam-ends towards the shore, now nothing but her keel, as she sprang wildly over and turned towards the sea, the bell rang; and its sound, the knell of those unhappy men, was borne towards us on the wind. Again we lost her, and again she rose. Two men were gone. The agony on shore increased. Men groaned, and clasped their hands; women shrieked, and turned away their faces. Some ran wildly up and down along the beach, crying for help where no help could be. I found myself one of these, frantically imploring a knot of sailors whom I knew, not to let those two lost creatures perish before our eyes.

They were making out to me, in an agitated way—I don't know how, for the little I could hear I was scarcely composed enough to understand—that the lifeboat had been bravely manned an hour ago, and could do nothing; and that as no man would be so desperate as to attempt to wade off with a rope, and establish a communication with the shore, there was nothing left to try; when I noticed that some new sensation moved the people on the beach, and saw them part, and Ham come breaking through them to the front.

I ran to him—as well as I know, to repeat my appeal for help. But, distracted though I was, by a sight so new to me and terrible, the determination in his face, and his look, out to sea—exactly the same look as I remembered in connection with the morning after Emily's flight—awoke me to a knowledge of his danger. I held him back with both arms; and implored the men with whom I had been speaking, not to listen to him, not to do murder, not to let him stir from off that sand!

Another cry arose on shore; and looking to the wreck, we saw the cruel sail, with blow on blow, beat off the lower of the two men, and fly up in triumph round the active figure left alone upon the mast.

Against such a sight, and against such determination as that of the calmly desperate man who was already accustomed to lead half the people present, I might as hopefully have entreated the wind. 'Mas'r Davy,' he said, cheerily grasping me by both hands, 'if my time is come, 'tis come. If 'tan't I'll bide it. Lord above bless you, and bless all! Mates, make me ready! I'm a-going off!'

I was swept away, but not unkindly, to some distance, where the people around me made me stay; urging, as I confusedly perceived, that he was bent on going, with help or without, and that I should endanger the precautions for his safety by troubling those with whom they rested. I don't know what I answered, or what they rejoined; but, I saw hurry on the beach, and men running with ropes from a capstan that was there, and penetrating into a circle of figures that hid him from me. Then, I saw him standing alone, in a seaman's frock and trousers: a rope in his hand, or slung to his wrist: another round his body: and several of the best men holding, at a little distance, to the latter, which he laid out himself, slack upon the shore, at his feet.

The wreck, even to my unpractised eye, was breaking up. I saw that

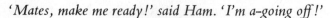

'Mates, make me ready!' said Ham. 'I'm a-going off!'

she was parting in the middle, and that the life of the solitary man upon the mast hung by a thread. Still, he clung to it. He had a singular red cap on—not like a sailor's cap, but of a finer colour; and as the few yielding planks between him and destruction rolled and bulged, and his anticipative death-knell rang, he was seen by all of us to wave it. I saw him do it now, and thought I was going distracted, when his action brought an old remembrance to my mind of a once dear friend.

Ham watched the sea, standing alone, with the silence of suspended breath behind him, and the storm before, until there was a great retiring wave, when, with a backward glance at those who held the rope which was made fast round his body, he dashed in after it, and in a moment was buffeting with the water; rising with the hills, falling with the valleys, lost beneath the foam; then drawn again to land. They hauled in hastily.

He was hurt. I saw blood on his face, from where I stood; but he took no thought of that. He seemed hurriedly to give them some directions for leaving him more free—or so I judged from the motion of his arm— and was gone as before.

And now he made for the wreck, rising with the hills, falling with the valleys, lost beneath the rugged foam, borne in towards the shore, borne on towards the ship, striving hard and valiantly. The distance was nothing, but the power of the sea and wind made the strife deadly. At length he neared the wreck. He was so near, that with one more of his vigorous strokes he would be clinging to it—when a high, green, vast hillside of water, moving on shoreward, from beyond the ship, he seemed to leap up into it with a mighty bound, and the ship was gone!

Some eddying fragments I saw in the sea, as if a mere cask had been broken, in running to the spot where they were hauling in. Consternation was in every face. They drew him to my very feet—insensible—dead. He was carried to the nearest house; and, no one preventing me now, I remained near him, busy, while every means of restoration were tried; but he had been beaten to death by the great wave, and his generous heart was stilled for ever.

As I sat beside the bed, when hope was abandoned and all was done, a fisherman, who had known me when Emily and I were children, and ever since, whispered my name at the door.

'Sir,' said he, with tears starting to his weather-beaten face, which, with his trembling lips, was ashy pale, 'will you come over yonder?'

The old remembrance that had been recalled to me, was in his look. I asked him, terror-stricken, leaning on the arm he held out to support me:

'Has a body come ashore?'

He said, 'Yes.'

'Do I know it?' I asked then.

He answered nothing.

But, he led me to the shore. And on that part of it where she and I had looked for shells, two children—on that part of it where some lighter fragments of the old boat, blown down last night, had been scattered by the wind—among the ruins of the home he had wronged—I saw him lying with his head upon his arm, as I had often seen him lie at school.

THE MYSTERIOUS MANSION

Honore de Balzac

About a hundred yards from the town of Vendôme, on the borders of the Loire, there is an old grey house, surmounted by very high gables, and so completely isolated that neither tanyard nor shabby hostelry, such as you may find at the entrance to all small towns, exists in its immediate neighbourhood.

In front of this building, overlooking the river, is a garden, where the once well-trimmed box borders that used to define the walks now grow wild as they list. Several willows that spring from the Loire have grown as rapidly as the hedge that encloses it, and half conceal the house. The rich vegetation of those weeds that we call foul adorns the sloping shore. Fruit trees, neglected for the last ten years, no longer yield their harvest, and their shoots form coppices. The wall-fruit grows like hedges against the walls. Paths once gravelled are overgrown with moss, but, to tell the truth, there is no trace of a path. From the height of the hill, to which cling the ruins of the old castle of the Dukes of Vendôme, the only spot whence the eye can plunge into this enclosure, it strikes you that, at a time not easy to determine, this plot of land was the delight of a country gentleman, who cultivated roses and tulips and horticulture in general, and who was besides a lover of fine fruit. An arbor is still visible, or rather the débris of an arbor, where there is a table that time has not quite destroyed. The aspect of this garden of bygone days suggests the negative joys of peaceful, provincial life, as one might reconstruct the life of a worthy tradesman by reading the epitaph on his tombstone. As if to complete the sweetness and sadness of the ideas that possess one's soul, one of the walls displays a sun-dial decorated with the following commonplace Christian inscription: "Ultimam cogita!" The roof of this house is horribly dilapidated, the shutters are always closed, the balconies are covered with swallows' nests, the doors are perpetually shut, weeds have drawn green lines in the cracks of the flights of steps, the locks and bolts are rusty. Sun, moon, winter, summer, and snow have worn the panelling, warped the boards, gnawed the paint. The lugubrious silence which reigns there is only broken by birds, cats, martins, rats and mice, free to course to and fro, to fight and to eat each other. Everywhere an invisible hand has graven the word *mystery*.

Should your curiosity lead you to glance at this house from the side that points to the road, you would perceive a great door which the children of the place have riddled with holes. I afterward heard that this door had been closed for the last ten years. Through the holes broken by the boys you would have observed the perfect harmony that existed between the façades of both garden and courtyard. In both the same disorder prevails. Tufts of weed encircle the paving-stones. Enormous cracks furrow the walls, round whose blackened crests twine the thousand garlands of the pellitory. The steps are out of joint, the wire of the bell is rusted, the spouts are cracked. What fire from heaven has fallen here? What tribunal has decreed that salt should be strewn on this dwelling? Has God been blasphemed, has France been here betrayed? These are the questions we ask ourselves, but get no answer from the crawling things that haunt the place. The empty and deserted house is a gigantic enigma, of which the key is lost. In bygone times it was a small fief, and bears the name of the Grande Bretêche.

I inferred that I was not the only person to whom my good landlady had communicated the secret of which I was to be the sole recipient, and I prepared to listen.

'Sir,' she said, 'when the Emperor sent the Spanish prisoners of war and others here, the Government quartered on me a young Spaniard who had been sent to Vendôme on parole. Parole notwithstanding he went out every day to show himself to the sous-préfet. He was a Spanish grandee! Nothing less! His name ended in os and dia, something like Burgos de Férédia. I have his name on my books; you can read it if you like. Oh! but he was a handsome young man for a Spaniard; they are all said to be ugly. He was only five feet and a few inches high, but he was well-grown; he had small hands that he took such care of; ah! you should have seen! He had as many brushes for his hands as a woman for her whole dressing apparatus! He had thick black hair, a fiery eye, his skin was rather bronzed, but I liked the look of it. He wore the finest linen I have ever seen on any one, although I have had princesses staying here, and, among others, General Bertrand, the Duke and Duchess d'Abrantès, Monsieur Decazes, and the King of Spain. He didn't eat much; but his manners were so polite, so amiable, that one could not owe him a grudge. Oh! I was very fond of him, although he didn't open his lips four times in the day, and it was impossible to keep up a conversation with him. For if you spoke to him, he did not answer. It was a fad, a mania with them all, I heard say. He read his breviary like a priest, he went to Mass and to all the services regularly. Where did he sit? Two steps from the chapel of Madame de Merret. As he took his place there the first time he went to church, nobody suspected him of any intention in so doing. Besides, he never raised his eyes from his prayer-book, poor young man! After that, sir, in the evening he would walk on the mountains, among the castle ruins. It was the poor man's only amusement, it reminded him of his country. They say that Spain is all mountains! From the commencement of his imprisonment he stayed out late. I was anxious when I found that he did not come home before midnight; but we got accustomed to this fancy of his. He took the key of the door, and we left off sitting up for him. He lodged in a house of ours in the Rue des Casernes. After that, one of our stablemen told us that in the evening when he led the horses to the water, he thought he had seen the Spanish grandee swimming far down the river like a live fish. When he returned, I told him to take care of the rushes; he appeared vexed to have been seen in the water. At last, one day, or rather one morning, we did not find him in his room; he had not returned. After searching everywhere, I found some writing in the drawer of a table, where there were fifty gold pieces of Spain that are called doubloons and were worth about five thousand francs; and ten thousand francs' worth of diamonds in a small sealed box. The writing said, that in case he did not return, he left us the money and the diamonds, on condition of paying for Masses to thank God for his escape, and for his salvation. In those days my husband had not been taken from me; he hastened to seek him everywhere.

'And now for the strange part of the story. He brought home the Spaniard's clothes, that he had discovered under a big stone, in a sort of pilework by the river-side near the castle, nearly opposite to the Grande Bretêche. My husband had gone there so early that no one had seen him. After reading the letter, he burned the clothes, and according to Count Férédia's desire we declared that he had escaped. The sous-préfet sent all the gendarmerie in pursuit of him; but brust! they never caught him. Lepas believed that the Spaniard had drowned himself. I, sir, don't think so; I am more inclined to believe that he had something to do with the affair of Madame de Merret, seeing that Rosalie told me that the crucifix that her mistress thought so much of that she had it buried with her, was of ebony and silver. Now in the beginning of his stay here, Monsieur de Férédia had one in ebony and silver that I never saw him with later. Now, sir, don't you consider that I need have no scruples about the Spaniard's fifteen thousand francs, and that I have a right to them?'

'Certainly; but you haven't tried to question Rosalie?' I said.

'Oh, yes, indeed, sir; but to no purpose! the girl's like a wall. She knows something, but it is impossible to get her to talk.'

After exchanging a few more words with me, my landlady left me a prey to vague and gloomy thoughts, to a romantic curiosity, and a religious terror not unlike the profound impression produced on us when by night, on entering a dark church, we perceive a faint light under high arches; a vague figure glides by – the rustle of a robe or cassock is heard, and we shudder.

Suddenly the Grande Bretêche and its tall weeds, its barred windows, its rusty ironwork, its closed doors, its deserted apartments, appeared like a fantastic apparition before me. I essayed to penetrate the mysterious dwelling, and to find the knot of its dark story – the drama that had killed three persons. In my eyes Rosalie became the most interesting person in Vendôme. As I studied her, I discovered the traces of secret care, despite the radiant health that shone in her plump countenance.

There was in her the germ of remorse or hope; her attitude revealed a secret, like the attitude of a bigot who prays to excess, or of the infanticide who ever hears the last cry of her child. Yet her manners were rough and ingenious – her silly smile was not that of a criminal, and could you but have seen the great kerchief that encompassed her portly bust, framed and laced in by a lilac and blue cotton gown, you would have dubbed her innocent. No, I thought, I will not leave Vendôme without learning the history of the Grande Bretêche. To gain my ends I will strike up a friendship with Rosalie, if needs be.

'Rosalie,' said I, one evening.

'Sir?'

'You are not married?'

She started slightly.

'Oh, I can find plenty of men, when the fancy takes me to be made miserable,' she said, laughing.

She soon recovered from the effects of her emotion, for all women, from the great lady to the maid of the inn, possess a composure that is peculiar to them.

'You are too good-looking and well favoured to be short of lovers. But tell me, Rosalie, why did you take service in an inn after leaving Madame de Merret? Did she leave you nothing to live on?'

'Oh, yes! But, sir, my place is the best in all Vendôme.'

The reply was one of those that judges and lawyers would call evasive. Rosalie appeared to me to be situated in this romantic history like the square in the midst of a chessboard. She was at the heart of the truth and chief interest; she seemed to me to be bound in the very knot of it. The conquest of Rosalie was no longer to be an ordinary siege – in this girl was centred the last chapter of a novel, therefore from this moment Rosalie became the object of my preference.

One morning I said to Rosalie: 'Tell me all you know about Madame de Merret.'

'Oh!' she replied in terror, 'do not ask that of me, Monsieur Horace.'

Her pretty face fell – her clear, bright colour faded – and her eyes lost their innocent brightness.

'Well, then,' she said, at last, 'if you must have it so, I will tell you about it; but promise to keep my secret!'

'Done! my dear girl, I must keep your secret with the honour of a thief, which is the most loyal in the world.'

Were I to transcribe Rosalie's diffuse eloquence faithfully, an entire volume would scarcely contain it; so I shall abridge.

The room occupied by Madame de Merret at the Bretêche was on the ground floor. A little closet about four feet deep, built in the thickness of the wall, served as her wardrobe. Three months before the eventful evening of which I am about to speak, Madame de Merret had been so seriously indisposed that her husband had left her to herself in her own apartment, while he occupied another on the first floor. By one of those chances that it is impossible to foresee, he returned home from the club (where he was accustomed to read the papers and discuss politics with the inhabitants of the place) two hours later than usual. His wife supposed him to be at home, in bed and asleep. But the invasion of France had been the subject of a most animated discussion; the billiard-match had been exciting, he had lost forty francs, an enormous sum for Vendôme, where every one hoards, and where manners are restricted within the limits of a praiseworthy modesty, which perhaps is the source of the true happiness that no Parisian covets. For some time past Monsieur de Merret had been satisfied to ask Rosalie if his wife had gone to bed; and on her reply, which was always in the affirmative, had immediately gained his own room with the good temper engendered by habit and confidence. On entering his house, he took it into his head to go and tell his wife of his misadventure, perhaps by way of consolation. At dinner he found Madame de Merret most coquettishly attired. On his way to the club it had occurred to him that his wife was restored to health, and that her convalescence had added to her beauty. He was, as husbands are wont to be, somewhat slow in making this discovery. Instead of calling Rosalie, who was occupied just then in watching the cook and coachman play a difficult hand at brisque, Monsieur de Merret went to his wife's room by the light of a lantern that he deposited on the first step of the staircase. His unmistakable step resounded under the vaulted corridor. At the moment that the Count turned the handle of his wife's door, he fancied he could hear the door of the closet I spoke of close; but when he entered Madame de Merret was alone before the fireplace. The husband thought ingeniously that Rosalie was in the closet, yet a suspicion that jangled in his ear put him on his guard. He looked at his wife and saw in her eyes I know not what wild and hunted expression.

'You are very late,' she said. Her habitually pure, sweet voice seemed changed to him.

Monsieur de Merret did not reply, for at that moment Rosalie entered. It was a thunderbolt for him. He strode about the room, passing from one window to the other, with mechanical motion and folded arms.

'Have you heard bad news, or are you unwell?' inquired his wife timidly, while Rosalie undressed her.

He kept silent.

'You can leave me,' said Madame de Merret to her maid; 'I will put my hair in curl papers myself.'

From the expression of her husband's face she foresaw trouble, and wished to be alone with him. When Rosalie had gone, or was supposed to have gone (for she stayed in the corridor for a few minutes), Monsieur de Merret came and stood in front of his wife, and said coldly to her:

'Madame, there is someone in your closet!' She looked calmly at her husband and replied simply:

'No, sir.'

This answer was heartrending to Monsieur de Merret; he did not believe in it. Yet his wife had never appeared to him purer or more saintly than at that moment. He rose to open the closet door; Madame de Merret took his hand, looked at him with an expression of melancholy, and said in a voice that betrayed singular emotion:

'If you find no one there, remember this, all will be over between us!' The extraordinary dignity of his wife's manner restored the Count's profound esteem for her, and inspired him with one of those resolutions that only lack a vaster stage to become immortal.

'No,' said he, 'Josephine, I will not go there. In either case it would separate us for ever. Hear me, I know how pure you are at heart, and that your life is a holy one. You would not commit a mortal sin to save your life.'

At these words Madame de Merret turned a haggard gaze upon her husband.

'Here, take your crucifix,' he added. 'Swear to me before God that there is no one in there; I will believe you, I will never open that door.'

Madame de Merret took the crucifix and said:

'I swear.'

'Louder,' said the husband, 'and repeat "I swear before God that there is no one in that closet."'

She repeated the sentence calmly.

'That will do,' said Monsieur de Merret, coldly.

After a moment of silence:

'I never saw this pretty toy before,' he said, examining the ebony crucifix inlaid with silver, and most artistically chiseled.

'I found it at Duvivier's, who bought it off a Spanish monk when the prisoners passed through Vendôme last year.'

'Ah!' said Monsieur de Merret, as he replaced the crucifix on the nail, and he rang. Rosalie did not keep him waiting. Monsieur de Merret went quickly to meet her, led her to the bay window that opened on to the garden and whispered to her:

'Listen! I know that Gorenflot wishes to marry you, poverty is the only drawback, and you told him that you would be his wife if he found the means to establish himself as a master mason. Well! go and fetch him, tell him to come here with his trowel and tools. Manage not to awaken any one in his house but himself; his fortune will be more than your desires. Above all, leave this room without babbling, otherwise –' He frowned. Rosalie went away, he recalled her.

'Here, take my latchkey,' he said. 'Jean!' then cried Monsieur de Merret, in tones of thunder in the corridor. Jean, who was at the same time his coachman and his confidential servant, left his game of cards and came.

'Go to bed, all of you,' said his master, signing to him to approach; and the Count added, under his breath: 'When they are all asleep – *asleep,* d'ye hear? – you will come down and tell me.' Monsieur de Merret, who had not lost sight of his wife all the time he was giving his orders, returned quietly to her at the fireside and began to tell her of the game of billiards and the talk of the club. When Rosalie returned she found Monsieur and Madame de Merret conversing very amicably.

The Count had lately had all the ceilings of his reception rooms on the ground floor repaired. Plaster of Paris is difficult to obtain in Vendôme; the carriage raises its price. The Count had therefore bought a good deal, being well aware that he could find plenty of purchasers for whatever might remain over. This circumstance inspired him with the design he was about to execute.

'Sir, Gorenflot has arrived,' said Rosalie in low tones.

'Show him in,' replied the Count in loud tones.

Madame de Merret turned rather pale when she saw the mason.

'Gorenflot,' said her husband, 'go and fetch bricks from the coachhouse, and bring sufficient to wall up the door of this closet; you will use the plaster I have over to coat the wall with.' Then calling Rosalie and the workman aside:

'Listen, Gorenflot,' he said in an undertone, 'you will sleep here tonight. But tomorrow you will have a passport to a foreign country, to a town to which I will direct you. I shall give you six thousand francs for your journey. You will stay ten years in that town; if you do not like it, you may establish yourself in another, provided it be in the same country. You will pass through Paris, where you will await me. There I will insure you an additional six thousand francs by contract, which will be paid to you on your return, provided you have fulfilled the conditions of our bargain. This is the price for your absolute silence as to what you are about to do tonight. As to you, Rosalie, I will give you ten thousand francs on the day of your wedding, on condition of your marrying Gorenflot; but if you wish to marry, you must hold your tongues; or – no dowry.'

'Rosalie,' said Madame de Merret, 'do my hair.'

The husband walked calmly up and down, watching the door, the mason, and his wife, but without betraying any insulting doubts. Madame de Merret chose a moment when the workman was unloading bricks and her husband was at the other end of the room to say to Rosalie: 'A thousand francs a year for you, my child, if you can tell Gorenflot to leave a chink at the bottom.' Then out loud, she added coolly:

'Go and help him!'

Monsieur and Madame de Merret were silent all the time that Gorenflot took to brick up the door. This silence, on the part of the husband, who did not choose to furnish his wife with a pretext for saying things of a double meaning, had its purpose; on the part of Madame de Merret it was either pride or prudence. When the wall was about half-way up, the sly workman took advantage of a moment when the Count's back was turned, to strike a blow with his trowel in one of the glass panes of the closet-door. This act informed Madame de Merret that Rosalie had spoken to Gorenflot.

All three then saw a man's face; it was dark and gloomy with black hair and eyes of flame. Before her husband turned, the poor woman had time

All three saw the man's gloomy face

to make a sign to the stranger that signified: Hope!

At four o'clock, toward dawn, for it was the month of September, the construction was finished. The mason was handed over to the care of Jean, and Monsieur de Merret went to bed in his wife's room.

On rising the following morning, he said carelessly:

'The deuce! I must go to the Marie for the passport.' He put his hat on his head, advanced three steps toward the door, altered his mind and took the crucifix.

His wife trembled for joy. 'He is going to Duvivier,' she thought. As soon as the Count had left, Madame de Merret rang for Rosalie; then in a terrible voice:

'The trowel, the trowel!' she cried, 'and quick to work! I saw how Gorenflot did it; we shall have time to make a hole and to mend it again.'

In the twinkling of an eye, Rosalie brought a sort of mattock to her mistress, who with unparalleled ardor set about demolishing the wall. She had already knocked out several bricks and was preparing to strike a more decisive blow when she perceived Monsieur de Merret behind her. She fainted.

'Lay Madame on her bed,' said the Count coldly. He had foreseen what would happen in his absence and had set a trap for his wife; he had simply written to the mayor, and had sent for Duvivier. The jeweller arrived just as the room had been put in order.

'Duvivier,' inquired the Count, 'did you buy crucifixes off the Spaniards who passed through here?'

'No, sir.'

'That will do, thank you,' he said, looking at his wife like a tiger. 'Jean,' he added, 'you will see that my meals are served in the Countess's room; she is ill, and I shall not leave her until she has recovered.'

The cruel gentleman stayed with his wife for twenty days. In the beginning, when there were sounds in the walled closet, and Josephine attempted to implore his pity for the dying stranger, he replied, without permitting her to say a word:

'You have sworn on the cross that there is no one there.'

THE MOONLIT ROAD

Ambrose Bierce

Statement of Joel Hetman, Jr.

I am the most unfortunate of men. Rich, respected, fairly well educated
and of sound health—with many other advantages usually valued by
those having them and coveted by those who have them not—I sometimes think that I should be less unhappy if they had been denied me,
for then the contrast between my outer and my inner life would not
be continually demanding a painful attention. In the stress of privation
and the need of effort I might sometimes forget the sombre secret ever
baffling the conjecture that it compels.

I am the only child of Joel and Julia Hetman. The one was a well-to-
do country gentleman, the other a beautiful and accomplished woman
to whom he was passionately attached with what I now know to have
been a jealous and exacting devotion. The family home was a few miles
from Nashville, Tennessee, a large, irregularly built dwelling of no
particular order of architecture, a little way off the road, in a park of
trees and shrubbery.

At the time of which I write I was nineteen years old, a student at
Yale University. One day I received a telegram from my father of such

urgency that in compliance with its unexplained demand I left at once for home. At the railway station in Nashville a distant relative awaited me to apprise me of the reason for my recall: my mother had been barbarously murdered—why and by whom none could conjecture, but the circumstances were these:

My father had gone to Nashville, intending to return the next afternoon. Something prevented his accomplishing the business in hand, so he returned on the same night, arriving just before the dawn. In his testimony before the coroner he explained that having no latch-key and not caring to disturb the sleeping servants, he had, with no clearly defined intention, gone round to the rear of the house. As he turned an angle of the building, he heard a sound as of a door gently closed, and saw in the darkness, indistinctly, the figure of a man, which instantly disappeared among the trees of the lawn. A hasty pursuit and brief search of the grounds in the belief that the trespasser was someone secretly visiting a servant proving fruitless, he entered at the unlocked door and mounted the stairs to my mother's chamber. Its door was open, and stepping into black darkness he fell headlong over some heavy object on the floor. I may spare myself the details; it was my poor mother, dead of strangulation by human hands!

Nothing had been taken from the house, the servants had heard no sound, and excepting those terrible fingermarks upon the dead woman's throat—dear God! that I might forget them!—no trace of the assassin was ever found.

I gave up my studies and remained with my father, who, naturally, was greatly changed. Always of a sedate, taciturn disposition, he now fell into a so deep dejection that nothing could hold his attention, yet anything—a footfall, the sudden closing of a door—aroused in him a fitful interest; one might have called it an apprehension. At any small surprise of the senses he would start visibly and sometimes turn pale, then relapse into a melancholy apathy deeper than before. I suppose he was what is called a nervous wreck. As to me, I was younger then than now—there is much in that Youth is Gilead, in which is balm for every wound. Ah, that I might again dwell in that enchanted land! Unacquainted with grief, I knew not how to appraise my bereavement; I could not rightly estimate the strength of the stroke.

One night, a few months after the dreadful event, my father and I walked home from the city. The full moon was about three hours above the eastern horizon; the entire countryside had the solemn stillness of a summer night; our footfalls and the ceaseless song of the katydids were the only sound, aloof. Black shadows of bordering trees lay athwart the road, which, in the short reaches between, gleamed a ghostly white. As we approached the gate to our dwelling, whose front was in shadow, and in which no light shone, my father suddenly stopped and clutched my arm, saying, hardly above his breath:

'God! God! What is that?'

'I hear nothing,' I replied.

'But see—see!' he said, pointing along the road, directly ahead.

I said: 'Nothing is there. Come, father, let us go in—you are ill.'

He had released my arm and was standing rigid and motionless in the centre of the illuminated roadway, staring like one bereft of sense. His face in the moonlight showed a pallor and fixity inexpressibly distressing. I pulled gently at his sleeve, but he had forgotten my existence. Presently he began to retire backward, step by step, never for an instant removing his eyes from what he saw, or thought he saw. I turned half round to follow, but stood irresolute. I do not recall any feeling of fear, unless a sudden chill was its physical manifestation. It seemed as if an icy wind had touched my face and enfolded my body from head to foot; I could feel the stir of it in my hair.

At that moment my attention was drawn to a light that suddenly streamed from an upper window of the house: one of the servants, awakened by what mysterious premonition of evil who can say, and in obedience to an impulse that she was never able to name, had lit a lamp. When I turned to look for my father he was gone, and in all the years that have passed no whisper of his fate has come across the borderland of conjecture from the realm of the unknown.

Statement of Caspar Grattan

Today I am said to live; tomorrow, here in this room, will lie a senseless shape of clay that all too long was I. If anyone lift the cloth from the face of that unpleasant thing it will be in gratification of a mere morbid curiosity. Some, doubtless, will go further and inquire, 'Who was he?' In this writing I supply the only answer that I am able to make—Caspar Grattan. Surely, that should be enough. The name has served my small

He was standing rigid and motionless in the centre of the illuminated roadway . . .

need for more than twenty years of a life of unknown length. True, I gave it to myself, but lacking another I had the right. In this world one must have a name; it prevents confusion, even when it does not establish identity. Some, though, are known by numbers, which also seem inadequate distinctions.

One day, for illustration, I was passing along a street of a city, far from here, when I met two men in uniform, one of whom, half pausing and looking curiously into my face, said to his companion, 'That man looks like 767.' Something in the number seemed familiar and horrible. Moved by an uncontrollable impulse, I sprang into a side-street and ran until I fell exhausted in a country lane.

I have never forgotten that number, and always it comes to memory attended by gibbering obscenity, peals of joyless laughter, the clang of iron doors. So I say a name, even if self-bestowed, is better than a number. In the register of the potter's field I shall soon have both. What wealth!

Of him who shall find this paper I must beg a little consideration. It is not the history of my life; the knowledge to write that is denied me. This is only a record of broken and apparently unrelated memories, some of them as distinct and sequent as brilliant beads upon a thread, others remote and strange, having the character of crimson dreams with interspaces blank and black—witch-fires glowing still and red in a great desolation.

Standing upon the shore of eternity, I turn for a last look landward over the course by which I came. There are twenty years of footprints fairly distant, the impressions of bleeding feet. They lead through poverty and pain, devious and unsure, as of one staggering beneath a burden—'Remote, unfriended, melancholy, slow.'

Ah, the poet's prophecy of me—how admirable, how dreadfully admirable!

Backward beyond the beginning of this *via dolorosa*—this epic of suffering with episodes of sin—I see nothing clearly; it comes out of a cloud. I know that it spans only twenty years, yet I am an old man.

One does not remember one's birth—one has to be told. But with me it was different; life came to me full-handed and endowed me with all my faculties and powers. Of a previous existence I know no more than others, for all have stammering intimations that may be memories and may be dreams. I know only that my first consciousness was of maturity in body and mind—a consciousness accepted without surprise or conjecture. I merely found myself walking in a forest, half-clad, footsore, unutterably weary and hungry. Seeing a farmhouse, I approached and asked for food, which was given me by one who inquired my name. I did not know, yet knew that all had names. Greatly embarrassed, I retreated, and night coming on, lay down in the forest and slept.

The next day I entered a large town which I shall not name. Nor shall I recount further incidents of the life that is now to end—a life of wandering, always and everywhere haunted by an overmastering sense of crime in punishment of wrong and of terror in punishment of crime. Let me see if I can reduce it to narrative.

I seem once to have lived near a great city, a prosperous planter, married to a woman whom I loved and distrusted. We had, it sometime seems, one child, a youth of brilliant parts and promise. He is at all times a vague figure, never clearly drawn, frequently altogether out of the picture.

One luckless evening it occurred to me to test my wife's fidelity in a vulgar, commonplace way familiar to everyone who has acquaintance with the literature of fact and fiction. I went to the city, telling my wife that I should be absent until the following afternoon. But I returned before daybreak and went to the rear of the house, proposing to enter by a door with which I had secretly so tampered that it would seem to lock, yet not actually fasten. As I approached it, I heard it gently open and close, and saw a man steal away into the darkness. With murder in my heart, I sprang after him, but he had vanished without even the bad luck of identification. Sometimes now I cannot even persuade myself that it was a human being.

Crazed with jealousy and rage, blind and bestial with all the elemental passions of insulted manhood, I entered the house and sprang up the stairs to the door of my wife's chamber. It was closed, but having tampered with its lock also, I easily entered, and despite the black darkness soon stood by the side of her bed. My groping hands told me that although disarranged it was unoccupied.

'She is below,' I thought, 'and terrified by my entrance has evaded me in the darkness of the hall.'

With the purpose of seeking her I turned to leave the room, but took a wrong direction—the right one! My foot struck her, cowering in a corner of the room. Instantly my hands were at her throat, stifling a shriek, my knees were upon her struggling body; and there in the darkness, without a word of accusation or reproach, I strangled her till she died!

There ends the dream. I have related it in the past tense, but the present would be the fitter form, for again and again the sombre tragedy re-enacts itself in my consciousness—over and over I lay the plan, I suffer the confirmation, I redress the wrong. Then all is blank; and afterwards the rains beat against the grimy window-panes, or the snows fall upon my scant attire, the wheels rattle in the squalid streets where my life lies in poverty and mean employment. If there is ever sunshine I do not recall it; if there are birds they do not sing.

There is another dream, another vision of the night. I stand among the shadows in a moonlit road. I am aware of another presence, but whose I cannot rightly determine. In the shadows of a great dwelling I catch the gleam of white garments; then the figure of a woman confronts me in the road—my murdered wife! There is death in the face; there are marks upon the throat. The eyes are fixed on mine with an infinite gravity which is not reproach, nor hate, nor menace, nor anything less terrible than recognition. Before this awful apparition I retreat in terror—a terror that is upon me as I write. I can no longer rightly shape the words. See! They——

Now I am calm, but truly there is no more to tell; the incident ends where it began—in darkness and in doubt.

Yes, I am again in control of myself: 'the captain of my soul'. But that is not respite; it is another stage and phase of expiation. My penance, constant in degree, is mutable in kind: one of its variants is tranquillity. After all, it is only a life-sentence. 'To hell for life'—that is a foolish penalty: the culprit chooses the duration of his punishment. Today my term expires.

To each and all, the peace that was not mine.

Statement of the Late Julia Hetman, through the Medium Bayrolles

I had retired early and fallen almost immediately into a peaceful sleep, from which I awoke with that indefinable sense of peril which is, I think, a common experience in that other, earlier life. Of its unmeaning character, too, I was entirely persuaded, yet that did not banish it. My husband, Joel Hetman, was away from home; the servants slept in another part of the house. But these were familiar conditions; they had never before distressed me. Nevertheless, the strange terror grew so insupportable that conquering my reluctance to move I sat up and lit the lamp at my bedside. Contrary to my expectation this gave me no relief; the light seemed rather an added danger, for I reflected that it would shine out under the door, disclosing my presence to whatever evil thing might lurk outside. You that are still in the flesh, subject to horrors of the imagination, think what a monstrous fear that must be which seeks in darkness security from malevolent existences of the night. That is to spring to close quarters with an unseen enemy—the strategy of despair!

Extinguishing the lamp I pulled the bedclothing about my head and lay trembling and silent, unable to shriek, forgetful to pray. In this pitiable state I must have lain for what you call hours—with us there are no hours, there is no time.

At last it came—a soft, irregular sound of footfalls on the stairs! They were slow, hesitant, uncertain, as of something that did not see its way; to my disordered reason all the more terrifying for that, as the approach of some blind and mindless malevolence to which there is no appeal. I even thought that I must have left the hall lamp burning and the groping of this creature proved it a monster of the night. This was foolish and inconsistent with my previous dread of the light, but what would you have? Fear has no brains; it is an idiot. The dismal witness that it bears and the cowardly counsel that it whispers are unrelated. We know this well, we who have passed into the realm of terror, who skulk in eternal dusk among the scenes of our former lives, invisible even to ourselves, and one another, yet hiding forlorn in lonely places; yearning for speech with our loved ones, yet dumb, and as fearful of them as they of us. Sometimes the disability is removed, the law suspended: by the deathless power of love or hate we break the spell—we are seen by those whom we would warn, console, or punish. What form we seem to them to bear we know not; we know only that we terrify even those whom we most wish to comfort, and from whom we most crave tenderness and sympathy.

Forgive, I pray you, this inconsequent digression by what was once a woman. You who consult us in this imperfect way—you do not understand. You ask foolish questions about things unknown and things forbidden. Much that we know and could impart in our speech is meaningless in yours. We must communicate with you through a stammering intelligence in that small fraction of our language that you yourselves can speak. You think that we are of another world. No, we have knowledge of no world but yours, though for us it holds no sunlight, no warmth, no music, no laughter, no song of birds, nor any companionship. O God! what a thing it is to be a ghost, cowering and shivering in an altered world, a prey to apprehension and despair!

No, I did not die of fright: the thing turned and went away. I heard it go down the stairs, hurriedly, I thought, as if itself in sudden fear. Then I rose to call for help. Hardly had my shaking hand found the door-knob when—merciful heaven!—I heard it returning. Its footfalls as it remounted the stairs were rapid, heavy and loud; they shook the house. I fled to an angle of the wall and crouched upon the floor. I tried to pray. I tried to call the name of my dear husband. Then I heard the door thrown open. There was an interval of unconsciousness, and when I revived I felt a strangling clutch upon my throat—felt my arms feebly beating against something that bore me backward—felt my tongue thrusting itself from between my teeth! And then I passed into this life.

No, I have no knowledge of what it was. The sum of what we knew at death is the measure of what we know afterward of all that went before. Of this existence we know many things, but no new light falls upon any page of that; in memory is written all of it that we can read. Here are no heights of truth overlooking the confused landscape of that dubitable domain. We still dwell in the Valley of the Shadow, lurk in its desolate places, peering from brambles and thickets at its mad, malign inhabitants. How should we have new knowledge of that fading past?

What I am about to relate happened on a night. We know when it is night, for then you retire to your houses and we can venture from our places of concealment to move unafraid about our old homes, to look in at the windows, even to enter and gaze upon your faces as you sleep. I had lingered long near the dwelling where I had been so cruelly changed to what I am, as we do while any that we love or hate remain. Vainly I had sought some method of manifestation, some way to make my continued existence and my great love and poignant pity understood by my husband and son. Always if they slept they would wake, or if in my desperation I dared approach them when they were awake, would turn toward me the terrible eyes of the living, frightening me by the glances that I sought from the purpose that I held.

On this night I had searched for them without success, fearing to find them; they were nowhere in the house, nor about the moonlit dawn. For, although the sun is lost to us for ever, the moon, full-orbed or slender, remains to us. Sometimes it shines by night, sometimes by day, but always it rises and sets, as in that other life.

I left the lawn and moved in the white light and silence along the road, aimless and sorrowing. Suddenly I heard the voice of my poor husband in exclamations of astonishment, with that of my son in re-assurance and dissuasion; and there by the shadow of a group of trees they stood—near, so near! Their faces were toward me, the eyes of the elder man fixed upon mine! He saw me—at last, at last, he saw me! In the consciousness of that, my terror fled as a cruel dream. The death-spell was broken: Love had conquered law! Mad with exultation I shouted—I *must* have shouted, 'He sees, he sees: he will understand!' Then, controlling myself, I moved forward, smiling and consciously beautiful, to offer myself to his arms, to comfort him with endearments, and, with my son's hand in mine, to speak words that should restore the broken bonds between the living and the dead.

Alas! alas! his face went white with fear, his eyes were as those of a hunted animal. He backed away from me, as I advanced, and at last turned and fled into the wood—whither, it is not given to me to know.

To my poor boy, left doubly desolate, I have never been able to impart a sense of my presence. Soon he, too, must pass to this Life Invisible and be lost to me for ever.

LORD BYRON
AND THE FAIRY QUEEN

Eleanor van Zandt

'Mad, bad and dangerous to know,' wrote Lady Caroline Lamb in her diary after observing Lord Byron at a ball. She had begged a friend to introduce her to the poet, although he told her that 'he has a club foot and bites his nails.'

'If he is as ugly as Aesop, I must see him,' she insisted.

Far from being ugly, he was extremely handsome. He was also the most celebrated man in London. His recently-published poem 'Childe Harold's Pilgrimage' had created a sensation. Its melancholic, introspective, yet pleasure-seeking hero (generally assumed by most people to be the poet himself) had totally captured the romantic imaginations of ladies of fashion. And *no* one had a more romantic imagination than Lady Caroline.

But when she finally saw Byron, surrounded by spellbound women, Lady Caroline had second thoughts. There was something disturbing about his unnaturally pale face, his penetrating eyes, his sensuous mouth—perhaps a slight suggestion of evil? She allowed the hostess to lead her towards Byron, then, when she was within a few feet of him, she abruptly turned away.

For Byron her rebuff was a challenge. Basically unsure of himself and acutely sensitive about his deformed foot, he could not endure such a snub. It was not because he found Lady Caroline particularly attractive. A woman, in his view, should be plump and placid. Lady Caroline was thin with a kind of elfin beauty, and her wide eyes revealed not only a lively intelligence but also a wilful streak, even a tendency towards hysteria. She was not his type. But she had refused to meet him, and Byron vowed that, by God, she would.

Caroline's lack of physical appeal in Byron's eyes was more than offset by her social position. Although a Lord by birth, he had lived most of his life on the fringes of society. She, by contrast, had been born into the most glittering circle of the aristocracy and had grown up mainly in the exciting atmosphere of Devonshire House, the London home of her aunt and uncle, the Duke and Duchess of Devonshire. The Duchess and her sister Lady Bessborough, Caroline's mother, were both charming, impulsive and extravagant, and they lived in a dizzy whirl of dances, card games and love affairs. Their children received affection but little supervision. Caroline's schooling was cut short on the advice of a doctor who feared it would place too great a burden on her high-strung temperament.

With this background, Caroline grew into a captivating, irrepressible young girl with a strong tomboyish streak. She loved to ride bareback and sometimes amused herself by dressing as a page—a costume that well became her slight figure and short golden curls. 'The Sprite', people called her, or 'The Savage' or more often 'The Fairy Queen'.

One person who found her irresistible was William Lamb, later Lord Melbourne, Queen Victoria's first Prime Minister. In his 20s, he possessed every quality needed to win a girl's heart: striking good looks, a fine mind, a sense of humour and a gentle, tolerant nature. Caroline returned his love, and in 1805 they were married.

Early in their marriage there were signs of storms to come. The first few days of their honeymoon were marred by the bride's becoming overwrought, then physically ill. A visit from Lady Bessborough calmed Caroline's nerves, and the young couple settled happily into what promised to be an idyllic married life

Delighting in his wife's intelligence, William set about educating her. They spent hours together, reading and discussing history, literature and philosophy. He also undertook to educate her in the ways of the world. Caroline was an innocent, for somehow, the social and political intrigues of Devonshire House had scarcely touched her consciousness; whereas the refinement of feeling and the idealism that also characterized her aunt and her mother had made a great impression on her. Like her mother, she was a devout Christian, and she was shocked by William's agnosticism as well as by his cynical worldliness.

'*He called me prudish,*' she wrote, '*said I was straitlaced—amused himself with instructing me in things I need never have heard or known, and the disgust I at first felt for the world's wickedness . . . in a very short time gave way to the general laxity of principles which, little by little . . . has been undermining the few virtues I ever possessed.*' William, she felt, had enough strength of character to steer a wise course for himself in a corrupt world; she, in her weakness, needed a strict code of behaviour.

If she was a bit wiser in worldly matters, Caroline was as prone as ever to romantic fantasies, and just as capricious and temperamental —qualities that William was beginning to find extremely trying. They began to quarrel; the quarrels grew more frequent. William— appalled at his own loss of self-control—began avoiding her company simply in order to prevent scenes. While he immersed himself in his parliamentary career, Caroline sought diversion in society.

One agreeable way of passing the time was waltzing. This fashionable new dance had society literally in a whirl. At Melbourne House the dancing began around noon and continued into the evening, with Caroline, as always, the centre of attention. 'A correct and animated waltzer,' commented the *Morning Post* approvingly.

But something in Caroline was never quite content with approval. It was more fun to shock people. An effective way of doing this, she discovered, was to cultivate new friends whose reputations were more than a little tarnished. This particularly annoyed her mother-in-law, Lady Melbourne. Lady Melbourne had had her share of lovers, but she had always conducted her affairs with discretion. Now her son's wife was hob-nobbing with Lady Wellesley and Lady Oxford, women who had cut themselves off from polite society by their scandalous affairs. As if that weren't enough, Caroline began a flirtation with Sir Godfrey Webster, a notorious young rake. As the friendship came to public notice, Lady Melbourne's indignation knew no bounds.

In time, Caroline drifted away from these questionable friends towards the world of Holland House, where the more intellectual aristocracy discussed literature with prominent men of letters. Fond of writing verses herself, Caroline responded warmly to the exotic, dramatic poetry of the day, with its concern for individual sensitivity. She always saw herself as a heroine, living on a plane far above her husband's mundane concerns. Inevitably, she discovered in Byron, the author of 'Childe Harold', a kindred spirit.

It was at Holland House that they finally met.

'I must present Lord Byron to you,' said Lady Holland, and this time Caroline did not turn away.

'This offer was made to you before,' said Byron, somewhat pompously; 'may I ask why you rejected it?'

Caroline's reply is unknown, but she did give Byron permission to call on her the following day.

When he arrived, she had just returned from riding and was chatting with two friends. 'I was filthy and heated,' she wrote later. 'When Lord Byron was announced I flew out of the room to wash myself. When I returned Rogers said, "Lord Byron, you are a happy man. Lady Caroline has been sitting here in all her dirt with us, but as soon as you were announced she flew to beautify herself."'

The second time he called she was alone, except for her little son Augustus. Byron charmed her with his attentions to the child, holding him on his lap for 'hours', she said. What woman can resist a dissolute man who has a soft spot for children—especially for her own child? By this time Caroline had no intention of resisting.

A few days later, Byron sent her an early rose and a carnation—then an exotic flower—with the pointed message, 'Your ladyship, I am told, likes all that is new and rare, for a moment.'

To this challenge Caroline wrote a long letter, in a formal, and literally 'flowery' style, containing a passage on 'the flower she most wishes to resemble', the sunflower, which 'having once beheld in its full lustre the bright and unclouded sun, that for one moment condescended to shine upon it, never while it exists could it think any lower object worthy of its worship and admiration.'

Byron might well have been put off by this effusive letter, but for some inadvertent encouragement from Caroline's mother. Alarmed at her daughter's growing involvement with the poet, which could only, she surmised, lead to trouble, Lady Bessborough made a point of telling him that Caroline's affections were engaged elsewhere (presumably not merely with her husband). She little suspected that this was the very thing to whet Byron's interest.

In that spring of 1812 the Byron-Lady Caroline affair was the talk of London. They were seen everywhere together—at parties, at the opera, driving in Hyde Park. Nearly every day Byron visited Caroline alone in her apartments on the first floor of Melbourne House—which, incidentally, no longer echoed to the strains of the waltz. Unable to dance himself, Byron professed himself shocked by this intimate new dance, and so Caroline gave it up. Letters and love tokens flew back and forth between Melbourne House and Byron's rooms in St James's Street.

By their actions the two proclaimed to the world that theirs was no ordinary love, such as ordinary people experience, but a *grande passion*. They scorned the discretion that marked lesser love affairs. When, occasionally, Byron alone was invited to a party, Lady Caroline would go and wait outside the house until the party broke up and he appeared; then the two would greet each other rapturously and ride off in his carriage.

Their jealousy matched their passion. Byron would make Caroline swear that she loved him more than William. Once, when she hesitated, he flew into a rage. 'My God, you shall pay for this!' he stormed; 'I'll wring that little obstinate heart!'

On another occasion, when they were at a dinner party together and Byron was being especially attentive to a beautiful woman sitting next to him, Caroline became so agitated that she bit through her glass. More than once, their mutual friend, the writer Samuel Rogers, returned home late at night to find Caroline pacing back and forth in his garden, waiting for him to patch up one of their many quarrels.

Sometime that summer the lovers went through a mock marriage ceremony. They exchanged rings and in a book wrote their 'marriage' vows, to which they signed their names. Caroline signed hers 'Caroline Byron'.

Nevertheless, by this time Byron was beginning to tire of the affair. From the beginning it was his ego, not his heart, that was involved. It had suited his 'image' to engage in a tempestuous love affair with another man's wife, particularly if the lady were of the *crème de la crème*.

But Caroline was becoming more than a bit wearisome. 'Little Mania', he called her in private. What's more, his own public role of 'Childe Harold' was becoming something of a hair shirt. No doubt he half believed himself to be a debauched and tragic figure, essentially an outcast from society, like his poem's hero. But in reality, his character was far more complex. He had a strong puritanical streak —the result of his early education in Scotland. Even more surprising, he longed for a tranquil, domestic life. Among his closest friends he was witty, high-spirited and fond of a joke.

He had very mixed feelings about women. On the one hand, he enjoyed their company; on the other, he despised them. All a woman needed to be content, he claimed, was a box of sweets and a looking-glass. Far from being a compulsive seducer of women, Byron simply took advantage of the endless opportunities that fame brought his way. He may have done the actual seducing, but in nearly every case the lady had first made it plain that she was ready to be seduced.

As he tired of Caroline's emotional demands, Byron found more congenial female company in the person of Lady Melbourne. There was a world of difference between the impassioned vows required by Caroline on the first floor of Melbourne House and the cool, witty conversation provided by her mother-in-law on the ground floor. For her part, Lady Melbourne savoured her new friendship for more reasons that one. It was extremely gratifying, at the age of 62, to be cultivated—if only platonically—by the most desirable young man in town. And it was even more gratifying to encourage him to break off his affair with Caroline.

There was nothing, at this point, that Byron wanted more; but he dreaded the scene that would inevitably result. In vain he tried to urge on Caroline a little self-control, hoping the relationship could be steered into calmer waters. But Caroline was convinced that he was the love of her life.

'You think me weak and selfish,' she wrote to him; 'you think I did not struggle to withstand my feelings. But it is indeed expecting more than human nature can bear. When I came in last night [to a party] —when I heard your name announced—the moment after I heard nothing more.'

She knew that Byron's feeling for her was waning. Suspecting—

rightly—that he was seeing other women, she disguised herself as a van-driver, stationed herself outside Byron's house and waited until she saw a woman enter it. Then, using some pretext, she got herself admitted to his rooms, where she revealed her identity. Embarrassing scenes of this kind only made Byron more determined to be rid of her.

In the midst of all these dramatics, Caroline's husband had, from the first kept a cool head. He knew Caroline well enough to realize that for her the *idea* of being in love with Byron was even more attractive than Byron himself. He also saw right through the poet's brooding 'Childe Harold' pose, and amused himself and infuriated Caroline by making fun of it. Given time, he thought, the whole business would blow over. He did not share the fears of Lady Bessborough that the two might elope. 'They neither wish nor intend going, but both like the fear and interest they create.'

Nevertheless, Lady Bessborough thought it wise to get Caroline out of London for a while, and she invited both Caroline and William to accompany herself and Lord Bessborough on a visit to their estates in Ireland. Caroline, predictably, raised objections. One morning in August Lady Bessborough called at Melbourne House and found it in confusion. Caroline had done something to annoy her father-in-law. When rebuked by him, she flew into a rage and threatened to go to Byron. 'Go and be damned,' replied the exasperated Lord Melbourne, 'But I don't think he'll take you.' At that, Caroline had dashed out of the house. Lord Melbourne shouted to the servants to follow her but she eluded them and disappeared into the crowds thronging Whitehall.

Lady Bessborough spent the day frantically driving round London trying to find her daughter. Byron, who had not seen her, promptly joined the search. That evening—after bribing and threatening the hackney coachman who had brought him a farewell note from Caroline—Byron finally traced her to the house of a surgeon in Kensington, where she was awaiting a stagecoach, planning to go to Portsmouth and sail on the first available ship, whatever its destination.

Pretending that she was his sister, Byron gained access to the house and managed to persuade Caroline to return with him to Cavendish Square, where her parents lived. There, the combined entreaties of Byron and Lady Bessborough eventually induced her to

She disguised herself as a van-driver and gained admittance to her room.

return to Melbourne House, where she received a gentle, kindly welcome from her husband and in-laws.

Caroline was considerably chastened—particularly by the effect of her attempted flight on her mother. During the search, the distraught Lady Bessborough had collapsed in a fit in her carriage, breaking a blood vessel, and the following day she was still very ill. The Bessborough housekeeper was so indignant that she sent Caroline a sharply-worded letter:

'O Lady Caroline, could you have seen her at that moment you surely would have been convinced how wickedly you are going on. She was perfectly senseless and her poor mouth drawn all to one side and as cold as marble we was all distracted even her footmen cried out *shame* on you for alas you have exposed yourself to all London— you are the talk of every groom and footman about Town.'

Though contrite, Caroline still begged that the trip to Ireland be delayed, or that she be excused, claiming that she was expecting a child. Then Byron himself left London for Cheltenham. Caroline's pregnancy proved imaginary, and early in September the Bessborough party, including William and Caroline set out for Ireland.

Ireland did little to improve Caroline's state of mind. One moment she would be dancing a jig, charming the villagers. A little later she would be lying on the floor kicking and screaming, while her long-suffering husband and mother tried to calm her . At other times she would lavish affection on her husband. Indeed, everyone remarked on her obvious devotion to him. 'When they say this to me,' wrote her mother irritably, 'I want to bellow.'

Throughout the two months she spent in Ireland, Caroline was in an agony of uncertainty about Byron. He had, at their parting, sent her a letter full of protestations of his love, signing it, 'Ever and ever, more than ever, Your most attached, Byron.' For a while his letters continued, then they stopped.

All the time, Byron was conducting a brisk correspondence with Lady Melbourne and sharing with her many a laugh over Caroline's bizarre behaviour. He had also become involved—in very different ways—with two other women.

Shortly after meeting Caroline the previous spring, Byron had also met her cousin Annabella Milbanke, Lady Melbourne's niece.

Attractive, noted for her intelligence and intellectual pursuits (Byron dubbed her the 'Princess of Parallelograms'), Miss Milbanke was also heiress to a large fortune—a notable asset in the eyes of the financially hard-pressed Byron. She, like most women, found him fascinating. He had 'a noble heart', she decided, but one 'perverted by unkindness', and she 'vowed in secret to be a devoted friend to this lone being'.

Encouraged by Lady Melbourne, Byron now paid court to Annabella in a half-hearted fashion. When he proposed, however, she turned him down, having decided that he did not possess the strength of character she required in a husband. Byron accepted the refusal with something approaching relief; he had found her a little too high-minded, despite the attractions of her 'placid countenance' and substantial fortune. Later, she was to re-open the friendship and deftly lead him towards a second proposal, with disastrous results.

But now, with Annabella out of the picture temporarily and Caroline in Ireland, Byron turned to Lady Oxford. Here was a woman who demanded neither lofty principles nor melodramatic gestures. She did, however, insist that he make a clean break with Caroline, and this Byron agreed to do.

Having heard nothing from Byron for weeks, despite her anxious letters, Caroline received, one day, a terse letter that opened with the words, 'I am no longer your lover,' and closed with the following admonition: 'As to yourself, Lady Caroline, correct your vanity which has become ridiculous—exert your caprices on others, enjoy the excellent flow of spirits which make you so delightful in the eyes of others, and leave me in peace.'

The effect on Caroline can be imagined. In her frenzy she seized a razor and tried to cut her throat, but was prevented from doing so by her mother. For the next two weeks Caroline lay in bed in a state of nervous collapse.

On returning to England in November she immediately resumed her frantic efforts to get Byron's attention. Though aware that she had lost his love—or what had passed for love—she seemed impelled to embarrass and exasperate him in every outlandish way she could devise. At the Melbourne country house, Brocket, she staged a ceremonial burning of all the love tokens he had given her, as well as copies of his letters. Little girls recruited from the nearby village of Welwyn were dressed in white and instructed to dance round the bonfire, while a page recited a poem specially written by Caroline for the occasion, which went, in part:

'Burn, fire, burn, while wondering boys exclaim,
And gold and trinkets glitter in the flame.
Ah, look not thus on me, so grave, so sad,
Shake not your heads, nor say the lady's mad.'

Shortly after the Brocket bonfire, Caroline realized that she no longer had a picture of Byron. So she forged a letter in his handwriting requesting his publisher, John Murray, to send him a portrait of himself that Byron had lent him. Caroline presented the letter to Murray, who handed over the portrait. 'I presume she got it by flinging his own best bound folio at his head,' wrote Byron to Lady Melbourne, exasperated, yet amused.

For a long time Caroline had been pleading to meet Byron again. Finally, worn down by her entreaties, he agreed. The interview seems to have been relatively tranquil. In her account of it, Caroline wrote, 'he looked sorry for me: he cried; I adored him still, but I felt as passionless as the dead may feel.'

Whether Byron cried is doubtful; his feelings towards her now bordered on hatred. He was not amused to learn that her pages' uniforms were adorned with buttons inscribed *Ne Crede Byron*, 'Do not believe in Byron,' a contradiction of his family motto, *Crede Byron*. A growing segment of London society was beginning to believe that he had treated Lady Caroline badly; his popularity was slipping.

As for Lady Caroline, she was hardly as resigned as she claimed. A few weeks after the interview, at a ball, she made a scene that had London buzzing for days afterwards. It was the first time for many months that she and Byron had met in public. When the dancing began she went up to him and said pointedly, 'I presume *now* I am allowed to waltz.' He told her she could do as she liked. A little later, passing her in a doorway, he whispered sarcastically, 'I have been admiring your dexterity.' This remark threw Caroline into a rage. Running into the upper room, she broke one of the glasses and began to slash her arms with the fragments. In the commotion that followed, Lady Melbourne succeeded in grasping Caroline's hands and subduing her—temporarily. A few moments later, freed from restraint, Caroline got hold of some scissors and again and again began slashing at herself. Again Lady Melbourne seized her, and soon Caroline was borne out of the room and taken home.

Byron, who had moved into another room of the house where the ball took place, claimed later that he was unaware of the episode. His expressions of concern for Caroline's health were tinged with irritation. 'If I am to be haunted with hysterics wherever I go and whatever I do,' he wrote to Lady Melbourne, 'I think she is not the only person to be pitied.'

To her sorrow and humiliation Caroline soon realized that she was now a social outcast. Before the ball, her violent scenes had taken place in private; now she had made a public spectacle of herself and brought shame on her family. Newspapers published accounts of the incident—'put not truly,' said Caroline. She had always lived secure in the assumption that people would tolerate any eccentric behaviour on her part—even admire her for it. To see the contempt in their eyes was unbearable.

Though pressed by his family to separate from Caroline, William stood by her loyally. He took her to Brocket and endured, with occasional flashes of temper, her wild swings from frenetic gaiety to uncontrolled rage and back again. The following year, he took her on a visit to Paris. There her spirits improved. Once more, she was the centre of attention—in some circles at least—and her vivacity and charm won her new admirers, including the Iron Duke.

When the Lambs returned to London, Caroline resumed her pursuit of Byron. Once, having slipped into his rooms while he was out, she wrote in one of his books, 'Remember me!' On discovering the message Byron penned a savage retort in two stanzas, the second of which read:

> Remember thee! Ay, doubt it not,
> Thy husband too shall think of thee,
> By neither shalt thou be forgot,
> Thou *false* to him, thou *fiend* to me!'

Early in 1815 Byron married Annabella Milbanke. Caroline took this event remarkably calmly—perhaps because at their last meeting Byron had 'showed me letters, and told me things I cannot repeat, and all my attachment went.'

It seems likely that the things he told her concerned his relationship with his half-sister Augusta. The exact nature of this relationship is still something of a mystery, but Augusta was, almost certainly, the only woman Byron ever truly loved. He was, he wrote, 'utterly incapable of *real* love for any other human being—for what could they be for me after *you*?'

He married Annabella in a desperate attempt to escape from his attachment to Augusta. Not surprisingly, the marriage failed. Annabella and her good intentions brought out the worst in Byron; he tormented her continually. For a year she endured his insults, his black depressions and violent rages, then she left him. Soon afterwards Byron left England for the Continent, where he flung himself first into a life of dissipation and later into the struggles for Italian and Greek independence. He also produced some of his best literary work.

Literary fame, of a sort, was also achieved by Caroline. Her mental instability had become more and more obvious, until finally, after she had injured one of her pages (though not seriously), William was persuaded by his family to start separation proceedings. But Caroline still knew how to get round him, and on the very day the document was to be signed, the two of them were reconciled. In the meantime, however, she had begun work on a novel—one in which she intended to settle a few scores. She worked on it feverishly, mainly at night, and finished it in a month. She then sent it to a publisher.

The publication of *Glenarvon* created a furore. Superficially a Gothic romance, full of gloomy castles, monsters, ghosts and assassins, it is really about Caroline, Byron, William, their families, friends and acquaintances. At the heart of its labyrinthine plot is the story of the love between Calantha, a tragic heroine, and the mysterious, doom-ridden Glenarvon. Both protagonists die in the end, as does Calantha's husband Lord Avondale. Despite the fantastic story, readers had no difficulty identifying the originals of the characters portrayed in it.

Lady Caroline's few remaining allies, apart from her own family, now deserted her. People snubbed her in public. As for the Lambs, they were beside themselves. To have their personal affairs published for all the world to read was the ultimate humiliation. Once more, William resolved on a separation.

Yet again, his kindheartedness prevailed. He could not desert Caroline when she was being reviled on all sides, even in the newspapers. 'Caroline,' he said, 'we will stand or fall together.'

For most of the next 12 years they lived together at Brocket. It was a harrowing existence. At times Caroline was composed, at times animated, but her rages grew increasingly frequent. One morning she smashed £200 worth of china. Sometimes she had to be forcibly confined to her room. Here, she had hung a portrait of Byron, an altar cloth and a crucifix. Once, while ill, she thought she saw Byron: 'I screamed, jumped out of bed . . . He looked horrible and ground his teeth at me, he did not speak . . .'

News of Byron's death in Greece, several years later, sent her into an hysterical fever that lasted for three months. By an unfortunate coincidence, on the first day she was well enough to go out driving she and William encountered a funeral procession—Byron's. When she learned later whose it was she suffered a relapse.

As the years passed, her mind continued to deteriorate. During lucid periods she wrote; two more novels—innocuous ones—were published. She visited and entertained aspiring young writers. She made several attempts to re-launch herself into society, but she cut a pathetic figure in her slovenly clothes, desperately flirting with any presentable young man available. At times she seemed poignantly aware that to a great extent she had brought about her own unhappiness. 'The slave of impulse—I have rushed forward to my own destruction.'

By a cruel irony the illness that killed Lady Caroline Lamb—the delicate 'Fairy Queen'—was dropsy, a disease that causes unsightly swelling in the body. Mercifully, her suffering was not prolonged, and she bore it bravely and quietly. When she knew she was dying, she whispered, 'Send for William—he is the only person who has never failed me.' Her husband returned from Ireland, where he had been conducting some government business, and was in time to comfort her before her tragic life came to a close.

THE STORY OF
THE BAGMAN'S UNCLE

Charles Dickens

'My uncle, gentlemen,' said the bagman, 'was one of the merriest, pleasantest, cleverest fellows that ever lived. I wish you had known him, gentlemen. If any two of his numerous virtues predominated over the many that adorned his character, I should say they were his mixed punch, and his after-supper song. Excuse my dwelling on these melancholy recollections of departed worth; you won't see a man like my uncle every day in the week.

'In personal appearance, my uncle was a trifle shorter than the middle size; he was a thought stouter, too, than the ordinary run of people, and perhaps his face might be a shade redder. He had the jolliest face you ever saw, gentlemen: something like Punch, with a handsomer nose and chin; his eyes were always twinkling and sparkling with good humour; and a smile—not one of your unmeaning, wooden grins, but a real merry, hearty, good-tempered smile—was perpetually on his countenance. He was pitched out of his gig once, and knocked, head first, against a milestone. There he lay, stunned, and so cut about the face with some gravel which had been heaped up alongside it, that, to use my uncle's own strong expression, if his mother could have revisited the earth, she wouldn't have known him. However, there he lay, and I have heard my uncle say, many a time, that the man said who picked him up that he was smiling as merrily as if he had tumbled out for a treat, and that after they had bled him, the first faint glimmerings of returning animation were, his jumping up in bed, bursting out into a loud laugh, kissing the young woman who held the basin, and demanding a mutton chop and a pickled walnut instantly. He was very fond of pickled walnuts, gentlemen. He said he always found that, taken without vinegar, they relished the beer.

'My uncle's great journey was in the fall of the leaf, at which time he collected debts for Tiggin and Welps, and took orders, in the north: going from London to Edinburgh, from Edinburgh to Glasgow, from Glasgow back to Edinburgh, and thence to London by the smack. You are to understand that his second visit to Edinburgh was for his own pleasure. He used to go back for a week, just to look up his old friends; and what with breakfasting with this one, lunching with that, dining with a third, and supping with another, a pretty tight week he used to make of it. I don't know whether any of you gentlemen ever partook of a real substantial hospitable Scotch breakfast, and then went out to a slight lunch of a bushel of oysters, a dozen or so of bottled ale, and a noggin or two of whiskey to close up with. If you ever did, you will agree with me that it requires a pretty strong head to go out to dinner and supper afterwards.

'But bless your hearts and eyebrows, all this sort of thing was nothing to my uncle! He was so well seasoned, that it was mere child's play. I have heard him say that he could see the Dundee people out any day, and walk home afterwards without staggering; and yet the Dundee people have as strong heads and as strong punch, gentlemen, as you are likely to meet with between the poles. I have heard of a Glasgow man and a Dundee man drinking against each other for fifteen hours at a sitting. They were both suffocated, as nearly as could be ascertained, at the same moment, but with this trifling exception, gentlemen, they were not a bit the worse for it.

'One night, within four-and-twenty hours of the time when he had settled to take shipping for London, my uncle supped at the house of a very old friend of his, a Baillie Mac something, and four syllables after it, who lived in the old town of Edinburgh. There were the baillie's wife and the baillie's three daughters, and baillie's grown-up son, and three of four stout, bushy-eyebrowed, canty old Scotch fellows, that the baillie had got together to do honour to my uncle, and help to make merry. It was a glorious supper. There were kippered salmon, and Finnan haddocks, and a lamb's head, and a haggis—a celebrated Scotch dish, gentlemen, which my uncle used to say always looked to him, when it came to table, very much like a cupid's stomach—and a great many other things besides, that I forget the names of, but very good things notwithstanding. The lassies were pretty and agreeable; the baillie's wife, one of the best creatures that ever lived; and my uncle in thoroughly good cue: the consequences of which was, that the young ladies tittered and giggled, and the old lady laughed out loud, and the baillie and the other fellows roared till they were red in the face, the whole mortal time. I don't quite recollect how many tumblers of whiskey toddy each man drank after supper; but this I know, that about one o'clock in the morning, the baillie's grown-up son became insensible while attempting the first verse of "Willie brewed a peck o'maut"; and he having been, for half an hour before, the only other man visible above the mahogany, it occurred to my uncle that it was almost time to think about going: especially as drinking had set in at seven o'clock, in order that he might get home at a decent hour. But, thinking it might not be quite polite to go just then, my uncle voted himself into the chair, mixed another glass, rose to propose his own health, addressed himself in a neat and complimentary speech, and drank the toast with great enthusiasm. Still nobody woke; so my uncle took a little drop more—neat this time, to prevent the toddy disagreeing with him—and, laying violent hands on his hat, sallied forth into the street.

'It was a wild gusty night when my uncle closed the baillie's door, and setting his hat firmly on his head, to prevent the wind from taking it, thrust his hands into his pockets, and looking upwards, took a short survey of the state of the weather. The clouds were drifting over the moon at their giddiest speed: at one time wholly obscuring her: at another, suffering her to burst forth in full splendour and shed her light on all the objects around: anon, driving over her again with increased velocity, and shrouding everything in darkness. "Really, this won't do," said my uncle, addressing himself to the weather, as if he felt himself personally offended. "This is not at all the kind of thing for my voyage. It will not do at any price," said my uncle very impressively. Having repeated this several times, he recovered his balance with some difficulty—for he was rather giddy with looking up into the sky so long—and walked merrily on.

'The baillie's house was in the Canongate, and my uncle was going to the other end of Leith Walk, rather better than a mile's journey. On either side of him, there shot up against the dark sky, tall, gaunt, straggling houses, with time-stained fronts, and windows that seemed to have shared the lot of eyes in mortals, and to have grown dim and sunken with age. Six, seven, eight stories high, were the houses; story piled above story, as children build with cards—throwing their dark shadows over the roughly paved road, and making the dark night darker. A few oil lamps scattered at long distances, but they only served to mark the dirty entrance to some narrow close, or to show where a common stair communicated, by steep and intricate windings, with the various flats above. Glancing at all these things with the air of a man who had seen them too often before to think them worthy of much notice now, my uncle walked up the middle of the street, with a thumb in each waistcoat pocket, indulging, from time to time, in various snatches of song, chanted forth with such good-will and spirit, that the quiet honest folk started from their first sleep, and lay trembling in bed till the sound died away in the distance; when, satisfying themselves that it was only some drunken ne'er-do-weel finding his way home, they covered themselves up warm and fell asleep again.

'I am particular in describing how my uncle walked up the middle of the street, with his thumbs in his waistcoat pockets, gentlemen, because, as he often used to say (and with great reason too), there is nothing at all extraordinary in this story, unless you distinctly understand at the beginning that he was not by any means of a marvellous or romantic turn.

'Gentlemen, my uncle walked on with his thumbs in his waistcoat pockets, taking the middle of the street to himself, and singing, now a verse of a love song, and then a verse of a drinking one, and when he was tired of both, whistling melodiously, until he reached the North Bridge, which, at this point, connects the old and new towns of Edinburgh. Here he stopped for a minute, to look at the strange irregular clusters of lights piled one above the other, and twinkling afar off, so high in the air, that they looked like stars, gleaming from the castle walls on the one side, and then Calton Hill on the other, as if they illuminated veritable castles in the air: while the old picturesque town slept heavily on, in gloom and darkness below: its palace and chapel of Holyrood, guarded day and night, as a friend of my uncle's used to say, by old Arthur's Seat, towering, surly and dark, like some gruff genius, over the ancient city he has watched so long. I say, gentlemen, my uncle stopped here, for a minute, to look about him; and then paying a compliment to the weather, which had a little cleared up, though the moon was sinking, walked on again, as royally as before: keeping the middle of the road with great dignity, and looking as if he should very much like to meet with somebody who would dispute possession of it with him. There was nobody at all disposed to contest the point, as it happened; and so, on he went, with his thumbs in his waistcoat pockets, like a lamb.

'When my uncle reached the end of Leith Walk, he had to cross a pretty large piece of waste ground, which separated him from a short street which he had to turn down, to go direct to his lodging. Now, in this piece of waste ground, there was, at that time, an enclosure belonging to some wheelwright, who contracted with the Post Office for the purchase of old worn-out mail-coaches; and my uncle, being very fond of coaches, old, young, or middle-aged, all at once took it into his head to step out of his road for no other purpose than to peep between the palings at these mails; about a dozen of which he remembered to have seen, crowded together in a very forlorn and dismantled state, inside. My uncle was a very enthusiastic, emphatic sort of person, gentlemen; so, finding that he could not obtain a good peep between the palings, he got over them, and sitting himself quietly down on an old axletree, began to contemplate the mail-coaches with a deal of gravity.

'There might be a dozen of them, or there might be more—my uncle was never quite certain on this point, and being a man of very scrupulous veracity about numbers, didn't like to say—but there they stood, all huddled together in the most desolate condition imaginable. The doors had been torn from their hinges and removed; the linings had been stripped off: only a shred hanging here and there by a rusty nail; the lamps were gone, the poles had long since vanished, the iron-work was rusty, the paint worn away; the wind whistled through the chinks in the bare woodwork; and the rain which had collected on the roofs, fell, drop by drop, into the insides with a hollow and melancholy sound. They were the decaying skeletons of departed mails, and in that lonely place, at that time of night, they looked chill and dismal.

'My uncle rested his head upon his hands, and thought of the busy bustling people who had rattled about, years before, in the old coaches, and were now as silent and changed: he thought of the numbers of people to whom one of those crazy, mouldering vehicles had borne, night after night, for many years, and through all weathers, the anxiously expected intelligence, the eagerly looked-for remittance, the promised assurance of health and safety, the sudden announcement of sickness and death. The merchant, the lover, the wife, the widow, the mother, the schoolboy, the very child who tottered to the door at the postman's knock—how had they all looked forward to the arrival of the old coach! And where were they all now?

'Gentlemen, my uncle used to *say* that he thought all this at the time, but I rather suspect he learnt it out of some book afterwards, for he distinctly stated that he fell into a kind of a doze as he sat on the old axletree looking at the decaying mail-coaches, and that he was suddenly awakened by some deep church bell striking two. Now, my uncle was never a fast thinker, and if he had thought all these things, I am quite certain it would have taken him till full half-past two o'clock, at the very least. I am, therefore, decidedly of opinion, gentlemen, that my uncle fell into a kind of doze, without having thought about anything at all.

'Be this as it may, a church bell struck two. My uncle woke, rubbed his eyes, and jumped up in astonishment.

'In one instant after the clock struck two, the whole of this deserted and quiet spot had become a scene of most extraordinary life and animation. The mail-coach doors were on their hinges, the lining was replaced, the iron-work was as good as new, the paint was restored, the lamps were alight, cushions and great coats were on every coach-box, porters were thrusting parcels into every boot, guards were stowing away letter-bags, hostlers were dashing pails of water against the renovated wheels; numbers of men were rushing about, fixing poles into every coach; passengers arrived, portmanteaus were handed up, horses were put to; and, in short, it was perfectly clear that every mail there was to be off directly. Gentlemen, my uncle opened his eyes so wide at all this, that, to the very last moment of his life, he used to wonder how it fell out that he had ever been able to shut 'em again.

'"Now then!" said a voice, as my uncle felt a hand on his shoulder. "You're booked for one inside. You'd better get in."

'"*I* booked!" said my uncle, turning round.

'"Yes, certainly."

'My uncle, gentlemen, could say nothing; he was so very much astonished. The queerest thing of all was, that although there was such a crowd of persons, and although fresh faces were pouring in every moment, there was no telling where they came from; they seemed to start up, in some strange manner, from the ground or the air, and disappear in the same way. When a porter had put his luggage in the coach, and received his fare, he turned round and was gone; and before my uncle had well begun to wonder what had become of him, half-a-dozen fresh ones started up, and staggered along under the weight of parcels which seemed big enough to crush them. The passengers were all dressed so oddly too—large, broad-skirted, laced coats with great cuffs, and no collars; and wigs, gentlemen,—great formal wigs and a tie behind. My uncle could make nothing of it.

'"Now, *are* you going to get in?" said the person who had addressed my uncle before. He was dressed as a mail guard, with a wig on his head, and most enormous cuffs to his coat, and had a lantern in one hand, and a huge blunderbuss in the other, which he was going to stow away in his little arm-chest. "*Are* you going to get in, Jack Martin?" said the guard, holding the lantern to my uncle's face.

'"Hallo!" said my uncle, falling back a step or two. "That's familiar!"

'"It's so on the way-bill," replied the guard.

'"Isn't there a 'Mister' before it?" said my uncle—for he felt, gentlemen, that for a guard he didn't know to call him Jack Martin, was a liberty which the Post Office wouldn't have sanctioned if they had known it.

'"No; there is not," rejoined the guard coolly.

'"Is the fare paid?" inquired my uncle.

'"Of course it is," rejoined the guard.

'"It is, is it?" said my uncle. "Then here goes—which coach?"

'"This," said the guard, pointing to an old-fashioned Edinburgh and London Mail, which had the steps down, and the door open. "Stop—here are the other passengers. Let them get in first."

'As the guard spoke, there all at once appeared, right in front of my uncle, a young gentleman in a powdered wig, and a sky-blue coat trimmed with silver, made very full and broad in the skirts, which were lined with buckram. Tiggin and Welps were in the printed calico and waistcoat-piece line, gentlemen, so my uncle knew all the materials at once. He wore knees breeches, and a kind of leggings rolled up over his silk stockings, and shoes with buckles; he had ruffles at his wrists, a three-cornered hat on his head, and a long taper sword by his side. The flaps of his waistcoat came half-way down his thighs, and the ends of his cravat reached to his waist. He stalked gravely to the coach door, pulled off his hat, and held it above his head at arm's length: cocking his little finger in the air at the same time, as some affected people do when they take a cup of tea. Then he drew his feet together, and made a low grave bow, and then put out his left hand. My uncle was just going to step forward, and shake it heartily, when he perceived that these attentions were directed, not towards him, but to a young lady, who just then appeared at the foot of the steps, attired in an old-fashioned green velvet dress, with a long waist and stomacher. She had no bonnet on her head, gentlemen, which was muffed in a black silk hood, but she looked round for an instant as she prepared to get into the coach, and such a beautiful face as she discovered, my uncle had never seen—not even in a picture. She got into the coach, holding up her dress with one hand; and, as my uncle always said with a round oath, when he told the story, he wouldn't have believed it possible that legs and feet could have been brought to such a state of perfection, unless he had seen them with his own eyes.

'But, in this one glimpse of the beautiful face, my uncle saw that the young lady had cast an imploring look upon him, and that she appeared terrified and distressed. He noticed, too, that the young fellow in the powdered wig, notwithstanding his show of gallantry, which was all very fine and grand, clasped her tight by the wrist when she got in, and

729

followed himself immediately afterwards. An uncommonly ill-looking fellow in a close brown wig and a plum-coloured suit, wearing a very large sword, and boots up to his hips, belonged to the party; and when he sat himself down next to the young lady, who shrunk into a corner at his approach, my uncle was confirmed in his original impression that something dark and mysterious was going forward, or, as he always said himself, that "there was a screw loose somewhere." It's quite surprising how quickly he made up his mind to help the lady at any peril, if she needed help.

'"Death and lightning!" exclaimed the young gentleman, laying his hand upon his sword, as my uncle entered the coach.

'"Blood and thunder!" roared the other gentleman. With this, he whipped his sword out, and made a lunge at my uncle without further ceremony. My uncle had no weapon about him, but with great dexterity he snatched the ill-looking gentleman's three-cornered hat from his head, and receiving the point of his sword right through the crown, squeezed the sides together, and held it tight.

'"Pink him behind!" cried the ill-looking gentleman to his companion, as he struggled to regain his sword.

'"He had better not," cried my uncle, displaying the heel of one of his shoes in a threatening manner. "I'll kick his brains out if he has any, or fracture his skull if he hasn't." Exerting all his strength at this moment, my uncle wrenched the ill-looking man's sword from his grasp, and flung it clean out of the coach window; upon which the younger gentleman vociferated "Death and lightning!" again, and laid his hand upon the hilt of his sword in a very fierce manner, but didn't draw it. Perhaps, gentlemen, as my uncle used to say, with a smile, perhaps he was afraid of alarming the lady.

'"Now, gentlemen," said my uncle, taking his seat deliberately, "I don't want to have any death, with or without lightning, in a lady's presence, and we have had quite blood and thundering enough for one journey; so, if you please, we'll sit in our places like quiet insides. Here, guard, pick up that gentleman's carving knife."

'As quickly as my uncle said the words, the guard appeared at the coach window, with the gentleman's sword in his hand. He held up his lantern and looked earnestly in my uncle's face, as he handed it in: when, by its light, my uncle saw, to his great surprise, that an

A young lady appeared at the foot of the steps.

immense crowd of mail-coach guards swarmed round the window, every one of whom had his eyes earnestly fixed upon him too. He had never seen such a sea of white faces, and red bodies, and earnest eyes, in all his born days.

'"This is the strangest sort of thing I ever had anything to do with," thought my uncle. "Allow me to return you your hat, sir."

'The ill-looking gentleman received his three-cornered hat in silence; looked at the hole in the middle with an inquiring air; and finally stuck it on the top of his wig, with a solemnity the effect of which was a trifle impaired by his sneezing violently at the moment, and jerking it off again.

'"All right!" cried the guard with the lantern, mounting into his little seat behind. Away they went. My uncle peeped out of the coach window as they emerged from the yard, and observed that the other mails, with coachmen, guards, horses, and passengers, complete, were driving round and round in circles, at a slow trot of about five miles an hour. My uncle burnt with indignation, gentleman. As a commercial man, he felt that the mail-bags were not to be trifled with, and he resolved to memorialize the Post Office on the subject, the very instant he reached London.

'At present, however, his thoughts were occupied with the young lady who sat in the farthest corner of the coach, with her face muffled closely in her hood: the gentleman with the sky-blue coat sitting opposite to her: and the other man in the plum-coloured suit at her side: and both watching her intently. If she so much as rustled the folds of her hood, he could hear the ill-looking man clap his hand upon his sword, and could tell by the other's breathing (it was so dark he couldn't see his face) that he was looking as big as if he were going to devour her at a mouthful. This roused my uncle more and more, and he resolved, come what come might, to see the end of it. He had a great admiration for bright eyes, and sweet faces, and pretty legs and feet; in short, he was fond of the whole sex. It runs in our family, gentlemen—so am I.

'Many were the devices which my uncle practised to attract the lady's attention, or, at all events, to engage the mysterious gentleman in conversation. They were all in vain; the gentleman wouldn't talk, and the lady didn't dare. He thrust his head out of the coach window at intervals, and bawled out to know why they didn't go faster. But he called till he was hoarse—nobody paid the least attention to him. He leant back in the coach, and thought of the beautiful face, and the feet, and legs. This answered better; it whiled away the time, and kept him from wondering where he was going, and how it was he found himself in such an odd situation. Not that this would have worried him much, anyway—he was a mighty free and easy, roving, devil-may-care sort of person, was my uncle, gentlemen.

'All of a sudden the coach stopped. "Hallo!" said my uncle, "what's in the wind now?"

'"Alight her," said the guard, letting down the steps.

'"Here!" cried my uncle.

'"Here," rejoined the guard.

'"I'll do nothing of the sort," said my uncle.

'"Very well, then stop where you are," said the guard.

'"I will," said my uncle.

'"Do," said the guard.

'The other passengers had regarded this colloquy with great attention; and, finding that my uncle was determined not to alight, the younger man squeezed past him, to hand the lady out. At this moment, the ill-looking man was inspecting the hole in the crown of his three-corned hat. As the young lady brushed past, she dropped one of her gloves into my uncle's hand, and softly whispered with her lips so close to his face, that he felt her warm breath on his nose, the single word "Help!" Gentlemen, my uncle leaped out of the coach at once, with such violence that it rocked on the springs again.

'"Oh! you've thought better of it, have you?" said the guard, when he saw my uncle standing on the ground.

'My uncle looked at the guard for a few seconds, in some doubt whether it wouldn't be better to wrench his blunderbuss from him, fire it in the face of the man with the big sword, knock the rest of the company over the head with the stock, snatch up the young lady, and go off in the smoke. On second thoughts, however, he abandoned this plan, as being a shade too melodramatic in the execution, and followed the two mysterious men, who, keeping the lady between them, were now entering an old house, in front of which the coach had stopped. They turned into the passage, and my uncle followed.

'Of all the ruinous and desolate places my uncle had ever beheld, this was the most so. It looked as if it had once been a large house of entertainment; but the roof had fallen in in many places, and the stairs were steep, rugged, and broken. There was a huge fire-place in the room into which they walked, and the chimney was blackened with smoke; but no warm blaze lighted it up now. The white feathery dust of burnt wood was still strewed over the hearth, but the stove was cold, and all was dark and gloomy.

'"Well," said my uncle, as he looked about him, "a mail travelling at the rate of six and half an hour, and stopping for an indefinite time at such a hole as this, is rather an irregular sort of proceeding, I fancy. This shall be made known; I'll write to the papers."

'My uncle said this in a pretty loud voice, and in an open unreserved sort of manner, with the view of engaging the two strangers in conversation if he could. But, neither of them took any more notice of him than whispering to each other, and scowling at him as they did so. The lady was at the farther end of the room, and once she ventured to wave her hand, as if beseeching my uncle's assistance.

'At length the two strangers advanced a little, and the conversation began in earnest.

'"You don't know this is a private room, I suppose, fellow?" said the gentleman in sky-blue.

'"No, I do not, fellow," rejoined my uncle. "Only if this is a private room specially ordered for the occasion, I should think the public room must be a *very* comfortable one." With this my uncle sat himself down in the high-backed chair, and took such an accurate measure of the gentlemen with his eyes, that Tiggin and Welps could have supplied him with printed calico for a suit, and not an inch too much or too little, from that estimate alone.

'"Quit this room," said both the men together, grasping their swords.

'"Eh?" said my uncle, not at all appearing to comprehend their meaning.

'"Quit the room, or you are a dead man," said the ill-looking fellow with the large sword, drawing it at the same time, and flourishing it in the air.

'"Down with him!" cried the gentleman in sky-blue, drawing his sword also, and falling back two or three yards. "Down with him!" The lady gave a loud scream.

'Now, my uncle was always remarkable for great boldness, and great presence of mind. All the time that he had appeared so indifferent to what was going on, he had been looking slily about for some missile or weapon of defence, and at the very instant when the swords were drawn, he espied, standing in the chimney-corner, and old basket-hilted rapier in a rusty scabbard. At one bound, my uncle caught it in his hand, drew it, flourished it gallantly above his head, called aloud to the lady to keep out of the way, hurled the chair at the man in sky-blue, and the scabbard at the man in plum-colour, and taking advantage of the confusion, fell upon them both, pell-mell.

'Gentlemen, there is an old story—none the worse for being true—regarding a fine young Irish gentleman, who being asked if he could play the fiddle, replied he had no doubt he could, but he couldn't exactly say for certain, because he had never tried. This is not inapplicable to my uncle and his fencing. He had never had a sword in his hand before, except once when he played Richard the Third at a private theatre: upon which occasion it was arranged with Richmond that he was to be run through from behind, without showing fight at all; but here he was, cutting and slashing with two experienced swordsmen, thrusting, and guarding, and poking, and slicing, and acquitting himself in the most manful and dexterous manner possible, although up to that time, he had never been aware that he had the least notion of the science. It only shows how true the old saying is, that a man never knows what he can do till he tries, gentlemen.

'The noise of the combat was terrific; each of the three combatants swearing like troopers, and their swords clashing with as much noise as if all the knives and steels in Newport Market were rattling together at the same time. When it was at its very height, the lady, to encourage my uncle most probably, withdrew her hood entirely from her face, and disclosed a countenance of such dazzling beauty, that he would have fought against fifty men, to win one smile from it, and die. He had done wonders before, but now he began to powder away like a raving mad giant.

'At this very moment, the gentleman in sky-blue turning round, and seeing the young lady with her face uncovered, vented an exclamation of rage and jealousy; and turning his weapon against her beautiful bosom, pointed a thrust at her heart, which caused my uncle to utter a cry of apprehension that made the building ring. The lady stepped aside, and snatching the young man's sword from his hand before he had recovered his balance, drove him to the wall, and running it through him, and the panelling, up to the very hilt, pinned him there, hard and fast. It was a splendid example. My uncle, with a loud shout of triumph, and a strength that was irresistible, made his adversary retreat in the same direction, and plunging the old rapier into the very centre of a large red flower in the pattern of his waistcoat, nailed him beside his friend. There they both stood, gentlemen: jerking their arms and legs about in agony, like the toy-shop figures that are moved by a piece of packthread. My uncle always said, afterwards, that this was one of the surest means he knew of for disposing of an enemy; but it was liable to one objection on the ground of expense, inasmuch as it involved the loss of a sword for every man disabled.

'"The mail, the mail!" cried the lady, running up to my uncle and throwing her beautiful arms around his neck; "we may yet escape."

'"*May!*" cried my uncle; "why, my dear, there's nobody else to kill, is there?" My uncle was rather disappointed, gentlemen, for he thought a little quiet bit of love-making would be agreeable after the slaughtering, if it were only to change the subject.

'"We have not an instant to lose here," said the young lady. "He (pointing to the young gentleman in sky-blue) is the only son of the powerful Marquess of Filletoville."

'"Well, then my dear, I'm afraid he'll never come to the title," said my uncle, looking coolly at the young gentleman as he stood fixed up against the wall, in the cockchafer fashion I have described. "You have cut off the entail, my love."

'"I have been torn from my home and friends by these villains," said the young lady, her features glowing with indignation. "That wretch would have married me by violence in another hour."

'"Confound his impudence!" said my uncle, bestowing a very contemptuous look on the dying heir of Filletoville.

'"As you may guess from what you have seen," said the young lady, "the party were prepared to murder me if I appealed to anyone for assistance. If their accomplices find us here, we are lost. Two minutes hence may be too late. The mail!" With these words, overpowered by her feelings, and the exertion of sticking the young Marquess of Filleto-ville, she sunk into my uncle's arms. My uncle caught her up, and bore her to the house-door. There stood the mail, with four long-tailed, flowing-maned, black horses, ready harnessed; but no coachman, no guard, no hostler even, at the horses' heads.

'Gentlemen, I hope I do no injustice to my uncle's memory, when I express my opinion, that although he was a bachelor, he *had* held some ladies in his arms before this time; I believe, indeed, that he had rather a habit of kissing barmaids; and I know that, in one or two instances, he had been seen by credible witnesses to tug a landlady in a very perceptible manner. I mention the circumstances to show what a very uncommon sort of person this beautiful young lady must have been, to have affected my uncle in the way she did; he used to say, that as her long dark hair travelled over his arm, and her beautiful dark eyes fixed themselves upon his face when she recovered, he felt so strange and nervous, that his legs trembled beneath him. But, who can look in a sweet soft pair of dark eyes without feeling queer? *I* can't, gentlemen. I am afraid to look at some eyes I know, and that's the truth of it.

'"You will never leave me," murmured the young lady.

'"Never," said my uncle. And he meant it too.

'"My dear preserver!" exclaimed the young lady. "My dear, kind, brave preserver!"

'"Don't," said my uncle, interrupting her.

'"Why?" inquired the young lady.

'"Because your mouth looks so beautiful when you speak," rejoined my uncle, "that I am afraid I shall be rude enough to kiss it."

'The young lady put up her hand as if to caution my uncle not to do so, and said—no, she didn't say anything—she smiled. When you are looking at a pair of the most delicious lips in the world, and see them gently break into a roguish smile—if you are very near them, and nobody else by—you cannot better testify your admiration of their beautiful form and colour by kissing them at once. My uncle did so, and I honour him for it.

'"Hark!" cried the young lady, starting. "The noise of wheels and horses!"

'"So it is," said my uncle, listening. He had a good ear for wheels and the tramping of hoofs; but there appeared to be so many horses and carriages rattling towards them from a distance, that it was impossible to form a guess at their number. The sound was like that of fifty brakes, with six blood cattle in each.

'"We are pursued!" cried the young lady, clasping her hands. "We are pursued. I have no hope but in you!"

'There was such an expression of terror in her beautiful face, that my uncle made up his mind at once. He lifted her into the coach, told her not to be frightened, pressed his lips to hers once more, and then advising her to draw up the window to keep the cold air out, mounted to the box.

'"Stay, love," cried the young lady.

'"What's the matter?" said my uncle, from the coachbox.

'"I want to speak to you," said the young lady; "only a word— only a word, dearest."

'"Must I get down?" inquired my uncle. The lady made no answer, but she smiled again. Such a smile, gentlemen!—it beat the other one to nothing. My uncle descended from his perch in a twinkling.

'"What is it, my dear?" said my uncle, looking in at the coach window. The lady happened to bend forward at the same time, and my uncle thought she looked more beautiful than she had done yet. He was very close to her just then, gentlemen, so he really ought to know.

'"What is it, my dear?" said my uncle.

'"Will you never love anyone but me—never marry anyone besides?" said the young lady.

'My uncle swore a great oath that he would never marry anybody else, and the young lady drew in her head, and pulled up the window. He jumped upon the box, squared his elbows, adjusted the ribbons, seized the whip which lay on the roof, gave one flick to the off leader, and away went the four long-tailed, flowing-maned black horses, at fifteen good English miles an hour, with the mail-coach behind them. Whew! how they tore along!

'The noise behind grew louder. The faster the old mail went, the faster came the pursuers—men, horses, dogs, were leagued in the pursuit. The noise was frightful, but, above all, rose the voice of the young lady, urging my uncle on, and shrieking "Faster! faster!"

'They whirled past the dark trees, as feathers would be swept before a hurricane. Houses, gates, churches, haystacks, objects of every kind they shot by, with a velocity and noise like roaring waters suddenly let loose. Still the noise of pursuit grew louder, and still my uncle could hear the young lady wildly screaming "Faster! faster!"

'My uncle plied whip and rein; and the horses flew onward till they were white with foam; and yet the noise behind increased; and yet the young lady cried "Faster! faster!" My uncle gave a loud stamp on the boot in the energy of the moment, and—found that it was grey morning, and he was sitting in the wheelwright's yard, on the box of an old Edinburgh mail, shivering with cold and wet, and stamping his feet to warm them! He got down, and looked eagerly inside for the beautiful young lady. Alas! there was neither door nor seat to the coach—it was a mere shell.

'Of course, my uncle knew very well that there was some mystery in the matter, and that everything had passed exactly as he used to relate it. He remained staunch to the great oath he had sworn to the beautiful young lady: refusing several eligible landladies on her account, and dying a bachelor at last. He always said, what a curious thing it was that he should have found out, by such a mere accident as his clambering over the palings, that the ghosts of mail-coaches and horses, guards, coachmen, and passengers, were in the habit of making journeys regularly every night; he used to add, that he believed he was the only living person who had ever been taken as a passenger on one of these excursions; and I think he was right, gentlemen—at least I never heard of any other.'

THE RIGHT ONE

Henry James

Miss Daisy Miller, a young lady from Schenechtady, New York, is staying at Vevey in Switzerland with her mother and younger brother, Randolph, when she first meets Mr Winterbourne. He is captivated by her, though a little puzzled by her unconventional behaviour (she spends a whole day with him, unchaperoned, visiting the Castle of Chillon), and he is delighted to learn that they may meet again in Italy.

When Winterbourne reaches Rome in January, he learns from his aunt, Mrs Costello, that the Millers have arrived. But Daisy has already earned the disapproval of the small American community by being seen alone with several young men—'fortune-hunters', Mrs Costello calls them—and she astonishes Mrs Walker, at whose house Winterbourne encounters the Miller family, by proposing to take a walk in the Pincian Gardens. . . .

'Alone, my dear—at this hour?' Mrs Walker asked. The afternoon was drawing to a close—it was the hour for the throng of carriages and of contemplative pedestrians. 'I don't think it's safe, my dear.' said Mrs Walker.

'Neither do I,' subjoined Mrs Miller. 'You'll get the fever as sure as you live. Remember what Dr Davis told you!'

'Give her some medicine before she goes,' said Randolph.

The company had risen to its feet; Daisy bent over and kissed her hostess. 'Mrs Walker, you are too perfect,' she said. 'I'm not going alone; I am going to meet a friend.'

'Your friend won't keep you from getting the fever,' Mrs Miller observed.

'Is it Mr Giovanelli?' asked the hostess.

Winterbourne was watching the young girl; at this question his attention quickened. She stood there smiling and smoothing her bonnet-ribbons; she glanced at Winterbourne. Then, while she glanced and smiled, she answered without a shade of hesitation, 'Mr Giovanelli—the beautiful Giovanelli.'

'My dear young friend,' said Mrs Walker, taking her hand, pleadingly, 'don't walk off to the Pincio at this hour to meet a beautiful Italian.'

'Well, he speaks English,' said Mrs Miller.

'Gracious me!' Daisy exclaimed, 'I don't want to do anything improper. There's an easy way to settle it.' She continued to glance at Winterbourne. 'The Pincio is only a hundred yards distant, and if Mr Winterbourne were as polite as he pretends he would offer to walk with me!'

Winterbourne's politeness hastened to affirm itself, and the young girl gave him gracious leave to accompany her. They passed downstairs before her mother, and at the door Winterbourne perceived Mrs Miller's carriage drawn up, with the ornamental courier whose acquaintance he had made at Vevey seated within. 'Goodbye, Eugenio!' cried Daisy, 'I'm going to take a walk.' The distance from the Via Gregoriana to the beautiful garden at the other end of the Pincian Hill is, in fact, rapidly traversed. As the day was splendid, however, and the concourse of vehicles, walkers, and loungers numerous, the young Americans found their progress much delayed. This fact was highly agreeable to Winterbourne, in spite of his consciousness of his singular situation. The slow-moving, idly gazing Roman crowd bestowed much attention upon the extremely pretty young foreign lady who was passing through it upon his arm; and he wondered what on earth had been in Daisy's mind when she proposed to expose herself, unattended, to its appreciation. His own mission, to her sense, apparently, was to consign her to the hands of Mr Giovanelli; but Winterbourne, at once annoyed and gratified, resolved that he would do no such thing.

'Why haven't you been to see me?' asked Daisy. 'You can't get out of that.'

'I have had the honour of telling you that I have only just stepped out of the train.'

'You must have stayed in the train a good while after it stopped!' cried the young girl, with her little laugh. 'I suppose you were asleep. You have had time to go to see Mrs Walker.'

'I knew Mrs Walker—' Winterbourne began to explain.

'I knew where you knew her. You knew her at Geneva. She told me so. Well, you knew me at Vevey. That's just as good. So you ought to have come.' She asked him no other question than this; she began to prattle about her own affairs. 'We've got splendid rooms at the hotel; Eugenio says they're the best rooms in Rome. We are going to stay all winter—if we don't die of the fever; and I guess we'll stay then. It's a great deal nicer than I thought; I thought it would be fearfully quiet; I was sure it would be awfully poky. I was sure we should be going round all the time with one of those dreadful old men that explain about the pictures and things. But we only had about a week of that, and now I'm enjoying myself. I know ever so many people, and they are all so charming.' When they had passed the gate of the Pincian Gardens, Miss Miller began to wonder where Mr Giovanelli might be. 'We had better go straight to that place in front,' she said, 'where you look at the view.'

'I certainly shall not help you to find him,' Winterbourne declared.

'Then I shall find him without you,' said Miss Daisy.

'You certainly won't leave me!' cried Winterbourne.

She burst into her little laugh. 'Are you afraid you'll get lost—or run over? But there's Giovanelli, leaning against that tree. He's staring at the women in the carriages: did you ever see anything so cool?'

Winterbourne perceived at some distance a little man standing with folded arms, nursing his cane. He had a handsome face, an artfully poised hat, a glass in one eye, and a nosegay in his button-hole. Winterbourne looked at him a moment and then said, 'Do you mean to speak to that man?'

'Do I mean to speak to him? Why, you don't suppose I mean to communicate by signs?'

'Pray understand, then,' said Winterbourne, 'that I intend to remain.'

Daisy stopped and looked at him, without a sign of troubled consciousness in her face; with nothing but the presence of her charming eyes and her happy dimples. 'Well, she's a cool one!' thought the young man.

'I don't like the way you say that,' said Daisy. 'It's too imperious.'

'I beg your pardon if I say it wrong. The main point is to give you an idea of my meaning.'

The young girl looked at him more gravely, but with eyes that were prettier than ever. 'I have never allowed a gentleman to dictate to me, or to interfere with anything I do.'

'I think you have made a mistake,' said Winterbourne. 'You should sometimes listen to a gentleman—the right one?'

Daisy began to laugh again, 'I do nothing but listen to gentlemen!' she exclaimed. 'Tell me if Mr Giovanelli is the right one?'

The gentleman with the nosegay in his bosom had now perceived our two friends, and was approaching the young girl with obsequious rapidity. He bowed to Winterbourne as well as to the latter's companion; he had a brilliant smile, an intelligent eye; Winterbourne thought him not a bad-looking fellow. But he nevertheless said to Daisy—'No, he's not the right one.'

Daisy evidently had a natural talent for performing introductions; she mentioned the name of each of her companions to the other. She strolled along with one of them on each side of her; Mr Giovanelli, who spoke English very cleverly—Winterbourne afterwards learned that he had practised the idiom upon a great many American heiresses—addressed her a great deal of very polite nonsense; he was extremely urbane, and the young American, who said nothing, reflected upon the profundity of Italian cleverness which enables people to appear more gracious in proportion as they are more acutely disappointed. Giovanelli, of course, had counted upon something more intimate; he had not bargained for a party of three. But he kept his temper in a manner which suggested far-stretching intentions. Winterbourne flattered himself that he had taken his measure. 'He is not a gentleman,' said the young American; 'he is only a clever imitation of one. He is a music-master, or a penny-a-liner, or a third-rate artist. Damn his good looks!' Mr Giovanelli had certainly a very pretty face; but Winterbourne felt a superior indignation at his own lovely fellow-countrywoman's not knowing the difference between a spurious gentleman and a real one. But Daisy, on this occasion, continued to present herself as an inscrutable combination of audacity and inno-cence.

She had been walking some quarter of an hour, attended by her two cavaliers, and responding in a tone of very childish gaiety, as it seemed to Winterbourne, to the pretty speeches of Mr Giovanelli, when a carriage that had detached itself from the revolving train drew up beside the path. At the same moment Winterbourne perceived that his friend Mrs Walker—the lady whose house he had lately left—was seated in the vehicle and was beckoning to him. Leaving Miss Miller's side, he hastened to obey her summons. Mrs Walker was flushed; she wore an excited air. 'It is really too dreadful,' she said. 'That girl must not do this sort of thing. She must not walk here with you two men. Fifty people have noticed her.'

Winterbourne raised his eyebrows. 'I think it's a pity to make too much fuss about it.'

'It's a pity to let the girl ruin herself!'

'She is very innocent,' said Winterbourne.

'She's very crazy!' cried Mrs Walker. 'Did you ever see anything so imbecile as her mother? After you had all left me, just now, I could not sit still for thinking of it. It seemed too pitiful, not even to attempt to save her. I ordered the carriage and put on my bonnet, and came here as quickly as possible. Thank heaven I have found you!'

'What do you propose to do with us?' asked Winterbourne, smiling.

'To ask her to get in, to drive her about here for half an hour, so that the world may see she is not running absolutely wild, and then to take her safely home.'

'I don't think it's a very happy thought,' said Winterbourne; 'but you can try.'

Mrs Walker tried. The young man went in pursuit of Miss Miller, who had simply nodded and smiled at his interlocutrix in the carriage and had gone her way with her own companion. Daisy, on learning that Mrs Walker wished to speak to her, retraced her steps with a perfect good grace and with Mr Giovanelli at her side. She declared that she was delighted to have a chance to present this genteman to Mrs Walker. She immediately achieved the introduction, and declared that she had never in her life seen anything so lovely as Mrs Walker's carriage-rug.

'I am glad you admire it,' said this lady, smiling sweetly. 'Will you get in and let me put it over you?'

'Oh, no, thank you,' said Daisy. 'I shall admire it much more as I see you driving round with it.'

'Do get in and drive with me,' said Mrs Walker.

'That would be charming, but it's so enchanting just as I am!' and Daisy gave a brilliant glance at the gentlemen on either side of her.

'It may be enchanting, dear child, but it is not the custom here,' urged Mrs Walker, leaning forward in her victoria with her hands devoutly clasped.

'Well, it ought to be, then!' said Daisy. 'If I didn't walk I should expire.'

'You should walk with your mother, dear,' cried the lady from Geneva, losing patience.

'With my mother dear!' exclaimed the young girl. Winterbourne saw that she scented interference. 'My mother never walked ten steps in her life. And then, you know,' she added with a laugh, 'I am more than five years old.'

'You are old enough to be more reasonable. You are old enough, dear Miss Miller, to be talked about.'

Daisy looked at Mrs Walker, smiling intensely. 'Talked about? What do you mean!'

'Come into my carriage and I will tell you.'

Daisy turned her quickened glance again from one of the gentlemen beside her to the other. Mr Giovanelli was bowing to and fro, rubbing down his gloves and laughing very agreeably; Winterbourne thought it a most unpleasant scene. 'I don't think I want to know what you mean,' said Daisy presently. 'I don't think I should like it.'

Winterbourne wished that Mrs Walker would tuck in her carriage-rug and drive away; but this lady did not enjoy being defied, as she afterwards told him. 'Should you prefer being thought a very reckless girl?' she demanded.

'Gracious me!' exclaimed Daisy. She looked again at Mr Giovanelli, then she turned to Winterbourne. There was a little pink flush in her cheek; she was tremendously pretty. 'Does Mr Winterbourne think,' she asked slowly, smiling, throwing back her head and glancing at him from head to foot, 'that—to save my reputation—I ought to get into the carriage?'

Winterbourne coloured; for an instant he hesitated greatly. It seemed so strange to hear her speak that way of her 'reputation'. He looked at her exquisite prettiness; and then he said very gently, 'I think you should get into the carriage.'

Daisy gave a violent laugh. 'I never heard anything so stiff! If this is improper, Mrs Walker,' she pursued, 'then I am all improper, and you must give me up. Good-bye; I hope you'll have a lovely ride!' and, with Mr Giovanelli, who made a triumphantly obsequious salute, she turned away.

Mrs Walker sat looking after her, and there were tears in Mrs Walker's eyes. 'Get in here, sir,' she said to Winterbourne, indicating the place beside her. The young man answered that he felt bound to accompany Miss Miller; whereupon Mrs Walker declared that if he refused her this favour she would never speak to him again. She was evidently in earnest.

Winterbourne was not in the best possible humour as he took his seat in Mrs Walker's victoria. 'That was not clever of you,' he said candidly. while the vehicle mingled again with the throng of carriages.

'In such a case,' his companion answered, 'I don't wish to be clever, I wish to be *earnest*!'

'Well, your earnestness has only offended her and put her off.'

'It has happened very well,' said Mrs Walker. 'If she is so perfectly determined to compromise herself, the sooner one knows it the better; one can act accordingly.'

'I suspect she meant no harm,' Winterbourne rejoined.

'So I thought a month ago. But she has been going too far.'

'What has she been doing?'

'Everything that is not done here. Flirting with any man she could pick up; sitting in corners with mysterious Italians; dancing all the evening with the same partners; receiving visits at eleven o'clock at night. Her mother goes away when visitors come.'

Winterbourne was silent for some moments; then he said, 'I suspect, Mrs Walker, that you and I have lived too long at Geneva!' And he added a request that she should inform him with what particular design she had made him enter her carriage.

'I wished to beg you to cease your relations with Miss Miller— not to flirt with her—to give her no further opportunity to expose herself—to let her alone, in short.'

'I'm afraid I can't do that,' said Winterbourne. 'I like her extremely.'

'All the more reason that you shouldn't help her to make a scandal.'

'There shall be nothing scandalous in my attentions to her.'

'There certainly will be in the way she takes them. But I have said what I had on my conscience,' Mrs Walker pursued. 'If you wish to rejoin the young lady I will put you down. Here, by the way, you have a chance.'

The carriage was traversing that part of the Pincian Garden which overhangs the wall of Rome and overlooks the beautiful Villa Borghese. It is bordered by a large parapet, near which there are several seats. One of the seats, at a distance, was occupied by a gentleman and a lady, towards whom Mrs Walker gave a toss of her head. At the same moment these persons rose and walked towards the parapet. Winterbourne had asked the coachman to stop; he now descended from the carriage. His companion looked at him a moment in silence; then, while he raised his hat, she drove majestically away. Winterbourne stood there; he had turned his eyes towards Daisy and her cavalier. They evidently saw no one; they were too deeply occupied with each other. When they reached the low garden-wall they stood a moment looking off at the great flat-topped pine-clusters of the Villa Borghese; then Giovanelli seated himself familiarly upon the broad ledge of the wall. The western sun in the opposite sky sent out a brilliant shaft through a couple of cloud-bars; whereupon Daisy's companion took her parasol out of her hands and opened it. She came a little nearer and he held the parasol over her; then, still holding it, he let it rest upon her shoulder, so that both their heads were hidden from Winterbourne. This young man lingered a moment, then he began to walk. But he walked—not towards the couple with the parasol; towards the residence of his aunt, Mrs Costello.

Mrs Walker's party took place on the evening of the third day, and in spite of the frigidity of his last interview with the hostess, Winterbourne was among the guests. Mrs Walker was one of those American ladies who, while residing abroad, make a point, in their own phrase, of studying European society; and she had on this occasion collected several specimens of her diversely born fellow-mortals to serve, as it were, as text-books. When Winterbourne arrived Daisy Miller was not there; but in a few moments he saw her mother come in alone, very shyly and ruefully. Mrs Miller's hair, above her exposed-looking temples, was more frizzled than ever. As she approached Mrs Walker, Winterbourne also drew near.

'You see I've come all alone,' said poor Mrs Miller. 'I'm so frightened; I don't know what to do; it's the first time I've ever been to a party alone—especially in this country. I ain't used to going round alone.'

'And does not your daughter intend to favour us with her society?' demanded Mrs Walker, impressively.

'Well, Daisy's all dressed,' said Mrs Miller, with that accent of the dispassionate, if not of the philosophic, historian with which she always recorded the current incidents of her daughter's career. 'She's got dressed on purpose before before dinner. But she's got a friend of hers there; that gentleman—the Italian—that she wanted to bring. They've got going at the piano; it seems as if they couldn't leave off. Mr Giovanelli sings splendidly. But I guess they'll come before very long,' concluded Mrs Miller hopefully.

Daisy came after eleven o'clock, but she was not, on such an occasion, a young lady to wait to be spoken to. She rustled forward in radiant loveliness, smiling and chattering, carrying a large bouquet and attended by Mr Giovanelli. Everyone stopped talking and turned and looked at her. She came straight to Mrs Walker. 'I'm afraid you thought I never was coming, so I sent mother off to tell you. I wanted to make Giovanelli practise some things before he came; you know he sings beautifully, and I want you to ask him to sing. This is Mr Giovanelli; you know I introduced him to you; he's got the most lovely voice and he knows the most charming set of songs. I made him go over them this evening, on purpose; we had the greatest time at the hotel.' Of all this Daisy delivered herself with the sweetest, brightest audibleness, looking now at her hostess and now round the room, while she gave a series of little pats, round her shoulders, to the edges of her dress. 'Is there anyone I know?' she asked.

'I think everyone knows you!' said Mrs Walker pregnantly, and she gave a very cursory greeting to Mr Giovanelli. This gentleman bore himself gallantly. He smiled and bowed and showed his white teeth, he curled his moustaches and rolled his eyes, and performed all the proper functions of a handsome Italian at an evening party. He sang, very prettily, half a dozen songs, though Mrs Walker afterwards declared that she had been quite unable to find out who asked him. It was apparently not Daisy who had given him his orders. Daisy sat at a distance from the piano, and though she had publicly, as it were, professed a high admiration for his singing, talked, not inaudibly, while it was going on.

'It's a pity these rooms are so small; we can't dance.' she said to Winterbourne, as if she had seen him five minutes before.

'I am not sorry we can't dance,' Winterbourne answered; 'I don't dance.'

'Of course you don't dance; you're too stiff,' said Miss Daisy. 'I hope you enjoyed your drive with Mrs Walker.'

'No I didn't enjoy it; I preferred walking with you.'

'We paired off, that was much better,' said Daisy. 'But did you ever hear anything so cool as Mrs Walker's wanting me to get into her carriage and drop poor Mr Giovanelli; and under the pretext that it was proper? People have different ideas! It would have been most unkind; he had been talking about that walk for ten days.'

'He should not have talked about it at all,' said Winterbourne; 'he would never have proposed to a young lady of this country to walk about the streets with him.'

'About the streets?' cried Daisy, with her pretty stare. 'Where then would he have proposed to her to walk? The Pincio is not the streets, either; and I, thank goodness, am not a young lady of this country. The young ladies of this country have a dreadfully poky time of it, so far as I can learn; I don't see why I should change my habits for *them*.'

'I am afraid your habits are those of a flirt,' said Winterbourne gravely.

'Of course they are,' she cried, giving him her little smiling stare again. 'I'm a fearful, frightful flirt! Did you ever hear of a nice girl that was not? But I suppose you will tell me now that I am not a nice girl.'

'You're a very nice girl, but I wish you would flirt with me, and me only,' said Winterbourne.

'Ah! thank you, thank you very much; you are the last man I should think of flirting with. As I have had the pleasure of informing you, you are too stiff.'

'You say that too often,' said Winterbourne.

Daisy gave a delighted laugh. 'If I could have the sweet hope of making you angry, I would say it again.'

'Don't do that; when I am angry I'm stiffer than ever. But if you won't flirt with me, do cease at least to flirt with your friend at the piano; they don't understand that sort of thing here.'

'I thought they understood nothing else!' exclaimed Daisy.

'Not in young unmarried women.'

'It seems to me much more proper in young unmarried women than in old married ones,' Daisy declared.

'Well,' said Winterbourne, 'when you deal with natives you must go by the custom of the place. Flirting is a purely American custom; it doesn't exist here. So when you show yourself in public with Mr Giovanelli and without your mother—'

'Gracious! Poor mother!' interposed Daisy.

'Though you may be flirting, Mr Giovanelli is not; he means something else.'

'He isn't preaching, at any rate,' said Daisy with vivacity. 'And if you want very much to know, we are neither of us flirting; we are too good friends for that; we are very intimate friends.'

'Ah,' rejoined Winterbourne, 'if you are in love with each other it is another affair.'

She had allowed him up to this point to talk so frankly that he had no expectation of shocking her by this ejaculation; but she immediately got up, blushing visibly, and leaving him to exclaim mentally that little American flirts were the queerest creatures in the world. 'Mr Giovanelli, at least,' she said, giving her interlocutor a single glance, 'never says such very disagreeable things to me.'

Winterbourne was bewildered; he stood staring. Mr Giovanelli had finished singing; he left the piano and came over to Daisy. 'Won't you come into the other room and have some tea?' he asked, bending before her with his decorative smile.

Daisy turned to Winterbourne, beginning to smile again. He was still more perplexed, for this inconsequent smile made nothing clear, though it seemed to prove, indeed, that she had a sweetness and softness that reverted instinctively to the pardon of offences. 'It has never occurred to Mr Winterbourne to offer me any tea,' she said, with her little tormenting manner.

'I have offered you advice,' Winterbourne rejoined.

'I prefer weak tea!' cried Daisy, and she went off with the brilliant

Giovanelli. She sat with him in the adjoining room, in the embrasure of the window, for the rest of the evening. There was an interesting performance at the piano, but neither of these young people gave heed to it. When Daisy came to take leave of Mrs Walker, this lady conscientiously repaired the weakness of which she had been guilty at the moment of the young girl's arrival. She turned her back straight upon Miss Miller and left her to depart with what grace she might. Winterbourne was standing near the door; he saw it all. Daisy turned very pale and looked at her mother, but Mrs Miller was humbly unconscious of any violation of the usual social forms. She appeared, indeed, to have felt an incongruous impulse to draw attention to her own striking observance of them. 'Goodnight, Mrs Walker,' she said; 'we've had a beautiful evening. You see if I let Daisy come to parties without me, I don't want her to go away without me.' Daisy turned away, looking with a pale, grave face at the circle near the door; Winterbourne saw that, for the rst moment, she was too much shocked and puzzled even for indignation. He on his side was greatly touched.

'That was very cruel,' he said to Mrs Walker.

'She never enters my drawing-room again,' replied his hostess.

Since Winterbourne was not to meet her in Mrs Walker's drawing-room, he went as often as possible to Mrs Miller's hotel. The ladies were rarely at home, but when he found them the devoted Giovanelli was always present. Very often the polished little Roman was in the drawing-room with Daisy alone, Mrs Miller being apparently constantly of the opinion that discretion is the better part of surveillance. Winterbourne noted, at first with surprise, that Daisy on these occasions was never embarrassed or annoyed by his own entrance; but he very presently began to feel that she had no more surprises for him; the unexpected in her behaviour was the only thing to expect. She showed no displeasure at her *tête-à-tête* with Giovanelli being interrupted, she could chatter as freshly and freely with two gentlemen as with one; there was always, in her conversation, the same odd mixture of audacity and puerility.

But she was evidently very much interested in Giovanelli. She looked at him whenever he spoke; she was perpetually telling him to do this and to do that; she was constantly 'chaffing' and abusing him. She appeared completely to have forgotten that Winterbourne had said anything to displease her at Mrs Walker's little party. One Sunday afternoon, having gone to St Peter's with his aunt, Winterbourne perceived Daisy strolling about the great church in company with the inevitable Giovanelli. Presently he pointed out the young girl and her cavalier to Mrs Costello. This lady looked at them a moment through her eyeglass, and then she said:

'That's what makes you so pensive in these days, eh?'

'I had not the least idea I was pensive,' said the young man.

'You are very much preoccupied, you are thinking of something.'

'And what is it,' he asked, 'that you accuse me of thinking of?'

'Of that young lady's, Miss Baker's, Miss Chandler's—what's her name?—Miss Miller's intrigue with that little barber's block.'

'Do you call it an intrigue,' Winterbourne asked—'an affair that goes on with such peculiar publicity?'

'That's their folly,' said Mrs Costello, 'it's not their merit.'

'No,' rejoined Winterbourne, with something of that pensiveness to which his aunt had alluded. 'I don't believe that there is anything to be called an intrigue.'

'I have heard a dozen people speak of it; they say she is quite carried away by him.'

Of the observation excited by Daisy's 'intrigue', Winterbourne gathered that day at St Peter's sufficient evidence. A dozen of the American colonists in Rome came to talk with Mrs Costello, who sat on a little portable stool at the base of one of the great pilasters. The vesper-service was going forward in spendid chants and organ-tones in the adjacent choir, and meanwhile, between Mrs Costello and her friends, there was a great deal said about poor little Miss Miller's going really 'too far'. Winterbourne was not pleased with what he heard; but when, coming out upon the great steps of the church, he saw Daisy, who had emerged before him, get into an open cab with her accomplice and roll away through the cynical streets of Rome, he could not deny to himself that she was going very far indeed. He felt very sorry for her—not exactly that he believed that she had completely lost her head, but because it was painful to hear so much that was pretty and undefended and natural assigned to a vulgar place among the categories of disorder. He made an attempt after this to give a hint to Mrs Miller. He met one day in the Corso a friend—a tourist like himself—who had just come out of the Doria Palace, where he had been walking through the beautiful gallery. His friend talked for a moment about the superb portrait of Innocent X by Velasquez, which hangs in one of the cabinets of the palace, and then said, 'And in the same cabinet, by the way, I had the pleasure of contemplating a picture of a different kind—that pretty American girl whom you pointed out to me last week.' In answer to Winterbourne's inquiries, his friend narrated that the pretty American girl—prettier than ever—was seated with a companion in the secluded nook in which the great papal portrait is enshrined.

'Who was her companion?' asked Winterbourne.

'A little Italian with a bouquet in his buttonhole. The girl is delightfully pretty, but I thought I understood from you the other day that she was a young lady *du meilleur monde*.'

'So she is!' answered Winterbourne; and having assured himself that his informant had seen Daisy and her companion but five minutes before, he jumped into a cab and went to call on Mrs Miller. She was at home; but she apologized to him for receiving him in Daisy's absence.

'She's gone out somewhere with Mr Giovanelli,' said Mrs Miller. 'She's always going round with Mr Giovanelli.'

'I have noticed that they are very intimate,' Winterbourne observed.

'Oh! it seems as if they couldn't live without each other!' said Mrs Miller. 'Well, he's a real gentleman, anyhow. I keep telling Daisy she's engaged!'

'And what does Daisy say?'

'Oh, she says she isn't engaged. But she might as well be!' this impartial parent resumed. 'She goes on as if she was. But I've made Mr Giovanelli promise to tell me, if *she* doesn't. I should want to write to Mr Miller about it—shouldn't you?'

A few days after his brief interview with her mother, he encountered her in that beautiful abode of flowering desolation known as the Palace of the Caesars. The early Roman spring had filled the air with bloom and perfume, and the rugged surface of the Palantine was muffled with tender verdure. Daisy was strolling along the top of one of those great mounds of ruin that are embarked with mossy marble and paved with monumental inscriptions. It seemed to him that Rome had never been so lovely as just then. He stood looking off at the enchanting harmony of line and colour that remotely encircles the city, inhaling the softly humid odours and feeling the freshness of the year and the antiquity of the place reaffirm themselves in mysterious interfusion. It seemed to him also that Daisy had never looked so pretty; but this had been an observation of his whenever he met her. Giovanelli was at her side, and Giovanelli, too, wore an aspect of even unwonted brilliancy.

'Well,' said Daisy, 'I should think you would be lonesome!'

'Lonesome?' asked Winterbourne.

'You are always going round by yourself. Can't you get anyone to walk with you?'

'I am not so fortunate,' said Winterbourne, 'as your companion.'

'Giovanelli, from the first, had treated Winterbourne with distinguished politeness; he listened with a deferential air to his remarks; he laughed, punctiliously, at his pleasantries; he seemed disposed to testify to his belief that Winterbourne was a superior young man. He carried himself in no degree like a jealous wooer; he had obviously a great deal of tact; he had no objection to your expecting a little humility of him.

'I know why you say that,' said Daisy, watching Giovanelli. 'Because you think I go round too much with *him*!' And she nodded at her attendant.

'Everyone thinks so—if you care to know,' said Winterbourne.

'Of course I care to know!' Daisy exclaimed seriously. 'But I don't believe it. They are only pretending to be shocked. They don't really care a straw what I do. Besides, I don't go round so much.'

'I think you will find they do care. They will show it—disagreeably.'

Daisy looked at him a moment. 'How—disagreeably?'

'Haven't you noticed anything?' Winterbourne asked.

'I have noticed you. But I noticed you were as stiff as an umbrella the first time I saw you.'

'You will find I am not so stiff as several others,' said Winterbourne, smiling.

'How shall I find it?'

'By going to see the others.'

'What will they do to me?'

'They will give you the cold shoulder. Do you know what that means?'

Daisy was looking at him intently; she began to colour. 'Do you mean as Mrs Walker did the other night?'

'Exactly!' said Winterbourne.

She looked away at Giovanelli, who was decorating himself with his almond blossom. Then looking back at Winterbourne – 'I shouldn't think you would let people to be so unkind!' she said.

'How can I help it?' he asked.

'I should think you would say something.'

'I do say something'; and he paused a moment. 'I say that your mother tells me that she believes you are engaged.'

'Well, she does,' said Daisy very simply.

A week afterwards he went to dine at a beautiful villa on the Caelian Hill, and, on arriving, dismissed his hired vehicle. The evening was charming, and he promised himself the satisfaction of walking home beneath the Arch of Constantine and past the vaguely lighted monuments of the Forum. There was a waning moon in the sky, and her radiance was not brilliant, but she was veiled in a thin cloud-curtain which seemed to diffuse and equalize it. When, on his return from the villa (it was eleven o'clock), Winterbourne approached the dusky circle of the Colosseum, it occurred to him, as a lover of the picturesque, that the interior, in the pale moonshine, would be well worth a glance. He turned aside and walked to one of the empty arches, near which, as he observed, an open carriage—one of the little Roman street-cabs—was stationed. Then he passed in among the cavernous shadows of the great structure, and emerged upon the clear and silent arena. The place had never seemed to him more impressive. One half of the gigantic circus was in deep shade; the other was sleeping in the luminous dusk. Winterbourne walked to the middle of the arena, to take a more general glance, intending thereafter to make a hasty retreat. The great cross in the centre was covered with shadow; it was only as he drew near it that he made it out distinctly. Then he saw that two persons were stationed upon the low steps which formed its base. One of these was a woman, seated; her companon was standing in front of her.

Presently the sound of the woman's voice came to him distinctly in the warm night air. 'Well, he looks at us as one of the old lions or tigers may have looked at the Christian martyrs!' These were the words he heard, in the familiar accent of Miss Daisy Miller.

'Let us hope he is not very hungry,' responded the ingenious Giovanelli. 'He will have to take me first; you will serve for dessert!'

Winterbourne stopped, with a sort of horror; and, it must be added, with a sort of relief. It was as if a sudden illumination had been flashed upon the ambiguity of Daisy's behaviour and the riddle had become easy to read. She was a young lady whom a gentleman need no longer be at pains to respect. He stood there looking at her—looking at her companion, and not reflecting that though he saw them vaguely, he himself must have been more brightly visible. He felt angry with himself that he had bothered so much about the right way of regarding Miss Daisy Miller. He turned away towards the entrance of the place; but as he did so he heard Daisy speak again.

'Why, it was Mr Winterbourne! He saw me—and he cuts me!'

What a clever little reprobate she was, and how smartly she played an injured innocence! But he wouldn't cut her. Winterbourne came forward again, and went towards the great cross. Daisy had got up; Giovanelli lifted his hat. Winterbourne had now begun to think simply of the craziness, from a sanitary point of view, of a delicate young girl lounging away the evening in this nest of malaria. What if she *were* a clever little reprobate? That was no reason for her dying of the *perniciosa*. 'How long have you been here?' he asked, almost brutally.

Daisy, lovely in the flattering moonlight, looked at him a moment. Then—'All the evening,' she answered gently. . . . 'I never saw anything so pretty.'

'I am afraid,' said Winterbourne, 'that you will not think Roman fever very pretty. This is the way people catch it. I wonder,' he added, turning to Giovanelli, 'that you, a native Roman, should countenance such a terrible indiscretion.'

'Ah,' said the handsome native, 'for myself, I am not afraid.'

The gentleman with the nosegay in his bosom bowed.

'Neither am I—for you! I am speaking for this young lady.'

Giovanelli lifted his well-shaped eyebrows and showed his brilliant teeth. But he took Winterbourne's rebuke with docility. 'I told the Signorina it was a grave indiscretion; but when was the Signorina ever prudent?'

'I never was sick, and I don't mean to be!' the Signorina declared. 'I don't look like much, but I'm healthy! I was bound to see the Colosseum by moonlight; I shouldn't have wanted to go home without that; and we have had the most beautiful time, haven't we, Mr Giovanelli! If there has been any danger, Eugenio can give me some pills. He has got some splendid pills.'

'I should advise you,' said Winterbourne, 'to drive home as fast as possible and take one!'

'What you say is very wise,' Giovanelli rejoined. 'I will go and make sure the carriage is at hand.' And he went forward rapidly.

Daisy followed with Winterbourne. He kept looking at her; she seemed not in the least embarrassed. Winterbourne said nothing; Daisy chattered about the beauty of the place. 'Well, I *have* seen the Colosseum by moonlight!' she exclaimed. 'That's one good thing.' Then, noticing Winterbourne's silence, she asked him why he didn't speak. He made no answer; he only began to laugh. They passed under one of the dark archways; Giovanelli was in front with the carriage. Here Daisy stopped a moment, looking at the young American. '*Did* you believe I was engaged the other day?' she asked.

'It doesn't matter what I believed the other day,' said Winterbourne, still laughing.

'Well, what do you believe now?'

'I believe that it makes very little difference whether you are engaged or not!'

He felt the young girl's pretty eyes fixed upon him through the thick gloom of the archway; she was apparently going to answer. But Giovanelli hurried her forward. 'Quick, quick,' he said; 'if we get in by midnight we are quite safe.'

Daisy took her seat in the carriage, and the fortunate Italian placed himself beside her. 'Don't forget Eugenio's pills!' said Winterbourne, as he lifted his hat.

'I don't care,' said Daisy, in a little strange tone, 'whether I have

Roman fever or not!' Upon this the cab-driver cracked his whip, and they rolled away over the desultory patches of the antique pavement.

Winterbourne—to do him justice, as it were—mentioned to no one that he had encountered Miss Miller, at midnight, in the Colosseum with a gentleman; but nevertheless, a couple of days later, the fact of her having been there under these circumstances was known to every member of the little American circle, and commented accordingly. Winterbourne reflected that they had of course known it at the hotel, and that, after Daisy's return, there had been an exchange of jokes between the porter and the cab-driver. But the young man was conscious at the same moment that it had ceased to be a matter of serious regret to him that the little American flirt should be 'talked about' by low-minded menials. These people, a day or two later, had serious information to give: the little American flirt was alarmingly ill.

Winterbourne went often to ask for news of her, and once he saw Mrs Miller, who, though deeply alarmed, was—rather to his surprise—perfectly composed, and, as it appeared, a most efficient and judicious nurse. 'Daisy spoke of you the other day,' she said to him. 'Half the time she doesn't know what she's saying, but that time I think she did. She gave me a message; she told me to tell you. She told me to tell you that she never was engaged to that handsome Italian. I am sure I am very glad; Mr Giovanelli hasn't been near us since she was taken ill. I thought he was so much of a gentleman; but I don't call that very polite! Anyway, she says she's not engaged. I don't know why she wanted you to know; but she said to me three times—"Mind you tell Mr Winterbourne." And then she told me to ask if you remembered the time you went to that castle, in Switzerland. But I said I wouldn't give any such messages as that. Only, if she is not engaged, I'm sure I'm glad to know it.'

But, as Winterbourne had said, it mattered very little. A week after this the poor girl died; it had been a terrible case of the fever. Daisy's grave was in the little Protestant cemetery, in an angle of the wall of imperial Rome, beneath the cypresses and the thick spring flowers. Winterbourne stood there beside it, with a number of other mourners; a number larger than the scandal excited by the young lady's career would have led you to expect. Near him stood Giovanelli, who came nearer still before Winterbourne turned away. Giovanelli was very pale; on this occasion he had no flower in his buttonhole; he seemed to wish to say something. At last he said, 'She was the most beautiful young lady I ever saw, and the most amiable.' And then he added in a moment, 'And she was the most innocent.'

Winterbourne looked at him, and presently repeated his words, 'And the most innocent?'

'The most innocent!'

Winterbourne felt sore and angry. 'Why the devil,' he asked, 'did you take her to that fatal place?'

Mr Giovanelli's urbanity was apparently imperturbable. He looked on the ground a moment, and then he said, 'For myself, I had no fear; and she wanted to go.'

'That was no reason!' Winterbourne declared.

The subtle Roman again dropped his eyes. 'If she had lived, I should have got nothing. She would never have married me.'

'She would never have married you?'

'For a moment I hoped so. But no, I am sure.'

Winterbourne listened to him; he stood staring at the raw protuberance among the April daisies. When he turned away again Mr Giovanelli, with his light slow step, had retired.

Winterbourne almost immediately left Rome; but the following summer he again met his aunt, Mrs Costello, at Vevey. Mrs Costello was fond of Vevey. In the interval Winterbourne had often thought of Daisy Miller and her mystifying manners. One day he spoke of her to his aunt—said it was on his conscience that he had done her injustice.

'I am sure I don't know,' said Mrs Costello. 'How did your injustice affect her?'

'She sent me a message before her death which I didn't understand at the time. But I have understood it since. She would have appreciated one's esteem.'

THE DREAM WOMAN

Wilkie Collins

I had not been settled much more than six weeks in my country practice, when I was sent for to a neighbouring town to consult with the resident medical man there, on a case of very dangerous illness.

My horse had come down with me, at the end of a long ride the night before, and had hurt himself, luckily, much more than he had hurt his master. Being deprived of the animal's services, I started for my destination by the coach (there were no railways at that time); and I hoped to get back again, towards the afternoon, in the same way.

After the consultation was over I went to the principal inn of the town to wait for the coach. When it came up, it was full inside and out. There was no resource left me, but to get home as cheaply as I could, by hiring a gig. The price asked for this accommodation struck me as being so extortionate, that I determined to look out for an inn of inferior pretensions, and to try if I could not make a better bargain with a less prosperous establishment.

I soon found a likely-looking house, dingy and quiet, with an old-fashioned sign, that had evidently not been repainted for many years past. The landlord, in this case, was not above making a small profit; and as soon as we came to terms, he rang the yard-bell to order the gig.

'Has Robert not come back from that errand?' asked the landlord appealing to the waiter, who answered the bell.

'No, sir, he hasn't.'

'Well, then, you must wake up Isaac.'

'Wake up Isaac?' I repeated; 'that sounds rather odd. Do your ostlers go to bed in the day-time?'

'This one does,' said the landlord, smiling to himself in rather a strange way.

'And dreams, too,' added the waiter.

'Never you mind about that,' retorted his master; 'you go and rouse Isaac up. The gentleman's waiting for his gig.'

The landlord's manner and the waiter's manner expressed a great deal more than they either of them said. I began to suspect that I might be on the trace of something professionally interesting to me, as a medical man; and I thought I should like to look at the ostler, before the waiter awakened him.

'Stop a minute,' I interposed; 'I have rather a fancy for seeing this man before you wake him up. I am a doctor; and if this queer sleeping and dreaming of his comes from anything wrong in his brain, I may be able to tell you what to do with him.'

'I rather think you will find his complaint past all doctoring, sir,' said the landlord. 'But if you would like to see him, you're welcome, I'm sure.'

He led the way across a yard and down a passage to the stables; opened one of the doors; and waiting outside himself, told me to look in.

I found myself in a two-stall stable. In one of the stalls, a horse was munching his corn. In the other, an old man was lying asleep on the litter.

I stooped, and looked at him attentively. It was a withered, woebegone face. The eyebrows were painfully contracted; the mouth was fast set, and drawn down at the corners. The hollow wrinkled cheeks, and the scanty grizzled hair, told their own tale of past sorrow or suffering. He was drawing his breath convulsively when I first looked at him; and in a moment more he began to talk in his sleep.

'Wake up!' I heard him say, in a quick whisper, through his clenched teeth. 'Wake up, there! Murder.'

He moved one lean arm slowly until it rested over his throat, shuddered a little, and turned on the straw. Then the arm left his throat, the hand stretched itself out, and clutched at the side towards which he had turned, as if he fancied himself to be grasping at the edge of something. I saw his lips move, and bent lower over him. He was still talking in his sleep.

'Light grey eyes,' he murmured, 'and a droop in the left eyelid – flaxen hair, with a gold-yellow streak in it – all right, mother – fair white arms, with a down on them – little lady's hand, with a reddish look under the finger-nails. The knife – always the cursed knife – first on one side, then on the other. Aha! you she-devil, where's the knife?'

At the last word his voice rose, and he grew restless on a sudden. I saw him shudder on the straw; his withered face became distorted, and he threw up both his hands with a quick hysterical gasp. They struck against the bottom of the manger under which he lay, and the blow awakened him. I had just time to slip through the door, and close it, before his eyes were fairly open, and his senses his own again.

'Do you know anything about that man's past life?' I said to the landlord.

'Yes, sir, I know pretty well all about it,' was the answer, 'and an uncommon queer story it is. Most people don't believe it. It's true, though, for all that. Why, just look at him,' continued the landlord, opening the stable door again. 'Poor devil! he's so worn out with his restless nights, that he's dropped back into his sleep already.'

'Don't wake him,' I said, 'I'm in no hurry for the gig. Wait until the other man comes back from his errand. And in the meantime, suppose I have some lunch, and a bottle of sherry; and suppose you come and help me to get through it.'

The heart of mine host, as I had anticipated, warmed to me over his own wine. He soon became communicative on the subject of the man asleep in the stable; and by little and little, I drew the whole story out of him. Extravagant and incredible as the events must appear to everybody, they are related here just as I heard them, and just as they happened.

*   *   *   *

Some years ago there lived in the suburbs of a large seaport town, on the west coast of England, a man in humble circumstances, by the name of Isaac Scatchard. His means of subsistence were derived from any employment he could get as an ostler, and occasionally, when times went well with him, from temporary engagements in service as stable-helper in private houses. Though a faithful, steady, and honest man, he got on badly in his calling. His ill-luck was proverbial among his neighbours. He was always missing good opportunities by no fault of his own; and always living longest in service with amiable people who were not punctual payers of wages. 'Unlucky Isaac' was his nickname in his own neighbourhood – and no one could say that he did not richly deserve it.

With far more than one man's fair share of adversity to endure, Isaac had but one consolation to support him – and that was of the dreariest and most negative kind. He had no wife and children to increase his anxieties and add to the bitterness of his various failures in life. It might have been from mere insensibility, or it might have been from generous unwillingness to involve another in his own unlucky destiny – but the fact undoubtedly was, that he had arrived at the middle term of life without marrying; and, what is much more remarkable, without once exposing himself, from eighteen to eight-and-thirty, to the genial imputation of ever having had a sweetheart.

When he was out of service, he lived alone with his widowed mother. Mrs Scatchard was a woman above the average in her lowly station, as to capacity and manners. She had seen better days, as the phrase is; but she never referred to them in the presence of curious visitors; and, though perfectly polite to every one who approached her, never cultivated any intimacies among her neighbours. She contrived to provide, hardly enough, for her simple wants, by doing rough work for the tailors; and always managed to keep a decent home for her son to return to, whenever his ill-luck drove him out helpless into the world.

One bleak autumn, when Isaac was getting on fast towards forty, and when he was, as usual, out of place through no fault of his own, he set forth from his mother's cottage on a long walk inland to a gentleman's seat, where he had heard that a stable-helper was required.

It wanted then but two days of his birthday; and Mrs Scatchard, with her usual fondness, made him promise, before he started, that he would be back in time to keep that anniversary with her, in as festive a way as their poor means would allow. It was easy for him to comply with this request, even supposing he slept a night each way on the road.

He was to start from home on Monday morning; and whether he got the new place or not, he was to be back for his birthday dinner on

Wednesday at two o'clock.

Arriving at his destination too late on the Monday night to make application for the stable-helper's place, he slept at the village inn, and, in good time on the Tuesday morning, presented himself at the gentleman's house, to fill the vacant situation. Here again, his ill-luck pursued him as inexorably as ever. The excellent written testimonials to his character which he was able to produce, availed him nothing; his long walk had been taken in vain – only the day before, the stable-helper's place had been given to another man.

Isaac accepted this new disappointment resignedly, and as a matter of course. Naturally slow in capacity, he had the bluntness of sensibility and phlegmatic patience of disposition which frequently distinguish men with sluggishly-working mental powers. He thanked the gentleman's steward with his usual quiet civility, for granting him an interview, and took his departure with no appearance of unusual depression in his face or manner.

Before starting on his homeward walk, he made some inquiries at the inn, and ascertained that he might save a few miles on his return by following a new road. Furnished with full instructions, several times repeated, as to the various turnings he was to take, he set forth on his homeward journey, and walked on all day with only one stoppage for bread and cheese. Just as it was getting towards dark, the rain came on and the wind began to rise; and he found himself, to make matters worse, in a part of the country with which he was entirely unacquainted, though he knew himself to be some fifteen miles from home. The first house he found to inquire at was a lonely roadside inn, standing on the outskirts of a thick wood. Solitary as the place looked, it was welcome to a lost man who was also hungry, thirsty, footsore, and wet. The landlord was civil and respectable-looking, and the price he asked for a bed was reasonable enough. Isaac therefore decided on stopping comfortably at the inn for that night.

He was constitutionally a temperate man. His supper simply consisted of two rashers of bacon, a slice of homemade bread, and a pint of ale. He did not go to bed immediately after this moderate meal, but sat up with the landlord, talking about his bad prospects and his long run of ill-luck, and diverging from these topics to the subjects of horseflesh and racing. Nothing was said either by himself, his host, or the few labourers who strayed into the tap-room, which could, in the slightest degree, excite the very small and very dull imaginative faculty which Isaac Scatchard possessed.

At a little after eleven the house was closed. Isaac went round with the landlord, and held the candle while the doors and lower windows were being secured. He noticed with surprise the strength of the bolts, bars, and iron-sheathed shutters.

'You see, we are rather lonely here,' said the landlord. 'We never have had any attempts made to break in yet, but it's always as well to be on the safe side. When nobody is sleeping here I am the only man in the house. My wife and daughter are timid, and the servant-girl takes after her missuses. Another glass of ale, before you turn in? – No! – Well, how such a sober man as you comes to be out of place, is more than I can make out, for one. – Here's where you're to sleep. You're the only lodger tonight, and I think you'll say my missus has done her best to make you comfortable. You're quite sure you won't have another glass of ale? – very well. Good night.'

It was half-past eleven by the clock in the passage as they went upstairs to the bedroom, the window of which looked on to the wood at the back of the house.

Isaac locked the door, set his candle on the chest of drawers, and wearily got ready for bed. The bleak autumn wind was still blowing, and the solemn surging moan of it in the wood was dreary and awful to hear through the night-silence. Isaac felt strangely wakeful. He resolved, as he lay down in bed, to keep the candle alight until he began to grow sleepy for there was something unendurably depressing in the bare idea of lying awake in the darkness, listening to the dismal, ceaseless moan of the wind in the wood.

Sleep stole on him before he was aware of it. His eyes closed, and he fell off insensibly to rest, without having so much as thought of extinguishing the candle.

The first sensation of which he was conscious, after sinking into slumber, was a strange shivering that ran through him suddenly from head to foot, and a dreadful sinking pain at the heart, such as he had never felt before. The shivering only disturbed his slumbers – the pain woke him instantly. In one moment he passed from a state of sleep to a state of wakefulness – his eyes wide open – his mental perceptions cleared on a sudden as if by a miracle.

The candle had burnt down nearly to the last morsel of tallow, but the top of the unsnuffed wick had just fallen off, and the light in the little room was, for the moment, fair and full.

Between the foot of the bed and the closed door, there stood a woman with a knife in her hand, looking at him.

He was stricken speechless with terror, but he did not lose the preternatural clearness of his faculties; and he never took his eyes off the woman. She said not a word as they stared each other in the face; but she began to move slowly towards the left-hand side of the bed.

His eyes followed her. She was a fair fine woman, with yellowish flaxen hair, and light grey eyes, with a droop in the left eyelid. He noticed these things and fixed them on his mind, before she was round at the side of the bed. Speechless, with no expression in her face, with no noise following her footfall, she came closer and closer – stopped – and slowly raised the knife. He laid his right arm over his throat to save it; but, as he saw the knife coming down, threw his hand across the bed to the right side, and jerked his body over that way, just as the knife descended on the mattress within an inch of his shoulder.

His eyes fixed on her arm and hand, as she slowly drew her knife out of the bed. A white, well-shaped arm, with a pretty down lying lightly over the fair skin. A delicate, lady's hand, with the crowning beauty of a pink flush under and round the finger-nails.

She drew the knife out, and passed back again slowly to the foot of the bed; stopped there for a moment looking at him; then came on – still speechless, still with no expression on the beautiful face, still with no sound following the stealthy foot-falls – came on to the right side of the bed where he now lay.

As she approached, she raised the knife again, and he drew himself away to the left side. She struck, as before, right into the mattress, with a deliberate, perpendicularly downward action to the arm. This time his eyes wandered from her to the knife. It was like the large clasp-knives which he had often seen labouring men use to cut their bread and bacon with. Her delicate little fingers did not conceal more than two-thirds of the handle; he noticed that it was made of buckhorn, clean and shining as the blade was, and looking like new.

For the second time she drew the knife out, concealed it in the wide

She drew the knife out and passed to the foot of the bed

sleeve of her gown, then stopped by the bedside, watching him. For an instant he saw her standing in that position – then the wick of the spent candle fell over into the socket. The flame diminished to a little blue point, and the room grew dark.

A moment, or less if possible, passed so – and then the wick flamed up, smokily, for the last time. His eyes were still looking eagerly over the right-hand side of the bed when the final flash of light came, but they discerned nothing. The fair woman with the knife was gone.

The conviction that he was alone again, weakened the hold of the terror that had struck him dumb up to this time. The preternatural sharpness which the very intensity of his panic had mysteriously imparted to his faculties, left them suddenly. His brain grew confused – his heart beat wildly – his ears opened for the first time since the appearance of the woman, to a sense of the woeful, ceaseless moaning of the wind among the trees. With the dreadful conviction of the reality of what he had seen still strong within him, he leapt out of bed, and screaming – 'Murder! – Wake up there, wake up!' – dashed headlong through the darkness to the door.

It was fast locked, exactly as he had left it on going to bed.

His cries, on starting up, had alarmed the house. He heard the terrified, confused exclamations of women; he saw the master of the house approach along the passage, with his burning rush-candle in one hand and his gun in the other.

'What is it?' asked the landlord, breathlessly.

Isaac could only answer in a whisper. 'A woman, with a knife in her hand,' he gasped out. 'In my room – a fair, yellow-haired woman; she jabbed at me with the knife, twice over.'

The landlord's pale cheek grew paler. He looked at Isaac eagerly by the flickering light of his candle; and his face began to get red again – his voice altered too, as well as his complexion.

'She seems to have missed you twice,' he said.

'I dodged the knife as it came down', Isaac went on, in the same scared whisper. 'It struck the bed each time.'

The landlord took his candle into the bedroom immediately. In less than a minute he came out again into the passage in a violent passion.

'The devil fly away with you and your woman with the knife! There isn't a mark in the bed-clothes anywhere. What do you mean by coming into a man's place and frightening his family out of their wits by a dream?'

'I'll leave your house,' said Isaac, faintly. 'Better out on the road, in rain and dark, on my way home, than back again in that room, after what I've seen in it. Lend me a light to get my clothes by, and tell me what I'm to pay.'

'Pay!' cried the landlord, leading the way with his light sulkily into the bedroom. 'You'll find your score on the slate when you go downstairs. I wouldn't have taken you in for all the money you've got about you, if I'd known your dreaming, screeching ways beforehand. Look at the bed. Where's the cut of a knife in it? Look at the window – is the lock bursted? Look at the door (which I heard you fasten yourself) – is it broke in? A murdering woman with a knife in my house! You ought to be ashamed of yourself!'

Isaac answered not a word. He huddled on his clothes; and then they went down the stairs together.

'Nigh on twenty minutes past two!' said the landlord, as they passed the clock. 'A nice time in the morning to frighten honest people out of their wits!'

Isaac paid his bill, and the landlord let him out at the front door, asking, with a grin of contempt, as he undid the strong fastenings, whether 'the murdering woman got in that way?'

They parted without a word on either side. The rain had ceased; but the night was dark, and the wind bleaker than ever. Little did the darkness, or the cold, or the uncertainty about the way home matter to Isaac. If he had been turned out into the wilderness in a thunderstorm, it would have been a relief, after what he had suffered in the bedroom of the inn.

What was the fair woman with the knife? The creature of a dream, or that other creature from the unknown world, called among men by the name of ghost? He could make nothing of the mystery – had made nothing of it, even when it was midday on Wednesday, and when he stood, at last, after many times missing his road, once more on the doorstep of home.

★   ★   ★   ★

His mother came out eagerly to receive him. His face told her in a moment that something was wrong.

'I've lost the place; but that's my luck. I dreamed an ill dream last night, mother – or, maybe, I saw a ghost. Take it either way, it scared me out of my senses, and I'm not my own man again yet.'

'Isaac! your face frightens me. Come in to the fire. Come in, and tell mother all about it.'

He was as anxious to tell as she was to hear; for it had been his hope, all the way home, that his mother, with her quicker capacity and superior knowledge, might be able to throw some light on the mystery which he could not clear up for himself. His memory of the dream was still mechanically vivid, though his thoughts were entirely confused by it.

His mother's face grew paler and paler as he went on. She never interrupted him by so much as a single word; but when he had done, she moved her chair close to his, put her arm around his neck, and said to him:

'Isaac, you dreamed your ill dream on this Wednesday morning. What time was it when you saw the fair woman with the knife in her hand?'

Isaac reflected on what the landlord had said when they had passed by the clock on his leaving the inn – allowed nearly as he could for the time that must have elapsed between the unlocking of his bedroom door and the paying of his bill just before going away, and answered:

'Somewhere about two o'clock in the morning.'

His mother suddenly quitted her hold on his neck, and struck her hands together with a gesture of despair.

'This Wednesday is your birthday, Isaac; and two o'clock in the morning is the time when you were born!'

Isaac's capacities were not quick enough to catch the infection of his mother's superstitious dread. He was amazed, and a little startled also, when she suddenly rose from her chair, opened her old writing-desk, took pen, ink, and paper, and then said to him:

'Your memory is but a poor one, Isaac, and now I'm an old woman, mine's not much better. I want all about this dream of yours to be as well known to both of us, years hence, as it is now. Tell me over again all you told me a minute ago, when you spoke of what the woman with the knife looked like.'

Isaac obeyed, and marvelled much as he saw his mother carefully set down on paper the very words that he was saying.

'Light grey eyes,' she wrote as they came to the descriptive part, 'with a droop in the left eyelid. Flaxen hair, with a gold-yellow streak in it. White arms, with a down upon them. Little lady's hand, with a reddish look about the finger-nails. Clasp-knife with a buckhorn handle, that seemed as good as new.' To these particulars, Mrs Scatchard added the year, month, day of the week, and time in the morning, when the woman of the dream appeared to her son. She then locked up the paper carefully in her writing-desk.

Neither on that day, nor on any day after, could her son induce her to return to the matter of the dream. She obstinately kept her thoughts about it to herself, and even refused to refer again to the paper in her writing-desk. Ere long, Isaac grew weary of attempting to make her break her resolute silence; and time, which sooner or later wears out all things, gradually wore out the impression produced on him by the dream. He began by thinking of it carelessly, and he ended by not thinking of it at all.

This result was the more easily brought about by the advent of some important changes for the better in his prospects, which commenced not long after his terrible night's experience at the inn. He reaped at last the reward of his long and patient suffering under adversity, by getting an excellent place, keeping it for seven years, and leaving it, on the death of his master, not only with an excellent character, but also with a comfortable annuity bequeathed to him as a reward for saving his mistress's life in a carriage accident. Thus it happened that Isaac Scatchard returned to his old mother, seven years after the time of the dream at the inn, with an annual sum of money at his disposal, sufficient to keep them both in ease and independence for the rest of their lives.

The mother, whose health had been bad of late years, profited so much by the care bestowed on her and by freedom from money anxieties, that when Isaac's birthday came round, she was able to sit up comfortably at table and dine with him.

On that day, as the evening drew on, Mrs Scatchard discovered that a bottle of tonic medicine – which she was accustomed to take, and in which she had fancied that a dose or more was still left – happened to be empty. Isaac immediately volunteered to go to the chemist's and get it filled again. It was as rainy and bleak an autumn night as on the memorable past occasion when he lost his way and slept at the road-side inn.

On going in to the chemist's shop, he was passed hurriedly by a poorly-dressed woman coming out of it. The glimpse he had of her face struck him, and he looked back after her as she descended the door-steps.

'You're noticing that woman?' said the chemist's apprentice behind the counter. 'It's my opinion there's something wrong with her. She's been asking for laudanum to put to a bad tooth. Master's out for half an hour; and I told her I wasn't allowed to sell poison to strangers in his absence. She laughed in a queer way, and said she would come back in half an hour. If she expects master to serve her, I think she'll be disappointed. It's a case of suicide, sir, if ever there was one yet.'

These words added immeasurably to the sudden interest in the woman which Isaac had felt at the first sight of her face. After he had got the medicine bottle filled, he looked about anxiously for her, as soon as he was out in the street. She was walking slowly up and down on the opposite side of the road. With his heart, very much to his own surprise, beating fast, Isaac crossed over and spoke to her.

He asked if she was in any distress. She pointed to her torn shawl, her scanty dress, her crushed, dirty bonnet – then moved under a lamp so as to let the light fall on her stern, pale, but still most beautiful face.

'I look like a comfortable, happy woman – don't I?' she said, with a bitter laugh.

She spoke with a purity of intonation which Isaac had never heard before from other than ladies' lips. Her slightest actions seemed to have the easy, negligent grace of a thorough-bred woman. Her skin, for all its poverty-stricken paleness, was as delicate as if her life had been passed in the enjoyment of every social comfort that wealth can purchase. Even her small, finely-shaped hands, gloveless as they were, had not lost their whiteness.

Little by little, in answer to his questions, the sad story of the woman came out. There is no need to relate it here; it is told over and over again in police reports and paragraphs descriptive of attempted suicides.

'My name is Rebecca Murdoch,' said the woman, as she ended. 'I have ninepence left, and I thought of spending it at the chemist's over the way in securing a passage to the other world. Whatever it is, it can't be worse to me than this – so why should I stop here?'

Besides the natural compassion and sadness moved in his heart by what he heard, Isaac felt within him some mysterious influence at work all the time the woman was speaking, which utterly confused his ideas and almost deprived him of his powers of speech. All that he could say in answer to her last reckless words was, that he would prevent her from attempting her own life, if he followed her about all night to do it. His rough, trembling earnestness seemed to impress her.

'I won't occasion you that trouble,' she answered, when he repeated his threat. 'You have given me a fancy for living by speaking kindly to me. No need for the mockery of protestations and promises. You may believe me without them. Come to Fuller's Meadow tomorrow at twelve, and you will find me alive, to answer for myself. No! – no money. My ninepence will do to get me as good a night's lodging as I want.'

She nodded and left him. He made no attempt to follow – he felt no suspicion that she was deceiving him.

'It's strange, but I can't help believing her,' he said to himself, and walked away bewildered towards home.

On entering the house, his mind was still so completely absorbed by its new subject of interest, that he took no notice of what his mother was doing when he came in with the bottle of medicine. She had opened her old writing-desk in his absence, and was now reading a paper attentively that lay inside it. On every birthday of Isaac's since she had written down the particulars of his dream from his own lips, she had been accustomed to read that same paper, and ponder over it in private.

The next day he went to Fuller's Meadow.

He had done only right in believing her so implicitly – she was there, punctual to a minute, to answer for herself. The last-left faint defences in Isaac's heart, against the fascination which a word or look from her began inscrutably to exercise over him, sank down and vanished before her for ever on that memorable morning.

When a man, previously insensible to the influence of women, forms an attachment in middle life, the instances are rare indeed, let the warning circumstances be what they may, in which he is found capable of freeing himself from the tyranny of the new ruling passion. The charm of being spoken to familiarly, fondly, and gratefully by a woman whose language and manners still retain enough of their early refinement to hint at the high social station that she had lost, would have been a dangerous luxury to a man of Isaac's rank at the age of twenty. But it was far more than that – it was certain ruin to him – now that his heart was opening unworthily to a new influence at that middle time of life when strong feelings of all kinds, once implanted, strike root most stubbornly in a man's moral nature. A few more stolen interviews after that first morning in Fuller's Meadow completed his infatuation. In less than a month from the time when he first met her, Isaac Scatchard had consented to give Rebecca Murdoch a new interest in existence, and a chance of recovering the character she had lost, by promising to make her his wife.

She had taken possession not of his passions only, but of his faculties as well. All the mind he had he put into her keeping. She directed him on every point, even instructing him how to break the news of his approaching marriage in the safest manner to his mother.

'If you tell her how you met me and who I am at first,' said the cunning woman, 'she will move heaven and earth to prevent our marriage. Say I am the sister of one of your fellow-servants – ask her to see me before you go into any more particulars – and leave it to me to do the rest. I mean to make her love me next best to you, Isaac, before she knows anything of who I really am.'

The motive of the deceit was sufficient to sanctify it to Isaac. The stratagem proposed relieved him of his one great anxiety, and quieted his uneasy conscience on the subject of his mother. Still, there was something wanting to perfect his happiness, something that he could not realise, something mysteriously untraceable, and yet something that perpetually made itself felt – not when he was absent from Rebecca Murdoch, but, strange to say, when he was actually in her presence! She was kindness itself with him; she never made him feel his inferior capacities and inferior manners; she showed the sweetest anxiety to please him in the smallest trifles; but, in spite of all these attractions, he never could feel quite at his ease with her. At their first meeting, there had mingled with his admiration when he looked in her face, a faint involuntary feeling of doubt whether that face was entirely strange to him. No after-familiarity had the slightest effect on this inexplicable, wearisome uncertainty.

Concealing the truth, as he had been directed, he announced his marriage engagement precipitately and confusedly to his mother, on the day when he contracted it. Poor Mrs Scatchard showed her perfect confidence in her son by flinging her arms round his neck, and giving him joy of having found at last, in the sister of one of his fellow-servants, a woman to comfort and care for him after his mother was gone. She was all eagerness to see the woman of her son's choice; and the next day was fixed for the introduction.

It was a bright sunny morning, and the little cottage parlour was full of light, as Mrs Scatchard, happy and expectant, dressed for the occasion in her Sunday gown, sat waiting for her son and her future daughter-in-law.

Punctual to the appointed time, Isaac hurriedly and nervously led his promised wife into the room. His mother rose to receive her – advanced a few steps, smiling – looked Rebecca full in the eyes – and suddenly stopped. Her face, which had been flushed the moment before, turned white in an instant – her eyes lost their expression of softness and kindness, and assumed a blank look of terror – her outstretched hands fell to her sides, and she staggered back a few steps with a low cry to her son.

'Isaac!' she whispered, clutching him fast by the arm, when he asked alarmedly if she was taken ill, 'Isaac! does that woman's face remind you of nothing?'

Before he could answer, before he could look round to where Rebecca stood, astonished and angered by her reception, at the lower end of the room, his mother pointed impatiently to her writing-desk and gave him the key.

'Open it,' she said, in a quick, breathless whisper.

'What does this mean? Why am I treated as if I had no business here? Does your mother want to insult me?' asked Rebecca, angrily.

'Open it, and give me the paper in the left-hand drawer. Quick! quick! for heaven's sake!' said Mrs Scatchard, shrinking further back in terror.

Isaac gave her the paper. She looked it over eagerly for a moment – then followed Rebecca, who was now turning away haughtily to leave the room, and caught her by the shoulder – abruptly raised the long, loose sleeve of her gown – and glanced at her hand and arm. Something like fear began to steal over the angry expression of Rebecca's face, as she shook herself free from the old woman's grasp. 'Mad!' she said to herself, 'and Isaac never told me.' With those few words she left the room.

Isaac was hastening after her, when his mother turned and stopped his further progress. It wrung his heart to see the misery and terror in her face as she looked at him.

'Light grey eyes,' she said, in low, mournful, awe-struck tones, pointing towards the open door. 'A droop in the left eyelid; flaxen hair with a gold-yellow streak in it; white arms with a down on them; little lady's hand, with a reddish look under the finger-nails. *The Dream Woman!* – Isaac, the Dream Woman!'

That faint cleaving doubt which he had never been able to shake off in Rebecca Murdoch's presence, was fatally set at rest for ever. He *had* seen her face, then, before – seven years before, on his birthday, in the bedroom of the lonely inn.

'Be warned! Oh, my son, be warned! Isaac! Isaac! let her go, and do you stop with me!'

Something darkened the parlour window as those words were said. A sudden chill ran through him, and he glanced sidelong at the shadow. Rebecca Murdoch had come back. She was peering in curiously at them over the low window-blind.

'I have promised to marry, mother,' he said, 'and marry I must.'

The tears came into his eyes as he spoke, and dimmed his sight; but he could just discern the fatal face outside, moving away again from the window.

His mother's head sank lower.

'Are you faint?' he whispered.

'Broken-hearted, Isaac.'

He stooped down and kissed her. The shadow, as he did so, returned to the window; and the fatal face peered in curiously once more.

★   ★   ★   ★

Three weeks after that day Isaac and Rebecca were man and wife. All that was hopelessly dogged and stubborn in the man's moral nature, seemed to have closed round his fatal passion, and to have fixed it unassailably in his heart.

After that first interview in the cottage parlour, no consideration could induce Mrs Scatchard to see her son's wife again, or even talk of her when Isaac tried hard to plead her cause after their marriage.

This course of conduct was not in any degree occasioned by a discovery of the degradation in which Rebecca had lived. There was no question of that between mother and son. There was no question of anything but the fearfully exact resemblance between the living, breathing woman, and the spectre-woman of Isaac's dream.

Rebecca, on her side, neither felt nor expressed the slightest sorrow at the estrangement between herself and her mother-in-law. Isaac, for the sake of peace, had never contradicted her first idea that age and long illness had affected Mrs Scatchard's mind. He even allowed his wife to upbraid him for not having confessed this to her at the time of their marriage engagement, rather than risk anything by hinting at the truth. The sacrifice of his integrity before his one all-mastering delusion, seemed but a small thing, and cost his conscience but little, after the sacrifices he had already made.

The time of waking from his delusion – the cruel and rueful time – was not far off. After some quiet months of married life, as the summer was ending, and the year was getting on towards the month of his birthday, Isaac found his wife altering towards him. She grew sullen and contemptuous: she formed acquaintances of the most dangerous kind, in defiance of his objections, his entreaties, and his commands; and, worst of all, she learnt, ere long, after every fresh difference with her husband, to seek the deadly self-oblivion of drink. Little by little, after the first miserable discovery that his wife was keeping company with drunkards, the shocking certainty forced itself on Isaac that she had grown to be a drunkard herself.

He had been in a sadly desponding state for some time before the occurrence of these domestic calamities. His mother's health, as he could but too plainly discern every time he went to see her at the cottage, was failing fast; and he upbraided himself in secret as the cause of the bodily and mental suffering she endured. When to his remorse on his mother's account was added the shame and misery occasioned by the discovery of his wife's degradation, he sank under the double trial, his face began to alter fast, and he looked, what he was, a spirit-broken man.

His mother, still struggling bravely against the illness that was hurrying her to the grave, was the first to notice the sad alteration in him, and the first to hear of his last, worst trouble with his wife. She could only weep bitterly, on the day when he made his humiliating confession; but on the next occasion when he went to see her, she had taken a resolution, in reference to his domestic afflictions, which astonished, and even alarmed him. He found her dressed to go out, and on asking the reason, received this answer:

'I am not long for this world, Isaac,' she said; 'and I shall not feel easy on my death-bed, unless I have done my best to the last to make my son happy. I mean to put my own fears and my own feelings out of the question, and to go with you to your wife, and try what I can do to reclaim her. Give me your arm, Isaac and let me do the last thing I can in this world to help my son, before it is too late.'

He could not disobey her; and they walked together slowly towards his miserable home.

It was only one o'clock in the afternoon when they reached the cottage where he lived. It was their dinner hour, and Rebecca was in the kitchen. He was thus able to take his mother quietly into the parlour, and then prepare his wife for the interview. She had fortunately drank but little at that early hour, and she was less sullen and capricious than usual.

He returned to his mother, with his mind tolerably at ease. His wife soon followed him into the parlour, and the meeting between her and Mrs Scatchard passed off better than he had ventured to anticipate, though he observed with secret apprehension that his mother, resolutely as she controlled herself in other respects, could not look his wife in the face when she spoke to her. It was a relief to him, therefore, when Rebecca began to lay the cloth.

She laid the cloth, brought in the bread-tray, and cut a slice from the loaf for her husband, then returned to the kitchen. At that moment, Isaac, still anxiously watching his mother, was startled by seeing the same ghastly change pass over her face which had altered it so awfully on the morning when Rebecca and she first met. Before he could say a word, she whispered with a look of horror;

'Take me back! – home, home again, Isaac! Come with me, and never go back again!'

He was afraid to ask for an explanation; he could only sign her to be silent, and help her quickly to the door. As they passed the bread-tray on the table, she stopped and pointed to it.

'Did you see what your wife cut your bread with?' she asked in a low whisper.

'No, mother; I was not noticing. What was it?'

'Look!'

He did look. A new clasp-knife, with a buckhorn handle, lay with the loaf in the bread-tray. He stretched out his hand, shudderingly, to possess himself of it; but at the same time, there was a noise in the kitchen, and his mother caught at his arm.

'The knife of the dream! Isaac, I'm faint with fear – take me away, before she comes back!'

He was hardly able to support her. The visible, tangible reality of the knife struck him with a panic, and utterly destroyed any faint doubts he might have entertained up to this time, in relation to the mysterious dream-warning of nearly eight years before. By a last desperate effort, he summoned self-possession enough to help his mother out of the house – so quietly, that the 'Dream Woman' (he thought of her by that name now) did not hear their departure.

'Don't go back, Isaac, don't go back!' implored Mrs Scatchard, as he turned to go away, after seeing her safely seated again in her own room.

'I must get the knife,' he answered under his breath. His mother tried to stop him again; but he hurried out without another word.

On his return, he found that his wife had discovered their secret departure from the house. She had been drinking, and was in a fury of passion. The dinner in the kitchen was flung under the grate; the cloth was off the parlour table. Where was the knife?

Unwisely, he asked for it. She was only too glad of the opportunity of irritating him, which the request afforded her. 'He wanted the knife, did he? Could he give her a reason why? – No? Then he should not have it – not if he went down on his knees to ask for it.' Further recriminations elicited the fact that she bought it a bargain, and that she considered it her own especial property. Isaac saw the uselessness of attempting to get the knife by fair means, and determined to search for it later in the day, in secret. The search was unsuccessful. Night came on, and he left the house to walk about the streets. He was afraid now to sleep in the same room with her.

Three weeks passed. Still sullenly enraged with him, she would not give up the knife; and still that fear of sleeping in the same room with her possessed him. He walked about at night, or dozed in the parlour, or sat watching by his mother's bed-side. Before the expiration of the first week in the new month his mother died. It wanted then but ten days of her son's birthday. She had longed to live until that anniversary. Isaac was present at her death; and her last words in this world were addressed to him:

'Don't go back, my son – don't go back!'

He was obliged to go back, if it were only to watch his wife. Exasperated to the last degree by his distrust of her, she had revengefully sought to add a sting to his grief, during the last days of his mother's illness, by declaring that she would assert her right to attend the funeral. In spite of all that he could do or say, she held with wicked pertinacity to her words and, on the day appointed for the burial, forced herself – inflamed and shameless with drink – into her husband's presence, and delared that she would walk in the funeral procession to his mother's grave.

This last worst outrage, accompanied by all that was most insulting in word and look, maddened him for the moment. He struck her.

The instant the blow was dealt, he repented it. She crouched down, silent, in a corner of the room, and eyed him steadily; it was a look that cooled his hot blood, and made him tremble. But there was no time now to think of a means of making atonement. Nothing remained, but to risk the worst until the funeral was over. There was but one way of making sure of her. He locked her into her bedroom.

When he came back, some hours after, he found her sitting, very much altered in look and bearing, by the bedside, with a bundle on her lap. She rose, and faced him quietly, and spoke with a strange stillness in her voice, a strange repose in her eyes, a strange composure in her manner.

'No man has ever struck me twice,' she said; 'and my husband shall have no second opportunity. Set the door open and let me go. From this day forth we see each other no more.'

Before he could answer she passed him, and left the room. He saw her walk away up the street.

Would she return?

All that night he watched and waited; but no footstep came near the house. The next night, overcome by fatigue, he lay down in bed in his clothes, with the door locked, the key on the table, and the candle burning. His slumber was not disturbed. The third night, the fourth, the fifth, the sixth passed, and nothing happened. He lay down on the seventh, still in his clothes, still with the door locked, the key on the table, and the candle burning; but easier in his mind.

Easier in his mind, and in perfect health of body, when he fell off to sleep. But his rest was disturbed. He woke twice, without any sensation of uneasiness. But the third time it was that never-be-forgotten shivering of the night at the lonely inn, that dreadful sinking pain at the heart, which once more aroused him in an instant.

His eyes opened towards the left-hand side of the bed, and there stood – The Dream Woman again? No! His wife; the living reality, with the dream-spectre's face – in the dream-spectre's attitude: the fair arm up; the knife clasped in the delicate white hand.

He sprang upon her, almost at the instant of seeing her, and yet not quickly enough to prevent her from hiding the knife. Without a word from him, without a cry from her, he pinioned her in the chair. With one hand he felt up her sleeve; and there, where the Dream Woman had hidden the knife, his wife had hidden it – the knife with the buckhorn handle, that looked like new.

In the despair of that fearful moment his brain was steady, his heart was calm. He looked at her fixedly, with the knife in his hand, and said these last words:

'You told me we should see each other no more, and you have come back. It is my turn now to go, and to go for ever. I say that we shall see each other no more; and *my* word shall not be broken.'

He left her, and set forth into the night. There was a bleak wind abroad, and the smell of recent rain was in the air. The distant church clocks chimed the quarter as he walked rapidly beyond the last houses in the suburb. He asked the first policeman he met, what hour that was, of which the quarter past had just struck.

The man referred sleepily to his watch, and answered, 'Two o'clock.' Two in the morning. What day of the month was this day that had just begun? He reckoned it up from the date of his mother's funeral. The fatal parallel was complete – it was his birthday!

Had he escaped the mortal peril which his dream foretold? or had he only received a second warning?

As this ominous doubt forced itself on his mind, he stopped, reflected, and turned back again towards the city. He was still resolute to hold his word, and never to let her see him more; but there was a thought now in his mind of having her watched and followed. The knife was in his possession; the world was before him; but a new distrust of her – a vague, unspeakable, superstitious dread – had overcome him.

'I must know where she goes, now she thinks I have left her,' he said to himself, as he stole back wearily to the precincts of his house.

It was still dark. He had left the candle burning in the bedchamber; but when he looked up to the window of the room now, there was no light in it. He crept cautiously to the house door. On going away, he remembered to have closed it; on trying it now, he found it open.

He waited outside, never losing sight of the house until daylight. Then he ventured indoors – listened, and heard nothing – looked into kitchen, scullery, parlour; and found nothing; went up at last into the bedroom – it was empty. A picklock lay on the floor, betraying how she had gained entrance in the night, and that was the only trace of her.

Whither had she gone? No mortal tongue could tell him. The darkness had covered her flight; and when the day broke, no man could say where the light found her.

Before leaving the house and the town for ever, he gave instructions to a friend and neighbour to sell his furniture for anything that it would fetch, and to apply the proceeds towards employing the police to trace her. The directions were honestly followed, and the money was all spent; but the inquiries led to nothing. The picklock on the bedroom floor remained the last useless trace of the Dream Woman.

★   ★   ★   ★

At this part of the narrative the landlord paused; and, turning towards the window of the room in which we were sitting, looked in the direction of the stable-yard.

'So far,' he said, 'I tell you what was told to me. The little that remains to be added, lies within my own experience. Between two and three months after the events I have just been relating, Isaac Scatchard came to me, withered and old-looking before his time, just as you saw him today. He had his testimonials to character with him, and he asked me for employment here. Knowing that my wife and he were distantly related, I gave him a trial, in consideration of that relationship, and liked him in spite of his queer habits. He is as sober, honest, and willing a man as there is in England. As for his restlessness at night, and his sleeping away his leisure time in the day, who can wonder at it after hearing his story? Besides, he never objects to being roused up, when he's wanted, so there's not much inconvenience to complain of, after all.'

'I suppose he is afraid of a return of that dreadful dream, and of waking out of it in the dark?'

'No,' returned the landlord. 'The dream comes back to him so often, that he has got to bear with it by this time resignedly enough. It's his wife keeps him waking at night, as he often told me.'

'What! Has she never been heard of yet?'

'Never. Isaac himself has the one perpetual thought that she is alive and looking for him. I believe he wouldn't let himself drop off to sleep towards two in the morning, for a king's ransom. Two in the morning, he says, is the time she will find him, one of these days. Two in the morning is the time, all the year round, when he likes to be most certain that he has got the clasp-knife safe about him. He does not mind being alone, as long as he is awake, except on the night before his birthday, when he firmly believes himself to be in peril of his life. The birthday has only come round once since he has been here, and then he sat up along with the night-porter. "She's looking for me," is all he says, when anybody speaks to him about the one anxiety of his life; "she's looking for me." He may be right. She *may* be looking for him. Who can tell?'

'Who can tell?' said I.

ONE OF THE MISSING

Ambrose Bierce

Jerome Searing, a private soldier of General Sherman's army, then confronting the enemy at and about Kenesaw Mountain, Georgia, turned his back upon a small group of officers, with whom he had been talking in low tones, stepped across a light line of earthworks, and disappeared in a forest. None of the men in line behind the works had said a word to him, nor had he so much as nodded to them in passing, but all who saw understood that this brave man had been intrusted with some perilous duty. Jerome Searing, though a private, did not serve in the ranks; he was detailed for service at division headquarters, being borne upon the rolls as an orderly. 'Orderly' is a word covering a multitude of duties. An orderly may be a messenger, a clerk, an officer's servant—anything. He may perform services for which no provision is made in orders and army regulations. Their nature may depend upon his aptitude, upon favour, upon accident.

Private Searing, an incomparable marksman, young—it is surprising how young we all were in those days—hardy, intelligent, and insensible to fear, was a scout. The general commanding his division was not content to obey orders blindly without knowing what was in his front, even when his command was not on detached service, but formed a fraction of the line of the army; nor was he satisfied to receive his knowledge of his *vis-à-vis* through the customary channels; he wanted to know more than he was told by the corps commander and the collisions of pickets and skirmishers. Hence Jerome Searing—with his extraordinary daring, his woodcraft, his sharp eyes and truthful tongue. On this occasion his instructions were simple: to get as near the enemy's lines as possible and learn all that he could.

In a few moments he had arrived at the picket line, the men on duty there lying in groups of from two to four behind little banks of earth scooped out of the slight depression in which they lay, their rifles protruding from the green boughs with which they had masked their small defences. The forest extended without a break toward the front, so solemn and silent that only by an effort of the imagination could it be conceived as populous with armed men, alert and vigilant—a forest formidable with possibilities of battle. Pausing a moment in one of the rifle pits to inform the men of his intention, Searing crept stealthily forward on his hands and knees and was soon lost to view in a dense thicket of underbrush.

'That's the last of him' said one of the men; 'I wish I had his rifle; those fellows will hurt some of us with it.'

Searing crept on, taking advantage of every accident of ground and growth to give himself better cover. His eyes penetrated everywhere, his ears took note of every sound. He stilled his breathing, and at the cracking of a twig beneath his knee stopped his progress and hugged the earth. It was slow work, but not tedious; the danger made it exciting, but by no physical signs was the excitement manifest. His pulse was as regular, his nerves were as steady, as if he were trying to trap a sparrow.

'It seems a long time,' he thought, 'but I cannot have come very far; I'm still alive.'

He smiled at his own method of estimating distance, and crept forward. A moment later he suddenly flattened himself upon the earth and lay motionless, minute after minute. Through a narrow opening in the bushes he had caught sight of a small mound of yellow clay—one of the enemy's rifle pits. After some little time he cautiously raised his head, inch by inch, then his body upon his hands, spread out on each side of him, all the while intently regarding the hillock of clay. In another moment he was upon his feet, rifle in hand, striding rapidly forward with little attempt at concealment. He had rightly interpreted the signs, whatever they were; the enemy was gone.

To assure himself beyond a doubt before going back to report upon so important a matter, Searing pushed forward across the line of abandoned pits, running from cover to cover in the more open forest, his eyes vigilant to discover possible stragglers. He came to the edge of a plantation—one of those forlorn, deserted homesteads of the last years of the war, upgrown with brambles, ugly with broken fences, and desolate with vacant buildings having blank apertures in place of doors and windows. After a keen reconnaissance from the safe seclusion of a clump of young pines, Searing ran lightly across a field and through an orchard to a small structure which stood apart from the other farm buildings, on a slight elevation, which he thought would enable him to overlook a large scope of country in the direction that he supposed the enemy to have taken in withdrawing.

This building, which had originally consisted of a single room, elevated upon four posts about ten feet high, was now little more than a roof; the floor had fallen away, the joists and planks loosely piled on the ground below or resting on end at various angles, not wholly torn from their fastenings above. The supporting posts were themselves no longer vertical. It looked as if the whole edifice would go down at the touch of a finger. Concealing himself in the debris of joists and flooring, Searing looked across the open ground between his point of view and a spur of Kenesaw Mountain, a half-mile away. A road leading up and across this spur was crowded with troops—the rear-guard of the retiring enemy, their gun barrels gleaming in the morning sunlight.

Searing had now learned all that he could hope to know. It was his duty to return to his own command with all possible speed and report his discovery. But the grey column of infantry toiling up the mountain road was singularly tempting. His rifle—an ordinary Springfield, but fitted with a globe sight and hair trigger—would easily send its ounce and a quarter of lead hissing into their midst. That would probably not affect the duration and result of the war, but it is the business of a soldier to kill. It is also his pleasure if he is a good soldier. Searing cocked his rifle and set the trigger.

But it was decreed from the beginning of time that Private Searing was not to murder anybody that bright summer morning, nor was the Confederate retreat to be announced by him. For countless ages events had been so matching themselves together in that wondrous mosaic to some parts of which, dimly discernible, we give the name of history, that the acts which he had in will would have marred the harmony of the pattern.

Some twenty-five years previously the power charged with the execution of the work according to the design had provided against that mischance by causing the birth of a certain male child in a little village at the foot of the Carpathian Mountains, had carefully reared it, supervised its education, directed its desires into a military channel, and in due time made it an officer of artillery. But the concurrence of an infinite number of favouring influences and their preponderance over an infinite number of opposing ones, this officer of artillery had been made to commit a breach of discipline and fly from his native country to avoid punishment.

He had been directed to New Orleans (instead of New York), where a recruiting officer awaited him on the wharf. He was enlisted and promoted, and things were so ordered that he now commanded a Confederate battery some three miles along the line from where Jerome Searing, the Federal scout, stood cocking his rifle. Nothing had been neglected—at every step in the progress of both these men's lives, and in the lives of their ancestors and contemporaries, and of the lives of the contemporaries of their ancestors—the right thing had been done to bring about the desired result. Had anything in all this vast concatenation been overlooked, Private Searing might have fired on the retreating Confederates that morning, and would perhaps have missed. As it fell out, a captain of artillery, having nothing better to do while awaiting his turn to pull out and be off, amused himself by sighting a field piece obliquely to his right at what he took to be some Federal officers on the crest of a hill, and discharged it. The shot flew high of its mark.

As Jerome Searing drew back the hammer of his rifle, and, with his eyes upon the distant Confederates, considered where he could plant his shot with the best hope of making a widow or an orphan or a child-less mother—perhaps all three, for Private Searing, although he had repeatedly refused promotion, was not without a certain kind of ambition—he heard a rushing sound in the air, like that made by the wings of a great bird swooping down upon its prey. More quickly than he could apprehend the gradation, it increased to a hoarse and horrible roar, as the missile that made it sprang at him out of the sky, striking with a deafening impact one of the posts supporting the confusion of timbers above him, smashing it into matchwood, and bringing down the crazy edifice with a loud clatter, in clouds of blinding dust!

Lieutenant Adrian Searing, in command of the picket guard on that part of the line through which his brother Jerome had passed on his mission, sat with attentive ears in his breastwork behind the line. Not the faintest sound escaped him; the cry of a bird, the barking of a squirrel, the noise of the wind among the pines—all were anxiously noted by his overstrained sense. Suddenly, directly in front of his line, he heard a faint, confused rumble, like the clatter of a falling building translated by distance. At the same moment an officer approached him on foot from the rear and saluted.

'Lieutenant,' said the aide, 'the colonel directs you to move forward your line and feel the enemy if you find him. If not, continue the advance until directed to halt. There is reason to think that the enemy has retreated.'

The lieutenant nodded and said nothing; the other officer retired. In a moment the men, informed of their duty by the non-commissioned officers in low tones, had deployed from their rifle pits and were moving forward in skirmishing order, with set teeth and beating hearts. The lieutenant looked at his watch. Six o'clock and eighteen minutes.

When Jerome Searing recovered consciousness, he did not at once understand what had occurred. It was, indeed, some time before he opened his eyes. For a while he believed that he had died and been buried, and he tried to recall some portions of the burial service. He thought that his wife was kneeling upon his grave, adding her weight to that of the earth upon his chest. The two of them, widow and earth, had crushed his coffin. Unless the children should persuade her to go home, he would not much longer be able to breathe. He felt a sense of wrong. 'I cannot speak to her,' he thought; 'the dead have no voice; and if I open my eyes I shall get them full of earth.'

He opened his eyes—a great expanse of blue sky, rising from a fringe of the tops of trees. In the foreground, shutting out some of the trees, a high, dun mound, angular in outline and crossed by an intricate, patternless system of straight lines; in the centre a bright ring of metal—the whole an immeasurable distance away—a distance so inconceivably great that it fatigued him, and he closed his eyes. The moment that he did so he was conscious of an insufferable light. A sound was in his ears like the low, rhythmic thunder of a distant sea breaking in successive waves upon the beach, and out of this noise, seeming a part of it, or possibly coming from beyond it, and intermingled with its ceaseless undertone, came the articulate words: 'Jerome Searing, you are caught like a rat in a trap—in a trap, trap, trap.'

Suddenly there fell a great silence, a black darkness, an infinite tranquillity, and Jerome Searing, perfectly conscious of his rathood, and well assured of the trap that he was in, remembered all, and nowise alarmed, again opened his eyes to reconnoitre, to note the strength of his enemy, to plan his defence.

He was caught in a reclining posture, his back firmly supported by a solid beam. Another lay across his breast, but he had been able to shrink a little way from it so that it no longer oppressed him, though it was immovable. A brace joining it at an angle had wedged him against a pile of boards on his left, fastening the arm on that side. His legs, slightly parted and straight along the ground, were covered upward to the knees with a mass of debris which towered above his narrow horizon. His head was as rigidly fixed as in a vice; he could move his eyes, his chin—no more. Only his right arm was partly free. 'You must help us out of this,' he said to it. But he could not get it from under the heavy timber across his chest, nor move it outward more than six inches at the elbow.

Searing was not seriously injured, nor did he suffer pain. A smart rap on the head from a flying fragment of the splintered post, incurred simultaneously with the frightfully sudden shock to the nervous system, had momentarily dazed him. His term of unconsciousness, including the period of recovery, during which he had had the strange fancies, had probably not exceeded a few seconds, for the dust of the wreck had not wholly cleared away as he began an intelligent survey of the situation.

With his partly free right hand he now tried to get hold of the beam which lay across, but not quite against, his breast. In no way could he do so. He was unable to depress the shoulder so as to push the elbow beyond that edge of the timber which was nearest his knees; failing in that, he could not raise the forearm and hand to grasp the beam. The brace that made an angle with it downward and backward prevented him from doing anything in that direction, and between it and his body the space was not half as wide as the length of his forearm. Obviously he could not get his hand under the beam nor over it; he could not, in fact, touch it at all. Having demonstrated his inability, he desisted, and began to think if he could reach any of the debris piled upon his legs.

In surveying the mass with a view to determining that point, his attention was arrested by what seemed to be a ring of shining metal immediately in front of his eyes. It appeared to him at first to surround some perfectly black substance, and it was somewhat more than a half inch in diameter. It suddenly occurred to his mind that the blackness was simply shadow, and that the ring was in fact the muzzle of his rifle protruding from the pile of debris. He was not long in satisfying himself that this was so—if it was a satisfaction. By closing either eye he could look a little way along the barrel—to the point where it was hidden by the rubbish that held it. He could see the one side, with the corresponding eye, at apparently the same angle as the other side with the other eye. Looking with the right eye, the weapon seemed to be directed at a point to the left of his head, and *vice versa*. He was unable to see the upper surface of the barrel, but could see the under surface of the stock at a slight angle. The piece was, in fact, aimed at the exact centre of his forehead.

In the perception of this circumstance, in the recollection that just previously to the mischance of which this uncomfortable situation was the result, he had cocked the gun and set the trigger so that a touch would discharge it, Private Searing was affected with a feeling of uneasiness. But that was as far as possible from fear; he was a brave man, somewhat familiar with the aspect of rifles from that point of view, and of cannon, too; and now he recalled, with something like amusement, an incident of his experience at the storming of Missionary Ridge, where, walking up to one of the enemy's emplacements from which he had seen a heavy gun throw charge after charge of grape among the assailants, he thought for a moment that the piece had been withdrawn; he could see nothing in the opening but a brazen circle. What that was he had understood just in time to step aside as it pitched another peck of iron down that swarming slope. To face firearms is one of the commonest incidents in a soldier's life—firearms, too, with malevolent eyes blazing behind them. That is what a soldier is for. Still, Private Searing did not altogether relish the situation, and turned away his eyes.

After groping, aimless, with his right hand for a time, he made an ineffectual attempt to release his left. Then he tried to disengage his head, the fixity of which was the more annoying from his ignorance of what held it. Next he tried to free his feet, but while exerting the powerful muscles of his legs for that purpose it occurred to him that a disturbance of the rubbish which held them might discharge the rifle; how it could have endured what had already befallen it he could not understand, although memory assisted him with various instances in point.

One in particular he recalled, in which, in a moment of mental abstraction, he had clubbed his rifle and beaten out another gentleman's brains, observing afterward that the weapon which he had been diligently swinging by the muzzle was loaded, capped, and at full cock —knowledge of which circumstance would doubtless have cheered his antagonist to longer endurance. He had always smiled in recalling that blunder of his 'green and salad days' as a soldier, but now he did not smile. He turned his eyes again to the muzzle of the gun, and for a moment fancied that it had moved; it seemed somewhat nearer.

Again he looked away. The tops of the distant trees beyond the bounds of the plantation interested him; he had not before observed how light and feathery they seemed, nor how darkly blue the sky was, even among their branches, where they somewhat paled it with their green; above him it appeared almost black. 'It will be uncomfortably hot here,' he thought, 'as the day advances. I wonder which way I am looking.'

Judging by such shadows as he could see, he decided that his face was due north; he would at least not have the sun in his eyes, and north— well, that was toward his wife and children.

'Bah!' he exclaimed aloud, 'what have they to do with it?'

He closed his eyes. 'As I can't get out, I may as well go to sleep. The rebels are gone, and some of our fellows are sure to stray out here foraging. They'll find me.'

But he did not sleep. Gradually he became sensible of a pain in his forehead—a dull ache, hardly perceptible at first, but growing more and more uncomfortable. He opened his eyes and it was gone; he closed them and it returned. 'The devil!' he said irrelevantly, and stared again at the sky. He heard the singing of birds, the strange metallic note of the meadow lark, suggesting the clash of vibrant blades.

He fell into pleasant memories of his childhood, played again with his brother and sister, raced across the fields, shouting to alarm the sitting larks, entered the sombre forest beyond, and with timid steps followed the faint path to Ghost Rock, standing at last with audible heart-throbs before Dead Man's Cave and seeking to penetrate its awful mystery. For the first time he observed that the opening of the haunted cavern was encircled by a ring of metal.

Then all else vanished, and left him gazing into the barrel of his rifle as before. But whereas before it had seemed nearer, it now seemed an inconceivable distance away, and all the more sinister for that. He cried out, and startled by something in his own voice—the note of fear—lied to himself in denial: 'If I don't sing out I may stay here till I die.'

He now made no further attempt to evade the menacing stare of the gun barrel. If he turned away his eyes an instant it was to look for assistance (although he could not see the ground on either side the ruin), and he permitted them to return, obedient to the imperative fascination. If he closed them, it was from weariness, and instantly the poignant pain in his forehead—the prophecy and menace of the bullet—forced him to reopen them.

The tension of nerve and brain was too severe; nature came to his relief with intervals of unconsciousness. Reviving from one of these, he became sensible of a sharp, smarting pain in his right hand, and when he worked his fingers together, or rubbed his palm with them, he could feel that they were wet and slippery. He could not see the hand, but he knew the sensation; it was running blood. In his delirium he had beaten it against the jagged fragments of the wreck, had clutched it full of splinters. He resolved that he would meet his fate more manly. He was a plain, common soldier, had no religion and not much philosophy; he could not die like a hero, with great and wise last words, even if there

The thought flashed into his bewildered mind that the rats might touch the trigger of his rifle.

were someone to hear them, but he could die 'game', and he would. But if he could only know when to expect the shot!

Some rats which had probably inhabited the shed came sneaking and scampering about. One of them mounted the pile of debris that held the rifle; another followed, and another. Searing regarded them at first with indifference, then with friendly interest; then, as the thought flashed into his bewildered mind that they might touch the trigger of his rifle, he screamed at them to go away. 'It is no business of yours,' he cried.

The creatures left; they would return later, attack his face, gnaw away his nose, cut his throat—he knew that, but he hoped by that time to be dead.

Nothing could now unfix his gaze from the little ring of metal with its black interior. The pain in his forehead was fierce and constant. He felt it gradually penetrating the brain more and more deeply, until at last its progress was arrested by the wood at the back of his head. It grew momentarily more insufferable; he began wantonly beating his

lacerated hand against the splinters again to counteract that horrible ache. It seemed to throb with a slow, regular, recurrence, each pulsation sharper than the preceding, and sometimes he cried out, thinking he felt the fatal bullet. No thoughts of home, of wife and children, of country, of glory. The whole record of memory was erased. The world had passed away—not a vestige remained. Here, in this confusion of timbers and boards, is the sole universe. Here is immortality in time— each pain an everlasting life. The throbs tick off eternities.

Jerome Searing, the man of courage, the formidable enemy, the strong, resolute warrior, was as pale as a ghost. His jaw was fallen; his eyes protruded; he trembled in every fibre; a cold sweat bathed his entire body; he screamed with fear. He was not insane—he was terrified.

In groping about with his torn and bleeding hand he seized at last a strip of board, and, pulling, felt it give way. It lay parallel with his body, and by bending his elbow as much as the contracted space would permit, he could draw it a few inches at a time. Finally it was altogether loosened from the wreckage covering his legs; he could lift it clear of the ground its whole length. A great hope came into his mind: perhaps he could work it upward, that is to say backward, far enough to lift the end and push aside the rifle; or, if that were too tightly wedged, so hold the strip of board as to deflect the bullet.

With this object he passed it backward inch by inch, hardly daring to breathe, lest that act somehow defeat his intent, and more than ever unable to remove his eyes from the rifle, which might perhaps now hasten to improve its waning opportunity. Something at least had been gained; in the occupation of his mind in this attempt at self-defence he was less sensible of the pain in his head and had ceased to scream. But he was still dreadfully frightened, and his teeth rattled like castanets.

The strip of board ceased to move to the urging of his hand. He tugged at it with all his strength, changed the direction of its length all he could, but it had met some extended obstruction behind him, and the end in front was still too far away to clear the pile of debris and reach the muzzle of the gun. It extended, indeed, nearly as far as the trigger-guard, which, uncovered by the rubbish, he could imperfectly see with his right eye. He tried to break the strip with his hand, but had no leverage. Perceiving his defeat, all his terror returned, augmented tenfold. The black aperture of the rifle appeared to threaten a sharper and more imminent death in punishment of his rebellion. The track of the bullet through his head ached with more intense anguish. He began to tremble again.

Suddenly he became composed. His tremor subsided. He clinched his teeth and drew down his eyebrows. He had not exhausted his means of defence; a new design had shaped itself in his mind—another plan of battle. Raising the front end of the strip of board, he carefully pushed it forward through the wreckage at the side of the rifle until it pressed against the trigger guard. Then he moved the end slowly outward until he could feel that it had cleared it, then, closing his eyes, thrust it against the trigger with all his strength! There was no explosion; the rifle had been discharged as it dropped from his hand when the building fell. But Jcrome Searing was dead.

A line of Federal skirmishes swept across the plantation toward the mountain. They passed on both sides of the wrecked building, observing nothing. At a short distance in their rear came their commander, Lieutenant Adrian Searing. He casts his eyes curiously upon the ruin and sees a dead body half buried in boards and timbers. It is so covered with dust that its clothing is Confederate grey. Its face is yellowish white; the cheeks are fallen in, the temples sunken, too, with sharp ridges about them, making the forehead forbiddingly narrow; the upper lip, slightly lifted, shows the white teeth, rigidly clinched. The hair is heavy with moisture, the face as wet as the dewy grass all about. From his point of view the officer does not observe the rifle; the man was apparently killed by the fall of the building.

'Dead a week,' said the officer curtly, moving on, mechanically pulling out his watch as if to verify his estimate of time. Six o'clock and forty minutes.

THE MIRACLE OF THE BLACK CANYON

Morley Roberts

In that part of British Columbia called the Dry Belt, where rain is seldom and scanty, the whole landscape looks barren and desolate.

The Black Canyon itself is not terrible or imposing. It is but a narrower space where the steep iron-bound banks are set close together; the rocks are not perpendicular, nor does a tormented river run at unfathomable depths beyond the sunlight. But about it is the very horror of dry barrenness—it is an unspeakable place of thirst. Not a tree gives a moment's shadow in the hot noon.

But in the sullen depths lay the gold of a world's generations, and men hungered, as they have always done, on the barren edge of the impossible, desiring the rainbow gold of a river of death.

On the north side of the canyon's upper end was a mighty bluff some three hundred feet high. At the very base of this bluff was a layer of sandstone soft enough to scoop out with a knife; under that again was a thin line of semi-crystalline fracture. In one place close to the swirling stream was a little hollow cave, in which it could be seen how the strata sloped to the river. When the stream was high the cave was hidden, but at a low stage it appeared black to those who looked across from the southern side.

A month before the miracle two men sat on the opposing bank, staring sombrely into the waters. 'This place is accursed,' said the younger of the two, 'and I feel like a damned spirit myself. We are cast out of the borders of the earth.'

The elder man, Harry Payne, smoked quietly. Yet even he kicked his heels against the rock on which he sat, and his brows were drawn down; his teeth clenched his pipe's heavy wooden mouthpiece.

'It's no good wailing and gnashing your teeth,' he answered; 'I don't, and I've more to draw me away than you. We must put the survey through somehow, and trust that a paradise will open up for us when the work's done.'

But the young fellow made queer, ugly faces.

'And in the meantime we must grit our teeth on alkali dust, and dig prickly pear spines out of our hands and feet, and oil the blisters on our noses, and thank God for giving us our beautiful work. Oh, Lord, what a fool a man is. Is it natural to work this way? By thunder, no! We take it on as we would old rye—just to get blind and not care. Then it's tumble into the blankets and sleep the sleep of the drugged. And next day again and again.'

He sprang up excitedly and pointed down into the river.

'And look, Quin—here, here right underneath us, there's enough gold to buy ease and power and peace for a man's long lifetime!'

'Boy,' said Quin solemnly, 'don't butt your brains out on the impossible. It's easier to rob the biggest bank in the States or out of them than to burgle here.'

But Harry lay down on his stomach, and stared into the river.

'If it were only mine—a little of it! I can see the gold at the bottom,' said he.

'It's all mixed with mud and sand,' answered Quin literally. 'You can see nothing. You'll be having the worst kind of gold-fever if you watch it. This is no sort of a place to get kinks in your brain. You mind yourself, boy. Think of something else. Come, let's go back to the camp and grub.'

Harry grunted uneasily, for he could hardly take his eyes from the selfish water.

They stumbled over the rocks to their white tents, and after dinner they slept, and woke feeling slimy all over and bad in their mouths; and then they smoked and growled and cursed the long hot day down into the west. For the misery of idleness was on them all, and the thoughts of far pleasure came to embitter them. Their day of rest was no boon. Even as they prayed for it to come so they were glad to see it go.

It was the same to them all; whether to Quin and Harry Payne, the bosses, or to Shaw and Liston and Willis, the men, the time was a burden.

'We've been here for years in this hell of dust,' growled Willis. And the others snarled at him and reduced his exaggeration to exact days. They quarrelled and spoke sick words, for the alkali in their throats dried up kindness. Even Quin was hard put to it not to jump on their necks.

'Damn you, men, what's the good of taking it so? Be men—not snarling cayoots! Did you come across the mountains to look for a soft seat? And did you reckon that the land of the Chinook was all roses? D'ye think I'm having a lovely time.'

'Do you really reckon there's much gold in this all-fired canyon, Mr Quin?' asked Shaw, the youngest of the crowd.

But Harry Payne answered him, and as he spoke in a high key the greed of wealth crept into the haggard lines of his young face, and avarice puckered his bloodshot eyes.

'Gold? Why, man, it's full of it! And away down to the end of the Fraser Canyon it's one long gold-trap—one almighty sluice-box!'

He rose and walked up and down like a caged bear. He took his hat off and threw it down to catch the cooler evening air upon his brow.

They were all sitting round the camp-fire; even the Chinese cooks were close by, and each squatted on a skillet or on an inverted empty tomato can. As their idle eyes followed Payne almost mechanically, the flames gleamed on lean, brown faces. Overhead the cool stars shone; there was a heavenly breath of air coming from the north. But Payne walked back and forth, back and forth, muttering. Presently he broke out again.

'Oh boys, but just think of it! Just to dam this river and turn the stream——'

'Where?' asked Quin sardonically.

'Where—where?' said Payne, with irritation. 'Why, it's just a dream! Turn it back through the hills, cut a tunnel for it, and run it into the Columbia.'

'Up-end it by hand,' cried Shaw, laughing—'shove it into the Peace River and capsize the stuff out!'

But Payne was set heavily in his fixed mind. He dreamed of it and spoke in his dreams. In his spare time he sneaked off to the river and sat opposite the great bluff. And now his child-like religion came back to him. He carried a Bible in his pocket, and read it at intervals. And a big notion was born in his brain. It grew marvellously, like a gourd—it overshadowed obstacles; he walked in foreseen triumph and prayed happily to God. It ran out of him in words—he talked to himself. And then a bitter revulsion came.

'I'm a weak, miserable, and sinful wretch! I hate myself and this place! And it holds me; but even when we shift further I shall be crawling down here again. I shall end in the river. It draws me; moth and flame—moth and fire. Gold in it, and ease and rest.'

He put his hand to his head and screamed. 'Oh, this awful, awful sun —it's in my brain and burns!' He crawled to the dangerous verge, and scooped up water in his hat and cooled his head.

On the bank he prayed. 'Oh, almighty God, be merciful unto me, and let me look into the bottomless pit of it, where I see the gold—the gold. Dry it up as thou didst the Red Sea, to let me pass through out of this bloody Egypt. Thrust the hills into it.'

And, looking up, he called in the noonday sun to the glaring northern bluff as if it were alive and aware, itself a god. He made a fetish of it— myths sprang in his rotting mind like toadstools on sick earth at hot midnight.

'Fall down, fall down, and stay the river!'

That night some teams camped close by. At one o'clock in the morning he went out and sneaked two boxes of dynamite from under the cover of a wagon. He cached his find carefully, and when he crawled into the open tent he laughed silently at Quin's peaceful face turned to the quiet moon.

In the morning before breakfast he wrote a letter to a store-keeper in Yale. He went out to work cheerfully, and spoke no more of the gold hidden in the canyon. But he never looked at Quin, and spoke hardly at all. On the fifth or sixth day a small parcel came for him, which he opened in secret. He put its contents in his breast-pocket, and grinned with joy.

But he trembled very strangely, and his hands shook. In all his limbs came a fleeting aura, as though something breathed upon him.

That very night he stole out of the quiet moonlit camp, and finding the hidden boxes, he carried them, slung together, with great labour up the river bank. He shook so much and his limbs seemed so little under his control that he had to rest every hundred yards; but at last he came to a broader, quieter portion of the stream across which a taut rope was stretched. A crazy boat built by some man as a first attempt lay in a rocky recess. It was made fast to the rope by sliding rings, and could be pulled across the dangerous ferry by another rope that lay in the water, while a coil made fast to the shore from which it started paid itself out of the stern as it went.

Payne put his dynamite in the boat and pulled himself across the swirling stream. He sang and chattered and laughed as he pulled. When he came to the further shore he took his burden again and stumbled painfully down stream under the high, round moon, which gave him his own shadow for a companion to which he could talk. And soon the great bluff loomed up, and then it hung over him, and blotted out the moon, blinding him for a minute with opaque shadows that grew transparent once more for his trembling, doubtful feet. He laid down his heavy burden and sought for the little cave, which looked like a black patch at noon from the river's further bank.

When he found it he returned for his boxes, and on laying them down in the cave's mouth he prised off the lids with a heavy knife. The cartridges lay there packed in sawdust. He took them out one by one and touched them lovingly.

'If only Quin and the boys knew,' he said aloud, and above the low perpetual hiss of the waters his voice echoed with his very accent, and went whispering down the canyon's gap. He looked up suspiciously with his head on one side like a listening bird, and, being reassured, he screamed a high-pitched laughter that came back mixed and mingled in a chorus of discord, and ran off chuckling inaudibly. But Payne now took no note of aught but the dreadful strength under his hands. At last he emptied the boxes. Then one by one he packed the cartridges into the recesses of the cavern. Yet he kept a single cartridge, and partly stripped off its covering.

'Now the fuse and the cap!' he muttered, and took from his pocket that which he had sent to Yale for. Pressing the end of the fuse in, he nipped the cap a little to make it hold, and, thrusting his fingers into the dynamite to make a deep hole, he put the cap in and squeezed the soft explosive about it again. He put the cartridge among the others, while the long length of fuse ran wormlike out of the cavern, the mouth of which he closed with broken rocks. He rose up and clasped his hands.

'Oh, God, be merciful to me—be merciful!'

As he turned, his quick mood changed; he laughed at the personal, hateful river, and then cursed it, laughing.

'I've done it! And now let them laugh. For the river shall be dry and the waters shall stand in a heap.'

He lay down on a flat rock which was under water in the early summer, and, rolling over like a caressed cat, he hugged himself with odd, choked chuckles. 'Tomorrow I'll do it. No; I'll keep it till Sunday— till Sunday; and all the week I will think what I shall do with the gold.'

He coiled up the loose end of the fuse, and hid it carefully from any man's sight, though he knew well that no man ever went there; and by three he was back in his camp-bed.

During the remainder of the working week he lived in concealed frenzy, cunning of look and speech. He calculated hugely the wealth that even one day's work in the dry canyon would make his. He saw the poor world at his feet, and trod on air.

When Quin woke on Sunday in the early dawn he saw the boy had gone. A note lay on the bed. 'What's this?' said Quin sleepily. As he deciphered it in the dusk he sprang up. The letter ran thus:

'Quin, mind what I say. For I know that the Lord of Hosts is behind me. This is what I say. The river and its gold, from the great bluff down to the Fraser, is mine. It is all mine—the gold and the bed of the river. And when the bed runs dry, as it will today, all that is taken out is mine. At six there shall be a sign and a wonder, and the miracle will happen. I have prayed. The big bluff will fall into the river. And the water will stand in a heap. And the children of Israel will find the gold. For their day's pay I will give them a hundredth part. Each day the same till the water returns. Amen.'

Quin ran out. 'Willis—Liston—Shaw!' he called, and the men came half naked from their tents. 'Payne's gone raving mad,' cried Quin; 'he's away, and has left me a letter saying that the bluff is going to fall into the river, and that the gold in the dry bed is his. Hunt for him, you! I'll go to the river myself.'

And in a few minutes he was on the edge of the rocks at the bank. He called hopelessly in the dim dawn, but he was answered faintly.

'Is that you, Payne?' he shouted.

Then he saw a dark figure sitting on the other side. 'It is I. Who calls the chosen one of God?'

Quin stamped on the iron rock. 'Don't be an accursed fool!' he cried. 'Come back, man! What's gone wrong with you? What the hell are you doing there?'

Payne rose and rebuked him. 'Do not blaspheme God, or the works of God. I have prayed for the waters to be stayed, and he has put the power in my hands. The river will run dry, and the gold is mine.' He threw his hands up into the air, crying, 'Mine—mine!'

'He's mad—mad!' said Quin.

'As you have come I will wait no more,' cried Payne, and he stooped down. Yet he rose again. 'Quin'!

'What?'

'Get you under cover, or run, for the bluff will fall into the head of the canyon even now.'

And Quin saw him light a match. It spurted flame in the shadow of the cave's mouth, and then he saw Payne run like a goat along the hazardous edge of the river. As he went he signed with his open hand to Quin to lie down, to go, to hide.

Suddenly there was a mighty crash. To Quin it seemed that he was lying on something hollow that had been smitten from below by a giant's hammer, and for a moment he felt sick; then rocks and gravel flew past him or splintered on his shelter; the air was full of sand and dust that choked and blinded him. He rose and staggered and fell down.

And meantime Payne, blind and mad with furious excitement, his mind spurting flame, his brain overturned, went screaming hand over hand across the river in the creaking boat.

'The dry places shall be filled with water and the rivers shall be dry places. For the sea is in the hollow of his hand.'

He ran headlong for the camp. The other men were lying half stunned near the river. The blast had smitten them as they went running.

'By the holy frost, what's happened?' cried Shaw when he rose.

And Liston scrambled to his feet. They found Willis insensible with a cut on his head, and while they were attending him Quin came up.

But the great bluff stood yet in its ancient place, though Payne's god had torn away a buttress and dug a mighty hole into the dipping strata. Though the surface of the bluff was more concave, yet it had not fallen for all the awful blow dealt its foundations. And by now the river ran blue once more; the yellow patch of the fallen debris had been swept down.

And to the four men came Payne, singing.

But as they stared at him open-mouthed, awed and uncertain, he looked past and above them, and saw the great bluff gleam out in the arisen sun. His face went distorted, and his left hand twisted to his ear uncontrollably; his eyes turned into his head, and he fell grovelling. In the aspect of his stricken face was a curse on the works of God and his ways. And within an hour he was raving on his bed in the fevered horror of madness, and the men were hard put to it to hold him down.

Meanwhile, from this place and from that, camp and house and ranch, men came to their disturbed camp to inquire as to the reason of the sound which had run across the plateau at dawn. They came galloping, and at noon there were thirty men with Quin opposite the rent and splintered bluff.

'Dynamite, for sure,' said one man, 'for the sound of it was like a sudden clap, not the lifting roar of powder, and powder would have hoisted the bluff off its roots.'

'Where did he get it?' asked Quin, who was bewildered. But none answered, and the various talk ran on.

'Did he reckon—the madman—that the river would be dammed by the bluff even if he had fetched it down?'

Quin nodded.

'By the powers,' cried an old miner, 'but it's an almighty notion, and only a crazy lunatic could have tried it!'

They argued hotly in the rising heat whether enough could come down to block the river, and, granted that were possible, how long the dam would hold against the increasing waters. Though some took one side and some the other, the very imagined chance of robbing the river-bed inflamed their minds, and the desire of wealth got hold of them all alike; and they stood for unnoticed hours in the burning sun, with the heat coming doubly from the rocks beneath, and from the mighty bluff opposing them.

'Hark!' cried one man suddenly.

'It is nothing,' said his neighbour.

'It is distant thunder,' said a third.

Suddenly the very earth beneath them shook like an ill-built house, and there came a crack like a heavy rifle-shot, and after it a great grinding noise, that stayed their blood and made them pallid.

'Look! Look!' cried Quin—'it moves—it moves!'

The man next him cried 'No, no,' but even as he spoke the overhung edge of the bluff split and fell roaring into the torrent, beating it into spray that blinded them, and in the spray were a million wild rainbows.

But when the spray died slowly down there was an increasing roar, in which shouted words were dumb gestures, and the whole mighty bluff moved.

'Run, run!' they mouthed, and some ran and stayed again, and some stood petrified.

And with a grinding noise that was a terror of itself, the whole higher half of the bluff and hill behind it went steadily into the river. Thrusting the water aside, it strove like a decree of God, strong of accomplishment, even to the shadowed rocks of the hither side. Through the narrowing gate the water foamed turbidly; but at last the gap closed, and the calm river stayed against the silent obstacle.

The men sighed, awe-struck, and again held their breaths. But then the desire of gold took them, and they ran all ways for all things that might help them to the riches under the sinking waters.

It laid hold of Quin too. 'Quick,' he cried to his men—'all our things —pots or pans or skillets—anything that will hold water or scoop mud! Quick, or these others will sweep the camp clean!'

They ran to their tents like wolves after a deer. They were the first back to the west end of the canyon, and they found the river empty save for pools. It was a ghastly, weedy chasm, difficult of access, slimy, hideous with crawling insects in the holes and crannies. Here and there a stranded bewildered fish flapped desperately. They dropped a rope and lariat in the gap, and slid down.

'It's share and share alike here!' cried Liston.

They agreed on the word spoken.

'Then let Shaw stay here and hoist the buckets.'

He went down and stripped there, throwing his shirt and jacket away.

'Is the most gold here?' asked Willis.

But they worked where they stood.

Then the men who had been with them galloped back with buckets and scoops and all things they could find. The news ran like fire in dry grass; women and children drove up in carts with their household utensils; each moment others dropped into the canyon; in half an hour the black banks hummed. The Siwashes and their Klootchmen came with the whites; Chinamen worked with them. And as the drying river told those down below, buggies came furiously driven to the richest place. All along to the Fraser, men were in the river-bed, greedy of sudden wealth.

And he who had wrought this, and accomplished the impossible hopes of toiling men, lay parched and fevered and all alone. His lips cracked and bled, and he yelled in a narrow tent of a great world opened to him.

'It's all mine—mine!' and the tent fly flapped idly in the heated air.

He sang the hymn, 'Praise God, from whom all blessings flow.'

But in the canyon they cursed awfully; and were afraid, toiling under the dam against which the waters rose and rose still. On its edge one more fearful than the rest had stationed his old mother, and she was shaken with terror for her son. She watched the water as one would watch fire at sea. 'See if it breaks out under. Say when it reaches the top,' they had told her.

As each increased his pile of the drift which held gold, suspicion grew, and with it fear. Men doubted their partners, and glared angrily at each other on slight provocations. But the greater fear above them of the rising water cooled most contentions. And yet in the midst of them was panic crouching, known, hidden and unseen. A chance palsied motion of the grey-haired woman on the dam sent them flying more than once. They returned, worked, and some prayed.

'Oh, God! Oh, God, how long?'

Then on the height of the piled earth there sprang a white figure naked to the bitter sun.

'It is mine—mine, and all the wealth of it from here down even to the river's mouth!'

And the mad hero of the slidden mountain chanted dreadful joy of his riches, urging his men beneath to labour. In their ears he was as the buzz of a fly. But behind him, and against the barriers, the very quiet waters rose inch by inch; each distant hill sent aid. For nature was outraged and robbed—her secrets laid bare. As the madman sang, the pressed waters penetrated into every crevice, seeking every way, while a white naked insect yelled articulate blasphemy against the making of the world and the laws that hold matter in space.

'It is mine, and strong for ever!'

But now the backed-up waters began to spread on the lower terrace above the natural river. Every moment brought more power to bear upon the unnatural barrier. Even the old woman saw it. She turned and clambered down to the ancient rocks, for the man whose fair flesh was scorching in the sun terrified her. 'My son! my son!' she wailed.

But her boy down below strove desperately as the others strove. Not a man but left bloody finger-prints on the rocks; some paddled in blood, who, cursing for want of things to carry the river drift away, had stripped off their long boots in desperation. The lust for gold sent them wild: some cheered, some sang.

But others looked up and said, 'How long?'

For themselves they worked, but for none other than their own, and natural mercy left them. At one rich ledge two tramps fought unnoticed. The stronger beat out the brains of the weaker, and robbed him of his stolen bucket.

And the white genius of this sudden black inferno yelled congratulations to the burning skies, praising the Lord with fevered incantations.

Once again the workers fled and returned, and fled again, to come back once more. But down below Quin and his fellows toiled unmoved.

'Oh, there's millions—millions here!'

They spat blood and sweat, and worked blackly grimed and half naked. But at the dam's dry foot the waters began to chuckle, and

On the height of the piled earth there sprang a white figure naked to the bitter sun. 'It's mine, mine!' he yelled.

turbid springs spurted suddenly. The mad boy looked not behind. 'It's mine—it's mine. Oh, God! Oh, God!'

Then he turned and saw the gleaming lake behind him. Thrusting his hands against the hot air, he cursed and commanded the encroaching waters, that rose even to the dam's height and began to pour over. The word ran like thunder in the echoing chasm, and the men fled, stricken with white fear. Some cried, 'No, no—not yet!' even as they ran.

And the miracle-worker cursed his God at the motion under his feet, at the fear of poverty returning, at the loss of unmeasured hope.

'It moves—it moves!' piped the idiot woman, who had lived out her mind's life in that awful hour; and she picked idly at the withered flesh of her dry hands.

But he who was above her heard, and shook his clenched hand at the clear sky. 'No, no, no!' he cried, as the canyon edge was crowded with his men.

They clambered up the hanging ropes; they fought desperately for foothold, and pulled down those who had advantage. Only the brained man lay motionless in the slime, while his slayer, fearful of some terrible return of sane justice, grinned sickly on the bank.

The the great dam moved and surged with a grating noise, while the rivulets below gushed dreadfully, and after one long-drawn moment of expectation it gave way, and, with a roar that drowned the cries of the maddened crowd, it yielded wholly to the river that swept back into its ancient channel for ever, or till the end of long generations yet unborn.

But in the bitter surge and lifted crest of it he who had wrought the miracle was borne down like a foam bubble unregarded.

And then the order of the natural world returned.

THE RETURN

Charlotte Brontë

During her year as governess at Thornfield Hall, Jane Eyre falls in love with her employer, Edward Rochester, and he with her. All preparations for their marriage are made, but the ceremony is halted abruptly by a stranger, who produces a witness to testify that Rochester already has a wife and that Mrs Rochester is living, isolated from the others, at the Hall. She is a lunatic.

Jane, torn between love and conscience, leaves Thornfield immediately.

Chance brings her, after three days of wandering in misery and starvation, to the house of Diana and Mary Rivers, who take her in and care for her. Their brother, St John, offers Jane the position of schoolmistress in the village of Morton, and she accepts with gratitude. When St John discovers that Jane's name is Eyre he reveals to her not only that she is related to the Rivers family, but that she is now an heiress.

One evening, as Jane is struggling to decide how to answer St John, who wants her to go to India with him as his wife, she thinks she hears Rochester's voice calling 'Jane! Jane! Jane!'. She leaves for Thornfield the next day, but finds, when she reaches the Hall, nothing but a charred ruin. She learns from the inn-keeper that Rochester's wife died in the fire—and that Rochester himself is now crippled and blind.

The manor-house of Ferndean was a building of considerable antiquity, moderate size, and no architectural pretensions, deep buried in a wood. I had heard of it before. Mr Rochester often spoke of it, and sometimes went there. His father had purchased the estate for the sake of the game coverts. He would have let the house, but could find no tenant, in consequence of its ineligible and insalubrious site. Ferndean then remained uninhabited and unfurnished with the exception of some two or three rooms fitted up for the accommodation of the squire when he went there in the season to shoot.

To this house I came just ere dark, on an evening marked by the characteristics of sad sky, cold gale, and continued, small, penetrating rain. The last mile I performed on foot, having dismissed the chaise and driver with the double remuneration I had promised. Even when within a very short distance of the manor-house, you could see nothing of it, so thick and dark grew the timber of the gloomy wood about it. Iron gates between granite pillars showed me where to enter, and passing through them, I found myself at once in the twilight of close ranked trees. There was a grass-grown track descending the forest aisle between hoar and knotty shafts and under branched arches. I followed it, expecting soon to reach the dwelling, but it stretched on and on, it would far and farther: no sign of habitation or grounds was visible.

I thought I had taken a wrong direction and lost my way. The darkness of natural as well as of sylvan dusk gathered over me. I looked round in search of another road. There was none: all was interwoven stem, columnar trunk, dense summer foliage—no opening anywhere.

I proceeded: at last my way opened, the trees thinned a little; presently I beheld a railing, then the house—scarce, by this dim light, distinguishable from the trees; so dank and green were its decaying walls. Entering a portal, fastened only by a latch, I stood amidst a space of enclosed ground, from which the wood swept away in a semicircle. There were no flowers, no garden-beds; only a broad gravel walk girdling a grass plot, and this set in the heavy frame of the forest. The house presented two pointed gables in its front; the windows were latticed and narrow, the front door was narrow too, one step led up to it. The whole looked, as the host of the Rochester Arms had said, 'quite a desolate spot'. It was as still as a church on a week-day: the pattering rain on the forest leaves was the only sound audible in its vicinage.

'Can there be life here?' I asked.

Yes, life of some kind there was; for I heard a movement—that narrow front door was unclosing, and some shape was about to issue from the grange.

It opened slowly: a figure came out into the twilight and stood on the step—a man without a hat. He stretched forth his hand as if to feel whether it rained. Dusk as it was, I had recognized him; it was my master, Edward Fairfax Rochester, and no other.

I stayed my step, almost my breath, and stood to watch him—to examine him, myself unseen, and alas! to him invisible. It was a sudden meeting, and one in which rapture was kept well in check by pain. I had no difficulty in restraining my voice from exclamation, my step from hasty advance.

His form was of the same strong and stalwart contour as ever: his port was still erect, his hair was still raven black: nor were his features altered or sunk: not in one year's space, by any sorrow, could his athletic strength be quelled or his vigorous prime blighted. But in his countenance I saw a change: that looked desperate and brooding— that reminded me of some wronged and fettered wild beast or bird, dangerous to approach in his sullen woe. The caged eagle, whose gold-ringed eyes cruelty has extinguished, might look as looked that sightless Samson.

And reader, do you think I feared him in his blind ferocity?—if you do, you little know me. A soft hope blent with my sorrow that soon I should dare to drop a kiss on that brow of rock, and on those lips so sternly sealed beneath it; but not yet. I would not accost him yet.

He descended the one step, and advanced slowly and gropingly towards the grass plot. Where was his daring stride now? Then he paused, as if he knew not which way to turn. He lifted his hand and opened his eyelids; gazed blank, and with a straining effort, on the sky, and toward the amphitheatre of trees: one saw that all to him was void darkness. He stretched his right hand (the left arm, the mutilated one, he kept hidden in his bosom); he seemed to wish by touch to gain an idea of what lay around him: he met but vacancy still; for the trees were some yards off where he stood. He relinquished the endeavour, folded his arms, and stood quiet and mute in the rain, now falling fast on his uncovered head. At this moment John approached him from some quarter.

'Will you take my arm, sir?' he said; 'there is a heavy shower coming on: had you not better go in?'

'Let me alone,' was the answer.

John withdrew, without having observed me. Mr Rochester now tried to walk about: vainly—all was too uncertain. He groped his way back to the house, and, re-entering it, closed the door.

I now drew near and knocked: John's wife opened for me. 'Mary,' I said, 'how are you?'

She started as if she had seen a ghost: I calmed her. To her hurried, 'Is it really you, miss, come at this late hour to this lonely place?' I answered by taking her hand; and then I followed her into the kitchen, where John now sat by a good fire. I explained to them, in few words, that I had heard all which had happened since I left Thornfield, and that I was come to see Mr Rochester. I asked John to go down to the turnpike-house, where I had dismissed the chaise, and bring my trunk, which I had left there: and then, while I removed my bonnet and shawl, I questioned Mary as to whether I could be accommodated at the Manor House for the night; and finding that arrangements to that effect, though difficult, would not be impossible, I informed her I should stay. Just at this moment the parlour-bell rang.

'When you go in,' said I, 'tell your master that a person wishes to speak to him, but do not give my name.'

'I don't think he will see you,' she answered; 'he refuses everybody.'

When she returned, I inquired what he had said.

'You are to send in your name and your business,' she replied. She then proceeded to fill a glass with water, and place it on a tray, together with candles.

'Is that what he rang for?' I asked.

'Yes: he always has candles brought in at dark, though he is blind.'

'Give the tray to me; I will carry it in.'

I took it from her hand: she pointed me out the parlour door. The tray shook as I held it; the water spilt from the glass; my heart struck my ribs loud and fast. Mary opened the door for me, and shut it behind me.

This parlour looked gloomy: a neglected handful of fire burnt low in the grate; and, leaning over it, with his head supported against the high, old-fashioned mantelpiece, appeared the blind tenant of the room. His old dog, Pilot, lay on one side, removed out of the way, and coiled up as if afraid of being inadvertently trodden upon. Pilot pricked up his ears when I came in: then he jumped up with a yelp and a whine, and bounded towards me: he almost knocked the tray from my hands. I set it on the table; then patted him, and said softly, 'Lie down!' Mr Rochester turned mechanically to *see* what the commotion was: but as he *saw* nothing, he returned and sighed.

'Give me the water, Mary,' he said.

I approached him with the now only half-filled glass; Pilot followed me, still excited.

'What is the matter?' he inquired.

'Down, Pilot!' I again said. He checked the water on its way to his lips, and seemed to listen: he drank, and put the glass down. 'This is you, Mary, is it not?'

'Mary is in the kitchen,' I answered.

He put out his hand with a quick gesture, but not seeing where I stood, he did not touch me. 'Who is this? Who is this?' he demanded, trying, as it seemed, to *see* with those sightless eyes—unavailing and distressing attempt! 'Answer me—speak again!' he ordered, imperiously and aloud.

'Will you have a little more water, sir? I spilt half of what was in the glass,' I said.

'*Who* is it? *What* is it? Who speaks?'

'Pilot knows me, and John and Mary know I am here. I came only this evening,' I answered.

'Great God!—what delusion has come over me? What sweet madness has seized me?'

'No delusion—no madness: your mind, sir, is too strong for delusion, your health too sound for frenzy.'

'And where is the speaker? Is it only a voice? Oh! I *cannot* see, but I must feel, or my heart will stop and my brain burst. Whatever, whoever you are, be perceptible to the touch, or I cannot live!'

He groped; I arrested his wandering hand, and prisoned it in both mine.

'Her very fingers!' he cried; 'her small, slight fingers! If so, there must be more of her.'

The muscular hand broke from my custody; my arm was seized, my shoulder, neck, waist—I was entwined and gathered to him.

'It is Jane? *What* is it? This is her shape—this is her size—'

'And this her voice,' I added. 'She is all here: her heart, too. God bless you, sir! I am glad to be so near you again.'

'Jane Eyre!—Jane Eyre!' was all he said.

'My dear master,' I answered, 'I am Jane Eyre: I have found you out— I am come back to you.'

I approached him with the half-filled glass. 'Who is this?' he demanded.

'In truth?—in the flesh? My living Jane?'

'You touch me, sir—you hold me, and fast enough: I am not cold like a corpse, nor vacant like air, am I?'

'My living darling! These are certainly her limbs, and these her features; but I cannot be so blest, after all my misery. It is a dream; such dreams as I have had at night when I have clasped her once more to my heart, as I do now; and kissed her, as thus—and felt that she loved me, and trusted that she would not leave me.'

'Which I never will, sir, from this day.'

'Never will, says the vision? But I always woke and found it an empty mockery; and I was desolate and abandoned—my life dark, lonely, hopeless—my soul athirst and forbidden to drink—my heart famished and never to be fed. Gentle, soft dream, nestling in my arms now, you will fly, too, as your sisters have fled before you; but kiss me before you go—embrace me, Jane.'

'There, sir—and there!'

I pressed my lips to his once brilliant and now rayless eyes—I swept his hair from his brow, and kissed that too. He suddenly seemed to arouse himself: the conviction of the reality of all this seized him.

'It is you—is it, Jane? You are come back to me, then?'

'I am.'

'And you do not lie dead in some ditch, under some stream? And you are not a pining outcast amongst strangers?'

'No, sir! I am an independent woman now.'

'Independent! What do you mean, Jane?'

'My uncle in Madeira is dead, and he left me five thousand pounds.'

'Ah! this is practical—this is real!' he cried: 'I should never dream that. Besides, there is that peculiar voice of hers, so animating and piquant, as well as soft: it cheers my withered heart; it puts life into it What, Janet! Are you an independent woman? A rich woman?'

'Quite rich, sir. If you won't let me live with you, I can build a house of my own close up to your door, and you may come and sit in my parlour when you want company of an evening.'

'But as you are rich, Jane, you have now, no doubt, friends who will look after you, and not suffer you to devote yourself to a blind lameter like me?'

'I told you I am independent, sir, as well as rich: I am my own mistress.'

'And you will stay with me?'

'Certainly—unless you object. I will be your neighbour, your nurse, your housekeeper. I find you lonely: I will be your companion—to read to you, to walk with you, to sit with you, to wait on you, to be eyes and hands to you. Cease to look so melancholy, my dear master; you shall not be left desolate, so long as I live.'

He replied not: he seemed serious—abstracted; he sighed; he half-opened his lips as if to speak: he closed them again. I felt a little embarrassed. Perhaps I had too rashly overleaped conventionalities; and he, like St John, saw impropriety in my inconsiderateness. I had indeed made my proposal from the idea that he wished and would ask me to be his wife: an expectation, not the less certain because unexpressed, had buoyed me up, that he could claim me at once as his own. But no hint to that effect escaping him, and his countenance becoming more overcast, I suddenly remembered that I might have been all wrong, and was perhaps playing the fool unwittingly; and I began to gently withdraw myself from his arms—but he eagerly snatched me closer.

'No—no—Jane; you must not go. No—I have touched you, heard you, felt the comfort of your presence—the sweetness of your consolation: I cannot give up these joys. I have little left in myself—I must have you. The world may laugh—may call me absurd, selfish—but it does not signify. My very soul demands you; it will be satisfied, or it will take deadly vengeance on its frame.'

'Well, sir, I will stay with you: I have said so.'

'Yes; but you understand one thing by staying with me; and I understand another. You, perhaps, could make up your mind to be about my hand and chair—to wait on me as a kind little nurse (for you have an affectionate heart and a generous spirit, which prompt you to make sacrifices for those you pity), and that ought to suffice for me, no doubt. I suppose I should now entertain none but fatherly feelings for you: do you think so? Come, tell me.'

'I will think what you like, sir: I am content to be only your nurse, if you think it better.'

'But you cannot always be my nurse, Janet: you are young—you must marry some day.'

'I don't care about being married.'

'You should care, Janet: if I were what I once was, I would try to make you care—but—a sightless block!'

He relapsed again into gloom. I, on the contrary, became more cheerful, and took fresh courage: these last words gave me an insight as to where the difficulty lay; and as it was no difficulty with me, I felt quite relieved from my previous embarrassment. I resumed a livelier vein of conversation.

'It is time some one undertook to rehumanize you,' said I, parting his thick and long uncut locks; 'for I see you are being metamorphosed into a lion, or something of that sort. You have a *faux air* of Nebuchadnezzar in the fields about you, that is certain: your hair reminds me of eagles' feathers; whether your nails are grown like bird's claws or not, I have not yet noticed.'

'On this arm I have neither hand or nails,' he said, drawing the mutilated limb from his breast, and showing it to me. 'It is a mere stump—a ghastly sight! Don't you think so, Jane?'

'It is a pity to see it; and a pity to see your eyes—and the scar of fire on your forehead: and the worst of it is, one is in danger of loving you too well for all this; and making too much of you.'

'I thought you would be revolted, Jane, when you saw my arm, and my cicatrized visage.'

'Did you? Don't tell me so—lest I should say something disparaging to your judgement. Now, let me leave you an instant to make a better fire, and have the hearth swept up. Can you tell when there is a good fire?'

'Yes; with the right eye I see a glow—a ruddy haze.'

'And you see the candles?'

'Very dimly—each is a luminous cloud.'

'Can you see me?'

'No, my fairy: but I am only too thankful to hear and feel you.'

'When do you take supper?'

'I never take supper.'

'But you shall have some to-night. I am hungry: so are you, I dare say, only you forget.'

Summoning Mary, I soon had the room in more cheerful order: I prepared him, likewise, a comfortable repast. My spirits were excited, and with pleasure and ease I talked to him during supper, and for a long time after. There was no harassing restraint, no repressing of glee and vivacity with him; for with him I was at perfect ease, because I knew I suited him; all I said or did seemed either to console or revive him. Delightful consciousness! It brought to life and light my whole nature: in his presence I thoroughly lived; and he lived in mine. Blind as he was, smiles played over his face, joy dawned on his forehead: his lineaments softened and warmed.

After supper, he began to ask me many questions, of where I had bee, what I had been doing, how I had found him out; but I gave him only very partial replies: it was too late to enter into particulars that night. Besides, I wished to touch no deep-thrilling chord—to open no fresh well of emotion in his heart, my sole present aim was to cheer him. Cheered, as I have said, he was: and yet but by fits. If a moment's silence broke the conversation he would turn restless, touch me, then say, 'Jane'.

'You are altogether a human being, Jane? You are certain of that?'

'I conscientiously believe so, Mr Rochester.'

'Yet, how, on this dark and doleful evening could you so suddenly rise on my lone hearth? I stretched my hand to take a glass of water from a hireling, and it was given me by you: I asked a question, expecting John's wife to answer me, and your voice spoke at my ear.'

'Because I had come in, in Mary's stead, with the tray.'

'And the enchantment there is in the very hour I am now spending with you. Who can tell what a dark, dreary, hopeless life I have dragged on for months past? Doing nothing, expecting nothing; merging night in day; feeling but the sensation of cold when I let the fire go out, of hunger when I forgot to eat; and then a ceaseless sorrow, and, at times, a very delirium of desire to behold my Jane again. Yes: for her restoration I longed, far more than for that of my lost sight. How can it be that Jane is with me, and says she loves me? Will she not depart as suddenly as she came? To-morrow, I fear I shall find her no more.'

A commonplace, practical reply, out of the train of his own disturbed ideas, was, I was sure, the best and most reassuring for him in this frame of mind. I passed my finger over his eyebrows, and re-marked that they were scorched, and that I should apply something which would make them grow as broad and black as ever.

'Where is the use of doing me good in any way, beneficent spirit, when, at some fatal moment, you will again desert me—passing like a shadow, whither and how to me unknown, and for me remaining afterwards undiscoverable?'

'Have you a pocket-comb about you, sir?'

'What for, Jane?'

'Just to comb out this shaggy black mane. I find you rather alarming, when I examine you close at hand: you talk of my being a fairy, but I am sure you are more like a brownie.'

'Am I hideous, Jane?'

'Very, sir; you always were, you know.'

'Humph! The wickedness has not been taken out of you, wherever you have sojourned.'

'Yet I have been with good people; far better than you: a hundred times better people; possessed of ideas and views you never entertained in your life: quite more refined and exalted.'

'Who the deuce have you been with?'

'If you twist in that way you will make me pull the hair out of your head; and then I think you will cease to entertain doubts of my substantiality.'

'Who have you been with, Jane?'

'You shall not get it out of me to-night, sir; you must wait till tomorrow; to leave my tale half told, will, you know, be a sort of security that I shall appear at your breakfast-table to finish it. By the by, I must mind not to rise on your hearth with only a glass of water then: I must bring you an egg at least, to say nothing of fried ham.'

'You mocking changeling—fairy-born and human-bred! You make me feel as I have not felt these twelve months. If Saul could have had you for his David, the evil spirit would have been exorcised without the aid of the harp.'

'There, sir, you are redd up and made decent. Now I'll leave you: I have been travelling these last three days, and I believe I am tired. Good-night.'

'Just one word, Jane: were there only ladies in the house where you have been?'

I laughed and made my escape, still laughing as I ran upstairs. 'A good idea!' I thought with glee. 'I see I have the means of fretting him out of his melancholy for some time to come.'

Very early the next morning I heard him up and astir, wandering from one room to another. As soon as Mary came down I heard the question: 'Is Miss Eyre here?' Then: 'Which room did you put her into? Was it dry? Is she up? Go and ask if she wants anything; and when she will come down.'

I came down as soon as I thought there was a prospect of breakfast. Entering the room very softly, I had a view of him before he discovered my presence. It was mournful indeed, to witness the subjugation of that vigorous spirit to a corporeal infirmity. He sat in his chair— still, but not at rest: expectant evidently; the lines of now habitual sadness marking his strong features. His countenance reminded one of the lamp quenched, waiting to be re-lit; and alas! it was not himself that could now kindle the lustre of animated expression: he was dependent on another for that office! I had meant to be gay and careless, but the powerlessness of the strong man touched my heart to the quick: still I accosted him with what vivacity I could.

'It is a bright sunny morning, sir,' I said. 'The rain is over and gone, and there is a tender shining after it: you shall have a walk soon.'

I had wakened the glow: his features beamed.

'Oh, you are indeed there, my skylark! Come to me. You are not gone, not vanished? I heard one of your kind an hour ago, singing high over the wood; but its song had no music for me, any more than the rising sun had rays. All the melody on earth is concentrated in my Jane's tongue to my ear (I am glad it is not naturally a silent one); all the sunshine I can feel is in her presence.'

The water stood in my eyes to hear this avowal of his dependence; just as if a royal eagle, chained to a perch, should be forced to entreat a sparrow to become its purveyor. But I would not be lachrymose: I dashed off the salt drops, and busied myself with preparing breakfast.

Most of the morning was spent in the open air. I led him out of the wet and wild wood into some cheerful fields: I described to him how brilliantly green they were; how the flowers and hedges looked refreshed; how sparklingly blue was the sky. I sought a seat for him in a hidden and lovely spot, a dry stump of a tree; nor did I refuse to let him, when seated, place me on his knee. Why should I, when both he and I were happier near than apart? Pilot lay beside us: all was quiet. He broke out suddenly while clasping me in his arms—

'Cruel, cruel deserter! Oh, Jane, what did I feel when I discovered you had fled from Thornfield, and when I could nowhere find you: and, after examining your apartment, ascertained that you had taken no money, nor anything which could serve as an equivalent! A pearl necklace I had given you lay untouched in its little casket; your trunks were left corded and locked as they had been prepared for the bridal tour. What could my darling do, I asked, left destitute and penniless? And what did she do? Let me hear now.'

Thus urged, I began the narrative of my experience for the last year. I softened considerably what related to the three days of wandering and starvation, because to have told him all would have been to inflict unnecessary pain: the little I did say lacerated his faithful heart deeper than I wished.

I should not have left him thus, he said, without any means of making my way: I should have told him my intention. I should have confided in him: he would never have forced me to be his mistress. Violent as he had seemed in his despair, he, in truth, loved me far too well and too tenderly to constitute himself my tyrant: he would have given me half his fortune, without demanding so much as a kiss in return, rather than I should have flung myself friendless on the wide world. I had endured, he was certain, more than I had confessed to him.

'Well, whatever my sufferings had been, they were very short,' I answered: and then I proceeded to tell him how I had been received at Moor House; how I had obtained the office of schoolmistress, etc. The accession of fortune, the discovery of my relations, followed in due order. Of course St John Rivers' name came in frequently in the progress of the tale. When I had done, that name was immediately taken up.

'This St John, then is your cousin?'

'Yes.'

'You have spoken of him often: do you like him?'

'He was a very good man, sir; I could not help liking him.'

'A good man. Does that mean a respectable, well-conducted man of fifty? Or what does it mean?'

'St John was only twenty-nine, sir.'

'"*Jeune encore*", as the French say. Is he a person of low stature, phlegmatic, and plain? A person whose goodness consists rather in his guiltlessness of vice, than in his prowess in virtue?'

'He is untiringly active. Great and exalted deeds are what he lives to perform.'

'But his brain? That is probably rather soft? He means well: but you shrug your shoulders to hear him talk?'

'He talks little, sir: what he does say is ever to the point. His brain is first-rate, I should think not impressible, but vigorous.'

'Is he an able man, then?'

'Truly able.'

'A thoroughly educated man?'

'St John is an accomplished and profound scholar.'

'His manners, I think you said, are not to your taste?—priggish and parsonic?'

'I never mentioned his manners; but, unless I had a very bad taste, they must suit it; they are polished, calm, and gentleman-like.'

'His appearance—I forgot what description you gave of his appearance;—a sort of raw curate, half strangled with his white neckcloth, and stilted up on his thick-soled high-lows, eh?'

'St John dresses well. He is a handsome man: tall, fair, with blue eyes, and a Grecian profile.'

(*Aside*) 'Damn him!'—(*To me*) 'Did you like him, Jane?'

'Yes, Mr Rochester, I liked him: but you asked me that before.'

I perceived, of course, the drift of my interlocutor. Jealousy had got hold of him: she stung him; but the sting was salutary: it gave him respite from the gnawing fang of melancholy. I would not, therefore, immediately charm the snake.

'Perhaps you would rather not sit any longer on my knee, Miss Eyre?' was the next somewhat unexpected observation.

'Why not, Mr Rochester?'

'The picture you have just drawn is suggestive of a rather too over-whelming contrast. Your words have delineated very prettily a graceful Apollo: he is present to your imagination—tall, fair, blue-eyed, and with a Grecian profile. Your eyes dwell on a Vulcan—a real blacksmith, brown, broad-shouldered; and blind and lame into the bargain.'

'I never thought of it before; but you certainly are rather like Vulcan, sir.'

'Well, you can leave me, ma'am: but before you go' (and he retained me by a firmer grasp than ever), 'you will be pleased just to answer me a question or two.' He paused.

'What questions, Mr Rochester?'

Then followed this cross-examination.

'St John made you schoolmistress of Morton before he knew you were his cousin?'

'Yes.'

'You would often see him? He would visit the school sometimes?'

'Daily.'

'He would approve of your plans, Jane? I know they would be clever, for you are a talented creature!'

'He approved of them—yes.'

'He would discover many things in you he could not have expected to find? Some of your accomplishments are not ordinary.'

'I don't know about that.'

'You had a little cottage near the school, you say: did he ever come there to see you?'

'Now and then.'

'Of an evening?'

'Once or twice.'

A pause.

'How long did you reside with him and his sisters after the cousinship was discovered?'

'Five months.'

'Did Rivers spend much time with the ladies of his family?'

'Yes; the back parlour was both his study and ours: he sat near the window, and we by the table.'

'Did he study much?'

'A good deal.'

'What?'

'Hindustani.'

'And what did you do meantime?'

'I learnt German at first.'

'Did he teach you?'

'He did not understand German.'

'Did he teach you nothing?'

'A little Hindustani.'

'Rivers taught you Hindustani?'

'Yes, sir.'

'And his sisters also?'

'No.'

'Only you?'

'Only me.'

'Did you ask to learn?'

'No.'

'He wished to teach you?'

'Yes.'

A second pause.

'Why did he wish it? Of what use could Hindustani be to you?'

'He intended me to go with him to India.'

'Ah! here I reach the root of the matter. He wanted you to marry him?'

'He asked me to marry him.'

'That is a fiction—an impudent invention to vex me.'

'I beg your pardon, it is the literal truth: he asked me more than once, and was as stiff about urging his point as ever you could be.'

'Miss Eyre, I repeat it, you can leave me. How often am I to say the same thing? Why do you remain pertinaciously perched on my knee, when I have given you notice to quit?'

'Because I am comfortable there.'

'No, Jane, you are not comfortable there, because your heart is not with me: it is with this cousin—this St John. Oh, till this moment, I thought my little Jane was all mine! I had a belief she loved me even when she left me: that was an atom of sweet in much bitter. Long as we have been parted, hot tears as I have wept over our separation, I never thought that while I was mourning her, she was loving another! But it is useless grieving. Jane, leave me: go and marry Rivers.'

'Shake me off, then sir—push me away, for I'll not leave you of my own accord.'

'Jane, I ever like your tone of voice: it still renews hope, it sounds so truthful. When I hear it, it carries me back a year. I forget that you have formed a new tie. But I am not a fool—go—'

'Where must I go, sir?'

'Your own way—with the husband you have chosen.'

'Who is that?'

'You know—this St John Rivers.'

'He is not my husband, nor ever will be. He does not love me: I do not love him. He loves (as he *can* love, and that is not as you love) a beautiful young lady called Rosamond. He wanted to marry me only because he thought I should make a suitable missionary's wife, which she would not have done. He is good and great, but severe; and, for me, cold as an iceberg. He is not like you, sir. I am not happy at his side, nor near him, nor with him. He has no indulgence for me—no fondness. He sees nothing attractive in me; not even youth—only a few useful mental points—Then I must leave you, sir, to go to him?'

I shuddered involuntarily, and clung instinctively closer to my blind but beloved master. He smiled.

'What, Jane! Is this true? Is such really the state of matters between you and Rivers?'

'Absolutely, sir! Oh, you need not be jealous! I wanted to tease you a little to make you less sad: I thought anger would be better than grief. But if you wish me to love you, could you but see how much I *do* love you, you would be proud and content. All my heart is yours, sir: it belongs to you; and with you it would remain, were fate to exile the rest of me from your presence for ever.'

Again, as he kissed me, painful thoughts darkened his aspect.

'My seared vision! My crippled strength!' he murmured regretfully.

I caressed, in order to soothe him. I knew of what he was thinking, and wanted to speak for him, but dared not. As he turned aside his face a minute, I saw a tear slide from under the sealed eyelid, and trickle down the manly cheek. My heart swelled.

'I am no better than the old lightning-struck chestnut-tree in Thornfield orchard,' he remarked ere long. 'And what right would that ruin have to bid a budding woodbine cover its decay with freshness?'

'You are no ruin, sir—no lightning-struck tree: you are green and vigorous. Plants will grow about your roots, whether you ask them or not, because they take delight in your bountiful shadow; and as they grow they will lean towards you, and wind round you, because your strength offers them so safe a prop.'

Again he smiled: I gave him comfort.

'You speak of friends, Jane?' he asked.

'Yes, of friends,' I answered rather hesitatingly: for I knew I meant more than friends, but could not tell what other word to employ. He helped me.

'Ah! Jane. But I want a wife.'

'Do you, sir?'

'Yes: it is news to you?'

'Of course: you said nothing about it before.'

'Is it unwelcome news?'

'That depends on circumstances, sir—on your choice.'

'Which you shall make for me, Jane. I will abide by your decision.'

'Choose then, sir—*her who loves you best.*'

'I will at least choose—*her I love best.* Jane, will you marry me?'

'Yes, sir.'

'A poor blind man, whom you will have to lead about by the hand?'

'Yes, sir.'

'A crippled man, twenty years older than you, whom you will have to wait on?'

'Yes, sir.'

'Truly, Jane?'

'Most truly, sir.'

'Oh! my darling! God bless you and reward you!'

'Mr Rochester, if ever I did a good deed in my life—if ever I thought a good thought— if ever I prayed a sincere and blameless prayer—if ever I wished a righteous wish—I am rewarded now. To be your wife is, for me, to be as happy as I can be on earth.'

'Because you delight in sacrifice.'

'Sacrifice! What do I sacrifice? Famine for food, expectation for content. To be privileged to put my arms round what I value—to press my lips to what I love—to repose on what I trust: is that to make a sacrifice? If so, then certainly I delight in sacrifice.'

'And to bear with my infirmities, Jane: to overlook my deficiencies.'

'Which are none, sir, to me. I love you better now, when I can really be useful to you, than I did in your state of proud independence, when you disdained every part but that of the giver and protector.'

'Hitherto I have hated to be helped—to be led: henceforth, I feel I shall hate it no more. I did not like to put my hand into a hireling's, but it is pleasant to feel it circled by Jane's little fingers. I preferred utter loneliness to the constant attendance of servants; but Jane's soft ministry will be a perpetual joy. Jane suits me: do I suit her?'

'To the finest fibre of my nature, sir.'

'The case being so, we have nothing in the world to wait for: we must be married instantly.'

He looked and spoke with eagerness: his old impetuosity was rising.

'We must become one flesh without any delay, Jane: there is but the licence to get—then we marry.'

'Mr Rochester, I have just discovered the sun is far declined from its meridian, and Pilot is actually gone home to his dinner. Let me look at your watch.'

'Fasten it into your girdle, Janet, and keep it henceforward: I have no use for it.'

'It is nearly four o'clock in the afternoon, sir. Don't you feel hungry?'

'The third day from this must be our wedding day, Jane. Never mind fine clothes and jewels, now: all that is not worth a fillip.'

'The sun has dried up all the raindrops, sir. The breeze is still: it is quite hot.'

'Do you know, Jane, I have your little pearl necklace at this moment fastened round my bronze scrag under my cravat? I have worn it since the day I lost my only treasure, as a memento of her.'

'We will go home through the wood: that will be the shadiest way.'

He pursued his own thoughts without heeding me.

'Jane! you think me, I dare say, an irreligious dog: but my heart swells with gratitude to the beneficent God of this earth just now. He sees not as man sees, but far clearer: judges not as man judges, but far more wisely. I did wrong: I would have sullied my innocent flower— breathed guilt on its purity: the Omnipotent snatched it from me. I, in my stiff-necked rebellion, almost cursed the dispensation: instead of bending to the decree, I defied it. Divine justice pursued its course; disasters came thick on me: I was forced to pass through the valley of the shadow of death. *His* chastisements are mighty; and one smote me which has humbled me for ever. You know I was proud of my strength: but what is it now, when I must give it over to foreign guidance, as a child does its weakness? Of late, Jane—only—only of late—I began to see and acknowledge the hand of God in my doom. I began to experience remorse, repentance, the wish for reconcilement to my Maker. I began sometimes to pray: very brief prayers they were, but very sincere.

'Some days since: nay, I can number them—four; it was last Monday night, a singular mood came over me; one in which grief replaced frenzy—sorrow, sullenness. I had long had the impression that since I could nowhere find you, you must be dead. Late that night—perhaps it might be between eleven and twelve o'clock—ere I retired to my dreary rest, I supplicated God, that, if it seemed good to Him, I might soon be taken from this life, and admitted to that world to come, where there was still hope of joining Jane.

'I was in my own room and sitting by the window, which was open: it soothed me to feel the balmy night-air; though I could see no stars, and only by a vague luminous haze knew the presence of the moon. I longed for thee, Jane! Oh, how I longed for thee both with soul and flesh! I asked of God, at once in anguish and humility, if I had not been long enough desolate, afflicted, tormented; and might not soon taste bliss and peace once more. That I merited all I endured, I acknowledged—that I could scarcely endure more, I pleaded; and the alpha and omega of my heart's wishes broke involuntarily from my lips in the words,—"Jane! Jane! Jane!"'

'Did you speak these words aloud?'

'I did, Jane. If any listener had heard me, he would have thought me mad, I pronounced them with such frantic energy.'

'And it was last Monday night, somewhere near midnight?'

'Yes; but the time is of no consequence: what followed is the strangest point. You will think me superstitious—some superstition I have in my blood, and always had: nevertheless, this is true—true at least it is that I heard what I now relate.

'As I exclaimed, "Jane! Jane! Jane!" a voice—I cannot tell whence the voice came, but I know whose voice it was—replied, "I am coming; wait for me"; and a moment after, went whispering on the wind the words, "Where are you?"

'I tell you, if I can, the idea, the picture these words opened to my mind: yet it is difficult to express what I want to express. Ferndean is buried, as you see, in a heavy wood, where sound falls dull, and dies unreverberating. "Where are you?" seemed spoken amongst mountains; for I heard a hill-sent echo repeat the words. Cooler and fresher at the moment the gale seemed to visit my brow: I could have deemed that in some wild, lone scene, I and Jane were meeting. In spirit, I believe, we must have met. You no doubt were, at that hour, in unconscious sleep, Jane: perhaps your soul wandered from its cell to comfort mine; for those were your accents, they were yours!'

Reader, it was on Monday night—near midnight—that I too had received the mysterious summons: those were the very words by which I replied to it. I listened to Mr Rochester's narrative, but made no disclosure in return. The coincidence struck me as too awful and inexplicable to be communicated or discussed. If I told anything, my tale would be such as must necessarily make a profound impression on the mind of my hearer: and that mind, yet from its sufferings too prone to gloom, needed not the deeper shade of the supernatural. I kept these things and pondered them in my heart.

'You cannot now wonder,' continued my master, 'that when you rose upon me so unexpectedly last night, I had difficulty in believing you any other than a mere voice and vision, something that would melt to silence and annihilation, as the midnight whisper and mountain echo had melted before. Now, I thank God! I know it to be otherwise. Yes, I thank God!'

He put me off his knee and only his last words were audible.

'I thank my Maker, that, in the midst of judgment, He has remembered mercy. I humbly entreat my Redeemer to give me strength to lead henceforth a purer life than I have done hitherto!'

Then he stretched his hand out to be led. I took that dear hand, held it a moment to my lips, and then let it pass round my shoulder: being so much lower of stature than he, I served both for his prop and guide. We entered the wood, and wended homeward.

THE SPECTRE BRIDEGROOM

Washington Irvine

On the summit of one of the heights of the Odenwald, a wild and romantic tract of Upper Germany that lies not far from the confluence of the Main and the Rhine, there stood, many, many years since, the Castle of the Baron Von Landshort. It is now quite fallen to decay, and almost buried among beech trees and dark firs; above which, however, its old watch-tower may still be seen struggling, like the former possessor I have mentioned, to carry a high head, and look down upon a neighbouring country.

The Baron was a dry branch of the great family of Katzenellenbogen, and inherited the relics of the property and all the pride of his ancestors. Though the warlike disposition of his predecessors had much impaired the family possessions, yet the Baron still endeavoured to keep up some show of former state. The times were peaceable, and the German nobles, in general, had abandoned their inconvenient old castles, perched like eagles' nests among the mountains, and had built more convenient residences in the valleys; still the Baron remained proudly drawn up in his little fortress, cherishing with hereditary inveteracy all the old family feuds; so that he was on ill terms with some of his nearest neighbours, on account of disputes that had happened between their great-great-grandfathers.

The Baron had but one child, a daughter; but Nature, when she grants but one child, always compensates by making it a prodigy; and so it was with the daughter of the Baron. All the nurses, gossips, and country cousins, assured her father that she had not her equal for beauty in all Germany; and who should know better than they? She had, moreover, been brought up with great care, under the superintendence of two maiden aunts, who had spent some years of their early life at one of the little German courts, and were skilled in all the branches of knowledge necessary to the education of a fine lady. Under their instructions, she became a miracle of accomplishments. By the time she was eighteen she could embroider to admiration, and had worked whole histories of the saints in tapestry with such strength of expression in their countenances that they looked like so many souls in purgatory. She could read without great difficulty, and had spelled her way through several church legends, and almost all the chivalric wonders of the Heldenbuch. She had even made considerable proficiency in writing, could sign her own name without missing a letter, and so legibly that her aunts could read it without spectacles. She excelled in making little good-for-nothing ladylike knick-knacks of all kinds; was versed in the most abstruse dancing of the day; played a number of airs on the harp and guitar; and knew all the tender ballads of the Minne-lieders by heart.

Her aunts, too, having been great flirts and coquettes in their younger days, were admirably calculated to be vigilant guardians and strict censors of the conduct of their niece; for there is no duenna so rigidly prudent, and inexorably decorous, as a superannuated coquette. She was rarely suffered out of their sight; never went beyond the domains of the castle, unless well attended, or, rather, well watched; had continual lectures read to her about strict decorum and implicit obedience; and, as to the men—pah! she was taught to hold them at such distance and distrust that, unless properly authorized, she would not have cast a glance upon the handsomest cavalier in the world—no, not if he were even dying at her feet.

The good effects of this system were wonderfully apparent. The young lady was a pattern of docility and correctness. While others were wasting their sweetness in the glare of the world, and liable to be plucked and thrown aside by every hand, she was coyly blooming into fresh and lovely womanhood under the protection of those immaculate spinsters, like a rosebud blushing forth among guardian thorns. Her aunts looked upon her with pride and exultation, and vaunted that though all the other young ladies in the world might go astray, yet, thank Heaven, nothing of the kind could happen to the heiress of Katzenellenbogen.

But however scantily the Baron Von Landshort might be provided with children, his household was by no means a small one, for Providence had enriched him with abundance of poor relations. They, one and all, possessed the affectionate disposition common to humble relatives; were wonderfully attached to the Baron, and took every possible occasion to come in swarms and enliven the castle. All family festivals were commemorated by these good people at the Baron's expense; and when they were filled with good cheer, they would declare that there was nothing on earth so delightful as these family meetings, these jubilees of the heart.

The Baron, though a small man, had a large soul, and it swelled with satisfaction at the consciousness of being the greatest man in the little world about him. He loved to tell long stories about the stark old warriors whose portraits looked grimly down from the walls around, and he found no listeners equal to those who fed at his expense. He was much given to the marvellous, and a firm believer in all those supernatural tales with which every mountain and valley in Germany abounds. The faith of his guests even exceeded his own. They listened to every tale of wonder with open eyes and mouth, and never failed to be astonished, even though repeated for the hundredth time. Thus lived the Baron Von Landshort, the oracle of his table, the absolute monarch of his little territory, and happy, above all things, in the persuasion that he was the wisest man of the age.

At the time of which my story treats there was a great family gathering at the castle, on an affair of the utmost importance: it was to receive the destined bridegroom of the Baron's daughter. A negotiation had been carried on between the father and an old nobleman of Bavaria, to unite the dignity of their houses by the marriage of their children. The preliminaries had been conducted with proper punctilio. The young people were betrothed without seeing each other, and the time was appointed for the mariage ceremony. The young Count Von Altenburg had been recalled from the army for the purpose, and was actually on his way to the Baron's to receive his bride. Missives had even been received from him, from Wurtzburg, where he was accidentally detained, mentioning the day and hour when he might be expected.

The castle was in a tumult of preparation to give him a suitable welcome. The fair bride had been decked out with uncommon care. The two aunts had superintended her toilet, and quarrelled the whole morning about every article of her dress. The young lady had taken advantage of their contest to follow the bent of her own taste; and fortunately it was a good one. She looked as lovely as a youthful bridegroom could desire; and the flutter of expectation heightened the lustre of her charms.

The suffusions that mantled her face and neck, the gentle heaving of the bosom, the eye now and then lost in reverie, all betrayed the soft tumult that was going on in her little heart. The aunts were continually hovering around her; for maiden aunts are apt to take great interest in affairs of this nature: they were giving her a world of staid counsel, how to deport herself, what to say, and in what manner to receive the expected lover.

The Baron was no less busied in preparations. He had, in truth, nothing exactly to do; but he was naturally a fuming, bustling little man, and could not remain passive when all the world was in a hurry. He worried from top to bottom of the castle, with an air of infinite anxiety; he continually called the servants from their work to exhort them to be diligent, and buzzed about every hall and chamber, as idle, restless, and importunate as a bluebottle fly of a warm summer's day.

In the meantime, the fatted calf had been killed; the forests had rung with the clamor of the huntsmen; the kitchen was crowded with good cheer; the cellars had yielded up whole oceans of *Rhein-wein* and *Ferne-wein*, and even the great Heidelberg Tun had been laid under contribution. Everything was ready to receive the distinguished guest with *Saus und Braus* in the true spirit of German hospitality—but the guest delayed to make his appearance. Hour rolled after hour. The sun that had poured his downward rays upon the rich forests of the Odenwald, now just gleamed along the summits of the mountains. The Baron mounted the highest tower, and strained his eyes in hopes of catching a distant sight of the Count and his attendants. Once he thought he beheld them; the sound of horns came floating from the valley, prolonged by the mountain echoes: a number of horsemen were seen far below, slowly advancing along the road; but when they had nearly reached the foot of the mountain they suddenly struck off in a different direction. The last ray of sunshine departed—the bats began to flit by in the twilight—the road grew dimmer and dimmer to the view; and nothing appeared stirring in it but now and then a peasant lagging homeward from his labour.

While the old castle of Landshort was in this state of perplexity, a very interesting scene was transacting in a different part of the Odenwald.

The young Count Von Altenburg was tranquilly pursuing his route in that sober jog-trot way in which a man travels toward matrimony when his friends have taken all the trouble and uncertainty of courtship off his hands, and a bride is waiting for him, as certainly as a dinner, at the end of his journey. He had encountered at Wurtzburg a youthful companion in arms, with whom he had seen some service on the frontiers: Herman Von Starkenfaust, one of the stoutest hands and worthiest hearts of German chivalry, who was now returning from the army. His father's castle was not far distant from the old fortress of Landshort, although a hereditary feud rendered the families hostile and strangers to each other.

In the warm-hearted moment of recognition, the young friends related all their past adventures and fortunes, and the Count gave the whole history of his intended nuptials with a young lady whom he had never seen, but of whose charms he had received the most enrapturing descriptions.

As the route of the friends lay in the same direction, they agreed to perform the rest of their journey together; and, that they might do it more leisurely, set off from Wurtzburg at an early hour, the Count having given directions for his retinue to follow and overtake him.

They beguiled their wayfaring with recollections of their military scenes and adventures; but the Count was apt to be a little tedious, now and then, about the reputed charms of his bride, and the felicity that awaited him.

In this way they had entered among the mountains of the Odenwald, and were traversing one of its most lonely and thickly wooded passes.

It is well known that the forests of Germany have always been as much infested with robbers as its castles by spectres; and, at this time, the former were particularly numerous, from the hordes of disbanded soldiers wandering about the country. It will not appear extraordinary, therefore, that the cavaliers were attacked by a gang of these stragglers in the midst of the forest. They defended themselves with bravery, but were nearly overpowered when the Count's retinue arrived to their assistance. At sight of them the robbers fled, but not until the Count had received a mortal wound. He was slowly and carefully conveyed back to the city of Wurtzburg, and a friar summoned from a neighboring convent, who was famous for his skill in administering to both soul and body. But half of his skill was superfluous; the moments of the unfortunate Count were numbered.

With his dying breath he entreated his friend to repair instantly to the castle of Landshort, and explain the fatal cause of his not keeping his appointment with his bride. Though not the most ardent of lovers, he was one of the most punctilious of men, and appeared earnestly solicitous that this mission should be speedily and courteously executed. 'Unless this is done,' said he, 'I shall not sleep quietly in my grave!' He repeated these last words with peculiar solemnity. A request, at a moment so impressive, admitted no hesitation. Starkenfaust endeavoured to soothe him to calmness; promised faithfully to execute his wish, and gave him his hand in solemn pledge. The dying man pressed it in acknowledgment, but soon lapsed into delirium—raved about his bride—his engagements—his plighted word; ordered his horse, that he might ride to the castle of Landshort, and expired in the fancied act of vaulting into the saddle.

Starkenfaust bestowed a sigh and a soldier's tear on the untimely fate of his comrade; and then pondered on the awkward mission he had undertaken. His heart was heavy, and his head perplexed; for he was to present himself an unbidden guest among hostile people, and to damp their festivity with tidings fatal to their hopes. Still there were certain whisperings of curiosity in his bosom to see this far-famed beauty of Katzenellenbogen so cautiously shut up from the world; for he was a passionate admirer of the sex, and there was a dash of eccentricity and enterprise in his character that made him fond of all adventure.

Previous to his departure, he made all due arrangements with the holy fraternity of the convent for the funeral solemnities of his friend, who was to be buried in the cathedral of Wurtzburg, near some of his illustrious relatives; and the mourning retinue of the Count took charge of his remains.

It is now high time that we should return to the ancient family of Katzenellenbogen, who were impatient for their guest, and still more for their dinner; and to the worthy little Baron, whom we left airing himself on the watch-tower.

Night closed in, but still no guest arrived. The Baron descended from the tower in despair. The banquet, which had been delayed from hour to hour, could no longer be postponed. The meats were already over-done, the cook in an agony, and the whole household had the look of a garrison that had been reduced by famine. The Baron was obliged re-luctantly to give orders for the feast without the presence of the guest. All were seated at table, and just on the point of commencing, when the sound of a horn from without the gate gave notice of the approach of a stranger. Another long blast filled the old courts of the castle with its echoes, and was answered by the warder from the walls. The Baron hastened to receive his future son-in-law.

The drawbridge had been let down, and the stranger was before the gate. He was a tall gallant cavalier, mounted on a black steed. His coun-tenance was pale, but he had a beaming, romantic eye, and an air of stately melancholy. The Baron was a little mortified that he should have come in this simple, solitary style. His dignity for a moment was ruffled, and he felt disposed to consider it a want of proper respect for the im-portant occasion, and the important family with which he was to be connected. He pacified himself, however, with the conclusion that it must have been youthful impatience which had induced him thus to spur on sooner than his attendants.

'I am sorry,' said the stranger, 'to break in upon you thus unseason-ably—'

Here the Baron interrupted him with a world of compliments and greetings; for, to tell the truth, he prided himself upon his courtesy and his eloquence. The stranger attempted, once or twice, to stem the torrent of words, but in vain; so he bowed his head and suffered it to flow on. By the time the Baron had come to a pause they had reached the inner court of the castle; and the stranger was again about to speak, when he was once more interrupted by the appearance of the female part of the family, leading forth the shrinking and blushing bride. He gazed on her for a moment as one entranced; it seemed as if his whole soul beamed forth in the gaze, and rested upon that lovely form. One of the maiden aunts whispered something in her ear; she made an effort to speak; her moist blue eye was timidly raised, gave a shy glance of inquiry on the stranger, and was cast again to the ground. The words died away; but there was a sweet smile playing about her lips, and a soft dimpling of the cheek, that showed her glance had not been unsatisfactory. It was impossible for a girl of the fond age of eighteen, highly predisposed for love and matrimony, not to be pleased with so gallant a cavalier.

The late hour at which the guest had arrived left no time for parley. The Baron was peremptory, and deferred all particular conversation until the morning, and led the way to the untasted banquet.

It was served up in the great hall of the castle. Around the walls hung the hard-favoured portraits of the heroes of the house of Katzenellenbogen, and the trophies which they had gained in the field and in the chase. Hacked corselets, splintered jousting spears, and tattered banners were mingled with the spoils of sylvan warfare: the jaws of the wolf and the tusks of the boar grinned horribly among crossbows and battle-axes, and a huge pair of antlers branched immediately over the head of the youthful bridegroom.

The cavalier took but little notice of the company or the entertainment. He scarcely tasted the banquet, but seemed absorbed in admiration of his bride. He conversed in a low tone, that could not be overheard—for the language of love is never loud; but where is the female ear so dull that it cannot catch the softest whisper of the lover? There was a mingled tenderness and gravity in his manner that appeared to have a powerful effect upon the young lady. Her colour came and went, as she listened with deep attention. Now and then she made some blushing reply, and when his eye was turned away she would steal a sidelong glance at his romantic countenance, and heave a gentle sigh of tender happiness. It was evident that the young couple were completely enamoured. The aunts, who were deeply versed in the mysteries of the heart, declared that they had fallen in love with each other at first sight.

He conversed in a low tone for the language of love is never loud.

The feast went on merrily, or at least noisily, for the guests were all blessed with those keen appetites that attend upon light purses and mountain air. The Baron told his best and longest stories, and never had he told them so well, or with such great effect. If there was anything marvellous, his auditors were lost in astonishment; and if anything facetious, they were sure to laugh exactly in the right place. The Baron, it is true, like most great men, was too dignified to utter any joke but a dull one: it was always enforced, however, by a bumper of excellent Hoch-heimer; and even a dull joke, at one's own table, served up with jolly old wine, is irresistible. Many good things were said by poorer and keener wits that would not bear repeating, except on similar occasions; many sly speeches whispered in ladies' ears that almost convulsed them with suppressed laughter; and a song or two roared out by a poor, but merry and broadfaced cousin of the Baron, that absolutely made the maiden aunts hold up their fans.

Amid all this revelry, the stranger-guest maintained a most singular and unseasonable gravity. His countenance assumed a deeper cast of dejection as the evening advanced, and, strange as it may appear, even the Baron's jokes seemed only to render him the more melancholy. At times he was lost in thought, and at times there was a perturbed and restless wandering of the eye that bespoke a mind but ill at ease. His conversation with the bride became more and more earnest and mysterious. Lowering clouds began to steal over the fair serenity of her brow, and tremors to run through her tender frame.

All this could not escape the notice of the company. Their gaiety was chilled by the unaccountable gloom of the bridegroom; their spirits were infected; whispers and glances were interchanged, accompanied by shrugs and dubious shakes of the head. The song and the laugh grew less and less frequent; there were dreary pauses in the conversation, which were at length succeeded by wild tales and supernatural legends. One dismal story produced another still more dismal, and the Baron nearly frightened some of the ladies into hysterics with the history of the goblin horseman that carried away the fair Leonora—a dreadful, but true story, which has since been put into excellent verse, and is read and believed by all the world.

The bridegroom listened to this tale with profound attention. He kept his eyes steadily fixed on the Baron, and, as the story drew to a close, began gradually to rise from his seat, growing taller and taller, until, in the Baron's entranced eye, he seemed almost to tower into a giant. The moment the tale was finished, he heaved a deep sigh, and took a solemn farewell of the company. They were all amazement. The Baron was perfectly thunderstruck.

'What! going to leave the castle at midnight? Why, everything was prepared for his reception; a chamber was ready for him if he wished to retire.'

The stranger shook his head mournfully and mysteriously: 'I must lay my head in a different chamber to-night!'

There was something in this reply, and the tone in which it was uttered, that made the Baron's heart misgive him; but he rallied his forces, and repeated his hospitable entreaties. The stranger shook his head silently, but positively, at every offer; and, waving his farewell to the company, stalked slowly out of the hall. The maiden aunts were absolutely petrified—the bride hung her head, and a tear stole to her eye.

The Baron followed the stranger to the great court of the castle, where the black charger stood pawing the earth and snorting with impatience. When they had reached the portal, whose deep archway was dimly lighted by a cresset, the stranger paused, and addressed the Baron in a hollow tone of voice, which the vaulted roof rendered still more sepulchral. 'Now that we are alone,' said he, 'I will impart to you the reason of my going. I have a solemn, an indispensable engagement—'

'Why,' said the Baron, 'cannot you send some one in your place?'

'It admits of no substitute—I must attend it in person—I must away to Wurtzburg cathedral—'

'Ay,' said the Baron, plucking up spirit, 'but not until to-morrow—to-morrow you shall take your bride there.'

'No! no!' replied the stranger, with tenfold solemnity, 'my engagement is with no bride—the worms! the worms expect me! I am a dead man—I have been slain by robbers—my body lies at Wurtzburg—at midnight I am to be buried—the grave is waiting for me—I must keep my appointment!'

He sprang on his black charger, dashed over the drawbridge, and the clattering of his horse's hoofs was lost in the whistling of the night-blast.

The Baron returned to the hall in the utmost consternation, and related what had passed. Two ladies fainted outright; others sickened at the idea of having banqueted with a spectre. It was the opinion of some that this might be the wild huntsman famous in German legend. Some talked of mountain sprites, of wood-demons, and of other supernatural beings, with which the good people of Germany have been so grievously harassed since time immemorial. One of the poor relations ventured to suggest that it might be some sportive evasion of the young cavalier, and that he very gloominess of the caprice seemed to accord with so melancholy a personage. This, however, drew on him the indignation of the whole company, and especially of the Baron, who looked upon him as little better than an infidel; so that he was fain to abjure his heresy as speedily as possible, and come into the faith of the true believers.

But, whatever may have been the doubts entertained, they were completely put to an end by the arrival, next day, of regular missives confirming the intelligence of the young Count's murder, and his interment in Wurtzburg cathedral.

The dismay at the castle may well be imagined. The Baron shut himself up in his chamber. The guests who had come to rejoice with him could not think of abandoning him in his distress. They wandered about the courts, or collected in groups in the hall, shaking their heads and shrugging their shoulders at the troubles of so good a man; and sat longer than ever at table, and ate and drank more stoutly than ever, by way of keeping up their spirits. But the situation of the widowed bride was the most pitiable. To have lost a husband before she had even embraced him—and such a husband! If the very spectre could be so gracious and noble, what must have been the living man? She filled the house with lamentations.

On the night of the second day of her widowhood, she had retired to her chamber, accompanied by one of her aunts, who insisted on sleeping with her. The aunt, who was one of the best tellers of ghost stories in all Germany, had just been recounting one of her longest, and had fallen asleep in the very midst of it. The chamber was remote, and overlooked a small garden. The niece lay pensively gazing at the beams of the rising moon, as they trembled on the leaves of an aspen tree before the lattice. The castle clock had just told midnight, when a soft strain of music stole up from the garden. She rose hastily from her bed and stepped lightly to the window. A tall figure stood among the shadows of the trees. As it raised its head, a beam of moonlight fell upon the countenance. Heaven and earth! She beheld the Spectre Bridegroom! A loud shriek at that moment burst upon her ear, and her aunt, who had been awakened by the music, and had followed her silently to the window, fell into her arms. When she looked again, the spectre had disappeared.

Of the two females, the aunt now required the most soothing, for she was perfectly beside herself with terror. As to the young lady, there was something, even in the spectre of her lover, that seemed endearing. There was still the semblance of manly beauty; and though the shadow of a man is but little calculated to satisfy the affections of a lovesick girl, yet, where the substance is not to be had, even that is consoling. The aunt declared that she would never sleep in that chamber again; the niece, for once, was refractory, and declared as strongly that she would sleep in no other in the castle: the consequence was that she had to sleep in it alone; but she drew a promise from her aunt not to relate the story of the spectre, lest she should be denied the only melancholy pleasure left her on earth—that of inhabiting the hamber over which the guardian shade of her lover kept its nightly vigils.

How long the good old lady would have observed this promise is uncertain, for she dearly loved to talk of the marvellous, and there is a triumph in being the first to tell a frightful story; it is, however, still quoted in the neighbourhood, as a memorable instance of female secrecy, that she kept it to herself for a whole week; when she was suddenly absolved from all further restraint by intelligence brought to the breakfast-table one morning that the young lady was not to be found. Her room was empty—the bed had not been slept in—the window was open—and the bird had flown!

The astonishment and concern with which the intelligence was received can only be imagined by those who have witnessed the agitation which the mishaps of a great man cause among his friends. Even the poor relations paused for a moment from the indefatigable labours of the trencher; when the aunt, who had at first been struck speechless, wrung her hands and shrieked out, 'The goblin! the goblin! She's carried away by the goblin!'

In a few words she related the fearful scene of the garden, and concluded that the spectre must have carried off his bride. Two of the domestics corroborated the opinion, for they had heard the clattering of a horse's hoofs down the mountain about midnight, and had no doubt that it was the spectre on his black charger, bearing her away to the tomb. All present were struck with the direful probability; for events of the kind are extremely common in Germany, as many well authenticated histories bear witness.

What a lamentable situation was that of the poor Baron! What a heartrending dilemma for a fond father, and a member of the great family of Katzenellenbogen! His only daughter had either been rapt away to the grave, or he was to have some wood-demon for a son-in-law, and, perchance, a troop of goblin grandchildren. As usual, he was completely bewildered, and all the castle in an uproar. The men were ordered to take horse and scour every road and path and glen of the Odenwald. The Baron himself had just drawn on his jack-boots, girded on his sword, and was about to mount his steed to sally forth on the doubtful quest, when he was brought to a pause by a new apparition. A lady was seen approaching the castle, mounted on a palfrey attended by a cavalier on horseback. She galloped up to the gate, sprang from her horse, and falling at the Baron's feet, embraced his knees. It was his lost daughter, and her companion—the Spectre Bridegroom! The Baron was astounded. He looked at his daughter, then at the spectre, and almost doubted the evidence of his senses. The latter, too, was wonderfully improved in his appearance, since his visit to the world of spirits. His dress was splendid, and set off a noble figure of manly symmetry. He was no longer pale and melancholy. His fine countenance was flushed with the glow of youth, and joy rioted in his large dark eye.

The mystery was soon cleared up. The cavalier (for, in truth, as you must have known all the while, he was no goblin) announced himself as Sir Herman Von Starkenfaust. He related his adventure with the young Count. He told how he had hastened to the castle to deliver the unwelcome tidings, but that the eloquence of the Baron had interrupted him in every attempt to tell his tale. How the sight of the bride had completely captivated him, and that to pass a few hours near her he had tacitly suffered the mistake to continue. How he had been sorely perplexed in what way to make a decent retreat, until the Baron's goblin stories had suggested his eccentric exit. How, fearing the feudal hostility of the family, he had repeated his visits by stealth—had haunted the garden beneath the young lady's window—had wooed—had won—had borne away in triumph—and, in a word, had wedded, the fair.

Under any other circumstances the Baron would have been inflexible, for he was tenacious of paternal authority and devoutly obstinate in all family feuds; but he loved his daughter; he had lamented her as lost; he rejoiced to find her still alive; and, though her husband was of a hostile house, yet, thank Heaven, he was not a goblin. There was something, it must be acknowledged, that did not exactly accord with his notions of strict veracity in the joke the knight had passed upon him of his being a dead man; but several old friends present, who had served in the wars, assured him that every stratagem was excusable in love, and that the cavalier was entitled to especial privilege, having lately served as a trooper.

Matters, therefore, were happily arranged. The Baron pardoned the young couple on the spot. The revels at the castle were resumed. The poor relations overwhelmed this new member of the family with loving-kindness; he was so gallant, so generous—and so rich. The aunts, it is true, were somewhat scandalized that their system of strict seclusion and passive obedience should be so badly exemplified, but attributed all to their negligence in not having the windows grated. One of them was particularly mortified at having her marvellous story marred, and that the only spectre she had ever seen should turn out a counterfeit; but the niece seemed perfectly happy at having found him substantial flesh and blood—and so the story ends.

THE CHIMAERA

Nathaniel Hawthorne

Once, in the old, old times (for all the strange things which I tell you about happened long before anybody can remember) a fountain gushed out of a hill-side, in the marvellous land of Greece. And, for aught I know, after so many thousand years, it is still gushing out of the very self-same spot. At any rate, there was the pleasant fountain, welling freshly forth and sparkling adown the hill-side, in the golden sunset, when a handsome young man named Bellerophon drew near its margin. In his hand he held a bridle, studded with brilliant gems and adorned with a golden bit. Seeing an old man, and another of middle age, and a little boy, near the fountain, and likewise a maiden, who was dipping up some of the water in a pitcher, he paused, and begged that he might refresh himself with a draught.

'This is very delicious water,' he said to the maiden, as he rinsed and filled her pitcher, after drinking out of it. 'Will you be kind enough to tell me whether the fountain has any name?'

'Yes; it is called the Fountain of Pirene,' answered the maiden; and then she added: 'My grandmother has told me that this clear fountain was once a beautiful woman; and when her son was killed by the arrows of the huntress Diana, she melted all away into tears. And so the water, which you find so sweet, is the sorrow of that poor mother's heart!'

'I should not have dreamed,' observed the young stranger, 'that so clear a well-spring, with its gush and gurgle, and its cheery dance out of the shade into the sunlight, had so much as one tear-drop in its bosom! And this, then, is Pirene? I thank you, pretty maiden, for telling me its name. I have come from a far-away country to find this very spot.'

A middle-aged country fellow (he had driven his cow to drink out of the spring) stared hard at young Bellerophon and at the handsome bridle which he carried in his hand.

'The water-courses must be getting low, friend, in your part of the world,' remarked he, 'if you come so far only to find the Fountain of Pirene. But, pray, have you lost a horse? I see you carry the bridle in your hand, and a very pretty one it is, with that double row of bright stones upon it. If the horse was as fine as the bridle, you are much to be pitied for losing him.'

'I have lost no horse,' said Bellerophon, with a smile. 'But I happen to be seeking a very famous one, which, as wise people have informed me, must be found hereabouts, if anywhere. Do you know whether the winged horse Pegasus still haunts the Fountain of Pirene, as he used to do in your forefathers' days?'

But then the country fellow laughed.

Some of you, my little friends, have probably heard that this Pegasus was a snow-white steed, with beautiful silvery wings, who spent most of his time on the summit of Mount Helicon. He was as wild, and as swift, and as buoyant, in his flight through the air, as any eagle that ever soared into the clouds. There was nothing else like him in the world. He had no mate; he had never been backed or bridled by a master; and for many long year he led a solitary and a happy life.

Oh, how fine a thing it is to be a winged horse! Sleeping at night, as he did, on a lofty mountain-top, and passing the greater part of the day in the air, Pegasus seemed hardly to be a creature of the earth. Whenever he was seen up very high above people's heads, with the sunshine on his silvery wings, you would have thought that he belonged to the sky, and that, skimming a little too low, he had got astray among our mists and vapours, and was seeking his way back again. It was very pretty to behold him plunge into the fleecy bosom of a bright cloud, and be lost in it for a moment or two, and then break forth from the other side.

Or, in a sullen rainstorm, when there was a grey pavement of clouds over the whole sky, it would sometimes happen that the winged horse descended right through it, and the grand light of the upper region would gleam after him. In another instant, it is true, both Pegasus and the pleasant light would be gone away together. But any one that was fortunate enough to see this wondrous spectacle felt cheerful the whole day afterwards, and as much longer as the storm lasted.

In the summertime, and in the beautifullest of weather, Pegasus often alighted on the solid earth, and, closing his silvery wings, would gallop over hill and dale for pastime, as fleetly as the wind. Oftener than in any other place, he had been seen near the Fountain of Pirene, drinking the delicious water, or rolling himself upon the soft grass of the margin. Sometimes, too (but Pegasus was very dainty in his food), he would crop a few of the clover blossoms that happened to be sweetest.

To the Fountain of Pirene, therefore, people's great-grandfathers had been in the habit of going (as long as they were youthful, and retained their faith in winged horses), in hopes of getting a glimpse of the beautiful Pegasus. But, of late years, he had been very seldom seen. Indeed, there were many of the country folks, dwelling within half an hour's walk of the fountain, who had never beheld Pegasus, and did not believe that there was any such creature in existence. The country fellow to whom Bellerophon was speaking chanced to be one of those incredulous persons.

And that was the reason why he laughed.

'Pegasus, indeed!' cried he, turning up his nose as high as such a flat nose could be turned up.

'Pegasus, indeed! A winged horse, truly! Why, friend, are you in your senses? Of what use would wings be to a horse? Could he drag the plough so well, think you? To be sure, there might be a little saving in the expense of shoes; but then, how would a man like to see his horse flying out of the stable window? – yes; or whisking him up above the clouds, when he only wanted to ride to mill?

'No, no! I don't believe in Pegasus. There never was such a ridiculous kind of horse-fowl made!'

'I have some reason to think otherwise,' said Bellerophon quietly.

And then he turned to an old grey man, who was leaning on a staff, and listening very attentively, with his head stretched forward, and one hand at his ear, because, for the last twenty years, he had been getting rather deaf.

'And what say you, venerable sir?' inquired he. 'In your younger days, I should imagine, you must frequently have seen the winged steed!'

'Ah, young stranger, my memory is very poor!' said the aged man. 'When I was a lad, if I remember rightly, I used to believe there was such a horse, and so did everybody else. But, nowadays, I hardly know what to think, and very seldom think about the winged horse at all. If I ever saw the creature, it was a long, long while ago; and, to tell you the truth, I doubt whether I ever did see him. One day, to be sure, when I was quite a youth, I remember seeing some hoof-tramps round about the brink of the fountain. Pegasus might have made those hoof-marks; and so might some other horse.'

'And have you never seen him, my fair maiden?' asked Bellerophon of the girl, who stood with the pitcher on her head, while this talk went on. 'You certainly could see Pegasus, if anybody can, for your eyes are very bright.'

'Once I thought I saw him,' replied the maiden, with a smile and a blush. 'It was either Pegasus, or a large white bird, a very great way up in the air. And one other time, as I was coming to the fountain with my pitcher, I heard a neigh. Oh, such a brisk and melodious neigh as that was! My very heart leaped with delight at the sound. But it startled me, nevertheless; so that I ran home without filling my pitcher.'

'That was truly a pity!' said Bellerophon.

And he turned to the child, whom I mentioned at the beginning of the story, and who was gazing at him, as children are apt to gaze at strangers, with his rosy mouth wide open.

'Well, my little fellow,' cried Bellerophon, playfully pulling one of his curls. 'I suppose you have often seen the winged horse?'

'That I have,' answered the child, very readily. 'I saw him yesterday, and many times before.'

'You are a fine little man!' said Bellerophon, drawing the child closer to him. 'Come, tell me all about it.'

'Why,' replied the child, 'I often come here to sail little boats in the fountain, and to gather pretty pebbles out of its basin. And sometimes, when I look down into the water, I see the image of a winged horse, in the picture of the sky that is there. I wish he would come down, and take me on his back, and let me ride him up to the moon! But, if I so much as stir to look at him, he flies far away out of sight.'

And Bellerophon put his faith in the child, who had seen the image of Pegasus in the water, and in the maiden, who had heard him neigh so melodiously, rather than in the middle-aged clown, who believed only in cart-horses, or in the old man, who had forgotten the beautiful things of his youth.

Therefore, he hunted about the Fountain of Pirene for a great many days afterwards. He kept continually on the watch, looking upward at the sky, or else down into the water, hoping for ever that he should see either the reflected image of the winged horse, or the marvellous reality. He held the bridle, with its bright gems and golden bit, always ready in his hand. The rustic people, who dwelt in the neighbourhood, and drove their cattle to the fountain to drink, would often laugh at poor Bellerophon, and sometimes take him pretty severely to task. They told him that an able-bodied young man, like himself, ought to have better business than to be wasting his time in such an idle pursuit. They offered to sell him a horse, if he wanted one; and when Bellerophon declined the purchase, they tried to drive a bargain with him for his fine bridle. Even the country boys thought him so very foolish, that they used to have a great deal of sport about him, and were rude enough not to care a fig, although Bellerophon saw and heard it. One little urchin, for example, would play Pegasus, and cut the oddest imaginable capers, by way of flying, while one of his schoolfellows would scamper after him, holding forth a twist of bulrushes, which was intended to represent Bellerophon's ornamental bridle. But the gentle child, who had seen the picture of Pegasus in the water, comforted the young stranger more than all the naughty boys could torment him. The dear little fellow in his play-hours often sat down beside him, and, without speaking a word, would look down into the fountain and up towards the sky, with so innocent a faith, that Bellerophon could not help feeling encouraged.

Now you will, perhaps, wish to be told why it was that Bellerophon had undertaken to catch the winged horse. And we shall find no better opportunity to speak about this matter than while he was waiting for Pegasus to appear.

If I were to relate the whole of Bellerophon's previous adventures, they might easily grow into a very long story. It will be quite enough to say, that, in a certain country of Asia, a terrible monster, called a Chimaera, had made its appearance, and was doing more mischief than could be talked about between now and sunset. According to the best accounts, which I have been able to obtain, this Chimaera was nearly, if not quite, the ugliest and most poisonous creature, and the strangest and unaccountablest, and the hardest to fight with, and the most difficult to run away from, that ever came out of the earth's inside. It had a tail like a boa-constrictor; its body was like I do not care what; and it had three separate heads, one of which was a lion's, the second a goat's, and the third an abominably great snake's. And a hot blast of fire came flaming out of each of its three mouths! Being an earthly monster, I doubt whether it had any wings; but, wings or no, it ran like a goat and a lion, and wriggled along like a serpent, and thus contrived to make about as much speed as all the three together.

Oh, the mischief, and mischief, and mischief, that this naughty creature did! With its flaming breath it could set a forest on fire, or burn up a field of grain, or, for that matter, a village, with all its fences and houses. It laid waste the whole country round about and used to eat people and animals alive, and cook them afterwards in the burning oven of its stomach. Mercy on us, little children, I hope neither you nor I will ever happen to meet a Chimaera!

While the hateful beast (if a beast we can anywise call it) was doing all these horrible things, it so chanced that Bellerophon came to that part of the world, on a visit to the king. The king's name was Iobates, and Lycia was the country which he ruled over. Bellerophon was one of the bravest youths in the world, and desired nothing so much as to do some valiant and beneficent deed, such as would make all mankind admire and love him. In those days, the only way for a young man to distinguish himself was by fighting battles, either with the enemies of his country, or with wicked giants, or with troublesome dragons, or with wild beasts, when he could find nothing more dangerous to encounter. King Iobates, perceiving the courage of his youthful visitor, proposed to him to go and fight the Chimaera which everybody else was afraid of, and which, unless it should be soon killed, was likely to convert Lycia into a desert. Bellerophon hesitated not a moment, but assured the king that he would either slay this dreaded Chimaera, or perish in the attempt.

But, in the first place, as the monster was so prodigiously swift, he bethought himself that he should never win the victory by fighting on foot. The wisest thing he could do, therefore, was to get the very best and fleetest horse that could anywhere be found. And what other horse in all the world was half so fleet as the marvellous horse Pegasus, who had wings as well as legs, and was even more active in the air than on the earth? To be sure, a great many people denied that there was any such horse with wings, and said that the stories about him were all poetry and nonsense. But, wonderful as it appeared, Bellerophon believed that Pegasus was a real steed, and hoped that he himself might be fortunate enough to find him; and, once fairly mounted on his back, he would be able to fight the Chimaera at better advantage.

And this was the purpose with which he had travelled from Lycia to Greece, and had brought the beautifully ornamental bridle in his hand. It was an enchanted bridle. If he could only succeed in putting the golden bit into the mouth of Pegasus, the winged horse would be submissive, and own Bellerophon for his master, and fly whithersoever he might choose to turn the rein.

But, indeed, it was a weary and anxious time, while Bellerophon waited and waited for Pegasus, in hopes that he would come and drink at the Fountain of Pirene. He was afraid lest King Iobates should imagine that he had fled from the Chimaera. It pained him, too, to think how much mischief the monster was doing, while he himself, instead of fighting with it, was compelled to sit idly poring over the bright waters of Pirene, as they gushed out of the sparkling sand. And as Pegasus came thither so seldom in these latter years, and scarcely alighted there more than once in a lifetime, Bellerophon feared that he might grow an old man, and have no strength left in his arms nor courage in his heart, before the winged horse would appear. Oh, how heavily passes the time, while an adventurous youth is yearning to do his part in life and to gather in the harvest of his renown! How hard a lesson it is to wait! Our life is brief, and how much of it is spent in teaching us only this!

Well was it for Bellerophon that the child had grown so fond of him, and was never weary of keeping him company. Every morning the child gave him a new hope to put in his bosom, instead of yesterday's withered one.

'Dear Bellerophon,' he would cry, looking up hopefully into his face, 'I think we shall see Pegasus today!'

And, at length, if it had not been for the little boy's unwavering faith, Bellerophon would have given up all hope, and would have gone back to Lycia, and have done his best to slay the Chimaera without the help of the winged horse. And in that case poor Bellerophon would at least have been terribly scorched by the creature's breath, and would most probably have been killed or devoured. Nobody should ever try to fight an earth-born Chimaera, unless he can first get upon the back of an aerial steed.

One morning the child spoke to Bellerophon even more hopefully than usual.

'Dear, dear Bellerophon,' cried he, 'I know not why it is, but I feel as if we should certainly see Pegasus today!'

And all that day he would not stir a step from Bellerophon's side; so they ate a crust of bread together and drank some of the water of the fountain. In the afternoon there they sat, and Bellerophon had thrown his arm around the child, who likewise had put one of his little hands into Bellerophon's. The latter was lost in his own thoughts, and was fixing his eyes vacantly on the trunks of the trees that overshadowed the fountain, and on the grape-vines that clambered up among their branches. But the gentle child was gazing down into the water; he was grieved, for Bellerophon's sake, that the hope of another day should be deceived, like so many before it; and two or three quiet tear-drops fell from his eyes, and mingled with what were said to be the many tears of Pirene, when she wept for her slain children.

But, when he least thought of it, Bellerophon felt the pressure of the child's little hand, and heard a soft, almost breathless whisper.

'See there, dear Bellerophon! There is an image in the water!'

The young man looked down into the dimpling mirror of the fountain, and saw what he took to be the reflection of a bird which seemed to be flying at a great height in the air, with a gleam of sunshine on its snowy or silvery wings.

'What a splendid bird it must be!' said he. 'And how very large it looks, though it must really be flying higher than the clouds!'

'It makes me tremble!' whispered the child. 'I am afraid to look up into the air! It is very beautiful, and yet I dare only look at its image in the water. Dear Bellerophon, do you not see that it is no bird? It is the winged horse Pegasus!'

Bellerophon's heart began to throb. He gazed keenly upward, but could not see the winged creature, whether bird or horse; because, just then, it had plunged into the fleecy depths of a summer cloud. It was but a moment, however, before the object reappeared, sinking lightly down out of the cloud, although still at a vast distance from the earth. Bellerophon caught the child in his arms, and shrank back with him, so that they were both hidden among the thick shrubbery which grew all around the fountain. Not that he was afraid of any harm, but he dreaded lest, if Pegasus caught a glimpse of them, he would fly far away, and alight in some inaccessible mountain-top. For it was really the winged horse. After they had expected him so long, he was coming to quench his thirst with the water of Pirene.

Nearer and nearer came the aerial wonder, flying in great circles, as you may have seen a dove when about to alight. Downward came Pegasus, in those wide, sweeping circles, which grew narrower and narrower still, as he gradually approached the earth. The nigher the view of him, the more beautiful he was, and the more marvellous the sweep of his silvery wings. At last, with so slight a pressure as hardly to bend the grass about the fountain, or imprint a hoof-tramp in the sand of its margin, he alighted, and, stooping his wild head, began to drink. He drew in the water with long and pleasant sighs and tranquil pauses of enjoyment; and then another draught, and another and another. For, nowhere in the world or up among the clouds, did Pegasus love any water as he had loved this of Pirene. And when his thirst was slaked, he cropped a few of the honey blossoms of the clover, delicately tasting them, but not caring to make a hearty meal, because the herbate just beneath the clouds on the lofty sides of Mount Helicon, suited his palate better than this ordinary grass.

After thus drinking to his heart's content, and, in his dainty fashion, condescending to take a little food, the winged horse began to caper to and fro and dance, as it were, out of mere idleness and sport. There never was a more playful creature made than this very Pegasus. So there he frisked, in a way that it delights me to think about, fluttering his great wings as lightly as ever did a linnet, and running little races, half on earth and half in air, and which I know not whether to call a flight or a gallop. When a creature is perfectly able to fly, he sometimes chooses to run, just for the pastime of the thing, and so did Pegasus, although it cost him some little trouble to keep his hoofs so near the ground. Bellerophon, meanwhile, holding the child's hand, peeped forth from the shrubbery, and thought that never was any sight so beautiful as this, nor ever a horse's eyes so wild and spirited as those of Pegasus. It seemed a sin to think of bridling him and riding on his back.

Once or twice Pegasus stopped and snuffed the air, pricking up his ears, tossing his head, and turning it on all sides, as if he partly suspected some mischief or other. Seeing nothing, however, and hearing no sound, he soon began his antics again.

At length – not that he was weary, but only idle and luxurious – Pegasus folded his wings, and lay down on the soft green turf. But, being too full of aerial life to remain quiet for many moments together, he soon rolled over on his back, with his four slender legs in the air. It was beautiful to see him, this one solitary creature, whose mate had never been created, but who needed no companion, and, living a great many hundred years, was as happy as the centuries were long. The more he did such things as mortal horses are accustomed to do, the less earthly and more wonderful he seemed. Bellerophon and the child almost held their breath, partly from a delightful awe, but still more because they dreaded lest the slightest stir or murmur should send him up, with the speed of an arrow-flight, into the furthest blue of the sky.

Finally, when he had had enough of rolling over and over, Pegasus turned himself about, and, indolently, like any other horse, put out his forelegs, in order to rise from the ground; and Bellerophon, who had guessed that he would do so, darted suddenly from the thicket, and leaped astride of his back.

Yes, there he sat, on the back of the winged horse!

But what a bound did Pegasus make when, for the first time, he felt the weight of a mortal man upon his loins! A bound, indeed! Before he had time to draw a breath, Bellerophon found himself five hundred feet aloft, and still shooting upward, while the winged horse snorted and trembled with terror and anger. Upward he went, up, up, up, until he plunged into the cold misty bosom of a cloud, at which, only a little while before, Bellerophon had been gazing, and fancying it a very pleasant spot. Then again, out of the heart of the cloud, Pegasus shot down like a thunderbolt, as if it meant to dash both himself and his rider headlong against a rock. Then he went through about a thousand of the wildest caprioles that had ever been performed either by a bird or a horse.

I cannot tell you half that he did. He skimmed straight forward, and sideways, and backward. He reared himself erect, with his forelegs on a wreath of mist and his hind legs on nothing at all. He flung out his heels behind, and put down his head between his legs, with his wings pointing right upward. At about two miles' height above the earth, he turned a somersault, so that Bellerophon's heels were where his head should have been, and he seemed to look down into the sky, instead of up. He twisted his head about, and looking Bellerophon in the face, with fire flashing from his eyes, made a terrible attempt to bite him. He fluttered his pinions so wildly that one of the silver feathers was shaken out, and, floating earthward, was picked up by the child, who kept it as long as he lived, in memory of Pegasus and Bellerophon.

But the latter (who, as you may judge, was as good a horseman as ever galloped) had been watching his opportunity, and at last clapped the golden bit of the enchanted bridle between the winged steed's jaws. No sooner was this done than Pegasus became as manageable as if he had taken food, all his life, out of Bellerophon's hand. To speak what I really feel, it was almost a sadness to see so wild a creature grow suddenly so tame. And Pegasus seemed to feel it so, likewise. He looked round to Bellerophon, with the tears in his beautiful eyes, instead of the fire that so recently flashed from them. But when Bellerophon patted his head, and spoke a few authoritative, yet kind and soothing words, another look came into the eyes of Pegasus; for he was glad at heart, after so many lonely centuries, to have found a companion and a master. Thus it always is with winged horses, and with all such wild and solitary creatures. If you can catch and overcome them, it is the surest way to win their love.

While Pegasus had been doing his utmost to shake Bellerophon off his back, he had flown a very long distance; and they had come within sight of a lofty mountain by the time the bit was in his mouth. Bellerophon had seen this mountain before, and knew it to be Helicon, on the summit of which was the winged horse's abode. Thither (after looking gently into his rider's face, as if to ask leave) Pegasus now flew, and, alighting, waited patiently until Bellerophon should please to dismount. The young man, accordingly, leaped from his steed's back, but still held him fast by the bridle. Meeting his eyes, however, he was so affected by the gentleness of his aspect, and by his beauty, and by the thought of the free life which Pegasus had heretofore lived, that he could not bear to keep him a prisoner, if he really desired his liberty.

Obeying this generous impulse, he slipped the enchanted bridle off the head of Pegasus and took the bit from his mouth.

'Leave me, Pegasus,' said he. 'Either leave me or love me.'

In an instant, the winged horse shot almost out of sight, soaring straight upward from the summit of Mount Helicon. Being long after sunset, it was now twilight on the mountaintop, and dusky evening over all the country round about. But Pegasus flew so high that he overtook the departed day, and was bathed in the upper radiance of the sun. Ascending higher and higher, he looked like a bright speck, and, at last, could no longer be seen in the hollow waste of the sky. And Bellerophon was afraid that he should never behold him more. But, while he was lamenting his own folly, the bright speck reappeared, and drew nearer and nearer, until it descended lower than the sunshine; and behold, Pegasus had come back! After this trial, there was no more fear of the winged horse making his escape. He and Bellerophon were friends, and put loving faith in one another.

That night they lay down and slept together, with Bellerophon's arm about the neck of Pegasus, not as a caution, but for kindness. And they awoke at peep of day, and bade one another good morning, each in his own language.

In this manner, Bellerophon and the wondrous steed spent several days, and grew better acquainted and fonder of each other all the time. They went on long aerial journeys, and sometimes ascended so high that the earth looked hardly bigger than – the moon. They visited distant countries, and amazed the inhabitants, who thought that the beautiful young man, on the back of the winged horse, must have come down out of the sky. A thousand miles a day was no more than an easy space for the fleet Pegasus to pass over. Bellerophon was delighted with this kind of life, and would have liked nothing better than to live always in the same way, aloft in the clear atmosphere; for it was always sunny weather up there, however cheerless and rainy it might be in the lower region. But he could not forget the horrible Chimaera, which he had promised King Iobates to slay. So, at last, when he had become well accustomed to feats of horsemanship in the air, and could manage Pegasus with the least motion of his hand, and had taught him to obey his voice, he determined to attempt the performance of this perilous adventure.

At daybreak, therefore, as soon as he unclosed his eyes, he gently pinched the winged horse's ear, in order to arouse him. Pegasus immediately started from the ground, and pranced about a quarter of a mile aloft, and made a grand sweep around the mountain-top, by way of showing that he was wide awake and ready for any kind of an excursion. During the whole of this little flight, he uttered a loud, brisk, and melodious neigh, and finally came down at Bellerophon's side, as lightly as ever you saw a sparrow hop upon a twig.

'Well done, dear Pegasus! well done, my sky-skimmer!' cried Bellerophon, fondly stroking the horse's neck. 'And now, my fleet and beautiful friend, we must break our fast. Today we are to fight the terrible Chimaera.'

As soon as they had eaten their morning meal, and drank some sparkling water from a spring called Hippocrene, Pegasus held out his head, of his own accord, so that his master might put on the bridle. Then, with a great many playful leaps and airy caperings, he showed his impatience to be gone, while Bellerophon was girding on his sword, and hanging his shield about his neck, and preparing himself for battle. When everything was ready, the rider mounted, and (as was his custom, when going a long distance) ascended five miles perpendicularly, so as the better to see whither he was directing his course. He then turned the head of Pegasus towards the east, and set out for Lycia. In their flight they overtook an eagle, and came so nigh him, before he could get out of their way, that Bellerophon might easily have caught him by the leg. Hastening onward at this rate, it was still early in the forenoon when they beheld the lofty mountains of Lycia, with their deep and shaggy valleys. If Bellerophon had been told truly, it was in one of those dismal valleys that the hideous Chimaera had taken up its abode.

Being now so near their journey's end, the winged horse gradually descended with his rider; and they took advantage of some clouds that were floating over the mountain-tops, in order to conceal themselves. Hovering on the upper surface of a cloud, and peeping over its edge, Bellerophon had a pretty distinct view of the mountainous part of Lycia, and could look into all its shadowy vales at once. At first there appeared to be nothing remarkable. It was a wild, savage, and rocky tract of high and precipitous hills. In the more level part of the country, there were ruins of houses that had been burnt, and, here and there, the carcasses of dead cattle strewn about the pastures where they had been feeding.

'The Chimaera must have done this mischief,' thought Bellerophon. 'But where can the monster be?'

As I have already said, there was nothing remarkable to be detected, at first sight, in any of the valleys and dells that lay among the precipitous heights of the mountains. Nothing at all; unless, indeed, it were three spires of black smoke, which issued from what seemed to be the mouth of a cavern, and clambered sullenly into the atmosphere. Before reaching the mountain-top, these three black smoke-wreaths mingled themselves into one. The cavern was almost directly beneath the winged horse and his rider, at the distance of about a thousand feet. The smoke, as it crept heavily upward, had an ugly, sulphurous, stifling scent, which caused Pegasus to snort and Bellerophon to sneeze. So disagreeable was it to the marvellous steed (who was accustomed to breathe only the purest air) that he waved his wings, and shot half a mile out of the range of this offensive vapour.

But, on looking behind him, Bellerophon saw something that induced him first to draw the bridle, and then to turn Pegasus about. He made a sign, which the winged horse understood, and sunk slowly through the air, until his hoofs were scarcely more than a man's height above the rocky bottom of the valley. In front, as far off as you could throw a stone, was the cavern's mouth, with the three smoke-wreaths oozing out of it. And what else did Bellerophon behold then?

There seemed to be a heap of strange and terrible creatures curled up within the cavern. Their bodies lay so close together that Bellerophon could not distinguish them apart; but, judging by their heads, one of these creatures was a huge snake, the second a fierce lion, and the third an ugly goat. The lion and the goat were asleep; the snake was broad awake, and kept staring about him with a great pair of fiery eyes. But – and this was the most wonderful part of the matter – the three spires of smoke evidently issued from the nostrils of these three heads! So strange was the spectacle, that, though Bellerophon had been all along expecting it, the truth did not immediately occur to him, that here was the terrible three-headed Chimaera. He had found out the Chimaera's cavern. The snake, the lion, and the goat, as he supposed them to be, were not three separate creatures, but one monster.

The wicked, hateful thing! Slumbering, as two-thirds of it was, it still held, in its abominable claws, the remnant of an unfortunate lamb – or possibly (but I hate to think so) it was a dear little boy – which its three mouths had been gnawing before two of them fell asleep!

All at once Bellerophon started as from a dream, and knew it to be the Chimaera. Pegasus seemed to know it, at the same instant, and sent forth a neigh that sounded like the call of a trumpet to battle. At this sound the three heads reared themselves erect, and belched out great flashes of flame. Before Bellerophon had time to consider what to do next, the monster flung itself out of the cavern and sprung straight towards him, with its immense claws extended and its snaky tail twisting venomously behind. If Pegasus had not been as nimble as a bird, both he and his rider would have been overthrown by the Chimaera's head-long rush, and thus the battle have been ended before it was well begun. But the winged horse was not to be caught so. In the twinkling of an eye he was up aloft, halfway to the clouds, snorting with anger. He shuddered, too, not with affright, but with utter disgust at the loath-someness of this poisonous thing with three heads.

The Chimaera, on the other hand, raised itself up so as to stand absolutely on the tip-end of its tail, with its talons pawing fiercely in the air, and its three heads spluttering fire at Pegasus and his rider. My stars, how it roared, and hissed, and bellowed! Bellerophon, mean-while, was fitting his shield on his arm and drawing his sword.

'Now, my beloved Pegasus,' he whispered in the winged horse's ear, 'thou must help me to slay this insufferable monster, or else thou shalt fly back to thy solitary mountain peak without thy friend Bellerophon. For either the Chimaera dies, or its three mouths shall gnaw this head of mine, which has slumbered upon thy neck!'

Pegasus whinnied, and, turning back his head, rubbed his nose

Bellerophon made a cut at the monster.

tenderly against his rider's cheek. It was his way of telling him that, though he had wings and was an immortal horse, yet he would perish, if it were possible for immortality to perish, rather than leave Bellerophon behind.

'I thank you, Pegasus,' answered Bellerophon. 'Now, then, let us make a dash at the monster!'

Uttering these words, he shook the bridle; and Pegasus darted down aslant, as swift as the flight of an arrow, right towards the Chimaera's threefold head, which, all this time, was poking itself as high as it could into the air. As he came within arm's length, Bellerophon made a cut at the monster, but was carried onward by his steed before he could see whether the blow had been successful. Pegasus continued his course, but soon wheeled round, at about the same distance from the Chimaera as before. Bellerophon then perceived that he had cut the goat's head of the monster almost off, so that it dangled downward by the skin, and seemed quite dead.

But, to make amends, the snake's head and the lion's head had taken all the fierceness from the dead one into themselves, and spit flame, and hissed, and roared, with a vast deal more fury than before.

'Never mind, my brave Pegasus!' cried Bellerophon. 'With another stroke like that, we will stop either its hissing or its roaring.'

And again he shook the bridle. Dashing aslantwise as before, the winged horse made another arrow-flight towards the Chimaera, and Bellerophon aimed another downright stroke at one of the two remaining heads as he shot by. But this time neither he nor Pegasus escaped so well as at first. With one of its claws the Chimaera had given the young man a deep scratch in his shoulder, and had slightly damaged the left wing of the flying steed with the other. On his part Bellerophon had mortally wounded the lion's head of the monster, insomuch that it now hung downward, with its fire almost extinguished, and sending out gasps of thick black smoke. The snake's head, however (which was the only one now left), was twice as fierce and venomous as ever before. It belched forth shoots of fire five hundred yards long, and emitted hisses so loud, so harsh, and so ear-piercing, that King Iobates heard them fifty miles off, and trembled till the throne shook under him.

'Welladay!' thought the poor king; 'the Chimaera is certainly coming to devour me!'

Meanwhile Pegasus had again paused in the air, and neighed angrily, while sparkles of a pure crystal flame darted out of his eyes. How unlike the lurid fire of the Chimaera! The aerial steed's spirit was all aroused, and so was that of Bellerophon.

'Dost thou bleed, my immortal horse?' cried the young man, caring less for his own hurt than for the anguish of this glorious creature, that ought never to have tasted pain. 'The execrable Chimaera shall pay for this mischief with his last head!'

Then he shook the bridle, shouted loudly, and guided Pegasus, not aslantwise as before, but straight at the monster's hideous front. So rapid was the onset, that it seemed but a dazzle and a flash, before Bellerophon was at close grips with his enemy.

The Chimaera by this time, after losing its second head, had got into a red-hot passion of pain and rampant rage. It so flounced about, half on earth and partly in the air, that it was impossible to say which element it rested upon. It opened its snake-jaws to such an abominable width, that Pegasus might almost, I was going to say, have flown right down its throat, wings outspread, rider and all! At their approach, it shot out a tremendous blast of its fiery breath, and enveloped Bellerophon and his steed in a perfect atmosphere of flame, singeing the wings of Pegasus, scorching off one whole side of the young man's golden ringlets, and making them both far hotter than was comfortable, from head to foot.

But this was nothing to what followed.

When the airy rush of the winged horse had brought him within a distance of a hundred yards, the Chimaera gave a spring, and flung its huge, awkward, venomous, and utterly detestable carcass right upon poor Pegasus, clung round him with might and main, and tied up its snaky tail into a knot! Up flew the aerial steed, higher, higher, higher, above the mountain peaks, above the clouds, and almost out of sight of the solid earth. But still the earth-born monster kept its hold, and was borne upward, along with the creature of light and air. Bellerophon, meanwhile, turning about, found himself face to face with the ugly grimness of the Chimaera's visage, and could only avoid being scorched to death, or bitten right in twian, by holding up his shield. Over the upper edge of the shield he looked sternly into the savage eyes of the monster.

But the Chimaera was so mad and wild with pain, that it did not guard itself so well as might else have been the case. Perhaps, after all, the best way to fight a Chimaera is by getting as close to it as you can. In its efforts to stick its horrible iron claws into its enemy, the creature left its own breast quite exposed; and perceiving this, Bellerophon thrust his sword up to the hilt into its cruel heart. Immediately the snaky tail untied its knot. The monster let go its hold of Pegasus, and fell from that vast height, downward: while the fire within its bosom, instead of being put out, burned fiercer than ever, and quickly began to consume the dead carcass. Thus it fell out of the sky, all aflame, and (it being nightfall before it reached the earth) was mistaken for a shooting star or a comet. But, at early sunrise, some cottagers were going to their day's labour, and saw, to their astonishment, that several acres of ground were strewn with black ashes. In the middle of a field there was a heap of whitened bones, a great deal higher than a haystack. Nothing else was ever seen of the dreadful Chimaera.

And when Bellerophon had won the victory, he bent forward and kissed Pegasus, while the tears stood in his eyes.

'Back now, my beloved steed!' said he. 'Back to the Fountain of Pirene!'

Pegasus skimmed through the air, quicker than ever he did before, and reached the fountain in a very short time. And there he found the old man leaning on his staff, and the country fellow watering his cow, and the pretty maiden filling her pitcher.

'I remember now,' quoth the old man, 'I saw this winged horse once before, when I was quite a lad. But he was ten times handsomer in those days.'

'I own a cart-horse worth three of him!' said the country fellow. 'If this pony were mine, the first thing I should do would be to clip his wings!'

But the poor maiden said nothing, for she had always the luck to be afraid at the wrong time. So she ran away, and let her pitcher tumble down, and broke it.

'Where is the gentle child,' asked Bellerophon, 'who used to keep me company, and never lost his faith, and never was weary of gazing into the fountain?'

'Here I am, dear Bellerophon!' said the child softly.

For the little boy had spent day after day, on the margin of Pirene, waiting for his friend to come back; but when he perceived Bellerophon descending through the clouds, mounted on the winged horse, he had shrunk back into the shrubbery. He was a delicate and tender child, and dreaded lest the old man and the country fellow should see the tears gushing from his eyes.

'Thou hast won the victory,' said he joyfully, running to the knee of Bellerophon, who still sat on the back of Pegasus. 'I knew thou wouldst.'

'Yes, dear child!' replied Bellerophon, alighting from the winged horse. 'But if thy faith had not helped me, I should never have waited for Pegasus, and never have gone up above the clouds, and never have conquered the terrible Chimaera. Thou, my beloved little friend, hast done it all. And now let us give Pegasus his liberty.'

So he slipped off the enchanted bridle from the head of the marvellous steed.

'Be free for everymore, my Pegasus!' cried he, with a shade of sadness in his tone. 'Be as free as thou art fleet!'

But Pegasus rested his head on Bellerophon's shoulder, and would not be persuaded to take flight.

'Well, then,' said Bellerophon, caressing the airy horse, 'thou shalt be with me as long as thou wilt; and we will go together, forthwith, and tell King Iobates that the Chimaera is destroyed.'

Then Bellerophon embraced the gentle child, and promised to come to him again, and departed. But, in after years, that child took higher flights upon the aerial steed than ever did Bellerophon, and achieved more honourable deeds than his friend's victory over the Chimaera. For, gentle and tender as he was, he grew to be a mighty poet!

A STORY OF SURVIVAL

Mark Twain

The Clipper ship Hornet *carrying locomotives and general cargo sailed out of New York harbour on 15 January 1866.*

Three-and-a-half months later her Captain (Captain Mitchell) and crew were caught up in one of the most remarkable stories of survival ever recorded.

At seven o'clock on the morning of the 3 May, the chief mate and two men started down into the hold to draw some 'bright varnish' from a cask. The captain told him to bring the cask on deck – that it was dangerous to have it where it was, in the hold. The mate, instead of obeying the order, proceeded to draw a can full of the varnish first. He had an 'open light' in his hand, and the liquid took fire; the can was dropped, the officer in his consternation neglected to close the bung, and in a few seconds the fiery torrent had run in every direction, under bales of rope, cases of candles, barrels of kerosene, and all sorts of freight, and tongues of flame were shooting upwards through every aperture and crevice toward the deck.

The ship was moving along under easy sail, the watch on duty were idling here and there in such shade as they could find, and the listlessness and repose of morning in the tropics was upon the vessel and her belongings. But as six bells chimed, the cry of 'Fire!' rang through the ship, and woke every man to life and action. And following the fearful warning, and almost as fleetly, came the fire itself. It sprang through hatchways, seized upon chairs, table, cordage, anything, everything – and almost before the bewildered men could realize what the trouble was and what was to be done the cabin was a hell of angry flames. The mainmast was on fire – its rigging was burnt asunder! One man said all this had happened within eighteen or twenty minutes after the first alarm – two others say in ten minutes. All say that one hour after the alarm, the main and mizzenmasts were burned in two and fell overboard.

Captain Mitchell ordered the three boats to be launched instantly, which was done – and so hurriedly that the longboat (the one he left the vessel in himself) had a hole as large as a man's head stove in her bottom. A blanket was stuffed into the opening and fastened to its place. Not a single thing was saved, except such food and other articles as lay about the cabin and could be quickly seized and thrown on deck. Thomas★ was sent into the longboat to receive its proportion of these things, and, being barefooted at the time, and bareheaded, and having no clothing on save an undershirt and pantaloons, of course he never got a chance afterward to add to his dress. He lost everything he had, including his logbook, which he had faithfully kept from the first. Forty minutes after the fire alarm, the provisions and passengers were on board the three boats, and they rowed away from the ship – and to some distance, too, for the heat was very great. Twenty minutes afterward the two masts I have mentioned, with their rigging and their broad sheets of canvas wreathed in flames, crashed into the sea.

All night long the thirty-one unfortunates sat in their frail boats and watched the gallant ship burn; and felt as men feel when they see a tried friend perishing and are powerless to help him. The sea was illuminated for miles around, and the clouds above were tinged with a ruddy hue; the faces of the men glowed in the strong light as they shaded their eyes with their hands and peered out anxiously upon the wild picture, and the gunwales of the boats and the idle oars shone like polished gold.

At five o'clock on the morning after the disaster, in latitude 2 degrees 20 minutes north, longitude 112 degrees 8 minutes west, the ship went down, and the crew of the *Hornet* were alone on the great deep, or, as one of the seamen expressed it, 'We felt as if somebody or something had gone away – as if we hadn't any home any more.'

Captain Mitchell divided his boat's crew into two watches and gave the third mate charge of one and took the other himself. He had saved a studding sail from the ship, and out of this the men fashioned a rude sail

★ John S. Thomas, 3rd mate.

with their knives; they hoisted it, and taking the first and second mates' boats in tow, they bore away upon the ship's course (northwest) and kept in the track of vessels bound to or from San Francisco, in the hope of being picked up.

In the few minutes' time allowed him, Captain Mitchell was only able to seize upon the few articles of food and other necessaries that happened to lie about the cabin. Here is the list: Four hams, seven pieces of salt pork (each piece weighed about four pounds), one box of raisins, one hundred pounds of bread (about one barrel), twelve two-pound cans of oysters, clams, and assorted meats; six buckets of raw potatoes (which rotted so fast they got but little benefit from them), a keg with four pounds of butter in it, twelve gallons of water in a forty-gallon tierce or 'scuttle butt,' four one-gallon demi-johns full of water, three bottles of brandy, the property of passengers; some pipes, matches, and a hundred pounds of tobacco; had no medicines. That was all these poor fellows had to live on for forty-three days – the whole thirty-one of them!

Each boat had a compass, a quadrant, a copy of Bowditch's *Navigator* and a nautical almanac, and the captain's and chief mate's boat had chronometers.

Of course, all hands were put on short allowance at once. The day they set sail from the ship each man was allowed a small morsel of salt pork – or a little piece of potato, if he preferred it – and half a sea biscuit three times a day. To understand how very light this ration of bread was, it is only necessary to know that it takes seven of these sea biscuits to weigh a pound. The first two days they only allowed one gill of water a day to each man; but for nearly a fortnight after that the weather was lowering and stormy, and frequent rail squalls occurred. The rain was caught in canvas, and whenever there was a shower the forty-gallon cask and every other vessel that would hold water was filled – even all the boots that were watertight were pressed into this service, except such as the matches and tobacco were deposited in to keep dry. So for fourteen days. There were luxurious occasions when there was plenty of water to drink. But after that how they suffered the agonies of thirst!

For seven days the boats sailed on, and the starving men ate their fragment of biscuit and their morsel of raw pork in the morning, and hungrily counted the tedious hours until noon and night should bring their repetitions of it. And in the long intervals they looked mutely into each other's faces, or turned their wistful eyes across the wild sea in search of the succoring sail that was never to come.

And thought, I suppose. Thought of home – of shelter from storms – of food and drink and rest.

The hope of being picked up hung to them constantly – was ever present to them, and in their thoughts, like hunger. And in the captain's mind was the hope of making the Clarion Islands, and he clung to it many a day.

The nights were very dark. They had no lantern and could not see the compass, and there were no stars to steer by. Thomas said, of the boat, 'She handled easy, and we steered by the feel of the wind in our faces and the heave of the sea.' Dark and dismal and lonesome work was that! Sometimes they got a fleeting glimpse of the sailor's friend, the North Star, and then they lighted a match and hastened anxiously to see if their compass was faithful to them – for it had to be placed close to an iron ringbolt in the stern, and they were afraid, during those first nights, that this might cause it to vary. It proved true to them, however.

On the fifth day a notable incident occurred. They caught a dolphin! And while their enthusiasm was still at its highest over this stroke of good fortune, they captured another. They made a trifling fire in a tin plate and warmed the prizes – to cook them was not possible – and divided them equitably among all hands and ate them.

On the sixth day two more dolphins were caught.

Two more were caught on the seventh day, and also a small bonita, and they began to believe they were always going to live in this extravagant way; but it was not to be; these were their last dolphins, and they never could get another bonita, though they saw them and longed for them often afterward.

On the eighth day the rations were reduced about one half. Thus – breakfast, one fourth of a biscuit, an ounce of ham, and a gill of water to each man; dinner, same quantity of bread and water, and four oysters or clams; supper, water and bread the same, and twelve large raisins or fourteen small ones, to a man. Also, during the first twelve or fifteen days, each man had one spoonful of brandy a day, then it gave out.

This day, as one of the men was gazing across the dull waste of waters as usual, he saw a small, dark object rising and falling upon the waves. He called attention to it, and in a moment every eye was bent upon it in intensest interest. When the boat had approached a little nearer, it was discovered that it was a small green turtle, fast asleep. Every noise was hushed as they crept upon the unconscious slumberer. Directions were given and hopes and fears expressed in guarded whispers. At the fateful moment – a moment of tremendous conse-quence to these famishing men – the expert selected for the high and responsible office stretched forth his hand, while his excited comrades bated their breath and trembled for the success of the enterprise, and seized the turtle by the hind leg and handed him aboard! His delicate flesh was carefully divided among the party and eagerly devoured – after being 'warmed' like the dolphins which went before him.

The eighteenth day was a memorable one to the wanderers on the lonely sea. On that day the boats parted company. The captain said that separate from each other there were three chances for the saving of some of the party where there could be but one chance if they kept together.

The magnanimity and utter unselfishness of Captain Mitchell (and through his example, the same conduct in his men) throughout this distressing voyage, are among its most amazing features. No disposition was ever shown by the strong to impose upon the weak, and no greediness, no desire on the part of any to get more than his just share of food, was ever evinced. On the contrary, they were thoughtful of each other and always ready to care for and assist each other to the utmost of their ability. When the time came to part company, Captain Mitchell and his crew, although theirs was much the more numerous party (fifteen men to nine and seven respectively in the other boats), took only one third of the meagre amount of provisions still left, and passed over the other two thirds to be divided up between the other crews; these men could starve, if need be, but they seem not to have known how to be mean.

After the division the captain had left for his boat's share two thirds of the ham, one fourth of a box of raisins, half a bucket of buscuit crumbs, fourteen gallons of water three cans of 'soup-and-bully' beef.

The captain told the mates he was still going to try to make the Clarion Isles, and that they could imitate his example if they thought best, but he wished them to freely follow the dictates of their own judgment in the matter. At eleven o'clock in the forenoon the boats were all cast loose from each other, and then, as friends part from friends whom they expect to meet no more in life, all hands hailed with a fervent 'God bless you, boys; good-bye!' and the two cherished sails drifted away and disappeared from the longing gaze that followed them so sorrowfully.

On the afternoon of this eventful eighteenth day two 'boobies' were caught – a bird about as large as a duck, but all bone and feathers – not as much meat as there is on a pigeon – not nearly so much, the men say. They ate them raw – bones, entrails, and everything – no single morsel was wasted; they were carefully apportioned among the fifteen men. No fire could be built for cooking purposes – the wind was so strong and the sea ran so high that it was all a man could do to light his pipe.

At eventide the wanderers missed a cheerful spirit – a plucky, strong-hearted fellow, who never drooped his head or lost his grip – a staunch and true good friend, who was always at his post in storm or calm, in rain or shine – who scorned to say die, and yet was never afraid to die – a little trim and taut old rooster, he was, who starved with the rest, but came on watch in the stern sheets promptly every day at four in the morning and six in the evening for eighteen days and crowed like a maniac! Right well they named him Richard of the Lion Heart! One of the men said with honest feeling: 'As true as I'm a man, if that rooster was here today and any man dared to abuse the bird, I'd break his neck!' Richard was esteemed by all and by all his rights were respected. He received his little ration of bread crumbs every time the men were fed, and, like them, he bore up bravely and never grumbled and never gave way to despair. As long as he was strong enough, he stood in the stern sheets or mounted the gunwale as regularly as his watch came round, and crowed his two-hour talk, and when at last he grew feeble in the legs and had to stay below, his heart was still stout and he slapped about in the water on the bottom of the boat and crowed as bravely as ever! He felt that under circumstances like these America expects every rooster to do his duty, and he did it. But is it not to the high honor of that boat's crew of starving men that, tortured day and night by the pangs of hunger as they were, they refused to appease them with the blood of their humble comrade? Richard was transferred to the chief mate's boat and sailed away on the eighteenth day.

The third mate does not remember distinctly, but thinks morning and evening prayers were begun on the nineteenth day. They were conducted by one of the young Fergusons, because the captain could not read the prayer book without his spectacles, and they had been burned with the ship. And ever after this date, at the rising and the setting of the sun, the storm-tossed mariners reverently bowed their heads while prayers went up for 'they that are helpless and far at sea.'

On the morning of the twenty-first day, while some of the crew were dozing on the thwarts and others were buried in reflection, one of the men suddenly sprang to his feet and cried, 'A sail! a sail!' Of course, sluggish blood bounded then and eager eyes were turned to seek the welcome vision. But disappointment was their portion, as usual. It was only the chief mate's boat drifting across their path after three days' absence. In a short time the two parties were abreast each other and in hailing distance. They talked twenty minutes; the mate reported 'all well' and then sailed away, and they never saw him afterward.

On the twenty-fourth day Captain Mitchell took an observation and found that he was in latitude 16 degrees north and longitude 117 degrees west – about a thousand miles from where his vessel was burned. The hope he had cherished so long that he would be able to make the clarion Isles deserted him at last; he could only go before the wind, and he was now obliged to attempt the best thing the southeast trades could do for him – blow him to the 'American group' or to the Sandwich Islands – and therefore he reluctantly and with many misgivings turned his prow towards those distant archipalagoes. Not many mouthfuls of food were left, and these must be economized. The third mate said that under this new program of proceedings 'we could see that we were living too high; we had got to let up on them raisins, or the soup-and-bullies, one, because it stood to reason that we warn't going to make land soon, and so they wouldn't last.' It was a matter which had few humorous features about it to them, and yet a smile is almost pardonable at this idea, so gravely expressed, of 'living high' on fourteen raisins at a meal.

The rations remained the same as fixed on the eighth day, except that only two meals a day were allowed, and occasionally the raisins and oysters were left out.

What these men suffered during the next three weeks no mortal man may hope to describe. Their stomachs and intestines felt to the grasp like a couple of small tough balls, and the gnawing hunger pains and the dreadful thirst that was consuming them in those burning latitudes became almost insupportable. And yet, as the men say, the captain said funny things and talked cheerful talk until he got them to conversing freely, and then they used to spend hours together describing delicious dinners they had eaten at home, and earnestly planning interminable and preposterous bills of fare for dinners they were going to eat on shore, if they ever lived through their troubles to do it, poor fellows. The captain said plain bread and butter would be good enough for him all the days of his life, if he could only get it.

But the saddest things were the dreams they had. An unusually intelligent young sailor named Cox said: 'In those long days and nights we dreamed all the time – not that we ever slept. I don't mean – no, we only sort of dozed – three fourths of the faculties awake and the other fourth benumbed into the counterfeit of a slumber; oh, no – some of us never slept for twenty-three days, and no man ever saw the captain asleep for upward of thirty. But we barely dozed that way and dreamed – and always of such feasts! bread, and fowls, and meat – everything a man could think of, piled upon long tables, and smoking hot! And we sat down and seized upon the first dish in our reach, like ravenous wolves, and carried it to our lips, and – and then we woke up and found the same starving comrades about us, and the vacant sky and the desolate sea!'

These things are terrible even to think of.

On the twenty-eighth day the rations were: One teaspoonful of bread crumbs and about an ounce of ham for the morning meal; a spoonful of bread crumbs alone for the evening meal, and one gill of water three times a day! A kitten would perish eventually under such sustenance.

At this point the third mate's mind reverted painfully to an incident of the early stages of their sufferings. He said there were two between-decks, on board the *Hornet*, who had been lying there sick and helpless for he didn't know how long; but when the ship took fire, they turned out as lively as anyone under the spur of the excitement. One was a 'Portyghee,' he said, and always of a hungry disposition; when all the provisions that could be got had been brought aft and deposited near the wheel to be lowered into the boats, 'that sick Portyghee watched his chance, and when nobody was looking, he harnessed the provisions and ate up nearly a quarter of a bar'l of bread before the old man caught him, and he had more than two notions to put his lights out.' The third mate dwelt upon this circumstance as upon a wrong he could not fully forgive, and intimated that the Portyghee stole bread enough, if economized in twenty-eighth-day rations, to have run the longboat party three months.

Four little flying fish, the size of the sardines of these latter days, flew into the boat on the night of the twenty-eighth day. They were divided among all hands and devoured raw. On the twenty-ninth day they caught another, and divided it into fifteen pieces, less than a teaspoonful apiece.

On the thirtieth day they caught a third flying fish and gave it to the revered old captain – a fish of the same poor little proportions as the others – four inches long – a present a king might be proud of under such circumstances – a present whose value, in the eyes of the men who offered it, was not to be found in the Bank of England – yea, whose vaults were not able to contain it! The old captain refused to take it; the men insisted; the captain said no – he would take his fifteenth – they must take the remainder. They said in substance, though not in words, that they would see him in Jericho first! So the captain had to eat the fish.

The third mate always betrayed emotion when he spoke of 'the old man.' The men were the same way; the captain is their hero – their true and faithful friend, whom they delight to honor. After the ordeal was over I said to one of these infatuated skeletons, 'But you wouldn't go quite so far as to die for him?' A snap of the finger – 'As quick as that! – I wouldn't be alive now if it hadn't been for him.'

About the thirty-second day the bread gave entirely out. There was nothing left, now, but mere odds and ends of their stock of provisions. Five days afterwards, on the thirty-seventh day – latitude 16 degrees 30 minutes north, and longitude 170 degrees west – kept off for the 'American group' – 'which don't exist and never will, I suppose,' said the third mate. They ran directly over the ground said to be occupied by these islands – that is, between latitude 16 degrees and 17 degrees north, and longitude 133 degrees to 136 degrees west. Ran over the imaginary islands and got into 136 degrees west, and then the captain made a dash for Hawaii, resolving that he would go till he fetched land, or at any rate as long as he and his men survived.

On Monday, the thirty-eighth day after the disaster, 'We had nothing left,' said the third mate, 'but a pound and a half of ham – the bone was a good deal the heaviest part of it – and one soup-and-bully tin.' These things were divided among the fifteen men, and they ate it all – two ounces of food to each man. I do not count the ham bone, as that was saved for the next day. For some time now the poor wretches had been cutting their old boots into small pieces and eating them. They would also pound wet rags to a sort of pulp and eat them.

After apportioning the hame bone, the captain cut the canvas cover that had been around the ham into fifteen equal pieces, and each man took his portion. This was the last division of food that the captain made. The men broke up the small oaken butter tub and divided the staves among themselves, and gnawed them up. The shell of the little green turtle, heretofore mentioned, was scraped with knives and eaten to the last shaving. The third mate chewed pieces of boots and spat them out, but ate nothing except the soft straps of two pairs of boots – ate three on the thirty-ninth day and saved one for the fortieth.

The men seem to have thought in their own minds of the shipwrecked mariner's last dreadful resort – cannibalism; but they do not appear to have conversed about it. They only thought of the casting lots and killing one of their number as a possibility; but even when they were eating rags and bone and boots and shell and hard oak wood, they seem to have still had a notion that it was remote.

Thomas and also several of the men state that the sick 'Portyghee,' during the five days that they were entirely out of provisions, actually ate two silk handkerchiefs and a couple of cotton shirts, besides his share of the boots and bones and lumber.

Captain Mitchell was fifty-six years old on the 12 June – the fortieth day after the burning of the ship. He said it looked somewhat as if it might be the last one he was going to enjoy. He had no birthday feast except some bits of ham canvas – no luxury but this, and no substantials save the leather and oaken bucket staves.

Speaking of the leather diet, one of the men told me he was obliged to eat a pair of boots which were so old and rotten that they were full of holes; and then he smiled gently and said he didn't know, though, but what the holes tasted about as good as the balance of the boot.

★   ★   ★   ★

At eleven o'clock on 15 June, after suffering all that men may suffer and live for forty-three days, in an open boat, on a scorching tropical sea, one of the men feebly shouted the glad tidings, 'Land ho!' The 'watch below' were lying in the bottom of the boat. What do you suppose they did? They said they had been cruelly disappointed over and over again, and they dreaded to risk another experience of the kind – they could not bear it – they lay still where they were. They said they would not trust to an appearance that might not be land after all. They would wait.

Shortly it was proven beyond question that they were almost to land. Then there was joy in the party. One man is said to have swooned away. Another said the sight of the green hills was better to him than a day's rations, a strange figure for a man to use who had been fasting for forty days and forty nights.

The land was the island of Hawaii, and they were off Laupahoehoe and could see nothing inshore but breakers. Laupahoehoe is a dangerous place to try to land. When they got pretty close to shore, they saw cabins, but no human beings. They thought they would lower the sail and try to work in with the oars. They cut the ropes and the sail came down, and then they found they were not strong enough to ship the oars. They drifted helplessly toward the breakers, but looked listlessly on and cared not a straw for the violent death which seemed about to overtake them after all their manful struggles, their privations, and their terrible sufferings. They said, 'It was good to see the green fields again.' It was all they cared for. The 'green fields' were a haven of rest for the weary wayfarers; it was sufficient; they were satisfied; it was nothing to them that death stood in their pathway; they had long been familiar to him; he had no terrors for them.

Two natives saw the boat, knew by the appearance of things that it was in trouble, and dashed through the surf and swam out to it. When they climbed aboard, there were only five yards of space between the poor sufferers and a sudden and violent death. Fifteen minutes afterward the boat was beached upon the shore, and a crowd of natives (who are the very incarnation of generosity, unselfishness, and hospitality) were around the strangers dumping bananas, melons, taro, poi – anything and everything they could scrape together that could be eaten – on the ground by the cartload; and if Mr Jones, of the station, had not hurried down with his steward, they would soon have killed the starving men with kindness. Jones and the Kanaka girls and men took the mariners in their arms like so many children and carried them up to the house, where they received kind and judicious attention until Sunday evening, when two whaleboats came from Hilo, Jones furnished a third, and they were taken in these to the town just named, arriving there at two o'clock Monday morning.

*   *   *   *

Each of the young Fergusons kept a journal from the day the ship sailed from New York until they got on land once more at Hawaii. The captain also kept a log every day he was adrift. These logs, by the captain's direction, were to be kept up faithfully as long as any of the crew were alive, and the last survivor was to put them in a bottle, when he succumbed, and lash the bottle to the inside of the boat. The captain gave a bottle to each officer of the other boats, with orders to follow his example. The old gentleman was always thoughtful.

The hardest berth in that boat, I think, must have been that of provision keeper. This office was performed by the captain and the third mate; of course they were always hungry. They always had access to the food, and yet must not gratify their craving appetites.

The young Fergusons are very highly spoken of by all the boat's crew, as patient, enduring, manly, and kindhearted gentlemen. The captain gave them a watch to themselves – it was the duty of each to bail the water out of the boat three hours a day.

The chief mate, Samuel Hardy, lived at Chatham, Massachusetts; second mate belonged in Shields, England; the cook, George Washington (Negro), was in the chief mate's boat, and also the steward (Negro); the carpenter was in the second mate's boat.

To Captain Mitchell's good sense, cool judgment, perfect discipline, close attention to the smallest particulars which could conduce to the welfare of his crew or render their ultimate rescue more probable, that boat's crew owe their lives. He had shown brain and ability that make him worthy to command the finest frigate in the United States, and a genuine unassuming heroism that [should] entitle him to a Congressional Medal. I suppose some of the citizens of San Francisco who know how to appreciate this kind of a man will not let him go on hungry forever after he gets there.

THE EXTRAORDINARY DOCTOR

Janet Sachs

Dr James Barry was discovered to be a woman on her death in 1865. During her lifetime, from her university years onwards, she posed as a man, and although there were comments about her feminine appearance, her true identity was never revealed. Most extraordinary of all, her career was spent as a surgeon in the army—that notorious seat of masculine pride and honour which would brook no intrusion by a mere female. She was retired from the army with the high-ranking post of Inspector-General of Hospitals in 1859.

What strange set of circumstances combined to force a little girl into boy's breeches, and to take up as nerve-racking a career as surgery? A set of surgeon's instruments in the early nineteenth century bore a close resemblance to a carpenter's tool-kit, and a lack of anaesthetics could not have added any enchantment to a surgeon's duty. An explanation has been pieced together but, like all explanations, has more than a few loose ends which remain to tease our curiosity.

One reliable clue to Dr Barry's origins is to be found in a note by her name in Edinburgh University's register 'known by Lord Buchan, nephew of Mr B, painter'. James Barry, alias Mr B, was a well-known eighteenth-century painter—an eccentric man who wore shabby clothes, had a quick temper, and whose reputation as a witty conversationalist gained him access to the literary and artistic circles of the day. In the last years of his life after having quarrelled with all the professors at The Royal Academy, he was living in poverty in a broken-down house and in no position to help his niece who most likely had arrived in London in 1805 with her mother, Mrs Bulkley.

Mr Barry had a friend in the shape of General Francisco de Miranda a Latin-American revolutionary in exile. His life-style was lavish and he owned one of the best libraries in London, where Mr Barry's little niece spent many a happy hour. The painter also had a patron in Lord Buchan, cousin to the King, and when Mr Barry died in 1806, Lord Buchan and the General determined to look after Mrs Bulkley and her two daughters.

A little girl's extraordinary interest in the large Latin tomes in the General's library must have indicated an exceptional intellectual ability. Lord Buchan believed in the equality of women and wished to provide the child with the kind of education that was open to little boys of his class, but not to girls. How was he to solve this problem? The solution, unfortunately, had to be a drastic one.

In the final month of the year 1809, a little girl enrolled at Edinburgh University as 'literary and medical student'. But this was no ordinary little girl: she was dressed in boy's clothing and signed herself James Miranda Steuart Barry. And what is more, if we are to believe the date she gave of her birth as 1799, she was the tender age of ten years old!

One cannot compare the medical training of today which takes some years to complete, with the scanty medical knowledge of the early nineteenth century. And the education system was so different then that boys often entered university at the age of twelve. Nonetheless, at the end of three years, a thesis had to be completed and a viva in Latin undertaken before a degree could be granted. And on top of this gruelling challenge, poor James Barry had to hide her identity for the first time and pose as a boy.

It was not much fun for the little girl. After a year her mother went back to London and James Barry had to carry on the pretence all by herself. She was a small, skinny child with a pale complexion to go with her red hair. Fear of discovery led her to shun the boys' rough and tumble existence; she only had one friend and could not even confide in him. There was only one thing she could do under the circumstances, and that was to study. And so she did—and very well. She passed her examinations with flying colours, despite her youth, and was the first girl to graduate MD (medical doctor) in Britain—if only Edinburgh had known it at the time!

Her next step was to join the army to become Hospital Assistant in the middle of 1813. Because of her youthful appearance, this appointment and her later postings did not go unchallenged—although had the medical authorities been more rigorous in the practice of their physical examinations, they might have discovered the root cause of their instinctive feelings of uncertainty. Either luck or Lord Buchan intervened and smoothed the way for Barry.

Throughout her life Barry was faced with difficulties when confronting authorities—although much of this was due to her own rebellious temperament. Her life was dedicated to her work—it would have been difficult for her to be otherwise. In many of the places she visited, she attempted to institute far-reaching reforms, not all of them, unfortunately, successful. The richest time of her life seems to have been the twelve years she spent in Cape Town, South Africa, arriving at seventeen, young, energetic and full of hope, and leaving, disappointed but not defeated.

Dr Barry was sent to Cape Town as Assistant-Surgeon to the garrison there. The intervening years' experience had given her confidence as well as promotion, and this was quite evident as she strutted around the wintry streets of Cape Town.

Barry was still small in stature and feminine-looking. She attempted to disguise this by inserting three-inch false soles in her boots and padding her shoulders with cotton wool, but observers seemed to be well aware of what she was trying to do.

She also loved to dress up and the male attire of the time gave her much more scope than it would today. For a start, as Assistant Surgeon she was expected to wear a scarlet tunic with a plumed cocked hat, spurs and a long sword by her side. When off duty she wore a coat whose cut and colour was always the latest fashion, with an embroidered satin waistcoat and tight-fitting knee breeches. Her image was important to her and this may have come as much from a natural desire to express herself in her dress as any attempt to exaggerate her 'maleness.'

Wherever she went during the day she was usually accompanied by a black servant, and a poodle called Psyche (of which she had a succession). This poodle would also keep guard in her room at night, curled up happily beside his mistress on her bed. Barry had strictly forbidden anyone to enter her room, and on the rare occasions when she had to share a room, she always requested the other inhabitant to leave while she dressed.

Socially Barry lived a very full life, with balls and outings and all the frivolous, enjoyable things that a privileged life of a nineteenth-century colonialist could offer. Of course, when summer came, there were many delightful outdoor activities from picnics to riding for miles in the foothills of the mountains or along the deserted beaches. This provided welcome relaxation for Barry, although she was constantly watchful of her disguise, and even cultivated a reputation with the ladies. The irony of her situation in this respect was amusing, but with a touch of real sadness, for Barry had no chance of ever forming a warm and open friendship with a member of her own sex.

Her entrée into society was not simply due to her position as an officer to the garrison, but more to her close relationship with the Governor of the Cape, Lord Charles Somerset. He had tremendous faith in the healing powers of this rather strange-looking doctor; these were to be demonstrated in 1818 when his Lordship became very ill. Dr Barry diagnosed his illness as 'typhus with dysentery' and his condition was so serious that there was a schooner ready to sail to England with news of his death. In a letter to the Governor of Malta thirty years later, Barry said that she had differed with the Inspector General over treatment and had managed to take sole possession of the case and thus bring about a recovery.

With the unfailing support of the Governor (she had been appointed Physician to the Governor's Household in 1817 and had accompanied him on an official tour of the Cape early in that year), with her name high up on the social list, with her extravagant dress and flirtatious manner, with a healthy garrison and little work to do, everything was set for Dr James Barry to have a high old time during her sojourn at the Cape. But Barry was not simply out to enjoy herself. What really stirred her was the plight of those who had not the means to help themselves, be they paupers, lepers or slaves. She had already set free one slave, Hermes, by paying his ransom and then arranging

The poodle kept guard in her room at night.

for the boy to join the household of Sir Jahleel Brenton, an anti-slavery supporter like herself. Her real chance to improve conditions came in 1822 when she was appointed Colonial Medical Inspector.

This post had only come into being six months beforehand. Previous to that the practice of medicine had been controlled by a Medical Board of doctors. All the power once shared among several men was to be vested in a single man—or as it turned out to be, woman.

A precarious balance had to be maintained throughout Barry's inspectorship between her own manner of doing things and what the authorities expected and approved. This is perhaps not unusual—a single individual who wishes to change things will always come up against bureaucracy or officialdom which are by nature conservative institutions. Sometimes this kind of restraint is necessary. But in all dealings with people diplomacy is required, and among Barry's many virtues, this was not one. This lack hindered and finally defeated her very courageous attempts to reform genuine grievances. One could excuse her by saying that in her youth she lacked wisdom, but this fault remained with her throughout her life, if tempered a little towards the end.

It must have been very difficult for her. In all areas of her life except work she was, to a greater or lesser extent, pretending to be something she was not—a fun-loving man-about-town—when really she was a serious-minded woman in constant fear of being discovered. But her work gave her the one opportunity to deal with a reality which truly interested her and which she could face without disguise. Therefore, to her more than most, it was particularly important that she achieve what she set out to do. Her overpowering desire to succeed blinded her to other people's points of view and she felt it very deeply when her tactlessness led to misunderstanding and eventually failure.

The first thing she tackled in her new position was the sale of drugs for, she said, 'to my certain knowledge, many persons have been poisoned by patent medicines given improperly.' This naturally impinged on the professional behaviour of both apothecaries and doctors. As Barry commented, 'Apothecaries were practising medicine, physicians were keeping shop and shopkeepers were selling drugs,' and such a state of affairs she was determined to remedy.

Although Barry wished to restrict the sale of medicines to licensed apothecaries, this was impracticable in country districts where there was no one but a doctor available. District physicians, therefore, were allowed to make up prescriptions. However she did manage by law to stop the apothecaries from acting as physicians. There were other reforms she introduced as well—those which showed her perspicacity in medical matters such as introducing a scheme for vaccination against smallpox for the total population of the Cape colony, and those based on her own humaneness. In the latter category fell her direction that doctors were to attend police, prisoners and paupers in their district, free of charge.

Then a Mr Charles Frederick Liesching applied to the Governor for a licence to practise as an apothecary and Dr Barry was asked to examine him. It happened that this young man had no formal qualifications although, to give him his due, he had served a five-year apprenticeship under two qualified men. It happened, too, that this young man was the son of the prison doctor, Dr Liesching, who very conveniently was selling drugs to the prison from the pharmacy he owned—a profitable situation from his point of view, but a situation which could lend itself to all forms of corruption. Therefore, Dr Barry's reply to the request to examine Mr Liesching was that since he had 'not any professional education, consequently no regular documents', it was impossible for her to recommend that he practise.

Automatically an appeal was sent to the Governor. In turn he asked for an interpretation of the law by the Chief Justice, who replied that on a technicality it would be possible that 'Leisching should be allowed to practise.'

Dr Barry would not recognize the Chief Justice's judgement over hers so Lord Somerset referred the case to the most powerful civil dignitary in the colony, Mr Denyssen, the Fiscal. He recommended that Barry examine Mr Liesching but Barry refused. The young man was then examined by a medical board set up by the Governor and duly granted his licence. The result of this was that Barry made two important enemies in the Fiscal and the Colonial Secretary, Sir Richard Plasket.

In the meantime, the little doctor had turned her attention to the leper colony which had the strange name of 'Heaven and Earth' although in reality it was nearer Hell. Situated at Swellendam, a seventy-mile journey from Cape Town, it had not often been officially visited and when Dr Barry made her first journey there in 1822, she found the lepers in a state of neglect. She was shocked into writing 'Nothing could excel the misery of the 120 lepers squalid and wretched beyond description.'

In the large area given over to the colony the lepers only used a small part. Their environment was spacious, the air was clean, the earth fruitful, and yet the lepers themselves had no hope of improving their lives. They were clothed in miserable filthy rags and their figures were so emaciated that Barry immediately enquired as to what they ate. Their diet turned out to be a meagre portion of porridge made from maize. Later she discovered that the three cows intended to supplement this diet had been taken from them. She immediately gave instructions that the amount of food given to the lepers be increased.

The medical attention they were given proved so scanty as to be almost non-existent. On entering the hospital Dr Barry found four lepers in such a wretched condition they could not move. No attempt had been made to comfort them and apart from one on a stretcher, they were lying on the floor nearly naked. The doctor who was supposed to be looking after them lived a good distance away and did not even visit them in the winter. The washing of wounds and dosing of salts was left to the one steward at the hospital, who obviously did not perform the unpleasant tasks very often.

Despite their condition, the lepers were made to work in the grounds. Dr Barry was not against them being occupied, but wished to change the spirit in which their labours were done. On her return to Cape Town she recommended that the fit lepers should be paid for working 'with a little wine, a few shillings or some tobacco or coffee so that they would cheerfully contribute to cultivate the soil to increase their own comforts.'

Dr Barry visited the colony again six months later in March 1823 when she found conditions much improved. However, she very sensibly suggested a change of diet which would include fruit and vegetables and milk. Apparently part of the disease is a display of appetite and Barry pointed this out, emphasizing that in no way should the lepers be deprived of food. She also wanted to engage some more nursing help.

Although the Governor approved her recommendations, there was little money available to put them into effect. In fact Barry herself was not able to visit the colony again until June because of the cost of providing horses. When she did return she was disappointed at the relapse that had taken place and drew up some new rules.

The basis of these rules was sound common sense. She put a tremendous emphasis on cleanliness, which we know is the basis of hygiene, but which was not a principle of good health in the early part of the nineteenth century.

She laid down that 'the bedding and clothing must be frequently changed and they must bathe twice a week at least. . . . The sores must be washed twice daily with tar water and dressed with tar plaster, the old plaster must be thrown away.'

The food was also to be clean and cooked well, salt was to be avoided and all fresh meat and vegetables to be encouraged.

As for the lepers themselves, the very ill were to be separated from the rest. She had noticed that there were some healthy children among the lepers who had not yet caught the disease. Barry suggested they be taken out of the colony altogether and, appealing to the practical officials back in Cape Town, she wryly pointed out that this would 'not only diminish the Government Expense, but also the children themselves would be rendered useful members of society.'

A missionary and his wife, Mr and Mrs Leitner, were in charge of the colony, and before long they were complaining to Lord Somerset of Dr Barry's 'interference' in their work. The fact was that in their zeal for converts they concentrated their energies on the spiritual concerns of the lepers and neglected their physical distress. Perhaps they were even willing to go along with Barry, despite the extra work, until she started demanding that they report to her once a week. Brother Leitner then took umbrage and sent in a stiffly worded letter of resignation. Knowing the difficulty he would have to find a replacement, the Governor refused to accept the resignation. Barry dropped her final request and the Leitners stayed, with a copy of Dr Barry's rules to look forward to fulfilling every day!

Dr Barry's interest in the lepers led to a rumour that she had adopted a little leper boy whom she kept in a beautiful garden surrounded by a high wall, where she used to visit him as often as she could. The story is a touching one but has never been proved.

In the nineteenth century, conditions in prisons, hospitals and lunatic asylums were appalling. It was with the help of humane people like Dr Barry that conditions were improved. She had been very disturbed by the town prison in Cape Town, where prisoners were kept in filthy conditions, were badly fed, and were flogged daily. All her pleas to the Governor to come and see for himself were in vain.

One day Dr Barry took Judge Kekewich, a friend of Lord Somerset, on a visit to the prison. They discovered a prisoner, Jacob Elliott, in a wretched state and marvelled that he was still alive. He was suffering from a broken thigh and could hardly move; his bed was the hard floor of the cell, and he had no medicine. He had little food and the filth in his cell was beyond belief. Judge Kekewich walked out in disgust.

This time Lord Somerset was forced into action. He immediately ordered the sick prisoner into hospital and later set up a sick bay at the prison. A committee was appointed to look into prison conditions.

Treatment of the insane has always given cause for concern and does so still today. In England the public used to go and stare at the antics of the lunatics in Bedlam with a lot less pity than one would feel gazing at a monkey in the zoo. Dr Barry's view of how to treat the insane was surprisingly modern. In a report of 1823 she advocated, as always, cleanliness and the basic comforts of beds and bedding. She had also taken care to examine all fifteen insane inmates of the hospital and found one patient with a head injury, and three *sane* patients among them. Above all she emphasized the need for a compassionate attitude to the mentally ill. The response to her report was a committee set up to investigate conditions in the town hospital.

The officials in Cape Town were becoming more and more irritated by the doctor's criticism. They did not like to appear as though they were not doing their duty and they certainly did not like her direct manner. However, she was protected by both the truth of her charges and the patronage of the Governor . . . until the case of Aaron Smith.

Aaron Smith was a sailor who had been taken into prison in a drunken state. There he was declared to be insane and Dr Barry was asked in to examine him so that he could be removed to the hospital. Barry very rightly declared the prisoner to be 'perfectly sane in mind'.

but added that he had been very badly beaten up by the police, and implied that Mr Denyssen, the Fiscal, was unable to control his own policemen.

The Fiscal, as mentioned before, was the highest civil dignitary in Cape Town. He and Dr Barry's other enemy, the Colonial Secretary, were responsible for her being summoned to Court to explain her report. Barry refused to attend. Summoned again, she attended because she was threatened with imprisonment if she did not, but she refused to give evidence. There then ensued a long wrangle whose eventual outcome was that the Colonial Secretary recommended that the position of Colonial Medical Inspector be abolished and be replaced by the old-style Medical Board.

Dr Barry, who was only doing her duty, was about to lose her job, although truth was on her side. It would be below her dignity, after the way she had been treated, to accept a seat on the new Medical Board. Not only that, her good reputation had been soiled—and this is what worried her most.

She resigned her post, and waited for the report of the Commissioners of Inquiry on the 'case of Dr Barry'. While admitting that her conduct during the affair had been tactless, they said that she had been unfairly treated and that her accusers should have remembered her 'integrity and zeal in bringing about reform of abuses'. They added that her 'professional talents and reputation were universally acknowledged', and thus restored to her what was most precious, her good name.

But Dr Barry's career in the Cape was, in essence, finished. Divested of her power, intensely disliked by all high officials, no longer protected by the Governor (who had recently retired), there was little she could do but carry on her military hospital duties. Despite her fears to the contrary, she was promoted by the army. In November 1827 Dr James Barry was gazetted Staff Surgeon and posted to Mauritius.

At twenty-nine the young doctor left the Cape. In her twelve years there she had done much to help those who were in need. At a very young age she had been appointed to one of the highest posts in the land, and all the while people had puzzled about this strange little doctor with the hands of a woman, but never really believed that the doctor could be female.

Dr Barry displayed tremendous courage while carrying on her battles despite the pressure of keeping up her disguise. She continued her extraordinary masquerade throughout her career and even until the day of her death in 1865.

THE GOLD-BUG

Edgar Allan Poe

Many years ago I became friendly with a Mr William Legrand. He had
once been wealthy but a series of misfortunes caused him to seek a new
home. He chose Sullivan's Island, near Charleston in South Carolina.

It is a strange island, mainly of sand and about three miles long and
never more than a quarter of a mile wide. Legrand built himself a small
hut at the eastern end, or more remote part, of this island. He was living
there when I first made his acquaintance. We soon became good friends.
He was well educated and had many books. His chief amusements were
shooting or fishing and collecting shells and bettles. He was usually
accompanied by an old Negro called Jupiter who, although a freed
slave, still felt it his duty to look after his young 'Massa Will', as he
called Legrand.

I had not visited my friend for some time and decided to call on him
about the middle of October. On reaching the hut I rapped on the
door. There was no answer so I let myself in and waited for him to
return. I sat by the fire, a most unusual sight in October on Sullivan's
Island. He and Jupiter arrived soon after dark and made me very welcome. Whilst Jupiter bustled about preparing supper, Legrand sat

opposite me. He seemed full of enthusiasm. He had found a new type of scarabaeus, or beetle, which he felt was entirely new.

I asked to see it but he told me he had lent it to a naval lieutenant, another enthusiast, for the night, and would send Jupiter down for it at sunrise. 'It is the loveliest thing in creation!' he said.

'What—sunrise?'

'Nonsense, no! The bug. It is of a brilliant gold colour—about the size of a large hickory-nut, with two jet-black spots at the top of its back and another, somewhat larger, at the base. The antennae are——'

'Dere ain't *no* tin in him, Massa Will,' Jupiter interrupted, in his strange manner of speaking. 'De bug is a gold-bug, every bit of him, inside and all, 'cept for his wing. Never felt half so heavy a bug in my life.'

Legrand suggested he made a drawing of the bug to give me some idea of its shape. He looked around for some paper, then said finally, 'Never mind, this will answer' and drew from his pocket a scrap of what I took to be very dirty foolscap. As he drew he told me of the brilliant and metallic lustre of the beetle's scales.

When he had done he handed the drawing to me, without rising. As I took it from him there came a loud growl and a scratching at the door. Jupiter opened it and a large Newfoundland dog bounded in and began to cover me with caresses. He knew me well for I had always made a fuss of him on previous visits. When his gambols were over I had my first chance to look at the drawing. I was rather puzzled.

'Well,' I said, after studying it for some minutes, 'this is a very strange scarabaeus. I've never seen anything like it before. It looks rather like a skull, or a death's head, than anything else.'

'A death's head!' he echoed. 'Oh—yes—well, it has something of that appearance on paper, no doubt. The two upper black spots look like eyes, eh? and the longer one at the bottom like a mouth—and then the shape of the whole is oval.'

We discussed it further and then I asked, 'But where are the antennae you spoke of?'

'The antennae?' queried Legrand, who seemed to be losing his temper. 'I am sure you must see them. I made them as distinct as they are in the original insect, and I presume that is sufficient.'

'Well, well,' I said, 'perhaps you have. Still, I don't see them,' and I handed back the paper. I was puzzled at the turn of affairs. His sudden ill-humour was odd, and as for the drawing of the beetle, there were positively no antennae to be seen. And the whole did bear a very close resemblance to a death's head.

He took the paper from me, very peevishly, and was about to crumple it, apparently to throw it in the fire, when a glance at it seemed suddenly to rivet his attention. The colour of his face appeared to change and he stared at the drawing very closely. Then he rose, seated himself on a sea-chest in the farthest corner of the room, and continued his close examination. Finally he took out a wallet, placed the paper carefully in it, then put both in a writing desk, which he locked.

He had lost his former ill-humour. Now he seemed absorbed in thought. This grew during the evening until, finally, I thought it best to leave. He did not press me to remain but, as I left, shook my hand with even more than his usual cordiality.

About a month later I received a visit at my home in Charleston from his man, Jupiter. He looked very upset and I feared that something had happened to my friend.

'Well, Jup,' I said. 'What is the matter now? How is your master?'

'Why, to speak de troof, him not so well as might be.'

'Not well! I am truly sorry to hear it. What does he complain of?'

'Dat's it! He never complains of nothin'—but him sick for all that.'

'Jupiter! Why didn't you say so at once?' and I listened while the good Negro began to tell me of his fears for his master. He then went on, 'Todder day he gib me de slip 'fore sun up and was gone for de whole of de blessed day.'

'Has anything unpleasant happened since I saw you?' I asked.

'No massa. There ain't been nothin' onpleasant *since* den—'twas *before* den I'm feared. 'Twas the berry day you was dare.'

'The what?'

'De bug. I'm berry certain dat Massa Will bin bit somewhere 'bout de head by dat gold-bug.'

'You think then that your master was really bitten by the beetle, and that the bite made him sick?'

'I don't think—I knows it. What makes him dream about gold so much if 'tain't because he was bit by the gold-bug?'

'How do you know he dreams about gold?'

''Cause he talks about it in his sleep—dat's how I knows.'

He then handed me a letter from Legrand. Although most of it chided me for not visiting the island sooner, it ended on an air of urgency. '*Do* come,' it said. 'I wish to see you *tonight*, on business of importance. I assure you that it is of the *highest* importance.'

How could I refuse such a summons? I went down to the wharf with Jupiter and saw, in the bottom of the boat, a new scythe and three spades. In answer to my question Jupiter replied, 'Massa Will insisted on my buying 'em for him in de town,' and that was all he knew.

When we reached the hut, Legrand was waiting for us. His face was pale and his deep-set eyes glared with unnatural lustre. We talked for a time and then he handed me the beetle, now in a glass case. It was an entirely new species. There were two round black spots near one extremity of the back, and a long one near the other. The scales were exceedingly hard and glossy, with all the appearance of burnished gold. Its weight was remarkable and I could well understand Jupiter's idea that it was of solid gold.

Legrand looked at it. 'That bug is to make my fortune, to reinstate me in my family possessions. I have only to use it properly, and I shall arrive at the gold of which it is the index.'

He assured me that he was not ill, adding, 'I am as well as I can expect to be under the excitement which I suffer. If you really wish me well, you will relieve this excitement.'

'And how is this to be done?'

'Very easily. Jupiter and myself are going on an expedition into the hills, on the mainland, and we shall need the aid of some person in whom we can confide. You are the only one we can trust. Whether we succeed or fail, the excitement which you now perceive in me will be equally allayed.'

We argued about this for a while and then, with a heavy heart, I agreed. We started about four o'clock—Legrand, Jupiter, the dog, and myself. Jupiter had with him the scythe and spades. I had charge of a couple of lanterns while Legrand contented himself with the scarabaeus, which he carried attached to the end of a bit of whipcord, and twirling it to and fro, with the air of a conjuror, as he went.

We crossed the creek at the head of the island by means of a skiff and, after about two hours, entered a region more infinitely dreary than any

yet seen. It was a sort of tableland, near the summit of an almost inaccessible hill, densely wooded and interspersed with huge crags. Deep
ravines, in various directions, gave an air of still sterner solemnity to the
scene. We finally reached the foot of an enormously tall tulip-tree,
which stood with some eight or ten oaks, on the level, and far surpassed
them all, and all other trees which I had then ever seen, in the beauty of
its foliage and form, in the wide spread of its branches, and in the
general majesty of its appearance.

When we reached this tree, Legrand turned to Jupiter and asked him
if he thought he could climb it.

'Yes, massa. Jup climb any tree he ebber see in his life.'

He was ready to prove this, but hesitated when Legrand told him to
take the gold-bug with him. Eventually he agreed, however, and began
the ascent of the huge tree. When he was about some sixty or seventy
feet from the ground Legrand shouted up to him to count the limbs
below him. When the Negro shouted down the number he ordered
him to go one limb higher, to the seventh. When this was done, Legrand
shouted out again, 'Now Jup, I want you to work your way out on that
limb as far as you can. If you see anything strange, let me know.'

Going very carefully, Jupiter edged his way along the seemingly
rotten branch and then we heard his terrified shriek.

'Lor-gol-a-marcy! What is dis here pon de tree?'

'Well!' cried Legrand, highly delighted, 'what is it?'

'Why, 'tain't noffin but a skull. Somebody bin left him head up de
tree, and de crows done gobble every bit of de meat off.'

'A skull, you say. Very well. How is it fastened to the limb?'

'Why dis berry curious sarcumstance. Dere's a great big nail in de
skull what fastens it on to de tree.'

Even more delighted now, Legrand shouted up to Jupiter to find the
left eye of the skull. This caused some argument for the Negro was
left-handed, but the problem, finally, seemed resolved. Legrand
shouted up, 'Let the beetle drop through it as far as the string will reach
—but be careful not to let go of the string.'

He did as he was told and the scarabaeus, glistening like a globe of
burnished gold in the last rays of the setting sun, hung clear of the
branches and, if allowed to fall, would have dropped at our feet. Legrand took the scythe and cleared a circular space some ten or twelve

The beetle hung clear of the branches, glistening like a globe of burnished gold in the last rays of the setting sun.

feet in diameter, just beneath the hanging insect. He then ordered Jupiter to let go the string and come down from the tree.

With great exactness Legrand drove a peg into the ground at the precise spot where the beetle had fallen and then, with Jupiter having used the scythe to clear away the brambles, set all three of us digging. We dug steadily for two hours, reaching a depth of five feet. Yet there was no sign of any treasure. We continued digging. Still nothing. Then suddenly Legrand strode up to Jupiter and hissed, 'You scoundrel. You infernal black villain. Speak, I tell you! Answer me this instant! Which—which is your left eye?'

The terrified Jupiter replied, hastily, 'Ain't dis here my lef' eye for sartain?'—and placed his hand on his *right* eye!

'I thought so. I knew it. Hurrah!' cried Legrand and led the way back to the base of the tree. He asked Jupiter, 'Was it this eye or that through which you dropped the beetle?' and he touched each of the other's eyes in turn.

''Twas this eye, massa—de lef' eye—just as you tell me'; and here it was his right eye that he indicated.

'That will do. We must try again.'

Legrand removed the peg which marked the spot where the beetle fell to a spot about three inches to the west of its former position. He took out a tape measure, which he had used before, and marked out a fresh spot several yards from where we had been digging.

Once again we all set to with the spades. After we had been at work for perhaps an hour and a half, we were interrupted by the violent howlings of the dog. He leapt into the hole, tore up the mould frantically with his claws and in a few seconds had uncovered a mass of human bones, forming two complete skeletons, intermingled with several buttons of metal, and what appeared to be the dust of decayed woollens. One or two strokes of a spade upturned the blade of a large Spanish knife and, as we dug farther, three or four loose pieces of gold and silver coin came to light. Legrand urged us to continue digging and the words were hardly uttered when I stumbled and fell forward, having caught the toe of my boot in a large ring of iron that lay half buried.

In ten minutes we had unearthed an oblong chest of wood, some three and a half feet long, three feet broad and two and a half feet deep. At first we found it difficult to open until we saw that the fastenings of the lid were two sliding bolts. These we drew back—trembling and panting with anxiety. In an instant, a treasure of incalculable value lay gleaming before us. As the rays of the lantern fell within the pit, there flashed upward a glow and a glare from a confused heap of gold and of jewels that absolutely dazzled our eyes.

A later examination showed that, within the chest, there was not a particle of silver. All was gold of antique date and of great variety. There were diamonds—some of them exceedingly large and fine—a hundred and ten in all, and not one of them small; eighteen rubies of remarkable brilliancy; three hundred and ten emeralds, all very beautiful; and twenty-one sapphires, with an opal. Besides all this there was a vast quantity of solid gold ornaments, crucifixes, censers, sword-handles and nearly two hundred superb gold watches.

When the intense excitement of the time had, in some measure, subsided, Legrand entered into full details of all the circumstances connected with it.

'You remember,' he said, 'the night when I handed you the rough sketch I had made of the scarabaeus. You recollect that I became quite vexed at you for insisting that my drawing resembled a death's head. I was about to crumple it up and throw it angrily into the fire.'

'The scrap of paper, you mean,' I said.

'No. It had much the appearance of paper, but when I came to draw on it I discovered it at once to be a piece of very thin parchment. My glance fell upon the sketch at which you had been looking when I perceived the figure of a death's head just where, it seemed to me, I had made the drawing of a beetle. I took a candle and, seating myself at the other end of the room, proceeded to scrutinize the parchment more closely. On turning it over I saw my own sketch on the reverse, just as I had made it. Yet I remembered, positively, that there had been *no* drawing on the parchment when I made my own sketch.

'I then thought back about the finding of the beetle. When I first picked it up it gave me a sharp bite which caused me to let it drop. Jupiter, with his usual caution, looked about for a leaf, or something of that nature, by which to take hold of it. It was then we saw the scrap of parchment, which I then supposed to be paper. It was lying half buried in the sand, a corner sticking up. Nearby was the remnants of the hull of what appeared to have been a ship's longboat. The wreck seemed to have been there for a very great while.

'Later, I established a kind of connection. There was a boat lying on a sea-coast, and not far from the boat was a parchment—*not paper*—with a skull depicted on it. The skull, or death's head, is the well-known emblem of the pirate.'

'But,' I interposed, 'you say that the skull was not on the parchment when you made the drawing of the beetle.'

'Ah, hereupon turns the whole mystery, although the secret, at this point, I had comparatively little difficulty in solving. You may remember you were seated near the fire as I handed you the parchment. Then Wolf, the Newfoundland entered, and leaped on your shoulders. With your left hand you carressed him and kept him off, while your right, holding the parchment, was in close proximity to the fire. It was the *heat* which had been the agent in bringing to light, on the parchment, the skull which I saw designed on it.

'I saw more. As I examined the parchment even more closely I saw, at the corner, the figure of a goat or kid. But why? Pirates have nothing to do with goats; that is for farmers. Then I realized. It was of the pirate chief, *Captain* Kidd. It was his stamp or seal.

'When you had gone, I held the vellum to the fire, but with no success. I then thought it possible that the coating of dirt might have something to do with the failure. So I carefully rinsed the parchment by pouring warm water over it, placed it in a tin pan, with the skull downward, and put the pan on a furnace of lighted charcoal. In a few minutes, the pan having become thoroughly heated, I removed the slips. To my inexpressible joy, I found it spotted in several places, with what appeared to be figures arranged in lines. Again I placed it in the pan and suffered it to remain another minute. On taking it off, the whole was just as you see it now.'

Here Legrand, having reheated the parchment, submitted it to my inspection. A whole collection of characters were rudely traced, in a red tint, between the death's head and the goat. The whole was obviously a cipher, but one far beyond my powers. The list of symbols read:

'53‡‡†305))6*;4826)4‡.)4‡) ;806*;48†8¶60))85;1‡(;:‡*8†83(88)5*†;
46(;88*96*?;8)*‡(;485);5*†2:*‡(;4956*2(5*—4)8¶8*;4069285) ;)6†8)
4‡‡;1(‡9;48081 ;8:8‡1 ;48†85 ;4)485†528806*81(‡9;48;(88;4(‡?34;48)4
‡;161 ;:188 ;‡?'

Consequently, Legrand began to carefully explain how he had solved the riddle. He first counted up the various characters, to see how many times each appeared.

'Now in English,' he said, 'the letter which most frequently occurs is *e*. As the predominant character in the code is 8, we will commence by assuming it to be the *e* of the natural alphabet. To verify the supposition, let us observe if the 8 be seen often in couples—for *e* is doubled with great frequency in English, in such words as "meet", "fleet", "speed", "seen", "been", "agree", etc. In the present instance we see it doubled no less than five times, although the cryptograph is brief.

'Let us assume eight, then, as *e*. Now, of all the *words* in the language, "the" is the most usual. On inspection we find no less than *seven* such arrangements, the characters being ;48. We may, therefore, assume that ; represents *t*, 4 represents *h*, and 8 represents *e*—the last now being well confirmed. Thus a great step has been taken.'

And so, step by step, Legrand explained how he had finally solved what he considered to be 'the very simplest series of cryptographs'. The final message said: '*A good glass in the bishop's hostel in the devil's seat forty-one degrees and thirteen minutes northeast and by north main branch seventh limb east side shoot from the left eye of the death's-head a bee-line from the tree through the shot fifty feet out.*'

Legrand then explained how he divided this sentence so that it at least made some sense. But only to him, for I said, 'Even this division leaves me still in the dark.'

'It left me also in the dark for a few days, during which I made diligent inquiry in the neighbourhood of Sullivan's Island for any building which went by the name of the "Bishop's Hotel"—for, of course, I dropped the obsolete word, "hostel". My search led me to the plantation, where I asked among the older Negroes of the place. At length, one of the most aged of the women said that she had heard of such a place as *Beesop's Castle*. But it was neither a castle nor a tavern, but a high rock. She showed me the place and I climbed up the side of the "castle". Then my eyes fell upon a narrow ledge in the eastern face of the rock. I had no doubt that here was the "devil's seat" alluded to in the message, and now I seemed to grasp the full secret of the riddle.

'The "good glass", I knew, referred to a telescope and the following phrases were intended for the levelling of the glass. After a great deal of trial and error I finally fixed my newly-bought telescope on a large tree that over-topped its fellows in the distance. It had a circular rift or opening in its foliage. In the centre of this rift I perceived a white spot. Adjusting the focus of the telescope I now made it out to be a human skull.

He smiled. 'Most of the rest you know,' he said.

'I suppose you missed the spot in the first attempt at digging, through Jupiter's stupidity in letting the bug fall through the right instead of through the left eye of the skull?'

'Precisely. This mistake made a difference of about two and a half inches in the "shot"—that is to say, in the position of the peg nearest the tree. Had the treasure been *beneath* the "shot", the error would have been of little moment; but the "shot", together with the nearest point of the tree, were merely two points for the establishment of a line of direction. Of course the error, however trivial in the beginning, increased as we proceeded with the line, and by the time we had gone fifty feet, threw us quite off the scent. But for my deep-seated impression that the treasure was here somewhere actually buried, we might have had all our labour in vain.'

'Now there is only one point which puzzles me,' I said. 'What are we to make of the skeletons found in the hole?'

'That is a question I am no more able to answer than yourself. There seems, however, only one plausible way of accounting for them. It is clear that Kidd—if Kidd indeed secreted this treasure, which I doubt not—it is clear that he must have had assistance in the labour. But his labour concluded, he may have thought it expedient to remove all participants in his secret. Perhaps a couple of blows with a mattock were sufficient, while his assistants were busy in the pit.

'Perhaps it required a dozen—who shall tell?'

LAURA

Saki

'You aren't really dying, are you?' asked Amanda.

'I have the doctor's permission to live till Tuesday,' said Laura.

'But today is Saturday; this is serious!' gasped Amanda.

'I don't know about it being serious; it is certainly Saturday,' said Laura.

'Death is always serious,' said Amanda.

'I never said I was going to die. I am presumably going to leave off being, Laura, but I shall go on being something. An animal of some kind, I suppose. You see, when one hasn't been very good in the life one has just lived, one reincarnates in some lower organism. And I haven't been very good, when one comes to think of it. I've been cruel and mean and vindictive and all that sort of thing when circumstances seemed to warrant it.'

'Circumstances never warrant that sort of thing,' said Amanda.

'If you don't mind my saying so,' observed Laura, 'Egbert is a circumstance that would warrant any amount of that sort of thing. You're married to him—that's different; you've sworn to love, honour and endure him: I haven't.'

'I don't see what's wrong with Egbert,' protested Amanda.

'Oh, I dare say the wrongness has been on my part,' admitted Laura dispassionately; 'he has merely been the extenuating circumstance. He made a thin, peevish kind of fuss for instance, when I took the collie puppies from the farm out for a run the other day.'

They chased his young broods of speckled Sussex and drove two sitting hens off their nest, besides running all over the flower beds. You know how devoted he is to his poultry and garden.'

'Anyway, he needn't have gone on about it for the entire evening and then have said, "Let's say no more about it", just when I was beginning to enjoy the discussion. That's where one of my petty vindictive revenges came in,' added Laura with an unrepentant chuckle; 'I turned the entire family of speckled Sussex into his seedling shed the day after the puppy episode.'

'How could you?' exclaimed Amanda.

'It came quite easy,' said Laura; 'two of the hens pretended to be laying at the same time, but I was firm.'

'And we thought it was an accident!'

'You see,' resumed Laura, 'I really *have* some grounds for supposing that my next incarnation will be in a lower organism. I shall be an animal of some kind. On the other hand, I haven't been a bad sort in my way, so I think I may count on being a nice animal, something elegant and lively, with a love of fun. An otter, perhaps.'

'I can't imagine you as an otter,' said Amanda.

'Well, I don't suppose you can imagine me as an angel, if it comes to that,' said Laura.

Amanda was silent. She couldn't.

'Personally I think an otter life would be rather enjoyable,' continued Laura; 'salmon to eat all year round, and the satisfaction of being able to fetch the trout in their own homes without having to wait for hours till they condescend to rise to the fly you've been dangling before them; and an elegant svelte figure—'

'Think of the otter hounds,' interposed Amanda; 'how dreadful to be hunted and harried and finally worried to death!'

'Rather fun with half the neighbourhood looking on, and anyhow not worse than this Saturday-to-Tuesday business of dying by inches; and then I should go on into something else. If I had been a moderately good otter I suppose I should get back into human shape of some sort; probably something primitive—a little brown, unclothed Nubian boy, I should think.'

'I wish you would be serious,' sighed Amanda; 'you really ought to be if you're only going to live till Tuesday.'

As a matter of fact Laura died on Monday.

'So dreadfully upsetting,' Amanda complained to her uncle-in-law, Sir Lulworth Quayne. 'I've asked quite a lot of people down for golf and fishing, and the rhododendrons are just looking their best.'

'Laura always was inconsiderate,' said Sir Lulworth; 'she was born during Goodwood week, with an Ambassador staying in the house who hated babies.'

'She had the maddest kind of ideas,' said Amanda; 'do you know if there was any insanity in her family?'

'Insanity? No, I never heard of any. Her father lives in West Kensington, but I believe he's sane on all other subjects.'

'She had an idea that she was going to be reincarnated as an otter,' said Amanda.

'One meets with those ideas of reincarnation so frequently, even in the West,' said Sir Lulworth, 'that one can hardly set them down as being mad. And Laura was such an unaccountable person in this life that I should not like to lay down definite rules as to what she might be doing in an after state.'

'You think she really might have passed into some animal form?' asked Amanda. She was one of those who shape their opinions rather readily from the standpoint of those around them.

Just then Egbert entered the breakfast-room, wearing an air of bereavement that Laura's demise would have been insufficient, in itself, to account for.

'Four of my speckled Sussex have been killed,' he exclaimed; 'the very four that were to go to the show on Friday. One of them was dragged away and eaten right in the middle of that new carnation bed that I've been to such trouble and expense over. My best flower bed and my best fowls singled out for destruction; it almost seems as if the brute that did the deed had special knowledge how to be as devastating as possible in a short space of time.'

'Was it a fox, do you think?' asked Amanda.

'Sounds more like a polecat,' said Sir Lulwroth.

'No,' said Egbert, 'there were marks of webbed feet all over the place, and we followed the tracks down to the stream at the bottom of the garden; evidently an otter.'

Amanda looked quickly and furtively across at Sir Lulworth.

Egbert was too agitated to eat any breakfast, and went out to superintend the strengthening of the poultry yard defences.

'I think she might at least have waited till the funeral was over,' said Amanda in a scandalized voice.

'It's her own funeral, you know,' said Sir Lulworth; 'it's a nice point in etiquette how far one ought to show respect to one's own mortal remains.'

Disregard for mortuary convention was carried to further lengths next day; during the absence of the family at the funeral ceremony the remaining survivors of the speckled Sussex were massacred. The marauder's line of retreat seemed to have embraced most of the flower beds on the lawn, but the strawberry beds in the lower garden had also suffered.

'I shall get the otter hounds to come here at the earliest possible moment,' said Egbert savagely.

'On no account! You can't dream of such a thing!' exclaimed Amanda. 'I mean, it wouldn't do, so soon after a funeral in the house.'

'It's a case of necessity,' said Egbert; 'once an otter takes to that sort of thing it won't stop.' 'Perhaps it will go elsewhere now that there are no more fowls left,' suggested Amanda.

'One would think you wanted to shield the beast,' said Egbert.

'There's been so little water in the stream lately,' objected Amanda; 'it seems hardly sporting to hunt an animal when it has so little chance of taking refuge anywhere.'

'Good gracious!' fumed Egbert, 'I'm not thinking about sport. I want to have the animal killed as soon as possible.'

Even Amanda's opposition weakened when, during church time on the following Sunday, the otter made its way into the house, raided half a salmon from the larder and worried it into scaly fragments on the Persian rug in Egbert's studio.

'We shall have it hiding under our beds and biting pieces out of our feet before long,' said Egbert, and from what Amanda knew of this particular otter she felt that the possibility was not a remote one.

On the evening preceeding the day fixed for the hunt Amanda

'I shall go on being something.'

spent a solitary hour walking by the banks of the stream, making what she imagined to be hound noises. It was charitably supposed by those who overheard her performance, that she was practising for farmyard imitations at the forthcoming village entertainment.

It was her friend and neighbour, Aurora Burret, who brought her news of the day's sport.

'Pity you weren't out; we had a quite good day. We found it at once, in the pool just below your garden.'

'Did you—kill?' asked Amanda.

'Rather. A fine she-otter. Your husband got rather badly bitten in trying to "tail it". Poor beast, I felt quite sorry for it, it had such a human look in its eyes when it was killed. You'll call me silly, but do you know who the look reminded me of? My dear woman, what is the matter?'

When Amanda had recovered to a certain extent from her attack of nervous prostration Egbert took her to the Nile Valley to recuperate. Change of scene speedily brought about the desired recovery of health and mental balance. The escapades of an adventurous otter in search of a variation of diet were viewed in their proper light. Amanda's normally placid temperament reasserted itself. Even a hurricane of shouted curses, coming from her husband's dressing-room, in her husband voice, but hardly in his usual vocabulary, failed to disturb her serenity as she made a leisurely toilet one evening in a Cairo hotel.

'What is the matter? What has happened?' she asked in amused curiosity.

'The little beast has thrown all my clean shirts into the bath! Wait till I catch you, you little—'

'What little beast?' asked Amanda, suppressing a desire to laugh; Egbert's language was so hoplessly inadequate to express his outraged feelings.

'A little beast of a naked brown Nubian boy,' spluttered Egbert.

And now Amanda is seriously ill.

THE ENCHANTED HORSE

Anonymous

The Nooroze, or the new day, which is the first of the year and spring, is observed as a solemn festival throughout all Persia.

On one of these festival days, just as the Sultan of Shiraz was concluding his public audience, which had been conducted with unusual splendour, a Hindu appeared at the foot of the throne, with an artificial horse richly adorned, and so spiritedly modelled, that at first sight he was taken for a living animal.

The Hindu prostrated himself before the throne and, pointing to the horse, said to the sultan, 'This horse is a great wonder: whenever I mount him, be it where it may, if I wish to transport myself through the air to the most distant part of the world, I can do it in a very short time. This is a wonder which nobody ever heard speak of, and which I offer to show your majesty if you command me.'

The Emperor of Persia, who was fond of everything that was curious, and who, notwithstanding the many prodigies of art he had seen, had never beheld or heard of anything that came up to this, told the Hindu that he was ready to see him perform what he had promised.

The Hindu instantly put his foot into the stirrup, mounted his horse with admirable agility, and when he had fixed himself in the saddle, asked the emperor whither he pleased to command him.

'Do you see that mountain?' said the emperor, pointing to it. 'Ride your horse there, and bring me a branch of a palm tree that grows at the bottom of the hill.'

The Emperor of Persia had no sooner declared his will than the Hindu turned a peg, which was in the hollow of the horse's neck, just by the pommel of the saddle; and in an instant the horse rose off the ground and carried his rider into the air with the rapidity of lightning to a great height, to the admiration of the emperor and all the spectators. Within less than a quarter of an hour they saw him returning with the palm branch in his hand; but before he descended, he took two or three turns in the air over the spot, amid the acclamations of all the people, then alighted on the spot whence he had set off. He dismounted, and going up to the throne, prostrated himself, and laid the branch of the palm tree at the feet of the emperor.

The emperor, who had viewed with no less admiration than astonishment this unheard-of sight which the Hindu had exhibited, conceived a great desire to have the horse, and said to the Hindu, 'I will purchase him of you, if he is to be sold.'

'Sire,' replied the Hindu, 'there is only one condition on which I can part with my horse, and that is the gift of the hand of the princess your daughter as my wife; this is the only bargain I can make.'

The courtiers about the Emperor of Persia could not forbear laughing aloud at this extravagant proposal of the Hindu; but the Prince Feroze-shah, the eldest son of the emperor and presumptive heir to the crown, could not hear it without indignation. 'Sire,' he said, 'I hope you will not hesitate to refuse so insolent a demand, or allow this insignificant juggler to flatter himself for a moment with the idea of being allied to one of the most powerful monarchs in the world. I beg of you to consider what you owe to yourself, to your own blood, and the high rank of your ancestors.'

'Son,' replied the Emperor of Persia, 'I will not grant him what he asked—and perhaps he does not seriously make the proposal; and, putting my daughter the princess out of the question, I may make another agreement with him. But before I bargain with him, I should be glad that you would examine the horse, try him yourself, and give me your opinion.' On hearing this, the Hindu expressed much joy, and ran before the prince, to help him to mount, and show him how to guide and manage the horse.

The prince mounted without the Hindu's assisting him; and, as soon as he had got his feet in the stirrups, without staying for the artist's advice, he turned the peg he had seen him use, when instantly the horse darted into the air, quick as an arrow shot out of a bow by the most adroit archer; and in a few moments neither horse nor prince were to be seen. The Hindu, alarmed at what had happened, prostrated himself before the throne. The sultan, in a passion, asked why he did not call him the moment he ascended.

'Sire,' answered the Hindu, 'your majesty saw as well as I with what rapidity the horse flew away. The surprise I was then and still am in deprived me of the use of my speech; but if I could have spoken, he was gone too far to hear me. If he had heard me, he knew not the secret to bring him back, which, through his impatience, he would not stay to learn. But, sire,' added he, 'there is room to hope that the prince, when he finds himself at a loss, will perceive another peg, and as soon as he turns that the horse will cease to rise, and descend to the ground, when he may turn him to what place he pleases by guiding him with the bridle.'

Notwithstanding all these arguments of the Hindu, which carried great appearance of probability, the Emperor of Persia was much alarmed at the evident danger of his son. 'I suppose,' replied he, 'it is very uncertain whether my son may perceive the other peg, and make a right use of it. May not the horse, instead of lighting on the ground, fall upon some rock, or tumble into the sea with him?'

'Sire,' replied the Hindu, 'I can deliver you from this apprehension, by assuring you that the horse crosses seas without ever falling into them, and always carries his rider wherever he may wish to go. And your majesty may assure yourself that if the prince does but find out the other peg I mentioned, the horse will carry him where he pleases. It is not to be supposed that he will stop anywhere but where he can find assistance, and make himself known.'

'Your head shall answer for my son's life, if he does not return safe, or I should hear that he is alive.' He then ordered his officers to secure the Hindu, and keep him close prisoner; after which he retired to his palace, dismayed that the festival of Noorozé should have proved so inauspicious.

In the meantime the prince was carried through the air with prodigious velocity. In less than an hour's time he ascended so high that he could not distinguish anything on the earth. It was then he began to think of returning, and conceived he might do this by turning the same peg the contrary way, and pulling the bridle at the same time. But when he found that the horse still continued to ascend, his alarm was great. He turned the peg several times in different ways, but all in vain. It was then he saw his fault, and apprehended the great danger he was in, from not having learnt the necessary precautions to guide the horse before he mounted. He examined the horse's head and neck with attention, and perceived behind the right ear another peg, smaller than the other. He turned that peg and presently realized that he descended in the same oblique manner as he had mounted, but not so swiftly.

Night had overshadowed that part of the earth over which the prince was when he discovered and turned the small peg; and as the horse descended, he by degrees lost sight of the sun, till it grew quite dark; insomuch that, instead of choosing what place he would go to, he was forced to let the bridle lie upon the horse's neck, and wait patiently till he alighted, though not without the dread lest it should be in the desert, a river or the sea.

At last the horse stopped upon some solid substance about midnight, and the prince dismounted very faint and hungry, having eaten nothing since the morning, when he came out of the palace with his father to assist at the festival. He found himself to be on the terrace of a magnificent palace, surrounded with a balustrade of white marble, breast high; and groping about reached a staircase, which led down into an apartment, the door of which was half open.

The prince stopped at the door, and listening, heard no other noise than the breathing of some people who were fast asleep. He advanced a little into the room, and by the light of a lamp saw that those persons were black mutes, with naked sabres laid by them: which was enough to inform him that this was the guard-chamber of some sultan or princess.

Prince Feroze-shah advanced on tiptoe, without waking the attendants. He drew aside the curtain, went in, and saw a magnificent chamber containing many beds, one alone being on a raised dais, and the others on the floor. The princess slept in the first and her women in the others. He crept softly towards the dais without waking either the princess or her women, and beheld a beauty so extraordinary that he was charmed at the first sight. He fell on his knees, and twitching gently the princess's sleeve, kneeling beside her, pulled it towards him. The princess opened her eyes, and seeing a handsome young man, was in great surprise, yet showed no sign of fear.

The prince availed himself of this favourable moment, bowed his head to the ground, and rising, said, 'Beautiful princess, by the most extraordinary and wonderful adventure, you see at your feet a suppliant prince, son of the Emperor of Persia; pray afford him your assistance and protection.'

The personage to whom Prince Feroze-shah so happily addressed himself was the Princess of Bengal, eldest daughter of the rajah of that kingdom, who had built this palace at a small distance from his capital, for the sake of the country air. She thus replied: 'Prince, you are not in a barbarous country—take courage; hospitality, humanity, and politeness are to be met with in the Kingdom of Bengal, as well as in that of Persia. I grant you the protection you ask—you may depend on what I say.'

The Prince of Persia would have thanked the princess, but she would not give him leave to speak. 'Notwithstanding I desire,' said she, 'to know by what miracle you have come hither from the capital of Persia in so short a time, and by what enchantment you have evaded the vigilance of my guards, yet as you must want some refreshment, I will postpone my curiosity, and give orders to my attendants to show you an apartment, that you may rest yourself after your fatigue, and be better able to answer my inquiries.'

The princess's attendants were much surprised to see the prince in the princess's chamber, but they at once prepared to obey her commands. They each took a wax candle, of which there were great numbers lighted up in the room; and after the prince had respectfully taken leave, went before and conducted him into a handsome hall; where, while some were preparing the bed, others went into the kitchen and prepared a supper; and when he had eaten as much as he chose, they removed the trays, and left him to taste the sweets of repose.

The next day the princess prepared to give the prince another interview, and in expectation of seeing him, she took more pains in dressing and adjusting herself at the glass than she had ever done before. She tried her women's patience, and made them do and undo the same thing several times. She adorned her head, neck, arms, and waist, with the finest and largest diamonds she possessed. The habit she put on was one of the richest stuffs of the Indies, of a most beautiful colour, and made only for kings, princes, and princesses. After she had consulted her glass, and asked her women, one after another, if anything was wanting to her attire, she sent to tell the Prince of Persia that she would make him a visit.

The Prince of Persia, who by the night's rest had recovered the fatigue he had undergone the day before, had just dressed himself when he received notice of the intention of the princess, and expressed himself to be fully sensible of the honour conferred on him. As soon as the princess understood that the Prince of Persia waited for her, she immediately went to pay him a visit.

After mutual compliments, the prince related to her the wonders of the magic horse, of his journey through the air, and of the means by which he had found an entrance into her chamber; and then, having thanked her for her kind reception, expressed a wish to return and relieve the anxiety of the sultan his father. When the prince had finished, the princess replied, 'I cannot approve, Prince, of your going so soon; grant me at least the favour I ask of a little longer acquaintance; and since I have had the happiness to have you alight in the Kingdom of Bengal, I desire you will stay long enough to enable you to give a better account of what you may see here at the court of Persia.'

The Prince of Persia could not well refuse the princess this favour, after the kindness she had shown him, and therefore politely complied with her request; and the princess's thoughts were directed to render his stay agreeable by all the amusements she could devise.

Nothing went forward for several days but concerts of music, accompanied with magnificent feasts and collations in the gardens, or hunting parties in the vicinity of the palace, which abounded with all sorts of game, stags, hinds, and fallow deer, and other beasts peculiar to the Kingdom of Bengal, which the princess could pursue without danger. After the chase, the prince and princess met in some beautiful spot, where a carpet was spread and cushions laid for their accommodation. There resting themselves, they conversed on various subjects.

Two whole months the Prince of Persia abandoned himself entirely to the will of the Princess of Bengal, yielding to all the amusements she contrived for him; for she neglected nothing to divert him, as if she thought he had nothing else to do but to pass his whole life with her in this manner. But he now declared seriously he could not stay longer, and begged of her to give him leave to return to his father.

'And, princess,' observed the Prince of Persia, 'that you may not doubt the truth of my affection, I would presume, were I not afraid you would be offended at my request, to ask the favour of taking you along with me.'

The princess returned no answer to this address of the Prince of Persia; but her silence, and eyes cast down, were sufficient to inform him that she had no reluctance to accompany him into Persia. The only difficulty she felt was, that the prince knew not well enough how to govern the horse, and she was apprehensive of being involved with him in the same difficulty as when he first made the experiment. But the prince soon removed her fear, by assuring her she might trust herself with him, for that after the experience he had acquired, he defied the Hindu himself to manage him better. She thought, therefore, only of concerting measures to get off with him so secretly, that nobody belonging to the palace should have the least suspicion of their design.

The next morning, a little before daybreak, when all the attendants were asleep, they went upon the terrace of the palace. The prince turned the horse towards Persia, and placed him where the princess could easily get up behind him, which she had no sooner done, and was well settled with her arms about his waist, for her better security, than he turned the peg, when the horse mounted into the air, and making his usual haste, under the guidance of the prince, in two hours the prince discovered the capital of Persia.

The prince would not alight in the palace of his father, but directed his course towards a kiosk at a little distance from the capital. He led the princess into a handsome apartment, where he told her, that to do her all the honour that was due to her, he would go and inform his

The prince turned the peg and the enchanted horse mounted into the air . . .

father of their arrival, and return to her immediately. He ordered the attendants of the palace, whom he summoned, to provide the princess with whatever she had occasion for.

After the prince had taken his leave of the princess, he ordered a horse to be brought, which he mounted, and set out for the palace. As he passed through the streets he was received with acclamation by the people, who were overjoyed to see him again. The emperor, his father, was holding his divan when he appeared before him in the midst of his council. He received him with tears of joy and tenderness, and asked him what was become of the Hindu's horse.

This question gave the prince an opportunity of describing the embarrassment and danger he was in when the horse ascended into the air, and how he had arrived at last at the Princess of Bengal's palace, the kind reception he had met with there, and that the motive which had induced him to stay so long with her was the mutual affection they entertained for each other; also, that after promising to marry her, he had persuaded her to accompany him into Persia. 'But, sire,' added the prince, 'I felt assured that you would not refuse your consent, and have brought her with me on the enchanted horse to your summer palace, and have left her there, till I could return and assure her that my promise was not in vain.'

After these words, the prince prostrated himself before the emperor to obtain his consent, when his father raised him up, embraced him a second time, and said to him, 'Son, I not only consent to your marriage with the Princess of Bengal, but will go myself and bring her to my palace, and celebrate your nuptials this day.'

The emperor now ordered that the Hindu should be fetched out of prison and brought before him. When the Hindu was admitted to his presence, he said to him, 'I secured thy person, that thy life might answer for that of the prince my son. Thanks be to God, he is returned again: go, take your horse, and never more let me see your face.'

As the Hindu had learned of those who brought him out of prison that Prince Feroze-shah was returned with a princess, and was also informed of the place where he had alighted and left her, and that the emperor was making preparations to go and bring her to his palace, as soon as he got out of the presence, he thought of being revenged upon the emperor and the prince. He mounted his horse, and without losing any time, went directly to the palace, and addressing himself to the captain of the guard, told him he came from the Prince of Persia for the Princess of Bengal, and to conduct her behind him through the air to the emperor, who waited in the great square of his palace to gratify the whole court and city of Shiraz with that wonderful sight.

The captain of the guard, who knew the Hindu, and that the emperor had imprisoned him, gave the more credit to what he said because he saw that he was at liberty. He presented him to the Princess of Bengal; who no sooner understood that he came from the Prince of Persia than she consented to what the prince, as she thought, had desired of her.

The Hindu, overjoyed at his success and the ease with which he had accomplished his villainy, mounted his horse, took the princess behind him, with the assistance of the captain of the guard, turned the peg, and instantly the horse mounted into the air.

At the same time the Emperor of Persia, attended by his court, was on the road to the palace where the Princess of Bengal had been left, and the Prince of Persia had gone ahead to prepare the princess to receive his father—when the Hindu, to revenge himself for the ill-treatment he had received, appeared over their heads with his prize.

When the Emperor of Persia saw the Hindu, he stopped. His surprise and affliction were the more terrible, because it was not in his power to punish so high an affront. He loaded him with a thousand threats, as did also all the courtiers, who were witnesses of so signal a piece of insolence and unparalleled artifice and treachery.

The Hindu, little moved with their threats, which just reached his ears, continued his way, while the emperor, extremely mortified at so great an insult, but more so that he could not punish the author, returned to his palace in rage and vexation.

But what was Prince Feroze-shah's grief at beholding the Hindu hurrying away with the Princess of Bengal, whom he loved so passionately! He returned to the summer palace, where he had last seen the princess, melancholy and broken-hearted.

When he arrived, the captain of the guard, who had learnt his fatal credulity in believing the artful Hindu, threw himself at his feet with tears in his eyes, accused himself of the crime which unintentionally he had committed, and condemned himself to die by his hand. 'Rise,' said the prince to him, 'I do not impute the loss of my princess to thee, but to my own want of precaution. But not to lose time, fetch me a holy man's habit, and take care you do not give the least hint that it is for me.'

The captain readily obtained such a habit and carried it to Prince Feroze-shah. The prince immediately pulled off his own dress, put the habit on, and being so disguised, and provided with a box of jewels which he had brought as a present to the princess, left the palace, uncertain which way to go, but resolved not to return till he had found out his princess, and brought her back again, or perished in the attempt.

In the meantime the Hindu, mounted on his enchanted horse with the princess behind him, arrived early next morning at the capital of the Kingdom of Kashmir. He did not enter the city, but alighted in a wood, and left the princess on a grassy spot, close to a rivulet of fresh water, while he went to seek for food. On his return, and after he and the princess had partaken of refreshment, he began to maltreat the princess because she refused to become his wife. As the princess cried out for help, the Sultan of Kashmir and his court passed through the

The sultan, addressing himself to the Hindu, demanded who he was and
wherefore he ill-treated the lady.

wood on their return from hunting, and hearing a woman's voice calling for help, went to her rescue.

The sultan, addressing himself to the Hindu, demanded who he was and wherefore he ill-treated the lady. The Hindu, with great impudence, replied that she was his wife, and what had anyone to do with his quarrel with her?

The princess, who knew neither the rank nor quality of the person who came so seasonably to her relief, exclaimed, 'My lord, whoever you are whom heaven has sent to my assistance, have compassion on me. I am a princess. This Hindu is a wicked magician, who has forced me away from the Prince of Persia, to whom I was going to be married, and has brought me hither on the enchanted horse you behold there.'

The Princess of Bengal had no occasion to say more. Her beauty, majestic air, and tears, declared that she spoke the truth. Justly enraged at the insolence of the Hindu, the sultan ordered his guards to surround him, and strike off his head, which sentence was immediately executed.

The sultan then conducted the princess to his palace, where he lodged her in the most magnificent apartment, next to his own, and commanded a great number of women slaves to attend her.

The Princess of Bengal's joy was inexpressible at finding herself delivered from the Hindu, of whom she could not think without horror. She flattered herself that the Sultan of Kashmir would complete his generosity by sending her back to the Prince of Persia when she would have told him her story, and asked that favour of him. But she was much deceived in these hopes; for her deliverer had resolved to marry her himself the next day; and for that end had issued a proclamation, commanding the general rejoicing of the inhabitants of the capital. At the break of day the drums were beaten, the trumpets sounded, and shounds of joy echoed throughout the whole palace.

The Princess of Bengal was awakened by these tumultuous concerts, but attributed them to a very different cause from the true one. When the Sultan of Kashmir came to wait upon her, after he had inquired after her health, he acquainted her that all these rejoicings were to render her nuptials the more solemn, and at the same time desired her assent to the union. This declaration put her into such a state of agitation that she fainted away.

The women slaves who were present ran to her assistance, though it was a long time before they succeeded in bringing her to herself. But when she recovered, rather than break the promise she had made to Prince Feroze-shah, by consenting to marry the Sultan of Kashmir, who had proclaimed their nuptials before he had asked her consent, she resolved to feign madness. She began to utter the most extravagant expressions before the sultan, and even rose off her seat as if to attack him, insomuch that he was greatly alarmed and afflicted that he had made such a proposal so unreasonably.

When he found that her frenzy increased rather than abated, he left her with her women, charging them never to leave her alone, but to take great care of her. He sent often that day to inquire how she did, but received no other answer than that she was rather worse than better.

The Princess of Bengal continued to talk wildly, and showed other marks of a disordered mind next day and the following, so that the sultan was induced to send for all the physicians belonging to his court, to consult them upon her disease, and to ask if they could cure her.

When the Sultan of Kashmir saw that his court physicians could not cure her, he called in the most celebrated and experienced of the city, who had no better success. He then sent for the most famous in the kingdom, who prescribed without effect. Afterwards he despatched to the courts of neighbouring sultans, with promises of magnificent rewards to any who should devise a cure for her malady.

Various physicians arrived from all parts, and tried their skill, but none could boast of success.

During this interval, Feroze-shah, disguised in the habit of a holy man, travelled through many provinces and towns, involved in grief, and making diligent inquiry after his lost princess at every place he came to. At last, passing through a city of Hindustan, he heard the people talk much of a Princess of Bengal, who had become mad on the day of the intended celebration of her nuptials with the Sultan of Kashmir. At the name of the Princess of Bengal, and supposing that there could exist no other Princess of Bengal than her upon whose account he had undertaken his travels, he hastened towards the Kingdom of Kashmir, and, upon his arrival at the capital, took up his lodging at a khan, where, the same day, he was informed of the story of the princess and the fate of the Hindu. The prince was convinced that he had at last found the beloved object he had sought so long.

Being informed of all these particulars, he provided himself with a physician's habit, and his beard having grown long during his travels, he passed the more easily for the character he assumed. He went boldly to the palace, and announced his wish to be allowed to undertake the cure of the princess to the chief of the officers.

Some time had elapsed since any physician had offered himself, and the Sultan of Kashmir with great grief had begun to lose all hope of ever seeing the princess restored to health, though he still wished to marry her. He at once ordered the officer to introduce the physician he had announced. The Prince of Persia being admitted to an audience, the sultan told him the Princess of Bengal could not bear the sight of a physician without falling into most violent transports, which increased her malady; and conducted him into a closet, from whence, through a lattice, he might see her without being observed.

There Feroze-shah beheld his lovely princess sitting melancholily, with tears in her eyes, and singing an air in which she deplored her unhappy fate, which had deprived her, perhaps for ever, of the object she loved so tenderly: and the sight made him more resolute in his hope of effecting her cure. On his leaving the closet, he told the sultan that he had discovered the nature of the princess's complaint, and that she was not incurable; but added withal, that he must speak with her in private and alone, as, notwithstanding her violent agitation at the sight of physicians, he hoped she would hear and receive him favourably.

The sultan ordered the princess's chamber-door to be opened, and Feroze-shah went in. As soon as the princess saw him (taking him by his habit to be a physician), she resorted to her old practice of meeting her physicians with threats and indications of attacking them. He made directly towards her, and when he was nigh enough for her to hear him, and no one else, said to her, in a low voice, 'Princess, I am not a physician, but the Prince of Persia, and am come to procure you your liberty.'

The princess, who knew the sound of the voice, and recognized his face, notwithstanding he had let his beard grow so long, grew calm at once, and felt a secret joy in seeing so unexpectedly the prince she loved. Feroze-shah told her as briefly as possible his own travels and adventures, and his determination to find her at all risks. He then desired the princess to inform him of all that happened to her, from the time she was taken away till that happy moment, telling her that it was of the greatest importance to know this, that he might take the most proper measures to deliver her from the tyranny of the Sultan of Kashmir. The princess informed him of all that had happened, and that she had feigned to be mad that she might so preserve herself for a prince to whom she had given her heart and faith, and not marry the sultan, whom she neither loved nor could ever love.

The Prince of Persia then asked her if she knew what became of the horse, after the death of the Hindu magician. To which she answered, that she knew not what orders the sultan had given; but supposed, after the account she had given him of it, he would take care of it as a curiosity. As Feroze-shah never doubted but that the sultan had the horse, he communicated to the princess his design of making use of it to convey them both into Persia; and after they had consulted together on the measures they should take, they agreed that the princess should next day receive the sultan.

The Sultan of Kashmir was overjoyed when the Prince of Persia stated to him what effect his first visit had had towards the cure of the princess. On the following day, when the princess received him in such a manner as persuaded him her cure was far advanced, he regarded the prince as the greatest physician in the world, and exhorted the princess carefully to follow the directions of so skilful a physician, and then retired. The Prince of Persia, who attended the Sultan of Kashmir on his visit to the princess, inquired of him how the Princess of Bengal came into the dominions of Kashmir thus alone, since her own country was far distant.

The sultan at once informed him of what the princess had related, when he had delivered her from the Hindu magician: adding that he had ordered the enchanted horse to be kept safe in his treasury as a great curiosity, though he knew not the use of it.

'Sire,' replied the pretended physician, 'the information which your majesty has given your devoted slave affords me a means of curing the princess. As she was brought hither on this horse, and the horse is enchanted, she hath contracted something of the enchantment, which can be dissipated only by a certain incense which I am acquainted with. If your majesty would entertain yourself, your court, and the people of your capital, with the most surprising sight that ever was beheld, let the horse be brought tomorrow into the great square before the palace, and leave the rest to me. I promise to show you, and all that assembly, in a few moments' time, the Princess of Bengal completely restored in body and mind. But the better to effect what I propose, it will be requisite that the princess should be dressed as magnificently as possible, and adorned with the most valuable jewels in your treasury.' The sultan would have undertaken much more difficult things to have secured his marriage with the princess, which he expected soon to accomplish.

The next day, the enchanted horse was by his order taken out of the treasury, and placed early in the great square before the palace. A report was spread through the town that there was something extraordinary to be seen, and crowds of people flocked thither from all parts, insomuch that the sultan's guards were placed to prevent disorder, and to keep space enough round the horse.

The Sultan of Kashmir, surrounded by all his nobles and ministers of state, was placed in a gallery erected on purpose. The Princess of Bengal, attended by a number of ladies whom the sultan had assigned her, went up to the enchanted horse, and the women helped her to mount. When she was fixed in the saddle, and had the bridle in her hand, the pretended physician placed round the horse at a proper distance many vessels full of lighted charcoal, which he had ordered to be brought, and going round them with a solemn pace, cast in handfuls of incense; then, with downcast eyes, and his hands upon his breast, he ran three times about the horse, making as if he pronounced some mystical words.

The moment the pots sent forth a dark cloud of smoke—accompanied with a pleasant smell, which so surrounded the princess that neither she nor the horse could be discerned—watching his opportunity, the prince jumped nimbly up behind her, and reaching his hand to the peg, turned it; and just as the horse rose with them into the air, he pronounced these words, which the sultan heard distinctly, 'Sultan of Kashmir, when you would marry princesses who implore your protection, learn first to obtain their consent.'

Thus the prince delivered the Princess of Bengal, and carried her the same day to the capital of Persia, where he alighted in the square of the palace, before the emperor his father's apartment. The solemnization of the marriage took place as soon as the emperor had made certain the ceremony would be pompous and magnificent.

After the days appointed for the rejoicings were over, the Emperor of Persia's first care was to name and appoint an ambassador to go to the Rajah of Bengal with an account of what had passed, and to demand his approbation and ratification of the alliance contracted by this marriage; which the Rajah of Bengal took as an honour, and granted with great pleasure and satisfaction.

THE FORGOTTEN MEDICAL WARRIOR

Ann M Currah

Two women, Elizabeth Blackwell and Elizabeth Garrett Anderson, are famous for their courageous battles to become medical doctors in the mid-19th century. At that time, the idea that young ladies should perform useful work outside their homes was considered ridiculous; any thought of well-brought-up ladies studying the health and ills of the *human body* would have been greeted with cries of horror.

In 1849 the young Englishwoman Elizabeth Blackwell became the first woman to qualify as a medical doctor at Geneva College in New York state. She then became the first woman to have her name inscribed on the British Medical Register, nine years later. Dr Blackwell provided the inspiration and example for Elizabeth Garrett Anderson, who qualified in Britain in a roundabout way, by becoming a licensed apothecary. In 1866 she too was listed in the British Medical Register.

A third pioneer doctor, who is almost a forgotten medical warrior in the fight to help women achieve first-class medical training, was Sophia Jex-Blake. The reasons why she is almost unheard of probably lie in her extraordinary character. She was a fighter who determined to engage in battle in public and, if necessary, in the law courts—both were male preserves in mid- and late-Victorian times. The two Elizabeths were always very conscious of preserving their feminine dignity and maintaining their respectability in Victorian eyes. Sophia was determined that women should have the legal right to enter medical schools as full-time students and to take the qualifying examinations for MD (Medical Doctor), even if seeking these rights created scandal.

Towards the end of her life, Dr Blackwell's sister Emily recalled the climate in which young women first sought to enter the medical profession:

'No one who was not alive sixty years ago can realize the iron wall hemming in on every side any young woman who wished to earn her own living or to do anything outside the narrowest conventional grooves. Such a woman was simply crushed. Those who were of a character not to be crushed without resistance had to fight for their lives, and their fight broke the way through for others to follow.'

Resistance, or even violence, could not and did not crush Sophia Jex-Blake.

Sophia was born on January 21, 1840, in the ancient English town of Hastings in Sussex. Her family were well-to-do and well-connected and her upbringing was that of a typical upper class English girl in early Victorian times.

She studied at Queen's College in London for three years, a rather advanced and intellectual pursuit for a young lady of her class and background. In 1865, the year in which the North finally won the American Civil War, she travelled to Boston in order to study American educational methods. While there she became friends with Lucy Sewell, a young doctor, and had a chance to inspect and learn about hospital work. She began to think that medicine might be a career which would suit her.

Before she returned to England, Sophia visited New York City and stayed at Elizabeth Blackwell's New York Infirmary for Women and Children, which became a registered medical school three years later in 1868. Sophia studied the work of Dr Rachel Cole, the first black woman doctor, who ran the Infirmary's 'sanitary visiting service', a pioneering welfare project which tried to teach New York City slum dwellers hygiene and to encourage mother and infant health care.

While Sophia was obviously fascinated by the medical care and facilities, she was not impressed by the living conditions for staff and students at the Infirmary. In response to Dr Blackwell's suggestion that she might try to bring back a group of English girls to study medicine when the Infirmary became a college she wrote, 'English ladies are not given to dine in kitchens on poor kitchen fare.' Despite this snobbery, when the college officially opened Sophia returned, but she rented more elegant living accommodation for herself outside the Infirmary walls.

Although Dr Blackwell felt that Sophia Jex-Blake had great potential, the student's stay was brief due to the death of her father in England. Perhaps this was fortuitous because America had by this time medical colleges for women in three big eastern cities, Boston, New York and Philadelphia. Even several men's colleges were admitting women medical students. For Sophia, the battleground was to be in Great Britain. Elizabeth Garrett was the only woman licensed to practice medicine in England as the Society of Apothecaries had closed their examinations to other women. There was fierce male opposition in the medical profession to women studying in hospitals or medical schools, so other girls were being prevented from following in Elizabeth Garrett's path.

In 1869, the year after her return from America, Sophia Jex-Blake was accepted as a full time student by the Senate of Edinburgh University, and was joined by six other girls who wished to study medicine. The acceptance of her studentship had come about as a result of her canvassing support among male students, professors, doctors and other influential acquaintances. At the time, it was considered a remarkable triumph and she was enthusiastically congratulated. Elizabeth Blackwell, who had journeyed to England to help encourage more women into a concern for health care and interest in medical matters, wrote to Sophia:

'It seems the grandest success that women have yet achieved in England.'

The congratulations and optimism over the future of medical training for women were sadly premature. Sophia Jex-Blake was about to face vicious opposition to her pursuit of a medical career.

Several months after she and her friends entered Edinburgh, Sir James Simpson, one of the leaders of the Faculty of Medicine who had encouraged and supported the women, died. The Faculty then came under the leadership of a Professor Christison and others who were directly opposed to the admission of women students. Although the Faculty attempted to make life more difficult for the women students, they kept on studying even though they had to pay expensive fees for private lectures in order to keep up with the prescribed courses. (Men students objected to having women attend the same lectures and classes.)

In a special chemistry examination, one of the women students achieved the highest mark and as a result should have been given the Hope Scholarship for Chemistry. The professor awarded the scholarship instead to a male student who had the next highest mark. This created a furore when newspapers discovered the refusal to award an academic distinction to a woman. *The Scotsman*, an influential newspaper, carried editorials denouncing the discrimination and arguing in favour of women medical students. Other national newspapers added fuel to the fire, some arguing for women and others denouncing them. Students and staff of Edinburgh University were up in arms and widely divided in their opinions as to whether women should be allowed to study under the Medical Faculty. Many professors refused to give lectures to Sophia and her female colleagues.

The publicity over the Hope Scholarship led to a riot at the Surgeon's Hall in which the gates were slammed as the women students approached. They were cornered by a howling mob of two hundred male students who pelted them with mud and refuse, shouted insults and obscenities and jostled them about until someone opened the gates and helped the women escape. Not surprisingly, the women were badly frightened and shocked, but the incident made them more determined to stay.

Many students and some of the University medical staff were outraged at the incident and sympathetic to the women. Sophia obtained information that Professor Christison's own personal assistant had been active in fomenting the riot and at a public meeting she accused him of helping to lead the riot with the approval of the Professor.

Christison promptly sued Sophia for libel and the case dragged through the law courts for two years before he won. He received only one farthing in damages, a laughably small sum for Sophia's supposed character assassination; this was both an insult and legal acknowledgement that although the libel had been proved it was fully justified.

In the next several years, life for the Edinburgh women students was difficult. They finally won a bitter battle over whether women should be allowed to attend real medical demonstrations in the Edinburgh Infirmary's wards. Eventually, Sophia realized that the University opposition was so strong that the women might be allowed to finish their studies, but would not be granted medical degrees.

Sophia took this matter to law and in 1872 it was judged that the women were legally entitled to complete their medical studies and to be examined for the MD degree. The University appealed against the judgement and in 1873 it was ruled that Edinburgh University had probably broken the rules of its charter by admitting women and so it was not legally bound to let them continue studies or take their degrees.

After four gruelling years and the vast expense of fighting court cases, Sophia and her friends finally had to give up their attempt to qualify at Edinburgh. She eventually obtained qualification at the University of Bern in 1877 and then obtained a licence to practice medicine in Great Britain from King's College and Queen's College of Physicians (The Royal College of Physicians), Dublin.

Sophia had become determined after her experiences in Scotland that women in Great Britain should have a medical school freely available that would provide both sound practical and distinguished academic medical training. With the encouragement and support of the Honorary Physician to King's College Hospital, Dr Anstie, and the Honorary Surgeon of St Mary's Hospital, Mr Norton, Sophia raised money and organized a medical school which opened its doors to more than a dozen young women in 1874 as the London School of Medicine for Women. The school had great difficulties in the first two years—no official medical examining body would agree to award its students degrees and no London hospital would agree to allow women students to receive clinical training.

Sophia and some of the distinguished governors of the school such as Lord Shaftesbury, the famous social reformer, decided an act of Parliament was required to guarantee women a legal right to medical training. With the support of Elizabeth Garrett Anderson, a friend from early student days in London, the Lord Privy Seal, members of Parliament and of the House of Lords were gradually won over to the

Over a hundred male students pelted them with mud and refuse.

cause. In 1876, a Bill was passed with little opposition which permitted all degree-granting medical institutions and bodies to admit women to their examinations despite any restrictions to the contrary in their ancient charters. This, in effect, gave women the legal right to receive MD degrees and licences to practice medicine and surgery.

Subsequently, the London School of Medicine for Women was placed on the official register of Medical Schools and a year later the Royal Free Hospital in London let women receive practical training in its wards.

Sophia had been the guiding light, source of energy, organiser and unofficial secretary to the new medical school, but when another official Honorary Secretary was appointed because the school's committee felt she was too forceful, strong-willed and liable to encourage the 'wrong sort of publicity', Sophia decided to leave for Edinburgh to set up medical practice. She did this successfully and also managed to found another medical school for women in 1886.

Sophia Jex-Blake died in 1912 (four years before women were granted the vote). Her brilliance, stamina and amazingly determined character had secured training in the medical profession for women. Perhaps if her fiery personality and fighting instincts had been tempered by some of the tactfulness of the two Elizabeths (who were always worried by Sophia's publicity garnering and ability to create scandal), she might have been remembered and honoured as they were.

Sophia's contemporaries thought of her as beautiful but snobbish, brilliant but rash—a useful warrior in the forefront of the battle but too tempestuous after the battles were over. Without her powerful, eccentric personality, the 19th century might have faded before women could have legally received medical training in Britain.

DICK TURPIN'S RIDE TO YORK

Harrison Ainsworth

The place of refreshment for the cockneys of Kilburn in the year 1737 was a substantial looking tenement of the old stamp with great bay windows and a balcony in front, bearing as its ensign the jovial figure of that lusty knight, Jack Falstaff.

It was here, on a day in late summer that same year, that two of the most famous highwaymen of the decade resumed an old friendship.

'Ha, Dick!' said one of them presently. 'You are off, I understand, to Yorkshire tonight. Upon my soul, you are a wonderful fellow. Here and everywhere at the same time. No wonder you are called the Flying Highwayman. Today in town, tomorrow at York, the day after at Chester. The devil only knows where you will pitch your quarters a week hence.'

Dick Turpin fingered his exuberant red whiskers and his keen grey eyes were smiling as he looked at his elegant friend. 'Perhaps,' said he, 'if you paid less attention to your riding-dress and more to the business in hand . . .' His words, though slightly malicious, were spoken with such an air of good humour that Tom King, better known as the Gentleman Highwayman, dismissed them with a languid wave of a well-manicured hand. 'But thank you for the compliment,' Dick went on, 'though to be sure it's no merit of mine. Black Bess alone enables me to do it, and to her be all the credit.'

'A glass to the best mare in England then,' cried Tom.

'I'll not refuse such a toast,' said Dick complacently, 'and after it we'll be on our way.'

After the toast to Dick's famous mare the two friends summoned the innkeeper.

'Order my horse—the black mare,' said Dick. 'We'll be in the garden.'

'And mine,' said King, 'the sorrel colt. Dick, I'll ride with you a mile or two on the road.'

Scarcely had the ostler brought out the two highwaymen's steeds when a post-chaise, escorted by two or three horsemen, drove furiously up to the door. The sole occupant of the carriage was a lady, whose slight and pretty figure was all that could be distinguished, her face being closely veiled.

The landlord, who was busy casting up Turpin's account, rushed to the summons of the lady in the carriage; a few hurried words passed between them, and the landlord pointed in the direction of the garden, whereupon the horsemen instantly dismounted.

'We have him now, sure enough,' said one of them exultantly.

'By the powers, I begin to think so,' replied another. 'But don't spoil all, Mr Coates, by being too hasty.'

'Never fear that, Mr Tyrconnel,' said Coates. 'I'm not an attorney for nothing!' And turning to the third horseman, he continued, 'We'll catch him, eh, Mr Paterson? We've got *you* now, the Chief Constable of Westminster, to back us. And now we've sprung the trap. He'll not leave without his mare!'

'We'll take them both,' said the chief constable. 'Tom King as well! We've long had an eye upon him—yes, we'll land him this time.'

'I'd rather you helped *us*, Mr Paterson. It's Turpin we want. Never mind King. Another time will do for him.'

'I'll take King myself,' said Paterson stubbornly. 'Surely you two, with the landlord and ostler, can manage Turpin amongst you.'

'I don't know about that,' returned Coates doubtfully. 'He's a devil of a fellow to deal with.'

'Take him quietly,' advised Paterson. 'Draw the chaise out of the way—Tom's fancy lady has played her part and will get her reward for giving us him on a plate—and tell the ostler to place their nags near the door. And now gentlemen,' he added, 'let's step aside a little. Don't use your firearms too soon.'

As if conscious of what was passing around her, and of the danger that awaited her master, Black Bess exhibited so much impatience, and plunged so violently, that it was with difficulty the ostler could hold her. 'The devil's in the mare,' said he. 'What's the matter with her? She was quiet enough a few minutes since. Soho! lass, stand!'

Meantime, preceded by the innkeeper, who was almost visibly trembling, Turpin and King advanced towards the door. At the unexpected sight of the constable each man rushed swiftly to his horse. Dick was up on the saddle in an instant and, stamping her foot upon the ostler's leg, Black Bess compelled the man, yelling with pain, to quit his hold of the bridle.

Tom King, however, was not so fortunate. Before he could mount his horse a loud shout was raised, one which startled the animal and caused him to swerve so that Tom lost his footing in the stirrup and fell to the ground. He was instantly seized by Paterson and a struggle commenced, King endeavouring, but in vain, to draw a pistol.

'Shoot him, Dick! Fire, or I'm taken!' cried King. 'Fire, damn you, why don't you fire?' He went on struggling desperately with Paterson, who was a strong man and more than a match for the lightweight King.

'I can't,' cried Dick. 'I'll hit you if I fire now!'

'Take your chance,' shouted Tom. 'Is this your friendship? Fire, I tell you!'

Thus urged, Turpin fired. The ball ripped up the sleeve of Paterson's coat but did not wound him.

Dick fired again but it was impossible for him to take sure aim. The ball lodged itself in King's breast. He fell at once.

Aghast at the deed he had accidentally committed, Dick remained for a few moments irresolute. He saw that King was mortally wounded, and that all attempts at a rescue would be fruitless. He hesitated no longer. Turning his horse, he galloped slowly off, little heeding the pursuit with which he was threatened.

Arriving at the brow of the hill, Turpin turned for an instant to reconnoitre his pursuers. Coates and Titus Tyrconnel he utterly disregarded, but Paterson was a more formidable foe, and he well knew that he had to deal with a man of experience and resolution. It was then, for the first time, that the thought of executing his extraordinary ride to York first flashed across his mind. His heart throbbed and he involuntarily exclaimed aloud, as he raised himself in the saddle, 'We'll do it, Bess, we'll do it!'

Then, aroused by the approaching clatter of his pursuers, Dick struck into a lane which lay on the right of the road and set off at a good pace in the direction of Hampstead.

'Now,' cried Paterson, as he saw Dick's move. 'Press forward, my boys. We must not lose sight of him for a second in these lanes.'

As Turpin was by no means desirous of inconveniencing his mare at this early stage, the parties preserved their relative distances. At length, after various twistings and turnings in that deep and devious lane, after scaring one or two farmers, and riding over a brood or two of ducks, after dipping into the green valley of West End, and ascending another hill, Turpin burst upon the gorsy, sandy and beautiful heath of London's Hampstead.

As he made for the lower part, it was here that the chase first assumed interest. Being open ground, the pursued and the pursuers were now in full view of each other, and as Dick rode swiftly across the heath, with the shouting trio hard at his heels, the scene was lively indeed.

To avoid Highgate Town, Dick struck into a narrow path and rode easily down the hill, but his pursuers were now within a hundred yards, and shouted to him to stand. Pointing to a gate which seemed to bar their further progress, Dick unhesitatingly charged it, clearing it in beautiful style. Not so with Coates's party, and the time they lost in unfastening the gate, which none of them dared to leap, enabled Dick to put additional space between them.

By now the whole neighbourhood was alarmed, and the shouts of 'Stop him! Stop him!' came at Turpin from all sides. On he rode with a pistol in each hand, his bridle in his teeth, and his fierce looks, his furious steed, and the boldness with which he pressed forward, bore down all before him.

As Dick approached the old Hornsey toll-bar with its high spiked gate, Paterson shouted exultantly, 'Shut the gate, man! We have him!'

The custodian of the turnpike swung the gate into its lock and held himself in readiness to spring upon the runaway, but Dick kept steadily on. He coolly calculated the height of the spiked gate. He looked to the right and to the left and saw that nothing better offered itself. He spoke a few words of encouragement to Bess, gently patted her neck, struck spurs into her sides—and cleared the vicious spikes by an inch!

Taking advantage of the time gained whilst his pursuers waited for the gate to be opened, Turpin rested Black Bess for a minute, then cantered easily along in the direction of Tottenham.

Little respite, however, was allowed him. Yelling like a pack of hounds in full cry, his pursuers were again at his heels. Indeed the whole countryside was up in arms; people were shouting, screaming, running, dancing and hurling every possible kind of missile at Black Bess and her rider. Dick laughed aloud at the clamour as he flew past, for the brickbats that were showered, thick as hail at his flying figure, fell harmlessly to the ground.

Away they flew, Dick and his gallant mare, like eagles on the wing, along the highway, and after them came Paterson and his men. But while their horses were streaming like water-carts, Black Bess had scarcely turned a hair.

What a horse she was, this heroine of a thousand stories of daring-do! A true thoroughbred, her sire was a desert Arab, renowned in his day and brought to England by a wealthy traveller. Her dam was an English racer, coal-black as Bess herself. How Turpin came into possession of such a horse is of little consequence, but now no sum on earth would have induced him ever to part with her. In Bess was united all the fire and gentleness, the strength and hardiness and endurance of the Arab, and all the spirit and fleetness of the racer.

Her smooth skin was polished jet, and not a single white hair could be detected in her satin coat. In make she was magnificent, every point was perfect, beautiful, compact, modelled for strength and speed. In Dick's eyes at least there was no horse in the world to match her—with her elegant little head, thin tapering ears closely placed together, and broad, snorting nostrils which seemed to snuff the wind with disdain.

Dick Turpin himself was no mean judge of horseflesh. He was the crack rider of England of his time—perhaps of any time—riding

Dick spoke a few words of encouragement to Bess and cleared the vicious spikes by an inch.

wonderfully light, and distributing his weight so exquisitively that his horse scarcely felt his pressure. He yielded to every movement made by the animal and became, as it were, part and parcel of itself. Thus he rode now and would always ride, no matter how hard the chase.

Confident in his mare's ability to out-distance any horse set against her, Dick made no attempt to ride away from his pursuers. He liked the fun of the chase, and would have been sorry to put a stop to his own enjoyment at such an early stage in the proceedings.

By now it was grey twilight. The mists of the coming night were weaving a thin curtain over the rich surrounding landscape. All the sounds and hum of that quiet hour were heard, broken only by the regular clatter of the horses' hoofs. Tired of shouting, the chasers now kept on their way in deep silence. Each man held his breath and plunged his spurs rowel-deep into his horse, but the animals were already at the top of their speed and incapable of greater exertion. Paterson, who was a hard rider and perhaps a shade better mounted, kept the lead. The rest followed as they might.

As for Bess, as the hours wore on, some fifty miles lay behind her and yet she showed no signs of distress. If possible, it seemed to Dick, she appeared fresher than when she started. He was intoxicated by her swiftness and her spirit. He shouted aloud to the night sky as the flints sparkled beneath his mare's hooves, and there was no thought in his head other than the glorious excitement of the chase.

As they entered the county of Huntingdon, and rode by the banks of the River Ouse, and then passed the bridge, Turpin heard the eleventh hour given from the iron tongue of St Mary's spire. In four hours they had now accomplished more than sixty miles!

A few drunken locals in the streets saw the horseman flit past, and one or two windows were thrown open; but he was gone, like a meteor, almost as soon as he appeared.

Huntingdon was left behind and once more, Dick was surrounded by dew-gemmed hedges and silent, slumbering trees, broad meadows, or pasture land with drowsy cattle or low-bleating sheep. But he spared them never a glance; all his thoughts were with his mare. At that moment he was willing to throw away his life in the hope of earning immortality for himself and Black Bess with this ride to York. He trembled with excitement, and Bess trembled under him.

Meanwhile, with unabated enthusiasm, Paterson and his men had pressed forward. A tacit compact seemed to have been entered into between the highwayman and his pursuers, that he was to fly while they were to follow. Like bloodhounds they kept steadily upon his trail; nor were they so far behind as Dick imagined.

At each post-house they passed they obtained fresh horses and, while these were saddled, a postboy was despatched to order relays at the next station. In this manner they proceeded after the first stoppage without interruption.

Eighty-odd miles had been covered, and it was now midnight—yet Turpin and his gallant mare had enjoyed no rest. Now, as he crossed the boundary of Northampton, Dick sought out a small wayside inn where the lad, who was the ostler there, could be trusted.

Riding up to the door of the stable, he knocked in a certain manner. After peering through a broken window, the lad came out, his hair full of hay. He gave Dick a sleepy but welcome salutation.

'Glad to see you, Captain Turpin,' said he. 'Can I do anything for you?'

'Get me a couple of bottles of brandy and a beefsteak, Ralph,' said Dick. 'And if there's no beefsteak to hand, raw meat will serve.'

'Raw meat?' echoed Ralph in surprise.

'That's what I want,' said Dick, unsaddling his mare. 'Give me a scraper. There, I can get a wisp of straw from your hair. Now run and get the brandy. Better bring three bottles. Uncork 'em, and let me have half a pail of water to mix with the spirit.'

'A pail full of brandy and water to wash down a raw steak! My eyes!' exclaimed Ralph, opening wide his mouth. But he went away immediately.

The most skilful groom in the world could not have bestowed more attention upon the horse of his heart than Dick Turpin now paid to his mare. He scraped, chafed and dried her, sounded each muscle, traced each sinew, pulled her ears, examined the state of her feet, and then finally washed her from head to foot in the diluted spirit, taking a thimbleful of the brandy to ease his own parched throat as he worked. And while Ralph was engaged in rubbing Bess down after her bath, Dick occupied himself in rolling the raw steak round the bit of his bridle.

'She will go as long as there's breath in her body,' said he, putting the flesh-covered iron within the mare's mouth.

The saddle being once more replaced, after champing a moment or two at the bit, Bess began to snort and paw the ground, as if impatient of delay. Knowing her indomitable spirit and power, Dick was still surprised at her condition, for, as he led her into the open space, her step became as light and free as when she started on her ride, and her sense of sound as quick as ever. Suddenly she pricked her ears and uttered a low neigh. A dull tramp was audible.

'Ha!' exclaimed Dick, springing into his saddle. 'They come!'

'Who comes, captain?' asked Ralph.

'The road takes a turn here, don't it?' asked Dick. 'It sweeps round to the right by the plantations in the hollow?'

'Ay, ay, captain,' answered Ralph. 'You knows the place, then?'

'What lies beyond the shed?'

'A stiff fence, a regular rasper! Beyond that—a hillside steep as a house. No 'oss as was ever shoed can go down it!'

'Indeed!' laughed Dick.

A loud hallo told Dick he was discovered, and he saw that Paterson and his friends had now been joined by a formidable enemy. This was Major Mowbray, with whom he had only recently crossed swords. The major, a superb horseman, was in the lead of the party.

No tall timber intervened between Dick and his pursuers, so that the actions of both parties were visible to each other. Dick saw in an instant that if he now started he should come into collision with the major exactly at the angle of the road, and he was by no means anxious to hazard such an encounter. He looked wistfully back at the fence.

'Come into the stable. Quick, captain, quick!' exclaimed Ralph.

'The stable?' echoed Dick, hesitating.

'Ay, the stable; it's your only chance. Don't you see he's turning the corner, and they are all coming. Quick, sir, quick!'

Dick, lowering his head, rode into the tenement, the door of which was most unceremoniously slammed in the major's face, and bolted on the other side.

'Villain!' cried Major Mowbray, thundering at the door. 'Come out! You are now fairly cornered at last—caught, like the woodcock, in your own trap. We have you. Open the door, I say, and save us the trouble of forcing it. You cannot escape us. We will burn the building down but we will have you!'

'What do you want, master?' asked Ralph from the lintel, blinking up at the major but keeping the door fast. 'You're clean mistaken. There be no one here.'

'We'll soon see that,' said Paterson, who had now arrived. Leaping from his horse, the chief constable took a short run to give himself impetus, and with his foot burst open the door. This being accomplished, in dashed the major and Paterson, but the stable was empty. A door was open at the back, and they rushed to it. The sharply sloping sides of a hill slipped abruptly downwards, within a yard of the door. It was a perilous descent to the horseman, yet the print of a horse's hooves was visible in the dislodged turf and scattered soil.

'Confusion!' cried the major. 'He has escaped us.'

'He is yonder,' said Paterson, pointing out Turpin moving swiftly through the steaming meadow. 'See, he makes again for the road—he clears the fence . . .'

'Nobly done, by heaven!' exclaimed the major. 'With all his faults, I honour the fellow's courage. He's already ridden tonight as I believe no man rode before. I would not have ventured to slide down that wall, for it's nothing else, with the enemy at my heels. What say you, gentlemen, have you had enough? Shall we let him go, or——'

'What says Mr Coates?' asked Paterson. 'I look to him.'

'Then mount, and off,' cried Coates. 'Public duty requires that we should take him.'

'And private vengeance,' returned the major. 'No matter! The end is the same. Justice shall be satisfied. To your steeds, my merry men!'

Once more on the move even the weary Titus forgot his distress. Major Mowbray and Paterson took the lead, but Coates was not far behind. They spurred on their horses furiously. When they reached Selby, they changed them at the inn, and learnt from the postboy that a toilworn horseman, on a jaded steed, had ridden through the town about five minutes before them, and could not be more than a quarter of a mile in advance.

'His horse was so dead beat,' said the lad, 'that I'm sure he cannot have got far, and if you look sharp, I'll be bound you'll overtake him before he reaches Cawood Ferry.'

Mr Coates was jubilant. 'We'll lodge him snug in York Castle before an hour, Paterson,' cried he, rubbing his hands.

'I hope so, sir,' said the chief constable, 'but I begin to have some doubts.

'Now, gentlemen,' shouted the postboy, 'come along, I'll soon bring you to him.'

The sun had just topped the eastern hills when Turpin reached the ferry of Cawood, and its beams were reflected upon the deep and sluggish waters of the Ouse. Wearily had he dragged his course to that point— wearily and slow. The powers of his gallant steed were spent, and he could scarcely keep her from sinking. Nine miles only lay before him and York, and that thought alone revived him. He reached the water's edge, and hailed the ferry-boat, which was then on the other side of the river. At that moment a loud shout reached his ears. It was the cry of his pursuers.

Despair was in Dick's eyes as he shouted to the boatman, telling him to pull fast. The man obeyed, but he had to breast a strong stream, and the boat was slow and heavy. He had scarcely left the shore when another cry was raised from the pursuers. The tramp of their horses grew louder and louder.

The boat had only reached the middle of the stream, and his captors were at hand. Quietly Dick walked down the bank, and as quietly entered the water. There was a plunge and horse and rider were swimming the river.

Major Mowbray was at the brink of the stream. He hesitated an instant, then urged his horse into the water. Coates, too, braved the current, but not Paterson. Very calmly he took out his pistol and, with his eyes on Turpin, calculated the chances of shooting him as he was swimming. 'I could certainly hit him,' he told himself. 'But what of that? A dead highwayman is worth nothing; alive, he's worth his weight in gold. No, I won't shoot him, but I'll make a pretence.' And he fired accordingly.

The shot skimmed over the water, but did not, as it was intended, do much mischief. It did, however, prove nearly fatal to the attorney. Alarmed at the report of the pistol, Coates drew in his rein so tightly that his horse instantly sank. A moment or two afterwards it rose, shaking its ears, and floundering heavily towards the shore, and such was the chilling effect of its rider's sudden immersion that Mr Coates now thought much more of saving himself than of capturing Turpin.

Dick, meanwhile, had reached the opposite bank and, refreshed by her bath, Bess scrambled up the banks of the stream to regain the road.

'I shall do it, yet!' Dick shouted. 'That stream has saved her. Away, lass! Away!'

Bess heard the cheering cry and answered to the call. She roused her energies, strained every sinew, and put forth all her remaining strength. Once more, on wings of swiftness, she bore Turpin away from his pursuers. Major Mowbray, who had now gained the shore, and made certain of securing him, saw him spring, like a wounded hare, from beneath his very hand.

'She cannot hold out,' said the major. 'That gallant horse must soon drop.'

'She be regularly booked, that's certain,' said the postboy. 'We shall find her on the road.'

Contrary to all expectation, however, Bess held on, and set pursuit at defiance. Her pace was as swift as when she started. But it was un-conscious and mechanical action. It wanted the ease, the lightness, the life of her former riding. She seemed screwed up to a task which she must execute. There was no flogging, no gory heel; but her heart was throbbing, tugging at the sides within. Her spirit spurred her onwards. Her eye was glazing; her chest heaving; her flank quivering; her crest again fallen. Yet she held on. 'She is dying, by God!' said Dick. 'I feel it——' No, she held on.

Fulford is past. The towers and pinnacles of York burst upon him in all the freshness, the beauty and the glory of a bright, clear, autumnal morn. The ancient city seemed to smile a welcome—a greeting. The noble minster and its serene and massive pinnacles, crocketed, lantern-like, and beautiful; St Mary's lofty spire, All-Hallows Tower, the massive mouldering walls of the adjacent postern, the grim castle, and Clifford's neighbouring keep—all beamed upon him 'like a bright-eyed face, that laughs out openly.'

'It is done—it is won,' cried Dick. 'Hurrah, hurrah!' And the sunny air was cleft with his shouts.

Bess was not insensible to her master's joy. She neighed feebly in

answer to his call, and reeled forward. It was a piteous sight to see her—
to mark her staring, protruding eyeballs—her shaking flanks. But,
while life and limb held together, she held on.

Another mile is past. York is near.

'Hurrah!' shouted Dick, but his voice was hushed. Bess tottered—
fell. There was a dreadful gasp—a parting moan—a snort; her eye
gazed, for an instant, upon her master, with a dying glare; then grew
glassy, rayless, fixed. A shiver ran through her frame. Her heart had
burst.

Dick's eyes were blinded, as with rain. His triumph, though achieved,
was forgotten—his own safety was disregarded. He stood weeping and
swearing, like one beside himself.

'And art thou gone, Bess!' cried he, in a voice of agony, lifting up his
mare's head, and kissing her lips, covered with blood-flecked foam.
'Gone, gone! And I have killed the best steed that was ever crossed!
And for what?' added Dick, beating his brow with his clenched hand—
'for what? for what?'

At that moment the deep bell of the minster clock tolled out the
hour of six.

'I am answered,' gasped Dick. *'It was to hear those strokes!'*

Turpin was roused from the state of stupefaction into which he had
fallen by a smart slap on the shoulder. Recalled to himself by the blow,
he started at once to his feet, while his hands sought his pistols; but he
was spared the necessity of using them by discovering in the intruder
the bearded face of his old acquaintance, the gypsy Balthazar. The
gypsy was dressed like a beggar and carried a large wallet upon his
shoulders.

'So it's all over with the best mare in England, I see,' said Balthazar;
'I can guess how it has happened—you are pursued?'

'I am,' said Dick, roughly.

'Your pursuers are at hand?'

'Within a few hundred yards.'

'Then why stay here? Fly while you can.'

'Never—never,' cried Turpin; 'I'll fight it out here by Bess's side.
Poor lass! I've killed her—but she has done it—ha! ha! We have won—
what?' And his utterance was again choked.

'I hear the tramp of horses, and shouts,' cried the gypsy. 'Take this wallet. You will find a change of dress within it. Dart into that thick copse—save yourself.'

'But Bess—I cannot leave her,' exclaimed Dick, with an agonized look at his horse.

'And what did Bess die for, but to save you?' rejoined Balthazar.

'True, true,' said Dick, 'but take care of her. Don't let those dogs of hell meddle with her carcass.'

'Away,' cried his friend. 'Leave Bess to me.'

Possessing himself of the wallet, Dick disappeared into the adjoining copse.

He had not been gone many seconds when Major Mowbray rode up.

'Who is this?' exclaimed the major, flinging himself from his horse and seizing the gypsy. 'This is not Turpin.'

'Certainly not,' replied Balthazar, coolly. 'I am not exactly the figure for a highwayman.'

'Where is he? What has become of him?' asked Coates in despair, as he and Paterson joined the major.

'Escaped, I fear,' replied the major. 'Have you seen any one, fellow?' he added.

'I have seen no one,' replied Balthazar. 'I am only this instant arrived. This dead horse lying in the road attracted my attention.'

'Ha!' exclaimed Paterson, leaping from his mount. 'This may be Turpin after all. He has as many disguises as the devil himself, and may have carried that goat's hair in his pocket.' So saying, he seized the gypsy by the beard and shook it roughly.

'The devil! Hands off!' roared Balthazar. 'By Salmon I won't stand such usage. Do you think a beard like mine is the growth of a few minutes? Hands off, I say.'

'Regularly done!' said Paterson, removing his hold of Balthazar's chin, and looking as blank as a cartridge.

'Ay,' exclaimed Coates, 'all owing to this worthless piece of carrion. If it were not that I hope to see him dangling from those walls' (pointing towards the castle), 'I should wish her master were by her side now. To the dogs with her.' And he was about to spurn the breathless carcass of poor Bess, when a sudden blow, dealt by the gypsy's staff, felled him to the ground.

'I'll teach you to molest me,' said Balthazar, about to attack Paterson.

'Come, come,' said the discomfited chief constable, 'no more of this. It's plain we're in the wrong box. Every bone in my body aches sufficiently without the aid of your cudgel, old fellow. Come, Mr Coates, take my arm and let's be moving. We've had an infernal long ride for nothing.'

'Not so,' replied Coates, 'I've paid pretty dearly for it. However, let us see if we can get any breakfast at the bowling-green, yonder—though I've already had my morning draught,' added he, looking at his dripping apparel.

'Poor Black Bess!' said Major Mowbray, wistfully regarding the body of the mare as it lay stretched at his feet. 'You deserved a better fate and a better master. In you, Dick Turpin has lost his best friend. His exploits will, henceforth, lack the colouring of romance which your unfailing energies threw over them. Light lie the ground over you, matchless mare!'

To the bowling-green the party proceeded, leaving the gypsy in undisturbed possession of the lifeless body of Black Bess. Major Mowbray ordered a substantial repast to be prepared with all possible haste.

A countryman in a smock-frock was busily engaged at his morning's meal.

'To see that fellow bolt down his breakfast, one would think he had fasted for a month,' said Coates. 'I envy him his appetite—I should fall to with more zest were Dick Turpin in his place.'

The countryman looked up. He was an odd-looking fellow, with a terrible squint and a strange, contorted countenance.

'An ugly dog!' exclaimed Paterson. 'What a devil of a squint he has got!'

'What's that you says about Dick Taarpin, measter?' asked the countryman, his mouth half-full of bread.

'Have you seen aught of him?' asked Coates.

'Not I,' mumbled the rustic. 'But I hears aw the folk hereabouts talk on him. They say as how he sets all the lawyers and constables at defiance, and laughs in his sleeve at their efforts to cotch him—ha, ha! He gets over more ground in a day than they do in a week—ho, ho!'

'That's all over now,' said Coates, peevishly. 'He has cut his own throat—ridden his famous mare to death.'

The countryman almost choked himself, in the attempt to bolt a huge mouthful. 'Ay—indeed, measter! How happened that?' asked he, as soon as he recovered speech.

'The fool rode her from London to York last night,' returned Coates; 'such a feat was never performed before. What horse could be expected to live through such work as that?'

'Ah, he were a fool to attempt that,' observed the countryman. 'But you followed belike?'

'We did.'

'And took him arter all, I reckon?' asked the rustic, squinting more horribly than ever.

'No,' returned Coates, 'I can't say we did. But we'll have him yet. I'm pretty sure he can't be far off. We may be nearer him than we imagine.'

'May be so, measter,' returned the countryman. 'But might I be so bold as to ax how many horses you used i' the chase—some half-dozen, may be?'

'Half a dozen!' growled Paterson. 'We had twenty at the least.'

'And I *one*!' Turpin said to himself—for he was the countryman!

LAST OF THE TROUBADOURS

O Henry

Inexorably Sam Galloway saddled his pony. He was going away from the Rancho Altito at the end of a three-month visit. It is not to be expected that a guest should put up with wheat coffee and biscuits yellow-streaked with saleratus for longer than that. Nick Napoleon, the big Negro cook, had never been able to make good biscuits. Once before, when Nick was cooking at the Willow Ranch, Sam had been forced to fly from his cuisine, after only a six-week sojourn.

On Sam's face was an expression of sorrow, deepened with regret and slightly tempered by the patient forgiveness of a connoisseur who cannot be understood. But very firmly and deliberately he buckled his saddle-cinches, looped his stake-rope and hung it to his saddle-horn, tied his slicker and coat on the cantle, and looped his quirt on his right wrist. The Merrydews (householders of the Rancho Altito), men, women, children, and servants, vassals, visitors, employees, dogs, and casual callers were grouped in the 'gallery' of the ranch-house, all with faces set to the tune of melancholy and grief. For, as the coming of Sam Galloway to any ranch, camp, or cabin between the rivers Frio and Bravo del Norte aroused joy, so his departure caused mourning.

And then, during absolute silence, except for the bumping of a hind elbow of a hound dog as he pursued a wicked flea, Sam tenderly and carefully tied his guitar across his saddle on top of his slicker and coat. The guitar was in a green duck bag; and if you catch the significance of it, it explains Sam.

Sam Galloway was the last of the troubadours. Of course you know about the troubadours. The encyclopedia says they flourished between the eleventh and the thirteenth centuries. What they flourished doesn't seem clear—you may be pretty sure it wasn't a sword; maybe it was a fiddlebow, or a forkful of spaghetti, or a lady's scarf. Anyhow, Sam Galloway was one of 'em.

Sam put on a martyred expression as he mounted his pony. But the expression on his face was hilarious compared with the one on his pony's. You see, a pony gets to know his rider mighty well, and it is not unlikely that cow ponies in pastures and at hitching racks had often guyed Sam's pony for being ridden by a guitar player instead of a rollicking, cussing, all-wool cowboy. No man is a hero to his saddle-horse. And even an escalator in a department store might be excused for tripping up a troubadour.

Oh, I know I'm one; and so are you. You remember the stories you memorize and the card tricks you study and that little piece on the piano—how does it go?—ti-tum-te-tum-ti-tum—those little Arabian Ten-Minute Entertainments that you furnish when you go up to call on your rich Aunt Jane. You should know that *omnes personae in tres partes divisae sunt*, namely: barons, troubadours, and workers. Barons have no inclination to read such folderol as this; and workers have no time: so I know you must be a troubadour, and that you will understand Sam Galloway. Whether we sing, act, dance, write, lecture, or paint, we are only troubadours; so let us make the worst of it.

The pony with the Dante Alighieri face, guided by the pressure of Sam's knees, bore that wandering minstrel sixteen miles south-eastward. Nature was in her most benignant mood. League after league of delicate, sweet flowerets made fragrant the gently undulating prairie. The east wind tempered the spring warmth; wool-white clouds flying in from the Mexican Gulf hindered the direct rays of the April sun. Sam sang songs as he rode. Under his pony's bridle he had tucked some sprigs of chaparral to keep away the deer flies. Thus crowned, the long-faced quadruped looked more Dantesque than before, and, judging by his countenance, seemed to think of Beatrice.

Straight as topography permitted, Sam rode to the sheep ranch of old man Ellison. A visit to a sheep ranch seemed to him desirable just then. There had been too many people, too much noise, argument, competition, confusion, at Rancho Altito. He had never conferred upon old man Ellison the favour of sojourning at his ranch; but he knew he would be welcome. The troubadour is his own passport everywhere. The workers in the castle let down the drawbridge to him, and the baron sets him at his left hand at table in the banquet hall. There ladies smile upon him and applaud his songs and stories, while the workers bring boars' heads and flagons. If the baron nods once or twice in his carved oaken chair, he does not do it maliciously.

Old man Ellison welcomed the troubadour flatteringly. He had often heard praises of Sam Galloway from other ranchmen who had been complimented by his visits, but had never aspired to such an honour for his own humble barony. I say barony because old man Ellison was the last of the barons. Of course, Bulwer-Lytton lived too early to know him, or he wouldn't have conferred that soubriquet upon Warwick. In life it is the duty and the function of the baron to provide work for the workers and lodging and shelter for the various troubadours.

Old man Ellison was a shrunken old man, with a short, yellow-white beard and a face lined and seamed by past-and-gone smiles. His ranch was a little two-room box house in a grove of hackberry trees in the lonesomest part of the sheep country. His household consisted of a Kiowa Indian man cook, four hounds, a pet sheep, and a half-tamed coyote chained to a fence-post. He owned 3,000 sheep, which he ran on two sections of leased land and many thousands of acres neither leased nor owned. Three or four times a year someone who spoke his language would ride up to his gate and exchange a few bald ideas with him. Those were red-letter days to old man Ellison. Then in what illuminated, embossed, and gorgeously decorated capitals must have been written the day on which a troubadour—a troubadour who, according to the encyclopedia, should have flourished between the eleventh and the thirteenth centuries—drew rein at the gates of his baronial castle!

Old man Ellison's smiles came back and filled his wrinkles when he saw Sam. He hurried out of the house in his shuffling, limping way to greet him.

'Hello, Mr Ellison,' called Sam cheerfully. 'Thought I'd drop over and see you awhile. Notice you've had fine rains on your range. They ought to make good grazing for your spring lambs.'

'Well, well, well,' said old man Ellison. 'I'm mighty glad to see you, Sam. I never thought you'd take the trouble to ride over to as out-of-the-way an old ranch as this. But you're mighty welcome. 'Light. I've got a sack of new oats in the kitchen—shall I bring out a feed for your hoss?'

'Oats for him?' said Sam derisively. 'No, sir-ee. He's as fat as a pig now on grass. He don't get rode enough to keep him in condition. I'll just turn him in the horse pasture with a drag rope on if you don't mind.'

I am positive that never during the eleventh and thirteenth centuries did baron, troubadour, and worker amalgamate as harmoniously as their parallels did that evening at old man Ellison's sheep ranch. The Kiowa's biscuits were light and tasty and his coffee strong. Ineradicable hospitality and appreciation glowed on old man Ellison's weather-tanned face. As for the troubadour, he said to himself that he had stumbled upon pleasant places indeed. A well-cooked, abundant meal, a host whom his lighest attempt to entertain seemed to delight far beyond the merits of the exertion, and the reposeful atmosphere that his sensitive soul at that time craved united to confer upon him a satisfaction and luxurious ease that he had seldom found on his tours of the ranches.

After the delectable supper, Sam untied the green duck bag and took out his guitar. Not by way of payment, mind you—neither Sam Galloway nor any other of the true troubadours are lineal descendants of the late Tommy Tucker. You have read of Tommy Tucker in the works of the esteemed but often obscure Mother Goose. Tommy Tucker sang for his supper. No true troubadour would do that. He would have his supper, and then sing for art's sake.

Sam Galloway's repertoire comprised about fifty funny stories and between thirty and forty songs. He by no means stopped there. He could talk through twenty cigarettes on any topic that you brought up.

And he never sat up when he could lie down; and never stood when he could sit. I am strongly disposed to linger with him, for I am drawing a portrait as well as a blunt pencil and a tattered thesaurus will allow.

I wish you could have seen him: he was small and tough and inactive beyond the power of imagination to conceive. He wore an ultramarine-blue woollen shirt laced down the front with a pearl-grey, exaggerated sort of shoe-string, indestructible brown duck clothes, inevitable high-heeled boots with Mexican spurs, and a Mexican straw sombrero.

That evening Sam and old man Ellison dragged their chairs out under the hackberry trees. They lighted cigarettes; and the troubadour gaily touched his guitar. Many of the songs he sang were the weird, melancholy, minor-keyed *canciones* that he had learned from the Mexican sheep herders and *vaqueros*. One, in particular, charmed and soothed the soul of the lonely baron. It was a favourite song of the sheep herders, beginning '*Huile, huile, palomita*', which being translated means, 'Fly, fly, little dove'. Sam sang it for old man Ellison many times that evening.

The troubadour stayed on at the old man's ranch. There was peace and quiet and appreciation there, such as he had not found in the noisy camps of the cattle kings. No audience in the world could have crowned the work of poet, musician, or artist with more worshipful and unflagging approval than that bestowed upon his efforts by old man Ellison. No visit by a royal personage to a humble woodchopper or peasant could have been received with more flattering thankfulness and joy.

On a cool, canvas-covered cot in the shade of the hackberry trees Sam Galloway passed the greater part of his time. There he rolled his brown paper cigarettes, read such tedious literature as the ranch afforded, and added to his repertoire of improvisations that he played so expertly on his guitar. To him, as a slave ministering to a great lord, the Kiowa brought cool water from the red jar hanging under the brush shelter, and food when he called for it. The prairie zephyrs fanned him mildly; mocking-birds at morn and eve competed with but scarce equalled the sweet melodies of his lyre; a perfumed stillness seemed to fill all his world.

While old man Ellison was pottering among his flocks of sheep on his mile-an-hour pony, and while the Kiowa took his siesta in the burning sunshine at the end of the kitchen, Sam would lie on his cot thinking what a happy world he lived in, and how kind it is to the ones whose mission in life it is to give entertainment and pleasure. Here he had food and lodging as good as he had ever longed for; absolute immunity from care of exertion or strife; an endless welcome, and a host whose delight in the sixteenth repetition of a song or a story was as keen as at its initial giving. Was there ever a troubadour of old who struck upon as royal a castle in his wanderings? While he lay thus, mediating upon his blessings, little brown cottontails would shyly frolic through the yard; a covey of white-topknotted blue quail would run past, in single file, twenty yards away; a *paisano* bird, out hunting for tarantulas, would hop upon the fence and salute him with sweeping flourishes of its long tail. In the eighty-acre horse pasture the pony with the Dantesque face grew fat and almost smiling. The troubadour was at the end of his wanderings.

Old man Ellison was his own *vaciero*. That means that he supplied his sheep camps with wood, water, and rations by his own labours instead of hiring a *vaciero*. On small ranches it is often done. One morning he started for the camp of Incarnación Felipe de la Cruz y Monte Piedras (one of his sheep herders) with the week's usual rations of brown beans, coffee, meal, and sugar. Two miles away on the trail from old Fort Ewing, he met, face to face, a terrible being called King James, mounted on a fiery, prancing, Kentucky-bred horse.

King James's real name was James King; but people reversed it because it seemed to fit him better, and also because it seemed to please his majesty. King James was the biggest cattleman between the Alamo plaza in San Antone and Bill Hopper's saloon in Brownsville. Also he was the loudest and most offensive bully and braggart and bad man in south-west Texas. And he always made good whenever he bragged; and the more noise he made the more dangerous he was. In the story papers it is always the quiet, mild-mannered man with light-blue eyes and a low voice who turns out to be really dangerous; but in real life and in this story such is not the case. Give me my choice between assaulting a large, loud-mouthed rough-houser and an inoffensive stranger with blue eyes sitting quietly in a corner, and you will see something doing in the corner every time.

King James, as I intended to say earlier, was a fierce, two-hundred-

'I'm putting up a wire fence, forty by sixty miles,' said King James, 'and if there's a sheep inside of it when it's done it'll be a dead one.'

pound, sunburned, blond man, as pink as an October strawberry, and with two horizontal slits under shaggy red eyebrows for eyes. On that day he wore a flannel shirt that was tan-coloured, with the exception of certain large areas which were darkened by transudations due to the summer sun. There seemed to be other clothing and garnishings about him, such as brown duck trousers stuffed into immense boots, and red handkerchiefs and revolvers; and a shotgun laid across his saddle and a leather belt with millions of cartridges shining in it—but your mind skidded off such accessories; what held your gaze was just the two little horizontal slits that he used for eyes.

This was the man that old man Ellison met on the trail; and when you count up in the baron's favour that he was sixty-five and weighed ninety-eight pounds and had heard of King James's record, and that he (the baron) had a hankering for the *vita simplex* and had no gun with him and wouldn't have used it if he had, you can't censure him if I tell you that the smiles with which the troubadour had filled his wrinkles went out of them and left them plain wrinkles again. But he was not the kind of baron that flies from danger. He reined in the mile-an-hour pony (no difficult feat) and saluted the formidable monarch.

King James expressed himself with royal directness.

'You're that old snoozer that's running sheep on this range, ain't you?' said he. 'What right have you got to do it? Do you own any land, or lease any?'

'I have two sections leased from the state,' said old man Ellison mildly.

'Not by no means you haven't,' said King James. 'Your lease expired yesterday; and I had a man at the land office on the minute to take it up. You don't control a foot of grass in Texas. You sheep men have got to git. Your time's up. It's a cattle country, and there ain't any room in it for snoozers. This range you've got your sheep on is mine. I'm putting up a wire fence, forty by sixty miles; and if there's a sheep inside of it when it's done it'll be a dead one. I'll give you a week to move yours away. If they ain't gone by then, I'll send six men over here with Winchesters to make mutton out of the whole lot. And if I find you here at the same time this is what you'll get.'

King James patted the breech of his shotgun warningly.

Old man Ellison rode on to the camp of Incarnación. He sighed many times, and the wrinkles in his face grew deeper. Rumours that the old order was about to change had reached him before. The end of free grass was in sight. Other troubles, too, had been accumulating upon his shoulders. His flocks were decreasing instead of growing; the price of wool was declining at every clip; even Bradshaw, the storekeeper at Frio City, at whose store he bought his ranch supplies, was dunning him for his last six months' bill and threatening to cut him off. And so this last greatest calamity suddenly dealt out to him by the terrible King James was a crusher.

When the old man got back to the ranch at sunset he found Sam Galloway lying on his cot, propped against a roll of blankets and wool sacks, fingering his guitar.

'Hello, Uncle Ben,' the troubadour called cheerfully. 'You rolled in early this evening. I been trying a new twist on the Spanish fandango today. I just about got it. Here's how she goes—listen.'

'That's fine, that's mighty fine,' said old man Ellison, sitting on the kitchen step and rubbing his white, Scotch-terrier whiskers. 'I reckon you've got all the musicians beat east and west, Sam, as far as the roads are cut out.'

'Oh, I don't know,' said Sam reflectively. 'But I certainly do get there on variations. I guess I can handle anything in five flats about as well as any of 'em. But you look kind of fagged out, Uncle Ben— ain't you feeling right well this evening?'

'Little tired; that's all, Sam. If you ain't played yourself out, let's have that Mexican piece that starts off with "*Huile, huile, palomita.*" It seems that that song always kind of soothes and comforts me after I've been riding far or anything bothers me.'

'Why, *seguramente, senor,*' said Sam. 'I'll hit her up for you as often as you like. And before I forget about it, Uncle Ben, you want to jerk Bradshaw up about them last hams he sent us. They're just a little bit strong.'

A man sixty-five years old, living on a sheep ranch and beset by a complication of disasters, cannot successfully and continuously dis-semble. Moreover, a troubadour has eyes quick to see unhappiness in others around him—because it disturbs his own ease. So, on the next day, Sam again questioned the old man about his air of sadness and abstraction. Then old man Ellison told him the story of King James's threats and orders and that pale melancholy and red ruin appeared to have marked him for their own. The troubadour took the news thoughtfully. He had heard much about King James.

On the third day of the seven days of grace allowed him by the autocrat of the range, old man Ellison drove his buckboard to Frio City to fetch some necessary supplies for the ranch. Bradshaw was hard but not implacable. He divided the old man's order by two, and let him have a little more time. One article secured was a new fine ham for the pleasure of the troubadour.

Five miles out of Frio City on his way home the old man met King James riding into town. His majesty could never look anything but fierce and menacing, but today his slits of eyes appeared to be a little wider than they usually were.

'Good day,' said the king gruffly. 'I've been wanting to see you. I hear it said by a cowman from Sandy yesterday that you was from Jackson County, Mississippi, originally. I want to know if that's a fact.'

'Born there,' said old man Ellison, 'and raised there till I was twenty-one.'

'This man says.' went on King James, 'that he thinks you was related to the Jackson County Reeveses. Was he right?'

'Aunt Caroline Reeves,' said the old man, 'was my half-sister.'

'She was my aunt,' said King James. 'I run away from home when I was sixteen. Now let's re-talk over some things that we discussed a few days ago. They call me a bad man; and they're only half right. There's plenty of room in my pasture for your bunch of sheep and their in-crease for a long time to come. Aunt Caroline used to cut out sheep in cake dough and bake 'em for me. You keep your sheep where they are, and use all the range you want. How's your finances?' The old man related his woes in detail, dignifiedly, with restraint and candour.

'She used to smuggle extra grub into my school basket—I'm speaking of Aunt Caroline,' said King James. 'I'm going over to Frio City today, and I'll ride back by your ranch tomorrow. I'll draw two thousand dollars out of the bank there and bring it over to you; and I'll tell Bradshaw to let you have everything you want on credit. You are bound to have heard the old saying at home, that the Jackson County Reeveses and Kings would stick closer by each other than chestnut burrs. Well, I'm a King yet whenever I run across a Reeves. So you look out for me along about sundown tomorrow, and don't worry about nothing. Shouldn't wonder if the dry spell don't kill out the young grass.'

Old man Ellison drove happily ranchward. Once more the smiles filled out his wrinkles. Very suddenly, by the magic of kinship and the good that lies somewhere in all hearts, his troubles had been removed.

On reaching the ranch he found that Sam Galloway was not there. His guitar hung by its buckskin string to a hackberry limb, moaning as the gulf breeze blew across its masterless strings.

The Kiowa endeavoured to explain. 'Sam, he catch pony,' said he, 'and say he ride to Frio City. What for no can damn sabe. Say he come back tonight. Maybe so. That all.'

As the first stars came out the troubadour rode back to his haven. He pastured his pony and went into the house, his spurs jingling martially.

Old man Ellison sat at the kitchen table, having a tin cup of before-supper coffee. He looked contented and pleased.

'Hello, Sam,' said he, 'I'm darned glad to see ye back. I don't know how I managed to get along on this ranch, anyhow, before ye dropped in to cheer things up. I'll bet ye've been skylarking around with some of them Frio City gals, now, that's kept ye so late.'

And then old man Ellison took another look at Sam's face and saw that the minstrel had changed to the man of action.

And while Sam is unbuckling from his waist old man Ellison's six-shooter, that the latter had left behind him when he drove to town, we may well pause to remark that anywhere and whenever a troubadour lays down the guitar and takes up the sword trouble is sure to follow. It is not the expert thrust of Athos nor the cold skill of Aramis nor the iron wrist of Porthos that we have to fear—it is the Gascon's fury—the wild attack of the troubadour—the sword of D'Artagnan.

'I done it,' said Sam. 'I went over to Frio City to do it. I couldn't let him put the skibunk on you, Uncle Ben. I met him in Summer's saloon. I knowed what to do. I said a few things to him that nobody else heard. He reached for his gun first—half a dozen fellows saw him do it—but I got mine unlimbered first. Three doses I gave him—right around the lungs, and a saucer could have covered up all of 'em. He won't bother you no more.'

'This—is—King—James—you speak—of?' asked old man Ellison, while he sipped his coffee.

'You bet it was. And they took me before the county judge; and the witnesses what saw him draw his gun first was all there. Well, of course, they put me under $300 bond to appear before the court, but there was four or five boys on the spot ready to sign the bail. He won't bother you no more, Uncle Ben. You ought to have seen how close them bullet holes was together. I reckon playing a guitar as much as I do must kind of limber a fellow's trigger finger up a little, don't you think, Uncle Ben?'

Then there was a little silence in the castle except for the spluttering of a venison steak that the Kiowa was cooking.

'Sam,' said old man Ellison, stroking his white whiskers with a tremulous hand, 'would you mind getting the guitar and playing that *"Huile, huile, palomita,"* piece once or twice? It always seems to be kind of soothing and comforting when a man's tired and fagged out.'

There is no more to be said, except that the title of the story is wrong. It should have been called 'The Last of the Barons'. There never will be an end to the troubadours; and now and then it does seem that the jingle of their guitars will drown the sound of the muffled blows of the pickaxes and trip-hammers of all the workers in the world.

THE TREASURE HUNT

Robert Louis Stevenson

Jim Hawkins, whose father kept the Admiral Benbow Inn, *discovers a map in the sea-chest of old Billy Bones and takes it to Squire Trelawney. It turns out to be a map giving details of the buried treasure of Captain Flint, a pirate with whom Bones has served. Squire Trelawney, taking with him Dr Livesey and Jim, fits out the* Hispaniola *at Bristol to find the treasure. The squire's careless talk, however, attracts the scheming Long John Silver, who persuades Trelawney to enrol him as ship's cook and to crew the schooner with his nominees. The latter are all cut-throats and mutineers, and Silver himself Flint's old quartermaster.*

Immediately on landing at Treasure Island the trouble starts. The squire, the doctor and Jim, together with a few loyal seamen, escape from the ship and shift for themselves on the island.

Jim discovers Ben Gunn, who has been marooned for three years; but returning from a hazardous journey round the island on the Hispaniola, which he has secured in North Islet, he falls into the hands of Silver and his gang. Silver now has possession of the map through a deal with the doctor, but the lack of success of his plans to this point has put him in danger from his unruly followers. The pirates, taking Jim with them, start on the treasure hunt and stumble across a skeleton.

Partly from the damping influence of this alarm, partly to rest Silver and the sick folk, the whole party sat down as soon as they had gained the brow of the ascent.

The plateau being somewhat tilted toward the west, this spot on which we had paused commanded a wide prospect on either hand. Before us, over the treetops, we beheld the Cape of the Woods fringed with surf; behind, we not only looked down upon the anchorage and Skeleton Island, but saw—clear across the spit and the eastern lowlands

—a great field of open sea upon the east. Sheer above us rose the Spy-glass, here dotted with single pines, there black with precipices. There was no sound but that of the distant breakers, mounting from all round, and the chirp of countless insects in the brush. Not a man, not a sail upon the sea; the very largeness of the view increased the sense of solitude.

Silver, as he sat, took certain bearings with his compass.

'There are three "tall trees",' said he, 'about in the right line from Skeleton Island. "Spyglass shoulder", I take it, means that lower p'int there. It's child's play to find the stuff now. I've half a mind to dine first.'

'I don't feel sharp,' growled Morgan. 'Thinkin' o' Flint—I think it were—has done me.'

'Ah, well, my son, you praise your stars he's dead,' said Silver.

'He were an ugly devil,' cried a third pirate, with a shudder; 'that blue in the face, too!'

'That was how the rum took him,' added Merry.

'Blue! well, I reckon he was blue. That's a true word.'

Ever since they had found the skeleton and got upon this train of thought they had spoken lower and lower, and they had almost got to whispering by now, so that the sound of their talk hardly interrupted the silence of the wood. All of a sudden, out of the middle of the trees in front of us, a thin, high, trembling voice struck up the well-known air and words:

'Fifteen men on the dead man's chest—Yo-ho-ho, and a bottle of rum!'

I never have seen men more dreadfully affected than the pirates. The colour went from their six faces like enchantment; some leaped to their feet, some clawed hold of others; Morgan grovelled on the ground.

'It's Flint, by——!' cried Merry.

The song had stopped as suddenly as it began—broken off, you would have said, in the middle of a note, as though someone had laid his hand upon the singer's mouth. Coming so far through the clear, sunny atmosphere among the green treetops, I thought it had sounded airily and sweetly; and the effect on my companions was the stranger.

'Come,' said Silver, struggling with his ashen lips to get the word out, 'this won't do. Stand by to go about. This is a rum start, and I can't name the voice: but it's someone skylarking—someone that's flesh and blood, and you may lay to that.'

His courage had come back as he spoke, and some of the colour to his face along with it. Already the others had begun to lend an ear to this encouragement, and were coming a little to themselves, when the same voice broke out again—not this time singing, but in a faint, distant hail, that echoed yet fainter among the clefts of the Spyglass.

'Darby M'Graw,' it wailed—for that is the word that best describes the sound—'Darby M'Graw! Darby M'Graw!' again and again and again; and then rising a little higher, and with an oath that I leave out, 'Fetch aft the rum, Darby!'

The buccaneers remained rooted to the ground, their eyes starting from their heads. Long after the voice had died away they still stared in silence, dreadfully, before them.

'That fixes it!' gasped one. 'Let's go.'

'They was his last words,' moaned Morgan, 'his last words above-board.'

Dick had his Bible out and was praying volubly. He had been well brought up, had Dick, before he came to sea and fell among bad companions.

Still, Silver was unconquered. I could hear his teeth rattle in his head; but he had not yet surrendered.

'Nobody in this here island ever heard of Darby,' he muttered; 'not one but us that's here.' And then, making a great effort, 'Shipmates,' he cried, 'I'm here to get that stuff, and I'll not be beat by man nor devil. I never was feared of Flint in his life and, by the powers, I'll face him dead. There's seven hundred thousand pound not a quarter of a mile from here. When did ever a gentleman o' fortune show his stern to that much dollars, for a boozy old seaman with a blue mug—and him dead, too?'

But there was no sign of reawakening courage in his followers; rather, indeed, of growing terror at the irreverence of his words.

'Belay there, John!' said Merry. 'Don't you cross a sperrit.'

And the rest were all too terrified to reply. They would have run away severally had they dared, but fear kept them together, and kept them close by John, as if his daring helped them. He, on his part, had pretty well fought his weakness down.

'Sperrit! Well, maybe,' he said. 'But there's one thing not clear to me. There was an echo. Now, no man ever seen a sperrit with a shadow; well, then, what's he doing with an echo to him, I should like to know? That ain't in natur', surely?'

This argument seemed weak enough to me. But you can never tell what will affect the superstitious, and, to my wonder, George Merry was greatly relieved.

'Well, that's so,' he said. 'You've a head upon your shoulders, John, and no mistake. 'Bout ship, mates! This here crew is on a wrong tack, I do believe. And come to think on it, it was like Flint's voice, I grant you, but not just so clear-away like it, after all. It was liker somebody else's voice now—it was liker——'

'By the powers, Ben Gunn!' roared Silver.

'Aye, and so it were,' cried Morgan, springing on his knees. 'Ben Gunn it were!'

'It don't make much odds, do it, now?' asked Dick. 'Ben Gunn's not here in the body, any more'n Flint.'

But the older hands greeted this remark with scorn.

'Why, nobody minds Ben Gunn,' cried Merry; 'dead or alive, nobody minds him.'

It was extraordinary how their spirits had returned and how the natural colour had revived in their faces. Soon they were chatting together, with intervals of listening: and not long after, hearing no further sound, they shouldered the tools and set forth again, Merry walking first with Silver's compass to keep them on the right line with Skeleton Island. He had said the truth: dead or alive, nobody minded Ben Gunn.

Dick alone still held his Bible, and looked around him as he went, with fearful glances: but he found no sympathy, and Silver even joked him on his precautions.

'I told you,' said he, 'I told you you had sp'iled your Bible. If it ain't no good to swear by, what do you suppose a sperrit would give for it? Not that!' and he snapped his big fingers, halting a moment on his crutch.

But Dick was not to be comforted; indeed, it was soon plain to me that the lad was falling sick; hastened by heat, exhaustion, and the shock of his alarm, the fever predicted by Dr Livesey was evidently growing swiftly higher.

It was fine open walking here, upon the summit; our way lay a little downhill, for, as I have said, the plateau tilted toward the west. The pines, great and small, grew wide apart; and even between the clumps of nutmeg and azalea wide-open spaces baked in the hot sunshine. Striking, as we did, pretty near north-west across the island, we drew, on the one hand, ever nearer under the shoulders of the Spyglass and, on the other, looked ever wider over that western bay where I had once tossed and trembled in the coracle.

The first of the tall trees was reached, and by the bearing proved the wrong one. So with the second. The third rose nearly two hundred feet into the air above a clump of underwood; a giant of a vegetable, with a red column as big as a cottage, and a wide shadow around in which a company could have manoeuvred. It was conspicuous far to sea on both the east and west, and might have been entered as a sailing mark upon the chart.

But it was not its size that now impressed my companions; it was the knowledge that seven hundred thousand pounds in gold lay somewhere buried below its spreading shadow. The thought of the money, as they drew nearer, swallowed up their previous terrors. Their eyes burned in their heads; their feet grew speedier and lighter; their whole soul was bound up in that fortune, that whole lifetime of extravagance and pleasure, that lay waiting for each of them.

Silver hobbled, grunting, on his crutch; his nostrils stood out and quivered; he cursed like a madman when the flies settled on his hot and shiny countenance; he plucked furiously at the line that held me to him and, from time to time, turned his eyes upon me with a deadly look. Certainly he took no pains to hide his thoughts; and certainly I read them like print. In the immediate nearness of the gold, all else had been forgotten; his promise and the doctor's warning were both things of the past; and I could not doubt that he hoped to seize upon the treasure, find and board the *Hispaniola* under cover of night, cut every honest throat about that island, and sail away as he had at first intended, laden with crimes and riches.

Shaken as I was with these alarms, it was hard for me to keep up with the rapid pace of the treasure hunters. Now and again I stumbled, and it was then that Silver plucked so roughly at the rope and launched at me his murderous glances. Dick, who had dropped behind us and now brought up the rear, was babbling to himself both prayers and curses, as his fever kept rising. This also added to my wretchedness, and, to crown all, I was haunted by the thought of the tragedy that had once been acted on that plateau, when that ungodly buccaneer with the blue face—he who died at Savannah, singing and shouting for drink—had there, with his own hand, cut down his six accomplices. This grove, that was now so peaceful, must then have rung with cries, I thought; and even with the thought I could believe I heard it ringing still.

We were now at the margin of the thicket and more light shone through the trees.

'Huzza, mates, all together!' shouted Merry, and the foremost broke into a run.

And suddenly, not ten yards farther, we beheld them stop. A low cry arose. Silver doubled his pace, digging away with the foot of his crutch like one possessed; and next moment he and I came to a dead halt.

Before us was a great excavation, not very recent, for the sides had fallen in and grass had sprouted on the bottom. In this were the shaft of a pick broken in two and the boards of several packing cases strewn around. On one of these boards I saw, branded with a hot iron, the name *Walrus*—the name of Flint's ship.

All was clear to probation. The cache had been found and rifled: the seven hundred thousand pounds were gone!

There never was such an overturn in this world. Each of these six men was as though he had been struck. But with Silver the blow passed almost instantly. Every thought of his soul had been set full-stretch, like a racer, on that money. Well, he was brought up in a single second, dead; and he kept his head, found his temper, and changed his plan before the others had had time to realize the disappointment.

'Jim', he whispered, 'take that, and stand by for trouble.'

And he passed me a double-barrelled pistol.

At the same time he began quietly moving northward, and in a few steps had put the hollow between us two and the other five. Then he looked at me and nodded, as much as to say, 'Here is a narrow corner,' as, indeed, I thought it was. His looks were now quite friendly; and I was so revolted at these constant changes that I could not forbear whispering, 'So you've changed sides again.'

There was no time left for him to answer in. The buccaneers, with oaths and cries, began to leap, one after another, into the pit, and to dig

Silver doubled his pace, digging away with his crutch like one possessed.

with their fingers, throwing the boards aside as they did so. Morgan found a piece of gold. He held it up with a spout of oaths. It was a two-guinea piece, and it went from hand to hand among them for a quarter of a minute.

'Two guineas!' roared Merry, shaking it at Silver. 'That's your seven hundred thousand pounds, is it? You're the man for bargains, ain't you? You're him that never bungled nothing, you wooden-headed lubber!'

'Dig away, boys,' said Silver, with the coolest insolence, 'you'll find some pignuts and I shouldn't wonder.'

'Pignuts!' repeated Merry in a scream. 'Mates, do you hear that? I tell you, now, that man there knew it all along. Look in the face of him, and you'll see it wrote there.'

'Ah, Merry,' remarked Silver, 'standing for cap'n again? You're a pushing lad, to be sure.'

But this time everyone was entirely in Merry's favour. They began to scramble out of the excavation, darting furious glances behind them. One thing I observed, which looked well for us: they all got out upon the opposite side from Silver.

Well, there we stood, two on one side, five on the other, the pit between us, and nobody screwed up high enough to offer the first blow. Silver never moved; he watched them, very upright on his crutch, and looked as cool as ever I saw him. He was brave, and no mistake.

At last Merry seemed to think a speech might help matters.

'Mates', says he, 'there's two of them alone there: one's the old cripple that brought us all here and blundered us down to this; the other's that cub that I mean to have the heart of. Now, mates——'

He was raising his arm and his voice, and plainly meant to lead a charge. But jest then—*crack! crack! crack!*—three muskets shots flashed out of the thicket. Merry tumbled head foremost into the excavation; the man with the bandage spun round like a teetotum and fell all his length upon his side, where he lay dead, but still twitching; and the other three turned and ran for it with all their might.

Before you could wink, Long John had fired two barrels of a pistol into the struggling Merry; and as the man rolled up his eyes at him in the last agony, 'George,' said he, 'I reckon I settled you.'

At the same moment, the doctor, Gray and Ben Gunn joined us, with smoking muskets, from among the nutmeg trees.

'Forward!' cried the doctor. 'Double quick, my lads. We must head 'em off the boats.'

And we set off at a great pace, sometimes plunging through the bushes to the chest.

I tell you, but Silver was anxious to keep up with us. The work that man went through, leaping on his crutch till the muscles of his chest were fit to burst, was work no sound man ever equalled; and so thinks the doctor. As it was, he was already thirty yards behind us, and on the verge of strangling, when we reached the brow of the slope.

'Doctor,' he hailed, 'see there! No hurry!'

Sure enough there was no hurry. In a more open part of the plateau we could see the three survivors still running in the same direction as they had started, right for Mizzenmast Hill. We were already between them and the boats, and so we four sat down to breathe, while Long John, mopping his face, came slowly up with us.

'Thank ye kindly, doctor,' says he. 'You came in in about the nick, I guess, for me and Hawkins. And so it's you, Ben Gunn!' he added. 'Well, you're a nice one, to be sure.'

'I'm Ben Gunn, I am,' replied the maroon, wriggling like an eel in his embarrassment. 'And,' he added, after a long pause, 'how do, Mr Silver? Pretty well, I thank ye, says you.'

'Ben, Ben,' murmured Silver, 'to think as you've done me!'

The doctor sent back Gray for one of the pickaxes, deserted, in their flight, by the mutineers; and then as we proceeded leisurely downhill to where the boats were lying, related, in a few words, what had taken place. It was a story that interested Silver; and Ben Gunn, the half-idiot maroon, was the hero from beginning to end.

Ben, in his long, lonely wanderings about the island, had found the skeleton—it was he that had rifled it; he had found the treasure; he had dug it up (it was the haft of his pickaxe that lay broken in the excavation); he had carried it on his back, in many weary journeys, from the foot of the tall pine to a cave he had on the two-pointed hill at the northeast angle of the island, and there it had lain stored in safety since two months before the arrival of the *Hispaniola*.

When the doctor had wormed this secret from him, on the afternoon of the attack, and when next morning he saw the anchorage deserted, he had gone to Silver, given him the chart, which was now useless—

given him the stores, for Ben Gunn's cave was well supplied with goats' meat salted by himself—given anything and everything to get a chance of moving in safety from the stockade to the two-pointed hill, there to be clear of malaria and keep a guard on the money.

'As for you, Jim,' he said, 'it went against my heart, but I did what I thought best for those who had stood by their duty. And if you were not one of these, whose fault was it?'

That morning, finding that I was to be involved in the horrid disappointment he had prepared for the mutineers, he had run all the way to the cave and, leaving the squire to guard the captain, had taken Gray and the maroon, and started, making the diagonal across the island, to be at hand beside the pine. Soon, however, he saw that our party had the start of him; and Ben Gunn, being fleet of foot, had been dispatched in front to do his best alone. Then it had occurred to him to work upon the superstitions of his former shipmates; and he was so far successful that Gray and the doctor had come up and were already ambushed before the arrival of the treasure hunters.

'Ah,' said Silver, 'it were fortunate for me that I had Hawkins here. You would have let old John be cut to bits, and never given it a thought, doctor.'

'Not a thought,' replied Dr Livesey cheerily.

And by this time we had reached the gigs. The doctor, with the pickaxe, demolished one of them, and then we all got aboard the other, and set out to go round by sea for North Inlet.

This was a run of eight or nine miles. Silver, though he was almost killed already with fatigue, was set to an oar, like the rest of us, and we were soon skimming swiftly over a smooth sea. Soon we passed out of the straits and doubled the south-east corner of the island, round which, four days ago, we had towed the *Hispaniola*.

As we passed the two-pointed hill we could see the black mouth of Ben Gunn's cave, and a figure standing by it, leaning on a musket. It was the squire, and we waved a handkerchief and gave him three cheers, in which the voice of Silver joined as heartily as any.

Three miles farther, just inside the mouth of North Inlet, what should we meet but the *Hispaniola*, cruising by herself. The last flood had lifted her, and had there been much wind, or a strong tide current, as in the southern anchorage, we should never have found her more, or found her stranded beyond help. As it was, there was little amiss beyond the wreck of the mainsail. Another anchor was got ready, and dropped in a fathom and a half of water. We all pulled round again to Rum Cove, the nearest point for Ben Gunn's treasure house; and then Gray, single-handed, returned with the gig to the *Hispaniola*, where he was to pass the night on guard.

A gentle slope ran up from the beach to the entrance of the cave. At the top the squire met us. To me he was cordial and kind, saying nothing of my escapade, either in the way of blame or praise. At Silver's polite salute he somewhat flushed.

'John Silver,' he said, 'you're a prodigious villain and impostor—a monstrous impostor, sir. I am told I am not to prosecute you. Well, then, I will not. But the dead men, sir, hang about your neck like mill-stones.'

'Thank you kindly, sir,' replied Long John, again saluting.

'I dare you to thank me!' cried the squire. 'It is a gross dereliction of my duty. Stand back.'

And thereupon we all entered the cave. It was a large, airy place, with a little spring and a pool of clear water, overhung with ferns. The floor was sand. Before a big fire lay Captain Smollett, and in a far corner, only duskily flickered over by the blaze, I beheld great heaps of coin and quadrilaterals built of bars of gold. That was Flint's treasure that we had come so far to seek, and that had cost already the lives of seventeen men from the *Hispaniola*. How many it had cost in the amassing, what blood and sorrow, what good ships scuttled on the deep, what brave men walking the plank blindfold, what shot of cannon, what shame and lies and cruelty, perhaps no man alive could tell. Yet there were still three upon that island—Silver, and old Morgan, and Ben Gunn—who had each taken his share in these crimes, as each had hoped in vain to share in the reward.

'Come in, Jim,' said the captain. 'You're a good boy in your line, Jim, but I don't think you and me'll go to sea again. You're too much of the born favourite for me. Is that you, John Silver? What brings you here, man?'

'Come back to my dooty, sir,' returned Silver.

'Ah!' said the captain; and that was all he said.

What a supper I had of it that night, with all my friends around me;

and what a meal it was, with Ben Gunn's salted goat, and some delicacies and a bottle of old wine from the *Hispaniola*. Never, I am sure, were people gayer or happier. And there was Silver, sitting back almost out of the firelight, but eating heartily, prompt to spring forward when anything was wanted, even joining quietly in our laughter—the same bland, polite, obsequious seaman of the voyage out.

THE PIT AND
THE PENDULUM

Edgar Allan Poe

I was sick—sick unto death with that long agony; and when they at length unbound me, and I was permitted to sit, I felt that my senses were leaving me. The sentence—the dread sentence of death—was the last of distinct accentuation which reached my ears. After that, the sound of the Inquisitorial voices seemed merged in one dreamy indeterminate hum. It conveyed to my soul the idea of *revolution*—perhaps from its association in fancy with the burr of a mill-wheel. This only for a brief period; for presently I heard no more.

Yet, for a while, I saw; but with how terrible an exaggeration! I saw the lips of the black-robed judges. They appeared to me white—whiter than the sheet upon which I trace these words—and thin even to grotesqueness; thin with the intensity of their expression of firmness—of immovable resolution—of stern contempt of human torture. I saw that the decrees of what to me was Fate were still issuing from those lips. I saw them writhe with a deadly locution. I saw them fashion the syllables of my name; and I shuddered because no sound succeeded. I saw, too, for a few moments of delirious horror, the soft and nearly imperceptible waving of the sable draperies which enwrapped the walls of the apartment. And then my vision fell upon the seven tall candles upon the table. At first they wore the aspect of charity, and seemed white slender angels who would save me; but then, all at once, there came a most deadly nausea over my spirit, and I felt every fibre in my frame thrill as if I had touched the wire of a galvanic battery, while the angel forms became meaningless spectres, with heads of flame, and I saw that from them there would be no help.

And then there stole into my fancy, like a rich musical note, the thought of what sweet rest there must be in the grave. The thought came gently and stealthily, and it seemed long before it attained full appreciation; but just as my spirit came at length properly to feel and entertain it, the figures of the judges vanished, as if magically, from before me; the tall candles sank into nothingness; their flames went out utterly; the blackness of darkness supervened; all sensations appeared swallowed up in a mad rushing descent as of the soul into Hades. Then silence, and stillness, and night were the universe.

I had swooned; but still will not say that all of consciousness was lost. Amid frequent and thoughtful endeavours to remember; amid earnest struggles to regather some token of the state of seeming nothingness into which my soul had lapsed, there have been moments when I have dreamed of success; there have been brief, very brief periods when I have conjured up remembrances which the lucid reason of a later epoch assures me could have had reference only to that condition of seeming unconsciousness. These shadows of memory tell, indistinctly, of tall figures that lifted and bore me in silence down—down—still down— till a hideous dizziness oppressed me at the mere idea of the interminableness of the descent. They tell also of a vague horror at my heart, on account of that heart's unnatural stillness. Then comes a sense of sudden motionlessness throughout all things; as if those who bore me (a ghastly train!) had outrun, in their descent, the limits of the limitless, and paused from the wearisomeness of their toil. After this I call to mind flatness and dampness; and then all is *madness*—the madness of a memory which busies itself among forbidden things.

So far, I had not opened my eyes. I felt that I lay upon my back, un- bound. I reached out my hand, and it fell heavily upon something damp and hard. There I suffered it to remain for many minutes, while I strove to imagine where and *what* I could be. I longed, yet dared not, to employ my vision. I dreaded the first glance at objects around me. It was not that I feared to look upon things horrible, but that I grew aghast lest there should be *nothing* to see. At length, with a wild desperation at heart, I quickly unclosed my eyes. My worst thoughts, then, were confirmed. The blackness of eternal night encompassed me. I struggled for breath. The intensity of the darkness seemed to oppress and stifle me. The atmosphere was intolerably close. I still lay quietly, and made effort to exercise my reason. I brought to mind the Inquisitorial proceedings, and attempted from that point to deduce my real condition. The sentence had passed; and it appeared to me that a very long interval of time had since elapsed. Yet not for a moment did I suppose myself actually dead. Such a supposition, notwithstanding what we read in fiction, is altogether inconsistent with real existence—but where and in what state was I?

A fearful idea now suddenly drove the blood in torrents upon my heart, and for a brief period I once more relapsed into insensibility. Upon recovering, I at once started to my feet, trembling convulsively in every fibre. I thrust my arms wildly above and around me in all directions. I felt nothing; yet dreaded to move a step, lest I should be impeded by the walls of a *tomb*. Perspiration burst from every pore, and stood in cold beads upon my forehead. The agony of suspense grew at length intolerable, and I cautiously moved forward, with my arms extended, and my eyes straining from their sockets, in the hope of catching some faint ray of light. I proceeded for many paces; but still all was blackness and vacancy. I breathed more freely. It seemed evident that mine was not, at least, the most hideous of fates.

And now, as I still continued to step cautiously onward, there came thronging upon my recollection a thousand vague rumours of the horrors of Toledo. Of the dungeons there had been strange things narrated—fables I had always deemed them—but yet strange, and too ghastly to repeat, save in a whisper. Was I left to perish of starvation in this subterranean world of darkness; or what fate, perhaps even more fearful, awaited me? That the result would be death, and a death of more than customary bitterness, I knew too well the character of my judges to doubt. The mode and the hour were all that occupied or distracted me.

My outstretched hands at length encountered some solid obstruction.

It was a wall, seemingly of stone masonry—very smooth, slimy, and cold. I followed it up, stepping with all the careful distrust with which certain antique narratives had inspired me. This process, however, afforded me no means of ascertaining the dimensions of my dungeon, as I might make its circuit, and return to the point whence I set out, without being aware of the fact, so perfectly uniform seemed the wall. I therefore sought the knife which had been in my pocket, when led into the inquisitorial chamber, but it was gone; my clothes had been exchanged for a wrapper of coarse serge. I had thought of forcing the blade in some minute crevice of the masonry, so as to identify my point of departure. The difficulty, nevertheless, was but trivial; although, in the disorder of my fancy, it seemed at first insuperable. I tore a part of the hem from the robe and placed the fragment at full length, and at right-angles to the wall. In groping my way around the prison, I could not fail to encounter this rag upon completing the circuit. So, at least, I thought; but I had not counted upon the extent of the dungeon, or upon my own weakness. The ground was moist and slippery. I staggered onward for some time, when I stumbled and fell. My excessive fatigue induced me to remain prostrate; and sleep soon overtook me as I lay.

Upon awaking, and stretching forth an arm, I found beside me a loaf and a pitcher with water. I was too much exhausted to reflect upon this circumstance, but ate and drank with avidity. Shortly afterward I resumed my tour around the prison, and, with much toil, came at last upon the fragment of the serge. Up to the period when I fell, I had counted fifty-two paces, and, upon resuming my walk, I had counted forty-eight more—when I arrived at the rag. There were in all, then, a hundred paces; and, admitting two paces to the yard, I presumed the dungeon to be fifty yards in circuit. I had met, however, with many angles in the wall, and thus I could form no guess at the shape of the vault; for vault I could not help supposing it to be.

I had little object—certainly no hope—in these researches; but a vague curiosity prompted me to continue them. Quitting the wall, I resolved to cross the area of the enclosure. At first, I proceeded with extreme caution, for the floor, although seemingly of solid material, was treacherous with slime. At length, however, I took courage, and did not hesitate to step firmly—endeavouring to cross in as direct a line as possible. I had advanced some ten or twelve paces in this manner, when the remnant of the torn hem of my robe became entangled between my legs. I stepped on it, and fell violently on my face.

In the confusion attending my fall, I did not immediately apprehend a somewhat startling circumstance, which yet, in a few seconds afterward, and while I still lay prostrate, arrested my attention. It was this: my chin rested upon the floor of the prison, but my lips, and the upper portion of my head, already seemingly at a less elevation than the chin, touched nothing. At the same time, my forehead seemed bathed in a clammy vapour, and the peculiar smell of decayed fungus arose to my nostrils. I put forward my arm, and shuddered to find that I had fallen at the very brink of a circular pit, whose extent, of course, I had no means of ascertaining at the moment. Groping about the masonry just below the margin, I succeeded in dislodging a small fragment, and let it fall into the abyss. For many seconds I hearkened to its reverberations as it dashed against the sides of the chasm in its descent. At length, there was a sullen plunge into water, succeeded by loud echoes. At the same moment, there came a sound resembling the quick opening, and as rapid closing, of a door overhead, while a faint gleam of light flashed suddenly through the gloom, and as suddenly faded away.

I saw clearly the doom which had been prepared for me, and congratulated myself upon the timely accident by which I had escaped. Another step before my fall, and the world had seen me no more. And the death just avoided was of that very character which I had regarded as fabulous and frivolous in the tales respecting the Inquisition. To the victims of its tyranny, there was the choice of death with its direst physical agonies, or death with its most hideous moral horrors. I had been reserved for the latter. By long suffering my nerves had been unstrung, until I trembled at the sound of my own voice, and had become in every respect a fitting subject for the species of torture which awaited me.

Shaking in every limb, I groped my way back to the wall—resolving there to perish rather than risk the terrors of the wells, of which my imagination now pictured many in various positions about the dungeon. In other conditions of mind, I might have had courage to end my misery at once, by a plunge into one of these abysses; but now I was the veriest of cowards. Neither could I forget what I had read of these pits—that the *sudden* extinction of life formed no part of their most horrible plan.

Agitation of spirit kept me awake for many long hours; but at length I again slumbered. Upon arousing, I found by my side, as before, a loaf and a pitcher of water. A burning thirst consumed me, and I emptied the vessel at a draught. It must have been drugged—for scarcely had I drunk before I became irresistibly drowsy. A deep sleep fell upon me—a sleep like that of death. How long it lasted, of course, I know not; but when, once again, I unclosed my eyes, the objects around me were visible. By a wild, sulphurous lustre, the origin of which I could not at first determine, I was enabled to see the extent and aspect of the prison.

In its size I had been greatly mistaken. The whole circuit of its walls did not exceed twenty-five yards. For some minutes this fact occasioned me a world of vain trouble; vain indeed—for what could be of less importance, under the terrible circumstances which environed me, than the mere dimensions of my dungeon? But my soul took a wild interest in trifles, and I busied myself in endeavours to account for the error I had committed in my measurement. The truth at length flashed upon me. In my first attempt at exploration I had counted fifty-two paces, up to the period when I fell; I must then have been within a pace or two of the fragment of serge; in fact, I had nearly performed the circuit of the vault. I then slept—and, upon awaking, I must have returned upon my steps—thus supposing the circuit nearly double what it actually was. My confusion of mind prevented me from observing that I began my tour with the wall to the left, and ended it with the wall to the right.

I had been deceived, too, in respect to the shape of the enclosure. In feeling my way, I had found many angles, and thus deduced an idea of great irregularity; so potent is the effect of total darkness upon one arousing from lethargy or sleep! The angles were simply those of a few slight depressions, or niches, at odd intervals. The general shape of the prison was square. What I had taken for masonry seemed now to be iron, or some other metal, in huge plates, whose sutures or joints occasioned the depression. The entire surface of this metallic enclosure was rudely daubed in all the hideous and repulsive devices to which the charnel superstition of the monks has given rise. The figures of fiends in aspects of menace, with skeleton forms, and other more really fearful images, overspread and disfigured the walls. I observed that the outlines of these monstrosities were sufficiently distinct, but that the colours seemed faded and blurred, as if from the effects of a damp atmosphere. I now noticed the floor, too, which was of stone. In the centre yawned the circular pit from whose jaws I had escaped; but it was the only one in the dungeon.

All this I saw indistinctly and by much effort—for my personal condition had been greatly changed during slumber. I now lay upon my back, and at full length, on a species of low framework of wood. To this I was securely bound by a long strap resembling a surcingle. It passed in many convolutions about my limbs and body, leaving at liberty only my head and my left arm to such extent that I could, by dint of much exertion, supply myself with food from an earthen dish which lay by my side on the floor. I saw, to my horror, that the pitcher had been removed. I say, to my horror—for I was consumed with intolerable thirst. This thirst it appeared to be the design of my persecutors to stimulate—for the food in the dish was meat pungently seasoned.

Looking upward, I surveyed the ceiling of my prison. It was some thirty or forty feet overhead, and constructed much as the side walls. In one of its panels a very singular figure riveted my whole attention. It was the painted figure of Time as he is commonly represented, save that, in lieu of a scythe, he held what, at a casual glance, I supposed to be the pictured image of a huge pendulum, such as we see on antique clocks. There was something, however, in the appearance of this machine which caused me to regard it more attentively. While I gazed directly upward at it (for its position was immediately over my own), I fancied that I saw it in motion. In an instant afterward the fancy was confirmed. Its sweep was brief, and, of course, slow. I watched it for some minutes, somewhat in fear, but more in wonder. Wearied at length with observing its dull movement, I turned my eyes upon the other objects in the cell.

A slight noise attracted my notice, and looking to the floor, I saw several enormous rats traversing it. They had issued from the well, which lay just within view to my right. Even then, while I gazed, they came up in troops, hurriedly, with ravenous eyes, allured by the scent of the meat. From this it required much effort and attention to scare them away.

It might have been half an hour, perhaps even an hour (for I could take but imperfect note of time) before I again cast my eyes upward. What I then saw confounded and amazed me. The sweep of the pendulum had increased in extent by nearly a yard. As a natural consequence, its velocity was also much greater. But what mainly disturbed me was the idea that it had perceptibly *descended*. I now observed—with what horror it is needless to say—that its nether extremity was formed of a crescent of glittering steel, about a foot in length from horn to horn; the horns upward, and the under edge evidently as keen as that of a razor. Like a razor also, it seemed massy and heavy, tapering from the edge into a solid and broad structure above. It was appended to a weighty rod of brass, and the whole hissed as it swung through the air.

I could no longer doubt the doom prepared for me by monkish ingenuity in torture. My awareness of the pit had become known to the inquisitorial agents—*the pit* whose horrors had been destined for so bold a recusant as myself—*the pit*, typical of hell, and regarded by rumour as the Ultima Thule of all their punishments. The plunge into this pit I had avoided by the merest of accidents, and I knew that surprise, or entrapment into torment, formed an important portion of all the grotesqueries of these dungeon deaths. Having failed to fall, it was no part of the demon plan to hurl me into the abyss; and thus (there being no alternative) a different and a milder destruction awaited me. Milder! I half smiled in my agony as I thought of such application of such a term.

What boots it to tell of the long, long hours of horror more than mortal, during which I counted the rushing oscillations of the steel! Inch by inch—line by line—with a descent only appreciable at intervals that seemed ages—down and still down it came! Days passed—it might have been that many days passed—ere it swept so closely over me as to fan me with its acrid breath. The odour of the sharp steel forced itself into my nostrils. I prayed—I wearied heaven with my prayer for its more speedy descent. I grew frantically mad, and struggled to force myself upward against the sweep of the fearful scimitar. And then I fell suddenly calm, and lay smiling at the glittering death, as a child at some rare bauble.

There was another interval of utter insensibility; it was brief, for upon again lapsing into life, there had been no perceptible descent in the pendulum. But it might have been long—for I knew there were demons

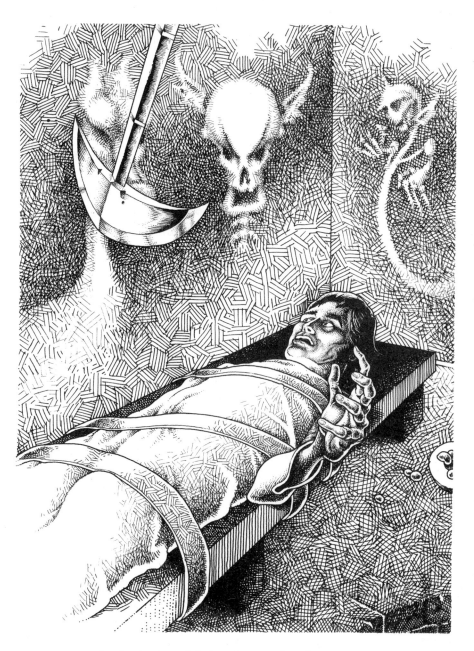

'Down, relentlessly down! I shrank convulsively at its every sweep.'

who took note of my swoon, and who could have arrested the vibration at pleasure.

Upon my recovery, too, I felt very—oh, inexpressibly—sick and weak, as if through long starvation. Even amid the agonies of that period the human nature craved food. With painful effort I outstretched my left arm as far as my bonds permitted, and took possession of the small remnant which had been spared me by the rats. As I put a portion of it within my lips, there rushed to my mind a half-formed thought of joy—of hope. Yet what business had *I* with hope? It was, as I say, a half-formed thought—man has many such, which are never completed. I felt that it was of joy—of hope; but I felt also that it had perished in its formation. In vain I struggled to perfect—to regain it. Long suffering had nearly annihilated all my ordinary powers of mind. I was an imbecile—an idiot.

The vibration of the pendulum was at right-angles to my length. I saw that the crescent was designed to cross the region of the heart. It would fray the serge of my robe—it would return and repeat its operations—again—and again. Notwithstanding its terrifically wide sweep (some thirty feet or more), and the hissing vigour of its descent, sufficient to sunder these very walls of iron, still the fraying of my robe would be all that, for several minutes, it would accomplish. And at this thought I paused. I dared not go farther than this reflection. I dwelt upon it with a persistent attention—as if, in so dwelling, I could arrest *here* the descent of the steel. I forced myself to ponder upon the sound of the crescent as it should pass across the garment—upon the peculiar thrilling sensation which the friction of cloth produces on the nerves. I pondered upon all this frivolity until my teeth were on edge.

Down—steadily down it crept. I took a frenzied pleasure in contrasting its downward with its lateral velocity. To the right—to the left—far and wide—with the shriek of a damned spirit! To my heart, with the stealthy pace of the tiger! I alternately laughed and howled, as the one or the other idea grew predominant.

Down—certainly, relentlessly down! It vibrated within three inches of my bosom! I struggled violently—furiously—to free my left arm. This was free only from the elbow to the hand. I could reach the latter, from the platter beside me, to my mouth, with great effort, but no farther. Could I have broken the fastenings above the elbow, I would have seized and attempted to arrest the pendulum. I might as well have attempted to arrest an avalanche!

Down—still unceasingly—still inevitably down! I gasped and struggled at each vibration. I shrank convulsively at its every sweep. My eyes followed its outward or upward whirls with the eagerness of the most unmeaning despair; they closed themselves spasmodically at the descent, although death would have been a relief, oh, how unspeakable! Still I quivered in every nerve to think how slight a sinking of the machinery would precipitate that keen, glistening axe upon my bosom. It was *hope* that prompted the nerve to quiver—the frame to shrink. It was *hope*—the hope that triumphs on the rack—that whispers to the death-condemned even in the dungeons of the Inquisition.

I saw that some ten or twelve vibrations would bring the steel in actual contact with my robe—and with this observation there suddenly came over my spirit all the keen, collected calmness of despair. For the first time during many hours—or perhaps days—I *thought*. It now occurred to me that the bandage, or surcingle, which enveloped me, was *unique*. I was tied by no separate cord. The first stroke of the razor-like crescent athwart any portion of the band would so detach it that it might be unwound from my person by means of my left hand. But how fearful, in that case, the proximity of the steel! The result of the slightest struggle, how deadly! Was it likely, moreover, that the minions of the torturer had not foreseen and provided for this possibility! Was it probable that the bandage crossed my bosom in the track of the pendulum? Dreading to find my faint, and, as it seemed, my last hope frustrated, I so far elevated my head as to obtain a distinct view of my breast. The surcingle enveloped my limbs and body close in all directions—*save in the path of the destroying crescent.*

Scarcely had I dropped my head back into its original position, when there flashed upon my mind what I cannot better describe than as the unformed half of that idea of deliverance to which I have previously alluded, and of which a part only floated indeterminately through my brain when I raised food to my burning lips. The whole thought was now present—feeble, scarcely sane, scarcely definite—but still entire. I proceeded at once, with the nervous energy of despair, to attempt its execution.

For many hours the immediate vicinity of the low framework upon which I lay, had been literally swarming with rats. They were wild, bold, ravenous—their red eyes glaring upon me as if they waited but for motionlessness on my part to make me their prey. 'To what food,' I thought, 'have they been accustomed in the well?'

They had devoured, in spite of all my efforts to prevent them, all but a small remnant of the contents of the dish. I had fallen into an habitual see-saw, or wave of the hand, about the platter; and at length the unconscious uniformity of the movement deprived it of effect. In their voracity, the vermin frequently fastened their sharp fangs in my fingers. With the particles of the oil and spicy food which now remained, I thoroughly rubbed the bandage wherever I could reach it; then, raising my hand from the floor, I lay breathlessly still.

At first, the ravenous animals were startled and terrified at the change—at the cessation of movement. They shrank alarmedly back; many sought the well. But this was only for a moment. I had not counted in vain upon their voracity. Observing that I remained without motion, one or two of the boldest leaped upon the framework, and smelt at the surcingle. This seemed the signal for a general rush. Forth from the well they hurried in fresh troops. They clung to the wood—they overran it, and leaped in hundreds upon my person. The measured movement of the pendulum disturbed them not at all. Avoiding its strokes, they busied themselves with the anointed bandage. They pressed—they swarmed upon me in ever accumulating heaps. They writhed upon my throat; their cold lips sought my own; I was half stifled by their thronging pressure; disgust, for which the world has no name, swelled my bosom, and chilled, with a heavy clamminess, my heart. Yet one minute, and I felt that the struggle would be over. Plainly I perceived the loosening of the bandage. I knew that in more than one place it must be already severed. With a more than human resolution I lay still.

Nor had I erred in my calculations—nor had I endured in vain. I at length felt that I was *free*. The surcingle hung in ribands from my body. But the stroke of the pendulum already pressed upon my bosom. It had divided the serge of the robe. It had cut through the linen beneath. Twice again it swung, and a sharp sense of pain shot through every nerve. But the moment of escape had arrived. At a wave of my hand my deliverers hurried tumultuously away. With a steady movement—

cautious, sidelong, shrinking, and slow—I slid from the embrace of the bandage and beyond the reach of the scimitar. For the moment, at least, *I was free.*

Free!—and in the grasp of the Inquisition! I had scarcely stepped from my wooden bed of horror upon the stone floor of the prison, when the motion of the hellish machine ceased, and I beheld it drawn up, by some invisible force, through the ceiling. This was a lesson which I took desperately to heart. My every motion was undoubtedly watched. Free!—I had but escaped death in one form of agony, to be delivered unto worse than death in some other. With that thought I rolled my eyes nervously around on the barriers of iron that hemmed me in. Something unusual—some change which, at first, I could not appreciate distinctly—it was obvious, had taken place in the apartment. For many minutes of a dreamy and trembling abstraction, I busied myself in vain, unconnected conjecture.

During this period, I became aware, for the first time, of the origin of the sulphurous light which illumined the cell. It proceeded from a fissure, about half an inch in width, extending entirely around the prison at the base of the walls, which thus appeared, and were completely separated from the floor. I endeavoured, but of course in vain, to look through the aperture.

As I arose from the attempt, the mystery of the alteration in the chamber broke at once upon my understanding. I have observed that, although the outlines of the figures upon the walls were sufficiently distinct, yet the colours seemed blurred and indefinite. These colours had now assumed, and were momentarily assuming, a startling and most intense brilliancy, that gave to the spectral and fiendish portraitures an aspect that might have thrilled even firmer nerves than my own. Demon eyes, of a wild and ghastly vivacity, glared upon me in a thousand directions, where none had been visible before, and gleamed with the lurid lustre of a fire that I could not force my imagination to regard as unreal.

Unreal! Even while I breathed there came to my nostrils the breath of the vapour of heated iron! A suffocating odour pervaded the prison! A deeper glow settled each moment in the eyes that glared at my agonies! A richer tint of crimson diffused itself over the pictured horrors of blood. I panted! I gasped for breath! There could be no doubt of the design of my tormentors. Oh! most unrelenting! Oh! most demoniac of men! I shrank from the glowing metal to the centre of the cell. Amid the thought of the fiery destruction that impended, the idea of the coolness of the well came over my soul like balm. I rushed to its deadly brink. I threw my straining vision below. The glare from the enkindled roof illumined its inmost recesses. Yet, for a wild moment, did my spirit refuse to comprehend the meaning of what I saw. At length it forced—it wrestled its way into my soul—it burned itself in upon my shuddering reason. Oh! for a voice to speak! Oh! horror! Oh! any horror but this! With a shriek, I rushed from the margin, and buried my face in my hands—weeping bitterly.

The heat rapidly increased, and once again I looked up, shuddering as with a fit of the fever. There had been a second change in the cell—and now the change was obviously in the *form*. As before, it was in vain that I at first endeavoured to appreciate or understand what was taking place. But not long was I left in doubt. The Inquisitorial vengeance had been hurried by my twofold escape, and there was to be no more dallying with the King of Terrors. The room had been square. I saw that two of its iron angles were now acute—two, consequently, obtuse. The fearful difference quickly increased with a low rumbling or moaning sound. In an instant the apartment had shifted its form into that of a lozenge. But the alteration stopped not here—I neither hoped nor desired it to stop. I could have clasped the red walls to my bosom as a garment of eternal peace. 'Death,' I said, 'any death but that of the pit!' Fool! Might I not have known that *into the pit* it was the object of the burning iron to urge me? Could I resist its glow? Or, if even that, could I withstand its pressure?

And now, flatter and flatter grew the lozenge, with a rapidity that left me no time for contemplation. Its centre, and of course, its greatest width, came just over the yawning gulf. I shrank back—but the closing walls pressed me resistlessly onward. At length for my seared and writhing body there was no longer an inch of foothold on the firm floor of the prison. I struggled no more, but the agony of my soul found vent in one loud, long, and final scream of despair. I felt that I tottered upon the brink—I averted my eyes ——

There was a discordant hum of human voices! There was a loud blast as of many trumpets! There was a harsh grating as of a thousand thunders! The fiery walls rushed back! An outstretched arm caught my own as I fell, fainting, into the abyss. It was that of General Lasalle. The French Army had entered Toledo. The Inquisition was in the hands of its enemies.

THE MUMMY'S FOOT

Theophile Gautier

I had entered, in an idle mood, the shop of one of those curiosity-venders, who are called *marchands de bric-à-brac* in that Parisian *argot* which is so perfectly unintelligible elsewhere in France.

You have doubtless glanced occasionally through the windows of some of these shops, which have become so numerous now that it is fashionable to buy antiquated furniture, and that every petty stockbroker thinks he must have his *chambre au moyen âge*.

There is one thing there which clings alike to the shop of the dealer in old iron, the wareroom of the tapestry-maker, the laboratory of the chemist, and the studio of the painter – in all those gloomy dens where a furtive daylight filters in through the window-shutters, the most manifestly ancient thing is dust; – the cobwebs are more authentic than the guimp laces; and the old pear-tree furniture on exhibition is actually younger than the mahogany which arrived but yesterday from America.

The warehouse of my *bric-à-brac* dealer was a veritable Capharnaum; all ages and all nations seemed to have made their rendezvous there; an Etruscan lamp of red clay stood upon a Boule cabinet, with ebony panels, brightly striped by lines of inlaid brass; a duchess of the court of Louis XV nonchalantly extended her fawn-like feet under a massive table of the time of Louis XIII with heavy spiral supports of oak, and carven designs of chimeras and foliage intermingled.

Upon the denticulated shelves of several sideboards glittered immense Japanese dishes with red and blue designs relieved by gilded hatching; side by side with enamelled works by Bernard Palissy, representing serpents, frogs, and lizards in relief.

From disembowelled cabinets escaped cascades of silver-lustrous Chinese silks and waves of tinsel, which an oblique sunbeam shot through with luminous beads; while portraits of every era, in frames more or less tarnished, smiled through their yellow varnish.

The striped breastplate of a damascened suit of Milanese armour glittered in one corner; Loves and Nymphs of porcelain; Chinese Grotesques, vases of *céladon* and crackle-ware; Saxon and old Sèvres cups encumbered the shelves and nooks of the apartment.

The dealer followed me closely through the tortuous way contrived between the piles of furniture; warding off with his hand the hazardous sweep of my coat-skirts; watching my elbows with the uneasy attention of an antiquarian and a usurer.

It was a singular face, that of the merchant – an immense skull, polished like a knee, and surrounded by a thin aureole of white hair, which brought out the clear salmon tint of his complexion all the more strikingly, lent him a false aspect of patriarchal *bonhomie*, counteracted, however, by the scintillation of two little yellow eyes which trembled in their orbits like two louis-d'or upon quicksilver. The curve of his nose presented an aquiline silhouette, which suggested the Oriental or Jewish type. His hands – thin, slender, full of nerves which projected like strings upon the finger-board of a violin, and armed with claws like those on the terminations of bats' wings – shook with senile trembling; but those convulsively agitated hands became firmer than steel pincers or lobsters' claws when they lifted any precious article – an onyx cup, a Venetian glass, or a dish of Bohemian crystal. This strange old man had an aspect so thoroughly rabbinical and cabalistic that he would have been burnt on the mere testimony of his face three centuries ago.

'Will you not buy something from me today, sir? Here is a Malay kreese with a blade undulating like flame: look at those grooves contrived for the blood to run along, those teeth set backwards so as to tear out the entrails in withdrawing the weapon – it is a fine character of ferocious arm, and will look well in your collection: this two-handed sword is very beautiful – it is the work of Josepe de la Hera; and this *colichemarde*, with its fenestrated guard – what a superb specimen of handicraft!'

'No; I have quite enough weapons and instruments of carnage – I want a small figure, something which will suit me as a paper-weight; for I cannot endure those trumpery bronzes which the stationers sell, and which may be found on everybody's desk.'

The old gnome foraged among his ancient wares, and finally arranged before me some antique bronzes – so-called, at least; fragments of malachite; little Hindoo or Chinese idols – a kind of poussah toys in jadestone, representing the incarnations of Brahma or Vishnoo, and wonderfully appropriate to the very undivine office of holding papers and letters in place.

I was hesitating between a porcelain dragon, all constellated with warts – its mouth formidable with bristling tusks and ranges of teeth – and an abominable little Mexican fetish, representing the god Zitziliputzili *au naturel*, when I caught sight of a charming foot, which I at first took for a fragment of some antique Venus.

It had those beautiful ruddy and tawny tints that lend to Florentine bronze that warm living look so much preferable to the gray-green aspect of common bronzes, which might easily be mistaken for statues in a state of putrefaction: satiny gleams played over its rounded forms, doubtless polished by the amorous kisses of twenty centuries; for it seemed a Corinthian bronze, a work of the best era of art – perhaps molded by Lysippus himself.

'That foot will be my choice,' I said to the merchant, who regarded me with an ironical and saturnine air, and held out the object desired that I might examine it more fully.

I was surprised at its lightness; it was not a foot of metal, but in sooth a foot of flesh – an embalmed foot – a mummy's foot: on examining it still more closely the very grain of the skin, and the almost imperceptible lines impressed upon it by the texture of the bandages, became perceptible. Those toes were slender and delicate, and terminated by perfectly formed nails, pure and transparent as agates; the great toe, slightly separated from the rest, afforded a happy contrast, in the antique style, to the position of the other toes, and lent it an aerial lightness – the grace of a bird's foot – the sole, scarcely streaked by a few almost imperceptible cross lines, afforded evidence that it had never touched the bare ground, and had only come in contact with the finest matting of Nile rushes, and the softest carpets of panther skin.

'Ha, ha! – you want the foot of the Princess Hermonthis,' – exclaimed the merchant, with a strange giggle, fixing his owlish eyes upon me – 'ha, ha, ha! – for a paper-weight! – an original idea! – artistic idea! Old Pharaoh would certainly have been surprised had someone told him that the foot of his adored daughter would be used for a paper-weight after he had had a mountain of granite hollowed out as a receptacle for the triple coffin, painted and gilded – covered with hieroglyphics and beautiful paintings of the Judgment of Souls,' – continued the queer little merchant, half audibly, as though talking to himself.

'How much will you charge me for this mummy fragment?'

'Ah, the highest price I can get; for it is a superb piece: if I had the match of it you could not have it for less than five hundred francs; – the daughter of a Pharaoh! nothing is more rare.'

'Assuredly that is not a common article; but, still, how much do you want? In the first place let me warn you that all my wealth consists of just five louis: I can buy anything that costs five louis, but nothing dearer – you might search my vest pockets and most secret drawers without even finding one poor five-franc piece more.'

'Five louis for the foot of the Princess Hermonthis! that is very little, very little indeed; 'tis an authentic foot,' muttered the merchant, shaking his head, and imparting a peculiar rotary motion to his eyes. 'Well, take it, and I will give you the bandages into the bargain,' he added, wrapping the foot in an ancient damask rag – 'very fine! real damask – Indian damask which has never been redyed; it is strong, and yet it is soft,' he mumbled, stroking the frayed tissue with his fingers, through the trade-acquired habit which moved him to praise even an object of so little value that he himself deemed it only worth the giving away.

He poured the gold coins into a sort of mediaeval alms-purse hanging at his belt, repeating:

'The foot of the Princess Hermonthis, to be used for a paper-weight!'

Then turning his phosphorescent eyes upon me, he exclaimed in a voice strident as the crying of a cat which has swallowed a fish-bone:

'Old Pharaoh will not be well pleased; he loved his daughter – the dear man!'

'You speak as if you were a contemporary of his: you are old enough, goodness knows! but you do not date back to the Pyramids of Egypt,' I answered, laughingly, from the threshold.

I went home, delighted with my acquisition.

With the idea of putting it to profitable use as soon as possible, I placed the foot of the divine Princess Hermonthis upon a heap of papers scribbled over with verses, in themselves an undecipherable mosaic work of erasures; articles freshly begun; letters forgotten, and posted in the table drawer instead of the letter-box – an error to which absent-minded people are peculiarly liable. The effect was charming, bizarre, and romantic.

Well satisfied with this embellishment, I went out with the gravity and pride becoming one who feels that he has the ineffable advantage over all the passers-by whom he elbows, of possessing a piece of the Princess Hermonthis, daughter of Pharaoh.

I looked upon all who did not possess, like myself, a paper-weight so authentically Egyptian, as very ridiculous people; and it seemed to me that the proper occupation of every sensible man should consist in the mere fact of having a mummy's foot upon his desk.

Happily I met some friends, whose presence distracted me in my infatuation with this new acquisition: I went to dinner with them; for I could not very well have dined with myself.

When I came back that evening, with my brain slightly confused by a few glasses of wine, a vague whiff of Oriental perfume delicately titillated my olfactory nerves: the heat of the room had warmed the natron, bitumen, and myrrh in which the *paraschistes*, who cut open the bodies of the dead, had bathed the corpse of the princess – it was a perfume at once sweet and penetrating – a perfume that four thousand years had not been able to dissipate.

The Dream of Egypt was Eternity: her odours have the solidity of granite, and endure as long.

I soon drank deeply from the black cup of sleep: for a few hours all remained opaque to me; Oblivion and Nothingness inundated me with their sombre waves.

Yet light gradually dawned upon the darkness of my mind; dreams commenced to touch me softly in their silent flight.

The eyes of my soul were opened; and I beheld my chamber as it actually was; I might have believed myself awake, but for a vague consciousness which assured me that I slept, and that something fantastic was about to take place.

The odour of the myrrh had augmented in intensity: and I felt a slight headache, which I very naturally attributed to several glasses of champagne that we had drunk to the unknown gods and our future fortunes.

I peered through my room with a feeling of expectation which I saw nothing to justify: every article of furniture was in its proper place; the lamp, softly shaded by its globe of ground crystal, burned upon its bracket; the water-color sketches shone under their Bohemian glass; the curtains hung down languidly; everything wore an aspect of tranquil slumber.

After a few moments, however, all this calm interior appeared to become disturbed; the woodwork cracked stealthily; the ash-covered log suddenly emitted a jet of blue flame; and the disks of the pateras seemed like great metallic eyes, watching, like myself, for the things which were about to happen.

My eyes accidentally fell upon the desk where I had placed the foot of the Princess·Hermonthis.

Instead of remaining quiet – as behooved a foot which had been embalmed for four thousand years – it commenced to act in a nervous manner; contracted itself, and leaped over the papers like a startled frog – one would have imagined that it had suddenly been brought into contact with a galvanic battery: I could distinctly hear the dry sound made by its little heel, hard as the hoof of a gazelle.

I became rather discontented with my acquisition, inasmuch as I wished my paper-weights to be of a sedentary disposition, and thought it very unnatural that feet should walk about without legs; and I commenced to experience a feeling closely akin to fear.

Suddenly I saw the folds of my bed-curtain stir; and heard a bumping sound, like that caused by some person hopping on one foot across the floor. I must confess I became alternately hot and cold; that I felt a strange wind chill my back; and that my suddenly rising hair caused my nightcap to execute a leap of several yards.

The bed-curtains opened and I beheld the strangest figure imaginable before me.

I beheld the strangest figure imaginable

It was a young girl of a very deep coffee-brown complexion, like the bayadère Amani, and possessing the purest Egyptian type of perfect beauty: her eyes were almond-shaped and oblique, with eyebrows so black that they seemed blue; her nose was exquisitely chiselled, almost Greek in its delicacy of outline; and she might indeed have been taken for a Corinthian statue of bronze, but for the prominence of her cheekbones and the slightly African fullness of her lips, which compelled one to recognise her as belonging beyond all doubt to the hieroglyphic race which dwelt upon the banks of the Nile.

Her arms, slender and spindle-shaped, like those of very young girls, were encircled by a peculiar kind of metal bands and bracelets of glass beads; her hair was all twisted into little cords; and she wore upon her bosom a little idol-figure of green paste, bearing a whip with seven lashes, which proved it to be an image of Isis: her brow was adorned with a shining plate of gold; and a few traces of paint relieved the coppery tint of her cheeks.

As for her costume, it was very odd indeed.

Fancy a *pagne* or skirt all formed of little strips of material bedizened with red and black hieroglyphics, stiffened with bitumen, and apparently belonging to a freshly unbandaged mummy.

In one of those sudden flights of thought so common in dreams I heard the hoarse falsetto of the *bric-à-brac* dealer, repeating like a monotonous refrain the phrase he had uttered in his shop with so enigmatical an intonation:

'Old Pharaoh will not be well pleased: he loved his daughter, the dear man!'

One strange circumstance, which was not at all calculated to restore my equanimity, was that the apparition had but one foot; the other was broken off at the ankle!

She approached the table where the foot was starting and fidgeting about more than ever, and there supported herself upon the edge of the desk. I saw her eyes fill with pearly-gleaming tears.

Although she had not as yet spoken, I fully comprehended the thoughts which agitated her: she looked at her foot – for it was indeed her own – with an exquisitely graceful expression of coquettish sadness; but the foot leaped and ran hither and thither, as though impelled on steel springs.

995

Twice or thrice she extended her hand to seize it, but could not succeed.

Then commenced between the Princess Hermonthis and her foot – which appeared to be endowed with a special life of its own – a very fantastic dialogue in a most ancient Coptic tongue, such as might have been spoken thirty centuries ago in the syrinxes of the land of Ser: luckily, I understood Coptic perfectly well that night.

The Princess Hermonthis cried, in a voice sweet and vibrant as the tones of a crystal bell:

'Well, my dear little foot, you always flee from me; yet I always took good care of you. I bathed you with perfumed water in a bowl of alabaster; I smoothed your heel with pumice-stone mixed with palm oil; your nails were cut with golden scissors and polished with a hippopotamus tooth; I was careful to select *tatbebs* for you, painted and embroidered and turned up at the toes, which were the envy of all the young girls in Egypt: you wore on your great toe rings bearing the device of the sacred Scarabaeus; and you supported one of the lightest bodies that a lazy foot could sustain.'

The foot replied, in a pouting and chagrined tone:

'You know well that I do not belong to myself any longer – I have been bought and paid for; the old merchant knew what he was about; he bore you a grudge for having refused to espouse him – this is an ill turn which he has done you. The Arab who violated your royal coffin in the subterranean pits of the necropolis of Thebes was sent thither by him: he desired to prevent you from being present at the reunion of the shadowy nations in the cities below. Have you five pieces of gold for my ransom?'

'Alas, no! – my jewels, my rings, my purses of gold and silver, they were stolen from me,' answered the Princess Hermonthis, with a sob.

'Princess,' I then exclaimed, 'I never retained anybody's foot unjustly – even though you have not got the five louis which it cost me, I present it to you gladly: I should feel unutterably wretched to think that I were the cause of so amiable a person as the Princess Hermonthis being lame.'

I delivered this discourse in a royally gallant, troubadour tone, which must have astonished the beautiful Egyptian girl.

She turned a look of deepest gratitude upon me; and her eyes shone with bluish gleams of light.

She took her foot – which surrendered itself willingly this time – like a woman about to put on her little shoe, and adjusted it to her leg with much skill.

This operation over, she took a few steps about the room, as though to assure herself that she was really no longer lame.

'Ah, how pleased my father will be! – he who was so unhappy because of my mutilation, and who from the moment of my birth set a whole nation at work to hollow me out a tomb so deep that he might preserve me intact until the last day, when souls must be weighed in the balance of Amenthi! Come with me to my father – he will receive you kindly; for you have given me back my foot.'

I thought this proposition natural enough. I arrayed myself in a dressing-gown of large-flowered pattern, which lent me a very Pharaonic aspect; hurriedly put on a pair of Turkish slippers, and informed the Princess Hermonthis that I was ready to follow her.

Before starting, Hermonthis took from her neck the little idol of green paste, and laid it on the scattered sheets of paper which covered the table.

'It is only fair,' she observed smilingly, 'that I should replace your paper-weight.'

She gave me her hand, which felt soft and cold, like the skin of a serpent; and we departed.

We passed for some time with the velocity of an arrow through a fluid and grayish expanse, in which half-formed silhouettes flitted swiftly by us, to right and left.

For an instant we saw only sky and sea.

A few moments later, obelisks commenced to tower in the distance: pylons and vast flights of steps guarded by sphinxes became clearly outlined against the horizon.

We had reached our destination.

The princess conducted me to the mountain of rose-coloured granite, in the face of which appeared an opening so narrow and low that it would have been difficult to distinguish it from the fissures in the rock, had not its location been marked by two stelae wrought with sculptures.

Hermonthis kindled a torch, and led the way before me.

We traversed corridors hewn through the living rock: their walls, covered with hieroglyphics and paintings of allegorical processions, might well have occupied thousands of arms for thousands of years in their formation – these corridors, of interminable length, opened into square chambers, in the midst of which pits had been contrived, through which we descended by cramp-irons or spiral stairways – these pits again conducted us into other chambers, opening into other corridors, likewise decorated with painted sparrow-hawks, serpents coiled in circles, the symbols of the *tau* and *pedum* prodigious works of art which no living eye can ever examine – interminable legends of granite which only the dead have time to read through all eternity.

At last we found ourselves in a hall so vast, so enormous, so immeasurable, that the eye could not reach its limits; files of monstrous columns stretched far out of sight on every side, between which twinkled livid stars of yellowish flame – points of light which revealed further depths incalculable in the darkness beyond.

The Princess Hermonthis still held my hand, and graciously saluted the mummies of her acquaintance.

My eyes became accustomed to the dim twilight, and objects became discernible.

I beheld the kings of the subterranean races seated upon thrones – grand old men, though dry, withered, wrinkled like parchment, and blackened with naphtha and bitumen – all wearing *pshents* of gold, and breastplates and gorgets glittering with precious stones; their eyes immovably fixed like the eyes of sphinxes, and their long beards whitened by the snow of centuries. Behind them stood their peoples, in the stiff and constrained posture enjoined by Egyptian art, all eternally preserving the attitude prescribed by the hieratic code. Behind these nations, the cats, ibises, and crocodiles contemporary with them – rendered monstrous of aspect by their swathing bands – mewed, flapped their wings, or extended their jaws in a saurian giggle.

All the Pharaohs were there – Cheops, Chephrenes, Psammetichus, Sesostris, Amenotaph – all the dark rulers of the pyramids and syrinxes – on yet higher thrones sat Chronos and Xixouthros – who was contemporary with the deluge; and Tubal Cain, who reigned before it.

The beard of King Xixouthros had grown seven times around the granite table, upon which he leaned, lost in deep reverie – and buried in dreams.

Further back, through a dusty cloud, I beheld dimly the seventy-two pre-Adamite Kings, with their seventy-two peoples – forever passed away.

After permitting me to gaze upon this bewildering spectacle a few moments, the Princess Hermonthis presented me to her father Pharaoh, who favoured me with a most gracious nod.

'I have found my foot again! – I have found my foot!' cried the Princess, clapping her little hands together with every sign of frantic joy: 'it was this gentleman who restored it to me.'

The races of Kemi, the races of Nahasi – all the black, bronzed, and copper-coloured nations repeated in chorus:

'The Princess Hermonthis has found her foot again!'

Even Xixouthros himself was visibly affected.

He raised his heavy eyelids, stroked his moustache with his fingers, and turned upon me a glance weighty with centuries.

'By Oms, the dog of Hell, and Tmei, daughter of the Sun and of Truth! this is a brave and worthy lad!' exclaimed Pharaoh, pointing to me with his sceptre, which was terminated with a lotus-flower.

'What recompense do you desire?'

Filled with that daring inspired by dreams in which nothing seems impossible, I asked him for the hand of the Princess Hermonthis – the hand seemed to me a very proper antithetic recompense for the foot.

Pharaoh opened wide his great eyes of glass in astonishment at my witty request.

'What country do you come from, and what is your age?'

'I am a Frenchman; and I am twenty-seven years old, venerable Pharaoh.'

'–Twenty-seven years old! and he wishes to espouse the Princess Hermonthis, who is thirty centuries old!' cried out at once all the Thrones and all the Circles of Nations.

Only Hermonthis herself did not seem to think my request unreasonable.

'If you were even only two thousand years old,' replied the ancient King, 'I would willingly give you the Princess; but the disproportion is too great; and, besides, we must give our daughters husbands who will last well: you do not know how to preserve yourselves any longer; even those who died only fifteen centuries ago are already no more than a handful of dust – behold! my flesh is solid as basalt; my bones are bars of steel!

'I shall be present on the last day of the world, with the same body and the same features which I had during my lifetime: my daughter Hermonthis will last longer than a statue of bronze.

'Then the last particles of your dust will have been scattered abroad by the winds; and even Isis herself, who was able to find the atoms of Osiris, would scarce be able to recompose your being.

'See how vigorous I yet remain, and how mighty is my grasp,' he added, shaking my hand in the English fashion with a strength that buried my rings in the flesh of my fingers.

He squeezed me so hard that I awoke, and found my friend Alfred shaking me by the arm to make me get up.

'Oh you everlasting sleeper! – must I have you carried out into the middle of the street, and fireworks exploded in your ears? It is after noon; don't you recollect your promise to take me with you to see M. Aguado's Spanish pictures?'

'God! I forgot all about it,' I answered, dressing myself hurriedly; 'we will go there at once; I have the permit lying on my desk.'

I started to find it – but fancy my astonishment when I beheld, instead of the mummy's foot I had purchased the evening before, the little green paste idol left in its place by the Princess Hermonthis!

THE PIPER AT THE GATES OF DAWN

Kenneth Grahame

The Willow-Wren was twittering his thin little song, hidden himself in the dark selvedge of the river bank. Though it was past ten o'clock at night, the sky still clung to and retained some lingering skirts of light from the departed day; and the sullen heats of the torrid afternoon broke up and rolled away at the dispersing touch of the cool fingers of the short midsummer night. Mole lay stretched on the bank, still panting from the stress of the fierce day that had been cloudless from dawn to late sunset, and waited for his friend to return. He had been on the river with some companions, leaving the Water Rat free to keep an engagement of long standing with Otter; and he had come back to find the house dark and deserted, and no sign of Rat, who was doubtless keeping it up late with his old comrade. It was still too hot to think of staying indoors, so he lay on some cool dock-leaves, and thought over the past day and its doings, and how very good they all had been.

The Rat's light footfall was presently heard approaching over the parched grass. 'O, the blessed coolness!' he said, and sat down, gazing thoughtfully into the river, silent and preoccupied.

'You stayed to supper, of course?' said the Mole presently.

'Simply had to,' said the Rat. 'They wouldn't hear of my going before. You know how kind they always are. And they made things as jolly for me as ever they could, right up to the moment I left. But I felt a brute all the time, as it was clear to me they were very unhappy, though they tried to hide it. Mole, I'm afraid they're in trouble. Little Portly is missing again; and you know what a lot his father thinks of him, though he never says much about it.'

'What, that child?' said the Mole lightly. 'Well, suppose he is; why worry about it? He's always straying off and getting lost, and turning up again; he's so adventurous. But no harm ever happens to him. Everybody hereabouts knows him and likes him, just as they do old Otter, and you may be sure some animal or other will come across him and bring him back again all right. Why, we've found him ourselves, miles from home and quite self-possessed and cheerful!'

'Yes; but this time it's more serious,' said the Rat gravely. 'He's been missing for some days now, and the Otters have hunted every-where, high and low, without finding the slightest trace. And they've asked every animal, too, for miles around, and no one knows anything about him. Otter's evidently more anxious than he'll admit. I got out of him that young Portly hasn't learnt to swim very well yet, and I can see he's thinking of the weir. There's a lot of water coming down still, considering the time of year, and the place always had a fascination for the child. And then there are—well, traps and things—*you* know. Otter's not the fellow to be nervous about any son of his before it's time. And now he *is* nervous. When I left, he came out with me— said he wanted some air, and talked about stretching his legs. But I could see it wasn't that, so I drew him out and pumped him, and got it all from him at last. He was going to spend the night watching by the ford. You know the place where the old ford used to be, in bygone days before they built the bridge?'

'I know it well,' said the Mole. 'But why should Otter choose to watch there?'

'Well, it seems that it was there he gave Portly his first swimming lesson,' continued the Rat. 'From that shallow, gravelly spit near the bank. And it was there he used to teach him fishing, and there young Portly caught his first fish, of which he was very proud. The child loved the spot, and Otter thinks that if he came wandering back from wherever he is—if he *is* anywhere by this time, poor little chap—he might make for the ford he was so fond of; or if he came across it he'd remember it well, and stop there and play, perhaps. So Otter goes there every night and watches—on the chance, you know, just on the chance!'

They were silent for a time, both thinking of the same thing—the lonely, heart-sore animal, crouched by the ford, watching and waiting, the long night through—on the chance.

'Well, well,' said the Rat presently, 'I suppose we ought to be thinking about turning in.' But he never offered to move.

'Rat,' said the Mole, 'I simply can't go and turn in, and go to sleep, and *do* nothing, even though there doesn't seem to be anything to be done. We'll get the boat out, and paddle up-stream. The moon will be up in an hour or so, and then we will search as well as we can—anyhow, it will be better than going to bed and doing *nothing*.'

'Just what I was thinking myself,' said the Rat. 'It's not the sort of night for bed anyhow; and daybreak is not so far off, and then we may pick up some news of him from early risers as we go along.'

They got the boat out, and the Rat took the sculls, paddling with caution. Out in mid-stream there was a clear, narrow track that faintly reflected the sky; but wherever shadows fell on the water from bank, bush, or tree, they were as solid to all appearance as the banks themselves, and the Mole had to steer with judgement accordingly. Dark and deserted as it was, the night was full of small noises, song and chatter and rustling, telling of the busy little population who were up and about, plying their trades and vocations through the night till sunshine should fall on them at last and send them off to their well-earned repose. The water's own noises, too, were more apparent than by day, its gurglings and 'cloops' more unexpected and near at hand; and constantly they started at what seemed a sudden clear call from an actual articulate voice.

The line of the horizon was clear and hard against the sky, and in one particular quarter it showed black against a silvery climbing phosphorescence that grew and grew. At last, over the rim of the waiting earth the moon lifted with slow majesty till it swung clear of the horizon and rode off, free of moorings; and once more they began to see surfaces—meadows widespread, and quiet gardens, and the river itself from bank to bank, all softly disclosed, all washed

The Rat and Mole stood worshipping at the Piper's feet.

clean of mystery and terror, all radiant again as by day, but with a difference that was tremendous. Their old haunts greeted them again in other raiment, as if they had slipped away and put on this pure new apparel and come quietly back, smiling as they shyly waited to see if they would be recognized again under it.

Fastening their boat to a willow, the friends landed in this silent, silver kingdom, and patiently explored the hedges, the hollow trees, the tunnels and their little culverts, the ditches and dry water-ways. Embarking again and crossing over, they worked their way up the stream in this manner, while the moon, serene and detached in a cloudless sky, did what she could, though so far off, to help them in their quest; till her hour came and she sank earthwards reluctantly, and left them, and mystery once more held field and river.

Then a change began slowly to declare itself. The horizon became clearer, field and tree came more into sight, and somehow with a different look; the mystery began to drop away from them. A bird piped suddenly, and was still; and a light breeze sprang up and set the reeds and bulrushes rustling. Rat, who was in the stern of the boat, while Mole sculled, sat up suddenly and listened with a passionate intentness. Mole, who with gentle strokes was just keeping the boat moving while he scanned the banks with care, looked at him with curiosity.

'It's gone!' sighed the Rat, sinking back in his seat again. 'So beautiful and strange and new! Since it was to end so soon, I almost wish I had never heard it. For it has roused a longing in me that is pain, and nothing seems worthwhile but just to hear that sound once more and go on listening to it for ever. No! There it is again!' he cried, alert once more. Entranced, he was silent for a long space, spellbound.

'Now it passes on and I begin to lose it,' he said presently. 'O, Mole! the beauty of it! The merry bubble and joy, the thin, clear, happy call of the distant piping! Such music I never dreamed of, and the call in it is stronger even than the music is sweet! Row on, Mole, row! For the music and the call must be for us.'

The Mole, greatly wondering, obeyed. 'I hear nothing myself,' he said, 'but the wind playing in the reeds and rushes and osiers.'

The Rat never answered, if indeed he heard. Rapt, transported, trembling, he was possessed in all his senses by this new divine thing that caught up his helpless soul and swung and dandled it, a powerless but happy infant, in a strong sustaining grasp.

In silence Mole rowed steadily, and soon they came to a point where the river divided, a long backwater branching off to one side. With a slight movement of his head Rat, who had long dropped the rudder-lines, directed the rower to take the backwater. The creeping tide of light gained and gained, and now they could see the colour of the flowers that gemmed the water's edge.

'Clearer and nearer still,' cried the Rat joyously. 'Now you 'must surely hear it! Ah—at last—I see you do!'

Breathless and transfixed the Mole stopped rowing as the liquid run of that glad piping broke on him like a wave, caught him up, and possessed him utterly. He saw the tears on his comrade's cheeks, and bowed his head and understood. For a space they hung there, brushed by the purple loosestrife that fringed the bank; then the clear imperious summons that marched hand-in-hand with the intoxicating melody imposed its will on Mole, and mechanically he bent to his oars again. And the light grew steadily stronger, but no birds sang as they were wont to do at the approach of dawn; and but for the heavenly music all was marvellously still.

On either side of them, as they glided onwards, the rich meadow-grass seemed that morning of a freshness and a greeness unsurpassable. Never had they noticed the roses so vivid, the willow-herb so riotous, the meadow-sweet so odorous and pervading. Then the murmur of the approaching weir began to hold the air, and they felt a consciousness that they were nearing the end, whatever it might be, that surely awaited their expedition.

A wide half-circle of foam and glinting lights and shining shoulders of green water, the great weir closed the backwater from bank to bank, troubled all the quiet surface with twirling eddies and floating foam-streaks, and deadened all other sounds with its solemn and soothing rumble. In midmost of the stream, embraced in the weir's shimmering arm-spread, a small island lay anchored, fringed close with willow and silver birch and alder. Reserved, shy, but full of significance, it hid whatever it might hold behind a veil, keeping it till the hour should come, and, with the hour, those who were called and chosen.

Slowly, but with no doubt or hesitation whatever, and in something of a solemn expectancy, the two animals passed through the broken, tumultuous water and moored their boat at the flowery margin of the island. In silence they landed, and pushed through the blossom and scented herbage and undergrowth that led up to the level ground, till they stood on a little lawn of a marvellous green, set round with Nature's own orchard-trees—crab-apples, wild cherry, and sloe.

'This is the place the music played to me,' whispered the Rat, as if in a trance. 'Here, in this holy place, here if anywhere, surely we shall find Him!'

Then suddenly the Mole felt a great Awe fall upon him, an awe that turned his muscles to water, bowed his head, and rooted his feet to the ground. It was no panic terror—indeed he felt wonderfully at peace and happy—but it was an awe that smote and held him and, without seeing, he knew it could only mean that some august Presence was very, very near. With difficulty he turned to look for his friend, and saw him at his side cowed, stricken, and trembling violently. And still there was utter silence in the populous bird-haunted branches around them; and still the light grew and grew.

Perhaps he would never have dared to raise his eyes, but that, though the piping was now hushed, the call and the summons seemed still dominant and imperious. He might not refuse, were Death himself waiting to strike him instantly, once he had looked with mortal eye on things rightly kept hidden. Trembling he obeyed, and raised his humble head; and then, in that utter clearness of the imminent dawn, while Nature, flushed with fullness of incredible colour, seemed to hold her breath for the event, he looked in the very eyes of the Friend and Helper; saw the backward sweep of the curved horns, gleaming in the growing daylight; saw the stern, hooked nose between the kindly eyes that were looking down on them humorously, while the bearded mouth broke into a half-smile at the corners; saw the rippling muscles on the arm that lay across the broad chest, the long supple hand still holding the pan-pipes only just fallen away from the parted lips; saw the splendid curves of the shaggy limbs disposed in majestic ease on the sward; saw, last of all, nestling between his very hooves, sleeping soundly in entire peace and contentment, the little, round, podgy, childish form of the baby otter. All this he saw, for one moment breathless and intense, vivid on the morning sky; and still, as he looked, he lived; and still, as he lived, he wondered.

'Rat!' he found breath to whisper, shaking. 'Are you afraid?'

'Afraid?' murmured the Rat, his eyes shining with unutterable love. 'Afraid Of *Him*? O, never, never! And yet—and yet—O, Mole, I am afraid!'

Then the two animals, crouching to the earth, bowed their heads and did worship.

Sudden and magnificent, the sun's broad golden disc showed itself over the horizon facing them; and the first rays, shooting across the level water-meadows, took the animals full in the eyes and dazzled them. When they were able to look once more, the Vision had vanished, and the air was full of the carol of birds that hailed the dawn.

As they stared blankly, in dumb misery deepening as they slowly realized all they had seen and all they had lost, a capricious little breeze, dancing up from the surface of the water, tossed the aspens, shook the dewy roses, and blew lightly and caressingly in their faces, and with its soft touch came instant oblivion. For this is the last best gift that the kindly demigod is careful to bestow on those to whom he has revealed himself in their helping; the gift of forgetfulness. Lest the awful remembrance should remain and grow, and overshadow mirth and pleasure, and the great haunting memory should spoil all the after-lives of little animals helped out of difficulties, in order that they should be happy and light-hearted as before.

Mole rubbed his eyes and stared at Rat, who was looking about him in a puzzled sort of way. 'I beg your pardon; what did you say, Rat?' he asked.

'I think I was only remarking,' said Rat slowly, 'that this was the right sort of place, and that here, if anywhere, we should find him. And look! Why, there he is, the little fellow!' And with a cry of delight he ran towards the slumbering Portly.

But Mole stood still a moment, held in thought. As one wakened suddenly from a beautiful dream, who struggles to recall it, and can recapture nothing but a dim sense of the beauty of it, the beauty! Till that, too, fades away in its turn, and the dreamer bitterly accepts the hard, cold waking and all its penalties; so Mole, after struggling with his memory for a brief space, shook his head sadly and followed the Rat.

Portly woke up with a joyous squeak, and wriggled with pleasure at the sight of his father's friends, who had played with him so often in past days. In a moment, however, his face grew blank, and he fell to hunting round in a circle with pleading whine. As a child that has fallen happily asleep in its nurse's arms, and wakes to find itself alone and laid in a strange place, and searches corners and cupboards, and runs from room to room, despair growing silently in its heart, even so Portly searched the island and searched, dogged and unwearying, till at last the black moment came for giving it up, and sitting down and crying bitterly.

The Mole ran quickly to comfort the little animal; but Rat, lingering, looked long and doubtfully at certain hoof-marks deep in the sward.

'Some—great—animal—has been here,' he murmured slowly and thoughtfully; and stood musing, musing; his mind strangely stirred.

'Come along, Rat!' called the Mole. 'Think of poor Otter, waiting up there by the ford!'

Portly had soon been comforted by the promise of a treat—a jaunt on the river in Mr Rat's real boat; and the two animals conducted him to the water's side, placed him securely between them in the bottom of the boat, and paddled off down the backwater. The sun was fully up by now, and hot on them, birds sang lustily and without restraint, and flowers smiled and nodded from either bank, but somehow—so thought the animals—with less of richness and blaze of colour than they seemed to remember seeing quite recently somewhere—they wondered where.

The main river reached again, they turned the boat's head upstream, towards the point where they knew their friend was keeping his lonely vigil. As they drew near the familiar ford, the Mole took the boat in to the bank, and they lifted Portly out and set him on his legs on the tow-path, gave him his marching orders and a friendly farewell pat on the back, and shoved out into mid-stream. They watched the little animal as he waddled along the path contentedly and with importance; watched him till they saw his muzzle suddenly lift and his waddle break into a clumsy amble as he quickened his pace with shrill whines and wriggles of recognition. Looking up the river, they could see Otter start up, tense and rigid, from out of the shallows where he crouched in dumb patience, and could hear his amazed and joyous bark as he bounded up through the osiers on to the path. Then the Mole, with a strong pull on one oar, swung the boat round and let the full stream bear them down again whither it would, their quest now happily ended.

'I feel strangely tired, Rat,' said the Mole, leaning wearily over his oars as the boat drifted. 'Its being up all night, you'll say, perhaps; but that's nothing. We do as much half the nights of the week, at this time of the year. No; I feel as if I had been through something very exciting and rather terrible, and it was just over; and yet nothing particular has happened.'

'Or something very surprising and splendid and beautiful,' murmured the Rat, leaning back and closing his eyes. 'I feel just as you do, Mole; simply dead tired, though not body-tired. It's lucky we've got the stream with us, to take us home. Isn't it jolly to feel the sun again, soaking into one's bones! And hark to the wind playing in the reeds!'

'It's like music—far-away music,' said the Mole, nodding drowsily.

'So I was thinking,' murmured the Rat, dreamful and languid. 'Dance-music—the lilting sort that runs on without a stop—but with words in it, too—it passes into words and out of them again—I catch them at intervals—then it is dance-music once more, and then nothing but the reeds' soft thin whispering.'

'You hear better than I,' said the Mole sadly. 'I cannot catch the words.'

'Let me try and give you them,' said the Rat softly, his eyes still closed. 'Now it is turning into words again—faint but clear—*Lest the awe should dwell—And turn your frolic to fret—You shall look on my power at the helping hour—But then you shall forget*! Now the reeds take it up—*forget, forget,* they sigh, and it dies away in a rustle and a whisper. Then the voice returns—

'*Lest limbs be reddened and rent—I spring the trap that is set—As I loose the snare you may glimpse me there—For surely you shall forget*! Row nearer, Mole, nearer to the reeds! It is hard to catch, and grows each minute fainter.

'*Helper and healer, I cheer—Small waifs in the woodland wet—Strays*

I find in it, wounds I bind in it—Bidding them all forget! Nearer, Mole, nearer! No, it is no good; the song has died away into reed-talk.'

'But what do the words mean?' asked the wondering Mole.

'That I do not know,' said the Rat simply. 'I passed them on to you as they reached me. Ah! now they return again, and this time full and clear! This time, at last, it is the real, the unmistakable thing, simple—passionate—perfect—'

'Well, let's have it then,' said the Mole, after he had waited patiently for a few minutes, half dozing in the hot sun.

But no answer came. He looked, and understood the silence. With a smile of much happiness on his face, and something of a listening look still lingering there, the weary Rat was fast asleep.

THE STRANGE CASE OF DOCTOR JEKYLL AND MR HYDE

R L Stevenson

In the month of October 1880, London was startled by a crime of singular ferocity, and rendered all the more notable by the high position of the victim. A maid-servant living alone in a house not far from the river had gone upstairs to bed about eleven. She was looking from her window when she saw two men talking in the street below. One was a tall, gentlemanly person with white hair; the other she recognized as a certain Mr Hyde who had once visited her master and for whom she had conceived a dislike. He had in his hand a heavy cane and was carrying it (as the maid described) like a madman. As she watched, the old gentleman took a step back, with the air of one very much surprised and a trifle hurt; and at that Mr Hyde broke out of all bounds, and clubbed him to the earth.

The next moment, with ape-like fury, he was trampling his victim under foot, and hailing down a storm of blows, under which the bones were audibly shattered and the body jumped upon the roadway. At the horror of these sights and sounds the maid fainted.

It was two o'clock when she came to herself and called for the police. The murderer was gone long ago, but there lay his victim in the middle of the lane, incredibly mangled. The stick with which the deed had been done, although it was of some rare and very tough and heavy wood, had broken under the stress of the cruelty and one splintered half had rolled into the neighbouring gutter. A purse and a gold watch were found upon the victim; but no cards or papers, except a sealed envelope which bore the name of Mr Utterson.

Mr Utterson, a lawyer, was taken to the body and identified the victim as Sir Danvers Carew. The police officer briefly narrated what the maid had seen, and showed the broken stick. Mr Utterson had already been surprised when the officer had mentioned that the maid had recognized the assailant as a Mr Hyde, but when the stick was laid before him he identified it for one that he had himself presented many years before to his friend, Dr Henry Jekyll.

'Is this Mr Hyde a person of small stature?' he inquired.

'Particularly small and particularly wicked-looking, is what the maid calls him,' said the officer.

As it happened, Mr Utterson knew the address of Hyde, for his client, Dr Jekyll, had made out a will in his favour, a will which Mr Utterson had helped draw up. He went to Hyde's address, a small house in a dingy street, but there was no sign of the man they sought. The two rooms which Hyde had occupied were well, almost elegantly furnished, but showed signs of having recently been ransacked. Clothes lay about the floor, drawers stood open, and in the hearth lay a pile of grey ashes, as though many papers had been burnt. The officer was highly delighted when, behind the door, the other half of the stick was found.

'You may depend upon it, sir. I have him in my hand,' he said, confidently.

Later that day, Mr Utterson found his way to Dr Jekyll's door, where he was at once admitted by Poole, the doctor's principal servant. He was shown into the doctor's laboratory—a place he had never visited before—and found Dr Jekyll seated by the fireplace, looking deadly sick. When Mr Utterson challenged him, he confessed that he had heard the terrible news of Sir Danvers' death and did not seem too surprised when his friend mentioned the name of Hyde, the man for whom the lawyer had altered the doctor's will. Yet he was obviously very upset. He pleaded with his friend, saying, 'I swear to God I will never set eyes on him again. I bind my honour to you that I am done with him in this world. It is all at an end,' and with that the lawyer had to be satisfied.

Time ran on. Thousands of pounds were offered in reward, for the death of Sir Danvers was resented as a public injury. But Mr Hyde had disappeared out of the ken of the police as though he had never existed. Although much of his past was unearthed, it seemed that from the time he had left the house in Soho on the morning of the murder he was simply blotted out. Gradually, as time drew on, Mr Utterson began to recover from his alarm and to grow more at quiet with himself. It was obvious that the mysterious Hyde had been an evil influence upon his friend the doctor for whom now, it seemed, a new life had begun. He renewed relations with his friends, became once more their familiar guest and entertainer, and while he had always been known for charity, he was now no less distinguished for religion. He was busy, he was much in the open air, he did good. His face seemed to open and brighten, as if with an inward consciousness of service, and for more than two months the doctor was at peace.

Yet by early January of the following year, all this was changed. The doctor's door was shut against Mr Utterson and his other old friend, also a doctor, Dr Lanyon. Soon afterwards Dr Lanyon took to his bed and in something less than a fortnight he was dead. He had left a letter on which, beneath his name, was written 'PRIVATE: for the hands of J. G. Utterson ALONE, and in the case of his predecease *to be destroyed unread.*'

The letter quoted at length another letter that the recently deceased had had from Dr Jekyll. It was, in fact, a cry for help. In it the doctor had said, 'I want you to postpone all other engagements for tonight— ay, even if you were summoned to the bedside of an emperor,' and begged him to drive straight to his house. There Poole, Dr Jekyll's butler, would be waiting for him together with a locksmith.

'The door of my laboratory is then to be forced,' the letter went on, 'and you are to go in alone, to open the glazed press on the left hand, breaking the lock if it be shut, and to draw out, *with all its contents as they stand*, the fourth drawer from the top or (which is the same thing) the third from the bottom. This drawer I beg of you to carry back with you to Cavendish Square exactly as it stands.

'That is the first part of the service : now for the second. At midnight, then, I have to ask you to be alone in your consulting room, to admit with your own hand into the house a man who will present himself in my name, and to place in his hands the drawer that you will have brought with you from my laboratory . . .'

Although almost convinced that his colleague was insane, Lanyon did as he was bid and, with the drawer intact as ordered, waited in his consulting room in Cavendish Square. Whilst he waited he examined the contents of the drawer, which seemed to contain various chemicals including a phial half full of a blood-red liquor.

Promptly at midnight, there came a gentle knocking on his door and he admitted the small man whom he found crouching against the pillars of the portico. When he led him into the light Dr Lanyon was able to examine him more closely. As the main letter said, 'This person was dressed in a fashion that would have made an ordinary person laughable. His clothes, that is to say, although they were of rich and sober fabric, were enormously too large for him in every measurement —the trousers hanging on his legs and rolled up to keep them from the ground, the waist of the coat below his haunches, and the collar sprawling wide upon his shoulders. Strange to relate, this ludicrous accoutrement was far from moving me to laughter. Rather, as there was something abnormal and misbegotten in the very essence of the creature that now faced me, this fresh disparity seemed but to fit in with and to reinforce it, so that to my interest in the man's nature and character there was added a curiosity as to his origin, his life, his fortune and status in the world.

'These observations, though they have taken so great a space to be set down in, were yet the work of a few seconds. My visitor was, indeed, on fire with sombre excitement.

' "Have you got it?" he cried. "Have you got it?" and so lively was his impatience that he even laid his hand upon my arm and sought to shake me.'

Dr Lanyon tried to curb the other's impatience and then said, 'There it is, sir,' and pointed to the drawer where it lay on the floor behind a table. The other sprang upon it then, turning, asked, 'Have you a graduated glass?'

Lanyon gave him what he asked and watched as the other measured

He reeled, staggered, clutched at the table and held on, staring with injected eyes, gasping with open mouth ...

out a few minims of the red tincture and added one of the powders. The mixture, which was at first of a reddish hue, began to brighten in colour, to effervesce audibly, and to throw off small fumes of vapour. Suddenly the compound changed to a deep purple, which faded again more slowly to a watery green. Lanyon's visitor, who had watched these changes with a keen eye, smiled, set down the glass upon the table, and then turned and looked upon the doctor with an air of scrutiny.

He offered him a choice. Either to be allowed to take the glass and go from the house without further talk, or, if the greed of curiosity had taken command of him, watch what would happen next.

'Sir,' said Dr Lanyon, 'you speak enigmas, and you will perhaps not wonder that I hear you with no very strong impression of belief. But I have gone too far in the way of inexplicable services to pause before I see the end.'

'It is well,' replied the visitor, 'Lanyon, you remember your vows. What follows is under the seal of our profession. And now, you who have so long been bound to the most narrow and material views, you who have denied the virtue of transcendental medicine, you who have derided your superiors—behold!'

He put the glass to his lips, and drank at one gulp. A cry followed. He reeled, staggered, clutched at the table and held on, staring with injected eyes, gasping with open mouth and as Lanyon watched there came a change. The other seemed to swell, his face became suddenly black, and the features seemed to melt and alter. The next moment Lanyon had sprung to his feet and leaped back against the wall, his arm raised to shield him from that prodigy, his mind submerged in terror.

'O God!' he screamed, and 'O God!' again and again. For there, before his eyes, pale and shaken and half fainting, and groping before him with his hands like a man restored from death—there stood Henry Jekyll!

The letter went on, 'What he told me in the next hour I cannot bring my mind to set on paper. I saw what I saw, I heard what I heard, and my soul sickened at it. And yet now, when that sight has faded from my eyes I ask myself if I believe it, and I cannot answer.'

The letter ended with, 'The creature who crept into my house that night was, on Jekyll's own confession, known by the name of Hyde and hunted for in every corner of the land as the murderer of Carew.'

How had this sad state of affairs come about? How was it that the highly respected Dr Jekyll had, by some strange means, also become the loathsome murderer known as Mr Hyde? The reasons for this were in his full statement, read when the whole sad business was finally at an end.

'I was born to a large fortune,' the statement began, 'endowed besides with excellent parts, inclined by nature to industry, fond of the respect of the wise and good among my fellow men and this, as might have been supposed, with every guarantee of an honourable and distinguished future. And indeed, the worst of my faults was a certain impatient gaiety of disposition, such as has made the happiness of many, but such as I found hard to reconcile with my imperious desire to carry my head high, and wear a more than commonly grave countenance before the public. Hence it came about that I concealed my pleasures; and that when I reached years of reflection, and began to look around me, and take stock of my progress and position in the world, I stood already committed to a profound duplicity of life.'

What he was saying was that to the world he was a staid, hardworking doctor; but he had a bad, almost evil side to his character, that no one else knew about. He had already concluded that almost everyone has such a dual personality—goodness mixed with occasional feelings of wickedness—but in his own personality he felt that this dividing line was more marked than usual. From this he had the thought—what would happen if he could actually separate these two opposite emotions? Could he, as a doctor and a chemist, actually do this?

The more he thought about the idea, the more absorbed he became. As he said in his statement: 'I hesitated long before I put this theory to the test of practice. I knew well that I risked death; for any drug that so potently controlled and shook the very fortress of identity might, by the least scruple of an overdose, utterly blot out that immaterial tabernacle which I looked to it to change. But the temptation of a discovery so singular and profound at last overcame the suggestions of alarm. I had long since prepared my tincture; I purchased from a firm of wholesale chemists a large quantity of particular salt which I knew, from my experiments, to be the last ingredient required; and, late one accursed night, I compounded the elements, watched them boil and smoke together in the glass, and when the boiling had subsided, with a strong glow of courage, drank of the potion.

'The most racking pains succeeded; a grinding in the bones, deadly nausea, and a horror of the spirit that cannot be exceeded at the hour of birth or death. Then these agonies began swiftly to subside, and I came to myself as if out of a great sickness. There was something strange in my sensations, something indescribably new and, from its very novelty, incredibly sweet. I felt younger, lighter, happier in body. I knew myself at the first breath of this new life to be more wicked, tenfold more wicked, sold a slave to my original evil, and the thought, at that moment, braced and delighted me like wine. I stretched out my hands, exulting in the freshness of these sensations and, in the act, I was suddenly aware that I had lost in stature.

'And hence, as I think, it came about that Edward Hyde was so much smaller, slighter, and younger than Henry Jekyll. Even as good shone upon the countenance of the one, evil was written broadly and plainly on the face of the other.'

He looked at himself in a mirror, noting the many differences between his two beings and then drank again, once more suffered the pangs of dissolution, and once more saw himself as Henry Jekyll.

Later he took and furnished the house in Soho to which Hyde was tracked by the police. He also announced to his servants that a Mr Hyde (whom he described) was to have full liberty and power about his own house. He then drew up a will so that if anything befel him in the person of Dr Jekyll, he could become Edward Hyde without loss.

He then began his strange, double life. No matter what he did outside the walls of his home he knew that he did not even exist! Let him but escape into his laboratory door, give him but a second to mix and swallow the draught that he always had standing ready, then, whatever he had done, Edward Hyde would pass away like a stain of breath upon a mirror. And there, in his stead, quietly at home, trimming the midnight lamp in his study, a man who could afford to laugh at suspicion ... would be Henry Jekyll!

But this was to end. Some two months before the murder of Sir Danvers he had been out on one of his adventures and had returned late. When he woke the next day he had an odd sensation. He looked about him. The room was as usual, nothing had changed. Yet something was wrong. Then he looked down on his hand. The hand of Henry Jekyll was large, firm, white and comely. The hand he saw was lean, corded, knuckly, of a dusky pallor and thickly shaded with a swart growth of hair.

He knew at once what had happened. He had gone to bed Dr Jekyll, he had awakened Edward Hyde. He managed to pass through the house—to the surprise of the servants—disappeared into his laboratory, and ten minutes later, Dr Jekyll was sitting down, with a darkened brow, to make a feint of breakfasting.

This was the beginning. He decided—for he was forced to make the choice—to let Hyde go forever and remain as the familiar, friendly doctor. For two months he led a life of severity and the pleasure of the company of his friends. Then he began to be tortured with longings and, as if he was Hyde struggling after freedom, once again compounded and swallowed the transforming draught.

It was on this night that he met and murdered the kindly, aged Sir Danvers. With a transport of glee, he mauled the unresisting body, tasting delight from every blow and it was not until weariness had begun to succeed that he was suddenly, in the top fit of his delirium, struck through the heart by a cold chill of terror. Seeing his life forfeit,

He mauled the unresisting body, tasting delight from every blow.

he fled from the scene, running to his little house in Soho, still gloating on his crime, yet still listening for the sound behind him of the steps of the avenger. He drank the draught, even pledging the dead man. Then the next moment, Henry Jekyll, with streaming tears of remorse, had fallen on his knees and lifted his clasped hands to God.

He realized that, never again, would the terrible Hyde be allowed to roam the streets, maiming and killing. He locked the door and ground the key under his heel. Enough was enough!

But it was not to be. One fine January day he sat quietly in Regent's Park, at peace with the world. And then he was filled with a horrid nausea, and the most deadly shuddering. He looked down His clothes hung formlessly on his shrunken limbs, the hand that lay on his knee was corded and hairy. A moment before he had been wealthy, beloved, the cloth being laid for him in the dining-room in his home. Now he was the common quarry of mankind, a known murderer.

He took a cab to a hotel he knew and wrote two important letters—one to Lanyon and one to his butler, Poole—then sent them out with directions they should be registered. He paced the room, desperately. Now it was no longer the fear of the gallows, it was the horror of being Hyde that racked him. He slept for a while then made his way back to his laboratory. This time it took a double dose to recall him to himself and six hours later, as he sat looking sadly into the fire, the pangs returned and the drug had to be retaken.

From that day it seemed that only by a great effort as of gymnastics, and only under the immediate stimulation of the drug, that he could continue to wear the countenance of Jekyll. If he slept, or even dozed for a moment in his chair, it was always as Hyde that he awoke. His very existence had become intolerable. It was then that he sat down to write his full statement, ending with: 'I am now finishing this statement under the influence of the last of the old powders. This then, is the last time, short of a miracle, that Henry Jekyll can think his own thoughts or see his own face (now how sadly altered) in the glass.

'Will Hyde die upon the scaffold? Or will he find the courage to release himself at the last moment? God knows; I am careless; this is my true hour of death, and what is to follow concerns another than myself. Here, then, as I lay down the pen, and proceed to seal up my confession, I bring the life of that unhappy Henry Jekyll to an end.'

Mr Utterson was sitting by his fireside when he was surprised to receive a visit from Poole. He soon learned from Dr Jekyll's butler that he suspected something was very wrong with the doctor. Would he come at once? Mr Utterson did not hesitate and the two men set out for the doctor's home. Reaching it, the butler led him through the house until they reached the door of the laboratory. He knocked upon it and announced that Mr Utterson had called to see him. A voice answered from within, 'Tell him I cannot see anyone.'

'Sir,' Poole asked, looking Mr Utterson in the eyes, 'was that the voice of my master?'

'It seems very changed,' replied the lawyer, very pale, but giving look for look.

'Changed? Well, yes, I think so. Have I been twenty years in this man's house, to be deceived about his voice? No, sir. Master's been made away with. He was made away with about eight days ago, when we heard him cry out upon the name of God. And *who's* in there instead of him, and *why* it stays there, is a thing that cries to heaven.'

The two men discussed the problem for some time, the butler insisting that, in his view, murder had been done by the person who had answered him through the door. He went further. He insisted that the *thing* inside the laboratory was the man he knew as Mr Hyde. He asked if the other had ever seen him.

'Yes,' said the lawyer, 'I once spoke with him.'

'Then you must know, sir, as well as the rest of us, that there was something queer about that gentleman—something that gave a man a turn—I don't rightly know how to say it, sir, beyond this; that you felt it in your marrow—kind of cold and thin.'

'I own I felt something of what you describe,' said Mr Utterson.

By now the lawyer's mind was made up. He called another male servant to help and told him that he and Poole were going to force their way into the laboratory.

'If all is well,' he said, 'my shoulders are broad enough to bear the blame. Meanwhile, lest anything should really be amiss, or any criminal seek to escape by the back, you and the boy must go round the corner with a pair of good sticks, and take your post at the laboratory door. We give you ten minutes to get to your stations.'

The ten minutes came to an end at last. 'Jekyll!' cried Utterson. with a loud voice. 'I demand to see you!' He paused a moment but there came no reply. 'I give you fair warning, our suspicions are aroused and I must and shall see you. If not by fair means, then by foul. If not of your consent, then by brute force!'

'Utterson,' said the voice, 'for God's sake, have mercy!'

'Ah, that's not Jekyll's voice—it's Hyde's!' cried Utterson. 'Down with the door, Poole!'

The other swung an axe he had taken from another room and the door leaped against the lock and hinges. A dismal screech, as of mere animal terror, rang from the other side. Up went the axe again and again, and it was not until the fifth blow that the lock burst in sunder and the wreck of the door fell inwards. The besiegers, appalled by their own riot and the stillness that had followed, stood back a little and peered in. There lay the room before their eyes in the quiet lamplight, a good fire glowing and chattering on the hearth, the kettle singing its thin strain, a drawer or two open, papers neatly set forth on the business table, and nearer the fire, the things laid out for tea. The quietest room, one would have said, and, but for the glazed presses full of chemicals, the most commonplace that night in London.

Right in the midst there lay the body of a man sorely contorted and still twitching. They drew near on tiptoe, turned it on its back, and beheld the face of Edward Hyde. He was dressed in clothes far too large for him, clothes of the doctor's bigness; the cords of his face still moved with a semblance of life, but life was quite gone; and by the crushed phial in the hand and the strong smell of kernels that hung upon the air, Utterson knew that we was looking on the body of a self-destroyer.

'We have come too late,' he said sternly, 'whether to save or punish. Hyde is gone to his account; and it only remains for us to find the body of your master.'

The two men searched the house but with no success. Finally, turning to the business table, they saw a large envelope bearing, in the doctor's hand, the name of Mr Utterson. The lawyer unsealed it and several enclosures fell to the floor. The first was a will, made out as before, but in place of the name of Edward Hyde the lawyer, with indescribable amazement, read the name of Gabriel John Utterson. He opened the next enclosure and read:

'My dear Utterson. When this shall fall into your hands, I shall

have disappeared, under what circumstances I have not the pene-
tration to foresee; but my instincts and all the circumstances of my
nameless situation tell me that the end is sure and must be early.
Go then, and first read the narrative which Lanyon warned me he
was to place in your hands; and if you care to hear more, turn to
the confession of

Your unworthy and unhappy friend, Henry Jekyll.'

'There was a third enclosure?' asked Utterson.

'Here, sir,' said Poole, and gave into his hands a considerable packet
sealed in several places.

The lawyer put it in his pocket. 'I would say nothing of this paper. If
your master is fled or is dead, we may at least save his credit. It is now
ten. I must go home and read these documents in quiet; but I shall be
back before midnight, when we shall send for the police.'

And Utterson returned home to read, with growing amazement,
Dr Jekyll's full statement together with an account of the change witnessed by Dr Lanyon. When he had finished, he arose with a sigh. The
mystery of Dr Jekyll and Mr Hyde had been explained—at last!